THE JADE DEMONS QUARTET

1: THE QUAKING LANDS

Kesira Minette Looked
into the Fangs
of Death

Molimo's entire body had altered into that of a wolf intent on ripping out her throat. Just as the beast leaped, Kesira dropped and rolled to one side. Hot breath and wetness gusted alongside her head as the wolf twisted in mid-leap, trying to bury teeth into her flesh.

Kesira stilled her harsh breathing and settled into fighting readiness. The Order of Gelya did not permit the use of steel weapons, but that did not mean she was unarmed. With only a stone-wood staff, she was better defended than if she possessed the finest sword.

In knowing she might die at any misstep lay Kesira's greatest strength. Her mind moved slower as she prepared for conflict. She did not anticipate the wolf's movements; she responded to them. She did not seek out weaknesses; she created them. Her staff rose as Molimo launched himself through the air, once more intent on tearing her throat to bloody ribbons.

THE JADE DEMONS QUARTET

2: THE FROZEN WAVES

Demons's Fury

The screams filled Kesira Minette's soul with searing acid. She resisted closing her eyes or putting her hands over her ears to block the farmer's hideous shrieks. To do so would give Ayondela too much pleasure. The jade demon sat on her throne of blue-white ice, sneering, her tusks gleaming with shining green. Ayondela tossed her head and sent a cascade of hair floating out gently; she had been lovely once, Kesira knew.

Only stark, ripping hatred showed now.

THE JADE DEMONS QUARTET

3: THE CRYSTAL CLOUDS

Kesira Minette Offered Up the
Small Baby
to Its Cowering Mother

"It is your baby, no matter who the father is,"
Kesira said. "You must tend him." The baby
looked well enough nourished, but the pale eyes
stared out at her with preternatural intelligence
more expected in a child ten times this one's
age. And there was no cry.

"Hell spawn!" shrieked Parvey Yera. "It is
demon spawn and I want nothing to do with it.
Or you!"

The sudden attack took Kesira by surprise.
One moment she had studied the small baby,
the next clawed fingers raked at her face. Only
instinct saved Kesira. She threw up one arm and
deflected the blow but lost her balance and
stumbled over a low table made from a rotting
log. Above her Parvey Yera straightened, a
gleaming axe in her hands.

Kesira watched in mute fascination as the
nicked blade began its descent, aimed directly
for her skull . . .

THE JADE DEMONS QUARTET

4: THE WHITE FIRE

The Demon's Wrath

"You dare use puny magicks against me? Against *me?*" Lenc strode out of the fire and brushed away burning debris from his shoulders and arms. "I will show you real magic!"

The demon clapped his hands. The thunder rumbling down the streets of Kolya deafened Kesira. She fell to her knees, sobbing with the pain lancing into her head. Even putting fingers in her ears failed to stop the hideous noise ripping away at her soul. And just when she thought it might be bearable, Lenc clapped his hands again.

And he laughed . . .

The Jade Demons Quartet

The Quaking Lands
The Frozen Waves
The Crystal Clouds
The White Fire

Robert E.
Vardeman

NEW ENGLISH LIBRARY
Hodder and Stoughton

First published in the United
States of America as four
separate volumes:
THE QUAKING LANDS © 1985
by Robert E. Vardeman
Published by Avon Books in
1985
THE FROZEN WAVES © 1985
by Robert E. Vardeman
Published by Avon Books in
1985
THE CRYSTAL CLOUDS ©
1985 by Robert E. Vardeman
Published by Avon Books in
1985
THE WHITE FIRE © 1986
by Robert E. Vardeman
Published by Avon Books in
1986

New English Library Paperback
edition 1987

Printed and bound in Great
Britain for Hodder and Stoughton
Paperbacks, a division of Hodder
and Stoughton Ltd., Mill Road,
Dunton Green, Sevenoaks, Kent
TN13 2YA. (Editorial Office: 47
Bedford Square, London WC1B
3DP) by Richard Clay Ltd.,
Bungay, Suffolk.

British Library C.I.P.

Vardeman, Robert E.
  The jade demons quartet.
  I. Title
  813'. 54[F]   PS3572.A714

ISBN 0-450-41351-9

1: THE QUAKING LANDS

Chapter One

"BAD OMEN, bad omen!" squawked the large *trilla* bird perched on Kesira Minette's shoulder. The woman turned to the luminescent green-feathered bird and stared into one beady black, white-rimmed eye.

"Nonsense," she said. "The day is fine. The trip has been without interruption. Our mission in the city went smoothly. Where is this bad omen?"

"The sky," replied the bird, tensing its claws and cutting into the woman's shoulder, even through the gray robe she wore. "Look to sky!"

Kesira glanced up and saw nothing unusual. Or rather, the only thing that struck the woman as unusual was the vividness of the sky. The blue was deeper than she had ever seen before, the few white clouds dotting the flawless perfection were puffy and billowing with goodness, perhaps promising easy spring rains, and drifting with gentle breezes as the demons played their unknown games with the elements.

She sighed and shook her head. Most times, Zolkan provided a fine traveling companion. Kesira asked for nothing more, whether in a human or a *trilla* bird. But Zolkan saw omens everywhere; he had ever since the

7

day six months earlier when he had flown into the Order of Gelya's sacristy and fallen asleep in a pile of vestments. Kesira had found Zolkan there, exhausted and more dead than alive, and had nursed him back to full health. Keeping a pet in the Order of Gelya was not forbidden by nunnery rules, but Dominie Tredlo discouraged such a show of concern for anything not pertaining to the order.

But Dominie Tredlo did not reside within the walls of the nunnery. As Senior Brother he traveled a circuit watching over both monastery and nunnery for the Order, and Kesira had kept Zolkan.

The *trilla* bird provided a new and amusing view of the world, one she had never encountered before.

The woman smiled as she thought of the nights she had lain awake listening to Zolkan's tales of flying high above even the loftiest mountains, peering down on mere mortals, and even demons, as they went about their business. None ever looked aloft, or so said Zolkan. The stories ranged from the touching to the ribald, and Kesira loved each and every one. She had taken to hungering for the experience of going out to see life away from the convent.

Kesira straightened her simple gray robes and worked at the blue cord encircling her waist until the knots were properly displayed in the front. Close-cropped brown hair insisted on poking out around the robe's cowl and she had never quite managed to keep her face composed in the imperturbable calm her instructors had so diligently taught. Once free of the confines of the Order, Kesira took in all with wide-eyed excitement, her lips curled into a perpetual smile of pleasure, and soft brown eyes dancing with delight as details paraded themselves before her. She could let her imagination have free rein and become what she was not, pretending to be even the Empress Aglanella in her royal court, entertained by jugglers and mages and chanteuses from far off Limaden.

Sequestered for most of her life, the young woman found even a street vendor in Blinn exotic and thrilling.

"The day is fine, Zolkan. Don't annoy me with your dire predictions."

"No prediction," the bird squawked. "Bad omen, many bad omens."

"Show me one."

"Shadows. Everywhere shadows."

"The sun shines brightly. Solid objects cast shadows. Are you telling me it is a bad omen that the sun is so warm and cheering after the long winter we suffered through? Or have you forgotten how your wings froze during the ice storm and you blundered into..."

"Bad omen," insisted Zolkan. The bird shifted position again and faced to the rear. Kesira took a quick glance behind, saw only empty road and continued on her way. While she enjoyed being away from the Order's high-walled nunnery and being trusted enough to fetch the lamp oil from Blinn merchants, Kesira knew of the brigands populating the hills. The stories the nuns whispered among themselves before falling into a deliciously terrified sleep put her on guard.

No nun of the Order of Gelya went unprotected. Gelya himself watched over them. But Gelya also decreed that each worshipper be self-sufficient in all ways. Kesira Minette knew how to defend herself, should the need arise. Slender fingers tightened on the stone-wood staff she used to help her along the road. The Order of Gelya forbade the use of steel weapons, those being sacred to another order, but Gelya smiled on rivers, stands of stone-wood trees and even on several roots and tubers and one very special wildflower which bore no formal name.

"It comes fast. Bad, bad," muttered Zolkan.

Kesira didn't know whether to pay heed to the *trilla* bird or not. Zolkan's perceptions of the world tended to be pessimistic and dire at the best of times.

Ahead she saw a small stone shrine. Her steady progress had brought her halfway back to the nunnery in ample time to arrive home well before sundown. But she ought to stop and pay obeisance to Gelya and meditate for at least an hour. To do so, Kesira considered, might delay her arrival until after the sun had slipped behind the jagged peaks of the Yearn Mountains to the west. The days were growing longer, but winter still jealously clung to the sun in the afternoon.

"Don't stop," the bird warned. Long wings extended

and beat at the back of Kesira's head. "Walk on. Hurry to home."

The *trilla* bird's insistence perversely convinced Kesira to stop and meditate, at least for a while. It never paid to allow Zolkan to have his way in everything or he became insufferable. And, Kesira admitted to herself, the spring day was too lovely to waste with senseless trudging.

"The time will fly by," she told the bird. "My meditations will be over before you know it."

"Danger stalks closer. Heavy foots."

"Feet," she corrected idly.

"Run! Flee!"

"Sit," Kesira said firmly, reaching up and grabbing Zolkan's claws in one hand. She removed the bird from her shoulder and placed him on a special stone perch outside the shrine. Beady black eyes glared at her.

"Leave and fly away. Not want to die."

"Do as you please. I will offer my prayers and then meditate. For one hour. No longer, but no less." Kesira turned without seeing how Zolkan accepted this dictate. The impatient flapping of the wings told her of the bird's indecision. Whatever made him so restive had also caused him to be overly protective of her. Kesira bowed her head, pulled back the simple cowl and entered the shrine.

Four dark red *renn*-stone walls, without windows or any other exit or entrance save the one through which she entered, protected the altar. A brown stone column hardly thicker than her arm rose up from the floor and on the small flat area atop it rested a single yellow-petaled wildflower with an ebony center. Kesira knew that this unnamed flower remained pure throughout the entire year, never wilting, always protected by the goodness of her patron Gelya.

She knelt before the altar, head bowed and eyes open. Focusing on the worn flagstone floor, Kesira allowed her mind to slip from one thing to another until all were passed by in favor of a single idea, a concept, a path. The wildflower provided the core but her mind wove about it an entire way of life, the way described by Gelya and to which she had devoted her life.

Peace, but not at the expense of honor.
Honor, but not to the detriment of duty.
Duty, but not if family comes to harm.
Harm, but only to maintain peace.

As she considered the wildflower—its delicately folded petals, the ebony vastness of the center containing pollen for bees, the patterns divulging the implications of life and death—Kesira's mind began to range farther afield, leaving her body behind. Her essence traveled beyond the confines of flesh and exulted in a freedom shared by few outside the Order of Gelya.

She roamed the corridors of infinity, sampling exquisite thoughts left behind like the discarded garments of ancestors dead a thousand years, studying and deciding, coming to conclusions, formulating new questions, and finding tranquillity.

Kesira shuddered slightly and returned to her body. It was ever thus. A mortal could not stand too much of that divine gift offered by Gelya. The meditation left her refreshed, relaxed; prepared for the final leg of her journey. She rocked back onto the balls of her feet and stood in a single smooth movement. Backing from the altar, she left the shrine.

Blinking in surprise, Kesira stared at the sky.

Once cobalt blue, it had transformed into a swirling, billowing blackness devoid of clouds or anything of substance. It was as if the very sky itself writhed in tortured agony, turning an inky, contorted countenance to the earth.

"Zolkan!" she cried out, when she failed to find the *trilla* bird on the perch where she'd left him. "Where are you?"

A flapping of wings rivaling heavy wardrum beats startled her. She spun, staff in hand, and pointed toward the sky. Zolkan braked to a halt and held himself motionless in the air above her, claws gripping the staff. Kesira tugged a bit and Zolkan's wings slowed their resonant movements to allow the *trilla* bird to settle once again on her shoulder.

"Bad omen. Told you so."

"What's happening?" she asked in confusion. Before she had meditated, the springtime weather had been perfect. Now, while the temperature remained constant and not a breath of winter air stirred, the heavens rippled with evil darkness. "Where's the sun? Zolkan, what did you see from aloft?"

"Omens. All bad." The bird's talons pierced the rough gray fabric of her robe and bit deeply into her flesh. Kesira felt the beginnings of bloody tricklings inside the robe. She was too distracted to tend to such minor wounds. Her attention fixed completely on the sky.

"Never have I witnessed such as this," she said, more in awe than fear. "The demons war among themselves."

"Truth! She sees truth!" cried Zolkan.

"What? Demons?"

"Bad omen. Jade omen."

Kesira shivered then, the clammy tendrils of fear brushing lightly at her senses. Only demons dared touch jade. For them it was a stone of power. For mortals it meant only ill luck and sickness and death—or worse.

"Let's get back to the nunnery," she said, swallowing incipient panic. The weather had not changed, even if the heavens bespoke evil. She would be able to make good time—and any other shrine along the road would be ignored. Kesira had worried about returning before sundown to avoid the brigands in the mountains. Now she worried about more than this, since no thief would venture forth with the sky in such an uproar.

For *any* to travel under such a sky was foolhardy.

But Kesira had nowhere else to go but back to the nunnery and her Sisters. In addition, more than ever they would need the oil she had purchased in Blinn. When day turned into night, the lamps burned longer hours. Duty drove her feet forward and kept her heart from quailing as the turbulence above her worsened.

"Jade," squawked Zolkan. "Jade sky!"

Kesira tried not to look above, but she knew the *trilla* bird was correct. Her peripheral vision showed *things* flowing in the sky, taking form and then ripping apart to form even more grotesque figures. And intermixed in the blackness came the tint she feared above all others. The pale green warned of demons warring— and demons and their concerns meant only sorrow for mortals.

"Rain!" cried Zolkan. "Beware rain!"

Kesira frowned. She felt no rain. Above weren't true clouds, but the doings of demons. The woman stopped and pushed back her cowl to better look at the bowl of the sky stretching from mountain peak to mountain peak. The huge vault, so devoid of color before, now sparkled with aurora. White shimmerings of gauzy veils pulled back and forth, as if opening the curtain on a celestial stage. But the veils hid nothing and revealed nothing. Their coronal dance intrigued Kesira, however.

"So lovely," she murmured. "I have never seen the demons' lights so active before. Only during the midwinter festival have I seen anything so stark and so lovely."

"Not pretty. Hide, hide!"

"Quiet, Zolkan. There's nothing to fear." Kesira sounded serene and confident, but inside she held in check the outright panic threatening to send her screaming along the road back to her Sisters. Her training had taught her restraint. Fear was the destroyer, panic the enemy of the mind. All of nature came together this day and she wanted to see it, to understand a minute portion more than she had, to conquer the part of her that tried to prevent this new knowledge from being accepted.

To know the forces of nature and the spirits driving them gave serenity. Only her ignorance gave birth to the irrational fears she felt.

"The aurora is so delicate appearing," Kesira said. "Ever changing, dancing on feathered feet across the sky. It brightens the darkness almost enough for us to see the road. Don't you agree this is the finest sight you've seen, Zolkan?"

The *trilla* bird said nothing.

Kesira watched the blazing display mount in intensity then fade away. When it returned with electric cracklings more appropriate to a thunderstorm, she shivered again. Some fears that the mind held at bay the body still reacted to instinctively. Kesira knew she would have to talk with Dominie Tredlo about this and attempt to transcend such physical slavery.

Kesira had trouble holding back the flood of terror when she saw the aurora changing from white to red—

and to green and blue and all the other colors of the rainbow. The discharges formed into sharp wands that battered one another and produced cascades of molten white.

"Demons," said Zolkan. "Battling for supremacy."

"Have you seen such as this before?" Kesira asked the bird. Talons gouged into her flesh once more. She turned and peered into one huge black eye not an inch from her own. The sharp, serrated beak opened and shut with a dull clack, hinting at brutal power beyond Kesira's comprehension. She had never done more than listen to the stories Zolkan offered up on the cold winter nights. Not once had she asked the bird of his origins or how he had come to blunder into the nunnery or even how he had come to be in such a debilitated condition. She had merely accepted. Now Kesira wondered just what Zolkan knew of this strange day's occurrences and whether the *trilla* bird was not somehow involved.

"Shelter. Take shelter. For a while," the bird urged. "Danger. Extreme danger awaits."

"Brigands?"

"Rain."

Kesira knew the bird disliked being wet, but rain had not bothered him like this before. She turned her steps toward the rocky precipice on her left to seek out a sheltering overhang. Off the road the going turned rougher, but Kesira kept on, the stones underfoot winking alive with colors reflected from above.

"There. Shelter."

She followed the line of Zolkan's wing and saw a small cave in the side of the cliff face. It took only a moment to work her way down through the loose rocks and into the shallow depression. Settling herself, Kesira said, "You never answered my question. Have you experienced anything like this before?"

"Heard, not seen," the bird informed her. "Terrible wars between demons. Jade rain!"

"What's that mean?" Kesira asked, feeling as much irritation toward herself as toward Zolkan for his faulty explanations. If only she had lived more, experienced more outside the walls of the Order of Gelya. But she hadn't. A dozen times, or perhaps once or twice more, she had been to the city of Blinn on errands. Few had spoken to her because she was a Sister of the Order of Gelya and the populace was composed of evil people, but still Kesira had been drawn to them perversely. She hoped that, when her apprenticeship ended, she might venture forth to carry the words of Gelya to some other city where the Order maintained small temples. To go to the City of Sin! Even the evil name brought forth unbidden excitement to Kesira. Most of the Sisters professed nothing but disdain for the idea of field work or prosyletizing the masses, preferring to remain away from the mainstream of society. But Kesira's curiosity drove her to find out more.

"Have you ever seen a demon?" she asked Zolkan.

"Yes."

Her heart almost stopped pounding and her throat constricted. It had never before occurred to her to ask Zolkan for such information.

"What are they like, the demons? Did you see Gelya?"

"Saw many. Not talk." Zolkan shook all over, loose feathers drifting softly downward as the bird continued to shake himself. He put his head under one wing and pretended to go to sleep. Kesira wanted to squeeze him until he answered. Never had she found anyone who claimed to know a demon.

Before the woman could speak, the very earth rumbled beneath her. Peering out, she saw the sky splitting into opposing factions. One gauzelike rainbow sword leaped across to engage another and another and still another until the sky burned with the fury of the battle. Shielding her eyes, Kesira watched in rapt fascination. And then fear crept into her as she saw the progress of the battle. It had begun past the Yearn Mountains, out on the plains and away from any populated centers. But the ebb and flow of the aerial duel came over the mountains and down the valley she traversed, and up the slopes of Mt. Lopurrian, where the convent snuggled close. Kesira couldn't tell for certain, but she thought the battle paused over the nunnery.

"Zolkan, we must hurry on. We must return and see if we can help. They need our oil."

Kesira took two steps out of the cave and saw the sky ignite. Huge columns of the purest jade green formed, aimed, and stabbed earthward—directly where the convent stood. And then the flickering white aurora returned, dancing and flicking from peak to peak, drifting to the valley floor, dazzling her eyes, sending cold rivers up and down her spine. A sickness mounted within her, more compelling than she felt every lunar cycle, more intense, less understandable.

"Something awful is happening!" she cried. Kesira winced as Zolkan tightened his grip on her shoulder. The bird held her back and for good reason. Tiny droplets of rain now fell, but rain unlike any she had ever seen.

"Jade rain!"

Kesira swallowed hard when she saw that the *trilla* bird was right. The drops pelting down from above were not water, but molten jade. They splashed against the rocks and burned with searing intensity. To be caught in an exposed location—out on the road or walking across a plain—would have meant slow, agonizing death.

Even as she spun to dive back into the cave, several of the drops struck her. One burned through her gray robe and found the flesh beneath. Another hissed as the skin on the back of her left hand charred. And another set a tiny watchfire in her brown hair. Sobbing, shaking, Kesira put out the fire by the painful expedient of yanking the lock from her head. Not for the first time did she curse the prohibition Gelya put on the use of iron implements, and she was not sufficiently advanced in the Order to merit an obsidian or flint knife.

Kesira dashed the smoldering lock of her hair to the cave floor and watched as green fire consumed it and sputtered out. She held her injured left hand to her body to prevent air from reaching that wound and, when the pain faded slightly, she opened her robe and saw the raw, burned spot just above her left breast where the other droplet of molten jade had struck.

"Omen," sighed Zolkan. "Good omen."

"I'm burned and you call it a good omen?" She shook her head. Sometimes the bird confounded her with its odd speech and even odder thought patterns. Still, Zolkan appeared to know far more of the demons and their doings than she did.

If only she could speak with the older Sisters in her Order! They were versed in such mysteries. They could tell her what she needed to know.

"Rain over," cawed Zolkan. "Hurry away. Back to Blinn."

"We're going to the nunnery."

"Please. No."

"What?" Kesira stopped and stared at Zolkan. She had never heard the bird say "please" before. Speech came awkwardly enough without adding words of politeness to further confound a listener's ear.

"Please. Do not go there."

"Why not?"

"Only death will be found."

"How do you know?"

"Demons war. Lenc is too strong."

"Lenc?" She tried to remember her lessons of the pantheon of demons. This name was unfamiliar. "Are you saying this Lenc is an enemy of Gelya?"

"Please. We go to Blinn?"

"We're returning to the convent." Kesira felt Zolkan start to flap his wings, to loft himself and fly off; then he settled back, his head rotating from side to side in obvious displeasure at her decision. Kesira didn't care at that moment if Zolkan went or stayed on his human perch. She had a duty to perform and, more than this duty, she felt the bond to the others in her Order drawing her back to the secluded buildings down the valley.

She picked up the pace until she almost ran. To either side of the road lay tiny fragments of jade. She saw no indication of the burning on dirt or rock where they lay—certainly nothing like the burning and pain she'd experienced when they struck her.

Above, the sky lost its rainbow colors and returned to inky blackness. No shapes writhed and danced. Only an infinite darkness without stars or light of any sort stretched from mountaintop to mountaintop. It was as if the sky sucked up light and heat and turned the world into a hellish, barren place for trapped souls awaiting death.

"Jade everywhere," grumbled Zolkan. "Bad omen."

Kesira saw increasing signs of destruction now. Huge furrows ran across the valley floor and into the rock of Mt. Lopurrian, as if a giant knife had gouged the earth. She swung the jars of lamp oil awkwardly and wondered if she should forsake them in exchange for more speed. Kesira tossed on the horns of this dilemma—obedience in carrying out her duty to a higher duty to her Order of Gelya.

Kesira knew they needed oil. With the skies blacker than night, it would be even more useful. She kept on, balancing the jars and trying to increase her pace even more.

"Jade. It glows!"

Kesira paled when she saw what Zolkan referred to. The tiny pieces of jade that had rained down had been inert—until now. As she ran closer and closer to the nunnery, the shards began to glow. Only a pale luminescence shone at first, but along the road she saw that the light from the jade pieces increased in intensity until they blazed brightly. It was a warning not to advance.

She dropped the jars of lamp oil, adjusted the blue cord knotted about her slender waist, gripped her stone-wood staff and started forward, the jade fragments on either side of the road lighting her way.

"Body. There!" squawked Zolkan. The bird flapped its wings and battered Kesira about the face until she stopped and looked. Alongside the road lay a man, arms twisted in odd directions and legs unnatural in the way they curled beneath him. Kesira glanced up the road toward the nunnery, then at the injured man. He stirred slightly, showing he still lived.

"Gelya, forgive my breach of duty," she muttered. Kesira hastened to the man's side—the youth's side, for he was even younger than she. His dark black hair lay in small cylinders formed by the blood seeping from a score of scalp wounds. His face carried the same number of tiny cuts and, even as she cradled his head, his eyelids flickered open. Eyes as dark as the sky itself peered up at her, without fear, without any discernible emotion.

"You are badly injured," she said. "I can do nothing for you. I will try to stop the worst of the bleeding, then go for help. My Order is only a short distance down the road. Do you understand?"

He nodded.

"Good," Kesira said, going about staunching what wounds she could. In spite of the blood and dirt on his face, Kesira found the youth appealing. Unmarked, he might even be handsome. His aquiline nose had escaped real injury and the high cheekbones hinted at royalty. Kesira had seen Emperor Kwasian once and he had the same facial structure, though she had not found him in the least attractive. The Emperor's haughty demeanor prevented that, but then he claimed to be descended from the demons and more divine than mortal.

Kesira winced as she studied the injuries the man had sustained to his arms and legs. She knew how to set bones, but the compound fractures were tricky and required more expert handling than she could give. Sister Enola was the Order of Gelya's healer. She would be able to cope with these limb-twisting injuries.

"There," Kesira finally said, after doing what was necessary. "I will bring back a litter and we'll get you to the nunnery."

The dark eyes blinked questioningly.

"The Order of Gelya," she said. "Gelya will aid you." She patted the man on his shoulder, hoping it wouldn't give him additional hurt when she wanted to convey only reassurance.

Fear came into his dark eyes or something so closely akin to it she could not call it anything else. But what puzzled Kesira was that the fear—concern?—directed itself at her.

"Gelya will protect you," she said again. Once more she got the reaction.

"Can you speak? What is your name?"

Lips opened to display an empty mouth. The tongue had been brutally ripped out. The greenish light cast by the glowing jade all about them made the tongueless mouth even more hideous to behold.

"I am sorry," she said. "I didn't know."

"Go to Blinn," urged Zolkan, who had perched silently the entire time Kesira had worked on the youth. "Three of us to Blinn. Now!"

"To the convent. We need to bring back help for him."

To the youth she said, "Rest now. I'll be back as soon
as I can. Rest." Her voice lulled him to the point that
his eyelids turned heavy and sank slowly over the fas-
cinatingly dark eyes. Kesira maintained the soothing
chant until the man slept quietly.

"Blinn," insisted Zolkan.

Kesira ignored the *trilla* bird and went on. As she
neared the convent, the bits of jade strewn about blazed
with eye-searing intensity. Kesira even felt their cold
radiance turning warmer, as if the heated fragments
sought to burn her further. But all this Kesira ignored.
Duty drew her onward.

She stopped in the middle of the road and simply
stared.

Where the high wall surrounding the nunnery had
been was now...dust. The huge blocks of *renn*-stone
had been turned into powder, as if struck by a huge
hammer blow. Mocking, the arch inscribed with the
Order of Gelya's name was left standing. Kesira swallowed hard and fought back the tears forming as she
went under the arch.

Destruction. Everywhere destruction. The buildings
of stone were all crumbled. Those of wood still stood,
but tiny fires burned here and there, showing the insides had been set ablaze while the exterior miracu-
lously escaped unscathed.

"Stone-wood sacred to Gelya," crowed Zolkan.

"A demon has attacked the nunnery?" Kesira asked.

"Lenc."

"This is unheard of. It can't be true!" Kesira rushed
forward, the paralysis that had gripped her suddenly
being cast off. From building to building she ran and
what she saw sickened her. Any structure made from
Gelya's sacred stone-wood remained intact, but the in-
teriors were uniformly scorched. Any stone building
had been razed.

And everyone Kesira found had died horribly. Sister
Enola, of the comforting smile and gentle hand, had
been dismembered and her parts strewn throughout the
dispensary before the fires had gutted the structure.
Sister Dana, her closest friend, sat with her back to a
stone-wood wall. The front of her body had been burned
away; the back was unscathed. Sisters Fenelia and Hedy

and Kai and all the others, dead, some of them burned beyond positive recognition. Kesira guessed as to their identities by reconstructing the afternoon meditations and where each was most likely to have been.

Kesira held back the rising gorge. Such a display was unthinkable and would dishonor not only her, but the memory of her Sisters and Gelya himself. She blinked away burning tears as she looked out over the destroyed nunnery. This place had been her life, her world, for fourteen years. Sister Fenelia had found her as a six-year-old wandering alone on the road, her parents killed by roving brigands. She had been formally accepted into the order when she was sixteen and for four years had studied the teachings of Gelya, learning and striving for the inner serenity and devotion required for attaining full status in the Order of Gelya.

Gone. Her world had been shattered and she didn't even understand why.

"Blinn. Go," insisted Zolkan.

"The altar," she said in an emotionless, shocky voice. "I want to see the altar. That which had been sacred to Gelya was untouched elsewhere. The altar will have survived."

Like one cut off from her senses, Kesira picked her way through the rubble and small fires burning in the debris and sought out the temple. It had been constructed of stone-wood and remained standing, but through the entryway she saw the unnatural whiteness of fire burning within.

Kesira stopped and peered inside. Four of her Sisters, all dead, knelt before the altar. Their faces were frozen in abject agony and their bodies permanently held in bondage to the white flame consuming the altar. Where once the nameless wildflower of Gelya had rested now danced a cold white flame. Kesira knew that to enter the temple meant suffering a fate like that of her Sisters.

She stared directly into the center of the white fire blazing so coldly and felt nothing. Not fear. Not hatred. Nothing. Kesira Minette had passed beyond simple emotion.

Chapter Two

KESIRA MINETTE turned and stumbled through the ruins
of the convent, unseeing, numb inside, not knowing or
caring about anything. Her blind footsteps took her to
a stone-wood structure that was hardly more than a
lean-to. She had spent much of her life inside this simple house, growing up, laughing, crying, meditating,
learning, finding friends, learning from Dominie Tredlo
of love and loving, finding others to share bed and
friendship.

Kesira went inside and found her straw-filled pallet
and lay down on it. Nothing else within the hut had
escaped destruction. All her belongings were singed and
charred and turned to ash. The rendering of her parents
done by Sister Dana had vanished in what had to be a
single puff of intense heat. Her ceramic sculptings had
been shattered. Of clothing there remained only burned
tatters.

The woman lay lack, eyes closed, and tried to meditate. Dominie Tredlo had taught her to overcome emotional storms, but none had been this severe since her
parents had been murdered. Kesira reached out for the
solace she'd always found before and it escaped her,

like sand through open fingers. The harder Kesira fought to retain the thread of her life, the more it knotted and broke into tiny fragments.

She didn't hear the heavy flapping of wings. She never saw Zolkan waddle into the hut and jump onto the scorched rung of a ruined chair.

"All gone," said the *trilla* bird. At Zolkan's words, she started, then forced herself back to a semblance of calmness.

"They're all dead," Kesira sobbed. Tears welled up. She fought them back and then stopped trying. Unashamedly she wept, for her Sisters, for the Order, for herself.

Zolkan began a soft crooning noise barely audible over the sound of her own sobs and the trip-hammering of her pulse in her head. She rolled onto her side, facing away from Zolkan, and gripped hard at the simple pillow on her pallet. Clutching it to her breast, Kesira fell into exhausted sleep.

The *trilla* bird's soothing, tuneless sounds fell to a whisper, less than a whisper, silence. Zolkan hopped to the ground and waddled out of the hut. The sound of powerful wings beating against the still twilight was lost on the sleeping Kesira.

She stood on a broad, featureless plain, all the world hers to inspect. Kesira turned north and saw legions marching, clouds of dust swirling about their heavily booted feet. To the east rose not one sun or two but dozens, burning brightly, blazing out to give an entire year's illumination in only one day. South? To the south lay only blackness, void, a soul-chilling emptiness that caused irrational panic to rise within her. But to the west lay true horror. From the west came the sounds of battle unlike anything the world had experienced.

Tremulous, Kesira looked over her right shoulder, then turned and faced the carnage squarely.

Demons, she moaned. *Demons battling demons!*

The ground beneath her shivered and began to stir like a beast awakening from a winter-long hibernation. Kesira tried to move and found her feet frozen to the spot. The small area of dirt all around her rippled with

insane life and began rising upward, to the sky, to a
point where Kesira stared down in abject fascination
on the battleground.

Demons fought one another, locked in individual
combat, but Kesira sensed sides forming, alliances being
negotiated and broken. This was no simple conflict.

Ayondela! screamed a male demon Kesira did not
recognize. The female demon named smiled and revealed inch-long fangs in an otherwise hauntingly
beautiful, delicately boned face. *Ayondela, I challenge
you. Never again will you work your intrigues!*

Lightning blasted forth from the male demon's hands.
Ayondela never flinched. The attack might never have
happened; Ayondela stood her ground in a sea of calm,
some protective magic turning aside the other demon's
most deadly thrusts.

My lover will deal with you! Ayondela acted as if the
other demon's taunts were little more than a fly buzzing
about her ears. But Kesira cried out in fear when she
saw Ayondela's fangs turning into the purest jade. The
female demon summoned powers far beyond those
understood by mortals. Kesira shielded her eyes by
throwing out her hands and turning her head—her
flesh turned transparent and her bones translucent. No
matter how she tried to look away from the ferocious
visage of Ayondela, Kesira saw.

She *saw* and she quaked inside.

Merrisen? bellowed the male demon. *You think I fear
Merrisen?*

Kesira felt the earth spinning around her, ever faster,
until she fell to her knees. The battle of demons spread
until it blotted out everything within her sight. And
Ayondela slowly sank to her knees, beaten down by the
male demon's awesome power.

Lenc, stop, stop or be banished! Another demon entered the boundless arena, one of commanding presence
and flashing eyes of pure jade.

Kesira tried to look away and couldn't. Something
inside her changed from fear to—what? The woman
tingled as she looked at the newcomer, savoring the
demon's sleek form, reveling in his authority, desiring
his sexuality.

The last to appear, eh, Merrisen? I did not think you

would allow Ayondela to bear the brunt of my attack.
The demon called Lenc spun from kneeling Ayondela
and sent fresh sheets of lightning slashing toward Merrisen.

Kesira wept for Merrisen. His noble features contorted with effort as Lenc used ploy after ploy to engage
him. Merrisen's responses to the renegade demon were
those of a superior to a subordinate, but Kesira's fear
mounted. This time she feared not for herself but for
Merrisen. The demon's jade eyes blazed with pure light,
honest light. Taller and more powerfully muscled than
most mortals, Merrisen fought in demonic ways. And
Kesira knew he was losing to Lenc.

She tried to warn Merrisen, to tell him of the error
of his defenses. She tried to focus clearly on Lenc and
find that demon's weakness to communicate to Merrisen, but her vision fogged and Lenc danced behind a
shimmering curtain that hid his features and actions.
All she saw was the repeated lightning attacks.

Goodbye, Merrisen, said Lenc.

You are premature, Merrisen said, the words grating
harshly.

Kesira tried to reach out to Merrisen, to warn him
that he was failing, just as Ayondela had failed, that
Lenc's trickery subverted whatever defenses he used.
Merrisen continued to stand firmly, a dominant figure
fending off Lenc's potent thrusts. But Kesira saw the
true attack coming in a more subtle fashion. By the
time Merrisen realized that something was amiss, it
was too late.

Lenc laughed, his booming cries echoing across all
eternity. Merrisen spun about, twisting and turning as
cold white flame burned at his feet, at his knees, at
waist and torso and finally at his noble head. Lost in
a pillar of arctic fire, Merrisen screamed and writhed
until Kesira wept for him. The doings of demons lay
beyond her ken, but Merrisen exuded goodness. A spark
of emotion bound her to Merrisen and caused the hurt
of his demise to be even greater for her.

*Die, Merrisen. Never again shall I bend my knee to
you!* Lenc's shimmering form stilled for the final death-
giving thrust.

The sky darkened, then turned to the purest jade

green. The pillar of white flame lapped about Merrisen's body and caused the demon intense agony. Lenc's magicks coalesced about Merrison and turned his enemy to jade, the precious gem sacred to the demons.

Kesira cried out as Lenc shattered Merrisen's body and sent the tiny shards cascading downward to the ground. But the woman held the outpouring of woe in check; she had seen Ayondela's slight motion the instant before Merrisen's destruction.

Kesira had never before seen a demon or even heard of Merrisen, but her heart had been captured by him in the span of a single human breath. The rain of green jade that had once been Merrisen's body fell in slow motion, but Kesira knew that Merrisen had not perished as Lenc believed. Ayondela had accomplished some small rescue.

Merrisen! Kesira called out, but she received no answer.

The woman stirred and thrashed about, her hand banging into the side of the hut. Bleary-eyed, she realized she had slept and dreamed. Pulling the thin blanket around her, Kesira rolled over on her pallet and went back to sleep.

The dreams were at an end. This time she rested body and spirit.

"Eat," ordered Zolkan, dropping the piece of burned meat into Kesira's lap. The woman sat up in her simple bed and looked at what had once been some animal's scrawny haunch. The sight sickened her; she couldn't help thinking of the incinerated bodies of her Sisters strewn about the convent.

"I don't want it," she said.

"Eat," said Zolkan. "Food and strength."

Reluctantly she nodded and picked up the meat. The taste offended her, but Kesira knew better than to go against Zolkan when he was in such a mood. Soon enough she had eaten the meat, broken open the bone and sucked forth the marrow and even licked off her fingers. She had been hungrier than she thought—or less fastidious.

"I had the oddest dream," she told the *trilla* bird.

"Demons fighting. I recognized Ayondela—no other demon sports such fangs."

"Others?" asked Zolkan, wings lightly flapping to
hold himself on the back of the solitary chair in the
room.

"Did I recognize any other demon? No," she said
slowly, remembering Merrisen. "But one was oddly
compelling. Only the sight of him made me feel—different."

"How?"

"That, Zolkan, is something I cannot tell you. Just
...different." Kesira fought back a wave of confusion
as she thought of Merrisen and his fight against the
other demon. Merrisen had been handsome beyond
compare, strong, yet unlike most demons. She knew
that with innate certainty. His ways were not devious.
Merrisen's honesty shone forth through the green-
glowing eyes like a lantern in the night.

"Who else?" squawked the bird. Both beady black
eyes fixed on her, shaking Kesira out of her reverie.
Still, forcing Merrisen's image from her mind was difficult. She felt as if a seed had been planted within her
simply by looking at him, and that seed was blossoming
into something special, something fine and wondrous.

"Lenc, they called him. I never saw him clearly. He
hid behind a curtain of heat."

"Curtain?"

"That's a poor description. In the desert to the east,
you've seen the heat radiating upward from the sand?
You know how it distorts shapes and alters your sense
of proportion?"

"More," demanded Zolkan. He blinked his heavily
lidded eyes and clacked the serrated edges of his beak,
urging Kesira to speak further about this.

"I never saw this demon Lenc. But Ayondela and
Merrisen. They were gorgeous."

"Omen? Premonition?" Zolkan jumped into the air
and beat his wings to land beside Kesira on the bed.
Twisting his head upward the bird studied her.

Kesira frowned. What did this matter to the *trilla*
bird? Zolkan had swept into her life and she knew so
little about him. His tales were witty and pungent, he
had flown over much of the world and had spoken of it

to her, and she knew next to nothing of him. Sister
Fenelia had told her, as a young child, of messengers
sent by the demons to warn and inform, but Fenelia
had also added that these were probably just folk tales.

Kesira wondered now. What *was* Zolkan?

"What more tell?" Zolkan repeated.

"I saw Ayondela and she was stunning," said Kesira,
remembering vividly now. "No mortal being was ever
so radiant or gorgeous. And perhaps no other demon."

"Merrisen?"

"Perhaps Merrisen," admitted Kesira.

"What of Merrisen!" squawked Zolkan. "Tell of Merrisen. Harmed?"

"Destroyed," Kesira said in a voice so low even she
barely heard it. "Lenc caught him in a pillar of cold,
white fire and turned him into pure jade. Then Lenc
shattered Merrisen and sent the pieces raining down..."
Kesira's eyes widened as she spoke.

"Raining down! The burning droplets of green rain!
That was Merrisen! I somehow dreamed of what happened to Merrisen. A vision," she said, mind racing.
"Sent by Ayondela, perhaps. She implied that she and
Merrisen were lovers." Kesira's heart skipped a beat
as she said that. All her training evaporated and she
envied Ayondela. The Order preached that envy was a
slayer of the soul, that jealousy had no rightful place
in the human heart, that inner tranquillity came only
through meditation and duty.

Kesira Minette had thought she had banished envy
and jealousy through the years of training. Now she
found they had only been hidden away, unused. She
envied Ayondela her apparent relationship with Merrisen. And more. Kesira was jealous of her, as if *she*
were Merrisen's lover and Ayondela a harlot.

"A true vision," said Zolkan. "Few are sent, even
fewer acted upon."

"Acted upon?" asked Kesira, shaking her head. "I
saw a battle among demons, nothing more. There is no
way I can act on anything I saw. If Merrisen has been
destroyed, there is nothing I can do. I saw what was,
not what will be." The woman looked around her simple
stone-wood hut, past Zolkan and out into the compound
of the Order.

Destruction lay everywhere she gazed. If her dreams had been true vision sent by Ayondela, there was nothing Kesira could do. Piece together the jade shards along the road and reform Merrisen? As absurd as this struck her, nevertheless hope flared for a moment in her breast. Then she shook her head. It had taken years of meditation to bring out her personal limitations; Kesira knew them intimately now. As much as she desired Merrisen, as much as she wished for the demon to again be whole, she saw no possible way of reuniting the jade pieces that had rained down.

Even if she succeeded in finding all the pieces—itself an impossibility—would Merrisen become reanimated? Would the handsome demon again flourish and love and...

Kesira forced it from her mind. She sighed deeply and heaved herself to her feet.

"Come along, Zolkan. We must leave. There is nothing here for us. Not now." Kesira looked at the temple as she emerged into the warm, sunlit day and shuddered. Inside burned the flame of Lenc. Had that demon destroyed the Order's patron, also?

"Gelya dead," said Zolkan. "Lenc has ambitions too great to contain."

"Gelya?" she asked in a vague voice. "Oh, yes, Gelya. I suppose you are right. Gelya would never allow another to usurp his domain."

"Gelya foolish," said the *trilla* bird with a hint of anger in his words.

"Don't say that," snapped Kesira. "He is—was—patron of my Order. As such, I owe him allegiance, obeisance. I have my duty to perform. Honor requires it."

"Gelya gone."

"I don't know that. I...I must be sure. I'll go to another nunnery and find out."

"All gone," insisted Zolkan. "Lenc grows too powerful. All Gelya's worshipers gone, too."

"I remain," Kesira said firmly. She packed what few pitiful items she could salvage. With the blanket rolled to hold precious little more than wisps of straw ticking, Kesira took her staff in hand and began marching down the road. Only once did she look back—and immediately regretted it. A tear formed in her eye and memories flooded over her like the crystal waves of an ocean.

"Wounded man in road," said Zolkan. "Needs you. Needs help. Remember him?"

Kesira's eyes went wide with horror. "Oh, Zolkan, I *had* forgotten! He might be dead by now. I left him to find Sister Enola. And she's dead." Kesira swallowed hard and forced her mind to calmness. Old meditation techniques came to her aid to ease the hurt caused by the memory.

"Need friends. Many friends, when Lenc comes."

"You think this demon will actually try to walk among mortals? Why? Demons live in realms far finer than this." Kesira waved her hand out over the valley, pointed to the mountains, indicated the small stream running quietly toward the River Pharna and thence to the ocean.

"Strange dealings occur," was all Zolkan said.

Kesira had no answer for that. It was as obvious as the fact she had lost home and friends and what security she had. Virtually without money, Kesira had no good prospects open to her. The Order had been more than family; it provided an anchor in the world.

"An anchor," she said aloud. "I still have it. Gelya might be dead, but his teachings live within me. I have more than my faith, I have training and will and ability."

Zolkan landed heavily on her shoulder and peered at her without saying a word, but somehow Kesira knew the bird agreed. Her human friends had perished through the demon's attack, but her feathered one supported her. With that thought, Kesira was amazed at how lightly she stepped down the road toward the spot where the injured youth had been.

"He's still alive," she said in wonder. "In spite of those hideous wounds, he lives."

"Tend him," said Zolkan, flapping off her shoulder to land on a nearby tree limb. From his perch, the *trilla* bird was able to survey both road and the tiny depression where the youth lay. Seeing him thus, Kesira knew no brigand could sneak up on them. Zolkan's eyes were almost as sharp as his talons and beak.

"I have so little knowledge," she said, wiping dirt from the youth's forehead. "And your wounds require so much."

Kesira Minette did not shirk from her self-imposed duties. She set the youth's fractured limbs, splinted them, bandaged the gaping wounds and then meditated to bring out from the depths of her mind lost snippets of medical lore. At first she tried too hard and nothing came. Then, relaxing fully, focusing on her inner self and entering the drifting state, Kesira floated along and allowed tiny bits of half-understood medical lore to bob to the surface. She followed the bouncing, dodging facts and slowly pulled them in, integrated them into wholes, discovered, reconstructed, learned.

When she opened her eyes and turned back to the injured man, Kesira knew more of what to do for him.

Slowly, the youth healed. All except for the missing tongue. To remedy that Kesira found no anodyne.

Kesira looked over at the youth, sitting cross-legged near the stream. She shook her head in wonder at how completely the wounds mended. While it had been more than a month since her nunnery had been destroyed by Lenc, Kesira knew such terrible injuries ought to have permanently crippled the youth. She said as much to Zolkan.

The *trilla* bird flapped wings and dangled upside down from an overhanging tree limb.

"Magicks," he suggested. "Left from destruction."

"You think he somehow taps into the power of a demon?"

The bird squawked and shook all over, dropping and righting itself expertly in midair to land feet first on the ground. Zolkan waddled about and finally hopped up to Kesira's shoulder, his beak just inches from her ear.

"He touches jade. It glows!"

She had seen the youth picking up and discarding the shards of jade lying around the area and had noted the strange response in the magical material.

"Perhaps you're right, that such contact heals him. It is a pity about his tongue. He seems such an intelligent boy."

"Man."

Kesira laughed at the bird. "It's all a matter of definition. But something is not right with him. I feel it. I try to get close to him and he draws away. Even after all this time, he still hasn't told me his name, much less anything of his past."

Kesira fell silent as the youth rose from his spot near the stream and came to join her. Their eyes met and Kesira fought away the sensation that she knew him. But that was not possible. The only place outside of the nunnery she had traveled for any length of time was Blinn, and she would have remembered him had they met.

Cleaned and mostly healed, the youth presented a fine figure. He stood a head taller than she, without the hint of stoop Kesira had begun to develop from long hours poring over tomes to learn the philosophy of Gelya. Muscles now rippled under only slightly scarred skin and dark eyes danced with intelligence and a humor forever hidden by the lack of tongue. Kesira thought he would have been a wondrous storyteller from the way he gestured and moved; without a tongue, he was a mere curiosity.

In the dirt he scratched out a small message indicating he had caught fish for their supper.

•"Good," Kesira said, smiling. She reached out and lightly touched his hand. He jerked it away. "Please," Kesira said, "don't be this way. You know Zolkan and I are friends. We would not have aided you were this not so."

He shook his head, a shock of raven hair falling forward. A quick toss of his head got the hair from his eyes.

"Friends?" asked Kesira, holding both palms out and turned toward the sky. The youth reached out and hesitantly placed his own hands atop hers. "Good. And thank you for the trust."

He pulled away his hands and immediately traced out characters in the dirt. Kesira moved beside him to better read what had been written. He looked up, fear etched on the handsome face as he hurriedly erased what had been there, only to construct new letters more carefully. At first the word made no sense, then Kesira smiled. For almost a month she had not known his name.

"You are Molimo?" she asked. He nodded vigorously. Giving of his name obviously accounted for a great deal of trust on his part. She knew this was not what he had first written, but this mattered little to her. Molimo might be a brigand with an Emperor's reward on his head. While she had a duty to the Emperor, she saw nothing wrong in aiding Molimo as long as she did not know for certain. Kesira had heard of cultures where names were used as weapons against their bearer, but such was not her creed. If Molimo worried about this, she had to respect his beliefs.

He wrote again. She gently rested a hand on his shoulder and said, "Yes, I am Kesira and this is my winged friend Zolkan."

She thought the *trilla* bird would speak up, but Zolkan stayed uncharacteristically quiet.

Kesira asked Molimo, "You were near my nunnery. Did you see what happened?" His reaction startled her. If he had been frightened, she would have understood. Or angry. That made sense to her. Anyone so badly injured by the demon's attack had to feel rage. But the response she sensed deep within Molimo was one of darkness, of impenetrable otherness. It was as if she peered into a deep well and caught only subliminal hints concerning what lay within.

He wrote simply, "I saw nothing."

"Did you lose your tongue at some earlier time? The wound seemed fresh."

"Then," Molimo wrote. Kesira trained her every sense on the youth. Molimo's reaction again struck a discordant note within her. Somehow, the demon Lenc had ripped out Molimo's tongue, had brutalized him and left him more dead than alive, and Molimo did not respond. His face remained composed, and Kesira saw no sign of nervousness about him. The only time she had, in fact, had been when he had first written his name in the dirt and erased it before she had the opportunity to read it.

"Are you a brigand? Is there a price on your head?" Molimo emphatically denied this.

Kesira considered Molimo and all she knew of him—

what little she knew of him. Meditation techniques sharpened her senses and allowed tiny hints to enter her brain that otherwise would have been missed. And always came the *feeling* of otherness.

"Did you belong to an Order? Were you a worshiper of any particular deity?"

A broad smile crossed Molimo's face. Kesira imagined the laughter rushing forth, deep and resonant from the depths of his thick chest—if he'd had a tongue to form the laugh. Molimo shook his head.

"Tell me of yourself. There is so much I want to know of you."

"Why?" Molimo wrote.

"Friends," cut in Zolkan. "We all alone like you."

Molimo considered this for a while, then slowly began writing in the dirt. Kesira read the tale one line at a time, erasing what she'd finished to provide Molimo with more room for further details.

"How awful!" she cried. "A geas by one of the demons?" She saw him bob his head quickly. "Lenc? The one who destroyed the convent?" Molimo's head almost came unhinged as he emphatically agreed to this.

"He victim, like us," said Zolkan. "Befriend him. Need him."

"I agree," said Kesira, her heart going out to the youth. "What is the nature of the geas? Do you know or is it something you have only sensed?" This accounted for the bleakness she'd found within Molimo, but did little to explain his acceptance of his situation.

Hand shaking for the first time, Molimo traced out the single word, "Kill!"

Kesira's eyes widened as she looked at what had been a handsome young man. The strong hand wavered amid a viscous flowing of flesh and reformed as a thin, hairy paw. The rest of the body altered even faster, transforming Molimo into a huge, slavering wolf. Kesira rocked back, staring into red-rimmed eyes and trying to keep her composure in the face of long, chipped, yellowed teeth.

Molimo rocked back on powerful haunches for the leap that would carry him to Kesira's vulnerable throat.

Chapter Three

KESIRA MINETTE looked into the fangs of death. Molimo's entire body had altered into that of a wolf intent on ripping out her throat. Just as the beast leaped, Kesira dropped down and rolled to one side. Hot breath and wetness gusted alongside her head as the wolf twisted in mid-leap trying to bury teeth into her flesh.

"Stop!" cried out Zolkan. The *trilla* bird flapped aloft and hovered a few feet off the ground. Kesira kept rolling and came to her feet, staff in hand, startled at the bird's courage on her behalf. It fluttered to and fro, keeping itself between her and the wolf—Molimo.

"I can handle this, Zolkan," she said in a soft voice. She stilled her harsh breathing and settled into fighting readiness. The Order of Gelya did not permit the use of steel weapons, but that did not mean she was unarmed. If anything, she was better defended than if she possessed the finest steel sword. With only stone-wood staff, Kesira could never feel overconfident against an enemy this strong and ferocious.

In knowing she might die at any slight misstep lay Kesira's greatest strength. Her mind moved slower and slower as she prepared for conflict. She did not antici-

pate the wolf's movements, she responded to them. She
did not seek out weaknesses, she created them. Molimo
launched himself full-length through the air, once more
intent on tearing her throat to bloody ribbons.

The staff rose and crashed squarely on the side of
the wolf's head. The sickening crunch of stone-wood
against skull and the vibration along the length of the
staff shook Kesira. She threw off such feeling and became—nothing.

Responding smoothly, moving well and using her
staff to full advantage kept the wolf at bay—and more.
Tiny bruises appeared and the gray fur became mottled
with streaks of red. Kesira forced herself not to think
of this animal as the youth she had nursed back to
health. Molimo had become submerged through the geas
laid upon him by Lenc and was not responsible for this
attack.

"Stop!" again shrieked Zolkan. Oddly, the bird's plea
stayed the wolf. Tongue lolling out one side of its mouth,
the wolf hunkered down and lay with its head on outstretched paws, as docile as any trained dog. But the
big, red-rimmed eyes peering up at her convinced
Kesira that the wolf was not tamed, but only waiting.

Zolkan flapped forward and landed inches in front
of the wolf's mouth. The beast revealed deadly fangs,
but the *trilla* bird paid them no heed.

"Careful, Zolkan," said Kesira. "The change is complete. You aren't talking to Molimo any longer. This is
a wild animal."

The *trilla* bird waddled forward, green-feathered tail
dragging in the dirt behind. He shoved his beak close
to the wolf's ear and began squawking in a manner
unfamiliar to Kesira. In the time she'd known Zolkan,
she thought she'd heard every possible sound the bird
could utter. This monologue combined the normal
squawks with a singsong lilt that hypnotized her. She
felt herself gliding along in the patterns revealed by
the nonwords, finding realms as yet unexplored in her
mind.

Kesira snapped out of the trance as her training
rose to the surface and provided a brief barricade for
Zolkan's sounds. She blinked and sat back, staff in hand,

and watched in wonder as Zolkan continued to soothe and beguile the wolf.

As quickly as the change had come upon Molimo, so did he return to human form. Kesira watched as features flowed and turned human. A panting, flushed Molimo lay on his belly, chin on forearms. Tears leaked from the corners of his eyes and dripped wetly to the ground where thirsty dust sucked them up.

"Molimo," cried Kesira, moving to kneel by him. "Are you all right? Did I hurt you?"

Tears of shame ran down Molimo's cheeks in steady rivers now. He hid his face.

"Don't be afraid—or embarrassed. This was not your doing. You are under a demon's spell."

He looked up, nodding as if his head was fastened to a spring. He quickly scribbled in the dirt, "Thank you for knowing. I cannot help myself."

"We are your friends. We understand," said Kesira, hand moving over his sweat-lank black hair. As she'd calm a wild animal, so Kesira calmed Molimo. He finally pulled away, rolled over and sat up, arms clutching his knees.

"You did well," spoke up Zolkan. "Good man. You good woman."

"Your bravery is appreciated, also, Zolkan. I had not expected you to come to my aid in such a way."

The *trilla* bird flapped to her shoulder and perched, one white-ringed eye close to hers. "Much happens in land. Must unite forces. Keep alert. Be brave."

Kesira helped Molimo down to the stream where she gently washed him clean of the new layer of dirt and blood she had helped put on him. The wounds inflicted by her staff were minimal, but certain bruises on his shoulders and hips and neck would begin to stiffen in a few hours. Kesira made a salve from the tubers sacred to Gelya and applied it to Molimo's black and blue spots. The youth shuddered slightly and curled up, a small smile on his lips. He slept.

Kesira quietly left him and went to a secluded spot with Zolkan.

She turned and looked at the bird and said, "What do you know of Molimo?"

"No tongue. Wolf changer. No more."

"You're lying to me. For the first time, Zolkan, I know you are lying."

"No lie!" protested the *trilla* bird.

Kesira did not argue with the bird. Zolkan's outlook on the world was broader than hers, more sophisticated due to greater experience, but she knew he lied to her. The *feel* of deception rang in her head as the bird spoke. She simply put this aside for further meditation.

"We are faced with new problems," she said.

"Molimo cannot control self."

"That is only one of them. I have meditated and do solemnly believe that Gelya has perished because of Lenc's attack. All that I have lived for is gone. His teachings remain as legacy, but the fountainhead is departed."

"True."

Kesira worried over the exact nature of Zolkan's knowledge. What did the bird know and conceal from her?

"I feel that, though Gelya is no more, the teachings are necessary and ought to be carried on. I propose we go to the City of Sin where the Order maintains a small chapel. Ranking members of the Order can advise me how to proceed."

"Join them in City of Sin?" squawked Zolkan.

"Yes," she said with an odd mixture of dread and anticipation. Never before had Kesira thought of traveling so far from the convent. Now, after the omens and the demon-strike and finding Molimo, she discovered that her haven had been a prison. She *wanted* to explore the world and find all she had missed because she had been held within the Order's *renn*-stone walls. Gone were security and enforced tranquillity; replacing them came a headier composition of excitement and change and renewed confidence in herself and her training.

"This is what Sister Fenelia meant," mused Kesira. "She said one day I would know peace instead of only being shown it."

"You believe this peaceful?" asked Zolkan, strong wings flapping in dismay.

"I believe I can cope with it. While within the Order I fantasized of being outside, but it was only a dream, a self-induced illusion. Now that I know I cannot return—ever—I find my training adequate, that I carry with me my own tranquillity. I do not need it forced upon me by others. It is mine!"

The *trilla* bird sputtered and took to wing. Kesira watched him leave, turning into a green dot against the cloudless sky and then vanishing altogether. His departure did not trouble her. She was complete within herself. Sister Fenelia and Dominie Tredlo and the others had forged well.

Kesira Minette returned to the side of the stream where Molimo slept, preparing their provisions for the trek to Chounabel, the City of Sin.

"Will you fly for a while?" Kesira asked irritably. "You're heavy enough and riding on my shoulder all these miles weighs me down." She glanced sideways at Zolkan, asleep with his head tucked under one wing. The woman knew the bird only feigned sleep; the normal tensing and relaxing of his talons when he slept hadn't occurred for miles. He had been awake and only wanted a free ride.

"Tired," the bird mumbled from under his wing.

"We've been on the road for over a week. Do you not think Molimo and I are tired, also? We've been eating nothing more than insects and half-ripe berries and we're still not clear of the mountains yet."

Even as Kesira complained, she felt a twinge of sorrow at leaving behind the Yearn Mountains. They were the place of her birth, her nunnery, all that had ever happened in her life. All too soon "home" would be behind her. Chounabel lay many more days' travel out on the Plains of Roggen, and Kesira longed for adequate food now, before tackling that foot-wearying distance. She also longed for some hope of being able to return to the Yearns after she had contacted the Order in the city. The food would be the easier to find.

"Let Molimo hunt."

"No!" she cried, adamantly opposed to Molimo shapechanging simply to hunt meat for her. Kesira loathed the sight of the transformed youth and believed that the more times Molimo changed, the harder it would be for him to return to human form.

"All eat."

"You get aloft and find us something, then," ordered Kesira. "Stop complaining and bring us some small game."

Pinions cracking, Zolkan spread his wings, shook so hard that a few green feathers floated to the ground, then launched himself. Kesira winced as the talons dug into her shoulder, but the relief of losing the *trilla* bird's bulk more than compensated for the tiny pain. She turned to see Molimo close behind, eyes on the soaring bird.

"A noble sight, isn't he, Molimo?"

The youth bobbed his head, then stopped, looked left and right and spun animallike to peer behind.

"Molimo, no!" she called. "Don't change form. Resist!"

He made gurgling noises and pointed behind them, but retained his human shape.

"What is it?" Kesira dropped the blanket in which she'd wrapped what pitiful provisions they carried. She rubbed her hands clean on her robe and hefted her staff.

She felt the pounding of hooves through the ground. Kesira guessed that at least five riders approached, perhaps more. On the trail to the plains she expected to find many fellow travelers, and perhaps even a caravan allowing itinerates to join. But this spring she encountered none on the road, contrary to all Dominie Tredlo had told her.

Kesira knew a bad omen without having to be told. And the riders came too hard, too fast, to be on legitimate business. They rode to overtake her.

"Molimo, go hide yourself. There, in that gulley. Hurry!"

The youth shook his head. He moved closer to her, bare arms gleaming in the bright noonday sunlight. Her heart reached out to him, and she felt a quickening of her pulse. Molimo's physical wounds still troubled him, but there was nothing wrong with his courage or devotion.

"Hey-up!" cried out the leading rider as he reined to a halt. Tall in the saddle, broad ashoulder and impressively thewed, the man said nothing to her as his cold blue eyes bored to the core of her soul.

Kesira turned aside this impersonal, even brutal stare. She feared no man.

"Good day, sir," she called out. "Are you and your men riding to Chounabel?"

The rider motioned for the six men with him to advance and dismount. While one held the reins, the other five approached Kesira on foot. Well out of range of her staff, they fanned out in a semicircle and stopped, hands on weapons.

"You need not fear me," Kesira said. "I am a nun of the Order of Gelya. I seek only peace. This is my friend, Molimo."

"Fear you?" roared the brigands' leader from astride his horse. "We don't *fear* you. We are going to *rape* you. There's been scant pickings since the skies poured forth their jade shit."

"Go on your way," Kesira said. Terror begged for release within her. Mind-calming rituals prevented any hint of panic from showing.

"She's a feisty one. We will enjoy using her for many days," said the man on the far right of Kesira. He wore a wolfskin cape tossed back over his left shoulder. Brass-studded leather straps crisscrossed his powerful chest and held a sheathed sword on either hip. He swaggered forward and raised his left fist above his head. "I, Kalash of Chounabel, do claim first use of this one." He swiveled from the hips, feet planted firmly, and looked up at his leader.

"You have done well for us," the leader said. "Does any dispute Kalash's claim to this one?"

Molimo made a half-choking noise, the best he could do without a tongue to properly articulate the words of anger he futilely tried to utter.

"Oh, look at this one. No tongue. Think he might be the young pup we slashed the tongue from last month?" Kalash laughed as if he'd made the best joke imaginable.

Kesira reached out and held Molimo back. "They *seek* to anger you—lose your temper and lose the battle. We have nothing to fear from them. Be calm."

"Do you stay calm when you feel a man inside you?" demanded Kalash. "Or are you a virgin? Will I be the first? A true feast you set before me, Baram."

The brigand chief smirked and silently indicated Kalash ought to take his prize.

Kesira stepped away from Molimo and spun her staff about her body, creating a solid wall of stone-wood. It spun and whirled and whistled through the air, never out of control, always directed toward Kalash. When one tip of the staff caught the brigand on the side of the head, he dropped to his knees and bellowed.

Baram said, "It is unlike you to allow such a slip of a girl to best you, Kalash. Perhaps Storn Ribcracker is a better choice for being first."

Kalash roared like a wounded bull and got to his feet. Kesira quickly stepped forward, staff swinging, and caught him behind the right knee. Again he tumbled to the ground—but this time he did not stay there. Kalash rolled and came to his feet, drawing both swords in a smooth snick-snick motion. For the first time, Kesira had doubts about her own ability. This man lived by dint of strength and fighting ability. If he had ever made a mistake he would have been sliced open and left for the dogs. That he stood menacing her now proved his skill with the twin swords.

Kesira glanced at Molimo and found her repose once more. Something about the youth engendered within her breast an almost maternal feeling of protectiveness. Molimo would lose more than his tongue if left to these brigands.

Fear conquered, Kesira fought, using the emptiness within her as an ally. She did not anticipate movement, she responded. Her defense proved too great for Kalash, and she soon backed him toward his horse, her staff singing its deadly song. He parried an overhead blow with crossed swords; in the same movement that brought the staff downward, Kesira spun and faced away from Kalash and lifted the other end of the staff so that it destroyed his groin.

He gave a choked gasp and fell face forward, unconscious.

Even before Kalash had been taken from the fray, the one named Storn advanced, holding a small round shield and sword against her staff. Kesira fought and eventually drove the butt end of her staff squarely into

Storn's eye, killing him amid a geyser of sundered eyeball and crimson blood.

The other three came for her simultaneously. Reaching the end of her physical strength, Kesira retreated—and despaired even more when she felt new hoofbeats vibrating through the ground. It wasn't enough to fell two of the brigands. More came to swell their rank.

Or did they?

The sight of Baram rising in his stirrups to peer out heartened her. Whoever rode in this direction was not part of the brigand band. But her flare of hope quickly faded into nothingness as she concentrated on the flow of battle. Holding three armed and well-trained fighters at bay proved increasingly difficult as they coordinated their efforts.

The one on the far right succeeded in getting a shield edge under her staff to swing it up and away. The brigand next to him rushed and caught Kesira around the waist, lifting her off her feet and throwing her heavily to the hard ground. His weight pinned her down—but for only a split second.

Kesira heard an inarticulate cry of rage as Molimo grabbed the brigand by the throat and lifted him bodily in a show of strength so impressive that the fight momentarily halted. Molimo tossed the brigand away with a crushed windpipe and turned to one of the two fighters left.

"Haieee!" cried the one who had so successfully used the shield against Kesira's staff. The shield edge rose and crashed into the point of Molimo's chin. The youth's dark eyes rolled up in his head, and he crumbled to the ground like a mud building melting in the rain.

"Now you are mine," gloated the surviving brigand, towering over her. Kesira kicked out and connected squarely with the man's kneecap, but to no avail. A brass greaves protected him. He dropped, pinning her to the ground.

Kesira's mind turned blank; no fear paralyzed her. She waited for the opportunity to strike out most effectively at eyes, at throat, at groin. The battle tactic had changed now and her blows changed with it.

Through the ground she felt the single horse thundering closer. Before she struck out to blind the man fumbling at her robe to expose her to his lustful advances, the rider crested a small rise. All eyes fixed on him, Kesira's included.

Sunlight glinted off the man's armored left arm and the sword so casually held in his right. A curiously formed steel helm protected both sides of his head, with a single protecting strip dropping between his eyes.

"Baram, isn't it? You are far afield today. You're intruding into my territory."

"Begone, Rouvin," bellowed Baram. "We came upon her first."

Kesira's heart almost exploded in her breast when she saw a spot of green moving along Rouvin's armored limb.

"Zolkan!" she cried.

The *trilla* bird took wing and hovered just out of reach of the brigands' waving swords. But it was the rider, Rouvin, who proved the most effective. With a loud battle cry, he put spurs to his horse's flanks and charged forward, long blade humming through the air. One pass removed Kesira's assailant's right ear, allowing her to finish him off with a single blow to the throat. But Rouvin never slowed his pace, galloping directly for Baram.

Their steel blades met and sent electric sparks blasting skyward. Kesira didn't see what followed, but Baram sagged in his saddle and fell forward, arms weakly holding onto his horse's neck. Rouvin laid the flat of his blade across the horse's rump and sent it racing across the plains.

Of the brigands left, Zolkan plucked the eye from one and the other took to his heels and fled.

Rouvin trotted back and mockingly bowed. "Good lady, it is my extreme pleasure to be of service to one so fair—and brave." Sharp blue eyes took in the brigands Kesira had felled before he had ridden to her rescue.

"My thanks, and those of my friends," she said. Kesira turned immediately to Molimo, who stirred weakly. She ran light, probing fingers over his chin and found the bone intact. It had been nothing more than the shock of the shield edge striking him that had knocked

Molimo unconscious. His ebony eyes flickered open. Kesira stroked his cheek, then stood to face Rouvin.

The rider dismounted and looked over the fallen thieves, taking their purses and whatever else struck his fancy. He caught Kesira's disapproving gaze and said, "It does them no good—and think on how they obtained it."

"Shouldn't the spoils be mine, by right of battle?" she asked.

"Can you take them from me?" he asked, his tone bantering, but a deadlier undercurrent running beneath the words.

"They are yours," Kesira said.

"Nonsense," Rouvin contradicted. "We split evenly."

"Even?" squawked Zolkan, fluttering down to rest on Rouvin's left arm. "My share?"

"Even yours, Zolkan."

"Did the bird summon you?" asked Kesira.

"In a manner of speaking. We got to talking, discovered mutual friends in Chounabel, your name dropped into the conversation and I rode to beg your permission to accompany you to the city."

"Beg?" Kesira said, one eyebrow arching.

"That is something of an error in wording," said Rouvin. "Rouvin the Stout never begs. For anything." His eyes hotly worked over the figure now only partially hidden by a tattered robe.

"I am Kesira, of the Order of Gelya," she said. "I am a nun on my way to Chounabel to seek out others of my sect."

Kesira almost laughed aloud when she saw Rouvin's face freeze at the mention of her religious order.

"Celibacy is not part of Gelya's teachings," she said. Rouvin's face once more flowed, this time into the lustful ways it had shown before. Kesira added, with just the right amount of disdain, "Promiscuity is not part of the teaching, either."

"We must discuss this further," said Rouvin. "For the moment, however, it is better that we ride quickly for Chounabel. Baram is sorely injured, but he has shown incredible resiliency in the past."

"You two are friends?" she asked.

"Friends?" he scoffed. "Mortal enemies is closer to

the truth. I wander the Roggen Plains, going from city to city. Baram seeks out only the weak and robs them."

"You professional savior?" Zolkan squawked from his vantage point just above Rouvin's elbow.

"That is an interesting description. Can a weary traveler be anything but grateful if I chase off Baram? Grateful in terms of gold and trinkets and—" Rouvin's deep blue eyes fixed on Kesira's beauty once again "—other prizes fit for the Emperor?"

"An exciting life you lead," Kesira said, helping Molimo to his feet. "Our friend is without a tongue. Brigands, no doubt. Or professional saviors."

Rouvin stared at the youth and frowned. Pushing back his helm for a clearer view, Rouvin studied Molimo as if he were a specimen awaiting identification by a botany student.

"He is familiar," Rouvin said. "What is his name?"

"Molimo," spoke up Zolkan, the name coming quickly to the bird's beak. "Good boy, good boy."

"Quiet, bird." Rouvin's gaze never wavered. Molimo returned it unflinchingly. "He is *very* familiar. When did you happen onto him?"

"Just after the demons fought," said Kesira. "You are aware of that battle? It brought down the walls of my Order."

"Aware?" laughed Rouvin. "Of course I am aware of it whenever demons battle. I am half-demon myself."

Kesira stiffened as she looked up at Rouvin. The blue eyes began to sparkle and dance—and shone forth with a faint green light.

Chapter Four

"A DEMON?" she asked in a voice barely audible. The way Rouvin's eyes glowed the telltale jade green left no doubt in Kesira Minette's mind, but the words had still escaped her lips unbidden.

"Half-demon," Rouvin admitted. "My mother is Ayondela and my father, well, he was a mercenary." A tinge of bitterness entered Rouvin's voice when he spoke of his father. "He had accepted assignment in an army Ayondela recruited."

"You are half-demon," Kesira said, accepting and trying to find the proper way of relating this fact to the man in front of her. "I know nothing of demons."

"Yet you are a student of Gelya, one of the foremost of all the demons," said Rouvin. "Granted, Gelya's a bit heavy on philosophy—or was. He is now dead."

"What is this battle that brings the demons back to this world?" asked Kesira. "Never have I heard of such a thing."

Rouvin laughed sharply, almost barking in derision. "You do not hear of it, but it happens all too often. The demons play among themselves and when that grows too tedious, they seek out mortals for a moment's diversion. They find us quite amusing, just like pets."

"But you are one of them."

Rouvin shook his head. "I am neither. I am stronger than most mortals, yet am not immortal. I carry the aspects of demon power and have no control of it. My eyes? You've seen them. That is the only outward sign I am other than mortal."

"Your mother taught you so little?" marveled Kesira. "No magicks, no spells?"

"Nothing. As soon as I slid from her body she discarded me. I was nothing more than a toy, an amusement to relieve the tedium of eternity. Still, I hold some small affection for her. She is, after all is said and done, my mother."

"A demon," said Kesira, still trying to decide what this meant.

Rouvin laughed, this time with genuine amusement, and said, "You have nothing to fear from me, little one. I am as mortal as any here."

"Little one?" snapped Kesira. "I am not your 'little one.'"

"And she has a temper." A smug grin crossed Rouvin's face.

Zolkan knew to take flight from Rouvin's arm the instant before Kesira kicked out and caught the man behind the ankle. Her timing was exact; his weight was shifting just as she moved. He sat down heavily, propped up on both his hands, a startled expression replacing the smugness.

"Do not ever call me that."

"My lady, I beg forgiveness." Rouvin looked about him and tensed slightly at what he saw. Kesira stood, ready for combat. The memory of those already fallen before he rode up came to Rouvin, but more immediate was the way Molimo stood, sinews in tight bunches along powerful forearms, and Zolkan, flapping overhead and darting about seeking the proper target for his sharp talons.

"Granted." Kesira reached out and grabbed Rouvin's arm, helping him to his feet.

"Will you ride to Chounabel with me?" he asked. "A party together attracts less...unwanted...attention."

"What you mean to say is that we're less likely to draw more brigands if they see you with us." Kesira smiled. "You are quite right in that. At least Molimo and I now have mounts."

Milling about were the horses left behind when the surviving brigands retreated. Molimo brought over a pair of sturdy animals, almost shyly handing the reins to Kesira. She frowned, trying to understand what flowed silently—and deeply—between Molimo and Rouvin. Molimo read more in the errant knight than Rouvin did in the tongueless youth, of that she was sure. But what?

They mounted, Zolkan flying ahead to scout the way. Kesira felt uncomfortable astride the horse, having to hike up her robe almost to waist level. She was only too aware of Rouvin's lustful eyes fastened on her long, slender legs.

"Did Zolkan summon you?" she asked, as much to take Rouvin's mind off her body as to gather information.

"He hunted the same game I did. We collided. That bird certainly has a salty vocabulary."

Kesira said nothing. To her Zolkan had never indicated anything of the sort.

"He told me of your plight and I decided to see if I could be of assistance." Rouvin smirked again. If Kesira had been afoot, she would again have knocked him to the ground, but on horseback she had great difficulty in guiding the animal where she wanted. "It is a good thing I came along when I did. You would have succumbed to Baram before too much longer. He's a fighter, that Baram."

"I would have died, not succumbed," said Kesira. "There is a difference. Honor would not allow me to surrender."

"Gelya taught well," said Rouvin. "I met that demon once. My mother thought highly of him. He required little from his worshipers, unlike some demons."

"You met him?" Kesira started to call Rouvin a liar, but the green glow had returned to the man's eyes. That erased any lingering doubt she might have had.

"Aye. I have met several of the demons. My mother

placed me with foster parents who raised me." A desolation sounded in his voice that startled Kesira.

"What happened to them?"

"Dead." Kesira said nothing, waiting for Rouvin to continue. There had to be more to the tale. And there was. Rouvin said, "Lenc killed them in one of his bids for supremacy. He thought destroying them somehow punished Ayondela for not aligning with him. To her they were nothing. To me...."

"I knew Gelya had died when I went into the temple and found a white flame burning on his altar," said Kesira. "Is this Lenc's sigil?"

"Of course it is. Gelya was not much of a fighter, but his assistance ofttimes turned the tide in favor of reason. Lenc killed him some time ago. And now there is none to stand against him."

"What does that mean?" Kesira asked. "The omens of the sky turning black at midday and the rain of jade—does this mean Lenc now rules the world?"

"Perhaps it does. Ayondela, I hear, still confronts Lenc. But Gelya, gone."

"How is this possible, if the demons are immortal?"

Rouvin laughed and looked at her. "You ask this, you, a nun? Recite your catechism."

"Don't mock me."

"Do it."

Kesira frowned, thinking on the appropriate teachings Gelya had handed down to the Order. Slowly, the answer dawned on her. She felt faint and weaved slightly in the saddle. Rouvin reached out and supported her until she pulled away, again able to ride unassisted.

"So you begin to understand," he said.

"But now?"

"Tell me all. See if the words do not match the facts."

Kesira felt her palms turning sweaty. She rubbed them on her robe and wiggled in the hard leather saddle. The woman found no comfort, in saddle or thoughts.

"The universe is comprised of five elements. First there came void, into which all other things fit. Filling void came the world, the solidity under our feet."

"Yes, yes," broke in Rouvin. "And following came the ocean, air and the fire burning in the sky and in our·heart. What then?"

"Those five elements comprise the universe. Then came the animals, wiggling and burrowing, swimming and flying. From their bodies came all humans."

"Us. Or rather, you," said Rouvin. "Go on."

"The demons entered the universe, stronger than mortals, possessing powers beyond our ken. They are the hybrid of human and animal."

"They are called immortal because they outlive humans, but are they truly without death?" Rouvin's face had hardened into a mask. Kesira was unable to decipher the emotions flowing within the man.

"Their time will pass. They can be slain by others of their kind, but their rule shall come to an end one day."

"Why are they called demons and not gods?"

"The gods," Kesira said, remembering fully the words of Gelya, "are yet to come. People show pettiness and pride, occasional flashes of nobility and true spirit. Demons are only humans with the traits magnified. Their passions are extreme."

"Their hate is intense," said Rouvin, "but so is their love."

"They form the ends of the spectrum with all of humanity between. But this intensity burns too brightly and will eventually die down, giving rise to the true gods."

"They will be humane and immortal, benevolent and able to do what is best for the people living past the Time of Chaos."

"Time of Chaos. The transition when demons and people die and the gods are born."

"This Time is near at hand," said Rouvin. "Whether it is because I carry within me the blood of my demon mother or something else, I truly feel it comes closer daily. We see the demons dying. Gelya killed by Lenc. And so recently, Merrisen also destroyed by Lenc. Or so I am told."

"Merrisen?" Kesira's heart nearly exploded at mention of the name. She remembered this demon all too well from her dream—her vision.

"Perhaps the greatest of the demons. My mother held true affection for him, and possibly he returned it. It is a sorrow I never had the chance to meet him."

"Are you so sure he perished?"

"You haven't been on the Plains of Roggen long, have you?" Rouvin looked about, then pointed. "There. Look sharp and tell me what you see."

Kesira blinked and shaded her eyes as she stared into the setting sun. Sinuous dark shapes flowed over the top of a rise and vanished. She tried to understand what she had seen and failed. Kesira told Rouvin this.

"So," he said in a harsh tone, "you do not know. I will tell you. That was probably human before the battle."

"Between Merrisen and Lenc?"

"The same one you witnessed. The jade pellets falling from the sky showed Merrisen's defeat. The demon was shattered and his parts strewn across the world. Lenc's desecration of your temple was little more than a flaunting of his victory. He had already defeated Gelya. Vanquishing Merrisen proved him invincible. The demons begin to die at one another's hand."

"But how does this explain the creature you pointed out?"

"Such magicks as the demons use are not easily contained. When one relies on the jade power, well, even this is beyond total control. Residual flows of power seep out and into the world. Those unfortunates trapped in the current...change."

"Change in what way?" Kesira demanded. Coldness welled inside her as she guessed at the answer.

"Humans become partly animal, animals become partly human. It matters little to the jade power. That is only a tool used poorly by the demons and the consequences of its misuse seldom concern them. What does matter is the creature created by the power."

Kesira looked quickly over at Molimo, who rode with eyes fixed straight ahead. He gave no indication of having heard Rouvin's explanation of his jade-induced affliction, but Kesira didn't see how he could have missed it.

"I kill them, each and every one," went on Rouvin. "They are pitiable, yes, but also treacherous and cunning. The only safe way of getting across these plains now is to kill first."

"But they are human."

"*Were* human," he corrected. "They are now fit only for slaughter. It is something I do well."

Kesira fell silent. She had fallen into the trap of thinking Rouvin human, like herself. He was not. The half-demon ancestry accentuated the passions blazing within him. She tried to imagine what he would be like, if she took him to her bed. Somehow, the image failed to form. Not that Rouvin was ugly. Quite the contrary. The sparkling blue eyes and his manner told of intelligence and wit, and she had seen some of his charm shining like a beacon in the night.

Strong, stronger than most men of her acquaintance, Rouvin was perfectly formed in body. Kesira had no doubt as to his bravery or even his sincerity. While his demeanor might change among others, Kesira viewed him as honest and even someone in whom she might place her trust.

And she had heard that demons' abilities in matters sexual were astounding—and very pleasing—for mortals. If Rouvin had inherited even half of this demonic prowess, he would be the best lover she might ever find.

Kesira still couldn't picture herself bedding with Rouvin.

Sending a chill up and down her spine came the unbidden thought of her lying with Molimo. Scarred, still mending in body and with some parts forever beyond healing, he appealed to her more on a sexual level. Kesira swallowed as she thought of his body above hers, moving with increasing fervor, then shape-shifting into a wolf, fangs snapping on her vulnerable neck, his furred underbelly pressing down on her breasts, her legs circling a strange lupine, kill-crazed beast.

"Is anything wrong?" asked Rouvin.

"Nothing," Kesira quickly lied. But what was wrong lay within her. She would prefer Molimo to Rouvin. Even if Molimo threatened to change into a wolf—or was her attraction for the youth *because* of that fear?

"The beasts will stay their distance. Until we stop for the night," said Rouvin. "They fear the hooves."

Kesira saw for the first time that brutal battle spurs had been placed on the horses' front feet. One savage kick would gut an enemy.

"Then they'll fear the campfire. But one of us must

tend it throughout the night to keep it from dying too low."

Kesira did not like the implication in what the man said. "How did you survive alone? Surely, you didn't force yourself awake every few hours to stoke the fire?"

"That I did," he said almost cheerfully. "Other times, I·let the fire die low and when the beasts crept up on me, I killed a few of them. The smell of blood drove the others wild. I'd move camp some distance away and it would take hours for them to finish feeding on their one-time comrades." Rouvin smiled. "That solution appeals most to me: Let them devour one another."

Kesira again looked at Molimo. The youth's eyes seemed riveted on the horizon and his ears clogged. But Kesira saw the tensesness in Molimo's shoulders and the way he fought to restrain himself. The woman knew Rouvin did not say these things to bait Molimo, but she wondered if Molimo understood. It would not do to have the youth turn into a wolf and seek vengeance on Rouvin while the man slept.

"Zolkan will be returning soon," she told Rouvin. "I'm sure he'll have found a suitable campsite for us. Ride on and prepare it. I wish to speak with Molimo."

"Speak at him, you mean." Rouvin kicked at his horse's flanks and trotted ahead when he saw the bright green dot in the sunset marking Zolkan's return. The *trilla* bird landed heavily on Rouvin's arm and jerked his feathered head to the right indicating his choice of resting spots. Rouvin motioned to Kesira, then went on.

When the half-man, half-demon was beyond hearing, Kesira turned to Molimo and asked, "Do you control the shape-shifting enough to keep from doing it while we ride with Rouvin? His feelings are intense against ones such as yourself."

A slow shake of the head gave Kesira the answer she'd dreaded.

Molimo began using his hands to convey the message of how little control he had over the shape-altering process. It was as Kesira had feared. Molimo did not seek out the wolf form; it was thrust upon him by the residual powers of the demons' combat, the potent geas Lenc had cruelly dispensed. Even worse, he knew all that happened while he wore the wolf's shape—and was powerless against the animal urges to kill.

Kesira reached out and lightly touched Molimo on the arm. "I am so sorry for you. But we will fight this affliction and conquer it. You and me."

Molimo gestured at her, then pointed off toward the spot where Rouvin had dismounted and already prepared camp.

Kesira shook her head and told Molimo, "No, nothing exists between Rouvin and me. I don't think it can. I like him, but nothing more. And I cannot explain why that is so."

Molimo's skeptical expression endeared him to her even more. Kesira bent over, precariously balanced in the stirrups, and kissed Molimo on the cheek.

"We still have several days' riding ahead. Let's rest tonight and garner our strength. And I want to meditate before eating."

She looked into Molimo's dark, fathomless eyes and saw stirrings of emotion within. But exactly what emotion it was eluded her.

She and Molimo dismounted and tied the horses' reins to a stake already planted by Rouvin.

"We're well protected from wind here. That rise cuts off most of the breeze coming from the west," he told her. "Firewood is scarce, though. And dried dung is seldom found on this part of the Roggen Plains, either. I might want to go kill a few of the half-beasts instead of trying to feed the fire throughout the night."

"Fire is adequate," Kesira said hastily. "You do not want to tire yourself needlessly. There might be other brigands on the road. Or Baram might return."

"Baram?" snorted Rouvin. "Hardly. He'll lick his wounds for a month before venturing out again, and even then he won't be so bold. There are other groups we might find, though. They make Baram look as if he'd just been weaned yesterday."

"You take such glee in that, don't you?"

"How else can a man live? Honor is all. There is no honor in simply surviving. One must put forth the effort to achieve. In that lies true duty, to the Emperor and to our individual patrons."

"What have you achieved for the Emperor?" asked Kesira, teasing.

Rouvin hunkered down as he worked to start the fire. When he got it blazing, he sat back and stared at her, as if appraising her reaction if he spoke. Finally deciding, he said, "I commanded a company of cavalry for two years. We had the finest record of any unit along the Sarabella front."

"I am not familiar with the Sarabella front."

"I am almost sorry that I am. The eastern barbarians had landed from a vast fleet. Hundreds of thousands of fighters, all superbly equipped and backed by those cursed ships.

"The battle began and Emperor Kwasian personally oversaw the first assaults launched to turn the barbarians back into the sea. In four months, almost a quarter-million fighters lost their lives, most of them ours."

Kesira said nothing. Dominie Tredlo had mentioned the war almost six years ago. For Kesira it had been little more than a vision seen through fog. In their secluded valley in the Yearn Mountains, the Order had experienced nothing out of the ordinary. They all had confidence in the Emperor and his troops, and that confidence had not been misplaced.

"You say we lost to the barbarians?"

"Hardly that. But too many died nobly and all too few lived to fight a second day. Emperor Kwasian moved to contain the barbarian army's advance. They were unable to advance and we were unable to push them back."

"The Sarabella front proved the turning point?" Kesira guessed.

An expression of both pride and sadness came to Rouvin. He nodded.

"What happened there?"

"We had too few men for a frontal assault. Each company ranged forth to chevy the barbarians, to cost them as many men as possible while taking as few casualties as possible on ourselves. For nine weeks we fought on the front, pushing them back past Sarabella, past Reun, back to the ocean. My company—what was left of it—stood and cheered as the barbarians swam

out to their ships and cast off to return to their home-
land in defeat."

"How many cheered" asked Kesira.

"My company was the largest. Eight of us threw
rocks and curses after the barbarians. We originally
had numbered two hundred."

"Why are you no longer in the Emperor's service?"

"Oh, I still serve Kwasian, but not in his cavalry. I
had reached the point where only death would gain me
another promotion."

Kesira understood this. Many positions in the Emperor's service were determined by heredity and social
standing. If Rouvin hoped to attain rank beyond that
which he had won, only his death would have allowed
the promotion. But although he no longer served in
uniform, all honorable citizens served the Emperor by
being productive and obeying imperial edicts without
question.

Before Kesira could speak, Rouvin twisted about, his
shortsword flashing from its sheath. He moved with
lightning swiftness and topped the rise protecting them
from the cold westerly wind. Seconds after he vanished
Kesira heard a scuffling in the dirt followed by an anguished inhuman cry of pain.

"Stay here, Molimo," she said, holding the youth back.
He strained until Zolkan flew over and rested on a
muscular shoulder, speaking to him in the singsong
that worked miracles. Molimo quieted.

Kesira hefted her staff and hastened up the hill.
Looking down from the crest she saw Rouvin surrounded by the half-human beasts. Some were partially
transformed into wolves, while others, snapping angrily at Rouvin's heels, were more doglike. Rouvin's
shortsword worked bloody tracks across one beast after
another, while his broadsword hacked larger circles in
the air and held back all but the man's chosen victim.

"Away!" shouted Kesira. "Flee!"

The creatures turned all-too-human faces toward her,
allowing Rouvin to slit two throats and skewer a third
beast through the shoulder. Rouvin had become a killing machine, reveling in the metallic copper smell of
blood. His powerful hands and forearms dripped gore

and his steel-tipped boots sank deeply into exposed sides as the man spun and twisted, kicked and thrust.

Kesira rushed up, staff spinning about her lithe body. One end of the staff connected with an apparently human head. The whimper coming from between those lips echoed vulpine across the plains. Kesira thrust the butt end of her staff and caught another man-beast in the belly, causing him/it to retch.

And then the carnage ceased. Rouvin's flashing swords had eliminated all opposition.

He stood with a smug expression on his face and said, "That's a dozen less of them. A good night's work. Thank you for your help, Kesira."

"Don't thank me," she said. "Never thank me for helping you slaughter like this."

Rouvin's face clouded with anger. "They stalked us. If we had not taken the battle to them first, they would have drunk our blood before sunlight again shone on the land. They are *not* human." He thrust his blades into the soft earth and wiped them clean, then stormed back to camp.

Kesira hurried after him, fearful of what she might find. The most potent of her mental calming chants failed to bring true serenity like the sight of Molimo sitting, in human form, with Zolkan still on his shoulder. If the dark-haired youth had form-shifted, there would have been no holding back Rouvin.

Molimo scratched out a question in the dirt.

"All dead," Kesira said softly. "Unlike you, they were trapped halfway through the transformation."

"My curse," wrote Molimo.

"Perhaps your salvation, too," the woman answered.

Rouvin sat on the far side of the fire, cleansing himself with sand and cleaning his blades properly. When he'd finished, he tended their horses. An hour later, fire blazing, he muttered, "Look after the wood. Keep the flames high while I get some sleep."

Rouvin pulled a blanket about his broad shoulders and rolled over. In a few minutes, deep, sonorous snoring mingled with the hissing and popping of the juniper-scented fire.

Kesira used the time to meditate. She allowed her mind to float, to drift, to not seek any answers while

it, indeed, did seek. The contradictions of life mingled
and flowed together, separated and were examined. She
drifted deeper into her mind and examined her life and
motives, her emotions and fears and loves.

Zolkan's talons on her shoulder returned her to the
world of a dying fire and Rouvin still sound asleep.

"What's wrong?" she asked the *trilla* bird.

"Molimo," came the muted answer.

Kesira turned and saw the transformation starting.
Molimo's face became furry, the jaw elongating and the
eyes sinking beneath bony ridges. Teeth jutted and the
body grew sleek.

The woman started to go to him to calm him, but
reason held her back. If Rouvin awakened now, his
quick swords would steal Molimo's life. Better to let
Molimo finish the shape change and then track him
down, soothe him, coax him back into human form.

Kesira watched Molimo snuffle about, snort and toss
his thin-skulled wolf's head, then lift his nose and take
in the scent-laden night breeze. Soundlessly, the wolf
bounded up the hill and vanished over it.

"Stay, Zolkan," she told the bird. "Keep Rouvin pa-
cified should he awaken."

"Help Molimo. Help him," was all the bird said.

Kesira leaned heavily on her staff as she made her
way after the wolf.

Chapter Five

Kesira Minette kept glancing over at Molimo as they rode toward Chounabel. She had found the man-wolf and coaxed him back, in spite of the obvious danger to herself. Zolkan had aided her somewhat, and this caused questions to rise in her mind as to the relationship between Molimo and the *trilla* bird. Zolkan acted protective of Molimo, far more so than she would have believed possible.

Kesira tossed such speculation away. *She* felt more protective of Molimo than she'd have believed possible. The Order of Gelya taught peace and benevolence, duty and honor. Somehow in all that she had sought refuge to keep from coming to grips with the fact that she was powerfully—physically—drawn to the tongueless youth.

"There," came Rouvin's deep voice. "There lies Chounabel. A splendid jewel lodged in the navel of this awful belly of the Empire."

Stretched out on all sides of Chounabel lay the richest grain-growing area in the land, and squatting in the center was the City of Sin. Kesira repressed a shudder at the mere thought of the city. The tales she had heard from her Sisters made it sound decadent, evil, totally depraved. Those of the Order assigned here worked like a hundred times their number simply to find a single convert to Gelya's teachings.

This might be the only temple remaining. Sadness replaced the illicit thrill Kesira had felt at seeing Chounabel for the first time. This new emotion filtered out much of her impression of the city. The spires rising into the azure sky weren't *that* outrageous. Lovely architecture and nothing more. The buildings themselves seemed functional enough. There didn't seem to be a pleasure house on every street corner nor were there people killing and raping one another in plain view in the middle of the day. If anything, now that Kesira studied Chounabel more, the City of Sin seemed little different from Blinn.

She told Rouvin this.

"Not so. This is the hub for many fine things not found elsewhere in the Empire. But you wouldn't be interested in such."

"Who can say?" she told the armored man.

"I will gladly show you sights most visitors to Chounabel never see." From his tone, Kesira guessed that the sights he referred to were primarily of himself. Kesira frowned, wondering what it was about him that failed to appeal totally to her. On the ride to the point, she had come to truly believe Rouvin was half-demon and possessed of attributes surpassing those of an ordinary mortal. He still bled when cut and would perish should the wound be grievous enough, but his strength was awesome and his wit and intelligence well above those Kesira had known, inside or outside the nunnery. Handsome and brave, Rouvin was more than most women would find in a lifetime of searching.

Kesira licked dry lips and looked at Molimo, who simply sat asaddle and stared at the City of Sin.

"Let's enter. I am weary of travel and would find the others of my Order."

"I, too, am eager to find lodging," said Rouvin. He took a deep breath and asked sidelong, his face forward, "Would you share them with me?"

Kesira shook her head and replied, "The needs of my Order come first."

"But you are not celibate?"

"Hardly," she said, smiling. "Gelya told us that suppression of natural urges was evil."

"If that's the case, Gelya must have found a soulmate in Chounabel," said Rouvin. He galloped forth, dust clouds rising from beneath his horse's hooves. Molimo and Kesira followed, Zolkan flapping diligently above them. They caught up with Rouvin at the outskirts of the city. Farmers toiled to prepare their fields for the first planting, now that winter's bite had left the land and spring's softer caresses had come. Some ran furrows while others cleared irrigation channels clogged by cold weather debris. A few turned curious heads to follow Kesira's passage, but most ignored her. Riders into Chounabel at any time of the year were many and travelers seldom produced much stir.

"This is the Street of Divine Satiation," said Rouvin, his blue eyes twinkling. His face was slightly flushed and Kesira thought even his lank hair had come alive at the prospect of being once more in Chounabel. "Your Order probably established its headquarters about a mile down the street and to the left of the Main Market."

"Do you head in that direction?" asked Kesira.

"No, dear lady, not unless you desire my company."

"Thank you for your assistance. The journey here was immeasurably more easy with you at our side."

Rouvin bowed as deeply as he could while on horseback; then, without another word, he turned his steed and trotted down a side street. With a small pang of loss, Kesira watched him until the knight errant vanished around a curve. She straightened and said to Molimo, "Let's seek out my Order."

Molimo bobbed his head, even as he looked left and right, up and around. Kesira smiled. The poor boy had probably never been in a city of any size and now he found himself in the fabled City of Sin. She walked her horse down the Street of Divine Satiation and discovered quickly why that name was appropriate. Everywhere she looked came the signs of appeal to the flesh. Food vendors with the finest, most delicate, rarest of culinary treats. Pleasure houses both discreet and bawdy, men and women enticing passersby to stop for a rapturous moment. Galleries of fine arts; pornographic pictures and sculptings from marble and dazzling orange *tulna* stone. No matter what indulgence she might want, it was presented openly, even boldly, along this major thoroughfare running the width of Chounabel.

The wealth of the city astounded Kesira. The people moving along the streets were well-clothed and even overfed, though she had to admit the sight of the dates from the Emperor's own garden grove, the *luria* fruit and the succulent sweetmeats tempted her sorely. Confronted with such treats every day, Kesira wondered how long it would take her to become a bloated pig.

"Molimo, it is a good thing we have no money. I might never reach our Order, otherwise. Oh, to sample such fine wares." With true longing she peered into an art gallery whose walls were studded with delicate etchings of ocean waves rushing against a shore, lifelike portraits of Empress Aglanella, haunting poems drawn with elegant calligraphy on parchment and framed with stone-wood.

Molimo reached out and lightly touched her arm, bringing Kesira back to her senses. She had been captivated by the otherworldliness of Chounabel.

"Thank you," she said, her hand momentarily covering Molimo's. "I may have to rely on you to keep me faithful to my vows." She laughed at his expression. "No, not of poverty. We won't starve, I assure you. But the Order doesn't seek riches without purpose. Gelya's teachings tell us to accumulate that which will aid."

Molimo pointed to a bookdealer.

"Knowledge for its own sake is worthless," she said, remembering well the lecture on this subject she had received from Sister Fenelia. "What good to know if there is not purpose to that knowing? Better to learn that which helps others—or yourself. To learn the ways of the farmer is important—for the farmer. For me, it would be pointless. Better I should find the lore necessary to help you recover from your . . . affliction."

Molimo glanced sharply at her, his dark eyes hard points. Kesira lost herself in his gaze. Something about the color struck her as different. It took several seconds before she realized the whites now carried a faint greenish tinge. These were not the green of demons' eyes, nor the green that had come to Rouvin's blue eyes when speaking of his mother, the demon Ayondela. Sea green, flecked with foam, Kesira thought. These were the sea eyes of one adrift in the world, bobbing about on waves of immense power and seeking a safe harbor.

Molimo pointedly turned from Kesira and jockeyed his horse slightly ahead of hers. She sighed. There was so much about Molimo she wanted to know, but he kept turning away from her. The woman winced as sharp talons cut into her left shoulder.

"Good city," said Zolkan. "But evil."

"Evil? You do not approve of the pleasure houses or..."

"Food vendors evil," insisted Zolkan. The *trilla* bird forced himself up and under Kesira's cowl so that only parts of his body peeped out. She felt the feathered head pressing close to her ear. "Eat birds."

"The food vendors sell fowls?"

"Sell *trilla* bird meat," Zolkan said glumly.

"I didn't know."

"Taste terrible. Cannibals."

Kesira smiled at that. "The only cannibals are those who eat others of their own kind."

"Barbarians," corrected Zolkan.

"Perhaps that," Kesira said.

They rode on, Zolkan hiding in the folds of her robe and Molimo leading the way. Reaching the Main Market, Kesira found everything she had seen in her mile-long ride along the Street of Divine Satiation—and much, much more. Stalls sold jewelry and services of every imaginable kind, including a few she found unimaginable and thoroughly disgusting; at the periphery of the Main Market Kesira found the first hints that not all were prosperous in Chounabel.

Beggars lined the sides of the immense market area and brought a choking response to Kesira. Blind, disfigured, hideously bent, they pleaded for the barest of notice, the smallest of coins. As Kesira rode, she saw not one citizen stop to give aid to any of the beggars.

"Molimo, I do not know if I like this city or not. There seems to be a putrid core to what appears a fine, lush, appealing fruit."

Molimo pointed to the right, down a small side street.
A sign dangled over a store front there that brought a
smile to Kesira's lips.

"Well done. This is the obvious spot to establish the
mission."

Molimo reached out and shook his head, pointed to
himself and shook his head even more vigorously. For
a moment, Kesira puzzled over the mute's reaction.

Zolkan spoke up, "No interest here for Molimo. Wants
to explore Chounabel. Let him find Rouvin."

Kesira smiled and said, "Very well, Molimo. Is that
truly your wish?" He nodded and his eyes danced with
energy, the green rims becoming more pronounced. "We
shall be here, should you want to rejoin us. If not, take
care." She leaned over and hugged Molimo, which
seemed to take the youth by surprise. He tensed for a
moment, then relaxed and hugged back. As they parted,
Kesira felt a curious reluctance to allow Molimo to go
like this.

Or to leave her side, at all.

"Learn caution through the misfortune of others,"
she said. Molimo smiled and turned from her, only once
glancing back to see if she still stood at the mouth of
the street leading to her mission or if she followed.

Kesira brushed a tear from her eye and said to Zolkan, "I shall miss him."

"Molimo must have freedom to explore," the *trilla*
bird said. "He will be cautious."

"I'd hate to think of anything more happening to
him," she said.

Kesira dismounted in front of her Order's headquarters, reached for the door and found it bolted.
Frowning, she rattled at the latch and tugged harder,
thinking the door might only be struck.

It was locked securely.

"I don't understand this," the nun said. "No Order's
mission is ever closed. Certainly not in the middle of
the day." Kesira moved around, looking for a window,
but the single window had been bricked up. She returned to the door, examined the lock and knocked
loudly, hoping to attract attention.

She did, but not of the sort she intended.

"What are you doing? Breaking into a mission?"

Guiltily, Kesira spun and faced three armed men. While their light armor showed different styles, all wore the red armband emblazoned with a white bar indicating service to the Emperor.

"I am a nun in the Order," Kesira said, speaking much too rapidly. The leader frowned, as if doubting such a wild tale.

"True!" squawked Zolkan, poking his head out from under Kesira's cowl. This sudden intrusion into the conversation caused one of the soldiers to draw his short-sword.

The leader held out a hand, staying the thrust. "A *trilla* bird?" he asked. "We see few of them in Chounabel."

"Eat us!" protested Zolkan. "You eat *trilla* birds in City of Sin."

"Some find the flesh a delicacy," admitted the officer. "I eat no meat."

"Good man," said Zolkan, bolder now.

"But my two comrades LOVE *trilla* bird meat." The officer laughed at Zolkan's outraged sputtering. "Be calm. I only joke."

"I seek out others of my Order." Kesira turned to indicate the lock on the door and the apparently empty building.

"There are few followers of Gelya in Chounabel," said the officer. "We always welcome newcomers." The look of appraisal he gave her made Kesira start to blush. She forced herself to meet his gaze evenly. The officer smiled, then laughed. "Let's be on our way," he told his men. "The lady needs to discover the fate of her faith."

Kesira started to ask what the soldier meant, but he wheeled and strutted off, the other two trailing in his wake.

"Eat birds? Barbarians!" screamed Zolkan after them. "Eat plants instead!"

"Quiet, Zolkan," Kesira said, distracted. "Let's find a place to stay. I have a few coins jingling in my purse. That ought to get us lodging, if we aren't too extravagant."

"Get room far from kitchen," Zolkan advised, when he saw Kesira heading toward a nearby public house. *"Far* away."

Kesira rented a room three flights up and at the back of the building, using some of the money Rouvin had stolen from the dead brigands. The room was small and austere, lacking any amenity or luxury, and smelled of heavy disinfectants. A hard bed covered with threadbare brown blanket provided the only furniture and a single rusty hook driven into the wall at eye-level provided closet space. Kesira sank to the bed and lounged back, as if this were the most luxurious palace in the Emperor's realm.

Zolkan flapped up and caught hold of the hook, balancing precariously.

"Crude," the bird observed.

"It suits me—and it is all I can afford. I had hoped to be able to stay with my Sisters at the chapel. Until I find them, I must stay here." Kesira lay back, eyes open, staring at the pockmarked ceiling. Bits of plaster had fallen and not been replaced; four or five different-colored coatings of paint were chipped and eroded away like strata of sandstone; bare, worm-eaten wood showed through in several places, giving the lie to any structural integrity claimed by the building's owners. But Kesira had seen worse. Gelya taught that physical luxury was transient and that true life came from within. To be content required only inner strength, not exterior goods.

She closed her eyes and drifted into deep meditation. Unbidden, Kesira began composing the next line of her death song, the composition that, when finished, would be the final testament to her life. Kesira had worked out only the first few words of the first line, but now inspiration flowed and a second line finished itself. Which was as it should be. Such a personal paen could not be forced; it welled up from an artesian source in her soul not examinable. All Kesira did was study the surface of the resulting stream and find those words which meshed with her life, her thoughts, her friends and enemies and experiences, her universe within and without.

Kesira allowed the grip of discovery to fade, and she lost the tenuous thread of concentration that wasn't concentration and slipped off to sleep.

* * *

"No one home," said Zolkan. "Find food. Hungry."

"If you don't keep quiet, someone will find *you* as food," Kesira said, only half-jokingly. The sight of the brilliantly plumed *trilla* bird on her shoulder provoked more than one offer to buy Zolkan. One or two of those offering were food vendors.

Kesira rattled the door to the mission and saw that it was as securely locked as the day before. She studied the sides of the building and found the walls bare. In back, however, Kesira came across the first sign that someone inhabited the small chapel: the garbage resting in the alleyway had been thrown out recently. The woman knocked on the back door and waited. Faint stirrings came from within. Kesira gripped her staff harder, not knowing what to expect as the door opened.

Brigands? Had they taken over Gelya's chapel? Or worse? Had the chapel been desecrated by the same demon responsible for destroying the nunnery?

Listless eyes peered forth and met her soft brown ones. Kesira read despair and even more in the woman's expression. Loss of faith echoed from every movement, every gesture, every facial tic.

"I am Kesira Minette, of the Order. I come from the Yearn Mountain nunnery seeking out others in Chounabel."

"Why?"

Kesira was taken aback. The woman inside the mission dressed in plain colors, white blouse with small ruffles at cuff and neck, a billowing beige skirt of some soft material and unpolished black boots. Her sandy hair floated in wild, unkempt disarray and she gave no indication of belonging to the Order of Gelya.

"The nunnery was destroyed by a demon. I alone escaped. I seek out my Sisters to join them."

The woman moved back from the door and made a vague gesture which Kesira took to mean that entry had been granted. Robes swishing, Kesira entered. Dimness fogged her vision for a few seconds, then hopelessness attacked. The chapel needed repairs, and this single back room provided the living quarters for four women, the one who had answered Kesira's knock and three others. Their vestments had been put away and all wore clothing more suitable for polite commerce along

Chounabel's streets. The altar, Kesira guessed, was in the nave.

She wasn't certain she wanted to see it. Not after finding her Sisters in such a state.

"I am Melonna," said one woman seated nearby. "I used to be the Sister of the Mission."

"Used to be?" asked Kesira, as gently as possible. All her Sisters moved lethargically.

"Gelya is dead. You did not know?"

"I suspect this to be the truth, but what is the difference? Are we not still entrusted with Gelya's teachings? Should we not seek out others and share this knowledge? Philosophy by itself is worthless; there must be action with it."

"You," said Melonna, "have learned well."

"And you have not? Is this why you no longer dress in Gelya's robes and cower in the backroom of a chapel as if all energy had fled your soul?" Kesira felt anger rising within her. These four violated all she held sacred in Gelya's teachings; they responded with despondency rather than action. "If Gelya is dead, does this alter the truth of all he has passed to us?"

"You are young," said Melonna. "That is your reason You have not seen what we have."

"*Oh?*" Scorn dripped from this single word. When Zolkan started to speak, Kesira reached up and crushed her hand into his beak to keep him silent. The bird felt the force of her anger and stilled rather than risk getting his neck broken.

At Melonna's gesture, they went into the nave. Pews marched back in silent rows, but Kesira's attention fixed on the altar. Where the wildflower sacred to Gelya had been now rested only gray ash.

"Gelya is dead. Our purpose fled when the flower burned," said Melonna in a voice like the ticking of a clock: level, regular and without discernible emotion.

Kesira approached the altar and felt coldness creeping into her. The ash on the altar threatened to replace her own faith. She fought it—and won.

"The demon Lenc is responsible. Gelya was too kind," Kesira said, "and perished. We must oppose Lenc."

"How?"

"With Gelya's teachings! We can take his words to

the people of Chounabel, let the teachings rush outward
like spilled water. Who can recover the water once it
has seeped into the soil? Let Gelya be remembered for
kindness and charity and strength, not Lenc for his
cruelty."

Melonna laughed and it was not a pleasant sound.
"You know so little. Chounabel isn't called the City of
Sin for naught. Many chapels exist here, but none is
successful. The people have no need for any teaching
when life is so easy, so pleasant, so diverting. Our re-
ligions bridge over bad times; in Chounabel there are
no bad times."

"Because of this sign, do you *know* Gelya is no more?"
demanded Kesira.

"He is gone."

"Allow me to cast the runes. On the altar." Kesira
quavered inside at her boldness. She had the gift of
future sight, or so said Sister Fenelia, but the cost was
extreme in terms of body and soul. But Kesira felt the
need to shake her Sisters from their current sorry state
and get them moving forward again, proselytizing, finding converts, instilling Gelya's message of harmony.

To do that, Kesira Minette would face any danger.

Without a word, Melonna went and brought back
the other three. They sat quietly in the front pew while
Kesira prepared herself for the arduous task of casting
the rune sticks. Outwardly, Kesira appeared calm, but
inside she quailed at the idea of what she was about to
attempt. She had never done this before—and without
Fenelia's quiet, solid support she wasn't certain she
could succeed.

The sight of the death-mask faces watching her convinced Kesira she had to try. If she couldn't salvage the
mission in Chounabel—couldn't salvage those who were
already inclined to believe Gelya's teachings—she was
lost in a world turning chaotic.

Gelya did not believe chaos was the natural state of
things, and neither did Kesira. She would have to show
her Sisters the true path once again.

"Here are the rune sticks," said Melonna, handing
over a small yellowed bone box. "It has been four years
since last they were used."

"May Gelya guide my hand."

"Gelya's dead," muttered one of the others, the first sound any had uttered since entering the chapel.

"That may be so, but his words still guide my hand. We walk through this world by faith, not sight." Kesira settled herself, composing her mind, allowing the meditation technique to smooth any ripples in her thought. She followed the narrow trail through her soul, up beautiful rises and down into ugly ravines, through them all, and emerged into a placid state where she was little more than a vessel containing something larger than herself.

She tossed the contents of the bone box on the altar. Five carved white splinters tumbled forth and landed amid the ash. Kesira, eyes still closed, passed her hand over the engraved rune sticks. Pulsations rose from them, burning her hand, causing blisters to form and messages to emerge from the muddle of her inner mind.

"Gelya is ... no more," she said. As if from a distance, she heard gusting sighs as the four who had been her Sisters let out pent-up breath. Kesira continued to pass her hand over the runes, enduring the physical damage to obtain the psychic knowledge.

She sorrowed at the answers she obtained from the runes. The Order of Gelya was no more. Of all those who had followed the gentle teachings, only she remained. The others had turned away, as Melonna and her Sisters had done—or were destroyed.

Kesira started to examine this destruction, then wavered in her resolve, allowing the force of the runes to carry her in other directions. More than a single demon's demise was revealed to her. She saw battles on a scale unlike anything she had ever imagined; death reigned supreme among the demons.

Immortal demons dying. Battles unimaginable to mortals raging, unchecked. Demons altering form and turning into solid pillars of jade. The order of the world changed.

Kesira railed at this. The time of man had passed with the coming of the demons. The time of the demons now passed, also, and she was a witness to the thinnest edge of it, the merest beginning. Before she sang the final line of her death song, Kesira saw, she would not only watch the passing of the demons but also be present at the birth of the gods.

The enormity of this shook her from her trance.

Sweat poured down her body and blinded her as it dripped from eyebrow into eye. She wiped it away, marveling that the hand she had passed over the runes showed no sign of the intense physical damage she'd thought it received.

"Gelya is dead. As we thought," said Melonna.

"That is true," said Kesira. "And I saw more."

The four appeared disinterested.

"I am now the sole member of the Order of Gelya." Kesira saw this did not affect the women, either positively or negatively. "I am entitled to wear the gold sash."

Melonna nodded, left and returned carrying it. Only the head of a mission or nunnery was allowed to wear the gold with the blue. Sister Fenelia had worn it; now Kesira wrapped it about her waist. The gold ribbon, thin silk, both inspired and enervated her. Kesira was alone in her belief, not in Gelya but in Gelya's teachings.

"This is a symbol that charity and kindness will never die," she said, more to herself than to the others.

"Heavy load," whispered Zolkan from her shoulder. "Heavy load."

Chapter Six

ZOLKAN'S WINGS fluttering about her face awoke Kesira just before dawn. She rolled over and for a heart-stopping instant did not recognize where she was. The woman finally remembered she had decided to save money and spend the night in the mission with the other four—whom she could no longer call Sisters. The few coins she had remaining hardly permitted her to do more than buy a loaf of bread and some cheese; indulging in a room, even at a hostelry as inexpensive as the one she'd found the night before, was beyond her means.

"Go," said Zolkan. "Do not like here."

Kesira reached up and stroked the topknot of particolored feathers. Zolkan began to coo, more like a dove than a *trilla* bird.

"Don't get your feathers up over this," she told him. "We are safe. Melonna and the others are no longer in the Order—only I am," she said, with infinite sadness. "But they are not going to harm us. Even you, my tasty little morsel."

Zolkan rubbed against her fingers, then pulled back. "Nothing more for us in Chounabel."

"You're right. But why leave now?"

"Now," insisted the bird.

Kesira lay on her pallet, thinking. She ignored Zolkan's talons trying to pull her up. The thick gray robe she still wore cushioned some of the gouging. Unbidden, her hand dropped to her waist and traced along the lines of her blue sash cord. All nuns in the Order wore this. Her fingers sought out the gold ribbon twining around with the blue cord. Only a few were permitted this honor.

And with the honor came duty. She had read in the runes the total collapse of the Order of Gelya. With their patron gone, the teachings were being forgotten all too quickly. Kesira could not permit that. She took her vows seriously and knew where true honor lay. Support of the Emperor, of family, of personal belief.

Kesira had scant cause or reason to oppose Emperor Kwasian. She had no family, not after the brigands killed her parents and Lenc destroyed her nunnery. Only innate belief remained. Kesira Minette had to be true to her own beliefs or life no longer carried meaning.

She rose, much to Zolkan's pleasure, but her footsteps carried her back into the chapel and away from the rear door that the *trilla* bird steered her toward.

"I must do this," she said to Zolkan.

"Too dangerous. Want to leave."

"I must. There are so many things I experienced only vaguely yesterday. I must find out more."

Kesira carried with her the worn box containing the sticks. She opened the box and stared for long minutes at the slender bits of bone with their runic carvings. Power exuded from these finger bones taken from deceased Sisters. Kesira looked at them—but saw *through* and *past,* and into other realms.

"Don't," pleaded Zolkan. "Leave now. Get from Chounabel by dawn."

Kesira ignored Zolkan and turned to the altar where the ash had been only slightly disturbed from the prior casting. She settled her mind and found the pathway, then cast the rune sticks. They sent up a cloud of gray ash that hung in the air like a desiccated morning fog. Kesira stared into the churning center of the ash cloud and *saw.*

"No," she heard Zolkan say, from far away. She calmed her mind for the journey before her. Though unphysical, it was a journey nonetheless. Kesira went forward, her mind reaching out for the tenuous threads of knowledge revealed by the cast rune sticks.

Movement. Demons rising, striving. Gelya taking up arms against his attackers.

Three demon attackers. The names came to Kesira painfully, with infinite agony.

"Lenc," she gasped out. "Lenc and Eznofadil and... and Howenthal!"

Kesira sagged forward, knocking over the altar and sending ash and rune sticks crashing to the floor. She dropped to hands and knees and panted like an animal trapped in the burning summer sun.

"Go," said Zolkan, softer now. "Leave Chounabel."

"Yes, Zolkan, we'll leave." Kesira looked up at the bird. He sat on the edge of the front pew. The woman had never been able to discern expression on his psittacine face. The hard buttons of black eyes bugged out on either side of his head and stared unblinkingly at her. Kesira had to ask, "Do you know?"

"Know," confirmed the *trilla* bird.

"How?"

"Just know."

"It's awful," Kesira said, moving so that she rested, her back supported by the wall behind the altar. Carefully picking up the fallen rune sticks, she returned them to their bone box and tucked it away in the folds of her gray robe.

"Leave now."

"Jade," she said, still stunned by all that had been revealed to her during the rune-cast. "Lenc, Howenthal and Eznofadil are attempting to conquer the other demons. All the others."

Zolkan said nothing. The bird sidestepped along the top of the pew, toward the door, in silent summoning. Kesira simply sat and tried to order what she now knew.

"The three were able to kill Gelya because they assumed the power of jade. They put tiny slivers of it under their tongues. They are becoming living jade beings!"

"Danger if you stay. Go now."

Kesira ignored Zolkan. "Their power is enhanced, and they killed Gelya. And I think I saw them kill the other demon, Merrisen. But why are they doing this? The jade shortens their lifespan. They burn with power; they also burn out more quickly. Not even a demon can withstand that for long."

"Jade evil."

"Yes, Zolkan, the jade is evil and it turns the three into something even more so. Why do they join in such an alliance, though? Their lot was good. Each has power. Why do they want more?"

She rose on shaking legs and steadied herself against the wall. As Kesira took a step she felt the grit of ash beneath her soles—the ash left from the wildflower sacred to Gelya. A single tear formed in her eye and dropped to the floor, mixing with the gray ash and turning into a thin paste. Kesira knelt and trailed the end of her gold sash in the dampened ash.

"May Gelya's teachings never die," she said solemnly.

She faced Zolkan and asked, "Are you ready to leave?"

"Now!"

"For the Quaking Lands," she said, the name almost burning the tip of her tongue.

"No! Where did you hear that name?" demanded the *trilla* bird.

"The three demons—Lenc, Eznofadil and Howenthal—killed Gelya in the Quaking Lands. I must go there. Some relic must remain, a symbol that will rekindle Gelya's teachings and allow me to oppose the other demons."

"You die if you fight Lenc."

"I suppose so," Kesira said, all energy drained from her. She fought even to stay awake. "What does it matter? Honor dictates this course for me. Lenc is primarily responsible for the death of my Order and my patron. Gelya and the Order were all I could claim as family."

"Revenge futile," pleaded Zolkan. "Start new chapel, recruit, do as you must. Avoid Quaking Lands!"

"I have never even heard of the Quaking Lands," she admitted. "But I will find them. Somewhere within their boundaries lies the answer to defeating Lenc."

"If powerful demon like Gelya cannot defeat Lenc, how can you?" asked Zolkan.

Kesira only shrugged. To this she had no answer. But she must try: honor dictated revenge for all that Lenc and the other two demons had done. The loss she felt was both more and less than personal. Gelya had given her a philosophy around which she had modeled her life. That philosophy lingered even though the propounder had perished, and of the demon Gelya, she felt scant loss. The demons prospered on a plane beyond that of mortals, and Kesira did not understand his motives. His death diminished her, but not as much as his life had elevated her.

Kesira Minette owed her patron what revenge she could exact on his murderers.

Melonna came into the chapel and saw the altar and its spilled contents. Her face paled, but she said nothing.

"Do you know of the Quaking Lands?" asked Kesira, not bothering to take the edge from her words. She felt only contempt for this woman and the other three. "Where might they be found?"

"Quaking land? I know nothing of such a place. Is it nearby?" answered Melonna.

"Zolkan and I are leaving. You may use the chapel as you see fit. Live here, sell it, do as you please."

"You will not return?"

Kesira shook her head and pushed past her former Sister. Even this brief physical contact caused her flesh to ripple with loathing. Kesira silently picked up her few belongings and left the mission, never even looking back.

"Get horse now?" Zolkan asked eagerly.

"Yes, and then we ride out of Chounabel. There's nothing to keep us here."

Kesira ransomed her horse from the public house's stable with the last few coins she had. Purse empty and heart leaden, she led the horse out and heaved a deep sigh of resignation at her fate. Kesira knew not where she rode, what lay in the Quaking Lands except death, and she had lost much since entering Chounabel.

Rouvin and Molimo had gone off on their own, she had finally accepted her patron's death and now she walked alone, burdened by knowledge she would as soon not have learned.

"It is truly said, Zolkan, that knowledge and sorrow are gained in equal measure."

"True," said the bird, hanging onto the saddle pommel with both claws.

Kesira considered mounting and riding quickly from the city, but good sense told her to allow the animal to rest as long as possible. Their journey would be difficult enough later on and she would need to rely on the animal's reserves then.

Street urchins bustled around her, playing a stick and ball game. Kesira barely noticed them until one bumped into her, falling down.

"Son, are you all right?" she asked, helping the child up. He was hardly more than eight or nine and was covered with dirt. As he rose, he fell heavily again, clutching at her gray robe for support. Kesira hoisted him into the air and gently put him on his feet. "There you are," she said. "On your way now."

The evil smile dancing on the child's face unnerved her. He turned and ran off down an alleyway.

"How strange," she said. "He acted as if...the rune sticks!" she cried. "He stole the box with the rune sticks!"

Feverish hands searched the folds of her robe for the bone box and found it missing. She swung up into the saddle, unseating Zolkan from his perch, and kicked the horse hard to send it racing down the alleyway after the urchin. Kesira had little hope of overtaking the boy; these streets wound about themselves and only those living in them could ever know every hiding place.

Terrified shrieks caught her attention and drew her down a narrow side street. What she saw filled her with a mixture of amusement and relief and fear.

The urchin who had stolen her box of rune sticks cowered against a brick wall, eyes wide with horror at the advancing wolf. The sleek gray animal moved ever closer, teeth snapping angrily, eyes narrowed to hunting slits.

"Molimo!" called out Kesira. "Don't harm him. Please, don't!"

The boy tried to escape by feinting right and dodging

left. Molimo was not fooled. The boy ran into opened jaws, and screamed. The jaws closed.

"Molimo!" again pleaded Kesira.

The boy choked and thrashed about, the powerful lupine teeth locked on his throat. In a few seconds, the struggles quieted, then stopped. The boy hung limply from Molimo's muzzle.

Kesira dropped to the ground and ran forward. "I told you to stop," she said, fearing the worst. But the boy had only passed out. Angry red teeth marks showed the pressure Molimo had exerted, but the skin wasn't broken. With his nose Molimo pushed forward the box containing the rune sticks.

"Thank you," Kesira said, somewhat contritely. Then, with more authority, "You shouldn't have savaged him like that. He's only a boy."

"Thief," said Zolkan.

"A boy thief," amended Kesira, "and not deserving of such brutal treatment." She swallowed hard when she saw the green-tinted wolf eyes narrow down again and the jaws tense. Molimo might be human, but in this form he had scant control over himself. "There, there," Kesira soothed, patting the huge gray head, "all is well. Calm yourself. Relax. Return to your human shape, Molimo."

Zolkan joined her, cawing and squawking in the singsong fashion that worked best with Molimo. In minutes, the transformation took hold and the human form predominated.

Molimo indicated that he was sorry for the trouble he had caused. Kesira hugged him to her breast, saying, "You have no control over this. Be tranquil and all will be well."

Molimo slumped forward and she felt the last vestiges of wolf depart his body.

"We're on our way out of Chounabel," Kesira said. "Will you accompany us? This time the journey will be hazardous. We go to the Quaking Lands."

Molimo's dark eyes sparked with flecks of bright green at the mention of the Quaking Lands. Zolkan squawked and fluttered above them in the narrow space between buildings, then landed on Kesira's horse once again. Molimo nodded slowly, reached out and grasped Kesira's hand in his. He almost crushed it.

"I *am* happy. I...I saw what happened to Gelya using a rune cast," she said to Molimo, "and during it I found I must go to the Quaking Lands. Do you know where they are? Can you guide us?"

Molimo nodded faster.

"Good!" Kesira found herself brightening. "You'll have to tell me more of them when we're on the road."

"Do not go to Quaking Lands!" pleaded Zolkan. Kesira frowned when she saw the look Molimo shot the *trilla* bird. Zolkan fluttered up and flew off above the rooftops.

"You haven't chased him off for good, have you?" she asked Molimo. "I've taken quite a liking to him. He may be noisy and more than a little self-centered, but he is a friend now."

Molimo shook his head to indicate that he thought Zolkan would return. Kesira wondered at the youth's confidence, then mounted and turned her steed back toward the Street of Divine Satiation and thence out of Chounabel.

Molimo vanished for a few minutes, then came galloping up beside her, scattering pedestrians in his wake. He smiled and indicated that they ought to leave. Kesira lost herself in thought as she rode the length of the street; the bazaar atmosphere with its throngs of people and myriads of products no longer captured her interest. The journey ahead occupied her—the dangers and the possible revenge on a demon.

Such was unheard of in her experience. No mortal plotted against the demons. And certainly not a demon with the jade power.

But, Kesira mused, *there has never been a demon killed, either.* Gelya lay dead—in the Quaking Lands?— and the other demon, Merrisen, had been slaughtered also by Lenc, Howenthal and Eznofadil. Those names rolled over and over in her mind, wondrous names evoking magicks beyond her pale of experience. Such commonplace sights as those offered by Chounabel—the City of Sin, indeed!—affected her but little.

"I am somewhat disappointed in Chounabel," she told Molimo. He cocked his head to one side, listening intently. "While I have hardly plumbed the depths of depravity here, I see little to protest. The Emperor's guard maintain a fair order, the people are prosperous and happy and well-fed, for the most part, and those few citizens I saw begging and stealing are such a small percentage of the total. Even the little waif who stole my rune sticks did so for the challenge rather than from real need."

Molimo gestured to the far side of town.

"I suppose there might be poverty and crime and decadence here, but I think Sister Melonna was right. Religion will not flourish if the people are otherwise content and have enough to eat." Kesira had heard tales of the guards oppressing the people, but those were only tales, she knew. Nowhere in the Empire was this likely to happen. Kwasian was beloved of the people and a great majority paid him homage by their obedience to the few laws he decreed.

Nowhere was that better seen than in Chounabel.

"Still, I must admit, being here is something of a thrill. We all need to think there are forbidden places, that there are evil doings we can sample, if only we are brave enough. The City of Sin! Awful things going on. Every street corner filled with decadence and crime."

Molimo pointed to a pair of harlots haranguing passersby. Most ignored them, but one or two stopped to barter price.

"Does that trouble you?" Kesira asked Molimo. "It shouldn't. Gelya said the sun also shines on them. They injure no one. Chounabel is as peaceful a city as poor, provincial Blinn." She chuckled and added, "The world loves the spice of wickedness. I do—I *did*. Let us keep the idea and accept the reality."

As they neared the end of the street and the spaces between shops widened to occasionally show a family dwelling in between, Kesira reined in. She frowned, feeling something amiss. She looked around and tried to figure out what gnawed at her senses.

Molimo touched her arm lightly, in concern.

"I don't know what it is," she said honestly. "A feeling. I ought not to depart Chounabel quite yet. But why not? Zolkan? He can take care of himself—he does easily."

Kesira turned in her saddle, studying the doorways
of the scattered businesses. The few houses were quiet
and the pedestrians showed no outward concern. Yet
Kesira grew increasingly edgy. Molimo lifted his chin
and pointed with it, not wanting to draw attention to
himself. Kesira glanced in the direction indicated, where
a squad of soldiers moved toward them along the street.

"They're looking for someone," Kesira said. The
bright red armbands with the white bar indicated they
were Imperial soldiers, not local peacekeepers out to
chevy a drunk or cutpurse.

Even as she spoke, Kesira turned to see Rouvin
pressed against a doorframe, eyes fixed on the soldiers.
He turned, smiled at her and waved, then flattened
even more as the soldiers drew even with her.

"May I be of assistance?" Kesira asked the officer
leading the soldiers.

He eyed her coldly. "Order of Gelya?" he asked.

"I have that honor and duty," she replied.

"The one we seek is no concern of yours," the officer
said, motioning to his men to continue their search.

"What has he done?" she asked. The officer studied
Molimo, obviously decided the youth did not fit the description of the hunted, and walked on without answering. To Molimo, Kesira said, "He seems intent on
his duty. And Rouvin is equally intent on evading him."

Rouvin slipped along the face of a wall, around the
building and out of sight.

"What should we do, Molimo? Go after Rouvin or
leave him and find our way alone?"

Even as she spoke, the cry went up from one of the
soldiers. The entire squad pulled forth their swords,
shifted shields on their arms, wheeled and started
in pursuit of Rouvin. Kesira and Molimo exchanged
glances, smiled broadly and spurred their horses onward, cutting across to a side street for easier travel.
There was no question now as to the right course of
action.

Chapter Seven

"LET HIM BE," cautioned Zolkan, clinging precariously to Kesira's shoulder. She heard the coarse gray robe rip slightly as the heavy *trilla* bird hung on for dear life. She didn't ask Zolkan where he'd been or where he'd come from so suddenly. Kesira had grown used to his odd comings and goings. The woman spurred her horse and took it around a corner, hoping to sight the fleet-footed Rouvin. The fugitive was nowhere to be seen, but the Emperor's guardsmen swarmed along the street, moving quickly and efficiently. "They get him soon," said Zolkan. "Do not interfere."

"Do you agree, Molimo?" she asked. The youth smiled and shook his head. Kesira laughed aloud. This added zest to life that had been missing before. What else remained for her? Order gone, patron dead, her Sisters worm-food, some crackbrained idea of going to the Quaking Lands—of which she had never heard and which would probably kill her—what else did Kesira Minette have but to seek some small adventure?

"Trouble," predicted Zolkan. The bird turned sullen and nestled himself into the flapping cowl. Kesira ignored him and kept a sharp watch for Rouvin. The man

had scant opportunity to make an escape. He had to be
hiding somewhere near.

"Molimo, find his horse," she ordered. "Get it ready.
When I find him, we'll want to leave Chounabel as
quickly as possible."

Kesira settled back and studied the street. The soldiers sought Rouvin in vain, but her quick eyes spotted
the man clinging to the eaves of a small taxidermy shop.
Rouvin kicked hard and pulled himself onto the roof
with a minimum of weapons clatter. The soldiers below
him never looked up; they were too intent on searching
each shop and house.

Rouvin waved to her, and Kesira gestured to tell the
man that rescue was at hand. Rouvin smiled and started
carefully along the roof top, then stopped dead in his
tracks. Kesira groaned inwardly. The officer in charge
had been as clever as Rouvin.

Both men stood on the same roof. Both drew weapons
simultaneously. And both attacked with stunning speed
and skill.

The harsh clash of steel weapons drew the attention
of the soldiers below. One pointed and soon the entire
squad gathered around to watch the fight between their
captain and the criminal they had sought so assidu-
ously.

Kesira sat astride her horse, viewing Rouvin's fight
with both admiration for the prowess and fear for his
reckless daring. The man seemed to have abandoned
all sense in every attack, yet Kesira knew enough about
swords and their use to appreciate how skilled Rouvin
was. The riposte, the quick parry and retreat, the ex-
plosive lunge—he did it all on the treacherous footing
afforded by the slanting rooftop.

"Get him!" yelled the officer. "Take him from behind!"

"Too much for you?" demanded Rouvin, slipping his
blade forward, then pulling it in a vicious slash that
almost opened the captain's gut. Blood trickled out
rather than flowed, only because the officer had slipped
and the blow missed by a fraction of an inch. "Where
is your honor? Aren't you enough of a warrior to handle
me all by yourself?"

Kesira knew Rouvin traveled on dangerous ground,

insulting the soldier's honor as he did, but the tactic worked. The captain became furious, lunged clumsily and Rouvin riposted perfectly. The tip of his blade slid along the soldier's arm and found a sheath in an exposed armpit. The captain's face lost all color and expression seconds before he stumbled and fell to his knees. Rouvin watched as the man toppled to the street below.

"He plays a dangerous game," Kesira said softly. "Can you aid him, Zolkan?"

"Why?"

"The soldiers are preparing to storm him. If enough attack at the same time, not even Rouvin can get away."

"Impale killers in Chounabel," the *trilla* bird said gruffly.

"Who knows what he did? The guard captain died in a fair fight. You could have seen it for yourself if you hadn't been hiding your head."

"No." The bird refused to budge.

"As Gelya taught, fortune rewards the brave."

"Do not interfere," squawked Zolkan, stirring about in her cowl. Kesira pulled a drawstring and trapped the bird within. Only incoherent sputterings issued forth.

"Rouvin needs our help," she said simply. "If you can't help, don't hinder."

Kesira pulled forth her stone-wood staff and leveled it as if she carried a lance. Taking a deep breath, calming herself and vowing to avoid the steel weapons, she lowered her head and kicked at the flanks of her horse. Galloping boldly, she caught one soldier in the side of the head with the butt end of her staff. Another soldier caught the side on his throat. Both went down in unstirring piles. Still another fell as she *thwacked!* him soundly with the staff. A fourth required a foot on the top of his head to convince him to make way.

"Rouvin!" she called. "Behind you!"

Rouvin dropped to one knee, pulled at his sword and sent the point directly backward. He caught one soldier in the groin. The Emperor's man gasped and cartwheeled off the roof.

"Move over!" Rouvin cried. "These people do not want to wish me good health and happiness!"

Kesira reined her steed around, using her staff further to fend off soldiers who had finally realized another danger had entered their ranks. Zolkan screeched, and the horse almost fell when Rouvin came hurling down off the roof to land squarely behind Kesira. The horse recovered and bolted. Kesira did nothing to control the gelding, knowing that the wildness provided as much defense as her staff or Rouvin's dextrous swordplay.

They thundered back down the street, wind whipping at Kesira's short brown hair and bringing tears to her eyes.

"Good timing," congratulated Rouvin. "I knew you wouldn't let me down."

Kesira grabbed one of Rouvin's hands clinging to her thigh and pulled it up to rest on her waist.

"I'm only saving your hide," she called back to him. "Keep your hands to yourself."

Rouvin laughed and Zolkan continued his raucous calls of anger and fear.

"There," Kesira said. "Ahead. Molimo has your horse. Let's not dally around here." Rouvin leaned around her and saw the youth holding the silver-studded reins of the big bay laden with the goods Rouvin had purchased—stolen?—while in Chounabel.

Kesira started to slow the headlong pace, but Rouvin applied his spurs to the gelding's side to keep it racing full tilt. With a movement more insane than adept, Rouvin leaped from Kesira's horse and onto the back of his own. The animal stumbled and went to one knee, then rose, snorting, and turned to eye the man indignantly.

"Back to the Plains of Roggen!" he cried. Kesira and Molimo paced him until their animals began to tire. Only then did Rouvin slacken the pace and allow them to walk their horses.

"What adventure," said Rouvin, taking in a deep breath and exhaling forcefully. "That is the way life is meant to be lived. Always on the knife edge of danger."

"Without danger, there can be no glory," agreed Kesira, "but what did you do to bring down so many of the Emperor's guard on you? Chounabel is virtually without laws, or so I have been told."

"The City of Sin," said Rouvin, "does have a few

peculiar ideas concerning propriety. Even here laws stalk the unwary. I seem to have violated one or two of them."

"All!" squawked Zolkan.

"Perhaps the bird is correct. I might have violated *all* of them. So be it. I hadn't intended returning to Chounabel any time soon."

"You stole?" asked Kesira. "That is a crime."

"Ah, but the stolen fruit is the sweetest," answered Rouvin. "But fear naught, lovely lady, there is nothing to offend you in my booty. In fact"—Rouvin bent over and dug into his saddlebags—"this might even amuse you."

He handed Kesira a small figurine of an armed and armored man. She took it hesitantly and stared at it. The detail of eyes and mouth, hair and fingers, was extraordinary.

"It's a mechanism of some refinement, much like myself," Rouvin said immodestly. "Squeeze just between the shoulders."

Kesira smiled when the warrior doll lifted his arm and shook the sword at her in mock menace.

"Press just a small bit lower." Rouvin watched as the sword dropped and the shield came up. "And at the small of the back." He laughed heartily at her embarrassment. The figurine's trousers parted and a long, lifelike male organ poked forth. "A swordsman of the finest kind. Just like me."

Kesira fought down her shame at responding in such an unseemly way. She was hardly a sophisticate, but neither was she a virgin who blushed at the slightest provocation. When she had told Rouvin that celibacy was not part of Gelya's vows, she had told the truth. Dominie Tredlo had introduced her to the ways between men and women and every trip to Blinn had provided that much more experience for her.

But this!

"The City of Sin," Rouvin said in a low, conspiratorial voice, "manufactures other mechanical devices of much more interest—and utility."

"I am not interested." Kesira thrust out the warrior doll in Rouvin's direction.

"A present," he said. "To remember me by. And when

you play with it, push the spot still lower. The figurine will march about in a most military fashion."

Kesira thanked him insincerely and put the doll into the folds of her tattered robe. "Do you think the soldiers will follow?" she finally asked.

"Perhaps so. Killing two of their rank is not likely to be forgotten soon."

"Two?"

"The captain on the rooftop, of course, and the other. It seems he had not learned the first rule of a game of chance."

"And what," asked Kesira, "is the first rule?"

"If you're going to cheat, do it well. He was clumsy and when the Sultan's Egg appeared twice in one hand, I knew he had extra cards in the deck." Rouvin smoothed his rumpled, wine-colored silk doublet and settled the light body armor into a more comfortable position. "He was no better a fighter than he was a card cheat."

"You killed him?"

"I only wanted my money back. And perhaps a bit more for punitive reasons," Rouvin added. "He thought, simply because he wore the Emperor's armband and was surrounded by a dozen of his comrades in arms, that he was invulnerable. He was wrong then, he is right now. Nothing more can be done to him."

"You killed him?" Kesira repeated.

Rouvin looked away over the farmlands surrounding them, then back along the road.

"It's best we part company. Let them come after me. You ride on to wherever you were heading. To the Yearn Mountains? To rebuild your nunnery?"

"The Order of Gelya is dead," Kesira said. She quickly explained the plight of the mission in Chounabel and how badly she felt the loss of all her Sisters, both to death and to apathy and fear.

"If not back to the Yearns, then where?" Rouvin asked.

"I cast the rune sticks," said Kesira, wondering if she dared tell this man about her divinations.

"You have the power?" he asked, almost in awe. "My mother told me only a handful of humans possessed it. Very rare. Even I, as half-demon, cannot accurately read the rune sticks. And I have tried, oh yes, I have tried. What did you find?"

Kesira composed herself before launching into the story of the two readings. "Lenc, Eznofadil and one other demon were responsible for Gelya's death."

"A demon alliance. Unheard of," mused Rouvin. "My mother Ayondela told me that all demons mistrust one another. As long as that condition holds, they ignore humankind and content themselves with petty intrigues. This sounds as if the three might vanquish the other demons and turn their unwonted—unwanted!—attention to us."

"The destruction of my Order shows this to be the case," said Kesira. "In my second casting I saw more. Molimo, Zolkan and I head for the place where I might be able to obtain some measure of revenge."

"Revenge? Against demons? Ha!" Rouvin laughed until he clutched his sides, tears running down his cheeks. "That's a rich jest—on *you!* No one gets revenge on a demon. No human, that is. And seldom another demon."

"We go to the Quaking Lands," Kesira said primly, offended by Rouvin's behavior. And she was astounded at the sudden change that came over him—from laughter to instant sobriety.

"What did you say?"

"If you ride to the east, you might avoid the Emperor's guard," she said. "Molimo and I ride on west. Gelya favored rivers. We can cross the Pharna River safely enough. Molimo points out that the Quaking Lands are only a week's ride farther."

"The Quaking Lands are forbidden," said Rouvin. His entire visage clouded over, and Kesira saw tendons standing in bold relief on his forearms as the man tensed. "To go there is suicidal."

"One might say the same thing about killing two officers in the Emperor's guard."

"I still live. They'll never catch me. Besides, I have enough sense to run when trouble nears. You walk knowingly into the jaws of destruction if you venture into the Quaking Lands."

"Molimo says nothing about such danger," she said.

"Molimo cannot say a damned word!" flared Rouvin.

Kesira knew then that the warrior was not feigning his displeasure with her decision. She read no fear in the man, but concern—for her?—poured forth.

"That was a cruel thing to say," she pointed out. "Molimo communicates well enough without speech. He knows the way. Zolkan can scout from above for us. There will be no trouble reaching the Quaking Lands."

"What was the third demon's name? The one in league with Lenc and Eznofadil?"

"Howenthal," she said. Now Kesira knew Rouvin did not fake concern. His face turned as white as bleached linen.

"Of the demons, Howenthal is the most dangerous to humans," Rouvin said. "He is not...rational."

"Is any demon?" she countered.

"Some are, more than others. My mother, though her ways were strange, was not irrational. She spoke highly of Merrisen and Gelya, both. Of Wemilat and a few others, also."

Molimo rode closer, straining to hear. Kesira reached out and rested a hand on the youth's shoulder. He smiled wanly at her, but his attention centered on what Rouvin said.

"Howenthal and the Quaking Lands are connected? How?" she asked.

"Howenthal rules this portion of the world. His powers are immense, but narrow in scope. He causes the very ground to tremble. When angered, Howenthal can bring down entire nations with his earthquakes. It is said that the Quaking Lands are a testing ground for him to practice. He is unsociable, scorning humans and most demon contact, and lives in a deep valley surrounded by unscalable mountains. The few paths into the valley are treacherous due to the quakings."

"So he is the one I must confront," she said. Rolling the name over and over on her tongue produced a bitter taste. This, more than anything else, convinced Kesira that the demon Howenthal was equally responsible for Gelya's death—and the subsequent death of the Order.

"Howenthal will destroy you. If you are lucky, you might reach the mouth of the valley. But the Quaking Lands are impassable, unless Howenthal allows it. And he won't."

"Have you ever seen him?"

"Once."

"And?"

"You ride to the west?" Rouvin asked.

"Tell me of Howenthal," Kesira demanded.

"Tell her," squawked Zolkan from his cloth prison. "Tell her and convince her to abandon foolish trip." Kesira reached back and loosened the drawstring on the cowl. A green feathered arrow shot into the sky, flapped hard, then settled onto her shoulder, where Kesira was developing calluses.

"If I say more, it will only firm her resolve," Rouvin said to Zolkan. "Will tales of Howenthal torturing helpless children affect her? No. Can I convince her that the Quaking Lands will churn her guts and cause one internal organ to grind against another until she dies horribly? No. Why, I cannot even persuade her of a simple thing like sharing my bed." Rouvin cocked his head to one side and asked, "Can I?"

"Your guesses are all correct. The answer is 'no' in every case."

"See, Zolkan. You try to change her mind."

Kesira cut off the *trilla* bird's protest. "We ride to the Quaking Lands. If Howenthal is even partially responsible for Gelya's demise, then I must avenge my patron. Nothing else remains to me."

"The world can be yours!" shouted Rouvin, his anger building. "What is this revenge you speak of? What does one mere mortal concern Howenthal? He is a *demon!* He destroys wantonly because he has the power to do so. What can you do against one such as he?"

Kesira shrugged. No answer for that occurred to her, but the rune cast had shown her what must be done. Honor and duty to her patron dictated as much. If she perished, she did so honorably in an attempt to discharge her belief in Gelya and his teachings. No warrior dying in battle would be able to claim more.

"A fool!" Rouvin cried. "I am guiding a fool across the River Pharna!"

"Oh?" she asked. "I thought you rode to the east—away from the river."

"Have you ever been near the Quaking Lands?" he asked. "No, I thought not. I have seen them."

"So has Molimo."

"I can warn you," Rouvin said. "I warn you now, but you don't listen. Perhaps when you see the danger, then you will listen."

"You will accompany us, then?" Kesira asked.

Rouvin sat sullenly, then jerked his reins and headed directly west, toward the River Pharna and beyond. Beyond to the Quaking Lands.

Kesira Minette rode and meditated, a way of easing the burden of the long miles they traversed. The Emperor's guard had made only a token effort to catch Rouvin, returning to Chounabel and the city's wiles after only a single day of pursuit. Kesira rode and considered what lay ahead—and what lay behind.

She examined her motives in this journey and always came to the same answer. Necessity pursued her and honor demanded this of her. Her serenity had been shattered by the violence of the warring demons; the aftermath of one of their battles had destroyed Gelya and the precious comfort afforded by the Order. Even worse, Kesira's place of solitude and peace had been ripped away. Long meditations only partially returned her to the tranquillity of her former life.

Kesira touched the gold ribbon around her waist. It became more than a symbol of the Order. It transformed her into a vessel of vengeance against Howenthal and Eznofadil and Lenc. The trio of demons had shattered her history. She was honor-bound to destroy their future.

Kesira rose up through the thick shrouds of her meditation when she felt a hand shaking her shoulder. She turned and saw Molimo's hard-set face.

"What's wrong?" she asked.

Molimo pointed to the ground. Kesira studied the dirt path they followed and eventually saw what the sharp-eyed youth had so easily spotted. The tracks of a small band of horses had passed this way within the past ten hours.

"The rain hasn't erased the tracks," she said aloud. "How near are they?"

Molimo held up four fingers, indicating four miles.

"Danger?" muttered Zolkan, pulling his head out from

a protecting wing. The bird slept while Kesira meditated. She felt her time was the better spent.

"Possibly. Rouvin is scouting ahead, but Molimo found tracks of—how many?"

The youth indicated six riders.

"Poor country. No brigands here," said Zolkan. "Danger lives close by."

"If they're not brigands, we don't have to worry," Kesira said.

Molimo shook his head violently and began working his way through a series of hand signs they had agreed upon. Kesira translated painfully.

"I hardly think we are in danger, Molimo. Certainly not from another religious order." She frowned when he continued to gesture. Kesira knew she missed all he meant to convey, but she was weary from long hours in the saddle and had little time for such nonsense.

"Get Rouvin," squawked Zolkan. "He tell of danger." The bird launched himself into the warm spring air and flapped noisily for a moment, then silently glided ahead, lost in the dusky sky.

Kesira and Molimo rode on in silence. By the time a shadowy figure drifted across the trail, the sun had set over the Pharna River and clouds boiled up from their resting spots around the Yearn Mountains. The night would again be filled with heavy rains.

"Zolkan told you?" asked Rouvin.

"Molimo spotted tracks. Six?"

"Eight, now. Two more joined the band where they camped near the river. We can only hope they move on soon. Otherwise we will lose days waiting for them to pass us by."

"Are you afraid of them? Molimo suggested they might be from some nearby religious order. Surely, they would respect my right to pass unmolested. I am the Senior Sister of Gelya now." Her hand stroked along the silken gold ribbon at her waist. It had taken Sister Fenelia fourteen years of diligent service to attain that honor; Kesira had gained it while hardly more than an apprentice. Kesira appreciated the burden.

"Molimo says much for one who can't speak," said Rouvin.

"Just because he doesn't have a tongue doesn't mean eyes and mind aren't sharp."

"Too sharp," said Rouvin.

"What of the band ahead of us?"

"They look to be of the Order of the Steel Crescent."

"I have never heard of this Order," said Kesira, trying hard to remember any mention that might have been made in her earshot. "No, I can't say I know of them."

"They are loyal to Howenthal because we near his territory. This Order worships only power—and Howenthal provides a clear example of raw power misused."

Kesira scoffed at the idea. Religious orders were not devoted to what the patron demon might do for them, but rather what the teachings of the individual patron offered them to apply to life. Gelya spoke eloquently of dutiful life and charity, doing for others honorably. She had no idea what Howenthal passed along to his followers, but a good teacher never engendered students such as suggested by Rouvin.

The man was obviously mistaken.

"Back," muttered Zolkan. "We go back along trail."

"We stay," Kesira said firmly. "And I think you overstate the case, Rouvin. You make these men sound evil."

Molimo tugged at her sleeve, but Kesira was beginning to warm to the subject.

"Gelya preached that true friendship is like his wildflower, slow to blossom but of long duration. Simply because you do not know these people, you think the worst of them."

Molimo tugged harder at Kesira's robe. She turned and, halfway toward the youth, saw the sharp glint of fading sunlight on steel. Kesira continued the slow circuit. They were ringed in by eight men, all with drawn swords.

"Good evening," she said pleasantly. Kesira knew this was a chance to prove to Rouvin how wrong he was. She jerked slightly as Zolkan took wing and shot into the sky. "Wait!" she cried, when one of the armed warriors started to unlimber a sling and knock Zolkan from the sky. "The *trilla* bird is harmless."

"Good meal," mumbled the one with the sling, but the dim light convinced him not to pursue Zolkan's flight.

"Who might you be?" demanded one of the men. He stepped forward. Only slightly taller than Kesira, the man appeared fragile. Thin arms and legs barely supported the armor he wore. Sandy hair poked out from under a plain cloth cap and a feeble attempt at growing mustache left the impression of a caterpillar crawling over his upper lip. The only thing that distinguished him was the faint network of bright pink scars all over his body. It was as if he had fallen into a flaming spider's web and had the pattern burned into his flesh.

"I am of the Order of Gelya."

"Gelya?" the man snorted. "Gelya's dead."

"I am aware of that," Kesira said, not liking his tone. Behind her she heard Rouvin moving slightly, positioning himself to draw his swords. Molimo stood at her side, arms limp—but the expression on his face worried Kesira the most. The distant gaze foretold of the transformation into wolf.

"There's a toll to be paid on this road. A big one." The man took another step forward and used the tip of his saber to lift the hem of her robe. Kesira kept her feet planted, but her stone-wood staff lightly tapped the sword away.

"Who are you to claim a toll on a public road?" she asked.

"We are of the Order of the Steel Crescent," he said. "I am Nehan-dir, leader of this fine band." Several ugly snickers echoed from the darkness.

"If you are likewise connected with an Order, then we share much in common."

"We'll share much more in common when you pay the toll demanded," he said. Nehan-dir lunged, his sword going straight and true for Kesira's throat. She tipped the staff slightly to one side; the sword deflected and passed harmlessly to the side. "Ho, a fighter. You'll make good sport for us. We have been o'erlong on the road."

"What sort of Order encourages such behavior?" she demanded.

"What sort?" said Nehan-dir, sneering. "The Order of the Steel Crescent worships power. Our patron sold us to another as if we were cattle. We abandoned both and sought out a new patron."

"And now they go from one to another, seeking only the powerful," cut in Rouvin.

"There is nothing wrong with power," said Nehan-dir, "as long as you use it."

Nehan-dir made some small gesture that only Rouvin saw. Kesira was taken by surprise when Rouvin shot past her, his swords slashing down toward Nehan-dir's head. The smaller man ducked the dual-edged blow and dodged backward.

"Take them!" he shouted.

The ring tightened about Kesira and the others.

Chapter Eight

"GET BACK!" cried Rouvin, shoving Kesira to one side. One of his swords met Nehan-dir's. Fat blue sparks leaped into the night, and the ringing of steel against steel almost deafened the woman. Kesira recovered and swung about, her staff whirling just below knee level. She tripped one of Nehan-dir's men and spun the staff in a quick overhead circle to land squarely on the top of another's head.

"I'm all right. How about yourself?" she asked. But Rouvin and Nehan-dir engaged in deadly swordplay. Kesira blinked in surprise at how quick—and how strong—the deceptively thin Nehan-dir proved to be. He was almost more than Rouvin could handle, and Rouvin was part demon.

Three men grabbed Molimo and flung him to the ground. Kesira whirled the staff around her, forming a protective curtain of stone-wood. She waded into the center of the tight knot of men around Molimo, forcing them away. From her point of view, she saved their lives. Molimo's face melted and reformed in a lupine snarl. The transformation, once begun, proceeded faster and faster. Molimo crouched on all fours, snapping and

snarling. With a sudden bound, the wolf-man vanished
into the night, leaving Kesira and Rouvin to fight for
their lives.

Kesira did not take the time to consider Molimo's
motives. As a beast, he lacked certain human logical
faculties and loyalties. She could not blame him if his
animal instincts told him to flee rather than stand and
fight.

Kesira admitted to herself that she'd take flight, too,
if the opportunity presented itself.

But it didn't.

She found herself facing a man armed with a spear.
The honed steel edge of the blade poked and prodded
for her body. Only quick and accurate staff work prevented him from skewering her. But Kesira weakened
under renewed assaults from the others. She faced three,
four, then five of the men. Eventually one took a heavy
hit to his shoulder, but succeeded in trapping the butt
end of her staff. Falling heavily, arm circling the staff,
he wrenched her weapon away and left her barehanded
facing the other four.

"This will be fun," said the man with the spear as
he advanced.

Kesira kept her mind in fighting calm, not antici-
pating, waiting only to react to the first misstep. It
came suddenly. She batted aside the spear with one
hand and drove forked fingers into the man's eyes.
Yowling in pain, he jerked away. She caught the spear
as he dropped it.

"Away!" called Rouvin. He had forced Nehan-dir to
a small ravine. The crusted edge gave way under Nehan-dir and sent the man toppling onto his back a few
feet below. Rouvin vaulted over the two that Kesira
had felled earlier, kicked his way through the four still
around her and the pair of them raced into the night.

From behind she heard Nehan-dir gasping for breath,
struggling to give orders to the others in the band.

"Keep running," panted Rouvin. "We've got to put
as much distance between us and them as possible. I
know the Order of the Steel Crescent. They don't give
up like the Emperor's guard did. They'll track us until
they die of old age—or until they catch us."

Kesira felt as if she was lumbering along, ungainly

and increasingly tired. When she could go on no longer, she reached down within herself and tapped on the reservoir of strength locked there and released it. She got a second wind and maintained the breakneck pace.

Rouvin finally found a spot he deemed adequate for taking a small rest. They huddled a few feet inside a cave opening and spoke in guarded tones.

"They'll be on our trail soon," Rouvin said. "We've got to keep going. Regain strength, keep moving. It's our only chance."

"Molimo is out there," said Kesira. "We might be able to communicate with him. And Zolkan. He flies."

"Don't count on them," said Rouvin, getting his labored breathing under control. He leaned back against the cold rock wall and closed his eyes. "We dare not give ourselves false hope. Only by depending totally on our own resources can we escape. If they aid us, fine. But do not rely on them."

"A good point," Kesira said.

"This is a fine mess you've got us into," Rouvin finally said, after a long pause.

"I?"

"Going to the Quaking Lands was suicidal. I told you that. Even the bird told you that. But did you listen? No, you have some crackbrained mission to perform."

"No one forced you to come along," Kesira said, fighting to keep her temper.

"Without me, Nehan-dir would have you trailing along behind his horse, a rope around your neck. I knew what you'd be up against. How could I allow you to unknowingly blunder into such?"

"You're not doing such a good job of it," she said. "We seem to have ended up on foot, without supplies or horses, or prospects to improve our lot. Those brigands pursue us, and we're still some weeks travel from the Quaking Lands."

"May my mother Ayondela take the Quaking Lands!" he shouted. "Forget them! Forget this revenge against the demons. They are too powerful. See how a handful of followers of the Steel Crescent cornered us like silly *prin* rats? We might as well have rolled over and exposed our bellies to them."

"Your voice carries farther after dark," Kesira pointed

out. "Should we build a signal fire for Nehan-dir to follow?"

Rouvin heaved a sigh and said, "If we press on, directly over this mountain, we'll be within a day's walk of the River Pharna. Cross it, get back to Chounabel. Or go north to Blinn. Anywhere!"

"I am going to the Quaking Lands," Kesira said with conviction. "You think I am so dishonorable that I allow adversity to stop me? Revenge will be mine. It *will!*"

Rouvin reached out and gripped her forearm. She jerked away, but he held on grimly. "Bringing Howenthal to account for his actions is beyond a mortal's grasp. Even I, as half-demon, know that there is little I can do to influence them. They are too powerful."

"Then you, as a half-demon, can leave. I, as a mere mortal, will do what I must."

"We'll die," he said.

"Leave, then. If I die, it will be honorably. What more can anyone ask from life?"

Rouvin released her arm and stood. "It's time we moved on. Nehan-dir will have rallied his men. After what we did to them, mercy will be far from their thoughts when they find us."

"If you are such a good warrior, why should they catch us?"

"Good is one thing," Rouvin said, "lucky is another. With you sucking at all good fortune, there is scant luck to go around."

They emerged from the depression in the side of the hill and began making their way up. The darkness formed a cloaking blanket; this worked for and against them. Kesira blundered often, foot slipping on a loose stone, her fingers missing a key grip. More than once Rouvin's demon-strong hand supported her. By the time they reached the summit of the hill, she was again exhausted and needed rest. Rouvin was in little better condition.

"I haven't scaled mountains for some years," he said. "When I rode for the Emperor, we had no call to go bounding up hillsides—at least, not on foot."

"And after?" she asked.

"I did some rock climbing," he said. "But obviously not enough."

"Why do you say that? You were as surefooted as a mountain goat. I felt as if both my feet were lodged in milk pails."

Rouvin pointed.

Kesira followed the line of his arm, past the finger and downhill. She felt coldness forming in the pit of her stomach. It required several minutes of effort to calm herself enough to speak.

"How did they find us so quickly?" she asked.

Rouvin shook his head.

"If we press on, what are our chances?"

"Not good," Rouvin said. "The way Nehan-dir follows tells me that there is more to his tracking ability than we know."

"A demon aids him?"

"Or a demon's magic. The Order of the Steel Crescent worship the strongest, no matter what demands are placed upon them. In return for such a tracking charm, Nehan-dir might have given much more than simple allegiance to Howenthal."

"I cannot believe that there are men so unfeeling that they follow only power," said Kesira. "Where is the control, the ability to use for good?"

"They propound different philosophies," Rouvin said. "You have not seen enough outside your nunnery to realize that most demons are not like your Gelya."

"Is your mother so different?" Kesira shot back.

"She is more like Howenthal than Gelya," admitted Rouvin. "Power is important to her, but she'd never allow such scum as Nehan-dir to worship her."

"How did the Steel Crescent come to be? Nehan-dir muttered that their patron had sold them? I didn't understand."

Rouvin urged her on down the side of the hill opposite to the approaching band of men. "Their Order began as a tribute to Tolek the Spare. Tolek, as a patron, lacked everything you found in Gelya or I find in my mother. He fell on hard times, gambled heavily and lost, and bartered away his worshipers for a parcel of land on a distant island and the cancellation of his debts."

"You mean a patron exchanged believers for worldly gain?" Kesira was aghast.

"Tolek never amounted to much, as a demon or a patron. Ayondela and Merrisen made him a laughingstock, and the demon who had accepted the worshipers soon discarded them."

"I've never heard of such a thing."

"It happens, but seldom. The Order of the Steel Crescent drifted, without guidance, without ruling principles or much honor, until Nehan-dir joined their rank. He rose swiftly by dint of arms. He reasoned that, since Tolek bartered them away, then they had the right to sell their services to whichever demon offered the most. Nehan-dir led the Order to become mercenaries."

Kesira couldn't answer. The shock at this revelation turned the foundations of her beliefs to dust. Sister Fenelia and Dominie Tredlo had often said Gelya was the finest of patrons because of his teachings, his devotion, his affection. Allusions both had made to other demons now came back to her; the other patrons were not only different, they were possessed of motives less than altruistic.

But to trade away worshipers?

"They have experienced grief, I am sure," said Kesira, "but what do they gain spiritually? How can Nehan-dir and the others find peace within themselves by selling their services?"

"I'm afraid you're going to be in a position to ask Nehan-dir personally," said Rouvin, his voice grim. "This path leads into a box canyon."

Kesira spun and looked back along their path. Walls rose on either side. To regain the mouth of the canyon would take considerable hiking—and time had run out. She saw the bouncing of lanterns as the Steel Crescent followers came down the trail after them.

"Can we scale the sides of the canyon?"

"In time, in daylight, after a night's rest," Rouvin said. "But I tire with every additional step. How do you fare?"

Kesira did not deny her exhaustion and lack of strength, but she did not give in to it, either. She accepted and tried to compromise with it.

"Which side, left or right, affords us the easiest climb?" she asked.

"The right," said Rouvin, examining both. Kesira

saw a glint of green in the man's eyes. The demon power seeped out now, nurturing him, replenishing his inhuman strength. He looked at her, and the eyes had returned to their natural blue. "I see better at night than most," he said. "The path is still a difficult one."

"I will not surrender like this. I must know I have tried everything possible."

He smiled at her, and she felt some measure of energy trickle back into her body. Without another word, Rouvin started up the sheer face of the softstone cliff, Kesira right behind. Many times on the climb she wished for a safety rope. Depending on Rouvin to glance back often and pull her up when needed presented a danger that would eventually catch up with her.

"Rest," she panted. "Let's tie ourselves together." Kesira started to unfasten her gold sash and the blue rope denoting belief in Gelya's teachings when a stone turned nearby.

"We can furnish the rope," came a voice out of the darkness.

Rouvin sprang to his feet, sword in hand. A whining sound, a dull crunch, and Rouvin sank to the ground unconscious.

"Kalam-rin is expert with the sling. Rouvin might awaken in the morning with nothing more than a cut on his temple," said Nehan-dir, walking forward. He unshuttered the lantern he carried. Cool yellow light spilled forth and bathed Kesira. She felt trapped in the beam, unable to move to either side.

"How did you know we would climb this side of the canyon?"

"I didn't," Nehan-dir said smugly. "I placed a few lanterns on your horses and started them down the canyon. Three of my men went up the rim on the far side, and I and the other two patrolled this side."

"We could have backtracked and gotten free?"

"Yes," Nehan-dir said, laughing nastily.

"By your count, I felled two of your men." Kesira tried to take what satisfaction she could in that knowledge. With swords drawn, the two men on either side of her had a great advantage, but their greatest lay in her exhaustion. Even lifting her arms proved a feat beyond her present strength. She had run as far as she could. They would be able to do with her as they pleased.

"The one you crowned with the staff is still unconscious and the one whose eyes you poked out is blinded. The other merely hobbles. You failed to break his kneecap."

"A pity," she said.

"Let us have her," said the one Kesira took to be Kalam-rin. A long cord dangled from his belt and he had the quick, nervous gestures of one accustomed to using the sling rather than the sword.

"We take her to the Citadel," he said.

"She's no celibate," protested the man. "Gelya's whores, we called them in Chounabel."

Kesira blinked as Nehan-dir swung his fist and connected squarely with the side of Kalam-rin's head. The man stumbled and fell heavily. His eyes glazed over, but he never passed out—quite.

"Touch her and Howenthal has a new sacrifice."

This snapped Kalam-rin from his haze. Frightened eyes peered up at the scrawny leader of the Order.

"Understand, worm?"

Kalam-rin's head bobbed up and down, threatening to fall off from the effort. Kesira studied Nehan-dir and marveled at his command over these men. All in the band appeared stronger and larger, yet they feared him. Whatever quality he had, it impressed these hardened warriors.

"What of Rouvin?" she asked.

"We'll bring him along, too. There's no need to cut his throat and leave him for the jackals." Nehan-dir laughed his harsh, nasty laugh and added, "He might provide a moment's diversion."

Kesira was pulled roughly to her feet and her hands securely bound behind her back. Rouvin was dragged along behind by Kalam-rin. Kesira's heart went out to Rouvin, but her mind concentrated on moving one foot in front of the other. She had passed beyond the point of physical boundaries and now moved by will alone.

Kesira Minette peered out the small barred window and into the courtyard as she had done since arriving at the Citadel four days earlier. Food appeared through a slot in the door and she saw signs of life without, at the periphery of the courtyard, but other than these tenuous bonds, she had been cut off from all humankind.

Kesira turned and stared at Rouvin. Being dragged unconscious for so many miles behind Kalam-rin had sorely injured the man. His back had been slashed to ribbons by sharp rocks and the bouncing up and down as they descended from the canyon rim had addled his wits. Rouvin had remained in a coma during the week's travel to the Citadel and the four days of incarceration.

"Whassit?" the man mumbled, trying to roll off his belly. Kesira went to him and held him down. She had force-fed him what she could, but he had grown increasingly weaker. Trying to restrain him before would have been futile; now she did it without much effort.

"You are recovering," she said. "Your wounds are healing slowly. Do you want something to drink?" She glanced at the fired clay jug containing tepid water. It was enough to gag a maggot, but would be better than nothing.

"Drink," he agreed.

Shortly, Rouvin pulled himself upright on the narrow wooden plank bunk slung from the wall by a pair of thick chains and rubbed hands over his eyes.

"I'm not dead," he finally said. "Dead must feel much better than this."

"We're prisoners in the Citadel."

"The Citadel? Oh, the Order of the Steel Crescent's chapel. Why didn't they kill us?" Rouvin's eyes focused sharply on Kesira.

"They have done nothing to me." Seeing his continued stare, Kesira added, "And I have agreed to nothing. This is curious. When we first met I thought Nehandir desired me sexually. He prevented his men from touching me in that fashion."

"Odd," muttered Rouvin. "There's more to this than I thought."

"Do you want some food? It isn't the best, but it is filling."

Rouvin ate and drank more of the water and eventually lumbered to his feet, stretching and moving about. He grimaced only once, when healing skin pulled too

tightly across his back. Kesira watched him in frank
admiration of his physique; muscles rippled in tightly
rolled bundles across his belly; his chest was thick; his
arms were those of a man half again Rouvin's size.
Truly, she believed he was part demon.

He walked to the tiny window and stared out.

"I see no one, only shadows hovering at the edges of
the courtyard," she told him. "But in the center is that
post. Do you know what it is?"

"That," said Rouvin, "is the Order's altar. A tiny chip
of jade rests atop the stake. It must signify their allegiance to Howenthal."

"The jade empowers Howenthal?" she asked.

"It augments an already immense power. This is more
symbolic than anything else," the warrior said. "It rep-
resents the Order's willingness to follow—for the moment."

"How awful," said Kesira, shuddering delicately. "To
barter yourself for gain. Where is the honor?"

"I don't know, but I suspect that jade chip allows
Howenthal to peer into the Citadel and keep an eye on
the goings on."

"That might explain why so few venture forth. They
do not wish to attract the demon's attention."

Rouvin nodded. He paced around the cell, running
his hands up and down his bare arms. Kesira had cut
off his fine doublet to cleanse his wounds; he was now
naked to the waist. The leather trousers he wore had
taken a beating, but had better protected his posterior
and legs.

"Have you tried the door?" Rouvin asked, examining
it carefully. "It hardly seems strong enough to be a cell
door. Maybe they locked us in a storeroom."

Rouvin reached out to touch the door and screeched
in agony as an invisible hand lifted him into the air
and casually tossed him into the far wall. Rouvin
smashed into the cold stone, his injured back bearing
the brunt of the force. He gasped and sat on the floor,
clutching himself, teeth chattering.

"That w-wasn't such a smart thing to do," he said.
"Magicks bar the way."

"I hadn't examined the door," said Kesira.

He stared at her, the question unspoken.

"I wouldn't leave without you," she answered him simply.

"Perhaps we can pry out the bars in the window," he said.

"I can open the door," Kesira said, looking at the simple wooden portal. She reached out and tugged at the latch. The door creaked open. A shimmering curtain blocked exit.

"That's not much of a help," Rouvin said sourly.

"If I move the curtain aside, can you get free?" she asked. Already she began the mind-calming exercises she had spent a lifetime learning. The reaching out would be simple; her mind need only be blank. To react rather than initiate, to find the weakness and use it. Those were the weapons of the mind she called on to combat the magical curtain pulled over the doorway.

Rouvin stood beside her. "Be careful not to alert Howenthal." His words fell on deaf ears. Kesira had lost herself totally in the endless maze of her own mind. Meditation became all. She surged and flowed with the tides of the universe, entered the currents and accepted.

As simply as drawing back a curtain, she moved the deadly screen and allowed Rouvin to pass.

"Now you! Hurry!" he urged.

But the woman wavered, her strength fading. She dropped to her knees and fought to retain control. It slipped from her and she rose up from her trance.

"It's gone," she said in a small, choked voice. "And I'm so tired. So tired." She began to curl up on the rocky floor and go to sleep.

"Kesira!" Rouvin called. But he saw his pleas would do no good. The woman had exhausted herself. He looked around, got bearings and hurried off down the corridor, feeling the pressure of time. Howenthal might sense the escape—after all, Rouvin carried some of the power of a demon within his breast.

Rouvin stopped and peered cautiously around a corner. Snoring loudly, asleep at a rude wooden desk, sat a grizzled old man. Rouvin walked on cat's feet to a point immediately behind the hunched-over man. He doubled his fist and smashed down with all his strength. His normal blow would have crushed the man's skull like a delicate ceramic bowl. As it was, in his debilitated state, Rouvin barely felt bone yield. The man crumpled and twisted to the floor.

"Now, what do I seek?" Rouvin said, going through the drawers. He found nothing. Searching his victim, he discovered a long jade rod. "This must be the key," he said, hefting it. Power exuded from the slender shaft and into his body. Rouvin felt better than he had since awakening in the cell.

Hurrying back, he stopped in front of Kesira's cell. The curtain of scintillant energy taunted him. Rouvin examined the edges of the curtain where it meshed with the stone, where it touched wood. A tiny hole with small burn marks around it caught his eye. Rouvin thrust the jade rod into it; the charge snapped his head back and turned his arm numb, but the magical curtain vanished.

He rushed into the cell and shook Kesira awake.

"We leave. Now," he said urgently. The intensity of his tone held Kesira long enough for her to stagger outside.

"You freed me," she said. "But how? I hardly know what I did to get you outside the curtain."

"This." Rouvin yanked the jade rod from the hole. The curtain returned. "Let's hope this confuses them long enough. I am leaving clues aplenty."

They went back to where the jailer lay unconscious. Rouvin pulled the man into an empty cell and used the jade rod to drop the deadly magic curtain over the doorway.

"How do we get out of the Citadel?" asked Kesira. She had recovered only slightly, and fought to keep from passing out again.

"In a hurry," Rouvin said. "Even this small use of magic might have alerted Howenthal."

They had started up the stairs into the keep when Kesira had to reach out and support herself against Rouvin's strong body.

"Sorry," she apologized. "My legs turned weak and watery."

The expression on his face snapped her to full alertness.

"I felt it, too," he said. "Come on, run!"

The ground trembled with the full anger of a demon, throwing them to hands and knees and preventing escape.

"Howenthal!" cried Rouvin. "He's found us out!"

Chapter Nine

"HOWENTHAL must've sensed the power used to open the cell door," Rouvin cried over the bull-throated roar of the earthquake still shaking the keep. "That's the only explanation."

"He might have been coming here anyway," said Kesira Minette, struggling to regain her feet. The ponderous and irrepressible movement of the world beneath her caused dizziness to come and go. She fought to remain on her feet. Even as the woman reached out to support herself against the stone wall, a new and more potent quake rumbled through the keep and casually tossed her to the stairs. She landed in a pile atop Rouvin.

In spite of the temblor, Rouvin rose up, carrying her with him. She felt the man-demon's body strain with intense effort as he made his way to the top of the stairs and opened the door leading out into the courtyard. Kesira blinked in surprise at the sight.

The post with the tiny chip of jade affixed to it was now bathed in harsh green light. While the world quaked angrily, the pillar and the jade stood rock-still.

"The altar," she muttered, pointing. Rouvin's attention flickered in that direction for the briefest of instants, then turned to the gateway leading from the Citadel of the Steel Crescent and into the countryside. Carrying Kesira piggyback, he trotted for the gate. Nowhere was there a guard or proselyte of the Order to be seen.

Just before they reached the gate, a new earthquake seized them and robbed Rouvin of his footing. He and Kesira tumbled down, arms flailing wildly for support that wasn't there. They were danced over the dirt like droplets of water on a hot skillet.

"Rouvin!" the woman cried. "We've got to get away. Now!"

Rouvin followed her gaze and paled. The area around the pillar now spun with a green whirlwind that spiraled ever higher into the sky with each mighty twisting. The eye-searing green took on deeper, richer hues, more solidity, gave the impression of a large body forming within its boundaries.

"Howenthal," Rouvin said in a choked voice. "He comes, drawn to the altar." The warrior rolled over onto his belly, then onto his back. This was the only way he could survey the courtyard. Legs provided scant support in the midst of the heavy quaking. "There," he said, pointing. "Get into that corridor."

"Safer outside. Roof will collapse," Kesira said.

"Howenthal is using the altar as a gateway. Do you want to be the first person he sees?"

Kesira didn't answer. She began wiggling forward, clawing at the dirt, moving toward the relative protection of the corridor. Never had she felt more helpless. Every attempt to stand resulted in failure. The intense shaking of the earth caused her insides to grind, organ against organ, and made her queasy. Closing her eyes did no good and watching as the world jerked about with them open made her even sicker. Kesira gritted her teeth and concentrated on attaining the doorway. And she did, just seconds before a gust of hot wind tugged at her robe and threatened to set it afire.

"At least the earthquake is over, even if the place did catch on fire," she said. Then Kesira turned and saw the truth. She swallowed hard as she gazed for the first time on a demon.

Howenthal the Groundcracker stood by the altar in the courtyard, a full head taller than she, broader, with rippling muscles and the darkest expression she had ever seen turning a handsome face into something evil, twisted and vicious.

"He always was one to demand full attention," whispered Rouvin. "Even to the point of fake theatrics." The warrior had moved behind her, his arms circling her body protectively. Kesira couldn't figure out if he did this to guard her or to keep her from doing something stupid like running into the courtyard and drawing Howenthal's attention.

"My followers, harken!" came the booming voice. Kesira threw up her hands to cover her ears. Every word grated on her inner ear and tore at her nerves. "Attend me! In the Great Hall I shall permit you to worship me!"

The ground rumbled with miniature earthquakes triggered by every footstep as the demon strode off to enter a groined archway on the far side of the courtyard.

"Always playing to his audience," grumbled Rouvin. "Just once I wish he would relax and be himself. Or maybe this is the way he is all the time. Scary idea."

"How many of the demons have you met?" Kesira asked, still awed by the sight of the more-than-human being.

"A fair number. My mother wasn't one to play favorites." Kesira looked at Rouvin, noting his bitterness. "But she had the good sense to never take Howenthal to her bed. His opinion of himself was too hungry even for her to feed."

"What do you think he has to say to his Order?"

Rouvin looked at her and shook his head. "What difference does it make? We're not lingering to partake of the afternoon tea. To stay longer than necessary is suicidal. When they find the guard I killed, every single warrior will be out scouring the countryside for us. I want to be far, *far* away when that occurs."

"But Howenthal," Kesira began.

"The demon's business is his own."

"Are these the Quaking Lands?" Kesira asked.

"At the edge," admitted Rouvin. "But the demon roves

over much of the terrain. Now let's be off. We can find horses and..."

"I would hear what Howenthal says," Kesira declared. "My destiny is entwined with his."

"You should be more careful in your choice of enemies," said Rouvin. "Howenthal does not take prisoners. There's no reason. Only inglorious death awaits any mortal foolish enough to cross him."

Rouvin started toward the stables. Kesira paused, then split away, intent on the archway where Howenthal had vanished. Rouvin ran to her and spun her around. She glared at him, brown eyes hot and angry.

"Go, if you will. Follow your destiny. I must stay and find out what I can. I *must.*"

"You mistake Howenthal for your Gelya. The demons' personalities are all different, drastically so. What traits humans have, the demons share—but more so. If there is human kindness, Gelya's kindness was a hundredfold more. And if there is human evil, Howenthal's is a hundred times *that.*"

Kesira considered, then said, "If I have learned from Gelya, I must use that knowledge. If I have not learned enough then I must seek out further information. Only through observing Howenthal can I gain it."

Rouvin mumbled under his breath, then indicated a smaller doorway to one side.

"Oh?" said Kesira.

"It leads to a balcony above the Great Hall. We can see Howenthal from there."

"And how do you know this?"

"I have seen plans for the Citadel. This place changes hands often. One Order occupies it, then another takes it over. When I rode for the Emperor all officers were required to learn the layout of this and a dozen other major strongholds."

"A wise man, the Emperor."

"You should emulate him." Rouvin roughly pulled Kesira along. All the while they stood in the courtyard, not a single living being showed himself. Kesira wondered if Howenthal's control over the Order of the Steel Crescent was so extreme that each member awaited their patron within the Great Hall—or if something more sinister dictated this oddly deserted area.

She followed Rouvin along narrow walkways and up ladders hardly more than holes cut into stone until they edged along a balcony perched at the very top of the ornately domed Great Hall. On a throne of pure jade sat Howenthal.

Again Kesira felt her breath taken away. In spite of the aura of evil surrounding the demon, there was also a majesty. She had the feeling that if Howenthal had chosen differently at some point, this evil would have turned into goodness. He sat on the throne, arms crossed over his massive bare chest. The demon wore only a light blue breechclout that contrasted with the jade green tint of his skin; in the light filtering from windows around the dome, the definition of his muscles became all the more apparent.

Kesira glanced over at Rouvin. The man-demon's build was superb. She had no word to describe Howenthal's.

"Nehan-dir!" cried the demon on the throne. The name reverberated and then echoed down a dozen corridors radiating from the Great Hall.

"Howenthal, I salute you." The scrawny leader of the band that had taken her and Rouvin prisoner bowed deeply before the demon's throne. "Your plan is successful at every turning. Mighty is our patron, Howenthal!"

The metallic clicking of swords being half-drawn, then rammed back forcefully into their scabbards drowned out any further words from the human leader.

"I am pleased, Nehan-dir," said the demon. Kesira noted that the words did not boom forth as they had before. Somehow, Howenthal moderated them, having achieved the effect he wanted.

"We live only to serve," said Nehan-dir. The man stood upright and jerked open his battered brown leather tunic. Kesira caught her breath at the sight. Cruelly burned into the sickly white flesh was a crescent-shaped wound. She couldn't imagine the suffering Nehan-dir had endured to be so branded.

Howenthal glanced around. Each member of the Order of the Steel Crescent similarly bared his or her chest and displayed the sigil.

"Why do they mutilate themselves?" whispered Kesira.

"To prove their devotion to the order. This is why the Steel Crescent has become so mercenary. Can you imagine showing your devotion to a patron by being branded in that fashion, then having the patron sell you to another?"

Kesira felt no sadness for the men and women assembled below, but a dread rose up that threatened to choke her. They could not be sane to mutilate their own flesh this way, then switch allegiances as the ebb and flow of power dictated. Where was the seeking, the truth, the foundation for their lives?

"Your sallies go well," said Howenthal. "As do mine. Gelya is dead." Kesira clenched her fists until the nails bit into her palms and drew tiny crescents of blood. She fought down the angry cry forming on her lips and forced calmness through meditation technique. "On every front, Eznofadil, Lenc and I triumph."

"Great is our patron, Howenthal!"

The cry went up around the hall. Only when it had died to a retreating whisper did the demon continue.

"Our most recent victory is over Wemilat the Ugly. He has been imprisoned in the center of the Quaking Lands. Never again will he oppose us. We shall rule undisputed!"

While the cheers from the Order of the Steel Crescent rose, Rouvin spoke quickly to Kesira. "Wemilat and Gelya had much in common. Their ideals were similar, even if their outward appearances were totally different."

"Why does Howenthal call this Wemilat 'the Ugly'?"

Rouvin laughed without humor. "Bodily, he is the least favored of all the demons. To compare him to a toad is insulting to all reptiles. But Wemilat's heart is good."

"Why hasn't Howenthal killed him, as he did Gelya?"

Rouvin said grimly, "It can only be inability. Wemilat is powerful, perhaps more so than Gelya. His very ugliness gives him a determination and ruthlessness lacking in some of the others of more pacific disposition. It is possible Howenthal and the others with him can't do more than imprison Wemilat."

"Then we must rescue him."

"The Quaking Lands," said Rouvin. The man shook his head tiredly, as if beset by a stubborn child. "You felt the earthquakes Howenthal uses to announce his arrivals. Those in the Quaking Lands are hundreds of times worse. The land buckles; huge ripples of dirt and stone crisscross it; nobody walks without being tossed down. Reaching Wemilat will not be easy—it might be impossible."

"You have heard Howenthal boasting of his successes. If we do nothing to stop him and the other two, they will conquer not only the other demons but all this world, as well. Would you prefer a demon ruler to a human one?"

Rouvin took in a deep breath, held it, then exhaled heavily. "Considering the demons' predilections, I choose Emperor Kwasian."

"Even over Gelya, I would so choose," said Kesira. "Humans can learn much from the demons. A patron must teach, not rule. We must govern our own affairs, just as demons must govern their own. It would be wrong for us to force ourselves on them; the other side of this coin is equally as wrong."

"Still," said Rouvin, "the Quaking Lands? This is foolhardy."

"You cannot suggest an ally better than Wemilat, can you? Would your mother Ayondela aid us?"

The snort Rouvin gave answered her question. Kesira started to further build her case for rescuing Wemilat when Howenthal's words rolled up and silenced Kesira instantly.

"Have you imprisoned her?" Howenthal asked of Nehan-dir. "This nun, Kesira Minette. Is she your prisoner?"

"She and her warrior companion are now in our dungeon, Howenthal," immediately answered the Order's leader.

"Within her lies the seed of defeat," said Howenthal. "I will interrogate her personally."

"Kesira," whispered Rouvin, frantic now with haste. "We must leave. Did you hear? Howenthal knows you by name!"

"But how?" she asked, stunned at this.

"Does it matter? If he goes to the dungeon and finds you gone, he'll bring the entire Citadel down around our ears. His anger is legendary, even among demons. We've got to escape."

Rouvin tugged at her robe and Kesira followed, her mind in an uncharacteristic turmoil over this turn of events. That Howenthal spoke her name explained the odd reaction when Nehan-dir had learned her identity before he captured her. At first, the man had seemed little more than a brigand, intent on finding his men some helpless woman to use for the night. After she had declared herself a nun in the service of Gelya, Nehan-dir's attitude had not altered at all, but he had overheard Rouvin call her by name. Kesira now realized he had only been fulfilling a command given him by his patron.

But what did Howenthal want of her?

"Rouvin," she said to the man's back, "I will not run. I want more from them. From Nehan-dir, from each and every one of the Steel Crescent. I want revenge."

"What have they done?" Rouvin didn't slacken his pace one iota.

"They are in league with Howenthal. That is enough. They imprisoned us. That is enough. But I fear their involvement in Gelya's death, the destruction of my nunnery, the ruination of all I hold precious in life: those things I believe the Order of the Steel Crescent is responsible for, in part; also."

"So you're declaring vengeance on them?" Rouvin seemed amused at the very idea.

"Yes."

"Fear naught, Kesira. Howenthal will wreak the revenge on them you crave. That demon is faithless. Nehan-dir and the others will find out their mistake in seeking his guidance soon enough."

"It must be mine alone," she insisted.

"Think of it this way. When Howenthal goes to the dungeons and finds you gone, who is he likely to blame? Nehan-dir, right? And Howenthal's temper is violent. He may destroy the Citadel and all within it simply because you thwarted him by escaping. He has done worse in the past. Isn't this vengeance enough?"

"No."

Rouvin tried a different tack. "If you're recaptured, there's no chance at all for revenge. We must get away from here. Then you can do what you like about the Order's survivors. But we've got to escape. There's no hope for revenge if we don't."

Kesira saw the wisdom in the man's words, even as she saw the logic he used against her. She had to admit to a feeling of helplessness. What could she do now against Howenthal? He was physically stronger than she—even stronger than Rouvin, if she was any judge. The demon moved with a litheness that bespoke great fighting prowess. And what magicks might the demon unleash if physical force did not prove enough for him to triumph?

Memory of the ground wobbling under her feet came back to Kesira and decided her course of action.

The woman pulled back her short brunette bangs and tucked them under the cowl of her robe. She tried to picture what she looked like and failed. The jolting around she'd gotten because of Howenthal's earthquake had rattled her more than she cared to admit. Recovery definitely seemed preferable to openly opposing the patron of the Steel Crescent.

"How do we get out of here?" she asked Rouvin.

"Through the courtyard again, to the stable and out. Keep a sharp eye out for guards—and watch animals."

"What sort of animals?"

"The Order is notorious for using small cats with poisoned claws. There will be no pets within the Citadel. Kill anything that approaches. And if you can't kill it, then run from it. Understand?" Rouvin's blue eyes bored into her softer brown ones. Kesira quailed, then firmed her resolve. Only when the man was satisfied that she was ready did he break off the gaze and stride boldly out into the dusty central courtyard. Kesira stayed a few paces behind, wishing she had her stone-wood staff.

They reached the stables before the first guard spied them. The man scowled, worked through the idea that no one was supposed to be here—but by this time Rouvin had reached out and grabbed the man by the throat. Lifting, muscles bulging and sinews standing in bas-relief on his forearms, Rouvin held the guard at arm's length, the poor wight's feet just inches away from the ground. The gurgling sounds quickly vanished, and the man hung limp in Rouvin's grasp. The warrior cast him aside, taking up the fallen sword and shield.

Without a word they entered the stable. Their horses had been cared for, coats gleaming, full troughs of grain in front of them. Rouvin hastily looked around for more guards, but Kesira had found something that drew her like a lodestone pulls iron.

"Our gear!" she called out.

"Get it," said Rouvin. "And be quick about it. Our luck can't last much longer."

As Kesira reached to pick up her precious staff, she froze. A slight sound, hardly more than the rustle of wind through the straw on the floor, alerted her. Brown eyes darting while she kept her head stationary, she caught sight of a creamy blur out of the corner of her eye. In full fighting frame of mind, Kesira blasted forward, grasped her staff and somersaulted, using the strong wood rod to push herself to her feet. The woman spun and faced her attacker.

Kesira held back the smile forming on her lips. She faced no formidable enemy. It was only a small housecat hissing and clacking its teeth at her. Then she remembered Rouvin's half-heard warning in the courtyard.

"Back," she said softly. "Don't come any closer."

The cat launched itself directly at her, claws out. Kesira's mind slipped from normal time and accelerated in full fighting mode now. Everything moved in slow motion; she saw details that otherwise would have been denied to her. Every hair on the cat's body stood out, distinct, an entity unto itself. The teeth were revealed in the miniature snarl: one tooth had been broken off. The claws drew her full attention when she saw the dark crimson substance coating them.

Bloat-fish poison, came the mental recognition. But even as she witnessed the cat in mid-leap, she was moving. Forcing herself against inertia, feeling that her movements came too slowly, Kesira twisted to one side and dropped the top of her staff to intercept the small, savage animal.

The slow motion snapped back into regular time when

her staff collided with the guard-cat's head. Fragile bones crushed, and the cat fell to the straw, twitching and mewing piteously. One final convulsion seized its small body before it lay, limp. Kesira dropped to her knees, panting heavily in reaction. Using the tip of her staff, she pressed down on one lifeless paw. The claws popped out.

"What's wrong?" demanded Rouvin, leading the horses out. "Poisoned?" he asked when he saw the animal.

"It might be bloat-fish poison."

"Nasty," said Rouvin. "The lungs would rupture and you'd drown in your own blood in seconds. At least you wouldn't linger."

"Our gear," she said, her voice shaky. How could such a common animal be perverted into something so deadly? "I found it."

"Load it on, then," he said. Rouvin nervously fingered the sword he'd stolen and moved the small round shield up and down his left arm until he found a spot where it rested comfortably.

He watched as she secured their belongings. When Kesira had mounted, he nodded, pointed with his sword toward the distant gate leading to the outer world, then put his bootheels to his horse's side. Rouvin raced forward as if he'd been shot from a catapult. Kesira followed at a pace only slightly less breathtaking.

"Aieee!" screamed Rouvin, using his sword on first one and then another guard who had blundered into the courtyard. "Kesira, out! Now. Get out of here. I'll keep them busy."

But Kesira found a squad of soldiers blocking her path. Using her staff, she knocked down the leader and momentarily disorganized the others, but her rearing horse prevented her from capitalizing on the confusion. By the time she had the animal under control, the nun found herself the target of three of the soldiers.

Kesira swung her staff and landed a solid blow on one woman's helm. The soldier went down and lay in the dirt, not moving. But the man who swooped on her from the left had the advantage of Kesira's awkwardness. Kesira had to swing her staff over the horse's back and use the weapon left-handed.

If a green bolt from above hadn't come crashing down, talons ripping, she would have lost her leg to the soldier's sword slash.

"Zolkan!" she cried. "Thank you!"

"Flee!" the *trilla* bird ordered. "Deadly here. Too deadly! Demons!"

Kesira reared the horse and let its hooves knock away the third soldier, but she saw this was a losing battle. More armed members of the Order spilled out of barracks and the Great Hall.

Zolkan twisted savagely and came away with a huge gobbet of shoulder muscle, which he dropped. The bird flapped hard and rocketed skyward. He had done all he could. It was now up to Kesira and Rouvin to save themselves, if they were adept enough.

"Ride!" ordered the warrior. His sword dripped a steady stream of blood and Kesira wondered how much of the gore spattered on his body belonged to him. It seemed impossible that Rouvin had escaped injury plowing through the soldiers arrayed against him.

Kesira *thwacked!* repeatedly with her staff, deflected several potentially serious sword cuts, and managed to get to a spot just in front of the gateway leading outside. The pleasant springtime day beckoned to her; the soft green of new grass, the budding trees and insanely blossoming flowers all told of a better existence. Her heart longed to go racing freely down the road and experience all this, and to be free of the Order of the Steel Crescent and Howenthal. She didn't know how they would escape the pursuit that Howenthal's followers would surely mount, but that was something to be dealt with in the future. For the moment, all the woman wanted was to win freedom from the Citadel.

"Rouvin, hurry!"

"Go on!"

"Not without you," she said. But just as she wheeled about to go to the man's aid, she felt the faint stirrings deep within the earth. Those slight temblors were quickly overshadowed by the resonant boom of Howenthal's voice.

"Escaped! How can she have escaped?"

That angry, deeply rumbling voice brought down small blocks from the loftiest spires of the Citadel. And

Howenthal's full wrath started the earthquake that caused the heavy spiked wooden gate to come smashing down.

She and Rouvin stared through the thick wood bars of the gate and out into the countryside. Their escape was blocked.

Chapter Ten

KESIRA MINETTE felt the potent quake build and build until she wanted to scream in fear.

She did scream, but no one heard. The sharp cracking of sundered stone, the agonized twisting of wooden beams, the ear-splittingly shrill shrieks of humans in pain all drowned out her feeble cries of fear. Her horse bucked and fell to one side, the earth pulled out from under. Kesira managed to keep the animal from pinning her leg to the ground by jumping free of the saddle at the last possible instant, but Kesira could not stand, either. She tumbled to the shivering ground, caught in Howenthal's anger.

Rouvin struggled to her side, having little better luck staying upright. Kesira saw his lips moving, but the words were drowned out by all the destruction being wrought around them. She made out, "The gate!"

Falling heavily to her stomach, she spun about until she faced the wooden gate that had barred their exit. Hope surged within her when she saw the Citadel's stone fortifications crumbling under the unstoppable force of the earthquake.

Rouvin's hand rested on her shoulder, featherlight.

She nodded as she understood what he wanted her to do. Leading her horse the best she could, often falling to her knees or watching helplessly as the horse did likewise, Kesira moved to the heavy spiked gate. The quake ripped forth once again and Howenthal's words rumbled above it all, "How can she have escaped?"

This pushed the last restraining block aside. The gate toppled ponderously, falling outward to land in what seemed to be absolute silence. Kesira realized she might have been deafened by the cacophony raging within the keep. But at the first sign of the quake letting up, she vaulted into her saddle again and urged the frightened horse on. The animal leaped over broken fragments from the gate, stumbled once on the loose gravel topping the road and then found running room to vent all its accumulated fear.

Kesira knew the wind was whipping past her face, ripping at her skin, turning lips into chapped, deadened rolls of flesh and causing her eyes to water constantly. But she didn't feel any discomfort.

She was free! Free, she rode with the wind and became one with the straining beast between her legs. She gripped it tightly with her knees, bent forward and patted the horse on the neck. The animal responded with a renewed burst of energy. Kesira thought that at any moment they would become airborne and fly across the countryside, soaring until they found the Quaking Lands.

Caught in the movement, Kesira let her mind drift freely, away from the concerns of Howenthal and pursuit by the Steel Crescent. Reeling senses filled her with wonder—and the second line of her death song completed itself. When the entire song was ready to be sung aloud, her life would be at a close. But now, she had only two lines and an indeterminate number left to compose.

"Rouvin!" she shouted. "How long can we keep up this pace?"

"Forever!" came the returning cry. "I know now what it feels like to be entirely a demon!"

She watched as he raced ahead of her, his steed reaching forward powerfully to propel them with a breathtaking speed. Kesira might believe Rouvin was more than half a demon, but odd feelings rose as she considered his silhouette. By accompanying her on this dangerous journey to the Quaking Lands, he had shown more courage than wisdom, yet she didn't think he expended himself carelessly simply to impress her. She read the message in his blue eyes, the set of his strong body, the way he acted around her. Rouvin loved her.

Why didn't she feel anything toward him?

Kesira rode and relaxed, flowing with her animal, and pondered this. Rouvin was interesting, quick of wit, unlike any man—or demon—she had ever before met. Handsome beyond her wildest imaginings, demon-strong, worldly, he was the sort that her younger Sisters talked about between themselves when the older Sisters had retired for the night. Rouvin was a fantasy figure embodied in flesh.

Kesira had to admit she liked Rouvin. Curious fantasies of being locked in his arms arose to taunt her, but that was all they were—fantasies. Yet how easily accomplished they would be. She knew he loved her, even though the time since they'd met was brief. Why didn't she feel more toward him, after he'd risked his life saving her, after all they had been through together?

"The Order sends out its cavalry," Rouvin shouted back to her. "We must slow our pace."

"Slow down?" she protested. "We ought to speed up!"

"Can't," Rouvin said. "The horses will explode their very hearts. Rest a little now, run more later, if the cavalry gets too close. We might be able to lose them if we're clever enough and dodge in and out of the mountains."

"I know the passes well enough," said Kesira, reining in but keeping the horse going forward at a brisk clip. "But we cannot go to the east."

"Why not? There's what little hope we have of losing the Steel Crescent."

"Ah, Rouvin, so quickly you forget. Or are you truly forgetting at all? The Quaking Lands lie to the west and it is westward I must go."

Rouvin looked at her, his handsome face solemn now. "This has been little more than a lark for you, Kesira," he said. "Howenthal's presence changes the game to one more deadly than amusing. You cannot openly oppose a demon. Even if Howenthal acted alone, your cause would be futile."

"The more reason to go west and into the Quaking Lands," she said firmly. "I agree that one, or two, cannot stand against a demon. But another demon might be able to, with our aid."

"You mean to free Wemilat?"

"Why not? He has ample reason to oppose Howenthal—and Lenc." The name of the latter demon caught in her throat. The vision of the pillar of white, polar fire burning at Gelya's altar had at first sickened her. Now it generated a cold anger that flared higher and higher with every remembrance.

"The ways of demons are their own. Believe me," Rouvin said earnestly. "I have some small knowledge of their dealings and double dealings. Even my own mother sought out devious ways when straightforward ones were easier. It is their nature."

"Are you equally as devious?" teased Kesira.

"I am only half-demon," Rouvin said stiffly. "There is no way I can live among demons. Life with humans is more interesting." Softening his tone, he added, "There is much to love among humans."

Kesira heaved a deep sigh. It was as she surmised. What was there about Rouvin that affected her so? If she had strong negative feelings, it would be more comprehensible, but she didn't. To her, the man-demon was only...neutral.

"With your help or without it, I go into the Quaking Lands to rescue Wemilat. I am sure he will consent to join forces."

"Do you think you can make the difference in a war between demons? What power do you possess that can turn the tide?"

Kesira thought for a moment before answering. "I am not sure. You said only a few humans can read the rune sticks. And back in the Citadel I managed to reach out and alter the spell controlling the prison door. How, I can't say, but I did."

"Simple tricks for a demon," scoffed Rouvin. "To a human, these are awesome, but the meanest of demons controls powers a thousand times vaster."

"There might be other skills I have that remain latent. Gelya could have nurtured them within me, but now I must seek out another who can teach me: Wemilat."

"What if you free him and he turns against you? It is possible. He is a demon, after all."

"Will I be any worse off? In the midst of life too many of us are dead. The end we all face is linked to the beginning; I feel my end will be noble in comparison to my birth."

"Do you see this or is it simply a conjecture?" demanded Rouvin.

Kesira shrugged. There was no answer to such a question. If her death amounted to nothing, life was better ended in this fashion than lived on in futility. But the woman thought that death held more meaning attempting to free Wemilat than dying fifty years later, after a lifetime of rationalizations. It was a more honorable death, a more meaningful attempt at life.

"I wish I understood more of you," he said glumly. "Tell me of Wemilat."

"There's not much more to say about him. I have seen him once or twice, but never spoke to him. All else is hearsay and odd snippets overheard during my mother's conversations."

"Is he an honorable demon?"

"He takes no worshipers," said Rouvin. "The idea seems to disgust him."

"Then he makes no point in detailing his philosophy or attempting to help those lesser creatures with his wisdom."

"Kesira, what the demons do, they do for their own selfish motives. For all I know, Howenthal may have imprisoned Wemilat because the two had a falling out over division of spoils. Or Wemilat may have crossed Howenthal. Who can say?"

Before Kesira could answer, the ground began to undulate. Eyes widening in fear, the nun watched as part of the countryside rose up like a giant ocean wave. Grass and dirt flew skyward and a rain of small stones pelted down on them. The wave rippled and came surging forward, driving them from their horses. The animals squealed in complete terror, and no amount of soothing on Rouvin's and Kesira's part quieted them.

"Howenthal," said Rouvin. "His quakes are weaker here but still potent enough. When we ride into the Quaking Lands, the intensity will double, triple, rise tenfold."

"He uses the quakes to slow us," said Kesira. "That must mean the Order of the Steel Crescent has riders close by."

"Their horses would be almost dead. Look at ours." Rouvin tugged at the reins and a tired bay raised its head. "We almost rode them into the ground escaping. Only pulling back when we did kept them from perishing under us."

"They have everything to gain by killing their steeds to reach us," said Kesira, considering the situation from her enemy's viewpoint. "All they need to do is slow us until another company of soldiers can overtake us. Every delay works in their favor and against us."

"You would have made a great strategist for the Emperor. Too bad we'll never live to see such an appointment."

Kesira settled her mind and fought to keep from panicking. With every nervous twitch of the ground she thought she felt the accompanying hammer of horses. And finally the woman convinced herself that the hollow, ringing sounds she heard were those made by galloping horses—many, many horses.

"Rouvin?" she asked, her hand reaching out to touch his arm.

"I hear," the man said. "We'd best prepare for another small fight. There can't be more than one or two of them, not this soon. Only the fastest of horses could have overtaken us."

They tethered the bay and the gelding to a small bush and then sought higher ground. If they had to fight, they wanted their opponents to fight uphill.

"Oh, no," moaned Kesira when she saw the number of the Steel Crescent's guard opposing them. "There are five, six—no, seven. All armed."

"And all tired, just as we are. Perhaps more so since they rode the harder," said Rouvin. He pulled forth his sword and examined the edge. "Too many nicks along it for good slashing. I'd best just thrust and pray that the blade doesn't break."

"At times I wish my Order allowed the use of steel weapons." The wood staff gave Kesira scant comfort now as she faced six men and a woman, all armed with shining steel swords and impossibly sharp daggers.

"You are the one who makes the Order's rules now," said Rouvin, lifting the gold ribbon around her waist with the tip of his sword. He dropped the ribbon and turned his back to her in preparation for the fight that would end their lives. "Make some new rules."

"Gelya forbade the use of steel in weapons."

"Why?"

"No one ever said. Not even Dominie Tredlo, and he often explained the more esoteric rules."

"When you see the chance, pick up a sword and use it."

Kesira said nothing as she watched the seven warriors circle the small hillock and begin the short climb upward. She knew that she wouldn't violate her dead patron's wishes, no matter how sensible it seemed to ignore them now. All her training had been with the staff, not edged weapons. Attempting to use an unfamiliar sword now might mean a quicker death.

Kesira Minette vowed that her death would be won dearly by those of the Steel Crescent.

Kesira's staff flashed out in a quick, short arc that caught the first fighter just below the kneecap. He stumbled, cursed and tried to get up. The butt end of her staff sent him tumbling back down the hill before he could recover. Kesira had to fight with less than her usual flair; passing the staff behind her posed grave problems for Rouvin, should she hit him. He had his hands full dealing with the three soldiers intent on skewering him. Kesira heard the clang of steel on steel and the slither as blades deflected off shields. But she found herself too engrossed in fending off the three determined fighters in front of her to think at all about how Rouvin fared.

"Surrender," demanded the single woman facing Kesira. "There will be no rape. You know that. Howenthal wants you intact."

"Howenthal will have to be satisfied with you, then!"

Kesira's stone-wood staff whirred through the air and
forced the woman of the Steel Crescent to vault over
it, but Kesira's quick wrist motion smashed the end of
her staff into the ground and sent it ricocheting back.
It struck the other woman hard on the breast. Her face
paled and she dropped to her knees.

"Bitch!" screamed one of the two fighters facing her.
He lunged clumsily, his sword point going off-line, and
Kesira broke his neck with her staff. But the remaining
warrior closed with her, and strong arms circled her
body, lifted her off her feet, threw her to the ground.
Her staff clattered down the hill.

Trained though she was in hand-to-hand combat,
Kesira found herself locked with an opponent stronger,
quicker and more knowledgeable. Her every ploy was
easily turned aside. As she made a strike for the man's
eyes, he easily trapped her hand and bent her wrist into
an unnatural angle. She shrieked, then bit back any
further sound of pain.

She'd give them no satisfaction on *that* score.

Standing above her was her captor, smiling broadly,
and the drawn-faced woman who gingerly held her
bruised breast.

"If Howenthal did not want you so, you'd be cooling
meat now, slut!" raged the woman.

Kesira said nothing; there was nothing to say.

As she stared upward, surprise crossed the face of
the man holding her in the wrist lock. His eyes turned
skyward and he began twisting toward the ground. Only
when a shower of blood rained down did Kesira realize
that the man had died almost instantly. Jerking free
of his dead hand, she came to hands and knees, then
to her feet.

Molimo, in his wolf form, stood astraddle the man
who had held Kesira. The soldier's throat had been
slashed open with a single pass of savage talons. Molimo's lips pulled back in a hideous snarl to expose vast
yellowed arrays of teeth. The woman of the Steel Crescent had sheathed her sword after Kesira's defeat. The
nearness of Molimo's body prevented her from pulling
it again; rather, she drew her dagger, hoping for a quick
thrust to a lupine heart.

"Molimo, no!" called Kesira, too late. The wolf jerked

to one side, avoided the thrust and closed powerful jaws on the woman's arm. Blood exploded as the artery was severed. Already pale from shock, the woman turned deathly white and died as Molimo savaged her exposed throat.

Rouvin limped over, supporting himself on his nicked sword. He simply stared at Molimo and said nothing.

"Quiet, now," Kesira soothed the wolf. "You can return to your normal form. Reverse the transformation now. Calm. Settle your mind. Calm, now, very calm." She edged toward Molimo and touched his blood-specked muzzle, the dripping jowls, the head where the ears still lay back in preparation for the kill. Soothing him took several minutes, but Kesira felt the tenseness flowing away, like water draining from a cracked clay jug.

Kesira clung to the wolf's neck, the not-quite-furry neck, the human neck as Molimo returned to his human self.

"Oh, Molimo, you saved me, but the cost to you. Your poor soul." A tear formed at the corner of Molimo's eye and trickled down. Kesira gently wiped it away, then turned and kissed the youth fully on the lips. She came alive in that moment, thrilling to the vibrancy of this man, the coppery taste of blood still on his lips, the illicit power locked within his loins. At any instant Molimo might transform back into a wolf and destroy her, but this only added to Kesira's feeling for him.

Awkwardly, Molimo pushed her away. Embarrassed then, Kesira pulled her robes straight and stood.

Rouvin watched, a dark expression clouding his handsome face.

"There will be more," he said. "Nehan-dir will not trust only one squad to stop us." For the first time he knew Molimo for what he was.

A loud squawk pulled Kesira's attention aloft. Against the dusky twilight sky came a green blur, the plummeting form of a *trilla* bird. She held out her arm and Zolkan landed expertly on it, his talons not even breaking her skin.

"They ride away. Nothing to fear, nothing to fear," Zolkan announced.

"How's that?" asked Rouvin. "This doesn't sound like

Nehan-dir. From all accounts, he's a shrewd one. He won't give up pursuit of us. Not easily."

"Not unless Howenthal ordered it," said Kesira. "Zolkan, where do the troops go?"

The *trilla* bird lifted one wing and pointed to the west.

"Into the Quaking Lands," she said with some satisfaction. "Howenthal fears us. He has ordered Nehan-dir to supply extra guards for Wemilat's prison."

"Absurd," snorted Rouvin. "We don't know that. They may be going to do any number of other things. Howenthal still wants us—*you*. He won't give up until he wins."

"Wemilat," said Zolkan, "needs more guards. Howenthal directs them to Wemilat's prison. Follow?"

"Yes, Zolkan, I want you to follow. Report back now and then or if there's any immediate danger to us. On your way, now." Kesira launched Zolkan into the air. The bird flapped powerfully and vanished into the evening sky, caught for a brief instant between the two smaller waxing moons.

"It's a trap," said Rouvin.

"Wemilat is already in one," Kesira pointed out. "Join us?"

With ill grace, Rouvin slammed his sword into its scabbard and bobbed his head in assent.

Fourteen days dodging Nehan-dir's troops had exhausted both Rouvin and Kesira, but the woman's iron determination kept them traveling deeper and deeper into the Quaking Lands. The valley Rouvin had told her of beckoned like a chute to the netherworld. Tall mountains rose on either side, unscalable mountains trapping them completely in a cul-de-sac. Only two directions were accessible—forward and back onto the plains where the Order of the Steel Crescent patrolled relentlessly. And ahead? Zolkan reported the company of Steel Crescent soldiers had reached their destination: Wemilat the Ugly's prison.

"What now?" asked Rouvin. "We know where they are, but we can't possibly launch an assault against so many. Zolkan reports forty soldiers guarding the mouth of the prison."

"And," Kesira added, "there's no way to tell how many more hide within the mountainside."

Howenthal had worked well to create the prison holding his adversary. The Quaking Lands had been ominously still as they had ridden over them. The land between the mountain peaks was gently rolling and afforded no hiding places—but no patrols had spotted them and the appellation of "quaking" did not seem to be true.

Rouvin had refused to comment when Kesira mentioned this.

They stood some distance away from the entry to Wemilat's rocky prison and tried to figure out the best way of reaching the trapped demon. Nothing suggested itself.

"Molimo?" asked Kesira. "Do your sharp eyes see anything we might have missed?" The youth shook his head, a shock of dark hair falling carelessly forward. He brushed it from his ebony eyes and took no further note of Kesira.

"Rouvin?" she asked.

"We can't fight that many. Perhaps if we started a rockslide, we might be able to remove a few of them."

"And close off the mouth of the prison. We must get *into* the mineshaft if we're to free Wemilat."

"Aren't we assuming too much?" asked Rouvin. "We're only guessing Wemilat is even in there. He might be anywhere. This might be a trap laid for us by Howenthal."

Molimo disagreed violently, shaking his head and pointing toward the mine. A deft finger traced out the letters in the thin, rocky soil, indicating he knew Wemilat was inside.

"It's nice one of us is so sure," said the warrior with ill grace. "I'm not."

"There might be some other entry point," said Kesira. "See how extensive the mining has been? Whatever they dug for, they must have honeycombed the mountains with tunnels. We might be able to find our way through them and get much closer to Wemilat."

"Farfetched," muttered Rouvin.

"But our only chance. You said we were no match for the two or three score of guards. And sending down an avalanche might seal Wemilat inside the mountain forever."

"Which shaft?" Rouvin asked, still not warming to the idea.

Molimo jerked at Kesira's patched gray robe and pointed out a tiny opening some distance away, but out of sight of the main entrance to the mines.

"That's as good as any," said Kesira. "Any objections, Rouvin?"

"Many. Let's send Zolkan in to scout for us. He's small, not likely to be seen, and can see much better in the dark than either of us. Birds also scent the deadly gases present in some mines."

"I don't know where he is. I haven't seen him all day."

"Convenient—for him."

"We can wait or we can act. I say, act."

"You're correct on that," said Rouvin. "Doing something wrong is better than doing nothing right. Especially when we're likely to be spotted sooner or later." He eyed the flat expanse of the Quaking Lands and frowned. Nothing had gone as he thought it should have. The legends of this place described horrific quakes; they had encountered not even a tiny trembling.

"Let's ride," said Kesira.

The three quickly made their way unseen toward the tiny mineshaft selected by Molimo. As they approached it, Kesira reined back and cocked her head to one side.

"Do you hear something?" she asked.

"No," said Rouvin, but both he and the woman turned to Molimo. The youth slapped his chest for attention and pointed out to the quiet, gentle vastness of the valley.

"Oh, no!" exclaimed Kesira.

An earthquake was aborning. It picked up the entire floor of the valley like a rug and sent the single wave rippling across at a speed too great to be believed. Anything trapped on the wavefront died, tossed into the air and smashed hideously when it returned to earth. And the wavefront was speeding directly toward them.

"The cave!" shouted Rouvin. "It's our only chance."

"We'll be crushed inside if the shaft collapses," protested Kesira.

"Inside, *now!*"

They rode with reckless abandon for the mouth of the mineshaft, hit the ground running and dove into the opening. Kesira spun and saw her gelding's fear-widened eyes; then the horse raced off. Replacing it was the tranquil blue of the sky—and then only the grays and browns of the ground as the Quaking Lands began living up to their name and reputation.

Timbers creaked and the very rock over their heads grated in protest as the quake struck.

Chapter Eleven

"THE VERY WORLD rises up to devour us!" cried Kesira
Minette. She cowered back, bumping into Rouvin. All
Kesira could do was hang onto her staff and stare at
the earth ripples advancing so quickly upon them. The
man swung her about and shoved her deeper into the
mineshaft.

"Run," he ordered. "We have no other chance."

"The horses...."

"Forget them!"

Dragging her along, Rouvin gave the woman no time
to worry about their steeds. Then Rouvin scooped up a
rude torch thrust into a crevice and clumsily lit it on
the run; it produced a sputtering, hissing, pale light
that barely illuminated their path. Molimo ran just
behind, his body blocking the sight of the incoming
wave of solid ground. When Howenthal's earthquake
hit, however, not even Molimo's protecting body kept
the effects away from Kesira.

The rumbling deep within the ground welled up and
tossed them from wall to wall. The timbers moaned
constantly, threatening to give way at any instant, and
the debris falling from the mine roof quickly caused

Kesira to choke and cough from the obscuring dust.
Rouvin continued to pull her along while Molimo
bumped into her repeatedly from behind, silently urging her to greater speed.

"The shaft's collapsing!" Kesira yelled above the din.
She held out her staff as if this would protect them from
harm.

Both men realized the danger and forced her to even
greater exertion. Kesira used her staff in her left hand
to help pull herself along; Rouvin's grip on her right
hand now bruised with its intensity. From behind came
the deep-throated rumbling as the mine fell in upon
itself, hungrily swallowing the tiny shaft.

Blinded by dust, unable to breathe, stumbling and
dodging the rocks pelting down from above, Kesira
thought she was going to die. Only Rouvin and Molimo
kept her moving onward.

"Which way?" cried Rouvin, coming to a "Y" in the
tunnel.

"How should I know?" she asked. "I've never been
here before."

"Use the talent that lets you cast the runes. Which
way?"

Kesira had no idea. She pointed right. Rouvin and
Molimo were off in a flash, carrying her along. And all
the while they ran, the earth battered at them, the floor
of the tunnel rising and falling—and the overhead
threatening to crush them to bloody pulp.

Another juncture, another decision.

Kesira pointed and Rouvin obeyed instantly. To
the woman one path was no different than another.
Why should the warrior assume she had some special
insight? If anyone did, it would be a man who was half-
demon. But Rouvin obviously depended on her judg-
ment, so she gave it willingly, whether or not she
believed in it.

"Rest, I need to rest," she panted. The air in this
portion of the shaft was musty and dank, as if the tunnel
was long unused. "My sides hurt."

"We must keep running," Rouvin demanded. "We
need to put more distance behind us."

From the shaft came ominous rumbling sounds, as
if the products of the earthquake stalked them like

some jungle beast. Kesira closed her eyes and felt fear rising to absorb her senses. Jungle beast. She mentally pictured a *chillna* cat, fangs bared, eyes narrowed to slits, strong hooked black talons waiting to rip and shred, sleek purpled fur laid back for the kill.

"Run!"

Kesira shook her head and said, "No more. I...I've had enough. Let me rest. Just for a moment." The nun turned to see Molimo staring at her, pleading in his dark eyes, now lightly rimmed with soft, glowing green. Fear rose within her, not for herself but for Molimo. She worried that the change was seizing control of him. She reached out and hugged him to her. The youth pushed her away, startling her. He pointed toward Rouvin.

"You, too, Molimo?" The dark head nodded vigorously. Molimo pointed back toward the valley—the Quaking Lands—and gestured once more that they should flee.

Kesira took a deep breath and obeyed. She had to reach deep within herself to find reserves that had been virtually drained. Too much had been heaped upon her. The capture by the Order of the Steel Crescent had been bad, the escape from Nehan-dir and the demon Howenthal even worse, and the flight across the country to the Quaking Lands had been the worst of all. And she had naively thought that nothing more could happen. Kesira ran for another ten minutes, then began to stumble more and more often. Even with her staff for support, her legs refused to carry her.

"We rest here," said Rouvin, sinking down. He stuck the torch into a rock niche and sat beneath it. Tiny sparks drifted down and alighted in his hair. He took no notice, even when a few of the sparks began little fires.

Kesira started to mention it, but Molimo's hand on her shoulder restrained her. The youth crossed to Rouvin and brushed his hand on the man's sweat-lank hair. The fires went out with minute smoking pyres marking their demise.

"Thank you," said Rouvin. "I hadn't noticed."

Kesira felt the tension between the two. Rouvin had been cool toward Molimo from the beginning, and

Molimo had avoided Rouvin at every turn. Just after they'd escaped from the Citadel and Rouvin had learned Molimo's secret, the tenseness had turned to more open hostility. She had hoped this small gesture on the boy's part would mark the start of a friendship. It didn't.

Molimo returned and carefully seated himself across from Kesira.

"Is there any way of telling where we are?" she asked Rouvin. "I picked the turnings at random."

"Not random," the man said. "I have the sense we moved toward the spot where Wemilat is imprisoned. We might not be more than a few hundred paces from him." Rouvin frowned when Molimo shook his head and began sketching in the powdery white dust carpeting the floor. Molimo drew a tracing showing their route and other, intersecting tunnels leading off toward where they'd seen Howenthal's guards posted. Kesira studied the drawing and decided they were almost a mile away.

"How do you know this, Molimo?" she asked.

The youth smiled and tapped the side of his head.

"He's more animal than human, that's how," said Rouvin with ill-disguised contempt.

"That's none of his doing." Kesira found herself speaking more harshly than she'd intended. The strain of being trapped within the dark coffin of the mineshaft wore on her more than she liked. She closed her eyes and tried a brief meditation technique to remove the anger she felt boiling within her. As before, when she had tried to reach for inner strength to augment her physical exertions, she succeeded only in part. Fear still remained, but its edge had been blunted.

"We'll never get out of this alive," said Rouvin. "We must confront Nehan-dir's guards, fight free of the mountain, then cross the Quaking Lands. Howenthal will never allow that. Why he let us in so easily is a question I cannot answer."

"Easily?" blurted Kesira. "You call the month's ride getting here easy?"

"It was. Howenthal spoke of you by name back in the Citadel. To him, you are important." Rouvin's voice softened as he added, "To me, you are very important."

"Please, Rouvin." Kesira looked away, her eyes dropping to Molimo's sketch. The distances appeared ac-

curately proportioned; there remained only a short mile
to Wemilat.

"Kesira, I want you to..." began Rouvin.

She cut him off. "What sort of mining operation did
they conduct here? The walls do not appear to be hacked
at, as if they sent forth minerals."

Rouvin sighed. "These are jade mines. The veins of
nephrite are of only passing interest to a demon like
Howenthal. He wants only the best jadeite." Rouvin
pointed and a tiny gleam of brilliant green shone at the
very top of the tunnel, a flicker of light from the torch
catching the exposed point of jade. "Howenthal has
mined them for a hundred years. The mountains on
either side of the Quaking Lands are worse than a
termite-ridden tree."

"None will venture down this tunnel?" asked Kesira.

"How should I know? The only reason I can see for
imprisoning Wemilat is because Howenthal was unable
to kill him outright. I suspect the human guards furnished by the Steel Crescent are only to prevent the
likes of us from gaining entry. Howenthal can magically hold Wemilat easily enough on his own."

"Then Howenthal fears us." Kesira's mind turned
this over and over. She had been stunned when the
demon had spoken her name back in the Citadel's Great
Hall. How had a nun's name from a destroyed Order
come to the demon's lips? The woman fingered the twin
bindings at her waist, the gold and the blue. Gelya had
perished. Had she been so beloved of her patron that
he mentioned her just prior to dying? Was this why
Howenthal—and Eznofadil and the accursed Lenc—
sought her?

Kesira fought to keep tears from beading at the corners of her eyes. She had lost so much; only revenge
drove her on. Revenge for Gelya and Sister Fenelia and
all she had known for much of her life.

"Howenthal fears nothing," said Rouvin with a grimness that extended far beyond the subject at hand. "We
have little choice, though. We must forge ahead if we
are ever again to see the light of day."

Molimo cut off any reply she might have made by
erasing his sketch in the dust and pointing to the guttering torch. The flambeau burned to within inches of

the bottom. In only a short while they would be without light.

"Can you see in the dark?" Kesira asked the youth. Molimo nodded. "We'd better get as far as possible before we have to depend on Molimo to guide us like blind men."

Rouvin scowled at such a prospect. Kesira eased some of the tension in the man by taking his arm and starting off. She glanced back over her shoulder. Molimo had a gentle smile on his lips, an approving smile, she thought.

The torch burned to smoldering embers in less than five minutes, plunging them into complete darkness.

"Molimo," she called out. "You must be our eyes now."

"A moment," said Rouvin, still chafing at the idea of being dependent on the man-wolf. Kesira felt Rouvin reach out, heard his hand rake over the roughness of the walls. She threw up her hands when dazzling light shone forth like a green beacon. Rouvin had found a tiny chip of jade and cradled it in his hand. Where it touched the palm, it glowed with eye-searing intensity.

Rouvin looked pleased, but Molimo's expression defied explanation. The youth's eyes had grown wider—from the dark, perhaps—and he stared without blinking into the jade chip. He trembled like a horse ready for a race, hypnotized by something transcendent. The faint greenish tinge in his eyes grew deeper, reflecting the jade light, Kesira thought.

"Now we can see perfectly well, even without the torch," said Rouvin. "The part of me where my mother's blood flows has seldom proven useful. But now, *now* it does!"

He strode off, sword clattering against the side of the mineshaft. Kesira and Molimo followed a pace behind, getting enough of the light to prevent stumbling.

They had gone only a short distance before Molimo let out a peculiar noise from deep within his chest. He stopped and snarled, more wolflike than human.

"Rouvin," cautioned Kesira. "Molimo's heard something."

"There's nothing. He imagines it." The man had barely spoken the words when Kesira heard a soft padding behind them. She spun, her staff perpendicular to the ground. She had been trained to deflect sword thrusts by a slight movement to one side with that staff; Kesira reacted instinctively now and the rusty axe skittered off the stone-wood shaft and smashed ringingly against the tunnel wall.

"Mother Ayondela, I don't believe this!" exclaimed Rouvin, turning to see what the commotion was about.

Kesira used her staff to drive back the creature—she dared not call it human, although in general outline it appeared to be. It had two arms and two legs and walked upright, but there any similarity to humanity ended. Slithering tendrils snapping about like pit vipers replaced fingers and toes. The body was hung with pale green moss, as if the body had lain overlong in a grave before rising to stalk her. But the face caused her gorge to rise—if she could call the front of the thing's head a face.

No eyes. Skin flaps closed over the eye sockets. No nose. Only a double slit, too high up to be true nostrils. No ears. Holes drilled with cruel force substituted for true human ears. And worst of all was the mouth. The circular pit opened to reveal not teeth, broken and yellowed, but more sinuous wormlike tendrils nervously casting about, occasionally reaching out past blackened lips.

The axe came up, this time starting at the creature's knees and aiming to split her from groin to head. Kesira overcame her shock enough to spin her staff around and take the blow fully against the wood. The impact knocked her back; she stumbled and fell into a heap on the floor. Only Rouvin's quick leap and accurate lunge saved her. His sword spitted the creature through the throat.

Even in death throes it did not go in a human fashion. It grabbed the wounded spot in its throat, stuck tendrils into the cut and bleated like a sheep. Rouvin drew back, slashed, lopped off an arm, slashed again and cut most of the way through the injured neck. Only then did the beast have the good grace to collapse to the floor, dead.

"What is it?" Kesira asked. Her voice came forth in a whisper. Her mouth felt as if it had been filled with cotton wool.

"One of Howenthal's miners. He does something to

his human captives, something magical, and changes them into creatures like that." Rouvin displayed none of the distaste Kesira experienced. If anything, he sounded emotionless, neutral, untouched. "They work better. Don't want to return to the surface like more human workers."

"It's awful!"

"There will be more," said Rouvin. This time a thrill entered his voice. Kesira felt nothing but shock at this. Rouvin enjoyed the killing. He had been sullen since entering the mineshaft, but now he positively sparkled with vitality. The man had found his element and again performed a useful task.

"If one found us, there'll be more. They roam the mines in packs, like dogs—or wolves." Rouvin stared accusingly at Molimo, as if the youth was responsible for this perverted creature's attack.

"Let's go," Kesira said in a shaky voice. "I have no desire to be around when its friends find it."

They continued on their way, Rouvin's step springy. He barely broke stride when a pair of Howenthal's monstrosities erupted from a side tunnel and attacked. One slash took the leading miner-beast across the chest; a second gutted the other. Rouvin went on, not even commenting.

"Awful," Kesira said, one hand hiding her mouth. Molimo pressed close to her, comforting her. But the woman saw the expression on the youth's face. He shared none of her revulsion at the sight of humans altered into something...inhuman.

But why should he? Kesira knew then some of the pain Molimo carried within his breast. These creatures' transformation was permanent. His was uncontrollable. In an odd fashion, they were brothers. Kesira didn't doubt that Molimo rejoiced for their killing and the freedom from the magicks binding them. Perhaps he sought similar surcease from the change-spell.

"Hai!" shouted Rouvin. He rushed forward into a small chamber, sword flashing left and right. He drew his dagger and fought with both weapons. Kesira forced herself to look. The opponents were all too human this time. One man's tunic gaped open where Rouvin's slash had split it; Kesira saw the cruel brand of the Steel

Crescent on the man's chest. She swung her staff and knocked him sprawling. Molimo finished him with a single twist of the neck.

"That's the lot," said Rouvin, standing. Kesira thought he was saddened by the fact. "We ought to be near the main tunnels. See?" He pointed to huge green spots lining the walls: jade.

"Does Howenthal need to imprison Wemilat in a cell of jade?" she asked.

"Never thought of it. Quite possible." Rouvin whirled in a complete circle and again faced her. "No more soldiers, no more miners. But Howenthal will not let only a handful protect his prize. Where is Wemilat? We've got to get him freed quickly or we might spend the rest of eternity buried under this slag heap."

Kesira felt the deep rumblings beneath her feet. Howenthal sent temblors throughout the Quaking Lands again. She had no idea how far underground they were, but this only put them closer to the source of the quakes. The woman turned in the direction that led deeper into the mountain. She pointed, her hand shaking.

"That way. I sense something. Something words cannot describe."

"You're the one who can read the runes," said Rouvin. He cared little for this, she saw. He wanted only to fight, to feel his muscles straining in mortal combat with another. The warrior had become a vital force, implacable and burning with passion. Kesira saw that he would never easily accept the teachings of Gelya.

Kesira walked as if in a trance, following Rouvin and his flashing sword. The man slew a dozen or more of Nehan-dir's soldiers and Howenthal's miner-beasts. She tried not to count. It was bad enough wading through the rivers of blood and gore produced by that strong arm and deft sword.

"Magicks," she said in a low voice. "I sense them all around. It's similar when I read the rune sticks. But this is a force, a force immeasurably stronger."

Kesira wiped sweat off her brow. The quaking of the tunnel had not stopped since they had encountered the Steel Crescent's guard. If anything, it had mounted in intensity. She heard the wood beams protesting mightily, and tiny stones occasionally fell from the rocky roof. If Howenthal kept up his activity, the entire mine shaft would fall down around her ears.

"Rouvin! Wait!" she called out. "Do not advance. Can't you feel it?"

"Feel what?" he said irritably. He moved with determination to seek out new adversaries to test his skill. "There's nothing here."

"There is." Kesira walked forward, Molimo at her elbow. She studied the seemingly empty tunnel for long minutes before she pointed out the thin line of green running across the floor, up both walls and joining overhead to form a continuous band.

"Jade," said Rouvin. "So what?"

Kesira reached out. Her fingertips crossed the invisible barrier and instant pain flashed throughout her body. She jerked away, stifling the scream of agony that formed on her lips.

"What happened?" Rouvin also reached out. He was unable to hold back his cry of pain.

"Howenthal guards this corridor with magicks beyond my understanding. I never learned those mysteries. Sister Fenelia might not have known them," said Kesira. "Yet, I feel..."

As she had done in the Citadel, Kesira stretched out her hands and let her mind fall freely through space and time. She became disconnected with body and reality. She was still in the mineshaft and she was *elsewhere* at the same time. Her gentle tinkerings caused a ripple in the magical curtain. Not much, but enough. She drew it aside. Not much. A tiny amount. But enough.

Molimo shoved Rouvin past, then gripped Kesira's arm and pulled her numbed body to the other side. Kesira shook and dropped to hands and knees. Sweat poured from her face and dripped into the rocky dust, which greedily sucked it up to give birth to a thin mud.

"The cell," came Rouvin's distant voice. Molimo helped her up, then she shook him off, preferring to depend on her staff. The stone-wood gave her both strength and support. It reminded her of Gelya's teachings, her vows, the intensity of her need for revenge against the demons responsible for all the destruction.

"Here, Kesira. Look." Rouvin sheathed his sword and

stood in front of the doorway into a small room carved
from the purest jade. Within it hunkered a creature
more grotesque than the miner-beasts they'd encountered in the tunnels.

Kesira flinched away, then controlled herself. The
creature within appeared to be little more than a toad.
Long legs bent beneath it, short arms dangled limply
from high on its chest. Hair like green seaweed had
been pushed back from a high, warty forehead. The nose
had been brutalized repeatedly, broken and never properly reset. The lips fluttered like waves on the ocean
and pulpy ears hung on either side of the head.

But Kesira looked into brilliant green eyes and *knew*.
This was no stupid beast. Great intelligence resided
within this ungainly frame. Wisdom. Kindness.

"Wemilat," she greeted.

"You must be Kesira, of whom they have spoken so.
I knew you would seek me out. How are you, my child?"

"You are not what I expected," she said honestly.

"My form does not please you?" A laugh both mocking and kind came from those bloated lips. "Nor does
it me, but I live with it." Wemilat staggered slightly
as a quake reverberated through the tunnels. "Howenthal grows impatient. He might even realize you have
reached this point. *No!* Do not attempt to enter my cell."

"I passed through another magical trap in the tunnels," Kesira said. "I can do likewise with this one."

"Stop!" Wemilat hopped forward until he was less
than five feet distant. "This is of a different nature.
Only one or two humans have ever had the power to
break a spell cast by a demon of Howenthal's power.
Even I am enervated."

"The jade?"

The demon nodded.

"Howenthal will bring the entire mountain down
around our ears if we don't get you free."

"We? Ah, yes, I see the others now. Rouvin," greeted
the demon. "It has been a long time. How is your mother
Ayondela? Well, I trust."

Rouvin nodded. Kesira wondered if awe held his
tongue or something more prevented the man from
speaking. He stood with his feet spread wide, as if to
defend a position against heavy attack.

"Why hasn't Howenthal killed you, as he did Gelya?" asked Kesira.

"Ah, you know of Gelya's death? Yes, you would," the demon said, those sharp eyes fixed on the twin sashes about her waist. "He lacks the power. For all my ugliness, I command much Howenthal and the others desire. Not only can he not slay me, he desires knowledge only I possess. So he holds me here."

Molimo moved forward and tugged at Kesira's robe. She turned and saw the youth's face shifting.

"Molimo, control yourself. Please," she begged. The transformation began and she could not take the time to calm him. Not for the first time she wished Zolkan were here. He had a way with Molimo that she envied.

"Your friend?" asked Wemilat, gazing at Molimo.

"He got caught in a rain of jade," she explained. "Can you do anything to help him? He...he changes form and cannot help himself."

"I help him?" Wemilat sounded both astounded and saddened. "There is nothing I can do, even were I freed of this jade prison."

"How do we get you out?" Kesira asked. The rumblings from the bowels of the earth became more and more emphatic. She worried that Howenthal had discovered the slain guards and worked to bring the entire mountain down.

"Only one path from this cell exists. And the cost is far too great for me to ask of any human." Infinite sadness gripped the hideously shaped demon.

"Tell me," Kesira demanded.

"A hero must die."

"What?" Kesira asked. Then events flowed too swiftly around her. Molimo shifted totally into wolf form. In the same instant, he leaped. Kesira caught the flash of Rouvin's sword as it whipped from its scabbard. He swung at the wolf.

Blood erupted from Rouvin's throat as Molimo's fangs sank deeply. Only then did Kesira scream.

Chapter Twelve

KESIRA MINETTE watched in horrified fascination as Rouvin waved his sword feebly at the attacking wolf. Huge globs of blood spurted forth as Molimo savaged the man's throat. Shaken, but finally free of her shocked paralysis, Kesira swung her stone-wood staff and struck Molimo on the flank. The dull thud did nothing to stop the wolf at his gory feast. Again Kesira swung, this time with all her strength. The blow missed target and smashed into Molimo's upper shoulder; she had aimed for the head.

Molimo rolled away, snarling. He faced her, eyes bright green and glowing with lupine hatred. He tossed his head and sent a shower of Rouvin's blood curtaining upward. Then the wolf advanced, fangs bared. Kesira gripped her staff and waited, remembering Gelya's teachings. She wouldn't be the first to attack, but she would respond to any mistake made by her attacker. Molimo's nature dictated that such a mistake had to occur.

"My brother, be still," came Wemilat's soft words. The wolf stopped, corded muscles quivering in his powerful shoulders. "The spell is shattered. I am free. You have done too much for me."

Kesira chanced a quick look toward the jade prison. Blood from Rouvin's severed throat trickled in a stream to a spot halfway through the doorway. There the blood sizzled and burned as if it had been tossed into a raging fire. But Wemilat now waddled through the barrier, unharmed.

"Peace," the demon repeated. "You have freed me."

Kesira's fingers turned bloodless and cold on the shaft of her stone-wood staff from the intensity of her grip. She tried to relax and failed. The three of them— Molimo, Wemilat and herself—were held as if caught in a diorama. The moment passed and Molimo sank to the ground, paws stretched in front of his bloody muzzle. But the green eyes still burned with anger and hatred.

She took a hesitant step toward the wolf, but Wemilat stopped her. "This is something I must attend to, my dear."

Kesira allowed Wemilat to move her gently out of the way. The wart-faced demon waddled forward on his impossible legs and stood before the wolf. Wemilat reached out with his toy hands and touched the top of Molimo's head lightly. The wolf whined and shook, then began to change back into a more human shape.

Kesira heaved a sigh of relief and turned to Rouvin's body. He lay sprawled gracelessly on the floor, his head canted at an impossible angle. She didn't have to check for a pulse to know he had died almost instantly under Molimo's ripping fangs.

"I am sorry," she said softly. "It should have been different between us. More. I don't know why it wasn't."

A particularly sharp earth tremor sent her sprawling across Rouvin's body. Blood soaked into her gray robe and spotted the gold ribbon around her waist. Kesira pulled away and sat cross-legged beside the corpse. There was so much they could have done together, and now the time had passed. A single tear left a salty track down Kesira's cheek. She reached up with a trembling finger and captured it. Reaching out, she transferred that single droplet to Rouvin's lips.

"That will not revive him. He is past all help, mortal or demon," said Wemilat.

"Burial," she said in a voice too hoarse to be her own. "We can give him a proper burial. Honor demands it. He was a hero."

"Do you feel the shaking?" asked Wemilat.

"What? Oh, yes, of course. But what's that got to do with burying Rouvin?"

"Howenthal is powerful. He sensed it the instant Rouvin's blood crossed the doorsill and rendered his binding spell impotent. Howenthal thinks to crush us all under the mountain."

"We can't just leave him," protested Kesira.

Molimo rose and stood over her. His midnight-black eyes no longer held the ferocious green light that had been on him, but Kesira saw something still not human within. The youth wiped away blood from around his mouth, then pointed.

"Our friend is correct," said Wemilat. "We must leave. Now. If we tarry, there will be no containing Howenthal."

"But he imprisoned you because you could do him harm. Do it now!"

Wemilat smiled wanly. "That is not the reason he trapped me. I can destroy him, perhaps. I need the proper moment, the proper power. But he could not destroy me outright—and that is why he imprisoned me. That and the knowledge he seeks." The toadlike demon tapped the side of his misshapen head. "Locked within here is the key he needs to reign supreme."

"Even over Lenc and Eznofadil?"

"Even over them."

"Use it against him. Against them. Destroy them all!" Kesira buried her face in her hands and wept, as much for herself as for Rouvin.

Molimo reached under her arms and lifted her to her feet. At first she struggled, turning away from the youth. Then Kesira's facade crumbled totally and the frustration and fear and pain of the past months rushed out. She emptied her soul as she clung to Molimo, the man who had so brutally slain Rouvin, and she felt closer to him than to any other in the world.

"The shaking grows," said Wemilat. "Howenthal will trap us if we do not leave."

"All right," Kesira said, struggling to get her runaway emotions under control. "I am sorry. Gelya would not have approved of such an outburst. It...it's not honorable."

"Gelya was a fool in many matters," said Wemilat. "We shall discuss this further. After we have left behind these odious quarters." The demon turned and his face rippled like a reflection in a pond as he stared at the jade prison.

"That's the way we came in," Kesira said, her mind shifting to concrete items that allowed her more complete control of herself. "We can backtrack, but we'll have to explore if we want to find a way outside. Our path in was closed behind us by one of Howenthal's quakes."

"In that direction lies only death and destruction for you," said Wemilat. "If the miners don't slay you, Howenthal will surely smash you with a quake. The shortest distance out of the mountain is...there." Wemilat pointed up and to the right, through solid rock.

"I'm supposed to just pass through the tons of stone and move like an underground river?" Kesira shook her head. The imprisonment had addled Wemilat's mind. Or perhaps this was simply a joke, an ugly joke matching his exterior.

"Why not? Take my hand. No, my dear, it will not corrode your fine skin." The demon reached out and seized her wrist before she could pull away. Molimo moved closer. His hand closed on Wemilat's other minuscule one so that the three of them formed a ring.

"Noooo!" shrieked Kesira as she felt as if she had stepped off a mountainside. She fell...up.

The tunnel's jagged rock ceiling loomed and then she passed *through* in some fashion she couldn't understand. Her meditations had sometimes allowed her to explore the world around her without need of a physical body, but this was not the mind/body separation she had achieved. As a whole being, Kesira Minette passed through rock she knew to be impenetrable.

Molimo squeezed her hand to comfort her. While she felt no fear, uneasiness was almost as terrifying.

"My dear, try not to resist so. I have little practice taking mortals with me on my jaunts to see this part of the inner world." Wemilat's words echoed within her skull. Her ears were not equipped to listen through solid rock.

"Feel the vibrations? Howenthal is responsible. His quakes̄ grow in intensity. Soon enough the entire maze of tunnels will come crashing down. When that happens, Rouvin will be given a grave vaster than any mortal can expect. It will be a fitting monument to a true hero."

Kesira tried to speak and found she did not know how. Instead, she slowly turned and studied the rock strata flowing by around her. She saw geologic evidence of past seas, of animals trapped and preserved in the softer layers, of erosion and building. Eons of history rushed by; she glimpsed pockets of jade, veins of gold, huge chambers filled with gases and petroleum. And all the while the trio flew upward on magical wings provided by Wemilat.

They burst into sunlight so bright that Kesira jerked free of Wemilat's tiny hand and shielded her eyes. The instant the connection broke, the three tumbled down. Wemilat caught himself on the froglike legs and hopped to one side to avoid being crushed by Molimo's falling body. Kesira stumbled away, squinting.

Her eyes adapted quickly, and she saw they stood atop the mountain. Below, stretching like a table surrounded with rocky chairs, lay the Quaking Lands. Across the planar surface raced a shock wave from an earthquake. It had barely struck the mountains on the far side when it reflected back, met a newly formed quake front and merged to give birth to still another. Any mortal caught on that expanse would have been tossed and battered beyond survival.

"Howenthal plays his little games," said Wemilat without satisfaction. "He sends out those poor fools who follow his banner and slaughters them for amusement. Wherein lies the thrill of killing mortals?"

Kesira's head snapped around and she stared at the grotesque demon. He spoke of killing humans as if they were flies. He did not approve, any more than most humans approved of torturing insects. But if one happened to die, where was the loss? For the first time it was driven home to her that demons cared but little for life. To an immortal, the concept of an ephemera must seem peculiar in the extreme.

"How do you feel about Gelya's death? And the death of the others?" she asked.

"Death is not something we dwell on," admitted Wemilat. "The whole notion is not one I fully comprehend."

"That's why Rouvin's death meant so little to you?"

"Hardly. I appreciated his sacrifice. Howenthal has a savage sense of humor to install a wardspell with such a release mechanism. Actually, I discerned the key only through great thought on the subject. Most of the other demons would never have considered such a key."

Again Kesira Minette had it driven home to her how little the demons thought of death.

"Did Rouvin mean something to you?" asked Wemilat, looking from her to Molimo. The raven-haired youth had walked a short distance away and peered out into the hazy distance.

"He was a friend," she said.

"And more?"

"That is no concern of yours." She did not flinch away from his direct gaze. The demon shrugged his sloping shoulders and waddled to a stone, where he hunkered down.

"I did not mean to pry. You and your wolf strike me as more of a matching."

"Molimo?" she asked, trying not to sound too intense. "I feel sorry for him. He was almost killed when Lenc destroyed my Order's nunnery. I nursed him back to health and feel an obligation toward him."

"It should flow in the other direction. He ought to be grateful to you for your services." Wemilat scratched himself with the toe of his left foot. The awkward motion appeared quite normal for the demon.

"How did you pass through solid rock?" Kesira asked, wanting to change the subject. She felt a light flush rising to her cheeks as she thought of Molimo. The feeling disquieted her.

"That? It was ever so simple, my dear. Each demon possesses a particular talent. Howenthal reaches into the ground and pulls at whatever he finds there. Earthquakes are the result. I reach into the ground, not with power or anger, but with finesse. My entire body is able to slip through the good earth even as a faint shadow slides through this fine spring breeze."

"What of Ayondela?" asked Kesira. "She was Rouvin's mother."

The grotesque head nodded slowly. "That she was. And a fine demon she is, too. Strange in many ways, but aren't we all?"

Kesira paid Wemilat scant attention now. She studied the set of Molimo's body. The youth appeared to be listening. Strain as she might, Kesira heard nothing. She shrugged it off. The young man's hearing proved more acute than hers on many occasions, no doubt the result of being able to transform into the hearing-sharp wolf. When Molimo spun, his gaze locked on a point not ten feet from her, Kesira also tensed. Molimo had given every indication of preparing for battle.

At the spot Molimo indicated, Kesira saw frost forming on the ground. The springtime grasses, green and struggling, turned brown and wilted before her very eyes. And above that spot rose a pillar of ice, solid, blue, impenetrable.

She clutched her staff and waited. "What form of devilment has Howenthal brought us?" she asked Wemilat.

"Not Howenthal, I fear," the ugly demon said in a tired voice. "The use of her name brought her to us. And she is a most unhappy person at this instant."

The pillar of ice exploded, sending frigid shards in all directions. Kesira threw up her arm and shielded her face. Tiny needles of bright ice lanced into her cheeks and forehead, in spite of robe and arm. Smarting, she lowered her arm and stared in open-mouthed amazement at what was revealed.

Standing on the spot, half a head taller than she, was a woman cloaked in a stunningly draped light blue gown. Partially revealed by the cunning design were large, firm breasts, a slender neck and a petite gold chain encircling it. The woman's patrician face troubled Kesira; she had seen her before and yet she hadn't. The more Kesira worried about it, the more confused she became.

The aquiline nose dominated the face. The small mouth was pulled into a tight knot of anger, and the blue eyes were no warmer than the polar icecap. Hair blacker than midnight spun past from her shoulders and fell to waist length; tiny sparkles of rainbows danced in the dark strands. Clutched in her right hand was a wand of blue-white that caught the brilliant sunlight pouring down on them like a warm syrup and turned it into winter.

"You know?" asked Wemilat of the newcomer.

"I felt it when Rouvin died. He called me a few minutes prior and I was unable to come immediately—but I died the instant he died."

"Really, Ayondela, such theatrics. You probably cared for your son, but you make it sound as if you actually loved him." Wemilat snorted contemptuously.

"I loved him!" she roared. The heavens shook with the echoes of her words. The ice scepter in her hand dripped chilled water to the ground; everywhere a drop touched, grass perished.

"You are Rouvin's mother?" asked Kesira, concern overcoming her fear. "I am sorry. He died to..."

"He *died!*" she raged. "And you are the bitch responsible for Rouvin's death. You!" The wand pointed toward Kesira. The nun clung to her stone-wood staff and forced calm upon her thoughts. Trying to cope with a raging demon accusing her of killing a son, Kesira had to exert her meditative techniques to the utmost to retain composure.

Wemilat hopped forward and interposed his body between the two. The frosty beam emanating from the wand struck the toadlike demon squarely. He brushed it aside as if it were of no consequence—to him, it was. Kesira didn't want to think what that column of cold might have done to a mortal.

"Cool off," Wemilat said. For a moment, he stood stock still, then he chuckled. "You can hardly be anything else but cool, can you, Ayondela? The ruler of all that is cold and dark, the one to whom passion comes so seldom."

"Silence, Wemilat. I do not know or care what your role is in this. *She* killed my son. My only son. For that she will die. Now!"

Again came the beam and again Wemilat deflected it, using his own contorted body as a shield.

"She is under my protection, Ayondela. I cannot allow you to harm her."

"You are a fool, Wemilat. I will destroy you if you don't give her over to me." As Ayondela talked, a ring of hoarfrost spread out from her feet. Kesira planted her staff firmly in the ground, refusing to give way to the creeping tide of ice.

"A fool I may be, but she has aided me. I now seek your assistance, too, Ayondela. Against Howenthal and Eznofadil and Lenc. You know what they do. They try to destroy the rest of us."

"She killed Rouvin."

Kesira swallowed hard at the tone the female demon used. There was no shred of sanity in those words. She had become totally fixated on one fact and one fact only. The nun did not speak in her own defense. Anything she said would be twisted by Ayondela and used against her. Best to let Wemilat try to reason with the grief-stricken demon.

Wemilat said quietly, "She is innocent. She tried to prevent it. If anything, I think she cared greatly for Rouvin."

"No," said Kesira, the word slipping unbidden from incautious lips. "I...I liked him. He was a staunch fighter and helped in my escape from those loyal to the Order of the Steel Crescent, but he was nothing more. Nothing more."

"You slew him," said Ayondela. The ice wand dripped a constant stream of death now. When the beam lashed out at Kesira, Wemilat tried to stop it and failed. Kesira felt the wan light strike squarely on her stone-wood staff. The wood turned icy, but the death she had believed locked within the attack never came. Wemilat forced the wand up and away, hitting Ayondela's hand.

"Gelya was her patron. You and Gelya were friendly," said Wemilat. "Could one of his pets ever harm one of yours?"

"Rouvin was my son!"

"Son, pet, whatever," said Wemilat. "They are only mortals. We have greater concerns, you and I. Howenthal imprisoned me. When he and the others are strong enough, they will come for you." The toadlike demon hopped closer to Ayondela until, straining, his face and hers were less than a foot apart. "Help me stop them now. They seek power over the world of mortals—and our deaths."

Ayondela might not have heard Wemilat for all the attention she paid him. "She killed Rouvin. She will die. And you, Wemilat, you are even worse. You take a mortal's side against another demon."

"Ayondela," he began.

"Howenthal has partaken of the jade," she said in an ominous tone.

"Ayondela, don't do this," said Wemilat. "The jade will destroy Howenthal and the others. It will take time, but they are doomed."

"The jade augments their power. As it will mine!" She reached into the folds of her gown and drew forth a tiny sliver of jade. From behind Kesira, Molimo made tiny gasping noises. The nun dared not turn to see what troubled the young man. Her troubled eyes were affixed on the demon's palm where the chip of jade lay glowing with a dull inner light.

Ayondela lifted it to her mouth and dropped the bit of jade under her tongue. Kesira winced as the green aura spread, slowly at first, then with a voracity matched only by famished predators, until the demon's entire body blazed with emerald glory.

"The power," Ayondela muttered. "I never thought it would be like this. So much power!"

"There's still time," pleaded Wemilat. The ugly demon waddled around Ayondela and reached out. He pulled back his tiny hand as if it had been burned. The aura prevented direct contact with the ice demon.

"Look," said Ayondela. She held out her hand. The flesh which had appeared so human a short time earlier now took on a hard veneer of jade. The woman was transformed visibly into a living statue shining with illicit power.

"Your death will follow," said Wemilat, his words measured and sad. "I am sorry for you, Ayondela, truly sorry."

"You are wrong, warty one," Ayondela said in her icy tones. "You should feel sorry for yourself. I will join with Howenthal and the others and we will pillage this world, ravage the mortals and conquer all!" Spinning to face Kesira, Ayondela said, "And you will be mine, slut. You will suffer unlike any mortal has suffered. You will rue the day you conspired to kill my only son."

Ayondela thrust her wand into the air high above her head. A cloud of vapor poured down over her, enveloping her green form, hiding her totally from sight. When a gentle spring breeze wafted over the rounded top of the mountain, only a circle of dead grass remained to show the demon had ever been present.

"I didn't kill Rouvin," said Kesira in a choked voice. "I didn't want him to die."

"Ayondela hates you," said Wemilat.

"There were only three demons to fight," said Kesira, "and now there are four. And it is my doing!"

Chapter Thirteen

"AYONDELA'S WRATH is stunning, is it not?" asked Wemilat. The toadlike demon hunkered down and played with tiny wisps of the brown grass where Ayondela had stood. "She never allowed things to fall into perspective. Perhaps I misjudged her, though. She might have loved Rouvin."

Molimo moved closer to Kesira and put his arm around her shoulders. She looked up into the young man's face and saw nothing but sadness there. She touched his hand, then pulled away.

"Does it matter whether or not she loved Rouvin?" asked Kesira. "The fact is that she had joined ranks with Lenc and the others."

"Ah, yes, Lenc," said Wemilat. The demon picked his broken teeth with one tiny fingernail. "You know of his role in destroying Gelya?"

"Of course." Feelings of helplessness surged upward again to overwhelm her. Kesira paced restlessly, her feet never quite touching the browned, dead area left by Ayondela's frosty presence. "Rouvin wanted to help me against him when we became involved with Howenthal and the Order of the Steel Crescent."

"You cast the rune sticks?" asked Wemilat. "I see within you much power, but it is not directed properly. I see you as a glowing spot, but the light is diffuse. Even during the peak of your meditation there is no focus."

Kesira shrugged. "Gelya's teachings are all I have left to guide me."

"I have few enough followers, and that is fine with me," said the misshapen demon. "Not many desire alliance with one such as myself, though I must say there are decided benefits."

"Such as?"

Wemilat laughed, his pendulous earlobes bobbing about with the motion of his head. "Alliance to any living demon surpasses that to one now dead," he said.

"Not so. If Gelya's teachings were revelations of truth, they remain so, whether or not he is dead."

"Absolute truth does not exist," said Wemilat. "Look at how Ayondela interprets the fact of her son's death. You believe Rouvin died for a purpose and not by your hand. Ayondela says the death is both senseless and your personal fault."

Kesira glanced over her shoulder at Molimo. The youth stood with hands hanging limply at his sides. His shoulders slumped and the expression on his face was one the woman failed to read. The part he had played in Rouvin's death wore him down, but Kesira didn't find it within herself to blame Molimo. The transformation that seized him lay beyond his control or desire. Just as the young man hadn't wanted the maiming brought him by the battle between demons, neither had he wanted to take Rouvin's life.

Or had he? Kesira's uneasiness mounted. The communication with Molimo never quite fulfilled her desire for complete knowledge of what he thought and felt. The change into wolf form had begun almost immediately upon learning of Wemilat's predicament, and Kesira realized nothing short of a demon's magic could have stayed Molimo from killing Rouvin.

Had the young man wanted to kill?

"Ayondela must listen," said Kesira. "If she will give me only a few minutes I can make her understand."

"You had a chance," said Wemilat. "Ayondela's mind

is closed to what you call facts. And would you trade Molimo for your own life?" The demon cocked his head to one side and studied her closely. The eyes bored into her very soul.

"Ayondela would understand. She's a demon, after all, and has to know what other demons' magicks can do to a mortal. Molimo cannot control his changes. He is under a geas cast by Lenc."

"If you were a mother and found your child dead, would that explanation satisfy you?" A shrewd look came into Wemilat's eyes.

"This is not a debate with points given for logic," she said.

"No," agreed the demon. "We speak of emotion and irrationality and how Ayondela has begun her transformation into a being of living jade. As long as the chip remains under her tongue, the change will continue, giving her more and more power, until she can no longer control it and she is destroyed. But until then, you have much to fear from her." Wemilat looked from Kesira to Molimo. "As do you, wolf spawn."

Molimo's hands clenched and inarticulate mutterings came from deep within his throat.

"I will go spy on Howenthal," said the demon. "Camp here or find some other place. It matters little. Now that I am attuned to you, I can find you later."

Before Kesira could speak, Wemilat began to sink into the ground. The last she saw of him was his seaweedy hair dragging along the ground, being sucked into the earth as if its owner had fallen into quicksand. Kesira went to the spot and gingerly tested the soil with her foot. Solid.

Molimo shook his head.

"I know. We can't follow," said Kesira. "But I wish there were something we could do. I hate waiting."

Molimo rubbed his stomach and pointed to his mouth.

"I'm hungry, too, now that you mention it. Do you want to hunt or should I?" Kesira still entertained misgivings about allowing the young man to venture forth on his own, especially when killing might be involved. She trusted Molimo the man totally. But she wisely doubted Molimo the wolf's ability to control his own actions.

Molimo smiled and patted her on the arm. He turned, but Kesira gripped his shoulder and spun him around. For a moment brown eyes locked onto black. They moved closer and lips met, tentatively at first, then with increasing ardor. Molimo broke off, almost guiltily. Then he smiled shyly and hurried off. Kesira tried to regain her breath and only succeeded in creating more of a turmoil within.

She sat heavily, trying to piece together all that had happened to her. She realized the emotional confusion muddied her thoughts so she began her meditative techniques, not closing her eyes but staring straight off into the cerulean blue sky vaulting over the Quaking Lands.

A loud squawk intruded on her serenity and sharp claws dug into her shoulder, finding the perch with uncanny accuracy.

"Zolkan, where have you been?"

"Flying. Danger everywhere. Eat *trilla* bird!"

"You're about my only companion. We rescued Wemilat and..."

"Rouvin dead. Stony gone dead." The bird shifted weight from side to side, pulling one talon free from entangling gray cloth. "Heard Steel Crescent guards."

"They know Wemilat's freed?"

Zolkan bobbed his head up and down.

"Have they begun searching for him?" Kesira worried about contacting the demon with this information. Howenthal and Ayondela might have already joined forces.

"For all. Even me!" The *trilla* bird shook himself and sent green- and blue-tipped feathers down to the ground in a rainbow shower. "Steel Crescent guards gather below." Zolkan used one wing to point to the deceptively peaceful Quaking Lands. "Nehan-dir commands now. Citadel closed down, all here, all rally to Howenthal. Big battle comes."

"They're ready to start the conquest for Howenthal." She tried to understand the jade demon's plan, how Nehan-dir and the Order of the Steel Crescent fit in, what the demon might do—with or without Ayondela's help. "They'll probably assemble their troops here, then march straight east and over the River Pharna."

"Conquer Chounabel?"

"It's a rich city," she said. "The Emperor would have
to commit most of his troops immediately if it appeared
that a demon aided the Steel Crescent."

"Emperor has aid. Demon Lalasa favors him."

"That may be what Howenthal wants. If Lalasa com-
mits her aid to Emperor Kwasian, the others might
have to take sides. This drives a wedge in demon ranks
and allows easier conquest."

"That, my dear, is part of the scheme," came Wemilat's now familiar squeaky voice. The demon rose up
through the ground as if on a movable platform. He
rested easily on the surface, which seemed to harden
beneath his feet.

"Zolkan tells of gathering troops."

"The *trilla* bird sees well."

"'Course I do. Need sharp eyes to catch food." Kesira
stroked the bird's head to calm him; the demon meant
to compliment, not insult him.

"What have you discovered, Wemilat?"

The demon squatted down and folded his tiny hands
on the bulging chest, looking contented with himself.
He began rocking gently and humming softly. Finally,
he snapped out of the small trance, as if just realizing
Kesira had spoken to him.

"Howenthal," he said by way of explanation. "He is
firmly ensconced in his pillar of jade." Wemilat clucked
his tongue and finished, "The similarities between his
flesh and that of his fortress are becoming more and
more obvious. All too soon the transformation to pure
jade will have seized Howenthal. He will be quite invincible then, at least for us."

"Kill now," suggested Zolkan.

"I fear you are correct," said Wemilat. "I do so wish
I had more time. To speak with others, to find the proper
ploys. But alas, it is not to be. Time presses us so."

"What will Howenthal do?" Kesira outlined her ideas
concerning the Steel Crescent's battle strategy.

"To force Lalasa to take sides, either for mortals or
with Howenthal," mused Wemilat. "A cunning enough
plan, but only if you do not understand the inner workings of Lalasa's mind. She will never side with Howenthal. No, this bold venture by the Steel Crescent is

military, pure and simple. Craft and devious plotting
are not included in the plan."

"What can we do?" asked Kesira. Zolkan craned his
head around to peer at the demon.

"You? Nothing more than you have done already,
seeing me out of that damnable jade prison. Now it is
I who must act." Wemilat heaved a human-sounding
sigh. "The job is beyond my skill, but I must try."

"Get others," said Zolkan. "Have them help."

"Many of those most closely aligned with me are
gone. Gelya, for instance. Berura-ko has not been heard
from for many weeks. I fear she has fallen victim to
one of the others, perhaps Eznofadil. There's ample evidence that Lenc and Eznofadil have imprisoned Noissa
and his human bride Leoranne. But where? Seeking
him out would take time that is already in short supply." Again Wemilat gusted the heavy sigh. "They have
been too effective, the power given them by the jade
too great."

"They've outsmarted you," said Kesira with more
bitterness than she intended.

"My dear, I cannot disagree. We grew complacent in
our personal power. None of us thought that others
wanted more. Why bother? But it has come to pass that
the three—four, if we dare to count Ayondela—may
end up the sole surviving demons and exercise control
over all this." Wemilat swept his hand out to encompass
the world.

"The lovely green seas, the vapors in the air, the
dear earth, even the elements raging across its face, all
theirs," Wemilat continued. "And we allowed it through
inaction."

"Time for Chaos," said Zolkan.

"How's that? No, not that," said Wemilat. "This is
not a point of transition between epochs. There will
always be demons. We are too strong for it to ever be
otherwise. No, there will *not* be gods rising from our
ashes."

Kesira said nothing. Gelya had spoken of the dy-
namics of evolution, the changes wrought from animal
to human to demon and the eventual progression that
some day would lead to god. One's species need not die
out totally to make room for the next, but the journey

appeared endless and had to happen sooner or later. She felt, even without casting her rune sticks, that Zolkan spoke truly. Chaos would seize the moment. The Time of Passing had come for the demons.

And for humans.

"I must act in this matter, and I am so woefully drained. Howenthal has seen to that. Spending time surrounded by the jade enervated me horribly," said Wemilat.

"What do you plan?" asked Kesira. She paid the demon little attention, her eyes fixed on Molimo. The young man paced nervously as if he had changed into wolf form and found himself caught in a cage. She wondered what ideas raced behind those green eyes, what schemes were born and died in the flash of a single thought. Not for the first time she wished he still could talk. Kesira knew the things Molimo might tell her would be wondrous indeed, and she didn't know why she believed that.

"I will beard Howenthal in his most secure spot. I will pass through the ground, edge my way through the wardspells shining forth due to the jade foundations of his castle and take him by surprise. Howenthal will rue the day he imprisoned Wemilat the Ugly!"

Kesira frowned. She heard the false conviction ringing in Wemilat's voice. The misshapen demon boasted too loudly and the plan lacked coherence.

Zolkan told Wemilat so.

The demon glared at the *trilla* bird, then laughed. "You are astute, my brightly feathered messenger. Howenthal's fortress is virtually impregnable. When I enter, no other demon may follow, due to the jade surroundings. Howenthal, I fear, controls powers vaster than even I might imagine."

"Demons cannot pass," said Zolkan, "but humans can?"

"And even a friend of the air," said Wemilat.

Zolkan protested loudly at that, wings battering Kesira about the head. She reached over and soothed the bird until he stilled.

"You want Molimo and me—and Zolkan—to mount an attack of our own while you ease through the ground and emerge within Howenthal's fortress?"

"Succinctly put, my dear," said Wemilat. "The dangers are vast, the rewards nonexistent. Even if we succeed in removing the danger posed by Howenthal, there are the other jade demons to confront." The inflection placed on the word "jade" told Kesira the loathing Wemilat placed on this blasphemy.

"We have to cross the Quaking Lands," she said, looking out over the plains below. "It'll take some time for us. We either have to steal horses or risk the journey afoot."

"Horses," Wemilat said firmly. "Definitely horses to cross that shivery, treacherous terrain. Even I risk damage traversing beneath the surface."

Kesira considered her role in this foolhardy attack. She saw Molimo studying her; from the corner of her eye she caught Zolkan's beady eye, too. The decision was hers to make. They would honor it and follow her to death, if necessary. Small tears formed in her eyes. She brushed them away, knowing such loyalty was truly rare.

"Gelya said that right was like the morning sun, blazing forever bright. Howenthal and the others must be stopped."

She wanted vengeance on Lenc, but to succeed in it she needed Wemilat's aid. Only by immediately pursuing Howenthal could she hope to win a more lasting alliance with the grotesque demon.

"You think yourself right?" asked Wemilat.

"I do. I *am*. We go immediately. How long before you will be able to penetrate Howenthal's fortress?"

Sloping shoulders hunched forward and Wemilat's entire body shivered. He finally looked up from the ground and said, "One full day, if I begin near the base of the supporting pillar. It will take much skill to enter by this route and the danger is immense because of the jade facade. I can do it no faster."

"Just as well," squawked Zolkan. "Quaking Lands not meant for travel."

"I wish we could fly above them, as you do," Kesira said. "But Molimo and I must choose more earthly routes."

"Let us leave," said Wemilat. "The sooner this battle is met, the sooner I may recuperate. I will accompany you to within a few miles, then sink beneath the surface."

They started, Kesira and Molimo walking at a steady, ground-devouring pace. Wemilat huffed and puffed and followed the best he could. Kesira felt sorry for the demon until she remembered his incredible powers. He was immortal—or virtually so—and commanded magicks far beyond her wildest imaginings. She considered this as they made their way down the side of the mountain and to the edge of Howenthal's Quaking Lands, but by the time they set foot on the deceptively quiet terrain, Kesira had made up her mind.

Gelya had spoken well: *Those with courage must also have faith.*

Kesira had the faith in her own strength, and that of Molimo and Zolkan. Even without Wemilat, they would conquer Howenthal.

Molimo hunted constantly, returning with small game. Kesira had moderated her worry over Molimo's tasting of blood and thereby transforming into wolf. With both Zolkan and Wemilat along, she knew Molimo's shape alterings could be reversed, if caught in time.

A full day into the Quaking Lands, the first true tremor rose up beneath them. Splits opened in the earth and threatened to swallow them whole. Molimo and Kesira clung to one another as they were tossed high into the air, only to smash hard into the ground. The process repeated itself with unflagging energy.

"Wemilat!" she cried. "Stop it!"

"Alas, my dear," came the demon's words, almost hidden under the deep thunder of the quake, "Howenthal's magicks in this outweigh mine. All we can do is weather the storm."

Kesira felt her guts turning to mush. Every temblor caused her teeth to grate together, her internal organs to beat one against the other. Standing proved impossible. The more she groped for support, the less she found. As quickly as the quakes had come, they passed.

She lay gasping on the ground. Weakly, Molimo helped her to her feet. Even with the youth and her sturdy staff, Kesira found walking difficult for a few hundred yards. Then strength returned until she felt almost normal once more.

"The shiverings sap the strength so," she said. Molimo nodded solemnly. "Is there no other way to Howenthal's fortress?" Molimo shook his head and pointed ahead.

Squinting, Kesira made out a dull, pulsating green glow in the far distance. Fog cloaked the valley they traveled, and sudden rises and drops in the elevation caused by earthquakes produced an effect similar to looking through heat haze in the desert. Everything in the distance shimmered and danced.

"Why does Howenthal do this? It must take considerable energy and trouble on his part," she complained.

"He is a boastful demon, our Howenthal," said Wemilat. "He counts this as a barrier keeping out the unworthy. Only the strongest survive to challenge him— and by the time they cross the Quaking Lands, how strong can they be, eh?"

Kesira didn't answer. Hunting was sparse and the ground quivering beneath her feet robbed her of all will to continue. Even if they arrived at the base of the jade-covered column where Howenthal perched, they'd be in poor condition.

She remembered the sight of Ayondela swallowing the jade chip and the awesome change that had occurred. How much power did Howenthal possess now that he had experienced the full force of the illicit jade for so many months?

Molimo jerked on her sleeve and pointed to the sky. A tiny green spot showed where Zolkan scouted. The crazy dips and dives the *trilla* bird made betold danger.

"I see," said Wemilat. "I fear there is a party out hunting, whether for us or merely patrolling is incidental."

"No cover," muttered Kesira, looking left and right. Tiny clumps of hardy shrubs sprouted to break the monotony of the plain but these provided scant hiding place. The land rippled into gullies where the continual quakes had ripped open earthy wounds; these gave them their only chance to hide.

Molimo already sprinted for the cover of an arroyo. Kesira trailed by a few paces and Wemilat brought up the rear. They found a ravine where wind erosion had added to the depth and forced themselves up and under a slight overhang. Kesira didn't believe they would escape detection, but they had to make the effort. Fighting every party of soldiers from the Steel Crescent meant eventual defeat.

"Can you aid us with your magicks?" she asked anxiously. The pounding of hooves came ever closer. Wemilat crouched down, his tiny hands folded over his bulging chest.

"To do so risks all," the demon said. "Howenthal might sense it. If I used my powers during one of his quakes, that might mask the effect. Dare I give us away in a simple encounter?"

"Not so simple," Kesira said grimly. Her knuckles turned white as she gripped her staff. The horses' hooves were right above them. Not ten feet away rode a half-dozen well-armed soldiers.

A deep growl caused Kesira to spin, and see Molimo change into wolf form. She reached out to stop him, but the animal lurched free of her grasp and darted into the center of the sandy-bottomed ravine. With a quickness totally inhuman, Molimo whipped around, crouched, then hurled himself up and out, directly at the riders. Frightened horses neighed and pawed the ground. Kesira shielded her eyes as a curtain of dirt and small rocks tumbled onto her. The sound of one rider being thrown spurred her into action.

She leaped out, staff swinging. The fire-hardened shaft struck one horse just above the knee, breaking the leg. The horse's rider toppled headlong into the ravine, the fall knocking the wind from his lungs. Kesira kicked the helmless man in the head and he lay deathly still. Above, Molimo had dispatched still another, ripping the man's groin into bloody tatters. But the remaining four recovered quickly, swords slithering from scabbards.

A saber cut sent Molimo scuttling away, whining in pain and anger. And the other three forced their mounts to the ravine floor.

Kesira found herself surrounded by a shining barricade of steel blade.

"A pretty prize we have in this one," said one man.

"*Alive,*" countered another. "Nehan-dir wants this one alive. For Howenthal!"

"The green prick gets everything," grumbled the first. Kesira took advantage of the small byplay to unseat the one. The flat of the leader's saber landed squarely on the top of her head, stunning her. She stumbled and fell to her knees, the world spinning crazily about her.

Trying to rise, failing, she saw through blurred eyes two men coming for her. The staff slipped from nerveless fingers.

And the ground exploded upward.

Shrieks rent the air. Then silence fell. Kesira sat heavily in the sandy pit, rubbing her head and returning to a semblance of normality. The world again came into focus and she saw that Wemilat had descended into the ground, only to rise up behind the two soldiers of the Steel Crescent. In some fashion—his magicks?—the demon had reached into the men's backs and ripped out their spines.

"Not unlike the technique I use for passing through solids," said Wemilat. He shook his tiny hands and blood droplets spattered into thirsty sand, leaving no trace.

"Molimo!" Kesira twisted to her feet and grabbed her staff. But her fears were groundless. Already the wolf changed back into human. She clutched the young man's body to hers as he silently sobbed in frustration at his lack of control. "It's all right," she soothed. "You saved us. Your strength is so necessary, but why must you suffer in this fashion?" She rocked him to and fro like a newborn until Molimo shoved her away.

"More!" came Zolkan's aerial warning. "More come. Flee! Flee!"

"Hurry, Wemilat," the nun cried. "We have horses now. Can you ride?"

"I must," answered the demon. "For surely I cannot walk. The drain on me is so intense when I do things like that."

Molimo and Kesira helped Wemilat into the saddle of one of the horses. She felt the demon's clammy, unnatural flesh and guessed at his exertions. He had never fully recovered from his imprisonment.

And now other soldiers dogged their footsteps. Even if they eluded them, what condition would Wemilat be in when they confronted Howenthal in his most secure place? Kesira Minette didn't want to consider that. The days already passed swifter than an archer's arrow.

What little advantage they had over Howenthal passed as quickly.

Chapter Fourteen

THE QUAKING LANDS shook with a palsy strong enough to toss Wemilat from the saddle. The demon took a nasty spill and was slow in regaining his feet.

"Are you hurt?" asked Kesira, concerned. She had noted the steady weakening in Wemilat since the encounter with the patrol. Although the demon rode well enough, it obviously posed a great strain for someone with his misshapen physique.

"Only physically," answered Wemilat. "In spirit I remain whole." The froglike legs propelled him upward where his toy hands caught the saddle horn and pulled futilely. Molimo quickly slid from his own horse and assisted Wemilat. The demon huffed and heaved and again rode astride his horse.

"Thank you, my brother," said Wemilat to Molimo. Kesira saw the silent communication flowing between the pair and felt envious. Somehow Wemilat tapped into Molimo's very soul and learned those dark secrets she longed to share. Molimo vaulted into his own saddle with a single lithe movement.

"Zolkan warns of Steel Crescent riders to the east." She stood in her stirrups, hoping to catch further sight

of the bird. The tiny green spot against the blue sky
had vanished once the *trilla* bird had passed along this
information. If no other of their party escaped, at least
Zolkan might after this had come to a conclusion.

Kesira shook herself for such defeatist thinking. They
would not fail. No matter that Wemilat had never recovered from his ordeal and visibly lost in strength. No
matter that Molimo was maimed, his tongue ripped
from his mouth. No matter that her patron had died at
a jade demon's hand. No matter what Howenthal did,
no matter how many of Nehan-dir's Order of the Steel
Crescent rode them down, no matter what, they would
triumph.

"Hope is the poor man's bread," she said softly.

Wemilat's hearing proved more acute than she'd
thought. The demon turned and speared her with an
angry look. She ignored him, falling into a meditative
state, sorting out all that had befallen her. Kesira rode
and kept her mind calm like a pellucid pond with a
single leaf floating on its surface.

The quakes subsided somewhat and they made better time, Molimo ranging far ahead to hunt and find
suitable camp spots. But the journey wore down Kesira;
she had a glimmering as to how this must affect the
demon clinging to his mount, with legs too long and
arms too short.

"The patrol is passing us," said Wemilat. "I sense
their anger, though. They have heard of the deaths of
their comrades."

"They are only mercenaries," said Kesira.

"Even mercenaries allow themselves to have friends.
And these of the Steel Crescent are, after all, following
their patron. In that they have a common bond, however
transient for them."

Kesira didn't point out that Nehan-dir and the others
sold themselves to the highest bidder. Whichever demon provided the greatest opportunity for power was
the one they pledged allegiance to. They had no conviction of philosophy, only of domination. As she rode,
the nun considered this aspect. Was it such a bad way
of approaching the world? It seemed to work, and Gelya
had preached pragmatism. If tact did not accomplish a

worthy end, perhaps a straightforward approach would. Did the Steel Crescent do anything she did not?

"They consider themselves quite moral, I am sure," said Wemilat, as if he had read her thoughts. "Bitterness is a part of their world view because of past dealings with demons less than honest, but for the most part those of the Steel Crescent see themselves as bettering their lot in precisely the same fashion the Emperor does."

"The Emperor has almost universal support. They do not," said Kesira.

"If Nehan-dir replaced Emperor Kwasian, would not the people support him?"

"If he were the Emperor, of course they would. But Nehan-dir's behavior would be altered by the throne. His commands would be tempered by the will of the people he governed."

"And if he did only what pleased *him*, people be damned?" asked Wemilat.

"How could anyone do that?" Kesira puzzled over the odd turn this had taken. Gelya had preached—honestly and accurately—that proper behavior garnered proper behavior. Any ruler who did not serve the best interest of the people failed and a new emperor arose to claim the throne. Where was the honor in enslaving those you ruled? "Do you think this is what Nehan-dir desires?"

"It is what Howenthal and the others desire. There is no way a human could depose one of them."

"True," said Kesira. "But would they wish to rule over the mundane workings of the human government?"

"Why continue? Let the humans starve. You are ephemera, hardly worth notice."

"Where is the honor in dominating gnats?" she asked. "I seek revenge on Lenc for what he did to my patron. Such is only right. Because Howenthal is aligned with Lenc, he, too, is implicated in Gelya's passing."

"Your motives are simple enough. Perhaps I cannot explain the need for raw power. Perhaps I do not fully comprehend it myself. After all, I and the others failed to see the black seeds burgeoning in Lenc, Howenthal and Eznofadil."

"They rule only to kill?" Kesira wrestled with the idea.

"They rule to prove to all humans that their very whim is law."

"Such ego," the nun said. "This goes counter to all Gelya has spoken and taught. Honor glows all the brighter that I oppose them."

Wemilat laughed, but the sound came out as weak as tepid tea. "Never allow your courage to flag, my dear. You will succeed."

"*We* will," Kesira said. The way Wemilat laughed again worried her; the demon sounded unsure of himself.

With the ring of scintillant green stone rising from the center of the Quaking Lands growing ever nearer, they all needed a full measure of confidence.

"That is Howenthal's fortress," said Wemilat. "Note the way the very clouds avoid the top of the jade spire. The walls of the fortress itself are simple stone, yet they repulse wind and rain and even the blue of the sky. He has gone far in denying his heritage for the power given him by jade."

A cold lump coalesced in Kesira Minette's belly as she stared at the castle sequestered firmly atop the jade column.

"How do Molimo and I get up the sides? They're as slick as glass, and the power of the jade probably gives ample protection against invaders."

"That is your problem. Mine is one of greater magnitude. How do I wend my way through the base, if the entire foundation is one solid plug of jade?"

"Can you partake of the jade, as Ayondela did?"

"No!" Wemilat's vehemence shocked Kesira. "I am sorry, my dear. This, to me, is tantamount to your believing an emperor must govern for the benefit of the ruled. It is insidious, this demonic source of power. Ideals warp and twist when the jade is misused. Howenthal thinks all is normal and natural and that he is clever in possessing what I and the others spurn."

"The jade burns him out?"

"It robs him of his longevity, but that is only part of the trap. Even as it augments his already considerable power, it drives him quite mad, I fear. My brother," said Wemilat softly and with infinite sadness, "how can you do such a thing?"

Zolkan cawed loudly and plummeted from the sky, almost knocking Kesira off her horse when he landed on her shoulder.

"Be careful," she cautioned. "You're hurting me with those talons."

"Troops," the bird said without preamble or apology. "Ride hard. Do it *now!*"

Kesira saw dust clouds rising to the left—and to the right rose the hummocks of earth showing how Howenthal ravaged the land with his quakes. She felt the slight tremors and knew that they might be caught like bugs in amber if another earthquake seized them. Even the horses, bred for and used to the Quaking Lands, shied away from the earth's uneasiness.

"Ahead," she ordered. "We must ride with the wind if we are to avoid them."

"Fast!" agreed Zolkan. The *trilla* bird launched himself, Kesira wincing at the pain it caused her. His takeoffs were scarcely better than the landings; tiny trickles of blood stained her gray robe from his clawing.

Molimo rode back and joined them. Somehow he had also spotted the soldiers on patrol and had come to warn her. Kesira flashed him a reassuring smile and wished her confidence matched it. Only when their horses began stumbling often and thick foam dotted their coats did Kesira rein in.

Wemilat tumbled from the saddle, looking more dead than alive. The toadlike demon simply lay on the ground, his entire body quivering and whimpering moans coming from his puffy lips.

"The quakes come," he sobbed. "They scramble the paths through the earth. How will I find my way? And the jade? It is blinding! All roads into Howenthal's fortress are sealed."

Kesira licked dried lips as she studied the jade column rising from the floor of the Quaking Lands. Even with mountaineering gear, scaling this peak would be impossible. She didn't doubt that the other side of the spire presented the same foreboding picture.

"We cannot get up, not in time to aid you," she said.

Molimo began scratching a message in the dirt. The

waves passing through shook tiny rocks and tried to obliterate his words. The young man wrote all the faster to avoid this erasure by earthquake.

"Molimo says that Howenthal is preparing for a massive invasion. Somehow, the Emperor has decided the Order of the Steel Crescent is a danger and has mounted two full legions on the edge of the Quaking Lands." She scowled, peering at Molimo. "How did you learn this?"

Molimo waved off this inquiry and let the deep vibrations of the ground shake down his words to make way for more.

"The attack will commence within the hour," the nun continued reading. "Emperor Kwasian does not lead the troops himself, but General Dayle does." Kesira gripped Molimo's shoulder and shook gently. "Tell me your source. This is information not even a score of spies could ferret out."

"Be content he has gleaned this fine information," said Wemilat. "I think that Lalasa inadvertently aids us. She and Howenthal have never been friendly, but some intrusion or another—or even common sense on Lalasa's part, an unlikely happening—has pushed her into this move."

"Emperor Kwasian sends his troops, not his patron."

"Would he launch such a campaign without a demonic ally? I think not. Certainly not against a religious order with as powerful a following as the Steel Crescent."

Kesira started to interrogate Molimo more closely when the young man leaped to his feet and pointed. Kesira wanted to cry in frustration. Wemilat's horse had sunk to the ground and now lay on its side, flanks heaving and eyes wide and wild. Even knowing as little about horses as she did, the woman saw this animal would be of no further use to them—now or perhaps ever.

"My horse is just as tired. We'll have to trade Wemilat off between us," she said to Molimo. The young man shook his head. Even as Kesira had spoken she knew where the truth lay. Their progress would henceforth be too slow. And too much of the Quaking Lands still separated them from the base of Howenthal's fortress.

She stood on legs turned rubbery from a new bout of ground shakes. Walking was out of the question.

"But how?" she asked.

"I feared this would happen," said Wemilat. "Seeing the jade-plated sides of the spire only makes my role more important."

"You'll have to give us an extra day to scale the peak," said Kesira.

"How?" Before she could answer, Wemilat rushed on. "That way of ingress is impossible to anyone. I see it too clearly now that we are closer. We must go together, you and Molimo and me."

"Through the ground? But the extra burden will tire you overmuch!"

Wemilat's baleful expression revealed more than Kesira desired to know. "That is so," the demon said, "but without you and Molimo, my attack will fail without question. Better to attempt it now, than to stay here for Howenthal's legions to find us."

Kesira still worried over this when Wemilat reached out and gripped her hand. From the other side Molimo seized her slender wrist. She felt the world turn to melted butter around her as the trio sank into the ground, propelled by Wemilat's demonic powers.

Kesira Minette felt as if she had been caught in this nonworld forever. The stone flowed around her like a solid breeze, yet she tried to touch it and failed. There was no spring breeze blowing the first hints of pollen or the humming of bees or warmth or . . . anything.

It mattered little if her eyes stayed wide open or she closed them. The magicks woven by Wemilat carried her through the bowels of the world and she could do nothing but accept. The woman knew the ugly demon held one hand and Molimo the other, but her flesh experienced no sensation of touch. Only a gauzy haze showed where the stone-wood staff rested in one hand. She had become cocooned in her own universe and that bubble floated at Wemilat's whim.

Now and again tiny sparkles of light dazzled her, but these were few and not enough to capture her attention. But the woman did sense a slackening in their progress after—how long? A minute? Hour? Millennium?

She tried to look with more than vision and succeeded partially. Heat soothed the top of her head, soothing because it was the only real tactile sensation since vanishing beneath the surface. The warmth mounted, grew, threatened to burn. Kesira twisted and turned to it. The heat boiled away the flesh of her face. She winced. But no pain attended the maiming.

With the suddenness of lighting in the twilight, they burst into a tiny room. Wemilat jerked away from both Kesira and Molimo and huddled in one corner of the chamber, his face averted. Molimo stood in the center of the room, covered in sweat and panting as if he had run miles. All Kesira could do was shake.

"I hadn't realized there was so much strain involved. There didn't seem to be before, when we left the prison." Neither of the others took notice of her.

She touched Molimo lightly, but he drew back, his expression one of extreme concentration as if listening for the time of his death. Kesira went to Wemilat and sat down beside the demon. Shock passed through her when she got a good look at him.

"You're hurt!" she cried.

"No, just so...tired. My strength began to fade quicker than I had anticipated. And the barrier. I failed to breach it. No strength left. I failed."

"Where are we? What barrier?" Kesira worried more for the demon's condition than their current plight. They seemed safe enough in this stony room. Her eyes adapted to the faint phosphorescent glow cast by moss growing close to the rock. This wasn't as much a room as it was a coffin. No opening led outward.

"You must have experienced something," said Wemilat. "A tingling? Visions? The taste of spring berries on your tongue?"

"Heat," she said. "There was some heat on my head. When I turned to it, I thought my flesh had boiled off."

"It affects each differently. That heat was the result of the jade barrier on which Howenthal built his fortress."

"But we got through all right," Kesira said. "We're here, aren't we?"

"Wherever here is," said Wemilat. "And no, we did not get through. I told you. My strength failed. I was too weak!"

The grotesquely shaped demon quivered and began to sob quietly. The sight of Wemilat's frustration at his failure disquieted Kesira more than anything else. She had not known what to expect from the attempt. But this? She sampled some of the futility and helplessness Wemilat drank so deeply of.

"We're safe from the tremors," she said, trying to find some bright point for hope.

Wemilat shuddered, his earlobes bobbing like fatty drops of rain. "Safe? Not even from the quakes. Howenthal casts them everywhere, even under his own fortress. They amuse him."

"We're trapped here?" she asked. A cold blanket of fear settled over Kesira. This chamber was far too small for the three of them to survive long. Even considering the paltry rations they carried, the air would soon grow stale and they would suffocate. Kesira swallowed hard. She could feel the air turning warmer, stuffier, less breathable by the second.

Closing her eyes, she slowed her breath rate and stilled the racing heart hammering so within her breast. The mind techniques taught by Gelya served her well.

"Good," said Wemilat. "You understand."

"Can't you use your magicks to get us out of here? Again through the rock walls? Just slip through?" She pressed her hand against the all-too-solid wall.

"I cannot even stand," said Wemilat. "I am drained and the brush with Howenthal's jade barrier robbed me of what strength I had left."

"Hack too high on the tree and chips fly into your face," said Kesira.

"Another of Gelya's teachings?" asked Wemilat, smiling wanly.

"Just something Dominie Tredlo said once."

"Your Dominie Tredlo lacked ambition. Without the attempt there can be no success. In my case, it was not that my reach exceeded my grasp as much as Howenthal's grasp was the stronger."

A snarl came from Molimo's lips. Kesira saw the

transformation take the young man again. All too soon a wolf stood slavering where once a man had been.

"Do nothing," warned Wemilat, a tiny hand touching Kesira's lips. "Let him rove."

The wolf swayed nervously, then began pacing from one side of the small room to the other. In minutes, Molimo began digging furiously, dirt and rock chips flying. Kesira marveled at the sight of wolfen claws pulling away stones and she marveled even more when a gust of air rushed into the chamber. A dust cloud rose and obscured even Wemilat nearby, but Kesira had to cheer.

"You did it, Molimo! You freed us!"

The dust began settling slowly and Kesira's glee abated. Molimo had gone.

"He seeks a path through the interior of the column, a way clear of jade. It might exist. It just might," said Wemilat.

"He'll be back, won't he?" She longed to join the wolf and race beside him, to protect him. Then Kesira laughed bitterly at that notion. In this form Molimo needed no human aid. He was stronger than a man, quicker, his senses more acute and, for all Kesira knew, the shape change also made Molimo more cunning. But as cunning as he might be, his basic nature was that of a wolf.

"Fear naught. He will return."

Kesira tried to help Wemilat stand and failed. The demon's strength had vanished as surely as mist in the morning sunlight.

"How are you going to deal with Howenthal in this condition?" she asked. "You're not able to walk, much less trade magicks with a demon of his power."

"The jade strengthens him," agreed Wemilat.

"Well? Do we have to rest here until you recover? There's little enough food and water, but we might be able to last for a day or two."

"That will not suffice," said Wemilat. "My weakness is not so much of the flesh as of—there is no way of truly describing it. The core of my being, the spot I tap for power, is drained. As the jade builds Howenthal's power, it saps mine."

"You're saying we have to get away from this fortress until you can recover?"

"There's no way out of the pillar," Wemilat said, "except for the way we entered. And I cannot carry even myself out."

"But there's got to be some way of building you back up. Otherwise, Howenthal will..." Kesira let the sentence trail. She felt betrayed by the ugly demon. They had come this far carrying the belief that he would be able to put up a fight against Howenthal. Now Wemilat told her this was not only impossible, but that they were trapped in the jade demon's fortress, perhaps for the rest of their very short lives.

"There is a way to regenerate myself," said Wemilat so softly that Kesira almost missed the words.

"What is it?"

"Do not sound so eager. For you, it might be too distasteful to consider."

"More so than dying without avenging Gelya's death? Or the death of Sister Fenelia and the others in my Order?"

"Perhaps."

Kesira wiped away the patina of dust and sweat on her forehead. Licking dried lips only transferred the grit to her teeth, but the nun ignored it. Her mind raced to find the path Wemilat hinted at.

"I don't understand," she said after long thought.

"You have a deep inner strength, my dear," said the demon. "There is a nobility of soul, a power of mind and spirit that make you indomitable. You might shatter as if made of glass, but you will not bend. In this you are stronger than steel, yet more fragile. I mention this to point out the danger to you."

"I might be destroyed by what you have in mind?" she asked. All of Gelya's teachings poured back to her now to keep fear from gnawing at her mind.

"That is so."

"But you think I might survive?"

"That is also so."

"What do you want me to do?"

Wemilat smiled and Kesira shuddered at the sight. It was more of a leer than a smile now. She knew what he would say.

"Demons infrequently—in the past—roamed the world and mated with humans because of this inner fire. You burn so brightly inside. This is perhaps why your lives are so short. The fuel that is within you is used so quickly. But demons can taste of this inner fuel and, for a time, burn as brightly ourselves."

Kesira said nothing. The blood drained from her face as she looked at Wemilat. The bloated belly, the froglike legs, the tiny arms and hands, the stark deformity of his face.

"Some humans seek out such contact with demons. I have no doubt Rouvin's father was of that sort. There is something to be gained by both."

"I am not celibate," Kesira said in a voice scratchy and thin.

"I am aware of that. Gelya was pragmatic, above all else, and one so lovely as you would find ample opportunity to take a lover. Perhaps even this Dominie Tredlo you've mentioned?"

She nodded. "The Senior Brother of our Order. And others."

"Your energy will be diminished for only a short while. Mine will be augmented for a longer period."

"I must do this," she said, more to herself than to Wemilat. "No personal consideration should stand in the way of duty to an honorable quest."

"Damn Gelya!" snapped Wemilat. "This is not something to be decided on the basis of a dead demon's homilies. You must *feel* your answer. You must *respond* fully or there will be no gain. Can you do that?"

Kesira began unloosening the twin sashes of gold and blue at her waist, then began pulling off her tattered gray robe.

Chapter Fifteen

A SCRATCHING SOUND alerted Kesira. She spun, staff in hand. A heartfelt sigh of relief passed her lips when she saw Molimo's human head poking through the hole his wolf form had dug in the wall. The young man gestured for her to follow.

"You've found a way to Howenthal's fortress?" she asked.

A dark-haired head bobbed. But she saw no expression of joy on the face. Molimo was racked with the same fears she was about this quest. She glanced back at Wemilat, who sat contentedly in the corner of the room. Kesira had barely spoken to the demon, nor had Wemilat encouraged it. He seemed lost in a world of his own thought. And all Kesira could think of was the price she had paid to stoke the fires burning so low within the misshapen demon.

"Molimo's found a path upward," she said, louder. "It won't do to wait any longer."

"I quite agree, my dear." Wemilat saw how she flinched at the term he used so carelessly. "We will triumph. I assure you of that."

His words did not cheer her. Never had she lain with

anyone not of her choosing, not of her desire. That Wemilat could be so confident only meant he lied to her to bolster her courage.

"It's not necessary to say what you don't feel," she said. "Your condition is much improved. I see that. Can you honestly battle Howenthal and win?"

Wemilat's eyes bored into her. He said, without the least hesitation, "Yes."

Kesira felt shame at doubting the demon, but the doubt continued even though he had told her he was able to defeat the jade demon. She had seen all that they had overcome reaching this point and knew it was only a fraction of what lay ahead.

Kesira carefully transferred as much of the phosphorescent moss from the walls to her staff and robe as possible. The light cast was dim, but her eyes had adjusted readily enough to the darkness to permit safe travel.

The woman scrambled through the small hole and out into the shaft Molimo had uncovered. Wiggling along on her belly, she followed Molimo to a larger chamber. From this juncture three tunnels radiated outward. They waited for Wemilat to join them, then the young man confidently strode down the central shaft. Kesira followed, finding the pace almost too fast for her.

"Your energy will return soon enough, my dear," said Wemilat.

She glared at him and redoubled her efforts. Kesira finally decided the problem lay not within her, but in the tunnel. Looking back she saw it fell off sharply. The woman had hardly been aware of the incline as she walked, but the twinges in her calves and ankles soon reminded her of it with every step.

Kesira refused to slow the pace and, as long as Molimo led the way, she was willing to follow. The man-wolf took turning after turning, sometimes forcing them to crawl belly down along narrow shafts and other times bringing them to vast chasms.

At one, Kesira stopped and asked, "Is this of Howenthal's doing?"

Molimo indicated that it was and Wemilat said, "These are test sites for Howenthal. He practices cast-

ing his quakes by shattering specific portions of his
supporting pillar."

"That sounds dangerous. What if he goes too far and
brings down his entire fortress? Jade is strong, but with
the right force used against it, even it will break."

"What cares Howenthal of this? If the entire of the
Quaking Lands is ruined, so what?"

Again Kesira saw the difference in attitude between
demon and mortal. Wemilat struggled to understand
her concern. To him she was hardly more than an insect
from whom he sucked needed nourishment.

"You are wrong," said Wemilat, again accurately
reading her thoughts. "You are much more, my dear.
It is a pity you are not a demon. Even among our rank
you would be truly special."

Before Kesira could answer, Molimo scooped up a
rock and heaved it down a side corridor. Kesira wobbled
a bit as she turned, balanced on the brink of the deep
chasm. She caught sight of the sides of the chasm, absolutely smooth as if they'd been slagged after coring.
She shifted her weight back to the rocky pathway and
recovered, back to the pit.

"No," she moaned. Kesira wished she had never
turned to see what advanced along the corridor Molimo
defended with thrown stones.

"More of Howenthal's miner-beasts," said Wemilat.
"We cannot tarry. Let Molimo hold them back while
we press on."

"We fight together, not separately," she said. "We
all die here or none of us does."

"Noble sentiments, but Molimo is better equipped to
do battle than we are, at this instant. Come, the real
courage is in continuing to live, not in dying."

Wemilat herded her along, his tiny arms surpris-
ingly strong now. Kesira looked at Molimo, who pulled
back his lips in a lupine smile. While she still felt like
a coward abandoning him, she allowed Wemilat to push
her down another cross tunnel. In a few minutes, the
sounds of combat were far behind them.

"Howenthal continually reforms the jade base for his
fortress," said Wemilat, as if he had adopted a profes-
sorial role in Kesira's education. "The different config-
urations focus power differently for him. Day by day,

he becomes more fully jade himself. I am certain he longs for the time when he can merge totally with this massive spire."

"How can he retain consciousness if he is turned entirely into jade?" Kesira asked.

"The power of jade is immense, but so is that of a demon."

"This entire spire isn't of jade. None of these tunnels is jade, for instance." Kesira ran her hand along the rough stone, trying to identify it. She failed. The rock lay in strata of varying hues of brown and cream.

"Only certain portions of the spire are jade, but the quantity is immense, perhaps the largest deposit in the world. Howenthal has hoarded the stone for years. We thought him strange, but not overly so. Many of us develop odd hobbies."

"Forever is a long time," she said sarcastically.

"It is," replied Wemilat, not noticing her tone. "Howenthal has sheathed the spire in jade, but the core remains ordinary rock. And the foundation of his fortress—pure jade at least a foot thick." Wemilat vented a snort and said, "He did that to keep the likes of me out, I am sure."

"He fears you so?"

"Howenthal becomes paranoid. Remember all I said about the corrupting influence of the jade? Howenthal flees shadows now. The more possessed by the jade he becomes, the more suspicious he grows."

"This is true of Eznofadil and Lenc, also?"

"I am sure. The one who has thought the process through will end up supreme."

"He will play off the fears of the others so that they destroy themselves," said Kesira, ideas forming. "And he will slay the victor of that conflict."

"Such has it been among mortals for all of time," said Wemilat. "Now the poison comes to us demons."

Kesira held out her hand and gripped Wemilat's shoulder. She silenced him and urged him to look behind. Looming there was an ominous black cloud, more impenetrable than the darkest night.

"What is it?" she whispered, feeling like an acolyte misbehaving during prayers.

"The same as the one in front of us," said Wemilat.

Kesira's brown eyes snapped forward. They were trapped between the two inky, boiling clouds of fog. And those clouds slowly billowed toward them.

"Are they dangerous?" she asked.

"*Anything* found in Howenthal's domain is deadly."

She searched the narrow stretch of tunnel they occupied for a way out. No side tunnels existed. Scratching with the end of her staff produced only dirty smears on the rock walls. Getting free this way would take days of effort—days they did not have.

The clouds moved closer and closer.

Kesira saw tiny blue sparks jumping from the points of contact between fog and rock. Attempting to pass through the blackness meant instant death.

She lunged forward, thrusting out with her staff. The tip of the stone-wood staff disappeared into the enveloping cloud and never came out. Kesira looked at the end of the staff and saw it shortened by several inches.

"Whether they live or not is a point I must ponder at some later time," said Wemilat. "For the nonce, I feel the need to avoid these. Do come with me, my dear." The demon seized her wrists and they melted through solid rock, to emerge in a parallel tunnel.

"They're gone," she panted. "Do you think they can pass through the wall, too?"

"I doubt it. We simply took a wrong turning. I do wish Molimo would catch up with us and reveal a better path upward."

Kesira shook in reaction, then controlled herself. Walking helped and finally she managed to ask, "Did the movement through the stone weaken you?"

"Not measurably. The trip was only a few feet. You must remember, my dear, I am used to doing that sort of thing all the time. It is only the proximity of the jade and the stay in that damnable prison that has weakened me." Wemilat smiled and added, "Thank you again for lending your...strength when I needed it most."

"Save your breath for Howenthal," she said, bitterness flowing back.

"Your name will live long for your sacrifice," said Wemilat. "Mortals do still compose odd songs about their heroes?"

"They—we—do," she said.

"And consider this another line in your death song," Wemilat said.

"You know of Gelya's death song?" she asked, startled.

"It is a fine idea. A compendium of all that has shaped you, put to song. The last line, no matter how long or short, is always exactly right. It is the only perfect thing a mortal can do."

"I never thought of it like that," she admitted. Kesira stopped, then pointed, shouting out, "Molimo! Here, Molimo!"

The youth had been trudging along ahead of them, unseen due to the numerous bends and twists in the tunnel. The long stretch they entered revealed him. The young man waited for them to catch up.

"Now we shall make better time," said Wemilat. "You scouted all the way up to Howenthal's foundations, didn't you?" A quick nod of the dark-haired head. "And the dungeons? There is a way through the plug of jade?" Another nod, more solemn. "But it's dangerous? Ah, what isn't here?"

Kesira saw the bloodstains on Molimo's clothing that hadn't been there before. He had battled and won against Howenthal's miner-beasts—and what other horrors?

Molimo had found enough of the green-glowing moss to cover his clothing, but she guessed he needed little light to make his way through the tunnels. Wolves had keen night vision and the likeness came all too readily to Molimo's finely sculpted features. Kesira watched as the youth changed into animal once again.

"Danger is near," said Wemilat, his eyes focused at infinity. "Howenthal sends down human guards for us. He must have sensed it when I traveled through the walls."

The first Kesira saw of the soldiers was a blazing torch held aloft. The light reflected off the crescent scar branded so cruelly into his chest.

"Yes," said Wemilat. "The Order of the Steel Crescent. I suspect Howenthal uses them to the exclusion of all other humans now."

"To do his dirty work," she said.

"To die for him."

Molimo had ceased snarling and now raced forward

on silent paws. The guards were distracted by the sputtering torch and billowing, greasy smoke filling the upper portion of the tunnel and didn't see him until it was too late. Savage jaws closed on one throat. Claws ripped at another man's arm, forcing a sword to be dropped. And again Molimo's fangs bit deeply to kill another.

By then, Kesira had joined the fray. Shorter than the men, she found her head just under the cloying smoke from the torches. She used this advantage as Molimo had done to attack. Two more guards dropped, never to rise again, as the tip of her staff found vulnerable areas in groin and throat and temple.

Molimo finished off the lone soldier who turned tail and ran. A swift leap, claws tearing and sudden death.

"The floor is slippery from all the blood," complained Wemilat. "Do let us hasten on. I believe the entry into Howenthal's fortress is close by. These men hadn't been long in the tunnels from the way they worried over the torches."

Kesira had the same impression. Molimo trotting by her knee, Wemilat just behind, the woman plunged onward and found the massive wooden door in a wall of pure jade.

"Hurry," said Wemilat. "I...I must get inside the fortress. Once inside the evil force cancels itself out, but here, oh, do hurry, my dear!"

Kesira pressed her hands against the door and shoved. It refused to give. Again she tried and again to no avail.

"It's barred on the inside," she said.

"Hurry," said Wemilat. The demon hunkered down between his long froglegs and shook like a leaf in an autumn storm.

She glanced at Molimo, then smiled. "The most obvious can be overlooked. Let's see if this works."

Kesira rapped loudly on the door and shouted, "Damn your withered balls, you son of a pig, let us in. The torches are going out. Hurry up, you leperous sons of..."

She had hardly started her eloquent cursing when she heard the rasping of wood against wood—the bar being withdrawn on the inside. As the ponderous door swung open, Molimo slipped through like a streak of brown quicksilver. Rapacious eating sounds echoed forth. Kesira swallowed and pulled open the door enough for herself and Wemilat.

On the floor behind the door lay a man with throat and most of his chest ripped away. Molimo hadn't been neat in his lupine destruction.

"Close the door," ordered Wemilat. "There, good. I...I feel better."

"Why is the force diminished within the fortress?" asked Kesira. "We must be totally surrounded by jade here."

"We are. Surely your lessons have not suffered so much? Or did not Gelya think simple laws of the universe worth teaching?" Wemilat held up his hand to silence her. "The force is similar to that of electricity. A sphere holding a charge shows none of it within its boundaries. Such it is here. For the most part." Wemilat staggered a little, then righted himself. "Howenthal plays with bits of jade, however. Let's not dally, shall we?"

They searched through the dungeons for a stairway up. Molimo found it and raced ahead, against Kesira's wishes. The man-wolf killed four on his way, two of them people Kesira thought were potential allies. Molimo had ripped their throats out through the bars of prison cells as they crowded forth to see what the furor was.

"Molimo is only true to his nature," said Wemilat, huffing and puffing along behind.

They burst onto what had to be a main level of the fortress. The sound of soldiers marching in cadence echoed through the long hallways and reverberated off the high arched ceiling.

"Impressive," said Wemilat, "but then Howenthal always showed a flair for architectural oddities."

"It's lovely," said Kesira, taking in the intricate beauty of the walls, floor and furnishings as she hurried along after Molimo. The wolf seemed to know where he was going and all she could do was trail along, hoping that the guards wouldn't spot them.

They entered the central area of the castle, an atrium rising fully fifty feet above them. The domed ceiling had been fashioned of stained glass and the scene depicted warring demons. Kesira didn't have to strain her imagination unduly to know the victorious demon represented Howenthal—the jade coloration proved as much. The rest of the atrium provided her with a taste of true elegance; ivy of various kinds trailed downward from diamond-encrusted pots; the furniture lavishly strewn about was all of the finest workmanship and built for a physique easily twice Kesira's; the murals on the walls and the intricate rug on the floor blended together in a coordinated panorama.

Leading from the atrium were a half-dozen corridors, each decorated in a different precious gem motif. And to her left stood immense wooden doors—the main gateway into this opulence.

For a moment, she was overwhelmed by the grandeur, then she spotted Molimo. Kesira took the steps up a spiraling staircase two at a time and launched herself forward in time to wrap arms around Molimo's neck. The wolf twisted and snapped at her, but the woman held on. When Molimo had settled down, she looked him squarely in the eye and said, "We cannot become separated from Wemilat. We cannot. He is our only hope. Understand?"

By this time Wemilat made it up the stairs and handed back Kesira's dropped staff.

"I feel Howenthal close by," the demon said. "Molimo has guided us well."

"Well enough, Wemilat, if you seek your executioner," came a booming voice. From across the atrium, standing on the balcony opposite them, was Howenthal.

The demon's flesh had turned entirely green. Jade green. It was as if a statue had come to life and moved and breathed and taunted them. And in those insane eyes, Kesira read no mercy at all.

"Wemilat," she said, not daring to look away from Howenthal. "Can you...?"

The ugly demon pushed his way to the railing and peered over it at their adversary. Somehow the comparison between the two did nothing to inspire confidence.

Howenthal was massively built, muscular, tall, handsome in his way—radiating intense power from his jade green form. Wemilat, toadlike, still shook from the exertion of walking up the stairs.

"Die, fool. And those insignificant mortals with you, they shall die also!"

Howenthal lifted a meaty green hand to carry out his threat.

Chapter Sixteen

GREEN FIRE exploded all around Kesira Minette. Flailing, she stumbled back and fell heavily over Molimo. From her supine position she saw Wemilat struggling to counter the magical hammerblow that had staggered her. The misshapen demon turned aside only a portion of Howenthal's attack; the rest crushed down on him, flattening his face and ripping off one pendulous ear.

"There, Wemilat," called Howenthal from across the atrium. "That improved your looks immensely. Shall we try for some more cosmetic changes?"

"Have you taken to boasting instead of doing?" asked Wemilat, hanging onto the railing for support. Kesira saw how drained the ugly demon was and wondered at him taunting Howenthal.

"I am able to do what I please," said Howenthal, laughing nastily. "Look at some of my handiwork."

Kesira blinked in astonishment. The emptiness of the atrium filled with movement, ghostly figures stirring and melting together, to reform newer and more solid scenes. And those scenes sickened her.

"The mortal Emperor thinks to stop my troops. See how I enjoin his forces?"

Graphically depicted were dismemberments and agonies so extreme Kesira tried to look away—but she found she couldn't. Some force of the scene, whether of Howenthal's doing or of her own inner perversity, kept her eyes affixed on all that happened. The blood, the human suffering, the myriad ways the demon found to torture.

"What do you get from this?" she called. "To you, we are nothing more than insects. Is there any sport in killing insects?"

"She has spirit, if not good sense," said Howenthal, eyeing Kesira. "Mortal, has no one ever taught you the proper way of behaving before your betters?"

Kesira had no chance to respond. Another of Howenthal's magical green fireballs erupted in front of her, smashing her into the marble wall, burning her silhouette into once white stone. She shuddered as fires consumed her skin, her every organ. Pain racked her body and she looked down, expecting to see only charred skeleton.

She was intact.

Only pain had visited her, not destruction. And there was the sound of Howenthal's mocking laughter.

"I do not wantonly slay, bitch. I see that you are the one I sought, who was revealed to me as being a danger. My rune casts have finally failed me. *You* pose no threat to me. I see that now," he said.

"You are cruel, evil," sobbed out Kesira. "No one slays like that. No one!" She pointed to the pictures of slain soliders, all wearing the red armbands with the white bar showing allegiance to the Emperor.

"There is a reason for these deaths." Again came the panorama of death meted out to the Emperor's troops. Kesira sucked in her breath when she recognized General Dayle, writhing on the ground, caught in the same vicious vise of pain Howenthal had employed on her. The armored warrior fought phantoms that existed only in his mind, but fearsome those ghosts must have been. His lips pulled back in a soundless snarl and he lashed out with fists in a futile attempt to force them away.

"The troops loyal to me—those of the Order of the Steel Crescent—will soon take the field," said Howenthal. "There will be little opposition. See? General

Dayle unwisely moved his legions to the edge of the
Quaking Lands."

The earth trembled and buckled, coughed and spewed
forth huge geysers of dirt and rock as the earthquakes
struck with stunning force. Every shockwave was followed by one ten times more deadly. Horses fell to the
ground, pinning riders. Riders drew swords but found
no enemy to slay. And all died, either from the inconceivable power locked in every tremor or from their
fellows. Howenthal's phantoms were unreal; the deaths
caused as the soldiers fought among themselves were
only too real. Kesira watched in sick fascination as the
Emperor's finest warriors battled one another, thinking
their comrades were the enemy.

"I enjoy visiting the quakes upon them," said Howenthal, his voice booming loudly in the hollow atrium.
"The power...suffuses my body." The jade demon held
aloft one clenched green fist. Sparks jumped from
knuckles in a constant display of raw power. Howenthal
turned and thrust his hand in Wemilat's direction. The
misshapen demon barely deflected the fireball.

"You weaken, Wemilat," chided Howenthal. "I had
hoped for a more worthy opponent, but then, with the
magicks at my command now, there are none."

In a low voice, Wemilat said to Kesira, "The visions
he has shown us are only a small part of what he will
do if he defeats us this day."

Kesira cringed as tinier but more vivid images formed
between her and the toadlike demon. She saw the death
of her nunnery reenacted, the deaths of Sister Fenelia
and the others, the way Molimo's tongue had been ripped
from his mouth and more—ever so much more. She
wept for the babies blasted apart by jade-driven magicks. Tears were not adequate for the lives sundered
and ruined by the ambitions of Howenthal and the others. Kesira saw the demon Lenc crushing out fleets of
ships for a moment's amusement and Howenthal sending waves of quakes rippling through crowded high-
ways, into slums, bringing down the most majestic
towers of the Empire.

She saw Emperor Kwasian and Empress Aglanella
pinned like butterflies to a board and Howenthal's
miner-beasts abusing them. And more. Always more.

The tragedies of lost lives, the pain of endless tortures, the ruin left and all because the demons had tasted of human ambition and partaken of the power-augmenting jade.

Kesira wrenched her eyes from the display given her by Wemilat and fixed her gaze on Howenthal. The jade demon cavorted about, cackling to himself over the misery wrought among General Dayle's troops. Every twitch of those sinewed hands brought a new and more devastating temblor to the Quaking Lands. And Howenthal *enjoyed* it.

That, more than anything else, caused Kesira's wrath to explode like one of the green fireballs.

"Howenthal was never stable," Wemilat said softly. "The damnable power of the jade has crazed him. Never again can he be made whole. The jade flows within him and there is no turning back."

"He wouldn't, even if he could," said Kesira, her anger rising more and more. She felt her face flushing and adrenaline pumping fiercely through her veins. Molimo moved closer, one hand resting on her shoulder. Wemilat also joined her, taking her hand in his tiny one. The three faced Howenthal.

Kesira never understood exactly what happened. The scenes of destruction still playing in the atrium evaporated when Wemilat launched his attack. Kesira supplied the driving force, that she knew. But something more rose within her—from within Molimo? She glanced at the young man and saw only intense concentration on his face. He gave no indication of anything unusual. Kesira turned back to Howenthal and the hatred she felt for him, the sheer disgust for all he had done to other mortals, the fear that he would rule the world unchecked by honor and decency.

All this poured through her and into Wemilat, who molded it into an attack that stunned Howenthal with its force.

The jade demon shook, as if caught by one of his own quakes. The vivid green of his body lightened when the full shock hit him. And he gripped the railing with both huge hands with such intensity that the wood gave way and splintered. For a long second, Kesira thought Howenthal would topple head over heels to the floor two stories below, but the jade demon regained his composure.

"So the frog has more than a little hop left within him," said Howenthal. But Kesira rejoiced. The demon's voice was almost ordinary in timbre now. Wemilat's attack had sapped much of the jade-given strength.

Wemilat did not bandy words. Another attack blasted into Howenthal's green skin. And another and still another. Kesira exulted at the sight of Howenthal's flesh turning from jadeite to nephrite to whiteish-green. And then all joy fled. Howenthal had found a small piece of jade and slipped it into his mouth. His color flowed back, and with it, all his endurance and power.

Such was the gift and the curse of jade.

"Know the full wrath of a true demon," raged Howenthal.

While Wemilat turned aside the brunt of the attack, Kesira withered as some of the potent fireball came through. And under her feet the balcony began to shimmy and shake.

"He's bringing down his own fortress," she whispered to Wemilat. The toadlike demon did not answer. Only Molimo's hand on her shoulder restrained her from prodding Wemilat to see if he still lived.

The quakes grew in intensity until Kesira was tossed about, unable to keep on her feet. The three maintained physical contact with great difficulty. And all the while they bounced about like marbles in a can being kicked, Howenthal laughed. The jade fed his hunger for power and turned him even more insane.

"Do you know fear yet, Wemilat? No? You shall. You and those mortals with you will all know gut-wrenching fear at my hand. To think I feared this Kesira Minette, a mere whore of Gelya's!"

The dome over the atrium three stories above them began to crack from Howenthal's magicks. Shards of crystal tumbled to the floor far below to smash with the intensity of bombs exploding. The very walls of the fortress split and showed the blue sky outside and the green jade foundations.

"Die, fools, you will die!" shrieked Howenthal.

Flapping down through the hole in the crystal dome came a feathered arrow of vengeance. Zolkan plummeted directly for Howenthal, talons lifted and beak ready to rend. The jade demon didn't see the *trilla* bird until it was too late to strike the bird from the air with a magical fireball.

Howenthal screeched as claws pulled at jade flesh and the serrated beak drove for the face. But Zolkan wasn't massive enough or strong enough to resist the blow given him. The bird tumbled through the air in a feathery cartwheel and crashed to the floor two stories below.

"Yours, Wemilat? You send pigeons to do your work?"

Kesira's emotions flared even higher, fed by what Howenthal had done to Zolkan. She cared for the foundlings she took in. For Zolkan. For Molimo. Even for the pathetic figure of Wemilat. For all his demonic power, even he was a castoff.

Gelya taught that there could never be too much charity. And Kesira knew all such would cease if Howenthal vanquished them this day.

One who was not an orphan came to mind, too. Rouvin. Poor, dead, heroic Rouvin who had died to free Wemilat and hardly knew it.

Even for Rouvin, she did this.

Power such as she'd never known welled up inside like a bubbling artesian spring, overflowed and overwhelmed Howenthal. The jade demon's look of surprise fed Kesira's desire to end the threat he posed to social stability, to the Emperor, to all the other Orders seeking ways of honorable living.

Howenthal's riposte came weaker than other attacks, but the vileness of it made Kesira want to retch. The jade demon worked on all her fears, her night terrors, her smallest weakness. This was the sort of battle she had never sought and now had to fight—a duel with herself using Gelya's teachings as a weapon for good.

The weakness became strength. Fears died. Howenthal retreated.

"Jade," came Zolkan's squawk from below. "He finds jade. Stop Howenthal *now!*"

Kesira saw that the *trilla* bird spoke the truth. Howenthal spun around and staggered toward a small alcove off the balcony. From within she saw jade gleaming

brightly. Zolkan fluttered up and landed on her left
shoulder. With Molimo's hand on her right, the stone-
wood staff held upright, and her hand firmly in Wemilat's, Kesira experienced an odd sensation of invul-
nerability. No matter they faced a demon capable of
tapping vast illicit sources of power. No matter that
Howenthal had brought down the fortress around their
ears. They were not stronger, perhaps, but they were
better. Their souls were unblemished by the blight in-
festing Howenthal.

"Now," murmured Wemilat. "Now comes the moment."

Kesira stiffened, summoning all she had—and finding a reserve that had been unknown to her. And she
needed it. They all did. Howenthal's attack smashed
into them like the blow of a war hammer. The power
of jade sucked at their wills, grasped at their honor,
tugged at their very minds.

More and more of the atrium crumbled away as Howenthal added to his attack. The forces he had trained
on the Quaking Lands were now directed solely at them.
It didn't matter. The four of them held firm and even
returned the jade demon's magicks.

"We go—now!" cried Wemilat.

The entire top of the fortress simply vanished under
the assault Wemilat launched. Howenthal sat heavily
on the block of jade; it pulsated wildly beneath him.
But no matter how he tapped into that block, Kesira's
will shunted it aside. Howenthal's magical thrusts and
quakings were robbed of their full potency. And Wemilat drove ever inward, seeking the weakest portions of
Howenthal's body.

"He cracks," said Zolkan. "Like a dropped statue, he
cracks!"

Kesira saw that the bird was right. A split opened
in Howenthal's head and ran to his neck. Other, spiderweb fissures opened in his bare chest. And still
Wemilat drove on, shoving the magical wedge of his
might ever deeper into the other demon's body.

"The very jade that gives him strength works against
him now," said Wemilat. "Howenthal cannot last much
longer. We have triumphed!"

"This cannot be!" shouted Howenthal. The jade demon turned toward Wemilat and pointed an accusing finger. A fracture caused the digit to fall to the balcony with a loud noise. The hand followed, then the arm up to the shoulder. Howenthal disintegrated.

"NO!"

With a convulsive surge of energy, the dying jade demon shrank into himself, then blasted apart, pieces of the mineral hurling outward.

"He's gone," muttered Kesira, exhausted. She had fed Wemilat all her anger, all her pride, all that made her human, and now she discovered that nothing remained within. She was used up—for the moment.

"Wemilat," said Zolkan. "Look to Wemilat."

"What?" Kesira's fogged mind cleared slightly and she looked around. Howenthal was truly gone; Molimo sat on the edge of the balcony, his eyes glazed over and his entire body shivering as if he ran a high fever. But it was to Wemilat she turned.

The ugly demon lay face down on the floor. Not a muscle twitched. She rolled him over, Zolkan watching from his perch on her shoulder.

"Not dead, not dead," the bird insisted.

Eyelids fluttered and revealed the large eyes. Puffed lips pulled back in a parody of a smile. One small hand reached out and lightly touched Kesira's cheek.

"You have done more than could be expected of you, my dear," the demon said. "Howenthal is no more. I felt his life force vanish, even as his jade body shattered."

"Are you all right? You're only tired, aren't you?" Concern flared within her.

"Yes, my dear, I am all right now. Now that Howenthal is gone." Wemilat shuddered violently.

"He dies," said Zolkan. "Look. He dies by inches."

"Not by inches, my feathery friend. By miles." Wemilat turned his attention back to Kesira. "Howenthal did not slay Gelya. You know this."

"Lenc was the one."

"Yes, Lenc. Stop him. And Eznofadil. You have seen the evil produced by the jade. Do not let their ambition enslave all of humanity, if not for yourself, then for my memory."

"You'll be all right," she said, knowing she lied as she spoke.

"You will be protected, my dear. By this." Wemilat reached up and weakly pulled away the tatters of Kesira's gray robe and exposed her left breast. With effort, he lifted his head until his lips pressed into the woman's warm, soft flesh.

Kesira cried out at the sharp jab of pain. Where Wemilat's lips had touched her breast was the pink imprint of the demon's lips. And inside Kesira experienced a warmth unlike anything she had ever felt. More intimate, more exciting, more demanding, the warmth flowed throughout her body.

"Wemilat dead," said Zolkan. "Going now, too."

Kesira saw what the bird meant. The demon's body turned liquid and started to flow. The ugly features vanished and soon only a damp spot on the balcony remained. Before another minute passed, this too had vanished.

Wemilat the Ugly had joined Gelya and the others of his kind.

Chapter Seventeen

KESIRA MINETTE stared at the spot where Wemilat the Ugly had lain. The emptiness mocked her. Vengeance against the jade demons had seemed easy, almost too easy, with Wemilat at her side.

She shuddered, thinking of that intimate moment spent with the misbegotten demon. Kesira had hated herself for that, even knowing how necessary it was to their quest.

"The quest," she said bitterly. How she had played the role, doing what honor had dictated. Her Order destroyed? Revenge was the obvious answer. And where had this led her? The woman looked around at the wrecked fortress that had once stood so proudly atop its jade-sheathed spire of stone. Not even the destitute would sleep within these walls now. Wind whipped restlessly through fissures in the walls and caused huge chunks to fall heavily. Each second she stayed on this shaky balcony increased her chances of perishing, too.

"Howenthal dead," said Zolkan. "Good work. We make good team."

"But the best of us is gone," Kesira said. She pointed to the spot where Wemilat had fallen.

"Best still here. Us. Wemilat never strong demon. Not like Gelya. Not like Merrisen." The *trilla* bird blinked its beady black eyes at her to see if the words had the desired effect. "Not even strong like you. Wemilat lost. We won."

"He died," she said, "but is that losing?"

Molimo tugged at her robe. She smiled weakly at the youth. He was covered with dust to the point of looking like a movable trash heap. Cuts on his face and chest had bled copiously and left thick, crimson mud splotches. Molimo didn't look like a winner. He looked like the loser. And what of her own appearance?

Kesira moved about until she found a shard of the crystal dome that had fallen during the battle. She held it up and studied herself. Kesira had to laugh.

"I'm even worse-looking than Molimo!" she cried. Then tears came and left salty tracks down her dusty cheeks. Zolkan's claws tightened on her shoulder, reassuring her. She settled herself and got better control of her emotions. "What would Gelya think, if he saw me now?" she asked.

Molimo tugged again at her robe and wrote, "Proud" in the dust on the floor.

"Thank you," Kesira said, meaning it with all her heart and soul.

Her hand drifted to the lip print left on her breast. The mark Wemilat had placed there glowed pinkly and the inner warmth lingered.

"Branded," said Zolkan. "Good mark. Protect you?" the bird asked, craning his neck around to look at Molimo. The young man nodded and Zolkan said more positively, "It will protect you."

"Will I need it?" asked Kesira.

"Lenc is unpunished for murdering Gelya."

"But how will I ever reach him? The other jade demons are gaining strength daily, and our hope is gone. Wemilat is no more. Can you face a demon and triumph? I know that I can't."

"Poor mortal," cawed Zolkan. "Poor, poor human."

"Don't mock me," Kesira snapped.

"Fight! Lenc and Eznofadil spread their poison, just as Howenthal did. You know horrors awaiting all mor-

tals. You must stop them. If not for your Order or for
your patron, then for self."

"What do you get me into, Zolkan?" she asked. The
bird was just a little too adamant about this for her
taste.

"You are the chosen one."

"Who has chosen me?" she asked, more curious than
mad now. "If you say someone's chosen me for this duty,
let them come forward now and tell me to my face."

"Look," said Zolkan.

In the emptiness of the atrium the horrors Howenthal had shown them reformed. Kesira blanched at the
sight.

"He still lives!"

"His evil still lives. And evil of Eznofadil and Lenc
grows. You can stop them. Do it!"

Kesira didn't have to ask if the *trilla* bird would aid
her. She knew he would. Hadn't he courageously attacked a jade demon during the height of battle? And
Molimo would stay with her. She saw the set to his firm
jaw, the lines of his muscles, the way he held himself.
He would die for her.

And she for him.

"The fight continues," she said, suddenly tired to the
bone and unable to even stand. "But how? With Wemilat gone, how do we fight?"

Zolkan didn't answer. Molimo traced out a single
name in the dust, then quickly erased it, but not before
Kesira had read what he'd written.

"Ayondela?" she asked. The man-wolf nodded. "We
have met," Kesira mused, "but the enmity is so great.
She thinks I killed Rouvin." Kesira looked at Molimo
and used all her control to hold back the accusation. If
he had been able to restrain his animal instincts, Rouvin might still be alive. But would they have found
another method of releasing Wemilat?

Kesira didn't know. Gelya taught that what was past
was history. Learn from it and embrace the future. Molimo had acted according to his nature and they had
reached this point living with the consequences.

"Will she listen?" the nun said aloud.

"We try," said Zolkan. The bird flapped his wings
and lifted from her shoulder. "Now we go. Order of Steel .

Crescent soldiers march to fortress. We want to be away before they arrive. Hurry!"

Kesira heaved herself to her feet and started down the broken staircase, stepping over debris and skipping past missing steps entirely. To speak with Ayondela would be risky, but less so than confronting either Eznofadil or Lenc. If she could persuade Ayondela not to join with the other two, to ally herself with the Emperor and against the jade demons, the war might be winnable.

How committed was Ayondela to the power of the jade? She was the most recent of its victims. There might still be hope.

"Rouvin died a hero. That ought to mean something to Ayondela," she said to Molimo. The youth nodded. "We can win her back to our side. I know it," Kesira said with mounting conviction. Already her mind formed ways of persuading the angry demon. The woman walked with scant attention to where she went. Let Zolkan and Molimo lead her now. She had important tactics to work out in her mind.

Kesira paused at the extreme edge of the jade pillar and looked down on the now quiescent Quaking Lands.

"These peaceful lands will be the symbol for our success," she said. "Gelya will guide us onward."

"To Lenc! To Eznofadil!" squawked Zolkan.

"To Ayondela," Kesira Minette added in a softer voice.

Molimo brought long lengths of rope and they began the hazardous journey down the sheer face of the jade pillar.

2: THE FROZEN WAVES

```
10 PRINT "FOR GORDON GARB"
20 GOTO 10
```

Chapter One

THE FRIGID WIND gusting from the southlands cut into Kesira Minette's face like jagged-edged razors. The woman pulled the cowl of her battered gray robe futilely around her face to prevent the tendrils of cold from sneaking in to torment her further. The wind acted as if it had a mind of its own, intent on punishing her for sinful deeds. Strands of short brown hair caught on the wind and whipped about in front of her eyes, almost blinding her.

"Hard to believe this is early summer," she said to the lump under her thin robe and heavier cloak. The large mound stirred. Heavy talons cut into her shivering flesh.

"Too cold. Want to go where warmth is," came the cracked words. Kesira nodded, even though the *trilla* bird hiding under the cloth couldn't see the motion. She worried about the fragile creature. Zolkan belonged in warmer climes where he might preen his brilliant green plumage and flutter in cloud-dotted, syrupy warm skies. For a tropical bird, this weather must be pure horror not even her robe and cloak could fend off successfully.

Kesira found the wind unbearable. It stunned her even more when she realized that this *was* summer, that the air should be as a lover's caress and the full yellow sun smilingly benevolent in its warmth. Winter had been driven off by spring's fine weather, but there the usual wheeling of seasons ceased.

The demon Ayondela brought the freezing winds, the ice storms, the sharp pinpricks of flesh turning to stone. And she delivered the punishment to the land because of Kesira Minette.

Kesira jerked about when something large and powerful

9

jiggled her elbow. Her stone-wood staff dropped to protect
her from a predator. She relaxed when she saw her traveling companion, Molimo.

"I am sorry," she said. "You startled me."

The young man's solemn expression didn't change. He
held out his hands, palms skyward, and shook his head.

"No luck hunting?" Kesira waited for him to acknowl-
edge what she had already surmised. The game, normally
plentiful along the Pharna River, had been killed by the
preternatural weather. Before the polar sentence passed,
much of the world might lie in permafrost graves.

Molimo edged closer. Kesira shuddered but opened her
cloak for him. The youth whirled in and immediately
closed it so that it enveloped both of them. Kesira's heart
beat a trifle stronger, Molimo's presence now warming her
with a rush of—what?

Love? Kesira did not discount this, though it struck her
as impertinent on her part. She was a nun of the Order of
Geyla. About her waist hung the knotted blue cord of her
Order and intertwined with that rode the gold ribbon
showing her to be Sister of the Mission.

The last Sister of the Mission, Kesira thought bitterly.
The world had turned inside out, normal becoming unusual and the horrible commonplace. Unthinkable deeds
had been committed, and all of her Order perished or wantonly abandoned their vows. The demons had begun a war
for dominance that entangled her repeatedly until she
sought only vengeance for a single life-changing atrocity.
When the demon Lenc had partaken of jade he began the
power of transformation into something more than demonic. Lenc hungered for control over the world and all
those on it.

For centuries the demons had remained aloof, encourag-
ing humans to worship them. Kesira had fallen in with the
Order of Gelya, and Gelya was a kind patron, free with his
wisdom and caring of his charges. Life had been simple
and good within the walls of the nunnery. If Kesira had
not been sent to the distant city of Blinn for lamp oil, she,
too, would lie charred with her Sisters. Of them all, she
alone had survived. And alone of them, she had sought out
other missions, only to find the teachings of her patron discarded in favor of carnal pursuits and, worse, the ways of

doubt. They had turned from Gelya and left her alone in the world to carry on their patron's work.

Molimo stirred. Kesira felt his arm circling her waist, pulling her closer. Not for the first time she wished the handsome, darkly complected man could speak, but his dumbness was another atrocity brought by the jade demons. Somehow, Molimo had become embroiled in a battle between two of the demons and had been caught in a rain of jade. The forbidden green mineral had burned and scarred his strong young body, and he lost his tongue to one of the demons.

Kesira had found him at the side of a road, battered almost to the point of death, and had nursed him to health. But even the healing skills learned in her twenty-two summers failed to alleviate the problem of Molimo's sundered tongue.

Or a deeper, more troubling problem.

Even though they had been through much together, Kesira felt a thrill of danger when Molimo was near. The jade rain had seared his physical body and destroyed the natural balances. Molimo often lost control of his human shape and altered into a wolf, uncontrolled and at the mercy of bestial urges.

She turned slightly, brown eyes meeting his ebony ones. Molimo shook his head the slightest amount, assuring her that he was not in danger of undergoing that transformation. Still, Kesira worried. If Molimo became too hungry, would his human feelings stay in control over his more elemental, animal urges? She would make a fine meal for a predator as strong and sleek as Molimo the wolf.

"Too cold, too cold," Zolkan complained. Kesira winced as the *trilla* bird tightened his grip on her shoulder. She reached up and stroked gently over the cloth-covered mound of bird, soothing and trying to reassure him.

"We will stop soon. We must. The storm grows fiercer. Never before have I felt such wrath in a southern-born storm in summer."

"Ayondela's doing. She brings this as warning."

"I fear you are right. This ought to give us even more incentive to reach her and speak with her, to tell her that her son's death was accidental."

Kesira bit her lip when she uttered those words. Beside her Molimo tensed.

"I meant no criticism, Molimo. You could not prevent it. Your other self killed her son. Rouvin's death served a vital purpose, also. It was not in vain."

Rouvin had been half-demon, his mother Ayondela and his father a warrior captain in the employ of the Emperor Kwasian. Demons sometimes left their arcane concerns and walked the lands seeking out diversions. Ayondela had found hers in Rouvin's father, and Rouvin had grown to be a fine figure of a man. Too brash, Kesira knew, but still devoted to that which is honorable.

"I only wish I could have loved him as he wanted," she said softly, more to herself than to either Molimo or Zolkan. Rouvin had died under Molimo's wolf fangs to free another demon.

At the memory of Wemilat the Ugly, Kesira lifted her hand and placed it over her left breast. The bright imprint of the demon's kiss still burned in her flesh, Wemilat's mark.

They had met and defeated Howenthal, one of the original trio of jade demons. Howenthal had shattered, exploded, turned to jade dust and, in so passing, had taken Wemilat also. Kesira mourned the loss of the froglike demon. He had been kind and opposed to the changes demanded by Lenc, Howenthal and Eznofadil.

Kesira swallowed hard. There were still three jade demons, even though Howenthal had perished. Ayondela had joined their rank because of Rouvin's death.

"I can convince her," Kesira said firmly. "I need only reason with her. She was once a patron held in great esteem by her worshippers. Forsaking honor to seek the power of jade is not her way."

Kesira closed her eyes to the icy gusts and let small tears leak out, freezing her eyelashes together. Molimo guided them as Kesira remembered that moment on the hilltop. The weather had been pleasant then, the blush of springtime bringing forth particolored flowers in wild profusion along the slopes. But Ayondela in her wrath had appeared, the icy blue scepter in hand. Every spot on the ground touched by the water dripping from that wand had wilted and died. The demon's anger had mounted, and she had partaken of the jade, placing a tiny chip under her tongue.

Kesira shivered, more from memory than cold. Fangs had grown even as Ayondela's complexion altered from flesh tones to a pale green. The circle of hoarfrost at her feet had expanded as the forbidden power of the jade insinuated itself through her body. Her powers had been augmented, but Ayondela had lost something of her sanity, too. The jade demanded its payment. In exchange for the heightened power, it robbed Ayondela of a considerable portion of her prodigious life span. How much, the nun didn't know, but Wemilat had told her that Ayondela's years were numbered as a mortal's now.

Kesira had no wish to meddle in the affairs of demons, but Ayondela's angry alliance with Eznofadil and Lenc threatened the world—and Kesira could never forget the death of her beloved patron. Gelya had stood for charity and peace, and had been destroyed by the other demons. While Gelya's teachings did not include revenge, they did not preclude it, either.

Kesira gripped her stone-wood staff even more firmly and bent her head to the wind. Zolkan protested with wordless squawks, but she ignored the *trilla* bird. He complained far too much.

But the tugging at her arm made her turn again, to look nose to nose with Molimo. The hard dark eyes bored into her softer ones. He opened the front of their shared cloak and pointed. Kesira almost fainted from the renewed assault of cold air on her body, but she saw what the man-wolf meant.

Shelter!

"We will soon be warm and dry, Zolkan," she told the bird. The uncomfortable shifting warned her that she'd better be right or Zolkan might rip off her left arm. Eyes watering constantly from the wind, Kesira forged ahead until the rocky outjut broke the cold grasp of the storm and let her breathe normally for the first time all day.

"Better," Zolkan confirmed. "But still cold. Freeze me, feathers and all."

Molimo agilely spun from the warm confines of the cloak and vanished. Kesira grabbed for his arm and missed. The youth vanished from sight, as if he had never existed.

Warily, Kesira followed and found an icy pathway leading into a cave. Molimo had already gathered a few pitiful twigs for a fire.

"The cave should stand us in good stead this night," she said. Molimo nodded, and Zolkan poked his head out from beneath the coarsely woven gray fabric of Kesira's robe. The green-plumed head craned around and one large black eye fixed on a ledge above their heads. With a squawk, Zolkan took to wing and landed adroitly on the shelf. He turned and surveyed Molimo's handiwork.

"Not enough. Need heat. Lot of heat."

Molimo paid the bird no heed and continued about the serious business of building the fire.

Kesira settled down and let the youth work. She found it difficult to keep her eyes off him. The sleek, bronzed flesh of his upper arms lay bare to the cold, yet he seemed not to notice. If anything, it only firmed the muscles rippling beneath his skin. When satisfied with the way he'd placed the twigs and dried branches, he rocked back on his heels and pointed. Kesira bent forward, her fire kit already in hand. A tiny vial held a white powder, which she gingerly sprinkled onto the wood. The sudden flare momentarily blinded her. When the dancing yellow and blue dots had vanished from her eyes, Kesira smiled.

The warmth of the fire came to her almost painfully. Rubbing her frostbitten hands and moving closer to the dancing flames helped. She relaxed even more, content.

"Never find Ayondela," the *trilla* bird declared. "All die here. All. No use to continue. Cold, too frigging cold." The bird launched off on a biting, salty description of how cold it was and how much colder it was likely to be. Kesira had never learned Zolkan's origins, but from the way the *trilla* bird swore, she guessed he had been the property of some sergeant in the Emperor's guard. Zolkan had flown into the Order's sacristy one winter's day two years ago, more dead than alive. Against Sister Fenelia's advice, Kesira had nursed the bird back to health.

Now Zolkan was her only link with those happier days—except for her unshakable faith in Gelya's teachings.

"If Rouvin hadn't died, Ayondela wouldn't have brought this foul winter down upon us," said Kesira. "But we must accept what has happened and work to change it. We must find her and persuade her of the danger, of the error in choosing the path she now follows."

"Impossible," grumbled Zolkan. "She is jade. She is evil."

To Kesira's surprise, Molimo shook his head vigorously. It was the first time she had seen him become so agitated over Ayondela. The youth traced words in the dust on the stony floor. Kesira read and as quickly Molimo erased them to make room for new words.

"Not so," Molimo wrote, his finger bending into an arch as he pressed down hard in his vehemence. "Ayondela is good. Zolkan is wrong. We must find her."

Kesira sighed. "Yes, I agree, but where might she have gone? All I know is that she is to the south." Kesira shivered. "To the now frigid south."

Molimo wrote more. "Isle of Eternal Winter."

Kesira frowned. She pulled her cloak tighter around her body and leaned forward, balancing herself on her staff.

"What is this Isle of Eternal Winter?" she asked, puzzled. She had been well schooled in Gelya's teaching by the Sisters, but parts of her education had been ignored. Geography was one. When an acolyte spent more time within the nunnery walls than without, why bother with learning more than necessary about the terrain surrounding the Order?

"Isle of Eternal Winter?" called Zolkan from his perch. "No! We never arrive. Oh, my feather oil is freezing. I shall surely perish in this cold. Die, I tell you!"

"What is it?" she demanded of Molimo.

"To the south," was all he wrote. Her eyes locked once more with his. The fathomless depths of the man's soul beckoned to her. Kesira felt herself being drawn in, tumbling, falling, spinning through infinite space. She jerked away, eyes averted to the campfire. Was this strange magnetism an aftereffect of being caught in the jade rain, or did it come with the shape transformation? Whatever caused it, it frightened Kesira a great deal.

Molimo started to write something more of Ayondela, then stopped. His ears twitched and his nostrils dilated. Fur popped out on his cheeks and bony ridges above his eyes buried those burning black eyes in deep pits. He shook all over and dropped to hands and knees—to his paws.

"Molimo, no!" the woman cried. She threw her arms around his neck, as if this would stop the shape change. If anything, it accelerated it. She found herself clinging to Molimo's clothing, the sleek gray wolf snarling and snapping at the wind just a few feet distant.

"Do not stop him. Let Molimo go," cautioned Zolkan. "His ears are sharp. He hears them on our trail."

"Them? Who do you mean?" she asked. Kesira had lost Molimo, at least for the moment. She turned to Zolkan, eyes hot and demanding. "Is there something you haven't told me?"

The *trilla* bird stuck its head under one huge wing. Kesira reached up and grabbed the wing, pulling it away from the bird's thick body. One beady eye peered out at her. Guiltily.

"Tell me, damn you."

"Gelya not like your word choice."

"Gelya taught that the sun also shines on the wicked." Kesira fought to control her anger. "It shines even on you, Zolkan, even though you have deceived me."

"No lies. I tell no lies."

"You haven't told me the truth. Where is the difference?"

The *trilla* bird said nothing.

"Who follows?" Kesira shook the bird; tiny pinfeathers drifted gently downward until caught by the cold drafts of air gusting around her ankles.

"Molimo thinks they are Order of Steel Crescent."

"But how? They were all destroyed in the Quaking Lands."

"No," contradicted the bird. "They sought Howenthal as patron, but many fled when we destroyed him. Nehan-dir and others still follow us."

Kesira hunkered down by the fire, hands automatically thrust out to the feeble warmth. The Order of the Steel Crescent was not a religious order but rather one of mercenaries. Their patron had sold them to a cruel demon in exchange for payment of gambling debts; this had warped their views. They followed only strength, gave their allegiance only to the patron promising the most. Howenthal

had done so and had recruited Nehan-dir and his mercenaries. Now that Howenthal was no more, Nehan-dir undoubtedly sought a new patron for his small but intensely
combative group.

"Why cannot they see that war is not inevitable, that it
comes only from the failure of human wisdom?" Kesira
had run afoul of Nehan-dir and the others in his Order and
knew they were driven by ambition as large as the entire
world. They saw in the jade demons the opportunity to
gain status, power, riches. For so long those of the Steel
Crescent had been outcasts. The woman couldn't imagine
what she would have felt if Gelya had sold her and all her
Sisters for debts. The demons possessed greater than human strength, longevity, and traits. Alas, with the intense
burning of the good came the venal. What magnified to ele-
vate the demons above humanity also magnified their
flaws.

"Nehan-dir will not parley," she said. "But why must he
seek our deaths?"

"Killed Howenthal."

"We had no choice in that," she said, her tone almost
pleading. "Howenthal wanted to reign over all the others,
to disturb the balance of the ages existing between demon
and mortal. The jade made him too greedy. Can't Nehan-
dir see that?"

"Sees only his own misfortune and that you are cause of
most recent setbacks," said Zolkan. The *trilla* bird shifted
from one foot to the other, the cold rock beginning to affect
his circulation. He sank down and let his bright green
feathers cover his feet. This satisfied him for the moment.
One eye fixed on Kesira.

"We should attempt to parley. We can . . ."

Kesira reacted instinctively. The scrape of leather
against stone alerted her in time to rise and swing up her
staff. The butt end caught the man squarely between the
legs. He let out an anguished, "ooophhh!" and dropped to
his knees, clutching his groin. Kesira brought the other
end of the staff about smartly, landing it squarely on the
back of the man's head. The dull *snap!* and the way his
head lolled forward at an unnatural angle told her she had
broken his neck.

Kesira stepped over the man's fallen sword, gingerly

moving it with her stone-wood staff. Gelya taught the evil of steel weapons; this finely wrought sword had brought only death to its wielder.

The nun examined the man and opened the front of his jerkin. Burned with cruel force into his left shoulder was an ugly half-moon of scar tissue. He had been a follower of the Order of the Steel Crescent.

"Are there more about?" she asked Zolkan.

"Molimo checks now. Maybe."

Kesira Minette turned and stamped her foot, a tiny cloud of dust rising. "Tell me. I know by your tone that you're holding something back. What is it, Zolkan?"

"More than Nehan-dir walks outside. Much more. Demons battle demons."

Kesira had never found out how Zolkan knew of these matters. Yet the *trilla* bird had intimate—and accurate—knowledge of so many demonic affairs that she never doubted him when he made his pronouncements.

"Molimo! He's outside!"

"Stop! Wait!" Over Zolkan's protests, Kesira bolted into the jaws of the storm once again to warn Molimo. He might betray himself in his animal form. Some measure of his intelligence fled with the change, replaced by strength and animal cunning. Against the jade demons those were feeble commodities.

Kesira rushed forth, then staggered as Zolkan landed heavily on her shoulder. She glared at the *trilla* bird, then opened her cloak and let him burrow underneath. Kesira did not tell Zolkan this, but she needed his reassuring presence. Dealing with demons lay far beyond the training of a nun, even a Sister of the Mission. Any words of encouragement or warning Zolkan might give would be appreciated.

It might mean their lives.

She stumbled into the wind, eyes watering anew. Of Molimo she found not a trace, although she did discover the dead soldier's horse tethered to the lee side of a low hill. Kesira mentally marked the location; it would be good to ride again. She and Molimo had run their horses to ground. The cold winds had finished them with wracking coughs that shook the noble animals all the way down to their hooves. Molimo had killed the animals out of mercy;

they had eaten well enough for the next week, even if the going had been slower afoot.

"Are there others of the Order of the Steel Crescent?" she asked Zolkan.

"How do I know?" The bird buried itself deeper under the coarsely woven fabric of her robe.

The thunder rolling through the hills stopped Kesira in her tracks. She looked up in time to see two demons atop a mountain. One she recognized as Eznofadil; he blazed with the inner light of the jade power. The other was human in appearance but definitely more than human. He withstood blast after fiery blast from the jade demon, turning aside the potent thrusts with easy contempt.

The contempt turned to fear when another demon joined Eznofadil.

"Ayondela!" cried Kesira, but the name was lost in the wind. The air turned noticeably colder and frost formed quickly on the woman's face. She had to continually brush it off to see how the battle progressed.

The tide turned against the unknown demon.

"Toyaga's power leaves him. Jade overwhelms him," said Zolkan.

"Toyaga?"

Zolkan said nothing. Kesira looked at the ebb and flow of the battle. Ayondela lifted her icy scepter and sent a hailstorm pelting down on Toyaga. The demon cringed; Eznofadil threw another of his lightning bolts. It struck Toyaga squarely in the chest and sent the demon staggering. Against either Ayondela or Eznofadil he might prevail. Their combined might—augmented by the green evil of the jade—proved too much.

Toyaga fled.

Kesira slumped when she saw Ayondela and Eznofadil so triumphant. She had no idea who this Toyaga was, but he opposed them and the evil they sought to impose on the world. They would upset the balance of the ages, to force their wills on humanity rather than allowing mortal rule and appropriate worship.

Numbed by the sight and the cold, Kesira responded too slowly when she heard steel being drawn from a sheath. Her stone-wood staff barely deflected the lunge. The sword passed so close to her head that a lock of brown hair fell away, severed cleanly by the honed blade. Zolkan emitted a frightened squeak, more like a *prin* rat than a bird.

Kesira stared into the set face of her adversary. Another mercenary of the Steel Crescent. Kesira saw the same triumph mirrored in his grizzled face that she had witnessed on Ayondela and Eznofadil's.

The man rocked back for the thrust that would pierce her heart and leave her body to freeze in the polar winds.

Chapter Two

GELYA HAD NOT taught the principle of honorable surrender. Kesira Minette's patron demon had preached a faith that looked through death, but also a tenacity to cling to life. Honor and duty were all. Acquiescence to death was not a part of that.

Kesira's staff came up to parry the sword blow. The impact knocked her flat on the ground, stunning her. Through dazed eyes she watched as the shiny blade rose above the man's helmeted head, his knuckles white as he gripped the hilt tightly.

Then the world turned red and warm.

She blinked, not sure what had happened. A trembling hand wiped blood from her eyes, but it was not her blood. Struggling to sit up, Kesira managed to push the heavy weight off her chest. The soldier's body slid off with a dull thud.

The woman wiped the last of the blood from her eyes and saw that the Steel Crescent soldier lacked a throat. Bloody ribbons remained of his flesh. And standing nearby, crimson trickling off his gray muzzle, stood Molimo. The wolf's green eyes blazed with hatred.

"Thank you," Kesira said softly, not wanting to frighten Molimo more than necessary. When the change came on him, his human conditioning fled. But Kesira had never satisfactorily determined how much remained. She took no chances.

Molimo snarled and advanced, fangs yellowed and sharp, yearning for still more blood.

A shrill squawk stopped Molimo. The wolf-man turned his mobile lupine head about to stare at Zolkan. The *trilla*

21

bird crawled out of his hiding place and began yammering at Molimo in a singsong that Kesira did not understand. The wolf turned and bolted into the gloom, illuminated only by occasional—natural—lightning bolts.

"Thank you," the woman sighed. "What is it you say to him when he is like this? You've spoken those words before."

"It's nothing," the bird said.

"Why won't you tell me? Aren't we friends? Haven't we been through so much together?"

"Cold. Feathers freeze to my body. Return to piss-poor cave."

Kesira levered herself to her feet using the staunch stone-wood staff. "Very well, but one day you *will* tell me."

Zolkan said nothing.

The fire had died to embers and required several minutes of tending to build back to its former cheering warmth. Kesira sat, warming herself. Zolkan waddled around the perimeter of the fire, long wings outstretched, bobbing in and out until his feathers began to singe. Only then was the *trilla* bird warm enough to take wing and settle down on the ledge high in the cave.

"Molimo returns," the bird announced.

Kesira waited, expecting to see the lean gray wolf with the insanely blazing green eyes. A naked, shivering man returned.

"Oh, Molimo. Here." She hurried to him with his discarded clothing. Even as she helped him dress, Kesira felt urges within her toward him—urges that she tried to deny. Not that Gelya taught celibacy; he said to suppress natural functions was as evil as exalting them. Yet it was wrong for her to desire Molimo in the ways she did. She had nursed him to health when he was vulnerable. She would be taking advantage of him even now, even with his body restored. The jade rains had left him afflicted and open to any kindness.

Kesira swallowed hard. The only victory over her love for Molimo might lie in flight.

The youth quickly dressed and sat by the fire. Zolkan squawked and fluttered and carried on the singsong speech. Molimo paid no heed. As suddenly as he had appeared, Molimo stood and left.

Kesira started to call after him, then stopped. Wherever he went, he would return. In less than ten minutes he did come back, arms laden with bloody clothing stripped off the fallen soldiers. Molimo sorted through it and passed over the smallest of the articles for Kesira to don.

"They hardly turn me into the Empress Aglenella's lady-in-waiting," said Kesira, pirouetting about in the too-large clothing. "And you," she said, having to laugh, "are hardly decked out as a courtier." If Kesira's new clothing flapped in the wind, Molimo's cut off circulation. The tightness of the fit made Molimo appear even stronger than he was. Bulges showed in places where none ought to have been and movement was restricted to the point of ripping the fabric as he bent down by the fire. But the added insulation against the frigid wind aided them both.

"Are there any more soldiers of the Steel Crescent awaiting us?" she asked.

Molimo glanced at Zolkan, then etched in the dust, "None. Those two were the only humans about."

"Only humans?"

"Demons walk now, too," Molimo wrote. "Eznofadil and Ayondela."

"And Toyaga," she added, wanting to see his response. A slight flicker crossed his dark eyes, but he might have been playing a game of three-match for all the information revealed. Molimo solemnly nodded.

"Tell me of Toyaga," urged Kesira. "Is he an ally?"

Molimo nodded, then wrote, "He and Merrisen were staunch friends."

"What is Toyaga's relation to Ayondela?"

"They were once lovers."

Kesira shook her head at this. It seemed all of the demons had been Ayondela's lover at some time. Many humans also, if Rouvin was any guide. The demons showed all the human traits but magnified, she reminded herself. Altruism and charity were there, but so was promiscuity and cruelty. Ayondela had to have spent more time seducing her lovers than Gelya did in teaching that kindness gave birth to kindness.

Her attention came back to Molimo. "Toyaga," the young man wrote, "was badly injured. The surviving de-

mons have not united against those of jade. Toyaga might
lead, if he were in a position to do so."

"How can we aid him?" asked Kesira. "Any opposition
to the evil brought by Lenc and the others is welcome."
The fire did not warm her as much as her passion for revenge. Lenc had killed her Sisters and robbed her of the
only sanctuary she had ever found in this world. A cold
white flame burned on Gelya's altar, the symbol of Lenc's
triumph.

"He is a demon. What can we do?"

"You and Zolkan seem to know more of them than I,"
said Kesira. "Do you have any ideas?"

Molimo stared at her, black eyes unreadable. He finally
shook his head.

"Then we must press on in our attempt to reach Ayondela and convince her that Rouvin's death was accidental
and that she should oppose Eznofadil and Lenc. And if she
won't fight them openly, then she ought to remain neutral."

Even as she said the words, Kesira knew the futility of
their quest. The jade insinuated itself into the demon's
body and took on a life of its own. Even as it gave, it took
power in full measure. The virtually immortal demons
would live out only a normal mortal's life span, but to Eznofadil and Lenc this had been worth it—or they did not believe they were burning themselves out in exchange for
the additional power.

For Ayondela, it had been the mad act of a moment's
wrath. That did not stop it from being permanent—and
evil.

Kesira wiped cold sweat from her forehead at the
thought that Lenc might be able to augment his already
awesome power with the jade and not perish. Did he hold a
secret way free of this trap?

She prayed to long-dead Gelya that this was not so.

Of Molimo she asked, "What is the Isle of Eternal
Winter? You and Zolkan mentioned it."

The man ran thick fingers through his lank hair before
sketching out the answer. Kesira saw the emotions playing on his normally impassive face. She wondered if
imparting such information took so much from him. It obviously did. But why?

"The Isle," he wrote, "is Ayondela's stronghold. Even though it lies to the warm south, the summit of the mountain on the Isle is always covered in snow and ice."

"And now? With her bringing this permanent winter on us?"

"Even the seas may be frozen," Molimo wrote. He licked his lips, then wiped his finger on the front of his too-small shirt, indicating he had nothing else to say.

"The day has been long, but tomorrow we ride," she said. Molimo nodded. Zolkan already slept, his head stuffed under one wing. Kesira looked from companion to companion, wondering what they shared. And why they excluded her from the knowledge.

She wrestled with troubled dreams that night, getting sleep but little rest.

Kesira Minette reined in the horse. It stood, snorting kinetic plumes of breath into the frosty morning air. She pointed far to the south and the tiny village huddled on the banks of the River Pharna. At the headwaters, in the Yearn Mountains, had been her nunnery. The river meandered across the Roggen Plains and hurried south to this spot some ten days ride from the Sea of Katad. "We can make the Order's lands in another day," Kesira said. Zolkan stirred restlessly on her shoulder, only his head peering out.

"Why bother?"

"Zolkan," she chided. "We seek those who worship Ayondela. If they can lend their prayers and pleas to their patron, this gives us even more chance to sway Ayondela."

The *trilla* bird sniffed loudly. His contempt for the idea carried all too well, but Kesira was not going to argue the issue with him.

Molimo kicked at the flanks of his horse and came abreast Kesira. The man-wolf pointed to tiny dust clouds dotting the plains between them and the Order.

"Horses?"

Molimo gestured that it might be soldiers of the Steel Crescent.

"Can we avoid them?" she asked. Even before Molimo silently nodded, she had mentally added, *We must.*

She tapped the reins against the horse's neck and

nudged the mare down toward the plains and the Order of
Ayondela. This approach appealed to her. Who better than
the demon's worshippers to intervene? They had to believe
in their patron and would recoil in horror when they discovered Ayondela had eaten the jade. If for no other reason, they would intercede to return Ayondela to her former
status, to keep change from coming too quickly.

Kesira held her head proudly as she rode, a prisoner to
hope.

Under the cover of nightfall, after a long, bitter day of
following ravines iced over and robbed of their summer's
bounty, they arrived at the side door to the Order's headquarters. Molimo had chosen their path well; not once had
they encountered a patrol of the Steel Crescent mercenaries.

"We should hurry in," Kesira said. "I am certain they
bar the gates when darkness becomes absolute."

Molimo did not stir. The expression on his face, the set of
his body, told Kesira he wanted to bolt and run. Fearing a
transformation into wolf, she reached out and gripped his
sleeve.

"Are you all right?" she asked anxiously. He nodded, his
eyes never leaving the walls of the Order. Ayondela had
done well by those in this abbey. The walls were well
tended and the grounds minutely cared for, a fact apparent
even though the frost clung so perniciously to the soil.
Shrubs and other low bushes lined the road leading to the
main gate and fruit trees scattered themselves about to
lend shade in a summer now aborted and a windbreak during stormy months.

"They will not harm you," Kesira said. "The Orders of
Gelya and Ayondela have much in common—had much in
common," she hastily corrected. "They preach goodness
and humility, not death and conquest."

This did not relax Molimo. Like a *renn*-stone statue Molimo sat in the saddle, staring sightlessly ahead.

Kesira tugged at the reins of Molimo's horse. It started
forward even as Molimo shook himself out of his stupor.
Kesira often wondered what scenes he saw through his
other-eyes, the half-human eyes and the half-wolf ones.

"Cold. Too cold," Zolkan complained. "Let's fly in."

"No," Kesira said, too sharply. The bird's powerful beak

clacked in response. "We must not give the impression of spying on them. All must be open when we approach."

"Do it soon. My feather oil is stiffening. Never fly again. Never!"

Kesira rode boldly to the gate and waved to a solitary figure atop the wall. The sentry stopped pacing and peered down, giving no challenge. Kesira called out, "We are travelers in need of a night's lodging. Can we avail ourselves of Ayondela's hospitality?"

"Where do you come from?"

Kesira rocked back in surprise. Her horse tried to shy but she held the mare firmly. When anyone approached the nunnery of Gelya asking for aid, they received it without question. She had assumed such was the case at the Abbey of Ayondela.

"It is cold and we are tired and hungry," she said. "I am a Sister of the Mission of the Order of Gelya."

"Gelya's dead," was the only response from the sentry.

"I know." Kesira didn't try to hold back the bitterness she felt, both at the fact of Gelya's murder and the attitude of the person within the walls.

"One moment."

Kesira, Molimo, and Zolkan waited impatiently as the figure vanished into the gloom. In the far west the sun dipped below the horizon and took what little heat had been in the air with it. The sunsets had been spectacular due to the ice crystals in the air, but for such beauty Kesira had little time. She would have preferred the gentler hues of summer to the vivid, precise visions cast across the ice clouds.

After what seemed an eternity in the gathering cold and dark, the gate creaked open to reveal a pair of hooded figures.

"I am Kesira Minette, of—" The figure on the right cut her off.

"We know. Our Brother has relayed your name. Why do you come here?"

"Can we discuss this inside, out of the wind?" A gust of wind caught at Kesira's tattered cloak and momentarily exposed Zolkan. The *trilla* bird was more used to jungle climes than arctic winds. He shivered without pause now.

The two shadow figures consulted, then stepped back,

pulling wide the gate. Kesira rode forward but Molimo hung back. She turned in the saddle and motioned for him to join her. With great reluctance, he did so. She failed to understand the problem.

The gate swung shut behind them. A heavy iron rod dropped into place, securely barring it.

"Do you have trouble with brigands?" she asked.

"There are many along the river with whom we have no desire to communicate." The robed figure threw back her cowl. Hair of spun copper reflected the pale light gleaming through kitchen windows. The face might have been lovely, but the scars on both cheeks marred any true beauty and left even the soul touched by the disfigurement.

"Forgive my lapse. We seldom admit visitors anymore. I am Abbess Camilia of Ayondela's Order." She executed a short bow.

"This is my friend, Molimo," Kesira said, indicating the man. His dark eyes took on a haunted appearance. Kesira hoped that this did not signal the change. Too many other-beasts roamed the plains now, the product of the battles between demons. Rouvin had hunted the other-beasts with the ferocity of a trapped leopard. As more and more of the half-creatures came into weary existence, this attitude might spread. Kesira prayed to Gelya that those of this Order did not similarly hunt those unable to control their form.

Kesira did not bother to introduce Zolkan. The *trilla* bird cowered within her robe. While it gave her a slightly hunchbacked appearance, neither the Abbess Camilia nor the Brother with her commented.

The Abbess made a small hand signal. The man returned silently to his solitary pacing along the top of the guard wall to keep watch for other unwanted travelers. Seldom had Kesira been made to feel more like a burden and less like a guest.

"All we need is space in your stables. We won't disturb your routine or rituals."

"The rituals are seldom performed in recent times," said the Abbess with a sigh.

"Then you know?"

Camilia spun so that Kesira could not see her face. Without a word, the Abbess walked to the kitchen door. She held it open, beckoning to Molimo and Kesira.

Not wishing to shiver in the cold longer than necessary, and fearing Zolkan might be at the end of his avian tolerances to cold, Kesira hurried forward. Molimo followed but more slowly. Once in the kitchen, Kesira relaxed. Everything reminded her of the kitchen where she had grown up, surrounded by her Sisters, given shelter and peace and all she might want to eat. The odors of roasting meat rose and made her mouth water, and while she wasn't certain, she thought she smelled a fruit pie baking. Where they had found fruit after such a treacherous turn in the weather, Kesira didn't know. It was enough for her to pretend they had an orchard nearby laden with fruits of all descriptions instead of the barren trees she had seen riding to the gates.

"Eat," said the Abbess, putting plates before Kesira and Molimo. She eyed Molimo strangely, her left hand resting on the red knotted rope about her middle. Camilia's fingers traced out the knots and worried at the very end of her Order's cord in a way that made Kesira uneasy.

"We thank you, but again, we do not want to put you to any trouble. Simple fare is all we ask, and a warm place to stay. With our horses in the stable will be fine."

"You are of Gelya's Order?" asked Camilia.

"Yes." Kesira took a deep breath. The Abbess served them generous portions of cooked meat and stewed greens. As was the custom, no drink accompanied the meal. Kesira flipped back her robe and allowed Zolkan to waddle forth. The *trilla* bird eyed the meat skeptically, then attacked the greens with vigor.

"We see few such birds," Camilia said, frowning. "When we do, they end up in our stewpots."

Without lifting his beak from the plate, Zolkan managed to squawk out, "Butchers. Cannibals."

"Do you know of Ayondela?" asked Kesira, her voice rising to drown out the bird's comment. "That she has partaken of the jade?"

"That's a lie!" raged Camilia. The Abbess slammed her hand down hard onto the table. Flatware leaped upward and Zolkan had to catch a particularly toothsome piece of vegetable in midair.

"I speak only the truth, only what I have personally witnessed," said Kesira.

"There are others who make this claim, but they lie, too!"

"No lie. Traveling across the land signs are everywhere. The jade rains are partially responsible for Molimo's lost tongue. He cannot speak. And," Kesira went on quickly, "we have witnessed demons battling. Eznofadil and Lenc, who murdered Gelya and devastated my Order, carry the telltale green hue."

"Ayondela would never turn away from her duties to her worshippers. We adore her as our patron. How can any demon forsake such love as that which we give so willingly?"

"Love sought," Kesira said gently, "is good, but given unsought is far better."

The Abbess said nothing more, her eyes hot coals betraying her continued anger at Kesira's insolence.

"We have seen the demons battling—and Ayondela taking the jade." Kesira got no response to this. She pushed on, fearing that she trod on treacherous soils now. "She became wroth over the death of her half-demon son, Rouvin."

"We have seen this. Ayondela has told us in our prayers of Rouvin's foul murder."

Kesira shot a hasty glance at Molimo. He sat as if paralyzed.

"But Ayondela has not told you of her alliance with Eznofadil and Lenc—and the jade?"

"No."

Kesira knew that Camilia thought she lied about this and resented it. "I can show you the truth of what I say."

Camilia made a vague motion with her hand indicating that Kesira could do whatever she wanted. Molimo tried to stir, but only managed to shift slightly in his seat. Zolkan waddled over to Molimo's plate and began gorging himself on the greens he found there, not caring what went on around him. Kesira sometimes admired the *trilla* bird's ability to focus in single-mindedly on nothing but food.

"The rune sticks. I will cast them and show you."

Kesira closed her eyes and settled into the timeless calm so like when passions are spent. Her mind floated and sank lightly, to touch the hidden passages within herself.

Kesira opened her brown eyes and stared at the table, only vaguely aware that others had filed into the room and now lined the walls. She reached beneath her robe and pulled forth the box containing the bone rune sticks. With a flourish she cast the sticks onto the table.

"This is the future," she intoned. "Those of you who can also read the runes, do so. You see what I see, that Eznofadil and Lenc defile our world. That their ambitions soar too high."

"Men would be demons, and demons would be gods," someone in the room said softly. "I see it in the rune sticks."

"There is more," said Kesira. Agile fingers traced over the fall of the sticks, interpreting the patterns, pointing out the message given her. "There were three demons who originally sought the illicit power granted by the jade. Howenthal is dead, in his fortress in the center of the Quaking Lands."

"Wemilat," said the one who had spoken before. "The demon known as The Ugly died in the battle with Howenthal."

"That is so," Kesira rushed on. "And Ayondela replaced Howenthal in the unholy trinity of jade."

"They would conquer all."

Kesira warmed to the interpretation. Whoever it was reading the runes over her shoulder aided her with the telling.

"They bring only misery to our world. We must petition Ayondela for succor. Have her return to the serene ways before Lenc and Eznofadil. She is not evil, but the jade turns her so."

"Ayondela," came the voice, louder this time. "She weaves in and out of this casting. The runes ... the runes."

"What do you read?" demanded Abbess Camilia.

Before Kesira could answer, the other spoke, firmly and accusingly. "This one. Kesira Minette of the Order of Gelya, she and the other were responsible for Rouvin's death and forcing our patron to forsake us!"

"Wait," cried Kesira. "That's not what happened. We—"

"The runes speak it," insisted the unseen speaker.

"They killed Rouvin and forced Ayondela to vengeance. Because of them Ayondela has brought perpetual snows and freezing winter during our growing season. They are our enemy. Give them to Ayondela and our wondrous patron will embrace us once again and turn the leaves green with the loving kiss of spring!"

Kesira launched to her feet, only to find her arms seized by strong hands. She struggled but there were too many for her to escape. Kesira heard Zolkan's outraged squawking as the *trilla* bird also fell to groping hands. Of Molimo, Kesira saw nothing. But from the lack of sound, she guessed he succumbed without a fight. He had been in that odd trance ever since sighting the Order's walls.

"To the dungeons," ordered Abbess Camilia. "We will pray to Ayondela all night if necessary, and tell her of our gift."

"Murderer." The single word rose from one set of lips, only to be taken up by all. As they shoved Kesira toward the stairs leading downward into the bowels of the earth, they chanted "murderer" over and over until she wanted to clap hands over her ears and shut out the sound.

The clanging of the heavy steel door to the cell came almost as a relief. At least now there was silence. Deathly silence.

Chapter Three

KESIRA MINETTE sat in the corner of the cell, knees pulled up to her chest and arms encircling them. Even this did not prevent the cold from seeping into her bones.

"We're out of the wind," she said.

"Still cold," Zolkan complained. The *trilla* bird fluttered around the tiny cell, barely able to get aloft before having to swerve to miss the stone walls. Watching his corkscrewing path made Kesira dizzy. The confusion of green feathers, blue wingtips and the rosy red plumage of his breast spun in wild circles that blended and blurred and gave her a headache. She closed her eyes and leaned back against the rough stone, fingers working over the knotted blue cord at her waist.

She had tried, but had not properly thought through her dilemma. If she could read the rune sticks, it stood to reason others could, also. Kesira had to admit the reading given by the Sister of Ayondela's Order had been all too accurate. But, like their patron, they had not given her a chance to explain.

All were too eager to accuse, then repent their error at leisure. She had to convince them that any mistake would be fatal, that there'd be no opportunity to change their minds later.

Kesira found some solace in her rituals. Peace descended and enfolded her in its velvet arms—or was it numbness?

"Escape from here. Not like this place. Too dark. No one can see my lovely plumage." Zolkan landed heavily against the bars in the cell door and clung with strong talons. Kesira heard the scraping of hard claw against steel. She didn't have to examine the bars to know that Zolkan's claws gave out before the tiniest of scratches had been made on the tempered bar.

"How do you recommend we do this?" she asked. "Zolkan? Molimo?"

The bird squawked in frustration and returned to circle nervously in the tiny airspace provided. But from Molimo there came not a sound, no movement, no indication that he even lived. Frightened at his complete lack of response, Kesira slid across the rough floor and sat beside him. He did not give any sign of noticing her.

His eyes were open and fixated on infinity. Only the slow up-and-down movement of his chest showed that he lived. Kesira passed her hand in front of his face to break the gaze, but failed to produce any hint of life.

"Molimo, what's wrong? We're not in a hopeless situation. Molimo!" She shook him as hard as she could. Only then did he stir—he pulled away from her.

"Zolkan, what's happened to him?" she asked the *trilla* bird. "I've never seen him like this before. It's as if he is stunned. Has he hit his head? Or"—cold fingers gripped at her heart—"is this part of the transformation?"

"Not losing humanity," said Zolkan, now grounded and waddling to where they sat. The bird launched himself to land heavily on Molimo's shoulder. The man paid Zolkan no heed. Zolkan began the singsong speech that excluded Kesira totally. She listened, trying to find some sense in what must be words. She failed. But the effect on Molimo was all she could have wished. Slowly the man's eyes focused and his head turned until his nose and Zolkan's beak rubbed.

"Bad breath," Zolkan said, sidestepping along Molimo's shoulder.

"Molimo, what is it?" asked Kesira.

He turned to her, a slight smile on his lips. A pile of dust provided his writing material.

"Evil all about us," he wrote. "We must not linger."

"This is hardly my idea of luxury to rival the Emperor's palace in Limaden," she said tartly.

This produced what passed for a laugh from the tongue-severed youth. He quickly sketched out, "Magicks abound.

Saps my strength. Can hardly move. We must escape *very* soon."

"How?"

Their eyes met, then Molimo began to write quickly. Kesira caught her breath and started to protest what he had written, then changed her mind. It was dangerous, and she did not approve, but Gelya had said that to believe only in possibilities was not faith but mere philosophy. She had to put her entire faith in Molimo and Zolkan. In no other way could they escape from this cell—and the imprisonment and death offered by the Abbess Camilia.

"Do it," she said quietly. "But hurry. I do not like to watch when you change."

Even as she spoke, Molimo's body flowed and rippled, breaking free of the shackles of human weakness. Replacing the sleek, tanned flesh were furred gray flanks, powerful jaws, and eyes as green as the jade they fought. Molimo gave voice to a low, heartful howl.

Zolkan took flight and hovered above, straining to maintain his position. "He is strong enough," the bird told her. Kesira had to believe. She had to.

Molimo arrowed forward in the narrow cell like a gray battering ram. The wolf's full weight—and more—struck the steel door. Kesira clutched at her belly and bent double as forces beyond her understanding hammered against the steel forbidden to followers of Gelya.

Kesira clapped her hands over her ears as the door blasted outward, jerked free of its hinges. The loud clanging filled the dungeons as the door smashed to the stone floor. Molimo stood on all fours, panting, head swiveling left and right, fangs bared. When he looked over his shoulder, Kesira had the eerie feeling that he might consider her for a meal. But the wolf trotted off, growling deep in his throat.

Zolkan fluttered to her shoulder. "He gives voice to the rage he cannot as human. To lack a tongue. He will pay for that. Of all indignities, that is worst. He will pay."

"Who?" asked Kesira. "Who cut out Molimo's tongue?"

But the *trilla* bird had taken wing and fluttered down the corridor after Molimo. Kesira rushed after them, feeling alone. However it was, those two shared a common bond that she did not understand. Worst of all, they did not take her into their confidence. She might have nursed Molimo to health after he had been caught in the jade rains, but he was chary with information about his past. She had thought it an aftereffect, just as the shape-change was. Now she wondered.

If Zolkan knew, Molimo did also. Where else might the bird have gotten the information? He had been with Kesira for almost two years—and she had nursed him back to health as she had Molimo.

She thought she was following them, but the corridor stretched, barren, in front of her. Barred cell doors stood on either side of the stone tunnel. Kesira ran to one and peered through. Inside huddled a skeleton with a chain fastened to what had once been a living neck. She shuddered. Had the Abbess Camilia ordered some poor creature imprisoned and then forgotten him? Or had they remembered?

Kesira pushed such thoughts from her mind. She spun about and stared into the other cell. A small child crouched in the middle of the enclosure, playing with a chitinous insect.

"Wait," she called to the child. "I'll get you out." Kesira looked about frantically for some way to open the barred door. The lock had long ago turned brittle with rust, but still presented a formidable barrier.

Her eyes came to rest on her stone-wood staff. Not even thinking why it was there or why she hadn't seen it previously, she hefted the staff and ran the end through the lock hasp. Using leverage, what strength remained to her and the full weight of her body, she broke the lock. Fumbling in her haste, she cast off the bar and threw open the door.

"You're free now," she said, her words trailing off when she saw the thing in the cell. It had been a small, abused child. Now it filled the small space with scales and bulging muscles and a mouth filled with multiple rows of glistening fangs. A bloated purple tongue lolled to one side and, Kesira saw, all the way to the beast's belly.

The roar deafened her. Without thinking, she raised her staff and found it had turned into smoke. The vapor drifted away and left her helpless in the face of this monster.

"Away," she said, beginning to back from it. Her mind fought for composure and control over her panic-wracked

body. She might get the door locked again. Bar the steel
plate. Find another lock.

The beast rushed.

Only instinct saved her. Kesira dived and twisted in
midair, landing heavily and rolling. She came to her feet,
the creature in the corridor behind her.

Kesira Minette ran for her life.

Panting, gasping for air in the musty dungeon, she
found herself making no headway. Her legs pumped furiously, and she stayed in place. As she slackened her effort,
she was drawn back toward the creature's huge mouth and
those long, savage fangs. Kesira grabbed out and tried to
find a hold along the wetly seeping stone walls. Her
fingertips turned bloody with the effort—and she failed to
slacken her inexorable backward pace.

"Go from strength to strength," she moaned out. "It is
Gelya's will. Use what lies within. Honor demands it. For
life!"

Kesira began running faster and faster and kept herself
just beyond the beast's snapping jaws. Hot red eyes burned
like embers in the thing's head and bloated white nostrils
dilated with the effort it expended.

Legs pumping, Kesira found the chance to calm herself.
Her mind regained control of her body. People failed not
from physical weakness, but from lack of resolve; hers
stiffened. She would not provide easy dinner for this creature locked away in Ayondela's cellars.

Even as she concentrated on escape, a cold wind gusted
across her back. She broke stride and fell facedown. She
rolled over, legs coming up to kick away the beast as it
sprang. No attack came.

Molimo and Zolkan stood in the corridor, the monster
gone as surely as her staff had turned to smoke and wafted
away.

"All right?" asked Zolkan. The bird waddled forward
and hopped onto her leg. She felt sharp, familiar talons as
it walked up to sit in her lap, one beady eye glaring at her.

"Did you see it? The monster chasing me?"

"Magicks everywhere. This place nexus for Ayondela's
wrath. Power turned inward and down into earth. Bad.
Cold, too." The bird fluttered up to her shoulder for a better purchase. "Get dirty. Will my feathers ever come

clean?" Zolkan stretched forth one long wing and shook it until tiny green and blue feathers from the tip fluttered free.

"But the monster," she said, giving way to uncontrolled shaking.

"Magicks," repeated Zolkan. "Brought on us by Ayondela." The bird craned his head around and looked at the wolf. The green eyes blinked. "Eznofadil's magicks," Zolkan corrected, as if he had been so informed by Molimo.

Molimo spun and trotted off, head low, nose sniffing here and there as he went. Kesira got to her feet and followed, amazed that she actually traversed the hallway now. She forced herself to glance into the cell with the skeleton.

The cell stood empty.

And the steel cell door through which the fanged thing had rushed was firmly closed, its cell empty, also.

"Magicks," she muttered. These were far from her lessons in the nunnery. Kesira considered it a major talent being able to cast the rune sticks and divine some small measure of the past—and future. Many had considered this valuable. Rouvin had commented several times on how few mortals possessed the talent.

Kesira would gladly trade it now for a sight of the sun, even if it were wreathed in icy clouds and freezing winds.

"Stay," Zolkan warned her. "Molimo must bear brunt of attack. His duty, his punishment."

"What?"

She skidded to a halt and saw the wolf at a crossing corridor, head jerking to and fro, jaws snapping at thin air. Kesira frowned when she saw faint disturbances in the air, ghostly patches of glowing light flitting over Molimo's head.

"What are they?" she asked, and even as she spoke, the ghosts took substance and attacked Molimo.

"No!" she shrieked. Zolkan gripped firmly on her shoulder, talons sinking to flesh. Powerful wings beat and held her back. Kesira tried to spin free, but found the *trilla* bird too firmly lodged for that.

"He more powerful. Wait. Wait."

Molimo fought the nightmare creatures. They shapeshifted constantly, flowing for advantage over the wolf. Molimo fought them the best he could. Strong jaws clamped firmly, only to find ghost flesh. The wolf howled and fought and succeeded in herding both the other-beasts into one corridor. This prevented them from attacking him simultaneously, but Kesira still doubted Molimo could win.

The beasts turned from snake to owl to leopard to *chillna* cat and back into gauzy white light as they strove for supremacy.

"Molimo draws them," said Zolkan. "They sense otherness in him and hate him for it."

"We must help."

"No. No way. Molimo strong. Molimo good."

Kesira ripped Zolkan free of her shoulder and ran to aid Molimo. The wolf never looked up, but one of the other-beasts did. In that instant, Molimo attacked and found firm throat to rip out in a bloody fountain. Kesira blinked as the hot life fluid spattered her. Molimo freed his victim and pounced on the remaining creature.

The other-beast turned to dancing specks of light and *popped* out of sight. Even as she stared at the bloody corpse on the floor, it evaporated like mist in the warming sun. Of the fight, only Molimo and the blood on Kesira's gray robe remained.

"We cannot battle this way," she told the wolf. "Molimo, come with me. We must leave this awful place."

The green orbs still carried kill-lust within them, but Molimo's tension went away and the powerful shoulder muscles relaxed from the spring he had planned to launch.

"How escape? Where go?" cawed Zolkan.

Kesira didn't know. She pointed at random down one of the corridors, then started off, the wolf and *trilla* bird tagging along. As she walked, her confidence mounted. One direction might be as good—or bad—as another. It depended on what use they made of all they discovered along the way.

But confusion returned when she came to another juncture and another and another. All looked identical. She was at the point of tears when she spotted stairs leading upward.

"There!" she cried. "We'll be aboveground in a moment."

"Magicks," muttered Zolkan. "Molimo says—"

Kesira had no chance to hear the warning. She took a single step forward and found herself lost in a fleshy, pulpy mass. Air cut off, she battled to make a tiny pocket in the juicy, fragrantly enveloping crush around her. Her lips brushed over the walls of her new prison; Kesira tasted fruit.

Lungs at the point of bursting, she pushed away her curiosity and battled, using arms and legs. As suddenly as the crush had come, it ended. She dropped to hands and knees in the small tunnel and gasped.

Kesira lifted her head and peered into the dimness when she heard the slithering sounds.

"Gelya, give me strength," she gasped out.

In the tight circular tunnel came the most odious sight she had ever seen. A worm as large as she wiggled along, pulling up its hindquarters and then thrusting itself forward. The nictitating membranes over its dim eyes fell in protection as it attacked. The toothless mouth opened and cilia groped to pull her deep into the gut of this creature.

Kesira struck out awkwardly, her fist hitting the worm's side. The eye membrane tightened in a protective measure, but the forward motion stopped. Kesira began backpedaling as fast as she could. In the tight confines of the tunnel—no doubt chewed by this worm—she couldn't turn around to make better speed.

The worm regained its courage or hunger and started forth again, mouth cavity opening and closing in an obscene parody of a human kiss.

"Go away!" she shrieked. "Leave me alone!"

A cross corridor saved her. The worm had tunneled back and forth through the odd substance imprisoning her. Again Kesira's lips brushed the walls of the tunnel and fruit flavor came to her. Most important was the chance to spin about and face away from the worm. The woman hurried down the cross corridor on hands and knees.

This presented a problem she had not considered. The worm quickly came up from behind her now, its cilia licking forth to touch her bare legs. Sticky fluids impeded her progress and soon held her back.

Kesira tried to kick and found her legs bound too tightly. She was being sucked into the worm's mouth, inch by slow, agonizing inch. When digestive fluids touched her feet, she screamed.

Her faith in Gelya's teachings never faltered; one maxim rose in Kesira's mind: *Faith without deed is worthless.*

Her fingers closed on the softness of the tunnel walls and pulled free gobbets of the pulpy meat. She thrust it at the worm with little effect. Then Kesira spied a dark, round pebble in the wall. As she slipped further into the worm's interior, the digestive fluids burning worse and worse at her legs, she grabbed for the seed. It popped free. Hard, heavy, it gave her a weapon.

Kesira cried, "Die, you foul beast, die!" as she pummeled the head and mouth with the seed. The worm recoiled, but did not loosen its hold on her. Kesira kept fighting. And then was explosively shot out of the worm.

For an instant she was too dazed to think. The seed still clutched in her hand, she struck feebly at the worm. But the beast had turned away and tried to reverse its direction in the tunnel.

Hideous gobbling sounds came from out of her sight, from behind the worm. Something ate it as it had tried to devour her.

Tears flowed down Kesira's cheeks, leaving behind salty, dust-streaked paths. She clutched the seed to her breast as if it were the most precious thing in the world. Watching the worm perish was not pleasant. Even more unpleasant was the sight when the last of the worm was gobbled up and she saw what had attacked.

"Molimo," she sobbed out. The wolf stood in the tunnel licking off the ichorous worm fluids from his muzzle. He had saved her life, but she wanted to be sick to her stomach. "I want out of here. What is this place?"

Molimo came to her. She recoiled from the rough tongue licking away the worm's digestive fluids still searing her feet and legs. Tiny holes had appeared in her gray robe and the gold sash about her waist had developed two tiny burns.

"It's as if we are trapped within a fruit, and that was a fruit worm. This is a seed and the walls are the meat." She frowned. Folk tales of maidens lost within the realm of a flower came back to her. Sister Fenelia had told her those stories when she was small. She had believed them possible, and the Sister had never disputed it.

"Magicks?" she asked. Molimo bobbed his head up and down.

"There is a way free," she said with growing determination. "If magicks placed us within the fruit, then we can win free because of faith. Nothing is stronger. Nothing. Not even steel."

Molimo did not appear impressed with her catechism. She crawled along the worm tunnel until she found a tight brown barrier that yielded like tough rubber.

"The skin of the fruit. We can get out here." She placed her feet against the soft walls and found some small purchase. Using her legs, she shoved against the skin. It stretched but did not break. Just as she neared the end of her strength, Molimo growled and savagely ripped at her feet. She jerked away and his fangs caught the tough skin. A ripping sound echoed along the pulpy tunnel, and a hole appeared in the skin.

Kesira blinked in surprise. They *were* in a fruit at the bottom of a bin, but if they crawled out would they remain this size?

The possibility they might meet another fruit worm decided Kesira. She boldly gripped the ragged skin and levered herself through. She shrieked as she emerged outside the fruit. Arms and head banged painfully against walls and door as she regained her normal size. When Molimo joined her they were jumbled together in an ungainly pile. And when Zolkan erupted from the tiny hole in the fruit the three of them more than filled the bin.

The door latch popped and they tumbled into the kitchen, landing on the floor.

Molimo scrambled to his feet first, nose sniffing the air, muscles bunched for attack. Zolkan fluttered up and alighted on the doorsill leading outside. Kesira finally got to her feet, legs wobbly. She saw her stone-wood staff leaning against the wall where she'd left it on entering the abbey's kitchen. Hesitantly, she took its cool length in hand, expecting it to turn to smoke.

The substantial weight of the staff comforted her.

"Go. Leave this magick-damned place," squawked Zolkan.

"I must speak with Camilia," the woman said. "There must be a way to convince her to implore Ayondela to change her ways."

"That fruit was demon trap," said Zolkan. "Molimo agrees. Eznofadil plays with these people. They worship Ayondela, but Eznofadil plays with them. Ayondela does not care."

Kesira nodded. "What you say is undoubtedly so. I must try to change Camilia's mind, however. An ally is better than an enemy."

"We go," said Zolkan. "Get ready to flee."

"Find Molimo some clothes first," commanded Kesira. "When he changes back into human form, we don't want him to freeze to death."

Molimo and Zolkan exchanged that damnable look that excluded her, then left without further discussion. Kesira settled herself and straightened her robe and cloak the best she could. Fruit juices and blood now added to its patchwork appearance.

She cautiously explored. When Kesira heard low chants of a ritual response, her footsteps quickened. All the Order would be gathered in the chapel. When Kesira found the sacristy and peered out onto the altar a coldness swept through her. She'd thought she had experienced the depths of despair when locked in the Order's dungeons but now the nun's spirit plummeted even further.

A cold white flame burned at the altar of Ayondela. The sigil of Lenc held the Order's full attention as they worshipped. They worshipped death and destruction, the end of the world and the establishment of a newer, crueler one.

The Abbess rose and addressed the assembly. "Sisters, Brothers, we find ourselves awakening to the dawn of a new day, a new era. Our patron Ayondela implores us to find new paths as we abandon the old. This flame is the symbol of our future, our hope!"

The chants were unfamiliar to Kesira, but she guessed they were part of the ritual established by Ayondela for her worshippers. They were being perverted now. The words called for harmony and faith.

The deeds would carry them to death and turmoil.

Kesira Minette gave up all hope of convincing Camilia that her patron had forsaken her Order and turned to the forbidden jade. The nun quietly slipped back to the kitchen and out into the wind's cold knife-thrusts. Somehow, even the inclement weather was more comforting than the scene she had just witnessed.

Kesira went to find Molimo and Zolkan and leave. If Ayondela's followers could not plead their case to their patron, Kesira saw no way other than meeting with Ayondela and personally trying to convince the jade demon of her error.

The wind felt even colder as the woman mounted her horse.

Chapter Four

THE TINY SHRINE provided some shelter from the raging blizzard. Gelid snowflakes hit with the fury of tiny, wet fists and made riding impossible. When Kesira had seen the isolated shrine, she had steered them for it, over Zolkan's protests. Now that they were within the confines of the shrine, she grew increasingly uneasy.

The *trilla* bird had been right about this place. Most Orders had a Brother or Sister responsible for alignment of buildings within the compound, and of the furniture within the buildings. Proper placement guaranteed good health, answered prayers, and imparted general prosperity to the occupants.

Everything within the shrine reeked of wrongness. As Kesira had knelt to begin her meditation, she had jerked about and glanced over her shoulder, certain that someone spied upon her. Only Molimo and Zolkan rested within the shrine, and they worked at spreading their blankets on the stone floor and tacking up a horse blanket in such a way that it cut off cold winds working through the doorless entryway.

"Wrong," complained Zolkan. "All wrong."

"I know," Kesira said. "But why? There is no danger lurking. I hear nothing but the wind and snow outside." She glanced up at the well-sealed roof. There was no danger of leaks allowing cold water to drip upon them this night. The sturdy stone walls fully thwarted the force of the south wind and the floor, while cold, was dry.

Kesira found herself unable to begin meditation. Restlessly, she rose, using her staff for support and paced the perimeter of the room searching for the cause of her nervousness. The altar stood unsullied by the white flame sent by Lenc to other altars she had seen—that of Gelya and also of Ayondela.

"Positions wrong," said Zolkan. "No planning. Makes me feel dirty."

"You always complain about being filthy," she told the bird, but conviction was not in her voice. She had the same sensation, and it did not please her. True, they had been on the trail for long days since leaving the Order of Ayondela and had found no time or place to bathe. The weather had grown progressively more bitter and made travel well nigh impossible.

The Sea of Katad lay, by Molimo's estimate, some six days travel to the east. They had crossed and recrossed the frozen Pharna River four times after fleeing from the abbey. Then the river had straightened and flowed like a hunting arrow, a sure sign that the sea was not far distant. All the while they had ridden they watched for soldiers of the Steel Crescent. They had seen none, though spoor abounded.

Sere bramble grass had been grazed, tracks in the iced-over snow indicated recent passage of dozens of cavalry, and Molimo had even sniffed out a lost dagger turning to rust in the inclement weather. The sigil on the handle showed clearly it had belonged to one of the mercenaries.

Kesira considered the possibility that not sighting the murderous riders had made her more upset during their ride to the sea. And the woman could not deny that she feared what they would find once Katad came into view.

The Isle of Eternal Winter.

Zolkan had tried to describe it, but Kesira had the impression the bird did so from secondhand information. From Molimo? How had the man-wolf given the bird such detailed descriptions? If he had written them out, why hadn't Molimo shared them with her? The few times they had been apart, Molimo had been in his wolf form and incapable of writing.

Kesira felt more cut off now than at any other time. Her Sisters dead, Molimo and Zolkan hiding information from her—she had nowhere to turn for solace.

Even worse, Kesira *feared* the Isle of Eternal Winter and Ayondela and Eznofadil and Lenc. True courage lay not in denying all fear, but in overcoming it. Kesira knew that there was nothing in the world she wanted to avoid more than meeting Ayondela to tell her the details of her son's death. Rouvin had been a doughty warrior, reckless and strong, handsome and endowed with more than human traits from his demon mother. Kesira thought mother and son shared much: defense of the weak; pride in accomplishment; ambition; ability.

She did not for an instant doubt they also shared fiery tempers. She had seen Rouvin's flare repeatedly, often in the midst of battle, when he turned into a juggernaut possessing berserk strength. Cooling had taken several minutes, usually long after the last foe lay slain.

Ayondela's immediate reaction to hearing of her son's death proved he had rightfully inherited the trait.

Kesira remembered how even Wemilat The Ugly had been forced to use extreme caution with the female demon.

"Must convince Ayondela," grumbled Zolkan. "Too cold for proper bath." The bird tried to preen his feathers and failed; the feather spines snapped from the cold and left bald patches. "Starving. No greens."

Molimo hurriedly wrote on a small tablet he had found somewhere in the Order of Ayondela's stable. He had erased their tally of hay and feed for their animals and now used it for his own communications. "The last you ate gave you diarrhea."

"Not my fault," said the *trilla* bird with a haughty upturn of his serrated beak.

"It wasn't Molimo's fault that my robe and cape have endured such indignity," said Kesira. She made brushing motions at the shoulder where Zolkan perched. "Whose could it be, then?"

"Greens poisoned. Only explanation."

"No poison," insisted Molimo, his stylus moving with assurance.

"What do you know?" demanded Zolkan.

All three fell silent when they heard wagons clanking. Molimo and Kesira went to the open entryway of the shrine and peered into the snowy distance. A fluke of wind opened a tiny patch and allowed them to catch sight of a large band of brown-garbed figures forcing their way into the teeth of the wind.

"They come here," said Kesira.

"Flee?" Molimo wrote.

"How?" she asked. "Our mounts are tired from battling the storm and we are in scarcely better condition. It is obvious they come here seeking shelter. Perhaps this shrine was erected by their Order, for they appear to be religious pilgrims."

"Hide?"

Kesira shook her head. "We must assume they mean us no harm."

"Bad place. Creepy," said Zolkan.

"I take that to mean you believe them to be somehow evil. We don't know that. Only our most recent experiences have us hiding from strangers and suspecting the worst of them. While true friendship is a tree that grows but slowly and needs constant nurturing, suspicion is far more apt to grow like a bitter weed." Kesira noted that the brown-robed men had moved closer so that their outlines were visible through even the heavily blowing snow. No trick of wind was required now to see them.

In spite of her confident words, Kesira gripped her staff a little tighter and widened her stance in case she had to defend herself. The tiny stone shrine would prevent more than a handful of armed men from engaging her and . . .

She shook off the panic engendered by the unknown men. It was truly as Gelya said: The less known, the more feared.

Molimo put away his tablet and stylus and pulled forth a sheathed sword. She had tried to dissuade him from carrying it, but her beliefs were not his. For Molimo the steel carried no religious burden. Gelya had taught that only the flexible survived, that the inflexible, like steel, snapped under stress. Or so Dominie Tredlo had told her. The Senior Brother of her Order had been unclear on this point and had allowed Kesira to invent her own rationale. When she had done so, he hadn't corrected her.

"Ho, who rests in this shrine?" came the loud hail from outside.

"Welcome, pilgrims," said Kesira. "We, too, are weary travelers. Where are you bound?"

The man pushed into the stone shrine and shook back his hood. The dark visage did not reassure Kesira as to the man's peaceful intentions. His hand rested on a dagger belted around his middle and she detected the telltale lumps of a sword beneath the robe. Heavy bony ridges raced above each eye, almost totally lost in the undergrowth of his black, snow-dotted eyebrows. Kesira wondered if the man had a neck; from all she could see his head seemed to be cruelly driven directly into his shoulders.

With a fluid grace that belied his heavyset build, he flitted around the room, returning with a broken smile on his lips. Kesira looked away from the yellowed, uneven teeth. She had liked it better when he tried not to be friendly.

"Just you two, eh?"

Kesira made a motion to silence Zolkan. The *trilla* bird settled down, obviously fuming at being overlooked.

"We are pilgrims on a holy journey to the Sea of Katad," she said. "And where are you and the others bound?"

"Mostly getting out of the weather," he said. "We hoped for warmer climes to the south. We travel along the banks of the Pharna to the sea, then farther along, praying that the storms lessen as we go."

Others crowded into the shrine now. Kesira noted that none of the men made any sign that they were in a holy place. Only when a smallish man in a robe of a different brown tint entered did Kesira believe they might be traveling monks. The man knelt quickly, head bowed, and went through a quick prayer too softly spoken for her to overhear.

"I am Senior Brother," the man said.

"Your Order?"

Frightened eyes darted to and fro, as if answering might bring down Eznofadil's full wrath.

The Senior Brother swallowed so hard Kesira saw his throat work as if fingers gripped it. His eyes continued to study his companions restlessly.

"Berura-ko," he said. For a moment, Kesira thought she had misheard. A particularly loud gust of wind had whistled through the shrine.

"A fine patron," she said. "Berura-ko and my patron were often partners in developing solutions to worldly problems."

"Who's that? Your patron?"

"Gelya." The Senior Brother slumped as if the weight of the world had been lifted from him.

"Gelya is dead," he said almost cheerfully. Kesira said nothing. The monk rushed on, "I did not mean it in the way you think. It . . . it is only that my patron is dead, also. Killed by the jade demons."

"Such rumors contain truth, then," Kesira said. "I had heard Berura-ko had perished, but I did not know."

"Lenc," the Senior Brother grated out. "Lenc did it."

Kesira started to tell the monk of their quest to find Ayondela, but Molimo's hand stayed her. She had to admit the wisdom in keeping her own counsel on this point. Silence never betrayed anyone.

"Your Brother said you journey to the Sea of Katad also," she said. "Perhaps we can join your band, until we sight the sea. Since we travel to the same point, I see no reason not to travel together."

"Nor I, nor I," said the monk, too quickly. He glared at the man without a neck, who smiled even more broadly. If Kesira had felt uncomfortable in the stone shrine before, she now felt openly fearful.

"Come, my dear, let us talk while the others fix a meal and prepare to bed down for the night. We have so much information about our respective Orders to exchange. Yes, I know it. I do."

The Senior Brother took her by the elbow and guided her away to a distant corner. For every snippet of worthwhile data the man imparted, he spent twenty minutes blithering about inconsequentials. Kesira was only too glad to beg off further conversation and slip into her blanket beside Molimo.

Molimo had written on his tablet, "Many of them are armed—not of Berura-ko."

Her hand rested on his arm. Molimo already slept. She silently mouthed, "I know." Sleep finally overtook the nun and she drifted along the pathways of her inner mind.

They had ridden most of the day, the Senior Brother staying close by Kesira's side. While the storm had blown over, the cold air cut to the bone and made Kesira even less willing to talk. But the monk chattered on, worse than Zolkan ever had.

"So glad to have you with us," he said for the hundredth time. "Livens up a dreary excursion. The others' faces get so tedious."

"As is yours," came Zolkan's muffled comment. Kesira thwacked the hidden bird with the palm of her hand.

"How's that?" asked the Senior Brother.

"Nothing. Just clearing my throat," Kesira said.

Molimo spurred up and rode on her other side. He pointed off to the left, the north, where rising columns of heat distorted the clear wintry air.

"We will have company soon," Kesira said.

"What? Where?" The monk swiveled about. When he caught sight of the approaching riders, he let out a wordless shriek that brought the man without a neck on the double.

"There," said the Senior Brother. "Brigands. I am sure of it."

The man nodded, put fingers in his mouth and emitted a shrill whistle. Their progress died as most of the monks broke ranks and pulled out wicked, well-used swords from beneath their robes.

"Th-these men are mercenaries traveling with us," stammered the Senior Brother. "W-without them we couldn't have got this far. So many brigands. So many."

"The cold's drove them out of their homes, more starvin' than whole," the mercenary said. His glacial eyes fixed on Kesira's trim form, visible when a quick gust of wind pressed her robe and cloak tightly against her body. "We give protection in exchange for occasional prayers."

Kesira said nothing. She wondered what else the mercenary took as pay. From the expression on the Senior Brother's face, she could guess.

A loud yell went along the front of their defensive line. The mercenaries charged in a ragged line, but even this ragtag advance threw the brigands into disarray. They were hardly experienced at thievery, Kesira guessed. It was as the one mercenary had said: These were not brigands, but farmers driven off their land by the unseasonably cold weather. By this time of year, they should have tilled and planted and been rewarded with the first green shoots poking above the well-tended soil.

That soil knew no cultivation; it lay frozen to a depth of

an inch or more. If Ayondela's frigid curse continued, the soil might perish totally.

"Th-they are very good at fighting. We of Berura-ko's Order do not fight at all. No," the Senior Brother said. In spite of the cold, sweat beaded his forehead. Kesira looked at him sadly. His patron had done a poor job of instilling in his followers the courage needed to face all the unpleasantness in the world.

One of the brigands fought past two mercenaries and rode toward her, screeching at the top of his lungs. Kesira eyed him, judged distances and speeds, then swung her staff. The butt end of the stone-wood shaft rammed hard into the attacking man's belly. Air gushed from his lungs, and he somersaulted out of his saddle. One foot caught in a stirrup, and he found himself being dragged along the frozen ground.

Kesira might have gone after him but another man, this one on foot, came at her. She brought the staff around in a vicious circle, smartly whacking him on the top of his head. He sank down without a sound.

"Molimo, no!" she called. Molimo settled back into his saddle, the wild expression passing. Kesira had cautioned him just in time. Another few seconds and he would have begun to change into wolf shape. As it was, only she knew the strain he endured to prevent the transformation.

"Run, you swine, run!" cried the mercenaries' leader. He strutted back and stared up at Kesira. "They've shown us their heel, the cowards." He thrust his bloody blade into the hard ground and drew it forth, cleansed.

"Let's stop for the day," the monk suggested. "We need to rest and recover from such a fierce battle."

"Fierce?" The mercenary laughed harshly. "This was not so fierce. Let me tell you about . . ." He went on with an increasingly ribald tale of his days fighting against Emperor Kwasian's army, then changing sides and fighting under the command of the Emperor's foremost commander, General Dayle.

Kesira grew tired of the man's boasting. She knew he did it only to impress her, but it only repulsed her. The mercenary took little notice. The tale took on its own rationale for existing, just by being told.

Camp was made and feeble fires started for fixing their

rations. From the depths of a huge saddlebag, the mercenary leader pulled forth a flask sloshing with liquid.

"Here," he said, thrusting it under Molimo's nose. "Take a pull on this. It'll loosen your tongue. For such a man, you don't have much to say for yourself."

"Don't talk to pederasts," came Zolkan's muffled words from under Kesira's cloak.

"What did you say?" The soldier jumped to his feet, hand on sword hilt.

"Calm yourself," said Kesira. "He said nothing. The wind spoke, nothing more." As if to verify her claims, a mournful howling drifted up from a distant ravine near the Pharna. The sound came almost like a voice begging.

"Drink," the mercenary ordered. Molimo tipped back the flask, making a face as the liquor burned down his gullet. The soldier laughed and grabbed the bottom of the bottle, turning it up again for Molimo.

"Better," the mercenary said. He downed a goodly portion of the liquor, and by the time he thought to offer some to Kesira, was roundly drunk.

"Filthy creature," murmured Zolkan. The *trilla* bird emerged from under Kesira's stained cloak and took to wing, the powerful downstrokes stirring snow all around. In seconds, Zolkan had vanished into the black night.

"Your traveling companion," said the soldier, slurring his words. "What did he say?"

Kesira looked at Molimo. The ebony eyes had glazed over. The potent beverage had dulled his senses more than she would have believed. It was as if the man had never sampled liquor before, much less a vintage this strong. Kesira would have thought it drugged if the soldier hadn't finished off the flask.

"He said the wine was strong," she said, smiling. Perhaps this would help Molimo lose some of his tension. Ever since they had joined with the band of monks and mercenaries, he had been keyed up and jumpy. She had feared he would turn into the wolf and, when he hadn't, she had begun to think the strain came from other repressed desires.

"He's walleyed drunk, that's what he is," laughed the soldier. He slapped Molimo on the shoulder. Molimo slumped to his blanket, snoring peacefully.

"It'll keep him warm through the night," said Kesira.

"Good, because he will need it."

"What do you mean?" Kesira frowned at the man's tone. It had turned vicious.

"You keep him warm a'nights, unless I miss my guess. But not this night. You sleep with a hero of the day's battle. You sleep with Civv Nimlaw and discover how good it can be!"

Kesira shoved him away. "Thank you, no," she said.

" 'Thank you,' the fine lady says," he mimicked. "You'll thank me the more when I've done with you."

"Stop it," Kesira cried. She drove a hard fist directly into the middle of Nimlaw's face. He twisted slightly at the last instant or she would have broken his nose. As it was, she felt the flesh under his eye tear and blood ran over her knuckles.

"You're the kind I like. Spirit. Not like the Chounabel whores. City of Sin, pigshit! There's no sin in that city. Too tame for the likes of me. I'm a hero."

Strong, thick fingers clamped on Kesira's upper arm. She winced in pain as she tried to fight free. But Nimlaw was a fighter trained in the most deadly school of all: life-or-death battle. She did little more damage to him as he pulled her closer.

"Molimo, help me," she begged. But the man snored gently on his blanket. The liquor had dulled his senses and left him unconscious. "Zolkan!"

"The demons won't hear you. Nothing but your cries of pleasure as I thrust my powerful sword into your sheath." He grabbed her between the legs. Kesira gasped in pain. "You like that, don't you, eh? You'll like it the more when—aieee!"

Kesira had been pressed close to the mercenary. Her groping hand fell on his dagger. She drew it and raked the sharp tip across his chest. A thin streak of blood dribbled into the cut fabric of his monk's robe. She tried to spin the dagger around and drive it into Nimlaw's chest, but he batted her hand away and her thrust missed.

"Hey, look at her!" came a voice from just beyond the circle of light cast by the campfire. "She's giving Civv a real fight. Fifty silver sovereigns on the vixen, that she holds him at bay for another five minutes."

The betting went around the circle, each mercenary feeding the next's need for a spectacle. Kesira was acutely aware of the eyes studying her, lewdly appraising her potential for use after their leader finished. Kesira would not be raped just once, but repeatedly.

"Zolkan!" she cried out.

"She brings down the wrath of her patron," said one.

"No, no," said another. "There is no demon named Zolkan. She is from the Shann Province. That's their women's way of saying, 'Oh, yes, Civv, you're such a man. Do it, do it!' "

Kesira struggled, but mercenaries came to hold her arms and legs spread-eagle.

"Senior Brother, please, in the name of Berura-ko, stop them! Please stop them!"

"Don't call for that toad," scoffed Nimlaw, hiking his robes. "He has no idea what to do with a woman. But I do."

"So show us, Civv. Show us," urged on the ring of soldiers.

"Let's see what I'm getting first," the mercenary leader said. He ripped open Kesira's robe to expose her breasts. They gleamed whitely in the flickering firelight. "See? She *does* want me."

"That's only the cold doing it, Civv. You're going to have to warm her up, from the inside!"

Again the taunting, hideous laughter. Kesira struggled, but with one burly soldier on each arm she had no chance to do more than wiggle.

"Our little virgin nun might not be a virgin," said Nimlaw. "Look at this." He ran his rough, blunt fingertip over Kesira's left breast, teasing it and tormenting her. She trembled when he touched the lip print left where Wemilat had kissed her. The demon's mark glowed with a pink inner light of its own. "She has marked herself so that I might know where to begin. How thoughtful."

Civv Nimlaw hunkered down and placed his lips directly over the demon's imprint. Kesira's bare flesh rippled at the light touch.

Then it vanished. She opened her eyes and saw the mercenary sitting upright, his eyes wide in horror. It was as if his worst nightmares had become real. He gasped and grabbed for his mouth, lips fluttering like a beached fish.

The shriek that rent the night was the last sound uttered by the soldier. He toppled over, dead.

Chapter Five

THE LAUGHING, JEERING mercenaries fell silent. Even the wind's continual moaning ceased. The soldiers stared at their fallen leader, alcohol-fogged eyes wide with fear.

"Civv?" one of them asked. He released Kesira's left arm. The woman jerked her right arm free. By this time the men holding her legs had released them, too. She sat up, pulling her robe across her. The spot over her breast where Civv Nimlaw had touched her burned like a forest fire, but the flames quickly cooled, just as the man's corpse did in the frigid night air.

"She killed him without touching him," said another.

"She's cursed. She killed Civv with a curse. She's a witch."

"A demon," murmured another, backing off. "She might be a demon sent to test us."

"She's no demon. She would have slain us all with lightning if she was. This one's mortal, just as we are. But she knows the magicks. The bitch killed Civv with 'em."

"Kill her," said another. The circle about Kesira began to contract once more. The mercenaries' fear had not gone, but their need for revenge—and to eliminate possible danger in their midst—overshadowed the ominous death of their leader.

Kesira grabbed her staff and swung. She connected with one's ankle and broke the bone. He howled in pain and hobbled away. She spun the staff around faster and faster, defending herself as best she could from a sitting position. When Kesira rolled and came to her knees, the fight became more vicious.

Swords had been drawn, and the men ringing her were

all blooded veterans. One lunge went by her head and barely missed laying open a gash that would have blinded her with her own blood.

"I'll put a curse on all of you. Your balls will fall off if you don't leave me alone," she cried.

"She killed Civv. Kill her," came the cold words from the tall mercenary assuming command. Kesira didn't know if he had been the second-in-command or merely promoted himself when he saw his leader lifeless on the ground.

Kesira fought to her feet, stumbling when she backed into Nimlaw's body. The firelight cast unearthly shadows on the dead man's face. The thick body had a curious flaccidity as if every bone had turned to dust. The eyes gaped wide and horrible, the last nightmare sights burned into the retinas. The mouth hung open, and the tongue lolled blackly. Kesira had not realized Wemilat had meant it when he placed the kiss upon her breast and told her the demon's mark would protect her.

The nun would gladly have traded a little of its killing power for strength in her right arm. She kept the soldiers at bay, but doing so tired her quickly. There were so many of them, and she was nearing nervous exhaustion.

Kesira made no excuses for her condition. Her spirit was at its lowest ebb. She was failing to live up to the high standards demanded by Gelya.

Kesira jumped a sword cut at her calves and tangled herself in her flapping robe. The woman hadn't had time to secure it properly, and it now trailed along the ground. She stepped out, planted her foot firmly on the cloth and tumbled forward. Even quick use of her staff did not keep her in a defensible position.

Facedown on the ground, she waited for the cold steel to skewer her body.

Instead a hot shower cascaded upon her.

Startled, Kesira reached up and touched the wetness. Blood. But she felt no pain. She rolled over and looked up in time to see one of the soldiers clutching his severed throat. Blood spurted darkly around his fingers, then turned redder as the cold winter's air touched it. The mercenary staggered a few feet, then fell, lifeless.

The deep-throated growling and the harsh snap of jaws

convinced Kesira that Molimo had come out of his drunken stupor and transformed into the savage wolf.

She found her feet again and took the time to properly fasten her robe. By then Molimo had come into the camp-fire light, muzzle caked with blood and green eyes flashing. The wolf head swayed to and fro almost like a snake's; the fangs, when Molimo struck, were as deadly, ripping and tearing instead of poisoning.

"She's enchanted him. She *is* a witch. Flee!"

The cry went up and the mercenaries faded off into the night. Kesira heard the thunder of hooves as they fled the scene of their defeat. They had faced armies and been victorious. Their leader had given them triumphs over dozens of brigands. He—and they—had fallen victim to a nun and a youth unable to control his shape.

"Molimo," she said softly, dropping to her knees and holding out her hands. "You do not have to stay in this form. You can change back into a man. You have done well, but do not stay like this."

It took all her willpower not to jerk away when the wolf snapped at her hand.

"Peace. Become tranquil. Force away the animal and return to humanity. You know the path. Think on Gelya's maxims, the ones I've taught you. Do it, Molimo. Do it for me!"

The green eyes filled with hatred and evil fire. The lips curled back to reveal the sharp fangs that had ended so many lives.

"Kill me if you will, but return to your human form." Kesira steadfastly faced Molimo.

The wolf cowered down, hindquarters tensing. The leap went past her, over her left shoulder. Kesira heard the wolf impact heavily on another. She turned and saw one of the mercenaries beneath the wolf. Molimo tried to savage the man's throat and failed. Teeth sank deeply into a protecting right arm.

Before Kesira could say a word, the man under Molimo's writhing, twisting gray body began to flow in a way all too familiar to the woman: The mercenary changed into a *chillna* cat. Powerful shoulders supported a drooping head; the creamy-furred belly vanished as the cat doubled up to use back claws on Molimo's exposed underside. Forepaws raked on either side of the wolf's flanks while jaws even stronger than Molimo's snapped and worked to find a death-hold on a slender lupine throat.

Molimo was batted off by a powerful blow and came to all fours, snarling and ready to continue the attack.

"Molimo, wait," Kesira ordered. The *chillna* was too powerful, too heavy for the wolf. The cats had been hunted almost to extinction because of their catholic tastes in meat. They cared little whether they ate horse, swine, or human—and, it was rumored, even dined on demon flesh when they could. They hunted alone, and only because of that had humans succeeded in eliminating them as a menace to city and farm.

Kesira swung her stone-wood staff with all the power left in her body. She had judged well. The butt end of her staff crashed into the *chillna* cat's throat. The animal choked and fell flat on its chest, wheezing noisily.

Before it regained its breath, Molimo flashed forward, little more than a gray blur. Teeth ripped at ear and jowl. The cat pawed weakly at the wolf. Kesira landed another, far weaker blow to the rounded top of the cat's head. The vibration along her staff shook her and forced her away, pain lancing into her shoulders and body.

This time Molimo's strike went directly to the target. The cat lay kicking feebly, its death throes pitiful in comparison to the heavily muscled body.

And, in death, a partial transformation occurred that sickened Kesira. The hindquarters remained feline but from the waist up, the mercenary reappeared. His naked flesh shone with sweat in the dim light. Much of his face had been ripped away, and his throat still drained a trickle of blood. The half-human, half-bestial creature would never again threaten anyone.

Kesira hoped that he—it—had found peace in death. But she doubted it.

Molimo licked blood from his muzzle, then sank down by the fire, the kill-lust gone from the green eyes. Whatever drove the wolf had been sated. For now.

"Wh-what's happened?" came the timorous voice of the Senior Brother of the Order of Berura-ko. "Oh, no. This is awful."

"Do you have digging tools?" Kesira asked. "We should give him a proper burial."

"I wouldn't touch it!"

"Get the shovel," she snapped. The meek man trotted off to obey. Kesira forced him to dig a grave. It was far too shallow, but the ground had frozen and any digging proved difficult. Kesira worried that animals might unearth the body, then pushed the thought from her mind. If they found a meal in the shape changer, perhaps it would be for the best. She did her duty and could do no more.

Kesira pulled the carcass into the grave the monk had dug, then motioned for the man to cover the body. He did so hastily, not wanting to prolong the chore.

She stared at the tiny mound of dirt covering the body. "Can honor mend a broken arm?" she asked softly. "Can honor keep the people from starvation? No. Then what is honor but emptiness?" She swallowed and wiped her lips. "Honor shows our path through life. I did not know you, changeling, but I do hope that your path was straight and lined with decency and good deeds."

"We should leave," said the Senior Brother. "There might be others like it coming."

Kesira looked around and saw Molimo sitting beside the fire, returned to his human shape. He had dressed hastily, putting his shirt on backwards. She doubted if the monk would notice this, or even ask how Kesira had killed such a powerful other-beast.

"They are demon spawns. The demons test us with them. We . . . we ought not to allow it."

"Complain to your patron," Kesira said viciously, knowing Berura-ko had perished by the jade demons' hands.

As had her patron.

"What happened to the mercenaries?" the Senior Brother asked. "They rode off. They can't just leave us. We . . . I . . . where is Civv Nimlaw? I want to speak with him. We had an agreement."

"You would see him?" Kesira said in a deceptively mild tone. "I think he is yonder. Just on the other side of the campfire."

The monk hurried off, muttering to himself. The muttering stopped. Kesira heard a sharp gasp, then, "He's dead. Foully slain!"

Kesira walked to the Senior Brother's side and laid a hand on his thin, stooped shoulder. "Your wonderful body-guard tried to rape me."

"You did this to him? But how? There's no mark on his body, but he obviously died in agony."

"I hope so."

"But you must be wrong. He wouldn't . . ."

"Rape a woman?" Kesira's brown eyes bored into the monk's watery blue orbs.

He quickly glanced away. "We should be on our way."

"We stopped to rest. I haven't yet slept—or been allowed to sleep," Kesira said primly. "We will do so now."

"But Civv. We should bury him, shouldn't we? The other-beasts. The real animals."

Kesira picked up the small folding shovel and silently handed it to the Senior Brother. He looked from the shovel to the mercenary leader's body and back. With shaky hands, he took the shovel and began work on a second grave, next to the one containing the other-beast.

"All is fuzzy," Molimo wrote on his tablet. "What happened?"

"You don't remember?" Kesira asked. Molimo shook his head. "Don't worry, then," she told him. "It is only the strong drink. You shouldn't partake of it in the future."

Molimo nodded. Kesira wondered if this was good advice. Anything that brought forgetfulness to the young man might be a blessing rather than a curse. Still, she had some idea that his lack of control over his shape came from the liquor. Not that he always managed to hold back the change even when he was clearheaded.

It was a terrible curse Molimo endured, she thought. Perhaps Ayondela might lift it when they spoke and all was straightened out. Perhaps.

With this running through her mind, Kesira Minette dropped off to sleep.

"The brigands," complained the monk. "They are everywhere. We cannot hold them off. We can't. Not without the mercenaries."

Kesira tired of hearing the man's whines. The monk's courage had died with his patron.

"No one's attacked in three days. And we are almost to the Sea of Katad. What do you do then?"

The monk looked about and bobbed his head up and down, as if it had come loose from his neck. The other monks in the party—all six of them still loyal in some fashion to their patron—rode apart and out of earshot.

"I think I shall go my separate way," the Senior Brother said, as if confiding a deep, dark secret. "There is nothing to hold me to my Order now that Berura-ko is dead."

"Does the death of a patron spell the death of the Order?" Kesira asked.

"Of course. The demon gave us purpose, continually fed us new ideas. The influx was required. Without Berura-ko, we are nothing."

"It takes no courage to die," Kesira said, "but it does take courage to live. You are forsaking all your patron taught. Because he is dead, does that make his teachings wrong?"

"Of course not, but . . ."

"Gelya's words were strong—and true. His death does not alter that. I am now the Sister of the Mission and carry on the teachings. If they were a proper course for patterning lives while Gelya lived, they are no less so now that he had been foully killed by the jade demons."

"You will draw their ire. Live small, and they will ignore you."

Kesira snorted, white clouds of crystalline air gusting under her nostrils. "Live small and you will be stepped on. Where is the honor in not trying to do your best in this world?"

"You think you can matter?" the monk shot back, his anger surfacing for the first time.

"Yes."

He shook his head. "I no longer wish to try. Let *them* go their own way." He indicated the other monks. "One of them will be selected as the new Senior Brother and who will remember me—or care?"

Kesira had pitied the man before. Now she felt only contempt; he had turned from all he had lived for. She wondered if the flaw lay in the monk or in Berura-ko's teachings. The nun knew little of other Orders and their beliefs, but she did know Gelya's preachings. They gave strength when she weakened, they provided strong guidance in what was proper and what was dishonorable. All the Senior Brother said smacked of faltering honor. While she might die trying to speak with Ayondela, the attempt would be bathed in honor.

Kesira Minette would do the proper thing. There was nothing more her patron could ask of her than this.

Zolkan circled above, giving voice to shrill cries of warning. She stood in her stirrups and peered out along the banks of the frozen river. At first she did not see what had alerted the sharp-sighted *trilla* bird.

Then she saw the four beasts scrabbling over the ice, coming from the far side of the Pharna.

"Molimo," she called back. "Is there a chance to outrun them?"

He shook his head, eyes fixed on the beasts. She knew from his expression that he recognized the creatures' otherness. His hands had curled into fists and he shook, not with cold, but with the strain of maintaining his human form. Kesira said nothing. She wished she could fight this battle for him, but it was not that easy. Molimo had to learn control.

If only he would pay more attention to Gelya's teachings. But the man didn't. It was as if he had a course of action of his own. Kesira wished he could speak of it so they could compare, discuss, argue.

"No, the demon spawn. No!" The monk sighted the creatures struggling toward their small band and panicked. He rode ahead, calling loudly to the other monks and leaving Kesira and Molimo behind.

It was all she had expected from the Senior Brother.

They had encountered only one group of other-beasts, the day after the mercenaries fled. Without much effort, they had outpaced the beasts. These approaching, however, were fleeter of foot—and more dangerously taloned and fanged.

"We find more and more, the closer we get to the sea," she observed. "Do you think these might be the product of Ayondela's activities?"

Molimo made a gurgling noise deep in his throat. She had heard it before.

"Lenc," she agreed. "Yes, it must be Lenc's doing. We

must kill them, yet it carries a burden of such sorrow." Kesira said no more. Molimo knew her conflict. She loathed the creatures while sympathizing with their plight. Even the man-wolf; Kesira fought against loving him, yet she had to. She had nursed him to health and cared for him then and now, but the sudden changes from man to wolf carried with them intense danger. Her love for him had to be muted by this consideration.

That did not stop her fear of the other creatures.

"Demon spawn, the monk called them. Do you think so?"

Molimo only shrugged. Whatever had produced this horrid configuration of man and animal was unnatural by its very nature.

"One day the world will return to its normal course. There will be demons content to stay apart from humans, giving only of their philosophy and charity, and there will be mortals, living out our span content with the knowledge there are others greater than we in the world. Gone will be the overweening ambition of demons striving to be gods and gone will be humans suffering for the vanity of demons."

Molimo stared at her strangely.

Kesira laughed without humor. "No, I don't truly believe that. We can never go back to the ways of our teachers. The Time of Chaos has seized our world and can never let go, not until there are gods to replace the demons."

Zolkan screeched from above, then plummeted earthward like a green arrow. Talons flashed and ripped the eyes out of the leading other-beast. The others rushed Kesira and Molimo.

Kesira's staff held two at bay. Molimo thrust with his sword and killed another. The creatures did not immediately renew their attack. Rather, they crouched just beyond weapon's reach and made odd, cooing sounds.

"Trap, trick. Don't approach," warned Zolkan. The *trilla* bird landed on the saddle just behind Kesira and gripped down. She heard his talons cutting through tough leather as the bird cleansed them of blood and gobbets of eye.

"Are they demon spawn or other-beasts?" she asked the bird.

"No difference."

"Demon spawn cannot change shape. The other-beasts are like . . ." Her words trailed off. Kesira had started to say, "Like Molimo."

"Both deadly. Leave them. Escape now."

"I will see what they want."

"NO!"

Kesira ignored Zolkan's warning and dismounted, staff in hand. As she approached cautiously she saw no hint that these were shape changers. The grime had become a part of their scaly hides, and their frightened looks bespoke long hardship. The unnatural winter took its toll on them, just as it did on the humans.

"I won't harm you. Can I help?"

One made a tiny gesture imploring her to come nearer. The beast pointed to an injured foot, turning black with gangrene.

"This one's hurt," she said. "I'll see what I can do."

"No, trap. Don't." Zolkan's voice turned into the sing-song speech that somehow communicated with Molimo.

Kesira turned her head and started to scold Zolkan. She saw Molimo flowing into his wolf form—and she sensed rather than saw the creatures rising up before her.

Molimo blasted past her, fangs reaching out for one of the beasts. It died in a messy flood of its own life fluids. The other struck out for Kesira, a talon raking her arm. She dropped her staff and gasped with pain. Green feathers exploded around her as Zolkan's wings beat at her attacker. This brief but furious defense allowed Molimo to dispatch another and finally the last of the demon spawn.

They lay on the ground, no hint of humanity coming to them in death.

"Not shape changers," said Zolkan, perching on Kesira's shoulder. "Always ugly. Always deadly."

"They might have been."

"Pity for shape changers gets you into trouble," the *trilla* bird said.

"It worked out well with Molimo," she pointed out.

"Special case. Molimo different."

"How?"

The bird took wing without answering, flapping powerfully and returning to his position aloft to scout.

Kesira sighed and started to coax Molimo back into human form. It wasn't necessary. The man had already donned his loose clothing and sat asaddle waiting for her.

"How is it that Zolkan can speak to you?" she asked.

Molimo only pointed. The monks had ridden hard and fast; to catch them would take some doing. Kesira worried over whether this was a reasonable course of action. Still, a group offered some safety. Together, they might frighten away the less bold of the beasts roaming the riverbanks in increasing numbers.

She put her curiosity aside and rode hard beside Molimo, glad for the feel of the cold air against her face. In less than an hour, they overtook the Senior Brother and the other monks.

Kesira started to speak to the monk, then changed her mind. What was there to say? Gelya taught that kindness gives birth to kindness. Kesira added that fear feeds on fear. The monks were proof of that.

"You outran them?" the monk finally asked.

"Yes," was all she said.

"They are treacherous. They . . . they gull you into traps. You should never show them mercy."

"I'll try to remember that," she said tartly.

They hadn't ridden another ten minutes when faint sounds echoed along the river from down a ravine.

"What was that?" asked Kesira. "It sounds like someone in pain."

"I heard nothing. Just the wind," the monk said too hastily.

"Which is it? Nothing or wind?"

"More beasts. They lay in wait to catch us."

"The cries are human," Kesira said, reining in her horse to hear better. "They come from that direction." She pointed off and to the right, down the ravine. "We should make sure that someone's not seriously injured."

"It's the beasts, I tell you." The monk almost screamed the words. "Leave them. You'll get us all killed."

"The cries sound very human," she said. Kesira glanced at Molimo, who shook his head. Even his sharp ears could not differentiate.

"We must make camp soon," said the Senior Brother. "If we make the cliffs near the Sea of Katad before dusk, we can get out of this awful wind."

"We must help whoever that is."

Zolkan fluttered down from his aerial station. Kesira winced as the bird dug talons into her shoulder. "Once today you find demon spawn. Just because monk is coward doesn't mean he is wrong now."

"It doesn't mean he is right, either, just because we were attacked by those poor creatures."

"Pity for other-beasts leads you astray," said Zolkan.

"Sympathy," she corrected. "Can we turn away if someone needs our aid? What is the difference if it is an other-beast? Perhaps we can help, as we did with Molimo. Or with a disgusting-looking mass of green feathers who flew into our sacristy, starving and more dead than alive."

Zolkan snorted. "Molimo good. Other-beasts not all good. And I not demon spawn." The bird sounded offended that she compared him with any of the creatures they had fought that day.

"The cries died down. That might be a human, not some poor soul trapped between animal and human."

"We ride on," said the monk."

"So ride and be damned by all the demons," she snapped. "We go to see if we can be of assistance." Kesira glared at Zolkan and Molimo. "At least *I* go. They can do as they please."

Zolkan launched himself and circled, but Kesira smiled when she saw the bird flying in the direction of the piteous and all too human sounds. And Molimo rode at her side.

Kesira might find disappointment or danger, but she knew where honor lay. She put the spurs to her horse and dropped down into the rocky ravine, bound for the source of the noise.

Chapter Six

THE MOANS AND CRIES turned into sobs. Kesira Minette spurred her horse faster, positive that this was not a trap set by one of the demon spawn or other-beasts. A human in pain needed her assistance.

The ravine walls towered above her and turned into a small canyon. The rocky floor made going slower than she would have liked, but it gave Zolkan a chance to scout ahead. Without his aerial reconnaissance, Kesira knew that her life would have been in much more jeopardy. She did not even slow the pace as the *trilla* bird came back, landing on her shoulder.

"Hut quarter-mile ahead," the bird announced. "No windows. Door off hinges. Looks dangerous."

"But did you *see* anything dangerous?"

Zolkan admitted that he had not.

"What did you hear?" she asked.

"More human cries, like you made when Gelya died."

Kesira said nothing to this. She faced straight ahead and rode with new determination. If the rising power of the jade demons brought forth unnatural creatures, so be it. She knew her duty. A human in danger required her aid.

She reined in less than a hundred yards from the hut Zolkan had sighted. Rude walls of split tree trunk required caulking. Wind whipped past and produced a mournful whistle in the holes between logs, but it was not this that she and Molimo had heard.

"Help me," came the faint words from inside. "Oh, Rael-lard, why don't you help me?"

Kesira dismounted and tethered the horse to a stubby

tree. Walking the distance to the hut might be dangerous, but she didn't want Molimo any closer than necessary.

"Stay with the horses," she said. "I'll be all right. Zolkan will serve as extra eyes for me."

"Why?" Molimo quickly wrote on his tablet. He erased the word by pressing the clay back into a flat surface, then quickly traced out a new question. "Why won't you let me help?"

Kesira couldn't give the man the real reason, though she knew he sensed it. If it were a human inside, she wanted to take no chances on Molimo shape-changing into a wolf. She had seen what happened when he spotted a helpless soul; that part of him dominated by the wolf spirit demanded the easy meal. Kesira wished the man-wolf was better able to contain the change urges.

"I'll be all right," she said.

"Trap?" he wrote.

"Zolkan will call for you if anything happens to me. No more argument. Stay with the horses. Be ready to ride, if the need arises. But I doubt that it will. Truly, Molimo." She took his right hand in both of hers and squeezed reassuringly.

Kesira saw the hurt in his dark eyes, but there was no easy remedy for it. She turned and walked toward the hut, eyes seeking out the slightest detail to indicate a trap and ears cocked for more of the sounds from within the hut. A steady sobbing came forth now.

Kesira hesitated a few yards from the hut and looked around. From the way the canyon formed, the sounds were caught by the walls and magnified many times over. The echoes bounced about and finally emerged down by the Pharna River where she had heard them. Atop the canyon walls stood lines of scraggly, stunted trees, failing in their bid to survive the inclement weather. By this time of year, the warmth ought to have coaxed them to full greenery, roots powerfully thrusting into rocky soil and seeking out ways of spreading seeds to the surrounding area.

With Ayondela's winter locking the land in a fatal grip, the trees stood like skeletal sentinels.

Around the hut evidence of the discouraging weather was even clearer. A barn, partially burned for firewood, held no trace of the animals that should have been inside.

Kesira guessed that they might have been eaten. What could have been a pleasant pasture stretching back along the canyon was now coated with dead grass, as brown as it had been in midwinter. The slopes of the hills farther back along the ravine hinted at good cropland in most years.

The ordinarily prosperous had become fatal.

Kesira used her staff to open the door even more. The sobbing noise inside stopped, but a new sound replaced it.

A cry, low and choked.

"Who's there?" Kesira called out. She stepped away from the door so that she wouldn't be silhouetted by the weak sunlight behind her. The woman heard muffled noises as if someone covered a baby's mouth to prevent further crying.

Zolkan circled above, sharp eyes watching her. She waved to the *trilla* bird. A squawk combining indignation at this and disgust with her drifted back down.

"I am Kesira Minette, Sister of the Mission of Gelya. Do you need help? Please, I want only to aid you, not harm you."

The cry sounded again. Kesira went through the door into the dank, almost freezing interior of the hut. As wan as the sunlight had been, it was still much brighter than the light within the hut. It took almost a minute for her eyes to adjust.

Kesira found herself staring at a scrawny woman holding a pathetic dagger.

"Get out. Leave us. My husband returns at any time. He'll kill you!"

"Why would he want to hurt me?"

Kesira's calm words did not soothe the woman. She broke down and cried, shudders wracking her frail body.

"How can I help?" Kesira asked again.

"He's been gone for almost a month. A whole month! He must be dead. Or . . . or he's left me." The woman became incoherent, trying to stop her tears and failing. She made tiny hiccuping noises as she moved about and sank down to a thin blanket spread on the floor.

"He's not abandoned you," Kesira said gently. "I am sure there is a reason for hope. Why did he leave?"

"To hunt. The farm's gone. We had to eat the animals

just to survive. Raellard said there'd be no crops this year. He was right. Cold. Always so cold."

"Raellard's your husband?" Kesira saw the woman make one quick jerky movement that she took to mean yes.

The interior of the hut had been stripped bare, everything flammable having been burned for warmth. Kesira heaved a sigh. It was a good thing the roof was constructed of sod or that would have gone also. The log walls were too thick for easy burning or the desperate woman might have tried to cannibalize them too.

"I heard your call for help. When did you last eat? I have some food in my trail kit. It won't be much but . . ."

"Food?" The woman broke down and cried. "I . . . I'm sorry. It's been so long."

"Why didn't you leave with Raellard?"

The woman's dish-sized eyes stared up at Kesira, then darted off to the far corner of the room. Curious, Kesira followed the haunted look.

"A baby!"

"No, leave it alone. Don't touch it," shouted the woman.

"But it's so thin. It's almost starved to death. Can he take some broth? No, I see that he can't. How old is he?" Kesira couldn't guess from the baby's condition. The infant might have been as old as a year—and starved—or newborn.

"He's not human," the woman declared. "Touch it at your own risk. He's evil, evil."

Kesira started to speak, then firmly clamped her mouth shut. The woman had gone out of her head with hunger. The baby appeared ordinary enough, except for the starvation.

"Awful things being birthed in the hills. They come down to our fields and prey on each other. Can't hunt nearby. Dangerous to leave the hut. They want me, oh yes, they want me. Nothing else to eat but me. And they won't get me. I'll show those hideous creatures."

Kesira held the baby close, giving it warmth and some comfort. "When was your son born? Not long ago?"

"A week. Took me that long to find out it wasn't human. It's an other-beast. Wants to devour me!"

Kesira went to the door and saw Zolkan waddling along

the ground just outside. She held the infant up for the *trilla* bird to see. She inclined her head in Molimo's direction to indicate that it was all right for him to approach. The bird squawked in protest at being used as a mere messenger, preened for a moment, then took two cumbersome steps and gracefully became airborne. Kesira went back into the hut.

"There is nothing wrong with your child. He is not a demon spawn. They are permanently locked in twisted animal form. Nor is he an other-beast."

"How do you know?" The woman fingered the knife she still held. "You might trick me."

Kesira saw that the woman was out of her mind with hunger and fear. While she wasn't certain anything would soothe the craziness, Kesira tried soft words and nonsense stories.

"I am a nun of the Order of Gelya. I am trained in such matters." She hoped that the slight quaver in her voice did not betray her. Until Lenc had destroyed her secure home, she had never once seen an other-beast. The rambling stories she'd been told by Dominie Tredlo and others amounted to little more than ghost tales meant to deliciously frighten the small child.

"You can see?"

"I cast the rune sticks and predict what will be," Kesira said, more truthfully. "I also have the talent of 'feel.' "

"What's that?" In spite of herself the woman had become intrigued and some of the madness left her.

"By touch alone I can tell if someone is demon cursed and might become a beast. Your son is not cursed."

"You might be one of them," accused the woman. "Yes, that's it. You are trying to gull me."

Molimo and Zolkan appeared in the door bearing food supplies. The woman cowered, forgetting the pitiful knife in her hand.

"This is Zolkan. As you can see, he is a *trilla* bird from Rest Province. The jungles there abound with them and it is said even Emperor Kwasian has a *trilla* bird as counselor on weighty matters."

"I have heard of such," the woman said.

"She thinks of me as stew meat. How disgusting,"

sniffed Zolkan. He hopped to Molimo's shoulder and used this perch to work his beak over dirtied feathers.

"The other is my friend Molimo. He lacks a tongue and cannot speak, but his heart is good."

Molimo dropped the food and pointed far up the ravine, past the snowy meadows and to the hills rolling away from the Sea of Katad. Zolkan supplied the words. "Molimo says danger comes down the slopes. We go to see."

"Must you leave?"

"Isle of Eternal Winter lies to east and south along coast. If we not back soon, go ahead. All danger to north now. Be wary."

"All right, Zolkan. May Gelya's blessing rest with you, Molimo."

"May Merrisen's," squawked the *trilla* bird.

They vanished from sight, leaving Kesira alone with the woman and her baby.

"Merrisen?" asked the woman.

"He was killed by the jade demons, as were Gelya, Wemilat, and Berura-ko and perhaps others of the demonic rank. A great war goes on for supremacy, a war not even the Emperor can fight."

The woman's hunger-enlarged eyes stared at Kesira. The nun didn't know if her words made any sense to her or if it even mattered.

"What is your name? If I am to help you, it would be nice to know."

"You told me yours, didn't you?" the woman asked. "And the others. You called them Zolkan and Merrisen."

"Zolkan and Molimo," corrected Kesira.

"I . . . I sit down." The woman slumped to her blanket, visibly wobbling about. The light-headedness passed and she said, "It's been three days since I had any food. I melt snow for water since our well's frozen over. Never been like this. Not in my recollection. Name's Parvey Yera."

Kesira almost missed the woman's name in the unconnected rambling. She had placed the baby back in its corner and had started preparing simple fare. She dared not give Parvey too much to eat or it would make the woman sick. Kesira remembered Zolkan's reaction when he had devoured all the greens at the Abbey of Ayondela.

"Gnaw on this," she said, giving Parvey a piece of stale

bread. The woman might have been Molimo wolfing down a portion of a recent kill. She gave the baby a few drops of water but it needed milk, and only from its mother might this be forthcoming.

The tiny fire would not burn for long. Parvey had exhausted all nearby wood but the few twigs were sufficient for Kesira to boil snow into hot water and to make a broth from meat in her provisions. This, too, Parvey slurped up greedily.

"Do you feel better?"

"More."

"Soon," said Kesira. "It'll take a while to fix. Have some more bread while it brews."

"Winter's so cold. Husband can't find food nearby. Baby came a month premature. He's supposed to be back by then."

Kesira had wondered why a man would leave a pregnant woman; this explained it. The cruel grip of winter had never relaxed, thanks to Ayondela. With food running low, the farmer had taken the chance of leaving his wife to bring back supplies, but the baby had arrived earlier than anticipated. It did not seem a pretty picture to Kesira.

"You expect your husband back soon?"

"Raellard's a good man," Parvey said, almost defensively. Kesira did not even hint that he might have gone seeking food and just continued on to Chounabel or Blinn or some other city, abandoning his wife and unborn child. Or that he might have fallen prey to the other-beasts roaming the territory in increasing numbers.

Kesira felt a weariness heavier than ever before settle over her. The suffering brought by the jade demons grew with every new day. Why had they not been content with the old order of things? But some always aspired to more power and the familiar had been disrupted for the ambitions of a few.

"More broth?" Kesira dished it out to Parvey Yera, who drank this with less of a famished air.

"Good."

"And your son? When might he dine, also?"

Parvey stared unseeing into the corner.

"He is human, not an other-beast. He deserves life."

"They came down from the meadows. Where they en-

tered our fields I do not know. They stalked me for days.
Killed one, I did. Rolled a rock down onto it from up there."
Parvey made a vague gesture indicating the top of the can-
yon wall above her hut.

"It is all past. You must look to the future."

"Why are there other-beasts? Where do they come
from?"

Kesira knew that Parvey didn't want a literal answer to
that. Kesira had seen how Molimo had been trapped in the
jade rain as a demon blew apart. That the other-beasts
were the product of demonic ambition wasn't the proper
answer to Parvey's question.

"I was told a tale when I was a very, very young acolyte
in my Order," said Kesira. "There is little truth in it, or is
there only truth? It is not for me to say."

"What story? I remember my mother telling me
stories."

"As you will tell your son," Kesira said, handing Parvey
another hunk of bread.

"Where do they come from?"

"In a time now past," Kesira began, "the Emperor desired a bridge built between two mountaintops so that he
could take his entire court from one to the other without
traversing the treacherous land between.

"The Emperor was a mighty ruler and commanded
many demons. Such power was envied, but because he was
the Emperor none opposed him. He ordered the demons to
build this fabulous bridge, but to only work at night because he found their visages horrible, and he did not wish
to frighten the Empress."

"These were other-beasts?" asked Parvey, her mind
being taken from her own plight.

"All were demons. There were no other-beasts—not yet.
The demons did not like being told they were hideously
formed, but the Emperor's command was not to be ignored.

"The demons toiled for many months, and the work was
still not finished. The task was monumental, even for ones
so skilled and using magicks no mortal might understand.
The Emperor became increasingly angry that they did not
complete their task and threatened them with severe punishment for disobeying his commands. He desired, above
all else, to be able to move from his winter palace to a sum-

mer palace cresting the far peak. Without the bridge to
speed his journey, he might spend most of the pleasant
months in travel."

Parvey, like a small child, sat and shook her head in
wonder at this. The Emperor's command was law. No one
disobeyed. To do so was totally unthinkable.

"What did they do? The demons?"

"Well," said Kesira, warming to the telling of her tale,
"they knew that working only in the darkness of night
would hinder them and keep them from finishing the
bridge speedily. They begged the Emperor to be allowed to
work during the daylight hours. He refused. His command
had to be obeyed exactly.

"One of the demons, more fearful of the Emperor's
wrath than the others, suggested recruiting human workers. The demons argued among themselves over this, but
finally decided to do as the fearful one said when the Emperor began punishing the demons for their failure. And it
was then that the other-beasts were born. The fearful demon placed a curse on the Emperor's human servants so
that they changed into hideous creatures at night. The
Emperor saw them hard at work and believed they were
only demons, unable to recognize them as his loyal retainers. And thus the bridge was finished."

"But the other-beasts," said Parvey. "What happened?"

"The demons were not pleased when the Emperor rode
across the bridge and never once thanked them for their efforts, but because he was the Emperor they were unable to
take revenge on him. Instead, they left the curse upon his
human servants. During the day they remained at the Emperor's side, loyal retainers, but at night they took on the
likeness of the animals and roved the land, seeking their
own revenge for being trapped in such hideous shapes."

"I had never heard this story."

Kesira smiled. She had embellished it a little from when
she heard it as a child. Sister Fenelia had been able to tell
the wildest stories and make them seem plausible to a ju-
venile mind. Then the smile faded as she considered the reality of the world. Molimo was no simple servant seeking
revenge on the demons for being forced to build a bridge
between mountains. Day, night, it mattered little when

the transformation occurred. It was a curse that scarred Molimo's very soul—a jade curse.

"Rest now," Kesira urged. "And when you awaken you'll feel much refreshed. Your son will want his meal then."

Parvey looked apprehensive at this. She still believed in her hunger-induced craziness that her son was an other-beast. Kesira wanted to reason with her, to tell her it made no difference. Even if the baby were an other-beast what might it turn into? It was only a mewling infant, unable to cause any true harm. But Kesira knew better than to even hint that the child might be cursed.

"Rest. All will be better when you have taken the edge off your fatigue."

Parvey lay down and slumped into heavy sleep almost instantly. Kesira went and covered her with the thin blanket. She wondered if this were all Raellard Yera had left the woman, or if Parvey had somehow burned heavier blankets for the brief warmth that they gave.

Kesira picked up the baby and noted its eyes were open. The child was so famished it did not even cry. Bones poked through the skin and made the burden as light as feathers. She doubted the tiny boy would have been able to survive much longer. Her heart went out to him as she rocked the baby to and fro and even slight twitches subsided. She only guessed that the boy slept rather than died.

After returning the infant to its grubby corner Kesira explored the tight confines of the hut but found nothing. The place had been systematically stripped while Parvey had fought for survival. Kesira looked closer at the knife Parvey had dropped and saw that what she had first taken for rust was blood.

Other-beast's blood?

"You are a noble woman," Kesira said softly, "to endure such bitter hardship. As Gelya said, adversity introduces you to yourself. But I only wish that the introduction had not been so lengthy or torturous for you."

Kesira settled down and began her meditations. Reaching inside, she found serenity and renewed her flagging spirit. But before she had gotten halfway through her rituals, a scraping noise from outside brought her fully alert.

Clutching her staff, Kesira rose and turned to the door

just as it was jerked open. She blinked at the sight confronting her. At first she thought it was a compost heap. Leaves and twigs moved as one in a huge mound. But the mound had legs and arms.

And the right arm waved about a spear with a gleaming, razor-sharp tip.

Before Kesira could speak, the mountain of debris lurched forward and sent the spear directly for her heart.

Chapter Seven

"THEY COME DOWN from mountains. We must stop them soon," urged Zolkan, in the shrill singsong speech Molimo understood. "Kesira will not be hurt by any within cabin."

Molimo stared back at the pathetic wood hut and wondered if the *trilla* bird only tried to comfort him. Kesira had found others to comfort and help, but she needed protection. And did not know it.

Where? Molimo directed to the bird. Zolkan spiralled upward and studied the terrain. The grain fields had fallen to hard-crusted snow, with only bare stalks poking through the ice. Heavy tracks crossing the field betrayed passage of the other-beast. Zolkan swooped down, sharp black eyes studying the ragged tracks for the most minute detail, then returned to Molimo.

"Only one. Must be a huge pile of shit. Big enough to eat my lovely tailfeathers." The bird twitched, fanning out his tail, then neatly refolded it behind him.

It stalks Kesira?

Zolkan bobbed his head up and down, then extended a wing in the direction taken by the stalking other-beast. "Changed from human to other in middle of field."

Molimo skirted the deserted grain field, choosing his path carefully. Even though his feet made slight crunching noises as they broke through the thin icy crust of the snow, the wind blowing against his face would muffle such sounds or carry them back down the ravine. His keen nose sniffed the wind, too, for any hint of the other-beast. When the fetid odor struck, Molimo made a face.

"Needs bath. Smells like shit," said Zolkan. "So do we. Long since I properly bathed. Too long. Look at me. A mess. Hungry, too." The large bird stretched its green-feathered wings more than a yard wide and batted them against the breeze. He seemed to hang just above Molimo's shoulder.

No change. Not yet. I now sense when it comes upon me.

"All right," said Zolkan, settling back down to his perch. The *trilla* bird didn't mind not flying; riding on a human's shoulder was far easier and allowed him to sleep. "You get horses and ride after beast?"

On foot. Better this way.

They stalked the other-beast and found it easier than anticipated. The creature had scented Kesira and the woman and child within the hut and had single-mindedly fixed on them as its dinner. It foolishly ignored all else. This proved its downfall.

The burly, lumbering creature emerged from behind a rock near the edge of the ravine. For an approach to the hut, it was well shielded. From Molimo's position, it was exposed and vulnerable.

Zolkan flapped his wings for balance, saying as quietly as he could, "Strong beast. Be careful."

Molimo studied the other-beast and the way it moved. Long, curved arms swung in front of it as it moved on its stubby hindlegs. Patches of its reddish brown fur had been torn away in other battles, and heroic fights they must have been. The vicious talons popping from the heavy paws promised nothing less than instant death to any careless enough to receive a blow. The short black muzzle was lined with broken yellow teeth and deep-set eyes peered steadfastly at its target.

The thick body rippled with fat and muscle—the hunting in this area had not been poor for all. The other-beast lurched forward, talons clicking against stone.

"Molimo?"

Zolkan, it comes on me. The force is too great to resist.

"A blessing, this time. Only your other self can destroy this shit pile monster."

Molimo shuddered and felt the cloak falling from his shoulders. Zolkan took to the air and hovered nearby, working furiously to maintain his position. The jerkin strained in all the wrong places. Shoulders narrowed and arms shortened; muscles became like steel wires. Molimo's nose twitched and hurt him as it elongated.

He snarled and shook free of the mortal clothing. Only his sleek gray coat stood between him and the biting wintry winds. And this was all the wolf needed. A second snarl died on his lips. When hunting he never made a sound to warn his prey. The rugged fight he'd have when he attacked this other-beast would require stealth and cunning—and all the strength locked in his lupine form.

Molimo vaulted easily to the top of a large boulder and hunkered down, waiting.

The other-beast came beneath him, passed his position. Molimo tensed his hind legs, then blasted forth into the air. His front paws raked feebly at the other's back, but his hurtling weight unbalanced his victim.

The other-beast slammed forward, doubling into a furry ball and trying to roll. Molimo's jaws clacked shut; succulent hot juices spurted as his teeth ripped at a heavily muscled arm and prevented those raking talons from ripping his belly open.

As quickly as he had attacked, the wolf danced back, crouched and waiting. The incautious beast opened from its defensive posture. Molimo exploded forward once again, teeth sinking into exposed throat—but the wolf paid the price. One arm might have hung useless but the other's strength was augmented with fear and fury.

One talon ripped at Molimo's flesh and caked his gray coat with his own blood.

Again the wolf danced away, but the fight was now on even terms. The other-beast, though wounded, had the advantage of bulk and power. It reared up and fell forward, almost crushing Molimo beneath its body. Snapping, snarling ferociously now, Molimo rolled free, shaken and unable to retaliate quickly. For the briefest of instants, Molimo had the chance to end the battle. The other-beast exposed the back of its neck to powerful jaws. But Molimo missed and the fight continued.

The wolf retreated steadily in the face of the other-beast's power and would have been backed into a small, rocky box had it not been for Zolkan. The *trilla* bird lanced down from the heavens, picking at ears and eyes, tweaking the bloodied nose, ripping at reddish fur and distracting the other-beast's attention whenever it began its attack on Molimo.

The wolf rested, regained strength, coordinated well with the *trilla* bird. This attack finished their adversary. The other-beast shrieked for as long as air passed through its throat. Then only frothy pink foam gushed forth. It kicked and clawed, but Zolkan and Molimo continued to chase it.

"Dead," said Zolkan. "And about time. My feathers are all dirty again."

The bird landed beside the carcass and waddled over. Zolkan burrowed into the fur and found a warm spot. He sighed, enjoying true heat for the first time in days. Riding on Kesira's shoulder, under the woman's cloak, provided some heat, but in recent days even this had not been enough for the feathered Zolkan.

Its body cools soon in this wind, Molimo told him.

"What does it matter? Nice now."

A wolfish growl came from Molimo. Zolkan poked his head up as the wolf began to rip at the softer portions of meat on the other-beast. In death parts of the creature had returned to human; these Molimo left and dined only on the fatty, animal parts. Zolkan sampled a bit of the flesh and spat it out.

"Your tastes are deteriorating, Molimo," the bird said. "This is awful. Piss-poor meat. Yaaaa!"

Halfway through the bloody feast, Molimo involuntarily shape-shifted back to human. Zolkan sighed and left his warm niche beneath the other-beast's arm. The bird took to wing and swooped down on Molimo's clothing. Scooping them up, the bird returned and dropped them near the shivering human.

"Dress," commanded Zolkan. "Not even demons can save you if you freeze to death."

Molimo wiped his body as clean as possible on the other-beast's fur, then quickly donned the clothing. His flesh had begun to turn bluish white with frostbite.

The wolf's hide has definite advantages to my bare skin, he told Zolkan.

"Too bad you cannot control change—or stop partway. Human with wolf fur. Ha!" The bird crowed at his joke.

It is needed in Ayondela's winter. How many die because of her curse?

Zolkan alighted on Molimo's shoulder and buried his body under the cloak. "Back to Kesira?"

When Molimo didn't answer, Zolkan craned his head around, sniffing, keen eyes studying the dark sky.

North, Molimo indicated. *There is trouble to the north. We must help.*

"Who?"

Toyaga struggles to regain his power. He does not fare well. We can help.

Zolkan nodded. "We can use allies. Even a brass-ass like Toyaga."

Molimo went to where the horses stood tethered. For a moment, he hesitated, thinking to see Kesira again before he rode off. He changed his mind and stepped into the stirrup cup, heaving himself onto the horse's back. The animal protested the weight, then settled down into an easy walk as Molimo turned the horse's head toward the north. To the east, past a line of high hills, lay the Sea of Katad. Behind, the River Pharna emptied into the sea. To the west rose the low mountains forming the other side of this once-lush valley.

But Molimo concentrated on the feelings he had about what lay to the north in a small box canyon. The demon Toyaga rested there, fending off the occasional attacks mounted against him. Toyaga's effort was futile, however. Molimo sensed the gathering strength soon to be applied against the solitary demon. None could withstand those forces, not even a demon.

Scout for us, Molimo commanded. *We need to ride fast, if we are to be of any use to Toyaga.*

"Any other-beasts in air?" asked Zolkan. "I have no wish to be gobbled up by aerial beasts."

Fly, said Molimo. *Let me worry on such matters.*

"Easy enough for you to say," grumbled Zolkan, but the *trilla* bird flew with deft wingbeats toward the north, guided by the diamond points of stars and the cold wind against his face. Soon even Molimo's sharp eyes lost sight of the bird.

Molimo flicked the horse's reins and started across the fields, into the low foothills and farther back into the twisting, turning maze of the low mountains hugging the coastline.

Molimo stood beside his horse, looking down into the canyon. Ragged upjuts of stone rose in their immaculate white raiment. The serenity tore at Molimo, pulling away tiny pieces of his very soul. How could such beauty hide the ugliness he knew was there? Crystalline flakes of snow gleamed through all the colors of the rainbow as sunlight caught the delicate branchings. He turned his view from the tiny to the large. The vastness of the mountains was as rocky arms cast outward to embrace him. At any other time he would have been content simply to stand and watch the eons pass by, marching in step with the geologic changes wrought in the very mantle of the planet.

"Toyaga fights well, but he weakens," reported Zolkan. The green bird landed on Molimo's saddle and looked the man-wolf in the eye. "Think he can help you?"

Can we help him is a more pertinent question, replied Molimo.

"There is only narrow trail down side of hill. Want me to go on and tell Toyaga you come?"

No. Molimo considered the matter from different aspects. *There is no need to warn those attacking him. Let our arrival come as a surprise to them.*

"Not possible. Toyaga battles another demon."

The demon is not of the jade. Her powers are vastly inferior, Molimo pointed out. *Eznofadil corrupts many, and lures Urray astray. She is not evil.*

"Yet," Zolkan amended, "Eznofadil corrupts her and lures her with promises."

He would slay her if she tried to use the jade. There is room for only one jade demon after all is finished. Such power as they seek cannot be divided.

"Ayondela fights only for revenge of her lost son. Rouvin meant all to her." The *trilla* bird took to wing and allowed Molimo to begin the tedious downward trek along the narrow path.

She cared little for Rouvin. This has been building for centuries with her. It disrupts the routine and makes her existence more thrilling. That is all. She lives only for the instant, like a mortal.

"Which she becomes because of the jade."

Molimo said nothing. Zolkan's assessment hit close to the truth. For all Ayondela's increased powers, her life span neared an end because of the toll taken by the jade. Eznofadil and Lenc paced themselves, allowing her to expend her energies. The true conflict would come between those demons—Eznofadil and Lenc—when the world lay hollow and conquered.

He did not want to see that conflict come, nor did Molimo want to see either of the pair emerge victorious and all-conquering. The damage to the world was bad enough without the gaping wounds that would be inflicted by civil war in demonic ranks.

Sounds of conflict came to Molimo's sharp ears halfway down the winding dirt path. At places he dismounted and walked his steed past narrows, taking a maddeningly long time. Molimo sensed the ebb and flow of power beneath him. The fight between Toyaga and Urray raged, and Toyaga was gradually weakening.

"Soon, hurry," urged Zolkan as Molimo gained the bottom of the path. "Not far. Toyaga needs you. Now!"

I know.

The *trilla* bird stopped his singsong speech. To warn Urray might prove fatal. Molimo trotted his horse across the frozen, rocky ground and halted a hundred yards distant. While he couldn't see the actual conflict, the energies flowing between the two demons were more than obvious. Streams of heat rose in thick, shimmering columns, melting snow to water that trickled away to join a small mountain stream. Wary animals came and lapped at the water, then darted away when they saw Molimo.

His full attention focused on the column of heat. At the base of that pillar stood two demons who had once been friends—and more.

"Need me?" asked Zolkan.

Molimo nodded curtly. The bird perched on his shoulder. Together, they approached the battleground. As they neared the titanic struggle, they could see that not only snow had melted. The very rocks turned viscid and tried to flow away from the punishments being exchanged.

Urray might have been attractive at one time. No longer. Her locks hung in thick orange strands that looked more like copper wire than hair. The female demon's body had thickened and huge brown spots dappled her skin. Fingers elongated into talons pointed at Toyaga. Worst of all, the once pretty Urray's face contorted into a mask of pure evil as she strove to destroy her former lover.

"Urray, will it make your lot easier if I simply submit?" asked Toyaga. The handsome demon spoke in measured tones, but rivers of sweat poured from his face and body, mingling with the molten stone at his feet and sending tiny clouds of steam aloft.

"You cannot," Urray screeched. "Or you would have done so."

"I loved you, my dear one," Toyaga said. "I still do. Is my death such a vital matter to you? Have Eznofadil and Lenc seduced you?"

"I see how their power grows. I want it for myself. They are not fit to rule the world. But I am. I will destroy them and pluck the fruits of victory for myself!"

"Vain," grumbled Zolkan. Molimo silenced the bird with a single gesture.

Toyaga had seen Molimo enter the small clearing and dismount; Urray's back was to him. Molimo approached silently, hand on sword. He judged distances, estimated his chances. Whether or not a single sword thrust would kill a demon had never been satisfactorily decided. All Molimo hoped for was to distract Urray enough so that Toyaga might finish the task. It was a desperate act, but it was all Molimo could do. Toyaga was nearing death at the female demon's hand.

"There is nothing wrong with allowing mortals to run their own affairs," said Toyaga. "We were a contented lot, we demons. We had our little intrigues and our grand plans. Why should we add the burden of their petty, fleeting lives to our concerns?"

"Power. I want the power."

"You want the feeling of power, of being important. You could have it, Urray," the handsome demon said. "Look at Lalasa. She has the Emperor's attention. Hundreds of thousands attend her every word. Perhaps millions. I have no way of knowing."

"Think of that magnified, Toyaga," Urray cried. "It will be mine. Now!"

Toyaga fell to his knees. The magicks surrounding him crushed in like jaws of a vise. Urray chortled in glee at her impending victory. She shaped the cosmic forces and brought them together around her victim, squeezing, closing ever tighter around Toyaga.

Molimo stood within sword range of the female demon. The brown spots marring her skin pulsed with the power that used her body as a conduit. Molimo doubted she knew the source of that power or, if she did, even cared. He set his feet for the thrust.

No, not now! he shrieked. Zolkan took to wing, talons slashing at the female demon as Molimo shape-shifted into wolf.

Urray shrieked in rage at being thwarted in her attempt to destroy Toyaga. She spun and sent sizzling waves of heat at the airborne Zolkan. The *trilla* bird squawked in protest as his feathers smouldered and started to burn. Zolkan tucked his wings and dived directly into a pool of water.

Feathers and water rained down on Urray.

And a wolf tore at her throat.

The female demon staggered back, flailing with her taloned hands. Molimo knew better than to retreat. The animal urges were fully upon him, all human control gone.

Long red channels opened on his flanks as Urray raked his sides. And then he fought only thin air. A gauzy haze hung about him until a gust of cold wind pulled it away. The wolf stood, tongue lolling with breath coming in sharp, short pants.

"My friend," said Toyaga, limping toward Molimo. "You have saved my life. In a way, you have not done me a favor. I meant it when I told Urray she could have my very life. Now I must heal and continue the fight against Lenc and Eznofadil." Toyaga sighed. "And even Ayondela, poor, lovely, misguided Ayondela."

Molimo snarled.

"This is a rare affliction," the demon said, placing one hand on the side of the wolf's head. Toyaga jerked the hand away before Molimo snapped it off with a powerful *clack!* of his jaws. "Rather, I meant that it was rare, before . . . before we entered the Time of Chaos."

Toyaga sighed more heavily and sat facing the wolf.

Green eyes bored into him, as if sizing him up for a meal. Toyaga continued speaking, as if he had not a care in the world.

"It is an epoch of our development I have no wish to see. Urray and I have been through so much together, and now she turns on me. Her very flesh boiled with the evil Lenc channeled through her. And she never knew he only used her as a vehicle for his power. Urray was a tool, and an expendable one. But you know that, don't you?"

Toyaga took the wolf's head between his hands and stroked over the gray fur.

"Careful," squawked Zolkan, waddling out of the pool. The *trilla* bird shook and sent water droplets into the air. They hung in space and refracted sunlight, cascading down a myriad tiny rainbows. "He cannot control change."

"I guessed as much. I fear there is nothing I can do to aid him in gaining such control." Toyaga pried open Molimo's mouth and peered within. "The human form lacks a tongue, too. That lies beyond the scope of what I can heal."

"Help him?" suggested Zolkan.

"Yes, but how? What gift can I pass to him that will not attract Lenc and the others prone to abusing the powers given them by the jade?" Toyaga thought aloud, being mindful to stay away from Molimo's sharp teeth.

"Stop other-beast changes," said Zolkan. "Stop them!"

"Sorry, my feathered saviour. That is beyond my powers. I was always the poet among the demons, giving an instant's relief from eternal tedium with a witty phrase or a tart word. Only recently has it been necessary for me to learn to do things like this."

With a casual touch of his hand, Toyaga reduced a rock to dust. He shook his head in dismay.

"A paean to the seasons, a praising of the sun and moon, a glorification of the gentleness as warm winds touch our cheek, those are so much more important to me. Still."

Molimo rocked back on his haunches and stared balefully at the demon.

Can you do nothing?

"Alas, my fellow rescuer, I cannot," Toyaga answered

the plea. "No, that is not so. I might be able to give you one
gift. How does it go? Yes, a ward well against being sniffed
out by evil, magical noses. Something to make you go
unnoticed by them, as if you did not exist.

> The world about me,
> There are no eyes.
> Freedom of the air and sky,
> I fade into nothingness."

Toyaga nodded slowly as Molimo shifted back into human form. "I see that this is far beyond my feeble talents
to stop. But the words for the ward spell. Can you remember them?"

Molimo nodded.

"They protect from being seen?" asked Zolkan.

Toyaga shrugged. "Perhaps. Perhaps it will protect
only from magicks set to detect your presence. I cannot
say for certain. Words and phrases and emotions have
engrossed me for centuries, not such tedious magical
pursuits."

Thank you. Molimo held out his hand.

Toyaga grasped it, then laughed. "Clothe yourself. You
will freeze your pecker off and then what good would you
be to the ladies, eh?"

"Help us," said Zolkan. "We go to Isle of Eternal
Winter. Confront Ayondela."

"I know," said Toyaga. "I felt it within his mind." The
demon stared at Molimo. "Such changes. Perhaps the
Time of Chaos is a good thing. I cannot keep up with the
changes; it is best I step out of the way and let those who
can have their chance. Perhaps the era of demons is over."
A tear rolled down Toyaga's cheek. He quickly brushed it
away.

"I must go to heal, to rest, to lie in repose until the words
fit themselves together. I write an epic poem for the Emperor."

"Jade demons. Help us!" implored Zolkan.

"That would be worthwhile," Toyaga said. "Finding the

proper scansion for the poem is even more so. I wish you luck. It is little enough that I can do for you."

Zolkan sputtered incoherently and started to fly at the demon. Molimo's quick grab snared the *trilla* bird in mid-air.

We will meet again, Molimo told the demon.

Toyaga said nothing. The pity in his eyes spoke more eloquently than words. Then the demon vanished.

Chapter Eight

THE SPEAR DROVE directly at Kesira Minette's midsection. She inclined her staff just a fraction of an inch and deflected the deadly tip. Kesira felt the cold steel near her skin and slice away fabric, but she had escaped injury.

This time.

The woman danced back, getting both hands onto her staff. The pile of leaves and twigs filled the entire doorway, blocking any possible escape. She had to stand and fight.

"What manner of beast are you?" she asked, hoping to distract it. The ploy failed. Again the spear came seeking her heart.

This time the nun was better prepared. Her stone-wood staff parried the haft of the spear, and she spun the other end up and into the midriff of the animated vegetation. The "oof!" that came when she connected solidly told her of the human hidden under all the camouflage. As the man staggered a step back, Kesira brought her staff whirling about and lunged with it. Although she lacked a knife tip like a spear, the hard, rounded end of the staff sank deeply into the leaves.

Mud, twigs, and small bugs flew everywhere. Her adversary sat down heavily, but the spear remained in his hand.

Kesira got out of the confining hut and emerged into the cold, wintry night. Stars gave what pathetic illumination they could through the thin layer of high cirrus clouds, but the moon cast a ghostly, ghastly light that allowed Kesira to see.

Leaves and bits of caked mud fell away from her fallen

attacker. She thought she saw eyes, nose, and mouth through the clinging debris. Human hands and feet stuck out from the compost. And the hand tightened again on the haft of the spear to prepare for another attack.

Kesira stepped forward and brought the staff around in a low arc that connected where the side of the head ought to be. Twigs snapped, leaves crushed, and mud flew in all directions—and the man slumped to the side, unmoving.

"What *is* this thing?" Kesira muttered to herself. She used her staff to flick away the spear, then knelt and tentatively pulled away the cloak of leaves. A thin, not unhandsome face emerged from beneath the grime and caked leaves. Too thin, Kesira thought, but with winter gripping the world in such a deadly hold this was to be expected. Even she was not as plump as she had been when living in the nunnery.

More of the camouflage peeled away to reveal the black and purple bruise growing on the side of the man's head. She ran light, testing fingers over the wound. The man winced but did not regain consciousness. As Kesira continued her examination the leaves and other earth products fell free. Once gone, all that remained was a man dressed in the style of a farmer.

Hip-high leather boots sorely needed tending. The shirt had once been intricately embroidered with scenes of demons cavorting on their way to the Emperor's court, but now hung in tatters, bright threads dulled and broken. The short, heavy mid-thigh pants were totally inappropriate for cold weather but that never stopped the farmers from wearing them. With the high boots, only a few inches of bare, hairy thigh was exposed to the elements.

Kesira examined the spear. The shaft had been well worn by many years of use; the tip was shiny, sharp, and recently manufactured. She peered more closely at it and saw the name of the weapons maker and the faint imprint "Limaden" beneath.

"The Imperial Armorer?" she wondered aloud.

"Aye, it is, and give that back!"

Kesira instinctively swung her staff and connected hard with the man's wrist. The crack indicated a painful blow, but nothing permanently damaging; no bones broke.

"You'll get it back when I am sure you won't harm any of us with it."

"What?"

"Are your ears still ringing from my blow?" Kesira asked. She had seen cases where even a light head blow turned a man's brain to jam. It had not been her intent to addle her compost heap attacker, but if it had happened she wanted to know.

"No, nothing of the sort. I want my weapon back. And an explanation. What do you mean that I'd harm 'us'?"

"You are in no danger," said Kesira, "as long as you do not attempt violence. Till I am sure you are peaceful, I keep your spear." She used her staff to knock him back to a sitting position on the ground. "And I ask the questions. You intruded on us, not the other way around."

"Where's Parvey?" the man demanded. "Is she safe?"

"Parvey?" Kesira said, hoping she put enough query into her voice to get information from the man.

"My wife! Parvey Yera. I'm her husband, Raellard."

"You have a strange way of entering a home," said Kesira. "Do you always barge in, spear thrusting?"

"It's my house, and I do as I please."

She had offended his farmer's sense of possession. Kesira apologized.

"Who are you?" he demanded.

"Kesira Minette, Sister of the Mission of the Order of Gelya."

"Quite a mouthful. What have you done to Parvey? I want to see her." Raellard's eyes narrowed. "She's not been harmed, has she? The baby's not due for another week yet."

"Your son decided to make an appearance early. He arrived last week."

"Last week! *Parvey!*" he yelled. "It's me, Raellard! Get out here this instant!"

"She's been quite ill. Starving, because you left her alone."

"I left because we were both starving. Had to find food."

"You look well enough nourished," observed Kesira. Even through the dirt still marring Raellard Yera, he did not seem to be in as bad a way as his wife or newborn son.

"Hard to hunt and do more than eat it when you've

killed it," he said. "Tried smoking some of it. Got a few tubers and roots I brought back. Enough to keep us going for a few more weeks. Maybe by then the damnable winter'll have let up."

"I doubt it," Kesira said.

"It's enough, if we don't get gluttonish about it."

"The winter," corrected Kesira. "I don't think the winter will ease. I'm sure you brought more than an adequate amount of food back for your family."

"Want to see her." Raellard turned surly. Kesira silently motioned for him to go into the hut. She kept the tip of her staff firmly atop his spear so that he couldn't take it, though. Kesira did not trust the man. But she had to smile, and only through real effort did she keep from laughing, as he made his way to the hut. He left behind a trail of mulch normally seen only in the deepest of forests.

Kesira doubted he would harm Parvey or the boy. If anything, he'd keep Parvey from killing the infant in the mistaken belief he was an other-beast. While Raellard Yera was inside, she went exploring. Following the trail of leaves back down the ravine and around a bend, she saw where Raellard had dropped his burden of foodstuffs. She pawed through the rude canvas bag and saw green, decaying meat and the tubers and other poor viands described. She hefted them to her shoulder, staggered a little under the weight and started back toward the hut.

Raellard Yera blocked her way.

"Stealing my food, are you?" he raged.

"Helping get it to your wife," Kesira said angrily. "Why steal such pathetic fare? I could eat my horse and do better." The horse whinnied in protest from a score of yards away where it stood tethered. "Not that I would," Kesira hastily added. While she couldn't be sure the horse understood, it was best not to take chances.

And she and Molimo had regretfully lived off their steeds before arriving at the Abbey of Ayondela.

Raellard shifted uneasily from foot to foot.

Kesira dropped the bag and said, "Since you're here, carry your own load." She stormed past him, heading to the house. He made a choking noise, then grunted as he picked up the sack and followed. Kesira entered the hut and went to Parvey.

"Are you all right?" she asked the frail woman. "That is your husband?"

"Yes, Raellard came back. With food. Real food." Kesira didn't gainsay this. What Raellard carried in the bag was hardly what she'd consider "real food," but if you're starving anything looks delectable. Kesira stroked Parvey's stringy hair, thinking that a hungry person wouldn't listen to reason or be moved by prayer.

"Here it is," Raellard called, heaving the bag through the door. The bag landed with a *thunk!* in the middle of the floor. The infant began whimpering feebly at the sudden noise.

Raellard stood and stared for a moment, shifting weight uncertainly from foot to foot. He rubbed his lips and finally said, "Do something. The boy's bawling."

"He's hungry," said Kesira. "Only Parvey can do something about that."

Parvey cowered back. "It's an other-beast. It'll change on me and hurt me."

Raellard frowned, a look of concern on his face. Kesira saw that this was beyond his powers to understand.

"The baby is human," said Kesira in the softest, most comforting voice she could muster. "He will not harm you. He loves you. And you love him, don't you, Parvey?"

The woman shook her head and flinched away as the baby cried again.

"Eat some of the good food Raellard's brought and you'll feel better," said Kesira. "Eat and then let your son eat."

Kesira had no desire to intrude. She left the hut and went back into the cold, still night while Raellard fixed a meal of the provender he had scrounged. Kesira stood, arms crossed, trying not to shiver with the cold as she stared up into the now clear blackness of the heavens. Demon lights, someone had called them, but Kesira doubted that.

While the demons possessed powers, creating such artistic limitlessness lay beyond their ken. The demons might be superhuman in many ways, but they were not gods and only a god might form the vista Kesira gazed upon.

She had often wondered why the stars were not more

perfectly aligned, put into patterns, given outlines of distinct and recognizable figures. Sister Dana had told her that the confusion made it impossible to sort out such figures and that this was a mark of inspiration on a god's part—infinity had been created from a handful of stars.

Kesira played the gáme now that she had when Sister Dana told her this. The woman tried to find pictures where none were. Animals, birds—she found a dozen twinkling stars that might have been Zolkan's profile. The thought of the *trilla* bird filled her with uneasiness. Molimo and Zolkan had gone off on their quest without really telling her why they went. She had sensed the presence of other-beasts nearby, but she also felt that this was only a part of why they'd left.

Food? Perhaps. But they could hunt together as easily as apart. She was no handicap and had proven it repeatedly.

Kesira's fingers traced over the bone box containing her rune sticks. If she cast, would it tell her the future? Her skill at this had improved dramatically. When she had lived in the nunnery, her ability had been minimal. Since Lenc had destroyed her patron and her world, the talent had burgeoned. Kesira had no way of telling if her readings were a product of her own skill or if some other force guided her hand, made the cast using her as a vehicle, sent her the interpretations.

"It was to keep warm," came the voice from behind her. Kesira spun, startled. "Sorry. Didn't mean to frighten you." Raellard stopped a few feet away from her.

"I was thinking of other things. It is my fault. What did you mean, it was to keep warm?"

"The leaves and mud. Couldn't get a decent fur off the animals I clubbed. All of 'em were poxy and hairless. The leaves and mud kept me warmer."

"They also served as a home for the insects." Kesira fancied she still saw the bugs crawling over the man's body in an undulating wave of browns and blacks.

"Good with the bad. Life's like that."

"You're not talking about the leaves and bugs now, are you?" Kesira asked.

"No. Parvey. My son. She still hasn't named him, and he's a week old. I told her I'd do it, but she got so upset I didn't say any more. Besides, that's the mother's responsibility. Not my place to even suggest it."

"Is she nursing him?"

"Finally. Not much milk, but then she's been starving herself. Enough food in there to keep her alive for a month."

"But not the three of you for a month," said Kesira.

"I eat more'n she does." The way Raellard said it was neither a boast nor a lament—it was simply stated fact. "Have to go out right away to do some more hunting about."

"And I must rejoin my party. We were traveling to the sea. They went north on a scouting trip."

"Nothing much to the north. Not the way to the sea, not for fifty miles unless you're up to crossing the coastal mountains. Only back down there, the way you came, maybe a day's ride on a horse." Raellard pointed toward the Pharna River.

"I'll be leaving in the morning. You won't have to worry about me interfering. Parvey will be just fine now that you're here."

"Leaving myself," said Raellard. "Can't afford to stay and nursemaid her. We'd both starve if I did."

"You can't just leave her."

"Can't take her and the boy with me, either, now can I? Weather's not so bad now, but another storm's moving in. Feel it in my joints. Stiff elbow always signals bad weather. Killing me now." Raellard held out his right arm and flexed his arm to emphasize the point.

"I may have hit it with my staff."

"Did," he agreed, "but this is a different kind of hurting." Raellard fell silent for a few minutes, then said, "You're good with that stick. Where'd you learn to use it?"

"I'm a nun. When my Order still thrived, I made many trips to Blinn for supplies." Kesira smiled wanly at her use of the word *many*. She had made only a few such trips, but to a young woman free of the confines of a nunnery, each one had been precious in its newfound freedom. Looking back, there seemed more than there actually had been.

"Brigands," said Raellard, nodding. "Had to fight 'em

off." He smiled almost shyly and added, "All the men, too, in this Blinn. Bet you had to fight them off, too."

"Thank you for the compliment," she said. "Truthfully, most of them would have nothing to do with me because I was a nun acolyte."

"Most?"

Kesira laughed. "I found enough who had no fear. Celibacy is not part of my vow to Gelya."

"Never had much time for such things," said Raellard. "The demons, I mean." Kesira wondered if the farmer blushed; she couldn't tell in the pale starlight. "No patron. Never found one that fit into what I believed, one who'd help me out."

"It usually works better patterning yourself to the patron's teachings," she admitted. "There is an order to life then. A system. A knowable pattern. The teachings make it easier to know where honor lies, what your duties are, your place in society."

"My place has been frozen away," Raellard said with a touch of bitterness.

"My friends and I are going to the Isle of Eternal Winter to speak with Ayondela. She is responsible for this prolonged winter. If we can convince her that she has made a mistake, summer might still reach us in time to keep many from starvation."

"Who are these friends of yours? Saw signs of them, but they're not around. Why'd they leave you all alone?"

"To tend Parvey," she said quickly. "And we will meet up again. The separation is a brief one."

Kesira stared down the valley, wishing for Molimo and Zolkan to ride into sight.

"Getting cold. Come back to the hut. Out of the wind."

"Thanks." Kesira started back when a sharp pain doubled her over. She gasped and fell to her knees, clutching her belly.

"What's wrong?" asked Raellard. The man hovered around her ineffectually, not touching her but wanting to help.

"Pain's going away. Been like this for a month or so," she said. "My cycle has turned irregular. Umm, it's easing more."

"Haven't been getting enough to eat," said Raellard. "You're as skinny as a rail."

"So much riding—and fighting," she said. "Those contribute to the problem. But I'm fine now." Sweat beading her forehead, Kesira rose on unsteady feet. The pain had been abrupt, a needle of fire ripping through her abdomen. She didn't push Raellard away when he put his arm around her and helped her to the hut.

"You can't go on alone," the man said. "I'll go with you in the morning. Together. For a while."

"There's no need."

"Owe you something for helping my wife. Parvey's not been right in the head for some time and you didn't have to even stop."

"I had to," Kesira said. "I couldn't let anyone suffer the way she was. Her cries carried all the way to the river."

"Then I can't let you go off feeling sickly like you do. It'll be just for a while, till I find good hunting."

"You must stay with Parvey. For a while until she's stronger. It'll be for your son's sake, too, Raellard. He needs a great deal of care now, being as sickly as he is."

"Shouldn't have come so early into the world," grumbled Raellard.

"But he did. You must stay with them."

"Duty's to see that they're fed. Can't do it here. Growing grain is 'bout all I know and I can't grow in frozen ground."

"We'll talk about it in the morning," said Kesira, having no intention of doing so. She would be off and away while Raellard Yera still slept. She would rejoin Molimo in a day or two and they could continue on to the Isle of Eternal Winter.

Kesira slumped down in the far corner of the rude hut and tried to sleep. She heard the muffled argument going on between Raellard and Parvey and wished she didn't, but there was no way for her to shut out the words.

Or the soft *click-click-click* of talons against the frozen ground outside. For a few minutes, Kesira wasn't sure she heard them. Then she sat up and strained. The pace was slow, sure, a four-footed animal's stride.

"Molimo!"

Kesira rose and went to the door, peering out through a

small crack. Her heart fluttered with joy when she saw a shadow-shrouded sleek gray body sniffing about outside. She pushed aside the door and slipped out.

"Molimo, where's Zolkan? It took you long enough to get back." The wolf wheeled and stared at her, as if he'd never seen her before. The mouth opened to reveal the sharp, flesh-ripping teeth.

"The Emperor take it! An other-beast!" cried Raellard Yera.

Kesira turned and saw the man, spear in hand, ready to cast.

"No, wait!" she exclaimed.

Raellard threw the spear with impressive accuracy. The sharp tip entered the wolf's shoulder; a last-instant twist prevented the point from entering too deeply. The animal vented a yowl of pain and turned angry eyes on Kesira.

"Get inside, damn you," Raellard ordered. "It's one of them other-beasts. Hungry lot will kill anything that moves."

"Don't bother me. Nothing is wrong," Kesira said.

The wolf pounced. She got her arm up and under the furred neck, forcing the snapping jaws away. Hot wolf breath gusted into face and drool dripped onto her arm.

"Molimo, stop it!" Kesira feared that the change had seized his mind and immersed him totally in the animal world.

She heard a grunt and felt the wolf tense. Hot fluids dribbled onto her arms and chest. The wolf rolled off her, kicking feebly. Raellard Yera had retrieved his spear and driven it with savage fury into the wolf's back.

"Broke his spine. Cut clean through it," the farmer said proudly. "But you shouldn't have stood there asking it to attack. Damnedest thing I ever saw."

Kesira paid no attention to the man. She got to her knees and cradled the wolf head in her lap. The sightless eyes studied the stars above. Already the body cooled in death.

"Molimo, no, no," Kesira sobbed.

"This'll feed Parvey good while I'm gone. Wolf meat's not the best-tasting, especially when it comes off an other-beast, but it'll have to do. We all have to make sac-rifices."

Raellard pulled her away from the carcass. Kesira went back into the hut, oblivious to all Parvey said, oblivious to the baby, oblivious even to her own tears leaving cold, wet tracks down her cheeks.

Chapter Nine

"DID TOYAGA HELP?" asked Zolkan. The *trilla* bird fluttered around just above Molimo's head and caused a severe downdraft from his wings that made the man duck and dodge.

Who can say? I feel no different. The changes still come upon me, and I can do nothing to stop them.

"Pity. Toyaga can be such a fool. Always mumbling his shit-pretty words. Had hoped he might give you release."

His ways are different, admitted Molimo. *But he is not a fool.*

Zolkan did not answer. He rose higher, and Molimo escaped from the cold winds gusting down at him. The dark-haired man sat in his saddle and peered out over the land. Such beauty, he thought, and it had been blighted. For the depths of winter it was beautiful. Snow banked gently along the north sides of low hills and shone with a brilliance in the weak sun that made him squint. The crisp, cold air invigorated even as it sapped the heat from his bones, but Molimo withstood it more easily than either Zolkan or Kesira might.

Kesira.

His thoughts turned to her. By now she would have found her way back to the Pharna River and might even have reached the Katad. From there it was but a short journey along the coast to the prominence from which the Isle of Eternal Winter was visible. Crossing the sea to reach the Isle might prove dangerous, but Molimo failed to see one single moment of the journey south from the Quaking Lands that hadn't been. Even before, before they had left Howenthal's castle.

Every instant had been dangerous.

The battle with Nehan-dir and those following the banner of the Steel Crescent had been deadly. Wemilat had died. A kind and good demon, dead. For him Molimo mourned. And for Toyaga and the others.

Even for himself. He felt the urge to cry out, to shriek his name and listen to the echoes along the canyon walls. The hills would turn afire with his words and sear off this accursed winter brought by Ayondela.

Only tiny squeaks emerged from deep in his throat. The ripped-out tongue would never be healed, not in this lifetime. The jade rains had seen to that. He turned cold inside thinking of his fear as the molten jade had pelted his skin. Then he had been able to cry out in rage and pain. And he had.

A guttural growl now escaped him, the closest to an expression of stark anger he could voice.

"Feel stirrings?" came Zolkan's words from above. "Weak, ever so weak. But not far." The *trilla* bird let loose a string of curses that captured Molimo's full attention.

He sniffed the air for spoor, listened to the tiny slithers and crunches and snaps of moving wildlife about him, even experienced a slight drop in the temperature of the air moving across his face. But he sensed what Zolkan had seen with his eyes through an inner discipline that even the jade rains sent by Lenc could not extinguish.

Former power is not far, he told Zolkan. *I cannot get an understanding of what sort of power, though. It might be anything—and it is long gone.*

Zolkan's atonal complaints showered down on him from above. The *trilla* bird refused to ignore this.

We go to explore, Molimo said tiredly. *Then we leave immediately to rejoin Kesira.*

"You care for her, don't you?" the bird cawed.

My feelings are complex, as always.

"Don't give me that pigeonshit," said Zolkan. "She is a good woman."

She follows Gelya's teachings faithfully. She is honorable and shoulders her responsibilities, as is her duty.

"You love her, don't you?"

That path leads only to disaster for us all. You know the reasons why it cannot be.

"There is nothing to lose, not now," said Zolkan. "If we convince or defeat Ayondela, curse is lifted. If we don't, what's to lose?"

The battle is against Ayondela, Molimo said slowly, considering every aspect of the confrontation to come, *but Eznofadil is at the heart of the fight. He drives Ayondela, he goads her on, he is the source of the woe befalling us.*

"I gathered as much from Toyaga," said Zolkan. "Eznofadil uses Ayondela as peasant-minor in his game of conquest."

No peasant piece was ever so powerful. Ayondela is a major participant, at least a vassal-superior on this board.

"Is the Emperor piece in jeopardy?"

Molimo nodded. The jade demons' power grew daily, and he saw only small segments of their overall plan. Lenc was cunning in recruiting others to do his work for him. Whether that came from the jade turning his very flesh to stone, Molimo did not know. He did know that Eznofadil had always been cunning. None of the other demons played the strategy game as well.

The twitching within his skull alerted him. He kicked at his horse's flanks and urged the animal up a small incline and into a heavily forested area on the hillside. His every sense strained for a trap. The other-beasts saw nothing wrong in attacking those of their own kind.

Even one such as I, he said ruefully.

"What about you?" came Zolkan's muffled words. The tree limbs hid the sky and muffled the *trilla* bird's words.

Nothing. It lies ahead.

"I see shrine. An open-air rock altar. Old, very old. Predates even shit-eating demons and crotch-scratching humans."

You are so eloquent, Zolkan. Why do you not speak to me the way you do to Kesira?

"She is offended. Can I hide my origins from you? Old Garbgo sailed too long with me. Stole me from birthing nest when I was only chick. All life spent listening to him as he sailed coast along Rest Province."

The heat rises from the altar. I feel it almost as if it were physical.

Zolkan did not reply. Even the flap of wings disappeared. Molimo knew the bird flew on to scout the area for

traps. As acute as his own senses were, the aerial reconnaissance provided by the bird proved invaluable. Many of
the other-beasts lost large portions of their human intelligence and forgot to hide from all possible pryings. Zolkan
spotted them easily.

The demon spawn were harder to trap or trick into revealing themselves. They were permanently locked into
their deformed bodies, the product of intercourse between
demons and animals. Molimo's gorge rose at the thought of
such perversion, but he was in no position to pass judg-
ment. Ayondela and a human had mated to produce Rouvin, a half-human, half-demon warrior of honorable deeds
and a needful death.

Molimo licked chapped lips as he thought of Rouvin. The
transformation had come upon him too quickly to warn
Kesira—and Rouvin had not known he walked shoulder to
shoulder with an other-beast. Molimo had shape-shifted
and ripped the warrior's throat out before Rouvin's blade
cleared its sheath. That the death had freed Wemîlat and
eventually led to Höwenthal's downfall did not absolve
Molimo's guilt in the matter.

He could not control the transformation in his body; he
had slain Rouvin. Those were the facts. As it was a fact
that Ayondela's rage froze the world.

The altar in the small clearing promised Molimo surcease from his uncontrollable affliction. While he doubted
he could reverse the effect of the jade rain upon his body,
Molimo did believe he might better control the change
when it occurred. With the energies locked and dormant in
this altar, he might be able to prevent unwanted transi-
tions from one form to the other.

Molimo dismounted and tethered his horse at the edge of
the wooded area. On foot he approached the altar. The
stillness enveloped him like a warm, gauzy blanket. No
wind. No sound. No odor, however faint. Each step he took
made him think he moved that much closer to the end of
the universe. Molimo wondered why no one had ever spoken of this place before.

He stood and stared at the rude stone block that served
as an altar. Faint dark brown stains marred the sides; the
top had been scoured clean by eons of wind and rain. The
slow march of seasons, hot to cold, cool to warm, had

cracked the stone and left fissures thick enough for a knife blade to penetrate. The living heart of the stone lay within.

Molimo stepped up and laid the palms of his hands on the surface. The stone warmed him in spite of Ayondela's winter. He closed his eyes and reached deep within himself.

. Faint tendrils tried to touch him, to stroke the most afflicted parts of him. Then they vanished in the mist and left him as he had been.

There must be power given if power is to be received, he said. *Life must be exchanged for life.*

In the forest Zolkan squawked. He turned and saw the *trilla* bird perched on a thick tree limb just above where he'd tethered his mount. Molimo did not ask. He knew that the bird could come no closer. Faint though it was, the vestigial power of the altar kept Zolkan away.

With some reluctance, Molimo lifted his hands and backed away from the altar. He left the zone of silence surrounding it and again heard and felt and smelled the world.

"It still lives," said Zolkan. "Cannot get too close or burn me alive."

There are only embers, explained Molimo. *But it might help me to fan those embers into a fire.*

"Whose altar?"

Molimo shook his head. He had no knowledge of any before the demons with power to command such as this. But that did not mean they had not existed. Molimo considered what he was about to do and worried; it might be an error to bring back those who had left. Already the jade demons caused woes throughout the world. What might these spirits do if he resurrected them?

Zolkan read his face accurately. "Death now, death later, what difference? We all die eventually. Even demons."

The mortals call demons immortal, mused Molimo, *but this is not so. Demons merely live extended lives. As in all things, this human trait is only magnified and lengthened and augmented.*

"Their deaths are that much more spectacular," pointed out Zolkan. "To die nobly." The bird shivered. "I prefer to die quietly and not disturb my inherent beauty." Zolkan spread his wings and postured for Molimo.

Molimo shuddered and started to loosen his cloak, jerkin, and trousers. He barely got them off before his body flowed and twisted and grew and diminished, turning him into a sleek-furred wolf with snapping jaws and blazing green eyes.

"Change is slowed. Your control improves," said Zolkan, keeping high on the denuded tree limb to prevent the wolf from dining easily at his expense.

Molimo skirted the frightened horse with its kicking hooves and ran into the forest, more alive than before. His senses heightened. Every movement thrilled him; every odor burned in his nose. He longed to savor the coppery heat of a fresh kill's blood. Muscles responding smoothly, Molimo ran through the woods and rejoiced in the hunt.

A rabbit fell to his quickness. Four *prin* rats. A smaller gazelle. Molimo caught and maimed them all, careful not to kill. His almost human part fought the animal urges to rip flesh from the bones and dine on the tough, stringy flesh, even as that same part tormented itself over the creatures' sufferings.

While he was stalking another rabbit, Molimo shape-shifted back to human. He skidded along the dirt on his face, the ice and rocks cutting his chest and belly. Painfully, he lifted himself up and brushed off the freezing dirt. The rabbit had stopped and now peered at him curiously, unsure why it still lived. The rabbit's ears came up and swiveled around in wonder. The wolf had vanished. All it found was a clumsy human.

Slower, as grateful for miracles as a rabbit can be, it hopped off to return to its burrow. Foraging could wait till evening. It needed to recover from the fright it had received.

"Clothes," Zolkan said. A cascade of Molimo's clothes came from the sky. The bird swooped and landed deftly. It waddled around and pecked at the smell-weed and other hearty plants thrusting through the thin, icy crust coating the earth.

That will make you sick. Stop eating it, Zolkan.

"Dress. I only sample. It tastes terrible, anyway." The bird spat out tiny pieces of the smell-weed. Molimo donned his clothing and looked around. The world had changed on him. No longer did he view it from a height of two feet.

"Game still kicks back there where you mutilated it," said Zolkan with some disgust in his voice. "Clean kills are better."

I need living creatures.

Zolkan said nothing to this. He flew off and perched on the tree limb again, once more viewing all that happened within the small clearing. This time his expression, if the beaked face could show such, was only of disdain.

Molimo lugged the carcasses of the living animals and placed them on the altar. All about him he felt the stillness that had been present before, but now came a tension unlike anything he'd experienced previously. Molimo arrayed the creatures on the stone block and stared at them. No ritual came to his lips; none would have worked.

"Get it over with," urged Zolkan. "It will be night soon enough and I have no desire to be caught here in darkness."

Molimo ran his forearm across his dried lips. He stared at the animals and then did what was necessary. His sword flashed. One head, two, all. Life fluids returned to the stone, seeping into the cracks, seeking out the heart of the altar.

The curious bubble of nothingness he stood inside began to hum and vibrate with subdued energy. Molimo widened his stance, sword still clutched firmly in hand. Unseen beings brushed his elbows, touched his face, toyed with him.

What are you? he asked.

No answer.

Ghostly, almost-living veils fluttered before his eyes, nature spirits returning to a joyful existence after slumbering for untold years. The stone of the ages took on a vibrancy unlike any stone Molimo had seen. The blood had ceased flowing from the animals' bodies, but the stone took up a heartlike beat. Pulsations rippled from one side to the other. Molimo did not find this alarming, but it definitely unsettled him.

What have I returned to life?

—Nothing.

What are you?

—Spirits. Of trees. Of grass. Of life itself.

They spun around Molimo, ethereal fingers touching his body, yearning to be whole once more. The animal blood had revitalized long-forgotten nature spirits. They took on more substance, and he made out their silhouettes. A small bush shook feathery white leaves to the ground, then vanished. A larger tree poked its limbs to the very sky, only to falter and evaporate like burned-off fog. A small rabbit coalesced and stared accusingly at Molimo. He did not recognize the animal, but guessed it might have been one he recently killed. It started to hop away; its feet sank through the ground. The rest of the body dissipated, smoke in the wind.

Can you give me the power I seek?

—We have returned, for a moment, but it is a sweet moment.

Help me!

Mocking laughter rang inside Molimo's head.

—You who are so powerful, you who still hold possession of your corporeal body need our help?

Molimo sank to his knees. His hands reached for the altar. The warmth he had found there before now almost burned him, but he did not flinch away.

For this brief moment, aid me. Please.

.—We can only try.

Molimo sucked in his breath when he felt lacy tendrils stroking over his face. The altar grew even hotter, a griddle for his flesh. Ghost fingers pressed his hands down to the stone. The pain lancing up his muscular arms and into his brain activated the transformation—and the change was aborted.

I did not change! he exulted. *Give me the power to hold back the shape changes. Please!*

Again he groaned as pain assailed him. The change to wolf began, then reversed. He retained his human form. Molimo dug down inside himself to find the mechanisms causing the change, the trigger that turned him beastlike, the trigger to be avoided.

—We weaken. This is strong. You are strong.

Try. Help me. I beseech you.

The spirits fluttered around him and began appearing and disappearing with increasing regularity. He saw small animals and large. Their spirits remained long after their bodies had been devoured by hunters, both human and nonhuman, to roam the woods seeking release or rebirth. They had found neither over the millenia.

Molimo allowed them to show him the corridors of his own mind and body, to examine spots hitherto blocked to him. But they could not give him the key to permanently lock his metamorphosis. Molimo railed at the idea of coming so close, only to fail. He fought and struggled, implored and cajoled them for help.

—You are mightier than the last who sought our aid.

Another has walked this path?

—A warrior named Piscaro.

Molimo had heard the legends of this mighty human warrior. He had died in service to the Emperor more than five hundred years ago. Songs told of his bravery and devotion to duty, soldiers raised their sons and daughters with his every deed ingrained so that they, too, might become great. And none dared speak evil of him, even to this day.

—He was a coward, before he came to this altar.

Molimo blinked in surprise. The spirits entering and leaving his body sensed his confusion.

—Before he summoned us, he was a weakling. In exchange for the life he imparted to us all too briefly, we gave him a part of us, a spirit indomitable and unbreakable.

His courage is legend.

—His courage comes from nature, a part of all that we are, a part of all that has been and has died.

Molimo continued his inner battle for domination over the jade-imposed shape alteration to wolf. He groaned and let the spirits aid him, but their help grew weaker and weaker. Molimo came no closer to conquering his problem.

Why do you hold back?

—You do well.

Molimo tried to lift his hands from the altar. This was not the same spirit that had come to him before. A different one, one of blackness and not light now seeped through him.

What are you? You are not the same.

—How astute.

The blackness welled inside him, forcing away the control he had so painstakingly learned. The spirits now boiling around him were of decay, of evil, the otherness of death that opposed life. The blood offering he had given to the altar no longer held the nature-life spirits.

Nature-death drew closer to him.

Away! Get away from me.

—When you summon a part, you summon the whole. Their time with you is past. Now comes our turn.

Molimo's battle became one of escape rather than self-understanding. The evil forces had almost tricked him into lowering all his defenses, as he had done for the other spirits. The altar turned cooler under his hands; the changing of polarities had occurred, but Molimo found himself unable to pull back and leave.

As surely as he had been held before, the power of death held him and sucked at his body and soul.

—You are a strong one. You will make an excellent addition to our rank.

No! I fight the jade power. I cannot give in to you.

—Piscaro did.

But the fainter voice of the life-spirit came. —Piscaro successfully fought and escaped. Do the same while you are able. Now. Fight, now, now. . . .

Molimo had watched as Kesira meditated, had gently touched her soul as she sank into the calm oceans of her deepest thoughts. He duplicated all the nun had done, found solace, found strength.

He slowly removed his hands from the frigid stone altar. Molimo was aware of the inky clouds enveloping him, but no worry tainted his thoughts. He was strong, he had his duty to do. Honor demanded that he face Ayondela and tell her of his responsibility in the death of her son.

The black spirits drew closer when they sensed his part in Rouvin's death.

Molimo rose to his feet.

He saw Zolkan wildly flapping in the tree, signalling to him to retreat. Unhurried, composed and able to hold darkness at bay, Molimo stepped away from the altar.

—You cannot leave. Please. Return. It will be long centuries before another comes to us. We want only to live again.

We all entertain hopeless fantasies, Molimo said. *This is yours. Rest in peace.*

He took another step. The tension around him mounted. Another step and another. The black tendrils slipped from his arms and legs and mind. With measured step, he returned to stand under the limb where Zolkan awaited impatiently.

"Evil. All around, evil. I feel it. My feathers fall out from it. I pile up shit under limb from fear for you."

Thank you, Zolkan. We can go.

"You got what is needed?"

Molimo only shook his head. The evil spirits had come as he felt control within his grasp. Now, he just did not know. But Molimo doubted he had full control over his shape alterings.

If nothing else, he had gained some insight. But would it do him any good if he found himself again locked within a wolf's body?

Molimo ducked the low branches of a tree and guided his horse to a more open trail. With luck, they might rejoin Kesira within a few days.

Chapter Ten

"KILLING THAT WOLF was a lucky thing," said Raellard Yera. "Keep Parvey in food for a while. Give her a warm blanket, too, even if'n there's not much time to cure the hide."

Kesira said nothing. She was too sick inside. The thought stuck in her mind and stung like a nettle: Molimo is dead.

"Don't think it was one of them other-beasts, either. This one looked to be well fleshed. Good body fat. Wolf meat's never been one of my favorites, neither for me nor the Emperor, but in this accursed weather, anything'll do, isn't that so?"

Kesira numbly nodded. She had grown to love Molimo. Not because she had nursed him back to health or because he carried the awful afflictions of the jade rain, but for his courage, his devotion, his sense of honor.

Molimo is dead. Feeding a woman already crazy with malnutrition. The winds felt colder to Kesira, the air a little more humid and stifling, the white snow too intensely brilliant, the world a grimmer place than it had just a few hours earlier.

"You all right? Not said a word."

"I have little to say, Raellard. Just meditating," she lied. "Performing the rituals was an important part of the Order of Gelya. But our patron's gone. All that remains of him are the teachings. And the ritual."

"Doesn't seem like much."

"No, it doesn't."

Kesira kicked at her horse's flanks and urged the mare to a faster walk. Being on foot, Raellard had to pump hard to keep up, but the man said nothing. His breath came more heavily now with the exertion. Kesira knew she punished him unfairly, but she didn't care.

Now and again her tear-fogged eyes turned to the perfect wintry clearness of the sky. She looked for some sign of Zolkan, the green of his feathers against the azure sky, the sound of his impassioned squawks as he protested some minor indignity to his feathers or his belly. Only the razor-slashing wind filled the day.

"Getting colder," observed Raellard. "Good to exercise hard. Keeps me warm."

Kesira reined in a little and slowed the pace to one that the man could more easily maintain. "Sorry," the nun said. She stared straight ahead, her cold-thickened fingers working over the blue knots in the cord around her waist. Occasionally Kesira touched the gold sash and resented the burden it placed upon her.

She might be the sole surviving—practicing—member of her Order. If Gelya's teachings were not to die, she had to recruit, to proselytize, to establish a new mission. Her Sisters in the nunnery were dead by Lenc's jade hand. Those in Chounabel had been seduced away from Gelya by the lure of the city and the mistaken belief that the Order had died with the patron. She was alone now in her faith.

Alone, without Molimo.

"I done something wrong. That's it. What was it? You don't want me along to chase off brigands? What is it?"

"Nothing, Raellard. I already told you that."

"More'n nothing. You were almost damn cheerful when we first met. You had fixed up Parvey and the boy. Now that you're away from them and with me, you don't make no more noise than a stalking leopard. Can't say that's nothing, now can I?"

"My journey seems destined to end in failure," she said. "I had a very fine ally, the son of Ayondela and a human warrior. He died. The demon freed by his death also perished. Now I . . . I fear for my friends who went to the north. I don't think they will return." A tear ran down her cheek, threatening to freeze against her skin.

"Why you want to talk to Ayondela? She's a crazy one. Always thought that, even when the weather was running warm."

"You know, then, that this is her curse for her son's death?" Kesira's wave encompassed the white countryside. In the distance, swirling above the Yearn Mountains, harsh black storm clouds were preparing another load of misery. Summer would be postponed still another week when that storm swept down the mountain slopes and across the Roggen Plains. Cities would be buried under the snow and the Pharna would freeze even more solidly, if that was possible.

A wink of vivid blue-white lightning confirmed Kesira's fear that this storm would be worse than the ones preceding it. Ayondela's power and wrath grew with every passing day.

"You able to deal with Ayondela all alone?" asked Raellard.

"I must. That seems to be the destiny cast for me. It is certainly my duty."

"Might be other people who'd follow along with you."

"You, Raellard? Thank you, but I can't ask that of you."

"You took care of Parvey, and you didn't have to."

"Gelya taught that kindness spawns kindness. But it is my burden that I cannot let people suffer, if I am able to help. I wanted nothing in return."

"Want to help, though. However I can."

"Escort me to the river, then go hunting for more food. In that you will have repaid me. Take care of Parvey and your son. Perhaps seek out a mission and ask after Gelya's teachings. There can be no better payment for me than that."

"Parvey's always been off in the head," Raellard said unexpectedly. "Even before. Before she got the notion the baby's an other-beast." The man scratched his stubbled chin. "You don't suppose she can be right about that, do you?"

"The son is yours."

"Don't know. Parvey's crazy. Might have taken up with a demon wandering by or even some weird creature out stalking around in the woods. Never could understand her."

"You're saying you don't think you're the baby's father?" Kesira frowned. This was a serious allegation. The sanctity of family ranked only under loyalty to the Emperor as a basis for their society. And even then . . .

"She's the mother, there's no doubting that. But I been gone lots trying to find food or something to hunt. The times I was back might not have been enough. Three others have died stillborn. It's a good piece of land I farm, but there's not been much other luck."

"Wait," Kesira said, coming fully alert. She had been away from her nunnery long enough to develop the feel Molimo referred to as "trail sense." Something stalked them.

"Can't say I mind you being skeptical on this," said Raellard.

"Quiet. Someone is behind us, hunting us."

Raellard fingered the worn shaft of his spear and looked around nervously. "Hate this. Don't mind it when I'm doing the hunting, but when they come after me, by all the demons, do I hate it."

Kesira used her superior height to slowly survey the terrain. They had left the hillier section where Raellard had his farm and reentered the ravine leading to the Pharna River. The bends in the ravine precluded spotting anyone behind. Kesira saw enough of the tall, stony banks to know they were relatively safe from attack in that direction. But ahead? The same problem lay ahead as behind: no visibility through the twists and turns.

"Let's step it up," suggested Raellard. "Might outpace them."

"Or wear ourselves out," Kesira said. "They might be herding us into a trap."

"Up the bank?"

"Why not?" said Kesira, not seeing any better solution. This would give them the advantage of high ground and increased ability to watch their surroundings.

The idea was fine, but Kesira had difficulty getting her horse up the steep bank. The ground had turned brittle with frost and broke under the horse's weight. Tiny avalanches showered them with stones and ice and left no easy way up.

"Go on," said Kesira. "You scout. I'll stay here with my horse and wait."

"We're not splitting forces. The only strength we have

lies in guarding one another's back. If you're right about going into a trap, they'll hit us from both directions."

"I might be wrong. There might be nothing—or just a solitary beast stalking us."

"Never go against a hunch. Besides, you said you have the ability to read runes. Might carry over into seeing the future without the sticks, don't you think?",

"Since the jade power came over the demons, it takes no seer to know that danger is everywhere." Kesira sighed, thinking of the lost innocent days past. She had traveled unescorted to Blinn. The occasional brigand proved little problem, and there had never been other concerns. Not like now. Not like it had been since the jade released half-creatures and demon spawn and held an entire world in icy bondage.

"Might backtrack and take it by surprise," said Raellard.

"Better to find a good place to make our stand and wait it out, whatever it might be."

"Here looks good to me." The man stared at the tall banks Kesira's horse had been unable to scale. Those provided a measure of lateral protection. From either direction they had an unobstructed view of almost fifty feet. This would prevent anything from creeping up on them unseen. "Just a matter of how long we wait."

"Not long," Kesira said.

They stood back to back, tension growing. No attack came. Kesira knew she might have been wrong. Her worry over Molimo's death might have confused the growing awareness of her surroundings. She found out how astute her feeling had been when the attack came—not from the floor of the ravine but from above, along the ravine's lip.

The first hint of danger came as snowflakes fluttered down wetly. Kesira brushed them away and stared at the cloudless sky, wondering where they had come from. The sight of the dirty snow heap rearing up brought an involuntary scream to her lips.

The heap lumbered to the edge of the ravine and launched into the air, falling directly for her. Kesira felt Raellard shove her to the ground. Only vaguely aware of all the man did, she cowered, sobbing. Wetness exploded around her. At first she thought it was blood, then saw it was melting snow.

Kesira rolled over, gripping her stone-wood staff, ready to rush to Raellard's aid. The man stood stupidly, the butt end of his spear firmly planted in the rocky soil of the ravine bottom. All around him lay fresh patches of fluffy snow.

"It vanished. It touched the tip of my spear and turned into a blizzard. Never seen anything like that, never, never."

"There's another!" Kesira cried. She struggled to her feet, staff protecting her head from anything thrown from above.

The mound of snow burst out into the air. Again, when it touched the tip of Raellard's spear, it blew apart in a frenzy of tiny eddies that whipped dirty snow around and deposited fluffy white banks. They stood knee-deep now.

"Let's get away from this spot. Whatever these snow creatures are, they aren't dangerous. But my feet are getting frostbitten." Kesira kicked free of the snow and found walking difficult.

Raellard destroyed another of the odd entities.

"Not like anything I ever saw."

Another hurtled downward and blasted apart around the pair. The snow banked up waist deep. Then it flowed, shifted by the wind, and came to mid-chest. Kesira fought against it. She saw the edge of the tiny snow field and wanted nothing more than to escape, but the hard gusts of wind kept blowing the snow against her, stopping her, holding her in the center of the heap.

"There's no demon cursed wind blowing!" shrieked Raellard. "I just saw there's none and yet more snow moved against me." The man thrashed furiously in a vain attempt to get free of the snow.

Kesira started to panic, then caught herself. Using the mind-settling techniques taught her over the years, she kept her composure enough to study this bizarre phenomenon. Another of the snow creatures fell heavily on top of them. She and Raellard were up to their necks now.

"They attempt to smother us," she said. "We must get to the edge."

"Trying. Can't move my arms all that good. Feet are

damn near frozen." He flailed about wildly and got nowhere.

More wet snow pelted down on them. Kesira barely kept
her head above the top of the snowbank. Another creature
and they would be totally buried. She moved her arms and
legs slowly, thinking to escape by slow inches. She had to
admit this was the best scheme because she made headway—but it wouldn't work. Another of the creatures
crashed down and plunged her into total darkness. Kesira
heard Raellard's muted groans and knew their time was
limited unless they somehow drove off the snow forming
their burial tomb.

Something nibbled at her mind. Drive off the snow. But
if the snow was somehow alive and endowed with rudimen-
tary intelligence, how could she do such a thing? These
were predatory animals. Of snow—and magic—but still
predatory.

Kesira drove her staff directly up into the snow above
her head. She began wiggling it and formed a tiny chim-
ney to admit the air. Through the snow tunnel she saw a
circle of blue sky. Not much, but enough to keep her going.
Failure came, not from physical weakness, but weakness
of the spirit.

Kesira Minette was strong.

She started digging for the blue sky and found another
blanket of white laid down. Again she poked her staff
through and got the air flowing, but she was that much
farther from her goal.

There had to be another way of escaping the deadly, cold
embrace of the snow.

Kesira reached down and found the pouch beneath her
robe. In it she carried the bone box with her rune sticks,
and the tiny vial of white powder for starting fires.

"Can't go much more," she heard Raellard cry. The muffled words told more than anything else. He was buried
and would soon suffocate. He might have only minutes—or
seconds—of air left.

Kesira did not hurry or fumble. Her movements were deliberate, precise. Her numbed fingers balked but she drove
them to their task. The glass vial of powder came into her
trembling hand. But what could she use for fuel?

The gold sash around her waist had been soaked, but it

was all she had easily available. She tied this to the end of her staff. Forcing it as far away from her face as possible, which amounted to little more than a foot, she poured the volatile powder onto the gold ribbon. Another mound of snow closed the air hole above.

Praying to her lost Gelya for patience, Kesira worried open a new hole.

The sash burst into flame. She winced, the sudden heat searing her eyebrows and hair. Swinging the staff away from her face the best she could, she felt the snow melting. Cold trickles ran down her body, inside her robe, over her face.

At first Kesira thought the tiny whimperings she could hear came from Raellard. Then she realized it was the snow beast, sobbing in agony because she melted its flesh.

Gaining a small chamber in the snowbank allowed her some small degree of movement. Kesira thrust the burning sash up and opened a tunnel to freedom. She scrambled up it, cutting toeholds in the snow as she went, using the burning sash to fend off more snow creatures throwing themselves to the top of the snowbank.

Gasping in the clear air, she settled to hands and knees, the staff stuck in the snow. The torch end blazed merrily as it fed on the air. She wiped away soot and water from her eyes and saw a spear tip poking through the snow a few feet away. Kesira wasted no time melting away the snow around it to reveal a cold and frightened Raellard Yera.

"Get out of there," she ordered. "The torch might go out at any instant."

Raellard scrambled to safety. A new blanket of snow fell around them, but the fire cut through its center and left them unharmed.

"Never seen beasts like that. Nothing but damned snow, but it was alive," muttered Raellard, backing away from the tiny mountain of snow in the center of the ravine. The snow left behind after Kesira's fiery attack began to flow together, a thing alive. It lumbered toward them, but Kesira held it away with her torch.

"Get my horse. Lead her down the ravine. We can outrun this thing now that it's lumped into a huge mound." She made tentative thrusts at the snow creature, but it had already lost interest. It began to split into smaller piles of snow, which moved off with a curious folding motion: They heaved up, fell down and flowed over the part on the ground. Repeating the motion provided slow but sure progress.

And that progress took the snow creatures away from Kesira and Raellard.

"They had enough, from the looks of it. So've I," admitted the man. "Never liked snow overmuch, and now I know why."

Kesira extinguished the burning sash by covering it with sand from the ravine floor. She hadn't wanted to ruin her symbol of her Order, but it had saved her life. Gelya had taught that only life brought hope; being dead availed no one of anything.

"It's not burned," said Raellard, more curious than frightened. He scratched his head and peered at her as if she had performed the miracle herself. "But I saw it burning."

"As did I. Gelya might be dead, but faith in his teachings works miracles," she said. "Minor miracles, but still evidence that all might again be well."

Kesira fastened the unharmed sash around her waist and motioned for Raellard to hurry. The man needed no second urging.

They traveled down the ravine, taking the left branch at every juncture for the rest of the day. By nightfall, they had reached the banks of the Pharna River—and the storm that had been brewing early in the day over the Yearn Mountains had ripped downward, smashing icy fists into anyone brave or foolish enough to stir.

"Shelter," Raellard called into the teeth of the high wind. "We need shelter and soon. I'm freezing my balls off."

Kesira set her mouth in a grim line but said nothing. All day she had ridden, wondering how to separate herself from Raellard's unwanted attention. He had been something of a solace by just being near, but the thought rose to the surface of her mind that this was the man who had killed Molimo. While Raellard's motives had been pure, the fact remained. He had killed Molimo.

"Toward the sea," she shouted. "There must be a traveler's shelter nearby. The Abbey of Ayondela maintained several along this stretch for their Order."

Whether those in the abbey still did was a question she could not answer. Ayondela had only recently been lured by the power of jade in her desire for vengeance. The shelters might stand as they had done for years.

"There," called out Raellard, pointing through the white veils pulled around them. A moment's unnatural calm allowed the snow to whirl in miniature tornadoes and leave a clear patch. The wooden structure had not fallen into disrepair.

Kesira dismounted and led her horse toward it. They pushed in and managed to bolt the door the best they could. The horse neighed and whinnied at being trapped within the small structure, but there was no proper barn, nor had Kesira expected to find one. Such huts as this were a boon to travelers, a blessing from Ayondela.

Now the female demon's blessing cancelled her curse: The hut protected them from the storm raging outside.

"No firewood," grumbled Raellard. "Wait Will get some."

"You'll be lost before you go ten feet," said Kesira. "The blizzard's force mounts by the minute."

Raellard peered outside, his body blocking the door. When he heaved it shut and fumbled the bolt back across the door, he solemnly acknowledged what she had guessed. It was death to be outside in this weather. Raellard turned and patted the horse on the neck, soothing her nervous pawings and snorts.

"Good animal," he said.

"Would it bother you to know that I took it from a dead mercenary?"

"Not overly. Where do you think I got this spear? Found it buried in another man's back. The weather drives men to do awful deeds. Can't say I much like it, but I accept it."

Raellard Yera slumped down and pulled his thin cloak tighter around him. He hadn't bothered to coat himself with a fresh layer of mud and stick leaves onto it for insulation. Now Kesira wished that he had. Hers was the only blanket worthy of the name. Even her cloak provided scant protection against the penetrating cold of the storm.

"We should eat," she said.

"Tomorrow. Eat too much too soon and we might run out of food before the storm lets up. We're likely to be here for a few days. Seen other ear-freezers like it. Too many times before, I seen them."

Kesira saw that he was right. She had to remember that Raellard had survived in this area for long weeks while she rode, relatively flush with food and drink, from the Quaking Lands.

She fought back tears once more as she thought of Molimo lying dead on the ground outside Raellard's hut, the spear thrust through his spine.

"You said you did rune sticks. Will you?"

"What?" The words dragged her back to reality. Kesira did not want to go.

"The rune sticks. You can read them?"

"Yes, I suppose so." She found the bone box and opened it. The rune sticks lay inside, gleaming a dull white in the faint light of the hut. Even as she touched the rune sticks, the light dimmed even more. They were soon dropped into almost complete darkness.

"About sunset," observed Raellard. "Storm cuts off the sunlight, too. Nothing to worry 'bout, unless there's no light when the morning comes."

"It makes reading the runes difficult."

"What else we got to do?"

She smiled wanly. With a quick turn of her wrist, Kesira sent the rune sticks sailing. They landed in a tangled heap at her feet. She hunkered down and began sorting through them.

"They're glowing," said Raellard, a touch of fear in his voice. "All by themselves, they're glowing."

Kesira was surprised to see that he was right. Never before had this happened. She read the fiery runes easily, without need of additional light.

"What do they say?" he asked. He crowded a bit closer, his eyes locked on the rune sticks.

Kesira said nothing as she mulled over the meaning of the runes. The way they stacked, the ones visible, the ones half-hidden, the ones she could not read, all went into her interpretation. And more. From deep within came stirrings of just how much more the nun read.

"I see demons battling jade demons. Toyaga. Toyaga

and Eznofadil. Toyaga is . . . The runes fade on me when I look too closely."

"What of this one? The one that burns brighter than the others?"

"That is a strange configuration," she said. "One I have not seen before. Thwarted plans, perhaps. Or a mistake. It is close to a pair of rune sticks that mean friendship."

"Mistaken friendship?" asked Raellard. "Who gets this reading?"

"Either of us," she said. "Or neither."

"What of the storm? Will we survive it?"

Kesira studied the lay of the sticks a while longer, then let out a tiny sigh of relief. "The storm will pass by midday tomorrow," she said. "This is the rune of immediate departure. And this one," she said, pointing to another brightly glowing one, "tells of reunion."

Hope flared within her. Reunion? With Zolkan, perhaps?

"And that one?" asked Raellard. "The one that stays unlit?"

"That one is death," she said. "It lies across all the others. All of them. We will meet only death in the coming weeks."

The gusting wind drowned out her words. She pulled her cloak tighter and lay down near her mare. The heat from the animal helped and, when Raellard lay beside her, she did not even protest. Like sheep in a circle, they huddled and kept warm and survived the freezing temperatures.

Kesira survived—for death later on?

Chapter Eleven

THE STORM-DARKENED SKY split apart with thunder and fierce violet lightning. The jagged bolt of eye-searing energy struck a tree not a hundred feet away from Molimo, boiled the sap within and sent the superheated juices exploding outward in all directions. Droplets of the burning amber fluid touched his clothing and set it afire, but what bothered Molimo most was the deafness. The clap of thunder had robbed him of hearing.

Zolkan clawed at his arm, almost in a frenzy of worry. Molimo reached up and stroked over the *trilla* bird's crested feathers. Molimo saw his friend's beak opening and closing. Words no doubt issued forth, but he heard none of them.

He pointed to his ears, then his mouth. The message was clear. Zolkan subsided, but still craned his head from side to side. When he began pecking at the back of Molimo's cloak, the man realized he was on fire. He spun the cloak around and saw minute pinpoints flare from the sudden gust of air past them. Rolling the cloak into a tight ball, he thrust it into a snowbank. Tiny hisses issued forth as the burning sap was extinguished.

". . . they fight again," he heard Zolkan saying.

My hearing returns, he indicated. *Yes, you are right. The jade demons make still another bid for power. I cannot understand the protagonists in this, however.*

"Toyaga?"

Possibly. I wish we could find Kesira.

"She rides on to Isle of Eternal Winter." The *trilla* bird squawked loudly and shook a wing. A bit of sap had stuck to the blue feathers at the tip. Molimo plucked the offending feather and cast it away. Zolkan thanked him with ill grace, unhappy at having his fine plumage destroyed in such an ignominious fashion.

This trail follows a different ravine to the Pharna. We will emerge less than a mile from the sea.

"She will be waiting," Zolkan assured Molimo. "I have scouted. She is no longer at hut with woman."

How do the woman and her baby fare?

"Well enough, from all signs. They eat. Woman spends much time hiding from shadows."

You mean in *shadows.*

"From. Very frightened. As we ought to be. Demons!" Zolkan lifted a wing and spread it; feathers momentarily illuminated by a lightning flash of frightening intensity. He pointed at a peak to the east. From it Molimo guessed the demons had a splendid view of the Katad Sea. But they did not sightsee. They fought. With magicks that bemused him. Never had he seen their like, but then never had he thought about one demon attacking another in this way.

Molimo felt increasingly as if he belonged to an epoch now dying before his very eyes.

Pillars of green sprang up, gutting the nighttime sky. Those shining columns protected two of the jade demons. But which two? Ayondela? Eznofadil? Lenc? What combination fought the solitary demon on that far peak?

When lightnings lashed out and struck at the fighting demon, Molimo knew the identity of one jade antagonist: Ayondela. She used the elements to freeze and attack. The lightning was only a byproduct of her blizzards and ice storms wracking the feet of the offending demon.

"It is Toyaga," said Zolkan. "Can you help?"

I see no way. If only there were. Molimo railed at his own inability to fight the demons. Even when they lacked their jade-enhanced powers, he was only as a mortal against their demonic strength.

"Battle goes against Toyaga."

Molimo saw the handsome demon as if they were only an arm's length apart. Toyaga fell heavily, face upturned to Ayondela. A smile crossed his lips. Whatever powers he called upon, they protected him from Ayondela's wrath—but barely. The probing ice scepter Ayondela carried in her hand battered at Toyaga's defenses. Frost formed on the ground and then turned into a small glacier. Toyaga slipped and slid, futilely striving for traction. He fell heavily over the brink of the mountain and tumbled into nothingness.

"He is lost."

But Toyaga had not exhausted all tricks. He spun and somersaulted in midair, held aloft by the high winds of the very storm Ayondela had summoned.

The other pillar of green light moved, pushing aside Ayondela. The female demon jerked about, her eyes glowing like intense green beacons. The fangs that had sprouted since partaking of the jade matched her eyes in hue and blazing brilliance.

A hand waved her aside, and, after fuming for a few seconds over it, Ayondela yielded to the other demon.

"Eznofadil."

Truly, it is. He goads Ayondela on, but wants to be responsible for the final kill. Toyaga will not survive.

Molimo found himself silently cheering as Toyaga righted himself and floated like a bird on a summer's thermal air current. The handsome demon wafted away as gently as a leaf when updrafts tossed him higher and higher, away from his jade foes. But Eznofadil had singled him out. A pass of a green hand brought Toyaga back to the edge of the mountain.

Toyaga took a desperate gamble—and won. He doubled up into a ball and lost the airfoil that held him aloft. He fell like a rock toward the base of the mountain. And at the last possible instant, he winked out of existence and *popped* back a few paces from Molimo and Zolkan.

"We meet again. I had not intended it to be so soon. I am sorry to lead them to you in this manner, but unless I occupy them otherwise, they will slay me." True sorrow crossed Toyaga's face. "I can only wish it had ended in some other fashion for you." Again the demon shifted away, leaving only footprints in the snow.

"We run. They come, we run!" urged Zolkan.

We can try, but it is useless if they pursue him. Take to wing, my friend, and find Kesira. She will tend your needs.

"You need help. Now!"

The shock wave announcing Ayondela and Eznofadil's arrival knocked Molimo off his horse. Zolkan grabbed fiercely on the man's shoulder and brought blood, then released his grip and fluttered off drunkenly. The *trilla* bird fell to the ground and struggled to rise to his feet. By this time two shimmery green pillars rose from the snowbank.

"What have we discovered, darling Ayondela?" asked Eznofadil with mock seriousness. "Why, I do think we have made a discovery far surpassing that of the annoying Toyaga."

"It is the wolf who was with the bitch," Ayondela cried.

"Yes, I do believe it is. Has the wolf killed any more of our offspring, do you think?"

Ayondela spun around and faced Eznofadil. The taller demon smiled and crossed thick arms over his chest.

"What do you say? This wolf killed Rouvin? How do you know that?"

"Ayondela, Ayondela, the jade imparts immense powers. I see the past, as well as the future. You will, too, when you have experienced more of its ineffable qualities." Eznofadil lightly bounced a jade chip from one finger to the next as a juggler at the Harvest Fairs might do.

In other circumstances, this might have amused Molimo. Not now. A wolf's snarl rose from deep within his throat. He padded forward, jaws clacking shut powerfully. The animal urge struck him full force. He leaped, fangs intended for Ayondela's throat.

Her jade fangs unexpectedly parried his. Fat sparks crawled into the night like drunken red roaches from the impact.

"How lovely. Jade against natural tooth. I must study this phenomenon more carefully," said Eznofadil. "You do well, Ayondela. Remember. The jade will not permit failure."

Molimo cowered back, snarling. His green eyes met Ayondela's equally green ones. Neither flinched. He leaped again, teeth sinking into her wrist. With her icy blue scepter, she batted him away.

"Foul creature!" Ayondela pointed the scepter at Molimo. Caught in a circle of intense polar cold, the wolf sank to the ground, stunned. His drool froze his jowls shut. Eyelids refused to open as fur and eyelashes froze together. His breathing became labored; the air flowed like syrup into his lungs.

The wolf tried to stand only to fall belly-down on the ground, legs splayed out on either side. His matted tail flopped feebly, and the cold inside slashed fiercely at his lungs.

"You do that so well, my darling," said Eznofadil. "But for a moment, release the wolf. I would gloat at his death."

"He killed Rouvin? You are sure?"

"Ayondela, you have such a fixation on your son. He was hardly worthy of a mother so caring and thoughtful." Eznofadil smirked as he studied Molimo. The wolf's green eyes glared their hatred, life slowly ebbing from his body. "A moment. No more."

Molimo howled with the cessation of the cold around him, but he was unable to move. His frostbitten paws hurt as much as if a million needles had been thrust into them. His nose burned with a fury that made him think he had nudged into a fire rather than cold. Worst of all, he had been drained of all energy. Molimo would not be able to attack again, now that Ayondela's spell had been lifted.

"You do not bleed?" Eznofadil asked solicitously of the female demon. "His teeth did not break skin?"

"How could they?" she said, anger fading. She thrust her bare wrist skyward. Lightnings arched down from the heavens and smote her fist. The green of her skin took on hues and highlights unnatural and unnerving. No trace of the wolf bite showed. "The jade protects me."

"It turns the flesh hard," said Eznofadil, as if lecturing. "Soon enough, you will be harder than any *renn*-stone statue. The jade protects its own."

Zolkan waddled over to where Molimo lay gasping for breath. The *trilla* bird cawed in the wolf's ear. Weakly struggling, Molimo got to his feet, wobbled and fell muzzle-down in the snow.

"Can you flee?" asked Zolkan.

Molimo shook his head.

"I distract them. Flee. You must. You must! To Kesira!"

Molimo fought to regain his feet again and once more failed. He wanted to tell the bird to save himself, that further effort was not possible on his part. But the green-feathered bird took to wing and circled above. Neither of the jade demons paid the bird any attention. Molimo tried to decide if they hadn't noticed or if they just didn't care. What could one lone fowl do to an invincible demon?

Eznofadil turned back to Molimo. "You understand too well what is happening, don't you, *wolf?*"

The demon taunted him with knowledge hidden from Ayondela. Eznofadil knew he was an other-beast. Molimo gathered what anger rested within the wolf-brain and directed it toward Eznofadil. He surged to his feet. While his legs were wobbly and weak, strength flowed once again. He recovered. And he would rip the greenish throat from Eznofadil, no matter that the jade veneer protected his soft tissues.

"There will be no attack," Eznofadil said softly, so that only Molimo heard. "She does not know you. Should I tell her? How great would Ayondela's wrath be then? The world plunged under a mile-deep glacier extending all over the planet?"

Molimo growled, low and deep in his throat.

"Ah, you see the problems with that, do you?" Eznofadil glanced at Ayondela. "She is but a moment's diversion. A useful tool and nothing more. She destroyed you for us, did she not? I really must speak to Lenc about this. He assured me that—"

Ayondela screamed as Zolkan arrowed down from above. Hard talons raked across her face, sought green-glowing eyes, caught on one of her deformed tusks. The *trilla* bird grabbed hold of the jade fang and twisted heavily in midair, using momentum and surprising strength to catapult Ayondela to the ground. She landed heavily, ice scepter falling from her grasp.

Zolkan flashed to it and hefted the wand in his talons. It weighed no more than a large rabbit. The bird took to wing, carrying Ayondela's symbol of power.

"Die, you miserable creature!" she screeched. The sky split asunder with the power of the storm she summoned to stop Zolkan. Molimo watched in helpless fascination as the green tint of the demon's skin darkened. The power of the jade possessed her spirit more and more. She hardly noticed when Eznofadil handed her the chip of jade he had been playing with. She slid it under her tongue; the hue deepened and her power grew.

And grew and grew.

Molimo wanted to call out to her, to tell her that she destroyed herself. Eznofadil and Lenc waited for her to die, a burned-out husk that had served their intermediate purposes. Ultimate rule would rest with either Eznofadil or Lenc, of that Molimo was certain. Ayondela would be discarded along the way.

"Return my scepter, filthy bird!" she called.

Rain and snow turned to ice in the air. Zolkan was buffeted violently, his escape with the scepter impossible. He dropped the wand into a snowbank and careened off, still caught in the windy fingers of the punishing storm.

"Ayondela," said Eznofadil, "why not retrieve your toy and return to the Isle of Eternal Winter? I shall be along shortly. After I have kicked this miserable cur a bit more."

"He killed Rouvin. You said so. He is *mine!* I will kill him. No one else. No one."

Eznofadil began to radiate an intense green light. He tapped into the power given him by the jade, and did so more effectively than Ayondela. Molimo caught the subtle power words of the spell Eznofadil employed on her.

"He is not the one who destroyed Rouvin. I made a mistake. Return to the Isle. I will join you soon. Go, darling Ayondela, and await me. Await me."

Ayondela fetched her scepter and vanished into the storm, not saying a word.

"She can be controlled, yet," said Eznofadil. "It becomes more difficult, however. The jade is a two-edged sword she has not mastered. Using it against her is so easy." Eznofadil looked down at Molimo. The wolf snarled.

"You would see what I will do to you? Yes?"

Eznofadil looked around and saw Molimo's horse nervously pawing the snow-packed ground some distance away. "That is a good model for my demonstration."

Eznofadil smiled, the lip curling into a sneer. He held out his hand, palm to the storm-wracked sky. The horse neighed and bucked, as if caught in a fence. Eznofadil slowly closed his hand. The horse let out a whine that sounded human as it intermixed with the thunder. Then the poor animal fell over, kicking feebly, its neck broken.

"So easy. Before the jade I moved small items. I cheated at three-match and dice. I even enjoyed moving about the rune sticks my followers cast. But you know all about moving the rune sticks, don't you, my dear friend?"

Molimo almost choked when the shape change again seized him and he shifted from wolf to human form.

"This is appropriate. Face death in your real form, not some surly wolf shape. Good-bye."

Eznofadil reached out, as he had done to Molimo's horse. Molimo felt invisible fingers around his neck, squeezing, cutting off wind, breaking fragile bones.

He refused to die easily, but struggle was impossible. The jade demon was invincible. But escape? Molimo grunted and croaked and made pathetic noises.

And he remembered what Toyaga had said to him. The spell. Toyaga had no idea what it might do, if anything.

> *The world about me,*
> *There are no eyes.*
> *Freedom of the air and sky,*
> *I fade into nothingness.*

At first, Molimo did not think anything had changed, that Eznofadil still choked him. Then he realized that the pressure at his throat had vanished as surely as a thirsty plant drinks rain water.

"Where are you?" raged the jade demon. "What did you do? Where are you!"

Eznofadil rushed forward to where Molimo stood. Molimo moved a few feet to the side and let the demon batter at thin air.

"You are full of tricks. Too full of them. I don't know where you went, but we shall find you. We shall!"

Eznofadil winked away, probably following Ayondela to the Isle of Eternal Winter.

Molimo wondered at the spell's effect until he heard Zolkan squawking above.

"Where go? Where are you?"

Even as Zolkan spoke, Molimo felt sharp pains in his gut. He grunted and doubled forward, panting like a wolf that has chased a rabbit overlong.

Zolkan landed on his shoulder, one beady black eye peering into his midnight black one. "A trick? You used trick on Eznofadil and vanished? Good!"

Good, Molimo agreed. *But he killed the horse. We have to walk now.*

"To Kesira?"

To Kesira, he agreed. Molimo staggered a bit and stumbled, but as he walked down the ravine, toward the Pharna River, his strength slowly reasserted itself. By the time he sighted the frozen expanse of the river, he felt confident that they might defeat the jade demons.

Almost.

Chapter Twelve

"THE ENTIRE WORLD comes to an end? Just like that?" asked Raellard Yera, frowning at such an idea. "Why do anything against the damned demons, then?"

"That's not what I said." Kesira leaned forward, her face flushed. She ignored the howling winds and the penetrating cold and even the way her horse stepped over her awkwardly inside the tiny rock shelter. She spoke passionately of her theology now, of belief, of that which drove her life forward.

"Thought you did," said Raellard. He looked skeptical at all she had told him.

"Let me go back and retell it. Perhaps this will be clearer. You know how the world came to be?"

Raellard shrugged. "It formed from the five elements."

"Yes, yes," she said, impatient to bypass such basics and get on with the telling. "Void, filling it came the world, the dirt beneath our feet, then covering it the ocean, above it air and burning in the air was fire. Each element is higher than the last, but not better."

"I don't understand."

"This is going astray from what I wish to say," said Kesira. "But quickly, the heirarchy of elements was established as I mentioned: void, substance, water, air, fire. Each added to the others before it, each gave new dimensions to the universe."

"The five comprise everything."

"Exactly, Raellard. Then came animals, then humans." Kesira swallowed and said, "Then came the demons. They are stronger than mortals and possess powers we do not share. It is said they can run all day and live forever."

"They are the product of human and animal," said Rael-lard. "I remember that much."

"True. They are a hybrid, with human traits accentu-ated and strengthened, while still retaining baser animal instincts and energies. If a mortal loves, a demon loves a thousand times more. If a human hates, a demon hates with the intensity of all in the world. And not all demons possess all traits. Some are very, very good, like Gelya, while others seek only to destroy."

"Ayondela."

"She is deluded. As a human may be led astray, so has she been by Eznofadil and Lenc."

"They are the evil ones."

"Yes," said the nun, thinking of how Lenc had so vi-ciously destroyed her Order. And her life.

"If they can be killed—and you said they were being killed—why call us mortals?"

"This is at the core of what I said to you. They are not truly immortal, meaning that they live forever, but their life spans are immense by human standards. Their time will soon pass. They can be killed by their peers, and their rule nears its end."

"The Time of Chaos," said Raellard, shivering. Kesira did not think it was from the cold. "All that is normal will be gone."

"Chaos will not last. Nothing lasts save change. The gods will rise to supplant the demons."

"What gods?"

Kesira shook her head. "Those of my Order argued this point. The best that could be decided is a progression simi-lar to that occurring when the demons came into being through offspring of animals and humans."

"Human and demon breeding will produce the gods? I don't want no part of this. I saw Ayondela—or what she's done to the land. Froze it. She must be a coldhearted bitch. What man could take her to his bed and enjoy it?"

"You did not know her son Rouvin. There was a majesty about him, something more than human and even more than demon, yet less than both. He was no god, but rather a failed god. He combined the lesser points of each rather than the greater."

"These demons couple with anything. I heard the stories."

"Rouvin told me that the Time of Chaos is when demons and humans die and the gods are born. I think he was wrong. Humanity survives and the demons perish—and then there will be gods."

"So? How is this any different from being under the thumb of a demon?"

"The gods will be different," she said with conviction. "They will be more humane, have higher principles, be dedicated to good works. The flaws of humanity will be erased and the best traits will remain, intensified, distilled, perfected."

"They'll bring us all we want to live off?" asked Raellard. "That would be paradise."

"Humans need to work to give themselves a sense of worth. Can you imagine how dull it would be not having the well-being of accomplishment from your toils?"

Raellard sighed. "I would give it a try. Not to break my back in the fields, not to starve because the crops failed through no fault of my own, not to have to scratch and scrabble out a meager living—I'd like to live as the Emperor for just a day."

Kesira shook her head, saying, "The Emperor's burdens are even greater. He has the welfare of all to consider. Only loyalty to him gives us the greatest good. The decisions he makes daily are far more difficult than working in a grain field. He must strive to hold the Empire together, so that we work united, to keep faith in him."

"My faith dims," said Raellard. "A hollow belly demands filling before any duty to the Emperor."

"This attitude is another sign that we enter the Time of Chaos."

She settled back, the rush of having a new pupil past now. Raellard was hardly as good as some of the acolytes who had recently joined the Order, but it did Kesira good to think she instructed, enlightened, brought new ideas to the man. Lenc tore at the very foundations of the empire when he destroyed the Orders and their patrons. Education became muddled and factions rose up to oppose authority.

She shuddered. Her hardest task since the advent of the jade demons had been working almost alone. Without her Sisters to bolster and succor her, Kesira felt lost. Zolkan and Molimo were more than friends for her; they had become her sole sources of support. Now even they were gone and she had to rely on a dirt farmer. Still, Kesira tried to tell herself, each citizen of the empire needed every other; Raellard needed her and she needed him.

Somehow, that did not seem right to Kesira, even though it should.

She dozed fitfully, dreaming of Molimo and Zolkan and even Wemilat and Rouvin. Kesira awoke to Raellard shaking her gently.

"What is it?"

"The storm," he said. "It's died down. We can be on our way to the Sea of Katad."

"There's no need for you to come with me," she said. "You wanted to hunt to supply your wife with food enough for the rest of the . . . summer." Kesira had a difficult time believing this weather might be called summer.

"Parvey's crazy as a wobble bug. Can't go back to her. Not soon. I promised to help you for all you did, and I will. Honor requires me keeping my word."

"You never gave your promise on this," Kesira said, but she saw where the conversation led and resigned herself to his company.

"Do now. Promise to help you get to Ayondela and stop this winter. Isn't this helping Parvey, too? I mean, get rid of the cold and grain grows again. Won't have to forage off the land and worry about wolves and the like."

The mention of wolves sent Kesira into a new depression. Molimo dead. His body slowly being eaten by the woman back in the hills. Kesira grew sick to her stomach but held down her rising gorge.

"We'll ride to the sea," she said. "By my reckoning we might not be more than a day or two distant."

"A day, no more."

Kesira led her horse outside. Again the weather had cleared to leave a brilliant azure sky with only traces of fleecy clouds whitely dotting it. She found it so difficult to believe that this ought to be warm and summery and lushly green with every imaginable plant in abundance. The snow fields extended across the Pharna, obscuring the banks of the river and the frozen surface. Kesira remembered tales of the river freezing as myths told to frighten; if the river ever had frozen solid this far to the south, it had been in days long past. Still, with every hardship comes an unsuspected benefit. Riding on the river itself provided easier going than through the snowbanks and drifted blockages formed by the high winds.

"Might fall through," Raellard observed when she told him of her intention.

"How thick is the ice?"

He shrugged.

"Find out. I'll wait. I promise not to take the horse out onto the river until you tell me."

Raellard returned a few minutes later. "Ice's thicker than I thought. I dug for ten minutes and got almost a foot down and still didn't break through to water. Must make the fish uneasy having a white roof over their heads."

"They might not even notice," she said. "Unless they like coming to the surface for sunning."

Kesira rode along, eyes flashing this way and that, alert for any movement along the banks of the river. She remembered all too clearly the beasts roaming the Roggen Plains—and the brigands. Times were hard for both man and beast. She and Raellard looked to be easy prey. The woman wanted to dodge or outrun any danger rather than prove that they were not going to give themselves up easily.

As hard as Kesira watched, Raellard was the one who spotted the spoor along the crest of a snowbank. He tugged at her arm and pointed, motioning her to silence.

Kesira immediately dismounted. While she might be able to see farther, she could also be seen more easily. She and Raellard went to examine the tracks. The nun didn't need the man to tell her that many mounted troops had passed by recently. The edges of the imprints were still crisp and sharp, not melted by sun or eroded by wind.

"A dozen. More," Raellard said. "Soldiers."

While it was a logical conclusion from the pattern left by the tracks, Kesira asked how he knew.

"The shoes on their mounts. All identical. Look." Raellard pointed to one imprint that had sunk through snow and found the dirt beneath. "A mercenary sigil."

Nervous sweat popped out on Kesira's forehead. She wiped it away before it cooled her too much. She recognized the pattern instantly.

The Order of the Steel Crescent.

"We're heading the same way as they," she said. "Down to the Sea of Katad."

"Might skirt around their flank," said Raellard, indicating a possible path to the north. "Or forge south and away from the river. They are doing as we do, using the iced river as a highway."

"Time works against us," Kesira said. She felt increasingly uneasy about how the winter gripped the world around her. "Ayondela must be convinced of her errors soon, or no one will survive."

"From all you say, will the other jade demons permit it to continue much longer?"

"There wouldn't be any humans left to rule, would there?" mused Kesira. "I had not considered that. They obviously encourage this for their own reasons." She considered the unnatural winter from this perspective, then shook her head. "We must reach Ayondela as soon as possible. How long can Parvey survive, even with the . . . additional food supply?"

"The wolf won't last more'n a week or two at the outside. The other stuff should last her that long and then some."

Raellard did not see her cringe when he mentioned the wolf.

Molimo.

"We go on, along the river. We can only hope that the Steel Crescent rides fast and for another destination."

"Not so fast. Horses are walking," Raellard pointed out.

She gestured for the man to continue. Kesira walked her horse now, to keep it quiet and to lessen the sound of its hooves on the hollow, ringing ice. By midday they had not caught sight of any other riders. They stopped for a brief meal.

As they ate, Raellard said, "Cast the rune sticks again. Let them tell us of danger."

Kesira already knew the danger. But she did as the man asked. The nun pulled out the bone box and opened it. The sticks lay inside, inert and unlike the night before. She cast them forth, letting them land on the ice.

"They're not glowing," Raellard accused. "What's wrong?"

"They are," she said, cupping her hands over the pile. "The sun robs them of much of their inner light."

"Read them."

"The rune sticks do not tell all. They can be cryptic." Even as she spoke, she studied the casual pattern formed. "They say I am wrong, mistaken. Again the friendship runes appear prominent." She looked up at Raellard, who munched at his ration with little evidence of intelligence showing. Wrong in friendship? Was she wrong in trusting Raellard? Did the runes tell her what she already knew, that Raellard had slain Molimo? Or did the runes mean something else? "There is little more to see. Clouded future. Blocked to me."

"Humph," was the only comment the man made.

They repacked their meager belongings into a sack slung over the saddle and stood. But Kesira froze when she heard the clank of metal on metal. She turned and saw the man standing atop the low rise by the river, hands on hips. Sun glinted off the steel of his armor and turned him into a shining, indistinct form.

"Can I believe my eyes?" came the mocking words. "Is this the woman who killed our patron in the Quaking Lands?"

Kesira gripped her staff and stepped away from her horse, ready to fight.

"You know this one?" asked Raellard.

"Nehan-dir, leader of the Order of the Steel Crescent. Yes, we've met before. Not pleasantly, either."

Others joined Nehan-dir on the hilltop. They stared down at the two, then laughed uproariously.

"What are you laughing at?" demanded Raellard. "What's so funny?"

"You, little man. A dirt farmer and a nun. We find that immensely funny."

"Come down here and I'll show you how funny it is!" Raellard waved his spear about ineffectually.

"Raellard, be calm. They are mercenaries."

"Never heard of this Order of the Steel Crescent," he grumbled. "Well, I have," he amended sullenly. "So what?"

Kesira prepared herself for battle, settling her mind, tensing and relaxing muscles to make sure she was loose and able to move quickly when the need arose. She did not bother explaining to Raellard Yera her horror at finding Nehan-dir here. The man had turned mercenary after his patron had sold him and all his followers to another demon in exchange for cancelling a gambling debt. Nehan-dir had rebelled; something within the man had snapped after being treated as little more than chattel. He and the others sought out only strong patrons, selling their services. Howenthal had hired them; they had worshipped Howenthal until Kesira destroyed the jade demon. She had no doubt that Nehan-dir now rode to the Isle of Eternal Winter to pledge allegiance to Ayondela. The Order of the Steel Crescent gravitated toward strength and the female demon's power gleamed whitely across the land. It made sense that Nehan-dir sought a patron not likely to be destroyed soon, who would grant him and his fellow mercenaries the security they had never gotten before.

"I would kill her," said one soldier. Nehan-dir turned and nodded, indicating that his permission had been given with pleasure.

The armored mercenary awkwardly came to meet Kesira in battle. The nun saw that her opponent was a woman, half a head taller, with a thick pink scar running diagonally across her forehead. As the mercenary drew her blade, Kesira attacked.

Her stone-wood staff whirled about in a blinding arc that ended squarely on the other's wrist. Bones snapped. The mercenary yelled in pain and twisted away. The staff rebounded and continued its journey in a circular orbit, landing behind the mercenary's knee. The woman crumpled to the ground, moaning.

"I have no desire to harm you," said Kesira, knowing this

would not work with Nehan-dir. Gelya had said that it was possible to purchase peace at too high a price, but she had to try.

"But I want to see your blood foaming in the snow," said Nehan-dir. "You robbed me of my patron. Howenthal was the perfect replacement, and you killed him."

"My patron is dead, also," Kesira said, widening her stance, waiting for Nehan-dir's attack.

"He died because he refused to walk the way of power. Alone, he died. Alone, you will die!"

Nehan-dir came down the slope and motioned to the woman, still clutching her broken wrist.

"She's mine! You promised!"

"You failed," Nehan-dir said coldly. "She is very quick, this little nun. You underestimated her." Nehan-dir bowed forward from the waist, hands above his head. The chain mail vest he wore slid over his head and landed in a heap at his feet. "Take my mail and wait with the rest. I'll show you how to deal with her."

Kesira attacked even as Nehan-dir spoke, but the man was wary. Her staff flashed through the air—to the spot where his head had been. He ducked, drew his dagger, and moved in to kill. She barely succeeded in getting her staff spun around her waist and back in front to parry the thrust for her belly. Kesira danced away.

"This will be interesting," said Nehan-dir. "I enjoy your death already."

She studied the small, scrawny man for some sign of weakness. Kesira saw it everywhere, yet she knew it was all illusion. His thin arms were strung with steel sinews. The spider web of scars across his face testified to the battles lost—and won. Sandy hair blew in wild disarray, making Nehan-dir look the part of a wild man. But his attacks came purposefully, deliberately, with measured power and always on target.

Kesira Minette fought for her life.

"Haieee!" Raellard Yera took the opportunity to attack. His spear darted for Nehan-dir's throat, caught the gorget and skittered away. The leader of the mercenaries stepped back, a surprised look on his face.

"The farmer can fight. Then fight!"

Nehan-dir attacked and snapped the point off Raellard's spear before Kesira could move. The farmer tumbled back onto his rear, sitting and staring stupidly at the skinny soldier towering above him. With only a dagger, Nehan-dir had defeated a man armed with a spear. All that had saved Raellard from a nasty cut on the thigh was the tough-leathered high top of his boot.

"Stay," Nehan-dir said to Raellard, as if speaking to a dog.

Kesira fought then, hard, pushing offensively, being forced into defensive postures. Nehan-dir smiled as he fought, enjoying the conflict. Freed of his chain mail he was as agile as Kesira and more highly trained in the ways of combat. Luck—not skill—kept her from perishing at the point of the man's dagger.

"Go on, slip and slide over the ice," he taunted. "It makes my kill all the easier."

"Nehan-dir!" cried one of the soldiers on the hill.

"Fool, can't you see I am busy?" Nehan-dir never took his eyes off Kesira. He had learned that her staff could deliver savage punishment and even death to the unwary.

The sounds of death echoed down from the hill. Nehan-dir took the chance to spin and look, then whirled back to face Kesira.

"Witch! How did you summon the demon spawn?"

Kesira was in a better position to see what happened to the mercenaries. Hideous creatures boiled upon them, snapping and clawing. The soldiers fought well, but there were too many of the demon spawn for them to evade.

Nehan-dir had to choose between killing Kesira and losing his followers or retreating.

"There will be another time, I hope," he said. "If not, I leave you to the demon spawn. May their bellies churn and bloat when they devour you!"

He hurried up the hill, dagger resheathed and sword hacking at the monsters. Kesira heard the shrill cries of pain as men and women were injured. Then came the thunder of hooves as the horses raced off.

Kesira and Raellard faced the thwarted demon spawn alone.

"This is a better death, in my eyes," said Kesira. "These creatures are at least true to their savage nature. Nehandir sells himself to the highest bidder."

She helped Raellard to his feet. With little more than their bare hands, they faced the half-dozen hungry beasts slithering down the hill toward them.

Chapter Thirteen

THE DEMON SPAWN stopped at the top of the hill and peered down at Kesira Minette. She took the brief respite in attack to settle herself. A moment's panic came when she realized how alone she was. Raellard Yera would prove little use in this battle. He was not up to fighting and might only get in her way. How she wished for Molimo or her Sisters in the Order. It was unnatural having to fight without someone's support near at hand.

The centermost demon spawn vented a roar that shook her. She quickly recovered, knowing that this cry was intended to frighten her into a mistake. The bulbous creature waddled down the hill, inch-long fangs snapping and clacking against the lower, solid dental plate. The beast appeared to be a combination of snake and bear with a goodly portion of vegetable added. It had the color and general shape of a turnip, the arms and shoulders of a bear and the fangs of a reptile; Kesira was not optimistic about the outcome of the fight.

She faced speed, strength, and ugliness.

"I will stop it!" yelled Raellard, rushing forward. He poked at the creature with his broken spear. One careless paw reached out and batted him away, as if he were nothing more than a minor annoyance. The demon spawn seemed to recognize Kesira as its primary opponent.

"Stay back from it," she cautioned. "It shows some small intelligence." Under her breath Kesira added, "More than you possess."

The others in the pack started down the hill, a frightening combination mixing both the animal and vegetable into a stew too odious to contemplate. Claws scratched and

146

teeth banged shut and the odors that assaulted their nostrils were almost worse than any physical attack. Raellard stumbled back to take up a spot at Kesira's side.

"We can run."

"Nehan-dir is no fool. He would have realized we were trapped by them. They will attack constantly until we are dead. How can we run from so many?"

"They look slow."

Even as he spoke, the bear-snake-turnip beast lashed out with a speed so blinding it took even Kesira by surprise. She lost the bottom four inches of her staff to sharp dental plates.

Almost by instinct, she brought the top of her staff down firmly on the top of the furred head. It bounced off impossibly thick bone. Kesira wasn't even sure the beast noticed.

Backpedaling, she swung and got the tip of her staff near the creature's eye. She lunged and missed.

"This isn't working," Kesira said, panting from exertion. "Nothing slows it. And the others . . ." The rest of the demon spawn slowly spread out in a fan shape and worked their way in toward the center where Kesira and Raellard fought. Kesira muttered constantly under her breath, half the time praying to long-dead Gelya and the other half cursing the demon spawn so intent on making her their supper.

She used staff and feet against the creature and only confused it. She had yet to produce a visible wound.

It lunged forward, snapping and clawing. Kesira had to retreat across the icy Pharna River. The woman slipped, caught herself, and maintained a semblance of balance. To fall now meant only death.

"What do we do? Never saw so many of the damn things." Raellard poked and prodded. He might as well have been scratching a pet's proffered ears. The demon spawn kept coming back for more.

Before Kesira could reply, a shrill squawk filled the air. The demon spawn hesitated. A new squawk, this one followed by singsong words Kesira recognized.

"Zolkan!"

The *trilla* bird alighted between her and the demon spawn. The incongruous face-off should have ended in the bird's death. One quick swipe of those powerful claws, a gobble and a swallow, even a misplaced step would have ended Zolkan's life. The brightly feathered bird snapped another command. The demon spawn looked up at Kesira. She thought she read sorrow in its bloodshot eyes before it turned and lumbered off. Zolkan kept squawking and flapping his wings. The other demon spawn reluctantly turned and followed their leader.

By the time the beasts had vanished over the hill, Kesira had regained her composure.

"Zolkan, thank you. How'd you find us?"

"How'd the bird do it?" broke in Raellard. "How'd you chase off those monsters?"

"They envy my innate good looks," Zolkan said haughtily. He turned away from Raellard and jumped up to Kesira's shoulder. He craned his neck around and one beady eye peered into the woman's soft brown eyes. "We must go to sea. Now. No time to waste."

"The Order of the Steel Crescent," Raellard broke in again. "What of them? They'll know we didn't get eaten and stop us."

"Lose this bumpkin," advised Zolkan.

"Please, he has helped me," she said, but her own thoughts had run along similar lines. As much as she detested—and even feared—being alone, Raellard was not fit company.

"Let him help from farther away."

"I stay with you," Raellard stoutly maintained. "Parvey can do all right for herself. She has plenty to eat. You said this weather can only be changed by talking to Ayondela."

A lump formed in Kesira's throat. Parvey Yera had plenty to eat. Molimo's body lay outside in the cold, waiting for new pieces of flesh to be hacked off and eaten. Tears poured down her cheeks.

"Travel. Now!" squawked Zolkan. The bird batted at her with his hard wings. "Necessary. No time for cries."

"You are right," the nun said. She quickly traced over the knots in the blue cord around her waist, said a traveler's prayer that helped settle her rampaging emotions, and then she mounted up. The horse slipped and slid on the ice, but the going was easier than amid the snowbanks lining the river.

"Nehan-dir rides to the north. Stay on south side of river," urged Zolkan. "Ride like wind!"

Kesira angled across the river, but she did not heed the bird's advice. Raellard panted and puffed hard to keep up with the pace she set. As long as he walked and she rode there would be a difference in speeds. Kesira was not going to abandon the man.

"More, faster. Pigeonshit! Hurry!"

"Zolkan!" she exclaimed, shocked. "Your speech!" She had heard the *trilla* bird speak like this before, when he had been recovering at the nunnery. The wild tales he had told had aroused her imagination, opened up the ideas that whole vistas existed in the world to which she was not privy. Zolkan had obviously belonged to a soldier or perhaps a sailor for many years and had been sold to a wealthy merchant, but the details had never been clear to Kesira.

"Ride!"

She smiled now. Having Zolkan back did more to bolster her flagging spirits than she might have thought. Several times she started to ask about Molimo, how the two had become separated, why Zolkan hadn't been nearby when Raellard killed the wolf, but she held back. Simply feeling the talons cutting into her beleaguered left shoulder was enough for the moment. When she was better able to assimilate the story, she would inquire.

The untimely frost of Molimo's death would eventually melt within her heart, and then she could ask for details. But not now. Not now.

"Up banks. Snow not too thick," the bird told her when they finally reached the far side of the Pharna. Here and there Kesira had seen thinner patches of ice, the river beneath making its desperate, frightened path to the sea. She had skirted those spots and made the journey longer than either she or Zolkan desired.

Raellard complained, "Snow's damn thick. Damn near knee-deep. Hard going."

"Climb up behind me," Kesira told him. "We can ride together to the top of the rise. Then we'll rest."

"No rest," grumbled Zolkan. "Must reach Katad Sea soon. Must."

"Why?"

The bird didn't answer. It only grumbled and complained to himself.

"What I want to know's how you drove off those demon spawn," said Raellard. "You faced 'em down but good. They took off, not scared but really dejected."

"That is a good question, Zolkan. You seemed to be able to speak to them."

"Can. Told them you taste bad. Told them truth."

Kesira laughed. It wasn't as much the humor of the situation as it was a release of tension for her. "You must have a silver tongue to get rid of them so easily."

"They're not too bright." Zolkan grumbled some more, and Kesira heard him add, "Like humans."

The *trilla* bird spent their rest period preening himself, then urged them on. Kesira insisted that she and Raellard take time to eat again, even though it had only been an hour since their last meal. Zolkan waddled about, muttering, pointing, screeching.

"Chew faster. Eat, eat," he grumbled. "You tell me I think only of food. Look at you. Getting fat!"

Kesira involuntarily reached to her waist and felt. No ring of fat there or on her hips or behind. Since leaving the nunnery she had been on abbreviated rations. With Ayondela's curse upon the land, there was scant chance anyone grew fat.

"Zolkan, what is so important about reaching the sea? We'll be there. Does it matter if it is now or an hour from now?"

The bird let out an aggrieved cry and took to wing. He fluttered and flopped about as a downdraft caught him, then he found the proper rising thermal and soared. Kesira watched as the green dot dwindled and finally vanished in the blue sky.

"We'd best ride as he says."

"What is that bird?" asked Raellard. "Never seen his likes before. Looks to be good stew meat. Flesh on the bones."

"Don't let Zolkan hear you say that. He gets upset when he hears of peddlers selling *trilla* meat."

"A *trilla* bird? Guess I have heard of them. From way to the south. Wonder if it's warm there. Like it ought to be."

"That, Raellard, is something I don't know. I'd guess that Ayondela has been thorough in her curse."

The rest of the day passed by in an endless band of white and cold. As they topped a hill, Kesira reined in and simply stared.

"What by all the demons is that?" asked Raellard, stumbling up to stand beside her horse. "It looks like it cuts open the soft underbelly of the sky."

"It does."

Kesira had never seen the Isle of Eternal Winter before. But she knew that it had never before sported that towering, flickering, cold white flame in its center. Lenc had left his mark on Ayondela's private island. What other points of her life did the jade demon also claim as his own?

"Look at that," said Raellard, awe in his voice.

"I am," she said in some irritation.

"Not the island or that funny flame. The sea. Look at it. It's froze in the damnedest way."

Kesira's eyes widened. Raellard's description did not do justice to the truth. The sea had frozen, but not in the manner of a lake or river freezing over. The very waves had been caught as they pounded against the shore and had quick-frozen. All the way to the Isle of Eternal Winter, the jagged waves thrust sharply upward, etched in ice. It was as if she looked at a picture from a book drawn with ice as a medium and snow the brush.

"How do we cross *that?*" she wondered.

Kesira spun about in the saddle when she heard rocks being dislodged on the side of the hill. Her first thought was that Nehan-dir and his mercenaries had found them. Then she saw the handsome young man with the dark, flowing hair and penetrating midnight eyes. Kesira felt faint and rocked slightly in the saddle, suddenly weak hands gripping the saddle horn for support.

"Molimo!"

The youth smiled and pointed toward the island.

"You're alive. How? He— you— it can't be!"

Molimo frowned, obviously not understanding her. Kesira vaulted from the saddle and let Raellard take the reins of the bucking horse. She threw her arms around Molimo's neck and almost toppled him over. Kissing him, then burying her face in his shoulder, she cried unashamedly.

His hands stroked at her short brown hair, then lifted her face. They just stared at one another. Kesira swallowed hard. It was as if Molimo spoke to her, not with words but deep inside. Almost.

She struggled to understand the words, the feelings. Zolkan's loud squawk broke the spell.

"No time for that. To Isle of Eternal Winter. Need to hurry. Ayondela's curse killing off world."

"I know, Zolkan, I know," she said, tiredness overtaking her now. "But I've got to know. Molimo, why aren't you dead?"

His eyes widened, then he smiled. Molimo reached into his pouch and pulled out the writing tablet and quickly wrote.

"I am quick—hard to kill a man-wolf."

Kesira glanced back at Raellard, who stood shuffling his feet in confusion. "That man killed a wolf and left it for his wife—the woman in the hut. I thought it was you."

"Not me. Must have been real wolf. Zolkan and I explored." Kesira saw him hesitate, as if he wanted to write more. He rubbed out what he had started, then penned, "The Emperor is being forced to retreat on all fronts and return to Limaden. Crops are failing everywhere. Animals dying. Demon spawn are appearing with greater frequency. Other-beasts, too. The natural order is dying—being killed."

Kesira noted that Molimo's hand trembled the slightest bit when he wrote that.

"Magicks abound, unleashed by jade," he continued after he had erased the other message. "Cold feeds the demon's magic, killing off opposition. Emperor being unable to fight means the empire is totally under their control."

"Is the winter worldwide?" she asked. Molimo nodded.

"Ayondela must be stopped." Kesira frowned. "Can the other jade demons duplicate her spell and return us to winter if we do succeed in getting her to lift the curse?"

Molimo hastily wrote, "No. Takes too much energy, even with jade supplementing them. They use her as tool to be discarded when no longer worthwhile. Go to Isle of Eternal Winter. Stop her."

"You're beginning to sound like Zolkan," Kesira said. She heaved a sigh. She hadn't considered getting to an island to be any problem. Find a boat, one used by fishermen, perhaps, and sail to the Isle of Eternal Winter. Kesira had forgotten that appealing and easy approach when she saw how the Sea of Katad had been frozen. It was as if Ayondela had looked out and snapped her fingers, casting everything in ice in a split second. Crossing those jagged, knife-edged waves would be deadly—and there were rank after rank of them all the way out to the island.

"How?" she asked.

Molimo indicated that it would be difficult, but that he had no real plan. Zolkan squawked, "Why not fly? But no. You humans lack proper appendages."

"Chop our way through the waves," said Raellard. "The only road's going to be one we make for ourselves."

"I'm afraid you're right," she said, mind beginning to turn over the possibilities open to them. "But how? We don't have that kind of equipment with us. Your spear tip is hardly useful and Molimo's sword is not going to do the trick for us for long. The edge will blunt."

Raellard fingered the spear he had retrieved. The shaft had broken about a foot under the steel tip and provided only a cumbersome knife. Kesira's staff was hardly the tool for this task.

She sank to the ground, her mind falling in upon itself. She calmed her turbulent thoughts and concentrated, just as she would to do a rune stick reading. Inspiration and genius often walked hand in hand. Barely had she begun to consider the various avenues to be taken getting to the Isle of Eternal Winter when Zolkan let out an anguished squawk.

"Order of Steel Crescent. They go to island. Now we can never reach Ayondela's stronghold."

Kesira rose lithely to her feet and peered out over the blinding white expanse of the frozen wave crests. Even at this distance Kesira made out Nehan-dir's thin figure and that of the woman whose wrist she had broken in combat. The others worked with shiny devices, turning them this way and that, striving for whatever the proper position was.

"What they doing?" asked Raellard. "Never seen a thing like them before."

Molimo wrote quickly. "The devices capture the sun and turn it against the ice."

"They're melting a path to the island using the sun?" Kesira frowned. "Where would Nehan-dir get such a contraption? He did not strike me as mechanician enough to build it."

"One of the jade demons," wrote Molimo. "But which one? Which is now Nehan-dir's patron?"

"Lenc," spoke up Zolkan. "His flame burns on island."

"But Eznofadil has been very active lately," wrote Molimo. The bird nodded solemnly. Kesira wondered what had happened after they left her and Parvey Yera at the hut.

"Could Ayondela have furnished them the machine?" she asked. "What she does and doesn't do is something of a mystery. She is too destroyed by her grief to think clearly."

"Eznofadil," said Zolkan with some conviction. "This is his doing. Feel it."

"So what's the difference who gave 'em the burning plate?" asked Raellard. "Knowing doesn't help us any."

"But Nehan-dir having it does," said Kesira, an idea beginning to germinate. "They melt a road to the island What's to keep us from traveling along that same path, after they've gone?"

"They'll see us." Raellard said it flatly.

"They work to reach the Isle of Eternal Winter by nightfall. We go out then. Can they see in the dark?"

"Demons can," muttered Raellard, not liking the idea of being on the ice after the sun set. "Be cold out there. Damn cold. Freeze our balls off, we will."

Zolkan screeched and landed on Kesira's shoulder. "Might work," the bird said. "I scout, you walk. No horse."

"Why not?" asked Raellard.

"Because the rider would rear up far above the waves." Kesira squinted into the glare again and said, "Those waves are about head-high. They provide ample cover for us as we go on foot, but not for a horse and rider."

"What does it mean to you?" asked Zolkan. "You don't ride. She does."

"Make getting away harder," was all Raellard would say.

Kesira shook her head. Already the farmer thought in terms of escape. While it might be prudent, she did not for an instant consider it. They had to reach Ayondela and convince her to lift her curse. Somewhere deep inside, Kesira had come to the conclusion that the only payment Ayondela would accept for this was a life.

Kesira would gladly give hers in exchange for the stolen summer's return.

"They cut through the waves as knife through water," said Zolkan. "Hate being in way of that. Singe your feathers, quick."

"We rest and wait for sunset," she said. "At the rate Nehan-dir is progressing, they will be at the Isle of Eternal Winter by then. And we can follow." She glanced from one to the other. Both men and the *trilla* bird agreed, each to a varying degree.

To Raellard she said, "You can return to Parvey. She needs you, and this isn't really your fight. Go, hunt, feed your family."

"Gave my promise," Raellard said, almost sullenly. "Can't back down." His face brightened. "Besides, I've always wondered how a demon lives. I'm curious about that house sitting atop the island."

Kesira laid a hand on his shoulder. "Thank you," she said. "We may need all the help we can get before we are finished this day."

She sat, meditated, watched the pale flickering of the cold white flame burning at the center of the island. It was twin to the one gnawing away at Gelya's altar back in her nunnery.

Soon enough, dusk cloaked the land and they gathered their belongings to begin the trek across the ice. Kesira almost turned and ran when she saw the razored waves rising head-tall along their mathematically precise rows. The melted area in front of her had lost its dazzling whiteness now that the sun had set.

She felt as if she marched between the teeth of some voracious beast and descended into its throat.

Silently, Kesira motioned for the others to start. Molimo stayed at her right and Raellard on her left, with Zolkan flying above. Even in the midst of such staunch friends, she did not feel more confident.

Chapter Fourteen

"THE BIRD KEEPING a sharp eye out for any stragglers?" Raellard Yera asked uneasily. "Wouldn't want to run into any of those soldiers. Not now, not in here."

Kesira shared the farmer's concern. She found herself glancing back over her shoulder, certain someone followed. No one did. A haunted feel about the ranks of waves made her wonder what had died so that this frozen tribute to Ayondela's power could exist. The endless motion of the surf against the beach had been stilled, yet the thwarted waves trembled under her feet and threatened to burst free at any moment. Or was this only imagination? Kesira knew only that she was getting colder and colder. Being in this ice forest robbed her of heat, sent tiny needles of pain up from the soles of her feet, made the slightest mistake painful as she brushed against the waves held in perpetual suspense.

"The Steel Crescent's contraption worked good," observed Raellard, running his hand over the edge of one wave and noting how it had been melted into a smooth curve. "We'd never be able to move so fast without this road already cut for us."

"Quiet," complained Zolkan from above. "I listen for movement. How can I hear with your grumblings disguising all?"

Kesira put her hand on Raellard's shoulder to comfort him. She understood that he spoke only from nervousness. The eerie expanse of water turned to ice gnawed at her courage, too.

They walked on briskly, making good time. Kesira had estimated almost two miles to the Isle of Eternal Winter and decided they had gone more than halfway in only an hour. They slipped and slid on the recently melted slick surface and studiously avoided the more dangerous areas on the edges of the waves.

But it was Molimo and not Zolkan who first alerted her to dangers other than those presented by the immobile sea.

The man spun and drew his sword, facing along the front of a series of waist-high waves. Kesira quickly moved to stand beside him, peering into the gloom. She heard before she saw.

Delicate chewing sounds. Then stronger vibrations in the ice. Finally an inky black mass erupted not ten feet away, bulling its way through the thick ice. Tentacles lashed toward her face; Kesira shoved out her staff and allowed the suckers to fasten on the stone-wood rod. But she made the mistake of hanging on, not allowing the creature its pleasure with her staff. It pulled her along the ice on her knees, shouting as she went.

"Stop it, Molimo, stop it!"

The man leaped forward, blade rising and falling in a short, vicious arc. Black fluids spurted from the severed tentacle. It did not release the staff.

"What is it?" she gasped out. Kesira fought to get to her feet, succeeding only in slipping and falling again. All the while she struggled to pry loose the tentacle from her staff. It was made from the wood sacred to Gelya and had been through much with her. More from sentiment than good sense, Kesira tried to retain it.

"Never saw anything like that before," came Raellard's quavering reply. Molimo continued to hack and thrust at the beast, forcing it to partially retreat back through the hole in the ice. He fought well, but the beast knew no fear. It squirted back through, new tentacles grasping out blindly.

One caught Molimo on the chest and batted him away as if he were an annoying insect buzzing around a giant's nose. Molimo skidded back into Raellard, sending them both down in a pile.

Kesira stood, ichor-dripping staff in hand. She faced the formidable black sea beast without Molimo's quick sword to aid her. One snaky tentacle passed near her head. She stood without moving. It took a few seconds, then seemed to home in on her. When the two tentacles whipped about, the woman acted without thinking. She dived over the waist-high barrier of the frozen waves and into the next rank running perpendicular to their path.

The tentacles swung up, then crashed down to grip her. The sharp leading edges of the waves neatly severed the groping appendages. Hot black fluid hissed and popped on the ice. Kesira rose up on her toes and swung her staff double-handed. It impacted so hard on the creature that Kesira lost her balance and went skidding along the icy surface in the pipeline of waves.

A muted shriek aimed at the clouds hiding the moon, then the beast sank back down into its hole. Kesira heard the water sloshing about the break in the ice. Silence descended. She watched in awe as the ragged hole mended itself, freezing quickly until no trace remained of the beast, except for the severed tentacles and the spots where black blood had steamed their way into the surface.

"Hurry, hurry," urged Zolkan. "Sounds have alerted Steel Crescent soldiers. Nehan-dir sends back one to check. Hurry."

Molimo motioned for her to follow. The man trotted off a few yards and hunkered down in the darkness between ranks of waves. Kesira saw his plan immediately; he hid, ready to ambush the scout.

"What're we supposed to do?" asked Raellard, confused. "If we go on, that thing might follow. Can't go back. So far to land. If it catches us . . ."

"Don't worry now. Get down. We have to make sure the scout does not report back."

"But if he doesn't, the soldiers'll know something is wrong."

"A good point. We have lost any hope for secrecy now. At best we'll gain a few minutes."

The sharp scraping of boots equipped with steel cleats rang out in the deadly night's silence. Kesira felt her heart hammering wildly. She stilled it by rituals but still her hand shook. She didn't know if anticipated discovery did this to her or if it was a reaction to the monster breaking through the ice.

"Behind bad luck comes good," she told herself. This was hardly anything Gelya would have taught—her patron did not believe in luck's existence. Good luck is born from hard work, Gelya taught. But Kesira needed comforting not available from the innumerable maxims she so glibly recited.

Strutting along came the woman whose wrist she had broken the day before. The warrior wore her right arm in a sling and her sword pulled around so that she might draw it left-handed.

Molimo gave her no chance to do more than gasp before he ran her through with his sword.

"Twice now that she was careless," said Raellard with no remorse. "More chance'n any I ever knew got." Molimo knelt and plucked the sword from the woman's belt and handed it to the farmer. Raellard stared at the fine steel blade as if it were a poisonous snake.

"Take it," said Kesira, heaving a deep sigh. "Gelya taught against the use of steel. I am bound by that; you are not."

"But I've never used a sword before. Hardly ever used more than a spear or knife."

"Take her knife, too," said Kesira. "Just think of the sword as a longer knife." Molimo glared at her, but the woman was beyond caring. Tiredness assailed her and forced her eyelids shut in spite of all that happened.

"Hurry, hurry, hurry," urged Zolkan. "No new scout has been sent, but will be soon if you don't hurry."

They raced along the notch carved in the waves, making better time now with the threat of discovery balanced over their heads. Kesira and Molimo had each taken one of the sets of cleats from the dead woman's boots. With the cleats on one foot, they skated along on the uncleated foot. Raellard scrambled along behind the best he could.

"Halt. Wait. Look up," came Zolkan's words. Kesira did not find the *trilla* bird aloft, but she knew he was there, watching out for them. Her eyes started low, among the waves—then paused for a moment. The direction of the wave crests had reversed.

"We're near the shoreline of Ayondela's island," she said, showing Molimo what she meant.

Kesira's attention turned up. She gasped. They had stumbled almost onto the beach of the island and had not known it. Rocky, dark cliffs towered above them, rising more than two hundred feet. Faint ghost light rimmed the cliff's top like ethereal lace, the product of the white flame burning in the center of the island. Dancing shadows flitted across the ice, ducking and dodging, belonging to nothing human.

"The path ends against the cliff," said Raellard, missing the beauty of the Isle of Eternal Winter. "May be a stairway up the face. Or even some ladder inside the rock. Saw that in a mine once. Went right up through a mountain to the top."

Crunching and gnawing sounds came from beneath Kesira's feet. She looked down. Through translucent ice she saw ominous dark figures moving. Cracks shattered the ice. She hurried forward, leaning heavily on Molimo as she did.

"More of the beasts eating upward," she said. He put an arm around her waist, and they worked their way closer to the base of the cliff. Only when they were sure that dirt stretched under the ice rather than water did they stop.

"Can't get up there, no way," said Raellard, scratching the stubble on his chin. "I'm no climber. Can't get up there, just can't."

As Raellard talked, Molimo studied the rock face. His grim expression told Kesira that Raellard had been right. When Molimo swung about, sword in hand, she was startled. The man peered past her, toward the acres of frozen crests.

A voice as deadly as the ice field said, "Kill them where they stand. All three of them."

Kesira spun and saw Nehan-dir a dozen yards away. A boulder had been rolled away from a cave mouth. The mercenaries with him drew swords and came forward—more than two dozen of them.

Kesira knew there was no way to fight them and live. Nor could they hope to run back into the notch cut through the waves. Already several of the soldiers cut off escape by that route.

"That one has Alir's sword. The misbegotten demon spawn killed her. I claim him for my own!"

Raellard stared in dumb fascination at the sword in his hand. He had never thought simply holding it would brand him as a murderer.

"But I killed no one," he blurted. "That one. He did it!"

Nehan-dir laughed. "See? They turn on one another. This is the loyalty preached by the weaker patrons. Not the strength of arms *our* patron espouses."

"Who is your patron now, Nehan-dir? Ayondela?"

An amused smirk crossed the scrawny soldier's scarred face. "Hardly. We serve Eznofadil."

Kesira drove back the first mercenary to reach her; Molimo gutted another. Raellard found himself flat on his back, a swordpoint at his throat.

Before the thrust came that would end his life, the very earth shook with the booming command, *"Wait!"*

The soldier staggered back, stunned by the vibrancy and power locked in that single word. All eyes turned to the top of the cliff. Standing there, bathed in luminous green, Ayondela stared at them.

"They are ours, mighty Ayondela," protested Nehan-dir. "Lord Eznofadil promised them to us."

"Bring them to my throne room. *Now,* sniveling worms!"

Her cold blue scepter pointed downward. A circle of wan light enveloped Nehan-dir. Ice formed on his sword, his flesh turned gray with frostbite and his eyelids matted shut as the fluids around his eyeball started to freeze.

"Do as she says, damn you all," Nehan-dir grated out from between chattering teeth.

Ayondela's wand moved back into the cradle of her left arm. Her fangs caught the light from the dancing white flame inland and her long, waist-length hair billowed out over the sheer drop as she turned and vanished from sight.

With ill-concealed disgust, Nehan-dir indicated that the three should be taken into the small cave from which the mercenaries had emerged. Kesira blinked at the glare inside. The very walls burned and molten rock dribbled down in sluggish rivers. Yellows and whites stabbed into her eyes and forced her to lift a hand to shade them.

"What causes this?" she heard Raellard ask somewhere behind her. The farmer grunted when one of the soldiers cuffed him on the side of the head.

She called out to the man, "Magicks, Eznofadil's magicks. He makes the interior burn even as Ayondela holds the outer world in frigid bondage."

Nehan-dir shoved her toward a crushed stone ramp leading upward. Kesira began to climb, taking the switch-backs one after another. After what seemed an eternity of heat and light, they emerged in front of a palace forged from blue-white ice glinting like a giant diamond.

"Ayondela's," Nehan-dir said, confirming what she suspected. "For whatever reason, she has always enjoyed being surrounded by ice. Frigid bitch. Who else would come to what should be a tropical island and turn it into her own Isle of Eternal Winter?"

"You don't like her," said Kesira.

"She has her uses. Eznofadil uses her."

"You worship the power he has?"

"Ayondela is a fool." Nehan-dir said nothing more as they walked along the path leading to the immense gates chiseled from a glacier. On either side of the walkway grew tiny white flowers, their blue centers glistening with ice crystals. Kesira stooped to pluck one of the flowers and jerked her hand back when she touched one.

"Cold, isn't it?" said Nehan-dir, smirking. "Everything is cold here. You will learn."

Kesira's brown eyes rose to the pillar of cold, heartless fire rising behind the palace. This provided the faint light suffusing the entire area.

"Lenc's doing. His bond with Eznofadil requires a symbol," said Nehan-dir, kicking at Kesira so she stumbled and fell headlong into the palace's entryway. Molimo tried to come to her aid, but a half-dozen swordpoints pricked his skin. He subsided.

"You show more intelligence than I'd've thought, mute one," said Nehan-dir. "Don't try to escape or help her. Ayondela's wrath will take its toll, I assure you."

Kesira looked around, awed in spite of herself. The entire structure had been carved from a single block of ice, yet the interior was warm. Paintings by both mortal and demon artists hung on the ice walls, furniture lined the corridor, all was sumptuous and elegant and expected—except for the ice construction.

Nehan-dir motioned. Twenty-foot-tall doors of clear ice swung back to reveal a huge audience chamber. Ayondela sat on a blue-white throne, scepter in hand. Kesira's heart pounded now. She had wanted an audience with the female demon, a chance to explain what had happened to

Rouvin. She knew she would get only a few words before the demon's wrath erupted and doomed them all. Kesira had to make every instant count.

"Faith and courage are partners," she muttered to herself. Molimo heard, turned partially toward her and smiled. Kesira hoped that he retained his human form long enough for her to explain. Otherwise . . .

"Mighty Ayondela, Mistress of the Isle of Eternal Winter, your humble servants bring these prisoners," said Nehan-dir, obviously loathing every formal word he spoke.

"Ayondela!" cried Kesira, dropping to give obeisance. The floor burned at her knees and turned her robe damp with melted ice. "I am guilty of your son's death. I killed Rouvin. Take me and lift the winter curse you've placed on the world."

Ayondela ignored her. The female demon's eyes blazed with jade light. Her scepter rose and she pointed it directly at Molimo.

"This one. He killed Rouvin."

"I am responsible," protested Kesira. A flick of the wand sent waves of chilling cold against Kesira's face. The nun fell forward, supporting herself on quaking hands, gasping for breath in the magical beam that turned even the air into a frosty liquid.

"He killed Rouvin," Ayondela repeated.

"I'm innocent," blurted out Raellard Yera. "Don't know anything about these two. Nothing. They . . . they kidnapped me!"

"Silence!"

Raellard cowered back, then straightened. "I am a loyal servant of the Emperor. Only he can speak to me in such a tone."

"Careful," Kesira cautioned. "She is not in her right mind."

Ayondela's fangs began to glow with the pale green inner light. She rose and her eyes flashed hotly.

"To the special room with them. And *him,*" the female demon said, indicating Raellard with her wand, "I want *him* to understand fear. It will be a good exercise to see how well the device works."

Nehan-dir's soldiers grabbed the farmer by the upper arms and lifted him onto his toes so he couldn't struggle effectively. They dragged him off. Raellard said nothing. The expression of contempt on his face told it all. He had shown a moment's weakness and loss of faith, then regained that part making him a man.

"Wait," Ayondela said, as the mercenaries started to escort Molimo and Kesira from the room. The demon's eyes narrowed as she looked hard at Molimo. "This one is familiar to me. Very familiar."

Kesira stumbled slightly when Ayondela said that. Currents flowed in the room that she did not understand. She saw Molimo's throat muscles moving, as if he spoke, and she thought she heard quick words. But that wasn't possible. Molimo's tongue had been cut out.

But what confused the female demon? She had been certain of Molimo's guilt in her son's murder.

"Never mind. Take them away."

Kesira saw the look of relief on Molimo's face and relaxed a little herself. Whatever had happened, the woman knew she'd not been a part of it. Molimo worked on his own escapes. They were led into the bowels of the ice palace. In spite of her plight, Kesira couldn't help but admire the intricate carvings in the walls, the way the floors had been delicately etched with patterns of birds and flowers and things pastoral and alien to this frigid environment.

"She wants you to see what her wrath can be like," said Nehan-dir. "While you do not deserve it, I offer you a chance for escape."

"What?" asked Kesira, immediately suspicious. "Why?"

Nehan-dir took a deep breath, as if trying to compose unsettled thoughts. "You are a worthy opponent in battle, better than many who carry steel swords and wear armor. For that, I offer you a quick death rather than entering there." His pale eyes betrayed a flicker of distaste for what Ayondela intended.

"You're offering to kill us cleanly so we won't have to endure Ayondela's tortures?" Kesira laughed. "A useless life is one that ends too early."

"Remember that when your mind burns and your soul cries out for release." Nehan-dir made a gesture and his soldiers obeyed. Molimo and Kesira were shoved into the cell.

The door slammed shut. A hissing sound came that at-

tracted Kesira's attention. Through the translucent walls
of the cell she saw some of the soldiers working with a bra-
zier and irons to melt shut the prison door.

"We're melted inside," she said to Molimo. He nodded.
"What did you do back in the throne room? To Ayondela? I
heard, or felt—it is difficult to describe the sensation—
words."

"These?" he wrote on his tablet, outlining the spell
given him by Toyaga.

"Not that, not exactly, but some of the words. I heard
them, as if you spoke. You didn't, did you?"

He shook his head sadly. Then Molimo wrote, "It is a
spell given me by a demon. It did not work over-well on
Ayondela. She had been told I was guilty, so the spell could
not be expected to function perfectly. Not against the
power of the jade."

"She recognized you, but she did nothing. She preferred
to take her revenge on poor Raellard."

Molimo vehemently denied this. Kesira had to agree.
Ayondela's wrath could not be sated with a single act of
sadism. Her insanity required her to punish the entire
world, choking it in snow and blinding it with storm. Kesira had missed her chance to plead guilty to the crime of
killing Rouvin. Now she and Molimo and Raellard and
probably everyone else were doomed.

"Why is this cell supposed to be so nasty?" she asked,
slowly walking around. Her hands found only slippery ice
walls and floor. The ceiling was of the same frigid material. "She traps us in the center of an ice cube, nothing
more."

Molimo took her by the shoulders and spun her around.
The look of concern in his eyes tore at her.

"I'll be all right," she said. "We are together. We can escape any cell. And remember, Zolkan is still free. He will
figure some way of getting us away from this awful place."
She put her arms around herself and shivered.

Then she screamed.

Melting through the wall came a beast of utter blackness. Its body rejected the material and embraced the nothingness of space. Midnight black pseudopods rippled forth
to surround her, to embrace her with lingering, painful
death.

Kesira shied away and bumped into Molimo. The expression on his face matched hers—and he stared in the opposite direction. Kesira couldn't look to see what menaced the man. Her own personal horror floated and fluttered and slithered to take her.

She screamed again.

Chapter Fifteen

THE ARMIES OF FROZEN waves marched ghostlike in the silvered moonlight beneath Zolkan like dutiful soldiers on parade. He wheeled about, spilled air under his left wing, and plummeted downward, only to swoop and soar upward again when he saw the Order of the Steel Crescent mercenaries closing in around Kesira and Molimo, swords prodding dangerously into their bodies. The *trilla* bird let out a squawk.

Find help, came Molimo's words. Then Zolkan heard nothing more.

"Help?" he complained to himself as his powerful wings took him toward the moon. "Help from where? Who is asshole stupid enough to help?" Even as the bird screamed this protest into the still night the answer came to him. His beak clacked open and shut, tasting the cool breezes, then he dipped his brightly crested head and started flying in earnest for the mainland.

The jagged ice fields that had once been the Sea of Katad disappeared under him, replaced by low hills, higher ones, real mountains. Zolkan spiraled about, looking, not finding. Tirelessly he continued his search until, just a bit before the sun reached its zenith, a pinpoint of brightness shone from the area near the Pharna River.

Zolkan clucked to himself and arrowed downward, a green-feathered messenger. He pushed hard against the air and braked, hanging almost stationary in the air above the decrepit traveler heating soup over a minuscule fire of dung chips. The derelict glared upward as Zolkan cut off his warming sunlight. An impatient wave indicated that

Zolkan should land. The *trilla* bird dropped like a stone and faced the man across the fire.

"He needs your aid," Zolkan said without preamble.

"How did you find me? I've taken pains to lose myself along the myriad paths of this lacy winterland." The man ran his slender, uncallused fingers through snow and sent the white powder high into the air. Sunlight caught the individual crystals and sent forth tiny rainbows from the intricate shapes.

"Toyaga, he needs you. You cannot turn from him."

The man sighed and ran a hand over his eyes, as if a mighty headache assailed him now. "How you found me is a mystery, but then you always were adept at being the messenger, weren't you, Zolkan?"

"Some easier to find than others. Necessity drove me. He is caught by Ayondela."

"I gave him what I could. Has the spell worked?"

"It worked," confirmed the bird. "He needs more than simple spell. You received aid; it is your duty."

"This is one of the damnable things I hate about *trilla* birds. You have such long memories. You put even a demon to shame."

"Dangerous. Eznofadil as well as Ayondela on Isle of Eternal Winter."

"Your quick tongue works to convince me to never go to the Sea of Katad."

"You ought to know opponents."

"Ah, I know my enemies. They define me, they give my life substance and bounds. I do know them, Zolkan." Toyaga chuckled. "I suppose that if I had no enemies it would be a sign that fair fortune has overlooked me, which is certainly not the case."

"You have enemies," confirmed Zolkan. "You also have friends."

"And duty to them, yes, yes, Zolkan. You need not remind one such as I of this." Toyaga lounged back and spooned some of the hot stew into his mouth. A dribble went down his chin. The bird canted his head to one side, trying to understand this demon.

"Oh, sorry," Toyaga said. "When I play a role, I immerse myself in it totally." He wiped the spill off with a quick swipe of his hand. "I thought to wander among the

unfortunate mortals for a while and find new inspiration
for an epic poem of struggle and suffering."

"We must hurry."

"I suppose the poem can wait. I am barely rested from
my last battle with Eznofadil and Ayondela. They are worthy foes." Toyaga heaved a sigh. "And you are so right. I
have worthy friends, as well. Let's go see if we cannot prevail in their behalf, eh?"

Zolkan's colorful, delicately formed crest fanned out in
the warm sunlight, then folded low. He hopped to Toyaga's
shoulder and waited. The trip back to the Isle of Eternal
Winter would be accomplished much faster than the flight
away.

The black arms reached around her. Kesira shrieked
and struck out with her fists. She found emptiness. The
inky vacuum sucked her forward, against the nothingness
of its chest. Kesira twisted and turned, then fell heavily to
the floor as the creature made a wild grab to ensnare her.
She tingled all over as the emptiness fell into itself and
vanished as suddenly as it had appeared.

The ice wall remained untouched, whole. Kesira turned
and stared at Molimo. The man had shifted into his wolf
shape, snarling and snapping at thin air. She reached out
to pat the wolf head, to calm him. He nearly took her hand
off at the wrist. Kesira showed no fear as the teeth closed
around her hand. One convulsive wolf twitch and she
would be without a right hand.

"I am you friend. We must stand together, Molimo. Together. Against Ayondela. Against the jade demons." She
betrayed no hint of pain as the teeth clamped down harder
on her flesh when she mentioned the jade demons.

"It is terrible to be alone. I know that—I know a bit of
what you feel. No parents, no family, the social hierarchy
missing. The Emperor is far away and there is little that is
honorable left in this part of the world."

The wolf's green eyes turned almost phosphorescent in
their intensity.

"We can make the difference, Molimo. You and I, together." The wolf twitched nervously, getting free of the
human clothing still hanging about its sleek, gray-furred
body. Kesira noted that Molimo did not release her hand.

"All my life I have been alone, even among my Sisters in the Order. I sense that it is similar with you. We are different, Molimo. We do not fit the easy, accepted pattern of society. I was an orphan." Kesira started to point out the details of Molimo's affliction, then stopped. With the wolf instincts in control, she did not want to play too much on his pain and hardship.

Kesira didn't know what it was. The feel of the hot saliva on her hand turning different, a small jerking movement of the tail, some other small sign—but she gently withdrew her hand from the wolf's mouth just as the shape shift back to human occurred. She heaved a sigh as Molimo reappeared, a look of anguish on his face.

"You cannot help it," she said softly. "I know. I understand."

Molimo dressed in silence. Kesira couldn't help but watch as his naked body became clothed. He was such a handsome man, strong, intelligent, gentle when in human form. Her mind touched on all the fantasies about him she'd had before and added one or two new ones. To have him in her bed, intimately next to her, making love, when he shape-shifted. Kesira shivered at the forbidden thought. What would it be like with a wolf? And, even worse, one of the afflicted other-beasts caused by the actions of the jade demons?

She flushed guiltily when Molimo glared at her. She wondered if he read her mind or simply disliked all that had happened to them.

"Are you all right?" she asked Molimo. A curt nod was the only answer she received. "What was that monster? It came through the walls."

Molimo found his tablet and scribbled in an almost illegible hand, "Might be able to follow it through. Try?"

Kesira wasn't sure if she wanted to try or not. "Yes," she finally said. Anything had to be better than freezing in the ice cell.

"Will summon beast again. I will slip behind, distract it, then you come."

"This sounds dangerous," she said. For a moment she thought on it, then laughed. "Of course it is dangerous. It is dangerous merely being here."

Molimo rewarded her with a wry smile. His eyes had returned to their usual midnight black, and he carried himself with dignity once more. Whatever affront she had given him had been forgotten—or forgiven.

"How are you going to summon it?"

He waved her to the side of the tiny cell. She pressed her back into the frigid wall and waited. Somewhere—at the fringes of her hearing?—sounded a shrill whistle. The noise irritated Kesira as much as it reminded her of the singsong speech Zolkan used to communicate in his fashion with Molimo. The woman started to ask Molimo about this when the back wall turned gray, then black.

The creature surged through the wall once more.

And again, just at the edges of her senses, Kesira heard snatches of the spell Molimo had mentioned to her.

The world . . .

. . . no eyes.

Freedom . . .

I fade . . .

Only snippets came, but she had no time to think about this. The nothingness beast ignored Molimo, blundered past and came for her, tentacles reaching.

"Go, Molimo," she cried. Kesira had no chance to see if the man-wolf obeyed or not. He had to. This was his plan. She found herself dodging the long, vaporous reach of the groping black tentacles. One passed through the side wall and snaked around, coming back at her from an unexpected direction. When it touched her flesh, it was disgustingly substantial.

Kesira ducked down low, yanked her arm free and slammed hard against the wall where the door into the cell had been, before the mercenaries had melted it shut. As she faced the monster, Kesira felt a pang of guilt. At this instant of danger she experienced selfishness. She thought only of herself.

This was Ayondela's true torture: In adversity Kesira lost sight of her goals, of her teachings. Gelya would not have been pleased.

The world lay under a blanket of ice, shivering to death, robbed of warm summer breezes. Zolkan might have his freedom, but the dangers outside the ice palace were as great as those within. And Molimo. Where had he gone? To his death? Kesira did not know. Theirs might be the greater need and all she could think of was a cold black tentacle brushing along her skin.

"Time to leave," she said softly. Pseudopods flowed toward her from both sides of the creature. Inadvertently her feet helped her—she slipped on the icy floor, the cleated right shoe giving way. She fell heavily and slid past the black nothingness of the creature through the wall into darkness so extreme she had to push down a pang of fear that she'd gone blind.

Here.

Kesira looked about her at the sound of the word. She got to her feet and saw Molimo ahead, beckoning to her. The blackness danced about his body, repulsed by some force.

"You spoke!" she cried. No answer came. Kesira knew she might have imagined the single word. But she wasn't sure. Everything had turned upside down in her world. She rushed to Molimo yet her journey seemed endless, a trip ten times the distance from her nunnery to the Emperor's capital. When she finally reached him, thankful arms out-thrust to embrace him, Molimo had gone.

"No!" she shrieked. "Don't leave me like this. You can't, damn you, Molimo, damn you!"

Kesira stood alone in the dark. The impact of her predicament struck her anew. She had gotten back on the right path in the ice cell when facing the vapor-tentacled beast. The proper course to follow was not to think of herself, but to consider others. She was a part of the universe; an important part, due to a quirk of circumstance. She had to believe this. She knew the danger from the jade demons and had a way to alleviate some of the heartache they carried with them.

Only through her interaction with Molimo—and Zolkan and Raellard and all the others—might she triumph.

Even as she again found this point, Molimo returned to her side. He took her arm and guided her among hidden obstacles.

"How can you see?" she asked. Her voice sounded curiously dull and muted. "Did you truly speak to me? Before?"

His eyes flashed but carried no assurance. That had to

come from within. She simply accepted that Molimo's vision in this light-sucking black void was better.

Laughter taunted her. Molimo hurried her along even faster. She stumbled many times, but kept moving. Wherever they went, it had to be better than this. But strive as they did, they couldn't outrun the mocking laughter. It came from everywhere, and from nowhere. Kesira put her hands over her ears and even this did nothing to stop it. The nun felt as if it rattled inside her brain, forcing its way out.

"What is causing that?" she moaned. "Stop it, Molimo. Make it stop."

"Yes, Molimo, make it stop," the voice said. Kesira recognized it instantly: Ayondela.

"This is only some new torture," Kesira said. The absence of certainty had been snipping away pieces of her sanity. Knowing allowed Kesira to hold to what little she possessed. Failure came not from weak flesh, but from weak spirit. Over and over she told herself this. Her resolve strengthened.

And Ayondela sensed it.

"You will not escape my ice prisons. Never!"

"Please, Ayondela, listen to me. For just a moment. Take my life, if you will, in payment for your son's life. But lift the curse. Let the seasons grow naturally."

"All you mortals must suffer. Rouvin died for all of you, you must all die for him!"

"That's not so," protested Kesira. She tugged at Molimo's grip. He seemed to want to keep her from drawing more of Ayondela's attention. This might be the only chance Kesira got to explain. If any thread of rationality persisted in Ayondela, Kesira had to appeal to it.

"Oh?"

"We have an ordered society, one of hierarchies and duties," Kesira said, "and everyone knows their place in it, but I acted on my own, without authority from anyone." Tears welled up in her brown eyes. "Lenc killed my Sisters, my patron, all who would give me guidance. I acted on my own out of revenge."

"The one with you," said Ayondela. "He is so familiar. Who is he? He . . . he is responsible for Rouvin's death. Someone told me this. Who?"

Kesira heard Molimo grunting and mumbling deep in his throat. An instant of dizziness assailed her. She reeled, then straightened. She thought she heard the snippet of poem again. Something about freedom and nothingness and no more eyes.

"Ayondela, take me. Free the world."

The female demon's response startled her. It was as if Ayondela had forgotten all that had been said.

"Come, look upon my vengeance. A part of him dies every second. How long will he last? Not long. Oh, no, not long now."

Glare blinded Kesira; Molimo seemed to have expected it and had already shielded his eyes with one hand. A vista opened before them that made Kesira suck in her breath and hold it. She had been giddy before. Now she stumbled and fell to one knee, unable to stand without vertigo seizing control of her senses.

She and Molimo floated high above the floor of Ayondela's audience chamber. The demon's throne stood off to one side. Behind the throne, through a window of frost and ice crystal flickered the cold flame of Lenc's sigil. Immediately below—hundreds of feet below—stretched the icy floor with rank after rank of soldiers standing rigidly at attention. Kesira saw that Nehan-dir commanded them. The leader of the Order of the Steel Crescent had bared his chest and exposed the cruelly burned half-moon symbolic of his Order. Even though she was far distant, she saw the expression on the man's scarred face as if he were only at arm's length. He enjoyed all that happened and would enjoy her death even more, now that she had refused him his chance to kill her quickly.

The cathedral-high roof of the throne room brushed Kesira's hair; Molimo had to stoop. At some unseen command, they drifted lower. Ayondela pointed with her wand of blue ice. The light dancing forth in waves carried Kesira's attention with it, past the rows of mercenaries, past Nehan-dir, past the elegant and elaborate appointments in the room to a small alcove.

Molimo's fingers bit into her arm. He understood what torture Ayondela visited upon Raellard Yera long before Kesira did.

Raellard's arms had been pulled out to either side of his

body and chained securely. The links of that chain glistened and shone a milky white. Like so much else in the palace, they were of steel-hard ice. His legs were similarly attached, making all but the slightest of movements impossible.

He shrieked and moaned loudly.

Eznofadil's burning device used by the soldiers to cut through the frozen waves on the sea was now aimed for different parts of the farmer's body. Light from Lenc's flame entered a tiny window above Raellard, struck the curved reflecting surface and magicks bent the feeble rays into ones able to inflict intense agony.

"They're burning him with it. But no charred flesh appears when the ray touches him." Kesira felt faint, both from the idea that nothing beneath her feet supported her and that she drifted a hundred feet above her death, and from the obvious suffering Raellard endured.

"The burning takes place inside, when Lenc's flame is used as a source of energy. Sunlight," Ayondela said with obvious distaste, "produces only intense heat. This produces intense pain."

"He is innocent. I am responsible for Rouvin's death."

Molimo shook his head.

"No, Molimo," she said earnestly. "I cannot let another suffer for what we did." He put his hand over her mouth to stifle her words. Kesira's eyes widened in surprise. Molimo was no coward hiding in the dark, fearing the slightest of sounds, cringing from his own heartbeats. Time and time again he had risked his life for her and had done so without an instant's hesitation. Kesira found it hard to believe he could be so insensitive to Raellard's suffering.

Raellard might be a miserable person or worthy of deification—to Kesira it made no difference. He was a human and he suffered for something she and Molimo had done. Fair or not did not matter. This was a question of honor and duty.

"Stop it!" she pleaded.

"Focus the beam to produce more pain," commanded Ayondela, lounging back on her icy throne, enjoying the suffering. A woman of the Steel Crescent came forth and tinkered with the settings, tipping the dish-shaped part slightly. Raellard's shriek of misery cut through Kesira's heart like a knife.

"Continue. Until he is dead. Then we begin on them." Ayondela's green eyes burned like phosphorus as she pointed her scepter at Kesira and Molimo. They drifted lower until their feet touched the icy floor.

Chapter Sixteen

RAELLARD'S SCREAMS FILLED Kesira Minette's soul with searing acid. She resisted closing her eyes or putting her hands over her ears to block the farmer's hideous shrieks. That would have given Ayondela too much pleasure. The jade demon sat on her throne of blue-white ice, sneering, her tusks gleaming with shining green. Ayondela tossed her head and sent a cascade of hair floating out gently; she had been lovely once, Kesira knew.

Only stark, ripping hatred showed now.

"No wound appears—they are all within his mind," Ayondela boasted. "This is a fine instrument for wreaking the vengeance I need. You will be next, Geyla's slut. And then . . . then . . ." Her voice trailed off.

Kesira frowned. Ayondela had started to indict Molimo, also. But the female demon had lost the chain of her thought. Kesira looked away, gratefully, from Raellard's suffering and turned to Molimo. His eyes had the bleak, desolate look she had seen there so many times. But a curious triumph that fluttered here and there confused her. A tiny portion of the poem-spell came to her mind again. She saw Molimo's throat muscles working, as if he intoned the spell, but the words came not to her ears but directly to her mind.

"How can you do this to a man who has done no harm?" Kesira demanded of Ayondela.

"No harm? He helped you kill Rouvin. He is guilty and now is being punished!"

"He is a poor farmer, whose family is starving to death by slow inches because of your curse. He knows nothing of Rouvin or the Quaking Lands or Howenthal."

"He must be taught, then," came a new voice, a deeper, more resonant one. Molimo and Kesira watched as a thick green pillar of whirling dust formed between them and Ayondela. The miniature tornado spun faster and faster until an explosion blasted the windy walls apart to reveal a tall, well-muscled, handsome Eznofadil. The greenish complexion glowed in the light of Lenc's flame, giving Eznofadil an alien aspect that made Kesira shiver.

"Reason with her," pleaded Kesira. "You know I was responsible. I will die for it, if only she lifts her curse."

"Why should she lift her cold touch on the world in exchange for your confession? She already *has* you. You, my dear Kesira Minette, will be destroyed. You and your friends." Eznofadil blinked as he stared at Molimo.

Molimo tried not to appear nervous, but Kesira felt tenseness in the man's body. He moved slightly, so that she shielded him from Eznofadil's direct stare.

"What's wrong?" she asked, almost in a whisper. "Do you fear them?"

Molimo nodded vigorously.

"But you've confronted them before. Why do you fear them now?"

"He is . . ." Eznofadil paused, confused as Ayondela had been. "Let your friend revel in his anguish. Let him anticipate all that will be done to his precious body—and yours, my dear—with this fine implement of mine. Have you seen it at work? Ah, I see your other friend already samples its exquisite delights." Eznofadil laughed. No humor was contained within that sound.

Molimo tugged at her arm. She saw he had retrieved his tablet and wrote swiftly.

"The spell muddles their thinking, but Eznofadil is too powerful for it to last long. Their attention must not fall upon me. If it does, *we are lost!*" Molimo ran a bold stroke under those words to emphasize the importance of all he wrote.

Kesira frowned, unsure of the man.

"He cannot last much longer, can he, Ayondela?" Eznofadil pointed one slender, green-nailed finger in Raellard's direction. "Five minutes? Or less?"

Even as he spoke, the pale light playing over Raellard's body centered on his belly. The man's left hand sprang free of his manacle; the heat of his fear and pain had melted through the ice bracelet.

"My guts are on fire," he whimpered. Raellard clutched at his stomach, made a curious coughing sound, then slumped. The light from Eznofadil's infernal device continued to stroke over the man's unmoving body. Finally Ayondela gestured. The woman behind the machine made a few movements and the pale light winked off.

"He is quite dead, painfully achieving that sorry mortal's fate," said Eznofadil. "Ayondela, I do believe the nun's . . . companion ought to enjoy the caresses next. He is overly nervous. It will take his mind off other matters."

Ayondela barked out an order. Nehan-dir gestured and a dozen of his followers seized Molimo. Kesira started to her friend's aid, but was driven back at swordpoint. She watched helplessly as the ice manacles were fastened on Molimo's arms and legs.

"Please don't do this. He has suffered enough."

"Oh?" asked Ayondela. "How is this? Can he suffer more than a mother shorn of her only son?"

"He can't cry out in pain for your enjoyment," Kesira said bitterly. "Someone has already cut out his tongue."

"The silent scream is often the best," said Eznofadil. "Commence with the ray."

Kesira felt pain as great as any Molimo might feel. She sobbed and fought and found herself trapped within a magical bubble. Every time she tried to look away, the encapsulating bubble turned her around to face Molimo's plight. His ebony eyes took on a haunted expression far worse than anything she had seen before. Molimo was trapped within himself, unable to communicate since his tongue had been severed. His arms and legs strained against the ice links, but those bonds held him firmly.

The light worked over his legs, thighs, groin. Molimo's mouth opened in unvoiced pain.

"I begin to tire of this," Eznofadil said. "Ayondela, my sweet, let me show the nun about. I promise to return with her in time to see his demise."

The leer on Ayondela's face numbed Kesira even more. The demons understood one another all too well. Eznofadil was not offering her a guided tour of the ice palace; more hinged on the request than she understood.

"Do so. Return within one hour. I doubt he will be able to last longer. Then it will be *her* turn." The scepter pointed directly at Kesira, sending needles of alternating heat and cold through her. "She will be made to last for at least a week. If I can draw it out to a month, all the better." Ayondela leaned forward on her throne and told Eznofadil, "Let her escape and it will be you suffering in the beam of the torture machine."

Eznofadil laughed lightly. "Never would I jeopardize such a valued ally's loyalty. She will be returned in one hour. After I have given her the full benefit of my expertise."

The bubble holding Kesira burst. She tumbled downward. Only force of will prevented her from screaming as she rushed toward the cold ice floor. Inches above the ground, another invisible force seized her and prevented her from being injured.

"So easy," Eznofadil said, "since I have walked the jade path. But then, so many things have become clear to me. Come. I want to share them." He made a careless gesture. Unseen hands lifted Kesira and hurried her along beside the jade demon.

"You only use her, don't you?"

"How's that? Ayondela?"

"Ayondela," said Kesira. "You taunt and torment her, make her bring the coldness to the land for your own reasons. What will you do when her need for revenge is past?"

"Feed it again. I think she has an infinite capacity for hating mortals. In spite of her protests, she and Rouvin's father were never in love. As much as can ever happen to a demon, she was seduced, raped, whatever term you wish to employ. This has caused a long-festering hatred of mortals. I rather suspect Ayondela was happy that you killed Rouvin." Eznofadil turned and stared curiously at Kesira.

"A nun did not kill such a warrior. Was it your friend—the one now enduring Ayondela's tortures—who killed Rouvin?"

Kesira said nothing, but her expression betrayed her.

"I feel as if I know—knew—that." Eznofadil frowned, thinking hard. "Can it be some spell at work, one I do not detect? While it is possible, I doubt any is of sufficient strength to befuddle me."

"No one except Lenc," she said, hoping to sow discord among the ranks of the jade demons.

"We have an agreement, Lenc and I. No, this is something more. Curious. I must look at your friend more carefully when we return. And he is dead."

The aura of green surrounding Eznofadil built in intensity, radiating like a gaseous envelope. Eznofadil's skin had not taken on the brittle appearance that Howenthal's had shown, but it differed greatly from normal skin, for either human or demon. The texture was somehow smoother, the strength tougher.

"You admire my . . . suntan?" Eznofadil smiled. "This is an alteration in my appearance I find distressing, but it is little enough to trade for the power I wield. Come. See what we do in the world. You owe it to yourself."

Kesira gasped as wind whipped around her body, catching the tattered gray robe and pulling it back as if she soared like Zolkan. Eznofadil strode out on the snowy ground, pointing to the far north where the Yearn Mountains rose majestically. The white blankets of winter covering them had never been more brilliant in sunlight.

"Those are but one facet of Ayondela's gemlike curse. I encourage such beauty. Don't you agree that the mountains are at their loveliest in winter? Can you deny such a glory to the world?"

"How did we get here?" Kesira wandered about, dazed by the sudden transition from the Isle of Eternal Winter to the Plains of Roggen. Kesira thought she recognized the location; Chounabel lay off to the southeast and Blinn nestled high in the mountains directly to the north. And to the north and west lay the Quaking Lands. The woman wondered if they still shivered and boiled with subterranean restlessness or if Howenthal's passing had stilled their temblors.

"You cannot expect a demon to waste time getting from one spot to the next. All of us are able to travel in this mode, to some degree or another. But only those of us who partake of the jade can bring along such valued guests." Eznofadil executed a mockingly formal bow in her direction.

"Ayondela thinks to change the seasons? This is beauty? The only beauty is in the hope that the following season brings something better. Summer melds into autumn and harvests. Winter allows rest for the work of the summer and fall. Spring breaks the monotony of storms and snow. Summer is filled with the exaltation of spirit from good, pleasing labor. Ayondela breaks the natural cycle and locks us into perpetual boredom."

"Boredom?" asked Eznofadil. "Do you find storms boring?"

Kesira tried to hold back her gasp of surprise as they again changed locations. Strong, cold winds tugged at her flesh, freezing and nipping and trying to tear it from her bones. Eyes watering, she looked down a sheer precipice to the world below. Kesira had no idea where Eznofadil had brought her.

"We are atop Mt. Pline. Perhaps you don't know it? The Emperor once had a summerhouse here." Eznofadil walked about, untouched by the fiercely raging storm. Occasional bolts of lightning lit his green skin and turned it into something truly evil. "The heat of Limaden drives him here every summer for rest. Normally, this place would be pleasant, a high meadow lush with grass and trees, a small brook. A spot of unsurpassed loveliness after winter releases its death's grip. I think Ayondela does the empire a service by forcing the Emperor to stay closer to his capital and tend to matters other than his own comfort."

Kesira pulled her tattered robe more tightly around her body, but it didn't help much—nor had any amount of shelter helped those servants of the Emperor's caught in the unnatural storms now raging. Kesira made out the snowy forms of a dozen men and women, frozen as stiff as marble statues, all lined up outside one of the sumptuous houses kept here for the Emperor's use. To Eznofadil their deaths meant nothing; the suffering of millions meant no more.

Kesira found herself unable to speak from the overwhelming realization of the demon's indifference to human misery. She stood and snow clogged her nose and mouth. Her eyes froze and heat seeped from her body, stiffening her.

She stumbled and fell as Eznofadil took her to another spot. While the cold winds did not blow as strongly here, she still felt the teeth of unnatural winter.

"Tropical isles fascinate me," said Eznofadil. "The Isle

of Eternal Winter used to be such, until Ayondela took possession. I do not understand her passion for ice and snow but it is useful to me. The mortals cringe and cower. When the curse is lifted, the one responsible will be a hero. They will honor me as their patron. With the power of jade to back me, I will rule all of the empire—and more!"

"Won't Ayondela and Lenc protest this small breach of your trust?"

"Protest? Why, Lenc strives to kill me, even as I do him. We are realists. There can be no quarter given, but it might benefit us both to join forces now and again. Ayondela is a tool, no more. I use her to act as a lightning rod for you mortals' fear and loathing. When she is no more, I will ride in, the conquering hero."

"You say you use Ayondela as your tool, but Lenc's flame burns on the island."

Eznofadil frowned. "It keeps him happy. I do nothing to oppose him openly. Not yet. My power grows to the point where I can destroy him without injury to myself."

"The jade doesn't protect you?" Kesira said, her voice cutting sarcastically. She had nothing more to lose. Molimo might be dead by now—Raellard certainly was. Kesira saw no way of freeing the world from Ayondela's grip or of destroying Eznofadil. Caustic comments gained her nothing but a sense of finally striking back. It was feeble and futile, but it instilled her with a small feeling of accomplishment.

"The jade is both a master and a servant. I cannot explain to you the transformation within me. With the others removed, I will be its total master and its hold over me will be as nothing."

"Is that all you want? Power to rule? Why, after so many millenia? The demons were revered and looked upon as great teachers, not despots. The Emperor ruled and all looked up to the demons. What has changed? Why do you seek direct dominance?"

"It has taken a long time for me to understand my destiny. Petty mortals rule for a few briefs moments before dying. I can give a unity of purpose to the world. I will. And," he said, shrugging, "all this breaks the monotony of my existence. It becomes dull living for such a long, long time."

"How can anyone think to bring himself happiness by

exercising power over another?" Kesira asked. "Gelya rightly taught that with power comes responsibility. Emperor Kwasian does not sleep soundly at nights worrying over the condition of his vassals. If you are to rule the world, can you worry over the lives of all the populace?"

"The will to power is strong," said Eznofadil. "It is more than an aphrodisiac. It is the ultimate aphrodisiac. I am happy to have discovered it."

The demon spun and looked out on the once-tropical island. A few people had gathered to see what disturbed the serenity of their afternoon nap. Eznofadil pointed. Four green pillars rose just outside the tight knot of natives. Shimmery curtains of light leaped out of the posts connecting one to the other. Screams came from within.

"It seems some of the mortals were caught by the diagonal sheets of energy," said Eznofadil, not really caring about their deaths. "Pity. But you wanted to see the cold removed from the land. Very well. For those lucky ones, it is."

Flames a thousand feet high leaped to sear the sky. The burning came so quickly none within the energy barriers had a chance to even cry out, as their friends had on being cut in two. Eznofadil watched with a clinical detachment that startled Kesira.

"You feel nothing for them," she said in a choked voice. "To you they are little more than insects."

"Less, actually," admitted Eznofadil. "Insects perform useful services. You mortals only clutter the landscape."

"And yet you want to rule us. Why?"

"Power is worthless unless it is used. While you are feeble, vain, venal, and shallow, you do have your uses. You mortals keep our existence from becoming unbearably boring."

Kesira paled when the demon turned toward her. His expression hadn't altered but the aura surrounding him deepened, as if the jade demanded even more mortal sacrifice.

"The ones like Ayondela are interesting, but mortals can be used and then discarded, with no more thought needed."

"The jade drives you now. Once, you were held in high

esteem by both the mortals who worshipped you and your peers. Don't you see how it changes you, Eznofadil?"

"For the better," the jade demon said. His eyes flashed wildly. He advanced, arms reaching for her. Kesira tried to run, to fight, to resist. Whatever Eznofadil did to her, it sucked away all power, if not her resolve. She stood as motionless as a statue, railing inside but outwardly immobile. Kesira almost fainted when the jade fingers lightly brushed across her cheek, her jawline, tracing back to the crease under her ear, lower. Wherever his digit touched, flesh burned—passionately.

Kesira sobbed as he parted her robe and discarded it. She stood naked to the waist as the demon moved closer, hands touching her now, sparking within her insane lust. She gasped and tried to thrust out her hips in wanton need.

"See what joys I can bring you?"

"The jade," she gasped.

"Gelya was a fool. He never visited his worshippers to learn what they might offer, other than feeble prayers and idiot looks of adoration for his parables."

The demon's outstretched finger drifted lower, teasing her, stirring passion within Kesira's loins unlike any she'd ever felt. Tears ran down her cheeks, and she failed to control them—or herself. All of the hours of meditation and control learned at such a cost abandoned her. Primal urges rose like inexorable tides within her moon-wracked body. Eznofadil jerked and the nun's robe fell off her hips to pile about her feet. She stood naked before him.

And she wanted the demon.

"This is nothing new to you, is it, my lovely one?" asked Eznofadil. "I see one of my colleagues has already sampled your delightful mortal wares." The tormenting finger traced over the mark on her left breast. Wemilat's kiss began to heat up, as if touched anew with a branding iron.

"My toadlike fellow demon must have done this to you." Kesira gasped. And felt nauseated when she realized she enjoyed it—wanted more. "Ah, he did, didn't he? And this?" The fingers stroked over her nude figure, stimulating, dipping deep and racing out once more until her body quivered with abject, forbidden need.

"No, you cannot do this to me. I forbid it!"

"The jade power demands it," Eznofadil said. "Now and again, I delve into a mortal's body and extract needed energy. Perhaps this is what Wemilat did. Perhaps he needed your energy to combat Howenthal? Yes, I think that must be what happened."

Kesira flushed with shame as Eznofadil moved even nearer. His smooth, hard body rubbed suggestively against hers. She commanded her legs to move; they remained rooted to the spot. Her arms did not lift. Eznofadil's spell dominated her totally.

"You must be a strange nun to enjoy ugly Wemilat's company and yet find mine detestable. We shall have to change that perception. You will tell me afterwards the difference. You cannot prefer him to me. You cannot."

Kesira knew the demon wove a spell of ponderous magicks around her, tangling her thoughts, confusing her emotions. How she wanted to be like Molimo in this instant, to change into a wolf and rip the demon's throat out! But she was held to his will, little more than the demon's slave.

"Yes, you do desire me now. I can tell." The hands brushed over her body, lewdly touching. "You will desire me with every fibre in that mortal body of yours even as I drain you and leave you a burned-out husk!"

His jade lips crushed into her flesh-and-blood ones. Kesira jerked against the potent spell holding her as hot arrows of desire lanced through her body. The demon's arms encircled her, held her, stroked over her nakedness.

The kiss broke off, leaving her gasping. Kesira dared not open her eyes. Eznofadil mistook this for true passion on her part.

"You warm to me. Perhaps I won't exhaust your vitality totally. Perhaps I will leave just a little to sample later, for a lightly erotic snack."

His lips again crushed down passionately on hers, then slipped lower, to her curving throat. To the deep valley between her breasts. The demon's insistent kisses set her ablaze within—and Kesira gasped, arching her back when Eznofadil's lips touched Wemilat's mark on her breast.

Through a veil of confusion, fear and unwanted lust, she remembered the brigand who had tried to rape her. He had put his lips to that spot and died.

Eznofadil was no mortal brigand.

Kesira gasped and hated herself as Eznofadil moved between her legs, having his way with her. The Kiss of Wemilat had not protected her this time.

Chapter Seventeen

KESIRA MINETTE stood motionless. Her mind reeled, but her body refused to respond to even her most desperate commands. Eznofadil had finished with her and stepped back. Fearfully, she opened her eyes, not knowing what she would see. The expression on the demon's face startled her.

She had expected to see contempt, or the remnants of lust, or triumph. All Kesira saw was confusion.

And that Eznofadil's lips had changed from their jade green color to a more normal flesh tone.

"What now?" she asked.

"I . . . I don't know." Eznofadil turned and started to wander off, then stopped. The jade demon's entire demeanor told Kesira that he had been deprived of his senses.

Even the spell holding her so firmly in place began to slip. The woman at first allowed the tingling sensation in her toes to remind her of her continued life, but then it spread, to ankles, past her cramped, knotted calves, up her legs. Strength flooded into her arms and body. Gasping with relief, she sank forward onto the cold ground, balancing herself on hands and knees. When the cold winds caused her to shiver, Kesira knew she had recovered from the paralysis inflicted upon her. Without asking Eznofadil's permission, she hastily put on her gray robe. Knotting the blue cord and tying the gold sash around her waist returned her to the known and made her more confident, in spite of all that the demon had done to her.

"What?" started Eznofadil, then recovered. He stared around him as if this island came as a complete surprise.

Kesira approached the demon warily. She had an idea as to what had happened to him, but she needed to know for certain. The brigand's leader had placed his lips over Wemilat's imprint on her breast and died horribly a few seconds later. But Eznofadil was neither human nor an ordinary demon. He had accepted the burden and gift of the jade stone, becoming incredibly powerful because of it. Wemilat's protection might not be powerful enough to kill Eznofadil, but it might have robbed him of his senses—at least for a while.

"Do you know who I am?" Kesira asked.

Eznofadil nodded.

"You know who your enemies are, don't you, Eznofadil, my demon lover?"

"Lover?" he asked, panic rising into his green eyes when he failed to remember what Kesira meant.

"Lover," she said firmly. "We are lovers, you and I. You are completely devoted to me." Kesira forced herself closer, her hand stroking over Eznofadil's lean, stone-hard body. She captured his hand and lifted it to her breast. He pulled back, but the movement did not show his true physical prowess. Kesira exposed her left breast with the lip imprint and pulled Eznofadil's hand directly over it.

"That feels good," the demon muttered.

"Yes," she said, hating herself, but hating Eznofadil even more. The fury of her emotions added strength to her limbs, to her conviction. Her strength flowed from his weakness. Kesira's control over Eznofadil grew. "We are lovers, and you will do anything for me."

"No," he said, but his negation carried no fire. Eznofadil was increasingly confused. He stared blankly at his hand and again tried to pull away. This time Kesira was strong enough to hold him. The jade green of his left hand had begun to lighten where the flesh touched Kesira's. The transformation back to more human-appearing flesh proceeded slowly, but it happened. His slightly parted lips took on highlights of pinks and reds, the green totally vanished. Such was the power of Wemilat's kiss.

"Yes," said Kesira. "I am in danger. You must help me. You want to. Only you, my demon love, can aid me now against my greatest enemy. Our *mutual* enemy."

"Who?"

Kesira held back the gloating she felt. "Ayondela. She desires me for her own. You would never willingly give me to her, would you? When it is only you I care for?"

"Never," the demon said. Animation returned to his voice. Kesira hoped that memory did not also come back with it.

"She wants me for her lover."

"No!"

"Then you must stop her, Eznofadil. Only you are strong enough. You can do it. For me. For me!"

"She cannot do this. I won't allow it."

"She thinks to bind me to her by hiding the world under a blanket of snow. This is wrong. I do not want it. You don't either, because it makes me unhappy."

"Why should I care?" asked Eznofadil, the confused expression returning. Kesira worried that the effect on the jade demon might be fleeting. She jerked his other hand to her breast and forced both into the pinkly glowing lip print there. "Why?" he asked again. "I do, though. I do care."

Eznofadil's hands had both returned to a more normal hue. The line of green began at his wrists now. The demon quaked and anger replaced the confusion.

"Ayondela cannot get away with this! She flaunts the power I have given her. How dare she! She must die!"

"Yes," said Kesira, emotions high now. "Destroy Ayondela. She must never be permitted to take me. I must be yours and yours alone." The woman played on what she hoped the demon believed deep down. She strove not to break the mood she wove about him, the mood engendered by the magicks of Wemilat's mark.

As quickly as they had arrived on the tropical island, they returned to the Isle of Eternal Winter. Kesira threw up one arm to protect her face from the glare. It was nearly noon and the sun shone off the snow with an eye-searing light. Somehow, the palely burning white flame reaching upward for the sky seemed to flicker as Eznofadil returned. Kesira prayed to Gelya—to any other patron willing to hear her—that this was not a warning device alerting Lenc that he might have defectors in his ranks.

"She is inside. You must stop her or she will take me."

"Stop her," said Eznofadil, as if in a deep trance. He turned and faced the side wall of the immense ice palace.

His hand lifted. For a moment, nothing happened. Kesira feared the demon had also forgotten the proper spells to cast, but it seemed only to be a function of his hands returning to their normal fleshiness. Power welled up and rushed forth in scintillant waves.

An entire wall of the palace vanished in hissing steam and flowing water. Eznofadil strutted forward toward the startled Ayondela, who sat on her throne off to one side of the new entryway into her palace.

Kesira trailed Eznofadil as he boldly stopped in front of the female demon.

"She is mine," he said.

"What do you mean?" roared Ayondela. "She is *not* yours. I will torture her to death!"

Eznofadil heard nothing past the refusal to turn Kesira over to him, body and soul. Already he summoned his power. The greenish aura about his body firmed and turned ominously darker. The sheet of energy radiating forth from his outstretched hands smashed against Ayondela's throne and melted it.

With a squawk more like a *trilla* bird than anything else, Ayondela jumped up, her blue scepter pointing. The next wave of Eznofadil's melting power was turned aside by the power of her own magicks.

"How dare you accost me like this in my own palace? How dare you?" Ayondela shrieked.

Kesira slipped around, fingers behind her and guiding her along the destroyed wall. Molimo hung in his ice chains across the room. To reach his side Kesira would have to boldly cross the expansive floor—and this looked impossible. Nehan-dir had summoned his soldiers the instant Eznofadil melted through the palace wall and ranked them to protect Ayondela. Seeing that it was the Order of the Steel Crescent's own patron, Nehan-dir hung back, watching and waiting.

But mostly the scarred man watched. Kesira could not hope for an instant of inattention from one such as Nehan-dir.

Molimo's head lifted and half-hooded eyes opened wider. Kesira's heart went out to him. How he had survived was a mystery. She saw the diabolical focusing device still at work on his body, inflicting pain he could not shriek

against, injuries as much to the soul as to the body. Kesira
covered her mouth with a shaking hand when she saw the
flickerings in those midnight black eyes turning to specks
of green.

"No, Molimo, please, no," she whispered. "Don't transform. They will kill you instantly if you do. Ayondela will
know. She will!"

Her words came from too far away to have been heard by
the man, yet Molimo understood. The green, dancing highlights faded; Molimo slumped against his chains. Kesira
skirted the central portion of the audience chamber, keeping her back to the frosty wall, and hoped to reach Molimo
unseen.

The commotion caused by the two arguing demons aided
her cause.

"You cannot come in here and accuse me!" shouted
Ayondela. She fended off another of Eznofadil's attacks
with a wave of her ice-blue scepter, then rose up to her full
height. The viridescent aura surrounding her made Ayondela appear as if she had cloaked herself in shimmering
mosses.

"You overstep your bounds," said Eznofadil. "I will
have her for my own. She wants no part of you." Eznofadil's hands shook as the greenish tint returned to them;
his lips stayed as pinkish as they had been after he first
planted them against Wemilat's mark. Kesira knew that
some of the jade demon's power had been sapped by his attack on her.

Strangely, what Eznofadil had lost she felt that she had
gained. Never stronger, never more daring, Kesira continued to make her way around the audience chamber to free
Molimo while the demons continued their exchange of
deadly magicks.

"You will hang beside him," came a low voice from behind her. Kesira spun to face Nehan-dir, his sword drawn
and ready to lunge. "I offered you a clean death. You refused. Now you will suffer your friend's fate." Nehan-dir
smiled crookedly. "I must admit to respecting him. Even if
he'd had a tongue, I don't believe he would have cried out.
He is brave—and foolish, like you."

Kesira did not wait for Nehan-dir to attack. She
launched herself forward, only to slip on the icy floor.

Arms flailing, the woman crashed into Nehan-dir. They both tumbled to the ground, arms circling one another. Kesira stayed on top, got her legs under her and drove a hard knee into the man's midriff. Nehan-dir gasped, turned on his side and vomited.

Kesira reached for the mercenary's steel sword, then stopped. Gelya's edicts against using such weapons returned to her. "We walk by faith, not by sight. I must not give up my faith." She took the few extra seconds to clamber to her feet and kick Nehan-dir as hard as she could. He groaned weakly. He would not oppose her soon.

Kesira looked up and saw others loyal to the Steel Crescent closing on her. She turned and rushed to where the soldier still played the pale light from the magical device over Molimo's body and limbs.

Kesira struck the woman and sent her to her knees, but the soldier came up with a dagger. Without thinking, Kesira swung the dish-shaped device around. The light winked out, but the hard edge caught the soldier on the arm. The wounded mercenary spun to avoid a harder contact; Kesira gave her no chance to recover.

"Molimo," she gasped out, going to him. The ice links around his ankles and wrists had turned his flesh a sickly grayish white with frostbite. "I'll free you."

He lifted his chin and indicated something behind her. Kesira looked over her shoulder and saw a dozen of the mercenaries closing on her, swords drawn. Nehan-dir had to be supported by two burly men, but he made gestures indicating attack.

Save yourself.

Kesira stood, stunned. "You spoke!" she cried. Then the nun realized Molimo had done no such thing. The torturing beam focused in the dish had burned his lips badly. Even if Molimo had had a tongue in his head, speech would have been impossible. "How?"

The soldiers came closer.

Kesira took a few precious seconds to compose herself, to achieve a level of concentration that might permit her to see new solutions to the problem of their escape. She opened her eyes and found nothing changed.

The ring of soldiers around her still threatened. Eznofadil and Ayondela traded strange magicks in the center of the audience chamber. Around them the ice walls and floor melted and refroze as first Eznofadil and then Ayondela attacked. The two demons were oblivious to anything else in the icy room.

"The dish," she said. "I can turn it on them."

The soldiers of the Order of the Steel Crescent now stood between her and the magical device.

"Get her," came Nehan-dir's choked words.

Kesira stood firmly, mind settled. Her only weapons might be hands and feet, but she would not die easily.

A loud squawk pulled her level, appraising gaze from the advancing soldiers to high up in the chamber where she and Molimo had floated only hours before. A bright green bird spiralled around, screeching and swearing.

"Zolkan!" she cried.

A thunderclap blasted the chamber, and the resultant heat bowled over the soldiers almost upon her. Kesira managed to protect Molimo the best she could, then saw it had been a mistake. Where she had not thrown herself in front of him, the heat had melted his manacles. Molimo's right arm and leg had been freed.

"You have gone too far this time, Ayondela," came a loud voice. Toyaga strode arrogantly and confidently into the chamber. "You, also, Eznofadil. You cannot imprison such as he." As Toyaga lifted his hand, both of the jade demons ceased their squabble and turned the full fury of their magicks against the intruder. Toyaga staggered under the impact of such torrential outpouring.

"No!" the handsome demon cried. "You will not triumph so easily."

He fought, but Kesira saw immediately that there was no possible way Toyaga might defeat the combined power of Ayondela and Eznofadil. Those two drove Toyaga ever backward, wore him down until his face turned a pasty, sickly white, battered his defenses inch by slow inch and closed on him.

The mercenaries got sluggishly to their feet. While they were still groggy, Kesira hit them low. She skidded along the floor on her belly and slammed into their still shaking legs. They went down heavily—and she found herself by the torture machine.

Kesira hazarded a quick look at Molimo, who shook his head and waved at her, as if trying to warn her.

"Get yourself free," she called to him. Molimo clumsily bent and brought a sword closer with one toe until he was able to wrap numbed fingers around the hilt and lift it. Kesira decided he was not in immediate danger; Toyaga was.

She spun the bulky dish around, trying to find some control on the back that fired the device, that sent out the punishing pale light. She frantically pulled levers and turned dials. Nothing happened. From above, Zolkan cursed loudly and fluidly, then hurtled down and perched on the top of the dish.

"Reflections only. They used Lenc's flame as source. You cannot turn it against them, not from here."

Ayondela saw Kesira. Horror widened Kesira's eyes as the female demon smiled wickedly, the fangs gleaming bright green now. The scepter rose and pointed directly at Kesira.

Reflection.

"Reflection!" she cried, spinning the dish around and pointing it directly at Ayondela. The demon's potent stream of cold impacted on the dish, fell into itself and rushed back—but not directly to Ayondela. Kesira had inadvertently turned the dish.

"Toyaga!" squawked Zolkan, trying to reach the woman's arm with his claws. But Kesira saw her mistake too late. She caught the demon battling to free her and Molimo squarely with the beam. Toyaga stiffened, then fell forward. He hit the ice floor and shattered as if he has been built from glass.

A hush descended on the chamber. Then confused mutterings came from the soldiers. But Ayondela showed no hesitation. She turned on Kesira, her scepter again spewing forth its frosty death message.

Kesira gasped, her entire body caught in the beam. She stiffened, joints freezing, limbs unable to move. More solidly than she had been held by Eznofadil's magicks, this frigid ray immobilized her.

Seeing only straight ahead, Kesira was treated to the heady sight of Ayondela spinning angrily and directing her attack against Eznofadil. The jade demon had paused only an instant in his attack—and he perished under the female demon's attack. As Kesira had done, Eznofadil stiffened and froze into position.

Kesira wanted to shout with joy as Ayondela went to Eznofadil, then swung her scepter with all her might. Pieces of jade that had been the demon blasted all over the room.

Eznofadil was dead.

And Kesira Minette was forever cradled in winter's embrace.

Chapter Eighteen

SORROW. LONELINESS. ISOLATION. SORROW.

Intense sorrow filled Kesira Minette as the cold crept through her body and froze through to the core of her being. She had failed, and she was all alone now. That would be her eternal punishment: unendurable solitude.

Eznofadil might have died, but Ayondela's curse still lay heavy on the world. The woman stared sightlessly into the ice chamber and drifted off to a deep, deep slumber. One day her spirit might return, and when it did she would carry the burdens laid upon her this day.

And they would be heavy. Heavy.

Light intruded on her sleepless dreams, assaulting her eyes, making her want to blink. The spell of ice and immobility held her too firmly to allow any movement whatsoever. Pain started at the backs of her eyes when she failed to shut out the light, and the pain spread.

Legs, arms, body. Kesira tried to scream; her voice had been frozen, too.

Resist, came the oddly distant command. It was both familiar and unknown to her. Kesira puzzled over this paradox. Only slowly did she remember. She had heard such a voice before, when she had entered the audience chamber with Eznofadil. It had seemed to her that Molimo had spoken. But that was impossible. He had no tongue. Yet it had been Molimo, of that she was sure. Another paradox. A world of them. Kesira wanted only to slip back into her dark repose.

"She thaws," came another familiar voice, this time to

her ears and not only her mind. Zolkan. It had to be the *trilla* bird. Pain again came, this time to her shoulder.

"Go 'way," she muttered. Her tongue had turned to rubber and filled her mouth totally. Simply swallowing presented problems too vast to be overcome. Again the pain, a familiar one. Zolkan's talons biting into her flesh. "Stop it," Kesira said more plainly.

"She returns to us," the bird said.

Light faded, flowed, turned into a crazy kaleidoscope of vivid colors. When the scene focused it was the one Kesira remembered last. The throne room.

Other memories rushed back to her. Eznofadil. Ayondela. Toyaga. Their battle.

"Molimo!" she cried. Misery rocketed through her but Kesira moved. The pain a companion, the woman moved, twisted, turned, got circulation flowing throughout her veins once more.

"She returns from land of frozen living," said Zolkan with some pleasure.

Molimo held her upright. Her legs no longer supported her easily. With tender care he lowered her to a sitting position on the icy floor.

"What happened? I saw Toyaga die. I . . . I focused Ayondela's spell directly on him."

"Stupid," said Zolkan. "Tried to warn you. Stupid shit."

"Zolkan!"

The *trilla* bird shut up, but did not look the least bit contrite.

"All right," Kesira said, sighing. "It was stupid of me. And Toyaga died, didn't he?" She read the answer on Molimo's face. True sorrow found a home behind those ebony-dark eyes. "I'm sorry. I only tried to help him." Molimo put a comforting hand on her shoulder, but Kesira was not comforted.

"Ayondela gone," said Zolkan. "Eznofadil died and she left palace screaming mad. Ordered all soldiers to accompany her."

Kesira saw the scene of the battle among the three demons. Toyaga had died, shattering like glass. Ayondela had turned instantly against Eznofadil and frozen the confused demon. He, too, had broken like a dropped clay pot. Tiny fragments of jade pulsed and shone across the floor—all that was left of Eznofadil.

"Where did Ayondela go?"

"Just left. Shrieks of betrayal."

"She might have gone to seek out Lenc," said Kesira. "Eznofadil had turned on her. She might fear Lenc will do the same."

"He will."

"You're right, Zolkan. He never intended for her to be a true ally. Eznofadil told me they only used her powers, that they held no place for her. Lenc is the true winner in this battle. Ayondela has eliminated a powerful foe in Eznofadil, perhaps the only one able to challenge Lenc for supreme control of the world."

"Winter gets colder outside."

"Her curse."

Molimo had retrieved his tablet. He wrote and held it up for Kesira to see. "You can lift the curse. Only you."

"But, Molimo, I tried," she said. "Ayondela wouldn't listen to me. She . . . she tried to torture you to death and would have done the same to me. Even at this, she wouldn't have been sated. Rouvin's death unbalanced her. She is running amok now."

"Not that," Molimo wrote. *"You* can lift the curse. You have the power. I feel it within you."

"What do you mean?"

Molimo hesitated, then wrote much slower than before, as if carefully choosing the words. "After you were with Wemilat, did you not feel different?"

Kesira's hand involuntarily went to cover the spot on her left breast where the ugly demon's kiss had been burned into her flesh. The woman could only nod.

"He drained power from you, but he also gave you some. The process is not one way."

"And?" she said, her voice cracking now. Kesira thought she knew what Molimo would write next.

"You were responsible for Eznofadil's confusion. He gained power from you, but it was not the kind he expected. You gained from him. More than you suspect."

Kesira wanted to cry in humiliation. Was it so apparent to Molimo what the jade demon had done to her? It had to be. She felt dirty, used, wretched beyond words.

"You have power of jade within you," spoke up Zolkan. The bird muted his voice, pitched it softer than Kesira had ever heard. She looked at him. A topknot of feathers fanned out, then folded flat against his head. Zolkan had always prided himself on his appearance; he badly needed cleaning now and seemed not to notice. He had been through much. He didn't complain.

And Molimo? He had suffered for long hours under the agony of the torture device wielded by the soldiers of the Steel Crescent. Raellard Yera had died. None of them had had an easy time. Why should she feel sorry for herself?

But Kesira did.

"I can't do anything. I don't feel up to it."

"Look." Zolkan reached over and bit down on her ear, twisting until she cried out. He jerked her head around so that she stared out the window above where Molimo and Raellard had been chained. The pale dancing flame still reached for the heavens, still burned with its unnatural coldness. The pale white fire taunted her, mocked Kesira for being weak, only a mortal, not worthy of a patron as knowing and kind as Gelya.

Gelya had taught that great works are accomplished not by strength of arm, but by perseverance. The body may be frail, but the will must be strong. Kesira trembled in her weaknesses, but her resolve firmed.

"I feel no different," she said.

"You are," wrote Molimo. "There is more within you than you realize. Reach for it. It won't fail you."

"What do I have to do? I can lift Ayondela's curse?"

"You can. The flame is keystone holding the spell together. Cause the flame to falter, and the power of nature reasserts itself."

Kesira stared at the leaping flame and wondered how she could ever disrupt its flow, even for an instant. Step into it?

No!

Kesira swung about, looking at Molimo. She thought he'd spoken, but he only wrote the word on his tablet.

"You can do it without destroying yourself."

"Show me."

She, Zolkan, and Molimo left the ruined ice palace and stood on the tiled walk circling the flame pit. No fuel fed the fire. No heat radiated outward. No living being might survive within the flame's boundary. Yet Molimo had confidence that she might be able to break its cycle.

"Lenc supplied this as more than symbol," said Zolkan. "It powers Ayondela's curse. If for even small instant flame dies, the world returns to normal."

"How do you know this, Zolkan?"

"Do it," was the only answer she got from the bird.

"But I don't know how. What is it I am supposed to do?" She closed her eyes and dropped into a meditative state. No matter what she would be called on to do, it all began from this point. Calm. Settling down. Tranquility. Thoughts moving in precise paths. Ideas popping up spontaneously.

Molimo took her hand. Zolkan moved closer to her cheek. She was no longer alone, not with them. She depended on them as they did on her. She was a part of something greater, something more complete than any individual could hope to achieve.

"They conquer who believe they can," she muttered.

The source of the white fire came to her in a dreamlike state. And more. She saw the magicks feeding it, how Lenc had established it to burn forever. Kesira was unable to create fire on her own, but she knew the mechanisms, the magicks, the driving forces.

But how to unlock them, how to undo all the jade demon had set into motion?

She needed a spell to shut off some of the cold fire.

From a distance, she heard the poem Molimo had shown her.

> The world about me,
> There are no eyes.
> Freedom of the air and sky,
> I fade into nothingness.

She embraced the spell, followed the magical threads,

found new ones. It became hers. Part of the flame wavered into the nothingness promised by the spell. The intensity of the fire wavered, but it did not go out completely.

Zolkan. Molimo. They were with her. In a curious way, so were all her Sisters, now long dead, their spirits claimed by Lenc. They burned within the flame; Kesira joined them with her spell of negation.

She stood watching even as she stood at a long distance, detached and watching herself. The dichotomy lasted for only a few seconds before Kesira felt whole again.

Kesira rubbed her eyes. The flame had vanished.

"It is done," said Zolkan.

"No," Kesira shrieked. "It's returning. Look!"

Fingers of coldness worked at the bottom of the pit, coalesced, then rushed upward once again to burn with frigid white intensity.

"The curse is no more," insisted Zolkan.

"He is right," wrote Molimo. "You interrupted the flow of power long enough. Let the flame burn now. It doesn't give energy to any spell."

Even as Molimo wrote, Kesira felt a warm wind blowing from the mainland. She looked out across the Isle of Eternal Winter to the frozen waves on the Sea of Katad and beyond to land. It was only her imagination, she knew, but the wind *did* carry the scent of summer with it.

"Storm," cautioned Zolkan. "We must leave now. Across sea before it melts. Too dangerous if icebergs still float."

Kesira walked to the edge of the precipice and stared down at the waves, still trapped in rigid formations below. But she looked forward just a few hours and saw the heating caused by summer robbing those frozen waves of their stiffness, letting them fall regularly into themselves, to smash on the beach with aquatic fury.

"We must get across them soon," she agreed.

But Kesira didn't see the trip back through the icy waves; she saw her own failure. Ayondela still raged against the death of Rouvin. Lenc still schemed to rule all the world, to pass from demon to god using the evil jade.

She had come so far, and so many had died. Her Sisters in the Order, Raellard—what of Parvey Yera and her son?—Toyaga and the others. All gone.

Kesira Minette called out to Molimo and Zolkan, but her words were swallowed by the wind.

3: THE CRYSTAL CLOUDS

For those printers' devils, Dale Goble and Mike Horvat

Chapter One

As KESIRA MINETTE placed one small foot on the rotting ice, she felt it give way. Cold water and knife-sharp edges raked at her leg as the nun tumbled forward, flailing futilely for balance. Strong hands caught her and pulled her upright, but the frigid water took its toll on her already depleted strength. She had been through so much. This new danger only drove her into further despair.

She needed to add one final verse to her personal death song, though, before succumbing. So much had happened; there was such a great need to put it all into the lyrics that would sum up her life's struggles and triumphs.

Kesira glanced back over her shoulder at the Isle of Eternal Winter towering above the ice-dotted water—the jade demon Ayondela's stronghold. Ayondela's power had been thwarted, and the dancing, cold white flame powering her evil momentarily extinguished to give the land back its normal summer warmth. And in that release from the potent magical spell Kesira found herself caught in a trap.

The nun and her companions, Molimo and the brilliantly plumed *trilla* bird Zolkan, had penetrated the fastness and fought the female demon—and won. To get to the Isle they had crossed the frozen waves of the Sea of Katad.

Now that frigid expanse thawed. Ice floes slammed together all around them, forcing Kesira and Molimo to agilely leap from one treacherous perch to another. Above, Zolkan circled, squawking instructions to them, seeking out the safest path, if any path across the melting sea might be considered safe.

Molimo's strong hands again pulled her upright. Kesira shivered as her immersed leg turned blue with frostbite. The man knelt and saw the deathly pallor of her legs. Gently he began kneading and massaging the flesh to restore circulation.

Another ice floe smashed into the one on which they stood. The impact almost knocked Kesira and Molimo into the deadly, freezing waters.

"Later, Molimo," she said, urging the handsome, dark-haired man to stand. Cold, black eyes bored into her softer brown ones. She might live to be a thousand and never understand what thoughts surged behind Molimo's eyes. Love? Anger? Triumph? Fear? And asking did no good. He had been trapped in a rain of deadly jade caused by two fighting demons, barely surviving it. One handicap he bore from the cataclysmic battle had been the loss of his tongue.

Kesira shivered and not from the cold. The other loss suffered by her friend bothered her even more. Molimo had scant control over his shape. One moment he stood a robust young man, intelligence shining in those dark eyes. The next he shape-changed into a green-eyed wolf with no humanity in the savage snap of strong jaw or rake of sharp claw.

"If we don't hurry, we'll be trapped out here. I never thought the summer could come so quickly after we broke Ayondela's spell," she said.

From on high came the oddly accented words, "Left! Go left. Many floes, but move quick. Quick!" Zolkan wheeled above, a spot of green against the vivid blue of the new summer sky. Warm sunlight dropped down on them like melted butter. Kesira had battled the jade demons Ayondela and Emperor Kwasian to restore that natural warmth, and now she cursed uncharacteristically, praying that the freed season hide its warm fingers for just a few more hours.

The heat from the revitalized summer sun accelerated the melting of the floes.

Another minor iceberg crashed into the one on which they stood, driving her to her knees.

"Jump," urged Zolkan. He squawked loudly, then began a singsong speech meant only for Molimo. How they communicated, Kesira did not know. A sudden jolt of jealousy passed; they excluded her. But whatever Zolkan told Molimo, the man-wolf understood and acted on it immediately. Kesira shrieked as Molimo lifted her and jumped to the next floe and the next and the next.

She started to relax by the time he'd made the jump to a third ice floe. And then his foot slipped on ice turned into slush. They fell heavily, sprawling over the blunted edges of the frozen, protruding waves on the floe.

"How much farther?" she asked, panting. Kesira tried to focus her eyes on the shore, safe land where they might rest. Sweat—or was it blood?—dripped down her forehead, blinding her. Never had the nun felt so tired.

Life in the convent had been easy for her, too easy. Prayers to her patron demon Gelya had occupied much of her time. Tending the fields and doing the chores required by those of her order had delightfully filled the rest of her day. Easy work, pleasant times, a bubble of serenity floating along in a menacing and disordered world held together only through faith in the Emperor and the rightness of Gelya's teachings.

Kesira fought back tears forming at the corners of her eyes. Her ordered life had been cast into brutal ruins by the jade demons and their insane urge to conquer all. For centuries there had been no conflict between demon and mortal. The demons were content to walk among their worshipers from time to time. Their petty indiscretions, their couplings with humans, their more-than-human failings and charities, made up the universe as it was. No human emperor challenged the demons, and in return, the demons occupied themselves with their own dealings, leaving rule of the world to mortals.

The infernal jade had changed all that. Howenthal, Eznofadil, and Lenc had partaken of the jade, augmenting their powers—and their cruelty. Their rule over other demons had grown pallid; they sought more. Their battles overflowed and involved humans. But even as the jade gave them incredible powers, it robbed them of others. No longer immortal, time pressed in on them.

Kesira, Molimo, and Zolkan had crossed the Quaking Lands to confront Howenthal, and slayed the demon with the aid of another. Kesira reached up to her left breast. Glowing warmly there, Wemilat's kiss reminded her of the ugly toad-demon's goodness. He had perished in the struggle; only his lip print remained to protect her.

Kesira closed her eyes and rested. So tired. The fight had gone on for so long. Molimo had killed Ayondela's half-mortal son and driven the female demon into the ranks of jade. And they had invaded the Isle of Eternal Winter, destroying Eznofadil. But Ayondela still lived. The curse of winter she brought to the land had been removed, but the female demon still sought revenge for her son's death.

Ayondela. Lenc. Only two jade demons remained now, but they might as well have been a legion. Kesira's body refused to stir. Every ounce of energy had been drained. She could not go on.

Sharp pain lanced into her left shoulder, and a hard, sharp beak ripped at her ear. "Move. Floes come apart. Move!" Zolkan squawked, and jerked his talons on her shoulder to force Kesira to her feet.

"Go away. So cold, so tired. Let me sleep. Sleep . . ."

Zolkan flew off, but the pain did not diminish. A hard slap knocked her head to one side. Kesira's eyes flashed open. Anger burned within her. None dared touch her. She reached for her stone-wood staff and failed to find it. Her hands balled into fists, ready to strike out. Molimo stood above her, watching, waiting. He swung again. Her quick hand deflected the blow and turned it against him. Catching his hand and bending it backward, using the weakness in the joint, Kesira forced the man-wolf to his knees.

For a brief instant she saw the ebony eyes flicker with green light. Fear of bringing on the transformation to wolf caused her to release her grip. Molimo rubbed his injured hand.

"I'm sorry," she said. "I didn't mean . . . you shouldn't have slapped me."

"I wanted to," Zolkan piped up, "but I have no hands. Molimo did right. Move! Get off ice! Now!" The *trilla* bird strutted about, stretching his wings and trying to preen. Ice crystals caught the bright summer sunlight and blasted it into rainbows off the bird's feathers. "Need food, need bath, and you prattle on about being tired." Zolkan snorted, then took to wing.

Kesira struggled to her feet and found the ice too weak to support her. A chasm opened between her and Molimo. The man lithely vaulted across and joined her on the smaller ice floe.

"Can we swim to shore?" she asked. Molimo imitated a man freezing to death. They were caught between disparate seasons. The summer heat melted the ice, but the sluggish seawater took longer to shed its winter cloak. They wouldn't be able to swim more than a dozen yards before the water sucked the warmth from their flesh.

"Then we jump," Kesira said. She paused for a moment, reaching deep within herself for the strength she knew resided there. Kesira almost panicked when she failed to find that reservoir. She had done so much, so much. . . .

The dull, leaden, soul-depressing sense of duty rose within her and forced her to make the next jump and the next and the next. Kesira slipped and slid on the melting ice, cutting hands and legs, tearing her gray robe to tatters, leaving behind bloody streaks on the polar white, melting the ice further with her hot tears. But she went on without thought of pausing.

She had a duty to her dead sisters to avenge their deaths by Lenc's hand. She had a duty to stop Ayondela. She had been so lucky in life that she owed all this and more. Kesira Minette would not shirk her duty to those she thought of as family, to Emperor Kwasian, to the memory of her dead patron.

Kesira struggled on until Molimo tugged at her robe. Her feet slipped and slid, finding no purchase. Her hands had long since turned numb, but they clutched and clawed and moved her onward. Molimo jerked harder, tearing her robe.

"On," she said in a weak voice, eyes closed. Only slowly did Kesira realize that she slipped not on ice but on wet sand, that her hand found solid rock instead of razor-edged ice upjuts. "We made it," she said in a voice mixing surprise and triumph.

Molimo quickly wrote in the sand.

"So close?" she asked. Molimo had indicated that Nehan-dir and others loyal to the Order of the Steel Crescent were nearby. Molimo nodded briskly, pointing toward the foothills running parallel to the Sea of Katad. In those winding, twisting canyons entire armies could hide without being seen. Kesira sighed. The agony never stopped for her.

They had dodged Nehan-dir and his mercenaries to reach the sea, had followed the soldiers of the Steel Crescent across the frozen waves, and had for a second time killed that order's patron.

"Worshiping only strength is not doing Nehan-dir much good," she said to Molimo.

"Nehan-dir angers now," came Zolkan's squawks. "Every time he gets new patron, you kill him. Both Eznofadil and Howenthal are dead."

"Three patrons lost," mused Kesira. "How sad." She had lost only Gelya, but her belief in his teachings remained unshaken. Nehan-dir and his followers sought out the demon offering the most and did not truly believe in anything more than the intoxication of power. It was hardly her fault that they had chosen so poorly on all occasions, because they sought patrons for all the wrong reasons. The Order of the Steel Crescent's first patron, Tolek the Spare, had traded them for money to pay off gambling debts with another demon. Kesira could sympathize with the hurt and rage of Nehan-dir and the others over that, but selling their swords to the jade demons amounted to a crime against humanity that no previous sorrow could ameliorate.

"Is Nehan-dir nearby?" she asked.

Molimo shook his head. Zolkan cocked his crested head to one side, as if thinking on it, then agreed that no imminent danger threatened.

"Let's return to Parvey Yera's hut, then," Kesira said.

"Why?" Molimo etched into the wet sand.

"Her husband died by Ayondela's hand. We owe it to the woman to tell her. Raellard Yera was our ally."

"We must avoid Nehan-dir," wrote Molimo.

"We have our duty. Family ties are of the utmost importance, even more than saving our own lives," Kesira pointed out. "Raellard might have been only a dirt farmer, but he died nobly and in our service. We owe his memory this much."

"To south. Go south. Ayondela is there. Do battle with her," urged Zolkan. "Let this be Yera's monument." Kesira ignored the *trilla* bird. He'd never liked Yera, not that she blamed Zolkan. Yera had been unable to grow his crops due to the magicks-generated winter laid on the land by Ayondela, and the man had turned to hunting. The sight of a green-plumed bird had almost been too much for a hungry farmer to bear. In some parts of the country *trilla* bird meat counted as a delicacy.

"We go to Parvey."

"Leave her," Molimo wrote. "She and her son are trouble."

"They've probably starved to death by now," said Kesira. "But do as you choose. I know where my duty lies." On shaky legs she started off for the steep slopes leading to the top of a hill. Once there, the nun decided that she might meditate and say her daily devotionals, then find the path back to the Pharna River and from there upriver to the ravine leading to the Yera cabin.

Kesira smiled but tried not to show any further emotion

when she heard Molimo stomping along behind her and felt the warm downdrafts caused by Zolkan's beating wings above. They, too, knew where their duty lay. All it took was a little goading on her part from time to time to remind them. By determined effort they ought to be able to reach Parvey Yera in three days.

It took five.

Molimo hung back and shook his head. Kesira looked at the pathetic hut and knew what she had to do. The coward's way out would be to do as Molimo hinted: leave without once confronting the woman inside the log cabin. And, even as Kesira knew she couldn't walk away, she wanted to acquiesce and let Molimo convince her.

He pulled out the writing tablet that he had somehow managed to keep with him throughout their ordeals and hurriedly scratched his message.

Kesira read it and shook her head. "We've come this far. We can't simply turn and walk away. We owe it to Yera, if not to the woman."

"She's crazy," Molimo wrote.

"Yes." Kesira knew the man was absolutely right. The few hours she'd spent with Parvey Yera before had convinced her that the woman had become demented, by hardship or a vagrant touch of the demons or something else. Whatever the cause, the effect proved the same. "But if she is, this is all the more reason to aid her."

"No aid. She *likes* to eat birds," complained Zolkan. "I see it in her beady eyes. Cannibal. She is cannibal!"

"She's not a cannibal, Zolkan. Even if she does like *trilla* bird meat. You'd be the cannibal if you ate your own kind's flesh." She felt the bird shudder and tense his talons. The pain lanced deep into her shoulder; her robe no longer provided any cushioning. The only consolation to having her gray robe in tatters lay in the warmth of the wind slipping through the rents. Where it had previously admitted vicious winter breezes, she now felt the languid softness of summer airs.

"Don't like her," the bird said, sulking. "Molimo doesn't, either."

Kesira took a deep breath and composed herself. She had never been the one to shirk onerous duties and wasn't about to begin now. On that road lay personal humiliation and the death of courage. Gelya had taught that inner triumph led to outer victory. Strong inside, strong in all things.

"Steel Crescent follows," said Zolkan.

"They've been on our trail ever since we washed up on the beach," Kesira said softly. "While they might find us if we linger overlong, I don't intend to be here more than a few hours."

"Ayondela is to the south. At Lorum Bay."

Kesira jerked her head around and stared at the *trilla* bird. "How do you know that? You haven't left my sight since we escaped the Isle of Eternal Winter."

Zolkan started to take wing rather than answer. Kesira grabbed him by the neck and held him back. Powerful wings beat at her face. She ignored them and dangled the bird by his neck.

"I'll give it a good crank unless you tell me. How do you know where Ayondela went?"

A hand on her shoulder made Kesira loosen her grip. Zolkan sputtered and flopped to the ground. The bird batted about, got to his feet, and then launched himself with powerful wing action. Molimo held up his slate.

"So *you* told him, eh?" Kesira said skeptically. "And how is it that you came by this interesting tidbit of information? You've not been out of my sight for an instant, either."

Molimo wrote quickly, but Kesira studied the man's face. Her heart gave an extra beat. So handsome, so strong. What a pity he had been caught in the battle between Lenc and Merrisen. She believed the jade illness that afflicted Molimo had been produced by the demon Merrisen's body shattering into millions of shards. Eznofadil had perished that way—and what horror resided in the tiny fragments of a truly evil demon's body?

Kesira forced her thoughts to other paths. It would take so little for her to love Molimo, and she dared not do so. His shape-changing was only a part of it. She had nursed him back to health and felt sorry for his tongueless condition. That had to be it, she told herself. Pity. She pitied the young man. He was a friend and nothing more, and could be nothing more until the jade demons were put to route.

And even then...

Molimo held up the tablet. On it he had written, "Ayondela and Lenc must join forces. Lenc still uses her for his own ends. He is not strong enough to rule without her—not yet."

"You're saying that with Eznofadil and Howenthal gone, Lenc will continue to play on Ayondela's hatred and sorrow over Rouvin's death?" Molimo nodded. "So? So how do you know she and Lenc are to the south? You said you told Zolkan."

"A guess," Molimo wrote. The expression on his face remained impassive, but Kesira had the innate feeling that he lied. The man-wolf had obtained the information in ways other than logic. This was but another mystery about him that would be cleared up one day. But not now.

"We will examine your guess more closely. After I have spoken with Parvey."

Molimo started to restrain her, but the cold look she shot him stayed his hand. He shrugged and settled down onto a stump outside the hut. Whatever she did, Kesira knew, she wasn't likely to convince Molimo to join her inside.

Nor did she want his company. What she had to do was better done alone. How can anyone tell a woman that her husband and the father of her child had perished?

"Parvey?" she called out. "Are you inside?"

A sound more like the scurrying of rats than the movements of a human echoed from inside. Kesira cautiously pushed aside the door. It had been pulled off its hinges and never repaired. That told Kesira more about the condition of the woman inside than anything else. The nun slipped past the door and peered into the dim, smoke-filled haze within the tiny cabin. Her eyes adjusted to the dark and allowed her to make out the huddled figure near the back of the hut.

"Parvey, do you remember me? Kesira Minette. I was here before, with Raellard."

"Raellard?" came the cracked voice. "My husband?"

"I have an additional sorrow for you." Kesira's voice came out in a choked whisper, barely audible. She did not want to be the one to tell the poor woman of her husband's demise, yet there was no other to do the sad task.

"Raellard's dead," came the emotionless voice before Kesira could speak. "I knew it. The whoreson's gone and died on me, leaving me with the demon spawn."

"Parvey!" Kesira said sharply. "Raellard died in a valiant effort to rid the world of Ayondela's curse. As you can see, the winter is lifting. Raellard helped accomplish that. He was a brave man." Kesira winced, thinking of how Raellard had died under Ayondela's tortures. No one deserved such a fate. No one.

"He left me. Me and that hideous creature." The emaciated woman held out a bony hand with a finger looking more like a talon. She pointed at the small bundle in the rear of the hut. The child stirred, pudgy hand gripping the threadbare blanket swaddling it. The entire time Kesira had been inside the cabin, the baby had not uttered a sound.

"That is your son, Parvey. He is your flesh—yours and Raellard's."

"Not Raellard's! Not his. No, no," the woman cackled. "Not his. Another's."

Kesira swallowed hard, her mouth filled with cotton. Raellard had mentioned that he thought the baby had been fathered by someone else. Kesira had passed it off as paranoia generated by famine. Could both this crazed woman and her husband share the same delusion? Or was it delusion at all?

"He was gone too much. Worked too many hours. And for what? Nothing!"

"Yera, your husband was a good man who knew his duty. He did all he could to feed you. It is the jade demons' curse that drove him off the land and afield to hunt." Kesira remembered the pitiful few items Raellard had returned with. Tubers, a rabbit—the wolf he had slain on the doorstep. Kesira saw no evidence of the wolf skin or anything more than had been in the cabin the last time she had visited here.

"It is your baby, no matter who the father is," Kesira said. "You must tend him." The baby looked well enough nourished, but the pale eyes stared out at her with preternatural intelligence more expected in a child ten times this one's age. And there was no cry.

"Hell spawn!" shrieked Parvey Yera. "It is demon spawn, and I want nothing to do with it. Or you!"

The sudden attack took Kesira by surprise. One moment she had studied the small baby, the next clawed fingers raked at her face. Only instinct saved Kesira. She threw up one arm and deflected the blow but lost her balance and stumbled over a low table made from a rotting log. Above her Parvey Yera straightened, a gleaming ax in her hands.

Kesira watched in mute fascination as the nicked blade began its descent, aimed directly for her skull.

Chapter Two

ALL KESIRA MINETTE saw was the crazed woman holding the ax. The edge of the weapon took on intense meaning for her, every nick and flaw magnified a million times over. In spite of this, in spite of the danger, Kesira found herself frozen and unable to avoid the blow.

"Die, demon lover, die!" shrieked Parvey Yera. Muscles tightened and the heavy blade descended.

Blood fountained over Kesira, blinding her. She let out a tiny gasp when she realized it was not her own. The nun wiped away the gore and heard the chewing, gnawing, wetly ripping sounds. Her stomach rolled over and threatened to lose what little it contained. Kesira held down her gorge and forced herself to a sitting position.

"Molimo, stop!" she cried. It was too late by far. The man-wolf had transformed totally to wolf and now fed on Parvey's scrawny throat. Blazing green eyes swung on Kesira, studied her, appraised her for a better meal than that offered by the undernourished woman now dead on the dirt floor. Even as Molimo's wildness surged, Kesira felt inner calm returning.

This peace communicated to the wolf more fully than mere words. The feral light faded in Molimo's eyes, and powerful muscles rippled under the gray fur before beginning the shape-change back to human. Molimo huddled on the floor near his victim, gasping for breath. Kesira went to him and put her arm around his bare shoulders, pulling him close. Blood soaked into her robe from his lips and chest; she took no note.

"It's all right, Molimo. You saved my life. She had been driven crazy by her ordeals. You saved me. It's all right." She rocked him to and fro as if he were a small child.

As the thought occurred to her Kesira turned, still hugging Molimo's naked form. The baby lay in the corner of the hut, pale eyes taking in everything. Not once had the baby cried out.

"Sit quietly for a while," she told Molimo. "Don't get upset over this. You saved me." Kesira didn't want him reverting to wolf form. Every transformation, she felt, committed him that much more to permanence as an animal. Seeing that Molimo rested, the nun picked up the infant. Wise, old eyes peered at her, perfectly focused. A tiny smile crossed healthy pink lips, then the baby stuck one thumb into his mouth and closed his eyes. In seconds he slept contentedly.

"What are you to do with that?" came Zolkan's grating words. "Leave it!"

"How can I leave him?" asked Kesira. Yet she agreed with Zolkan's implied question of being able to care for the infant. He hardly ate the fare of a seasoned traveler—Kesira herself had been living on little more than tough jerked meat and the occasional root or tuber these past five days' journey from the coast. Dodging Nehan-dir's soldiers had added to the necessity of hurried meals and forced marches. How could a newborn possibly survive such hardship?

Thoughts of giving up her pursuit of Ayondela and Lenc flitted across the fringes of Kesira's mind. Battling the jade demons might eventually prove impossible. She had considerable luck so far, destroying two of them—but the cost! Tears welled at the corners of her eyes as she stared down at the sleeping infant in her arms. This little one's mother and father had died because of Ayondela's wintery curse. And others? Their names were legion, those who were even noted in passing. Even greater numbers had died with no one to mourn their deaths.

"Gelya," the woman said softly. "Why did they have to slay you also? You could guide me now."

Zolkan squawked loudly for her attention. "It will die, no matter what we do," the *trilla* bird declared.

"You might be right. But we must try."

"Needs mother's milk," insisted Zolkan. "Nowhere to get it. Do it a favor by killing it."

To Kesira's surprise Molimo reacted strongly. A croak came from his sundered mouth, and he slammed his fist into the palm of his other hand. Hurriedly Molimo left and returned, pulling on his clothing and scribbling away on his tablet. Kesira looked over the man's shoulder as he wrote.

"The boy goes with us," Molimo wrote with bold, forceful strokes.

"You are right," said Kesira, "but without milk he cannot live very long."

"There is a way." Molimo's words seemed to burn with a phosphorescent fire. Kesira blinked and the effect died.

"What way? I can't supply it." Kesira frowned when Molimo bobbed his head up and down. She smiled gently and shook her head. "My friend, there are some things you do not understand." Not for the first time, Kesira had the feeling that Molimo's education in wordly matters had been neglected. On some topics he showed incredible astuteness, but on others the abysmal ignorance made her want to laugh. Even as a nun locked away most of her life in a convent, she had experienced more of life than Molimo.

Or perhaps his mind had become addled through hardship and the awful wounds inflicted on him by the jade rain. More than his tongue might have been lost.

Again Molimo shook his head. With gentle fingers so different from the wolf's claws he reached out and pulled open her gray robe. The fabric had reached the limits of its endurance and tore, in spite of the light touch. Molimo exposed her left breast where Wemilat the Ugly had kissed her. The lip print pulsed warmly, pinkness spreading from the imprint throughout her breast.

"I don't understand," she said.

Molimo turned the baby so that she held it in her left arm, her nipple close to the infant's mouth. Those hauntingly old eyes opened, and a tiny hand reached out. Kesira sighed softly when she felt the lips working against her flesh.

"So nice," she said, more to herself. Louder, to Molimo, she said, "The baby will be disappointed."

Molimo shook his head vehemently. And Kesira understood why. Stirrings deep within her breast caused her to clutch the infant more closely to her body. Ineffable sensations built inside her, bringing a peace and contentment she had seldom found even in her deepest meditations.

Milk flowed from the breast kissed by Wemilat's lips.

"How did you know, Molimo?" she asked.

"Must leave. Nehan-dir will find us," protested Zolkan. The *trilla* bird vented a loud caw, then fell into the singsong speech directed at Molimo. Kesira listened for several minutes. Whatever went on between the two, both understood, and they came to a conclusion.

"Well?" asked Kesira.

"We might elude Nehan-dir if we cross mountains to Lorum Bay."

"Lorum Bay? You mentioned that before. How do you— or Molimo—know Ayondela is there?"

"Lorum Bay is on southernmost rim of Sea of Katad. We must hurry to leave behind Nehan-dir."

Kesira frowned. Zolkan had not answered her question, and she sensed that the *trilla* bird wasn't likely to, either. When he wanted, he could become very evasive. The infant had gone back to sleep after a quiet belch or two, and not even Zolkan's flapping seemed destined to keep him awake.

"Staying clear of the mercenaries is important," Kesira said, "but we have no plan once we find Ayondela. I had hoped to persuade her that Rouvin's death was accidental, that she should oppose Lenc. But there is little chance for either now. Ayondela is too firmly addicted to the power given her by the jade."

"We have killed Howenthal and Rouvin; we can kill Ayondela and Lenc," wrote Molimo.

"You make it sound so simple." Kesira rocked the baby gently. "We must find a home for him before continuing on against the demons. Do you suppose there'll be somewhere in Lorum Bay that will take him in?"

With the advent of the jade demons life had become cheap. Entire cities had perished and more would follow. Why should anyone want to burden himself with a newborn when personal survival was so difficult? Kesira had seen how her order's mission in Chounabel had fallen into ruin. The sisters had forsaken Gelya's teachings and succumbed to the city's carnal lure. Kesira touched the dirty yellow sash circling her waist—the symbol of the Sister of the Mission.

Of all those who had once followed Gelya, only she remained true. The virtue of prosperity was temperance, which Gelya taught. But never had her patron mentioned that the virtue of adversity is fortitude, a much more heroic value. She had endured so much, and so much more lay ahead if she were to avenge the demon Lenc's cruelties.

"The Steel Crescent mercenaries still seek us," wrote Molimo.

"I know," she said quietly, not wanting to disturb the infant. "I wonder what his name is? Raellard said that Parvey hadn't named him. I wonder if she did, while we were on the Isle?"

Molimo shrugged. Kesira looked at the man curiously. His dark hair had become matted with blood from the slain woman, but more than this held her attention. Around the baby Molimo seemed uneasy, as if such a small one could threaten him.

"Are you afraid of what you might do to the child?"

she asked him. "That you will shape-change and harm him?"

Molimo shook his head. Zolkan fluttered down and perched on the man's shoulder, beady black eyes fixed on her. The *trilla* bird squawked and said, "How can we travel with it holding us back? Nehan-dir will kill us all!"

"Then we *all* die together," Kesira said firmly.

"Madness," complained Zolkan. "And no time even to properly bathe. Awful weather, cruel humans wanting to eat *trilla* birds, and I am forced to stay dirty."

"You forgot to mention hungry," added Kesira, smiling at Zolkan.

"That too. Very hungry. No fit food anywhere. And Steel Crescent chases us. Nehan-dir will have my feathers for headdress!"

Kesira put the baby down into his threadbare blanket and tucked the corners in around him. While Ayondela's curse had been lifted from the land, touches of wintry cold remained to stalk unwittingly exposed soft flesh. Even as she made certain that the baby was warm, Kesira felt cold tendrils of air whipping at her rags. The gray robe of her order no longer provided any protection at all.

She undid the knotted blue cord proclaiming her a sister and then took off the gold sash, laying them aside.

"Parvey no longer needs covering," she said. "Poor though it is, her clothes look like Empress Aglenella's compared to mine." She rummaged through small boxes and pulled out what might be most useful. Kesira almost dropped the wolfskin skirt Parvey Yera had fashioned from the beast killed by Raellard. The fur, the coloring and texture, the size all were so close to that which Molimo became.

"Hurry," said Zolkan. "I would fly. The air cleanses my feathers."

"You just don't like being shut up in this tiny hut," said Kesira. But she didn't blame the bird. Staying here longer than necessary wore on her nerves. Too many unpleasant things had occurred for her to enjoy this place. Parvey's cooling body only accentuated the problems that had been born here.

Kesira's eyes darted to the sleeping infant. He smiled slightly in sleep, hands balled into tiny fists. No sound other than gentle breathing came to her sharp ears. Would he ever cry? Was the baby capable of such emotion, after all that had happened to his parents?

Kesira stripped off her robe and discarded it.

"Molimo, you don't have to go," she called out as the man turned to leave. "We have no secrets from one another. And this is hardly the first time you've seen me unclothed." Still, her nude body affected him. Molimo flushed and averted his eyes. Kesira almost enjoyed the uneasiness she caused in him. The nun wasn't being cruel, but her own emotions about him were brought into sharper focus.

If he had turned and taken her in his arms, Kesira Minette would not have resisted.

"Must go," Molimo scribbled on his tablet. He darted out the door before she could stop him.

Sighing, the woman dressed in Parvey's discarded clothing. The wolfskin skirt swung easily around her waist, and a fine embroidered cotton blouse slid sensuously against her skin. Parvey had done fine needlework—the shirt Raellard had worn attested to that. Thinking of him, Kesira dug further and found a worn pair of calf-high boots that had belonged to the man. By stuffing pieces of her robe into the toes Kesira could wear the boots with minimal discomfort.

"Almost ready," she said. She picked up the knotted blue cord and fastened it around her waist, then added the gold sash. These were little enough reminders of her upbringing, the teachings of Gelya, the trials she had been through, and the ones still in her future. As long as she held onto the wisdom passed on to her by Gelya, she had a chance. Lose sight of that and only failure awaited her.

Kesira sighed and sat down on the rotted stump and stared at the slain body of Parvey Yera. So many good people had died. Kesira felt cold anger building within her. She did not blame Molimo for this death; full guilt lay on Ayondela and Lenc. The jade demons' curse had frozen the land and stolen away summer crops. Raellard had died, Parvey had died, her entire mission had perished. And what of the cities? Kesira saw no way for them to have endured the bleakness of a winter lasting twice as long as usual. They depended heavily on farm produce, and the farms had failed.

"Your son will see better days without the jade demons," she promised Parvey.

A scratching sound at the door caught her attention. Molimo hesitantly entered, a look of relief on his face when he saw her fully clothed. He thrust out his tablet for her to read.

"Zolkan flies far to get such information," she said after scanning it. The *trilla* bird had sighted the outriders of the Steel Crèscent near the Pharna River, a full day's travel distant. They had time to rest, eat, and still be away before Nehan-dir's soldiers found their spoor.

Molimo held up a small rabbit he had clubbed. He pointed outside to indicate that he had a cooking fire started and that Kesira should join him. She checked the baby, then left the hut. The cool air outside hit her like a hammer blow, but she rejoiced in it after the musty cabin interior.

While Molimo fixed the simple meal Kesira fingered the battered box containing the bone rune sticks that were her due as a sister of the Mission of Gelya. She had thrown the rune sticks several times and had been uncannily accurate in her predictions. It was as if the demons aided her—those demons still opposing the power of the jade.

Molimo indicated that she should do another casting. With hardly a glance at the box Kesira upended it and flicked her wrist to send the rune sticks out in a fan-shaped pattern. They fell into the dust, many touching and one atop another.

The man-wolf lifted one eyebrow questioningly. Kesira hardly noticed him. Her eyes darted over the rune sticks, picking out meaning from the arcane scramble.

"Ayondela *is* to the south," she said in a low voice. "You might be right that we will find her at Lorum Bay. There is mention of water and ships and . . . and a peninsula in our future. Danger. I don't understand that. Storms and jade-spawned treachery."

Molimo gnawed on one of the rabbit's haunches, breaking open the femur and sucking out the marrow. His dark eyes fixed on Kesira rather than on the rune sticks she read.

"Inside my head," the woman said in a voice almost too low to be audible, "stirrings, as if someone speaks to me." Her fingers lightly traced over the carved sticks. "Ayondela is our enemy and we must destroy her. And Lenc. He uses her as a cat's-paw. He . . . he . . . oh, accursed sticks!"

Tears of frustration ran down her cheeks. The meaning came to her—almost. Kesira sensed more lurking in this casting of the runes and knew that she'd failed in her interpretation of it. All she got was information she already had: *of course* Ayondela was her enemy; Lenc *had* to be the one who destroyed Gelya and her mission.

"It's so murky, so unclear. Like chaos." Kesira stopped and swallowed hard. "It is as if the Time of Chaos is at hand." Her brown eyes lifted to lock with Molimo's darker ones. The man-wolf paled slightly and covered his discomfort by handing over the remainder of the roast rabbit.

"It is not an easy thing to consider," she said, taking the meat. "First there was void and dirt and air and water and fire, then animals, then humans, and then from the coupling of animals and humans came the demons."

Molimo stared into the crackling fire, pushed in a few more pungent twigs, and jerked away when a spark landed on his skin. Kesira saw that he did not want to consider that they might be poised on the brink of a new age.

Animals and humans mated to give birth to the demons, those creatures with accentuated traits. Stronger, longer-lived, more intelligent—and more venal and meddlesome

and stupid also. Humans ruled themselves while the demons watched with haughty, virtually immortal, disdain.

Until the Time of Chaos, the passing of the demons.
The mating of humans with demons to produce gods. Where
the best and worst of humanity rested within the demons,
the new gods would possess only the finest traits. So proclaimed the myth. But the birthing of the gods was supposed to be attended by upheaval and destruction and
calamity for humans. The demons would not easily relin-
quish their position in the cosmos.

"Dark soon," said Zolkan. The *trilla* bird flapped hard,
braked to a halt, and landed on Kesira's shoulder. She
winced as his claws cut into her shoulder. She vowed to
make a small pad for the bird before she left. Otherwise
he would savage her shoulder to the point of incapacity.

"The mercenaries are still arrayed along the river?" she
asked.

"We must be gone before dawn," said Zolkan. "Nehan-
dir is no fool—and he is angry. He will kill you this time."

Kesira said nothing. She went into the hut and took up
the infant, cradling him in her arm. "My little one," she
cooed. "What should I name you? Even an orphan deserves
a name."

Then Kesira swallowed hard. Her parents had been
killed by brigands. Without Sister Fenelia and the order
to take her in, Kesira would have perished. She looked
down into the baby's pale eyes. The debt she owed to her
sisters would be repaid by taking care of this infant. Kesira
could do no less: it was her duty.

"Leave it," said Zolkan. "We must go quickly. It will
hinder us."

"He is coming with us. I'll have to fashion a sling of
some sort to carry him." Kesira heaved a sigh. "And I
wish I had my stone-wood staff. It helps make the miles
go by easier."

Molimo extinguished the fire and pointed to the lee side
of the hut. Like her, he had no wish to spend the night
within the cabin. They unrolled their thin blankets and lay

down. Kesira soon heard Molimo's slow, regular breathing. He rested easily.

For her, sleep proved more elusive. The stars popped out, one by one, and wheeled about to form their cold, crystalline constellations set in the velvety blackness of night. The baby in her arms, Kesira eventually drifted off to a troubled sleep, doubts assailing her.

"Far behind us. We outrace them," squawked Zolkan. The bird perched on the pad Kesira had fashioned for him on her left shoulder.

"I wonder," Kesira said. "This seems too easy."

Molimo frowned and motioned for her to explain. The way for the past week had been anything but easy. At every turn they had to avoid Nehan-dir's soldiers. The weather warmed, melting the ice and snow but turning the ground into a quagmire that made walking a continual sucking, clutching struggle. And even with Zolkan's aerial reconnaissance, the path over the mountains and back to the Sea of Katad had not been easy. Before, they had followed the River Pharna to the sea. That path had been closed to them with the posting of Steel Crescent sentries along the way.

The hills turned into mountains, and even the passes required substantial outpourings of energy to traverse. With the infant strapped to her breast Kesira kept up with Molimo well enough, but if the man hadn't cut her a new staff of Gelya's sacred stone-wood, she would have faltered and lagged far behind.

"Nehan-dir must know where we're heading. Why do his soldiers hang back? On horse they could ride us down in a day. I feel that they are herding us."

"To sea?" protested Zolkan. "Our escape lies there. Why would Nehan-dir want us to escape?"

"His troops might come up the coast to meet us," wrote Molimo, awkwardly scribbling while they continued their brisk pace. "They would catch us between two patrols."

"Hardly needed," scoffed Zolkan. "Are we so dangerous to them?"

Kesira had to laugh. "We must be. Haven't we killed two of the jade demons? Aren't we responsible for lifting the curse of winter from the land?" She sobered, thinking of the ordeal endured on the Isle of Eternal Winter. She had used magicks far beyond her understanding when she had interrupted the burning of the cold white flame powering Ayondela's curse. For the briefest of instants Kesira had altered the flow of energy, and that had broken the spell.

"He seeks our blood because we slaughtered his patrons, nothing more," said Zolkan. But the *trilla* bird's words came slowly, indicating that he didn't really believe it. They all knew Nehan-dir still sought a patron of strength—and that the most likely replacement for Howenthal and Eznofadil would be Lenc.

Molimo grabbed Kesira by the shoulder and shook. He pointed along the ridge. Past a jumble of rocks she saw the chalky white cliff face and the heaving green waves of the Sea of Katad.

"We've made it," she said with a sigh of relief. Before, she had looked over that vast expanse and seen nothing but waves frozen in midroll, paralyzed in their unceasing assault on the sandy beaches. Now the waves came smoothly, breaking with ear-numbing force and filling the air with white froth and a sharp, salty tang.

"Down there. To right. Soldiers. Many soldiers. Nehan-dir's!"

Kesira didn't need Zolkan's identification to know who those armed mercenaries followed. One carried a long, thin green banner emblazoned with a crescent moon. She had seen similar designs burned into the vulnerable flesh of those loyal to the Order of the Steel Crescent.

"Wait," she said. She cinched up the straps holding the baby. A fat little hand reached up and gripped the edge of the cloth. Those eyes stared at her, too wise, too knowing. Not once did the infant emit even the tiniest of cries. She laid her hand atop the boy's head, more to reassure herself than to soothe the imperturbable baby.

"If we reach the beach unnoticed, we might find a fisherman to take us south to Lorum Bay," wrote Molimo, sketching quickly in soft dirt at their feet.

"We can only try. Zolkan, keep us informed of their movement. And try not to be too obvious about your spying."

The *trilla* bird harumphed and then became airborne. Strong green wings carried him outward on updrafts, rising and spiraling away from them. Kesira and Molimo began their descent, following a path down the face of the limestone cliff. By the time they reached the beach, both were winded.

It as then that Zolkan swooped down with the bad news.

"Nehan-dir himself rides this way. Flee! You have less than five minutes!"

Kesira frantically looked up the beach, imagining the mercenaries rounding an outjutting rock, banner flying, steel weapons gleaming in the morning sunlight. To go in that direction was suicidal. Just considering the climb back up the cliff face made her shake with weakness. No amount of urging would get them far enough away; but the only alternative was surrender.

"Up, once more up," she said. Molimo pointed. High above, on the brink where they had stood only an hour before, she spotted the sharp, hard points of metal weapons reflecting down to them. "They'll catch us between the jaws of their infernal war machine," she said.

Molimo started off down the beach, the only way open to them. Less than a hundred yards of trudging through the soft sand convinced Kesira that they were doomed. Her stamina fled, and she felt the thunder of hooves through the very ground.

When the loud cry rose from up the beach, she knew Nehan-dir had spotted them.

"To left," came Zolkan's squawking command. "A sandbar. You must go out to sea!"

Kesira almost balked. To walk out on the sandbar, out past the protecting curve of this small inlet, only stranded them. She glanced down at the baby. A tiny smile darted across his lips, and the eyes told her that she could not simply give up.

"If it means an added minute of life, let's make the most of it," she said. Kesira Minette sloshed through the shallow water and found the sandbar firm underfoot. Toward the watery horizon they walked, to find a place to make their final stand.

Chapter Three

"How far does it go?" cried Kesira. She looked back over her shoulder, fearful that Nehan-dir and his troopers had reached the juncture of sandbar and beach. The mercenary leader seemed in no hurry to cut off their escape. His company rode with painful slowness, covering little more terrain with every passing moment than Kesira and Molimo did on foot.

Molimo motioned for her to keep running. The water splashed up and into her calf-high boots, wetting the hem of her wolfskin skirt. But even in this panicky retreat Kesira found a touch of beauty. The seawater dotted Molimo's hair, and the sun sent its rays through the droplets in a spectrum of color. It was as if Molimo had been elevated to Emperor and wore a crown of liquid jewels.

The man stopped suddenly. Kesira crashed into him, arching her back so that her shoulders collided with his, protecting her small ward. The baby stirred restlessly, eyes accusing.

"There, there," she said. "It'll be all right. I promise." Even as she spoke Kesira knew how futile it was to give any hope. Her only consolation was that the infant was too young to understand more than her soothing tones. The nun only hoped that her words soothed; the panic rising within her made her want to scream in anguish.

To Molimo she said, "Why are you stopping?"

He dropped to his knees, the sea rising and falling

restlessly around his thighs. They had reached the end of
the sandbar. To go farther meant swimming for their lives.

Kesira turned and faced back toward the beach, her
hand turning cold on her stone-wood staff.

"I'm glad you made this for me. Only the wood sacred
to Gelya makes a good staff." The short time she'd used
this staff, she had broken the butt end and peeled back
splinters on the sides. One solid blow from a steel sword
would break it. Still, Kesira had nothing better to use to
defend herself, and Gelya forbade the use of edged steel
weapons.

Molimo rested his hand on her shoulder, then dropped
it to the infant.

"I'd forgotten," she said, ashamed of her lapse. "Help
me sling the baby onto my back." But Molimo didn't help
her. He swung her around and pointed out to sea, a curious
croaking sound coming from his throat. And high above,
hardly more than a green spot in the azure sky, Zolkan
spiraled and vented his singsong words for Molimo.

Kesira squinted into the sun, trying to make out what
attracted her friends' attention. Then she saw it. A small
fishing boat, hardly more than an overgrown rowboat,
hove into view.

"Zolkan!" she cried. "Get help. Get them to rescue us!"

Kesira was momentarily blinded as the green speck
crossed the face of the sun. The churning of water as
Nehan-dir's riders followed them along the bar spun her
back around.

"We are lost," she said in despair. Remove hope, and
only fear remained. Kesira reached down inside herself,
calling on the training she had received throughout her
life. Settling her emotions, finding strengths, conquering
weaknesses, she prepared for the battle. Not easily would
the Order of the Steel Crescent take her. They would find
that her patron's teachings burned brightly within her breast.
She might be the last, but her memory would endure after
this day.

The banner came ever nearer. Beside the bearer rode a

man dressed in steel-plate armor. Even at this distance Kesira recognized the spiderworks of scarring on Nehan-dir's face. The man hung a helmet from a cord on his saddle, then gestured for the banner bearer to hold position. Nehan-dir came closer until his horse nervously pawed at the fetlocks-deep water only a dozen paces distant.

"You have led us a merry chase," he said without preamble. "Do you now prepare to die?"

"I do not fear death," she answered truthfully. "Kill me if you will. I only ask that the life of this baby be spared."

Kesira had not been able to re-sling the infant. He still nestled peacefully against her breast.

"Where did you come across this foundling?" the warrior asked.

"His parents are both dead. One was tortured to death by Ayondela."

"Ah, yes, the dirt farmer. He died well enough. No disgrace in his passing. This is the sprig from his tree, eh?"

"You will spare the boy?"

"Of course not," snapped Nehan-dir. "After what he did to insure Eznofadil's death? After all you have done to disgrace my order?"

Kesira saw the flush rising to Nehan-dir's face, turning the webbing of pink scars a brighter hue than the rest of his flesh. He drew forth his sword and held it high, then brought it down, tip pointing directly at Kesira. The man holding the banner lowered his staff until the fabric trailed in the water. The pounding of that horse's hooves as he charged forward to impale them on the spear tip drowned out even the surf's restless action against the distant shore.

Molimo shoved Kesira aside at the last possible instant. With a move too swift for her to follow, the man-wolf twisted aside and allowed the spear to pass by harmlessly. Strong hands gripped the shaft and bent it groundward to bury it in the soft sand. The rider catapulted from the saddle and landed with a huge splash.

"Fool!" raged Nehan-dir.

The mercenary leader charged. Kesira felt herself sinking into a curious fugue state, with everything around her moving slowly. Try as she would, though, this increased awareness did not turn into increased speed on her part. She moved as if dipped in treacle.

The energy is within you. Use it, came soft, distant words from deep within her mind. Kesira's calm momentarily broke at the mental intrusion—from where?—but she recovered and found that the words acted as a key to parts of her hitherto untapped psyche.

She perceived with great precision that her senses had sped up—and she moved at a rate equal to them.

Nehan-dir's horse charged by her. Kesira spun lithely and thrust out her staff, catching the horse between the front legs. The scissoring of those legs as the horse ran proved to be its undoing. Fragile bones snapped against wood, and the horse nose-dived into the water, struggling in pain and panic. It kicked and threw Nehan-dir free, before slipping into deeper water. Its devastated front legs doomed it to swift, noisy drowning.

Kesira's senses slowed. She straightened, holding only fragments of her staff. Nehan-dir flailed around in the shallow water along the sandbar, the heavy plate armor weighing him down.

"Like a turtle on its back," she said. A booted foot pushed the mercenary after his horse. Yelping and grabbing futilely for her leg, Nehan-dir slid off the side of the sandbar toward deeper water. The soldier saw the danger and stopped trying to grapple with Kesira and began fumbling at the leather straps holding on his carapacelike armor.

"Molimo," the woman said softly, "help the man along."

Molimo's sword rose and fell in a bright arc. The ringing impact of sword tip against armored chest produced fat blue sparks that leapt outward to expire in the sea with a loud hiss.

"Stop—don't—damn your eyes, let me get to my feet

so I can die like a man!" Nehan-dir spun around, but Molimo's sword followed his every movement.

"Finish him, Molimo," ordered Kesira. "The others have seen and are coming. I want him dead before they arrive. I refuse to give him the pleasure of witnessing our death."

The Steel Crescent mercenaries had dismounted and taken off their own heavy armor before advancing along the submerged sandbar. As Kesira watched Molimo went to finish off Nehan-dir.

"You damned other-beast," raged Nehan-dir, struggling with the leather straps on his armor as he slipped deeper and deeper into the water. Waves lapped around him, making the small man sputter. Molimo's sword slashed out— and missed when the mercenary slid into the water, his head vanishing under the churning surface.

Kesira glanced over her shoulder. Molimo poised, knee-deep in the water, waiting for the soldier's head to reappear so he could lop it off. The woman sighed. Such was to be their fate when the others of the Steel Crescent reached them. She placed one gentling hand on the baby's cheek. Those haunting eyes looked up at her, as if saying, "I understand. You did what you could. No one can ask more."

Kesira clenched the shattered remnants of her staff and set her feet wider apart. Where the strength and speed she'd found before had come from, Kesira had no inkling. But it had aided her once. It could be summoned again.

A loud squawk captured her attention. Flying in tight circles overhead, Zolkan sailed down wordlessly. The sound of water lapping against a boat hull caught her attention. Kesira turned to see a small skiff less than a dozen yards away. The sailor at the oars rowed furiously, cursing as he came. Zolkan swooped down to land heavily on her shoulder. Kesira hardly noticed the weight this time.

"They aid us. Good people. Eat fish, not birds."

"The fishermen in the boat?" Kesira squinted into the

sun and saw the larger fishing boat bobbing some distance away.

"Good people. Good. Get in boat. Help sailor row. Hurry, hurry!"

"You're always in too much of a rush, Zolkan," she chided. But Kesira's own haste to get to the skiff was almost unseemly. Her own death would come one day; it hardly mattered anymore when that day was. But the baby's life stretched in front of him. Kesira felt she owed him as much as she could deliver.

"Molimo, come," Zolkan cawed.

The man-wolf was obviously torn between waiting for Nehan-dir to surface, so that he could finish off the mercenary, and joining Kesira in the skiff. When his dark eyes fixed on the dozen warriors pounding through the water toward him, he abandoned all hope of seeing Nehan-dir's head separated from his torso. Molimo sloughed through the water, then swam the last few yards. Kesira and Zolkan both struggled to pull the heavily muscled young man into the boat.

"Can't expect me to do all the rowing, now can yer?" complained the sailor. "Take an oar and row as if yer life depended on it." The sailor cast a jaundiced eye on the soldiers just now arriving at the tip of the sandbar. His expression indicated that he counted them out as any real opposition. All he wanted to do was return to the fishing boat and ply his trade.

Molimo dropped onto the seat beside the sailor and gripped the oar. Four smooth pulls took them far beyond the range of the Steel Crescent. None appeared eager to leave even the tenuous contact with land and swim after the fleeing nun and her friends.

Zolkan perched on the stern of the boat and shouted obscenities at the soldiers.

"Yer friend here, he's got quite a filthy mouth on him," observed the sailor.

"Shut up and row, you pile of pigeon shit. They still might come after us," said Zolkan.

Even as the *trilla* bird spoke a hand gripped the rotted wood side and tried to capsize the skiff. The sailor yelped and flailed about, and Molimo was thrown to one side, off-balance. Only Kesira reacted. Again, from deep within, she found the odd speed within slowness to respond with superhuman quickness. The remaining piece of her stone-wood staff amounted to little more than a stake. Kesira lifted it and brought it down directly into Nehan-dir's hand.

Nehan-dir shrieked and kicked, further rocking the boat. His other hand swung a dagger, but with his right hand injured he couldn't maintain his grip. He slipped off and thrashed about in the water, trying to pull out the wood spike and stay afloat at the same time.

"Bitch! You will suffer for a thousand days! I'll see that Lenc uses you for—"

Nehan-dir sputtered as Zolkan swooped low and clawed at his face. Only by submerging did the Steel Crescent's leader succeed in avoiding new facial scars.

"Fish-faced enemy of decency," grumbled Zolkan, re-alighting on the stern of the boat. By this time both the sailor and Molimo had recovered. They bent their backs and rowed, making the small skiff glide across the water with impressive speed.

Only when they touched against the hull of the larger fishing boat did Kesira relax. The soldiers still stood at the end of the sandbar shouting curses and promising death and torture. She watched as two of them rescued their leader and led Nehan-dir off to be bandaged.

"Come on up, milady. You look the worse for wear, you do." The captain of the small boat thrust out a gnarled hand for Kesira. Gratefully she let the man lift her the few feet to the boat's heaving deck. "Breezing up a mite, she is. Have to get 'er turned into the wind or ship some water."

The man was short, hardly taller than Kesira herself, but what he lacked in height he more than made up for in bulk. A heavy sea jacket strained at the seams to hold in the muscle, and his bandy legs showed long years at sea. His rolling gait exactly matched the boat's motion so that

Kesira felt she danced around while the captain and his ship stayed perfectly stationary. It made her increasingly queasy.

"Still, it's a good thing to be on the sea again, storm or no. That blasted winter kept the entire Sea of Katad froze over, it did. Never seen its like. And I ast my old da about it, I did. He never saw the like, neither."

"Thank you for rescuing us like this." Kesira perched against the rail and swallowed hard. The boat's surging motion made her seasick.

"Think nothing of it. When your bird landed and spoke with us, we knew what had to be done. A pleasure to do it, mark my words."

"Yer letting that damn feathered menace run the *Foul*, if yer ast me," grumbled the sailor who had rowed them to the boat.

"No one's asking you, bilge." The snap of authority entered the captain's words. Perhaps he commanded only a small fishing boat, but he was captain and brooked no rebellion in his ragtag ranks.

Zolkan landed beside Kesira and asked, "Met captain yet?"

"Of course," she said, wondering at the bird's lapse. The *Foul*'s captain stood not five feet away.

"Not *him*," Zolkan said disdainfully. "Captain. Him." One vivid green wing extended and pointed toward a cross bracing where another *trilla* bird sat, surveying the world as if he owned it.

Kesira smiled a little at the sight of the other bird. This explained what the sailor meant when he took the captain to task for letting the "damn feathered menace" run the boat.

"Name's Yinzan," said Zolkan. "Not a bad sort but aggressive. Very opinionated."

"You mean, this Yinzan doesn't always agree with you," said Kesira. She had to laugh now.

The other *trilla* bird fluttered down to perch beside Zolkan. Beak to beak, particolored crests furling and unfurling, they chattered away in shrill notes, ignoring Kesira. She heaved herself to her feet and lurched off to find the captain. He worked to get the sails furled against the wind's increasing force.

"Captain, is there a place where I might get out of the spray?"

"The wee one's needin' his lunch, is that it?" asked the weathered man. He peered down at the infant, then frowned, as if looking into a charnel pit. "Down there. Take my cabin, such as it is."

Kesira wondered at his reaction, then shrugged it off. She sat on the edge of the hard bunk and brought the baby out, holding him up so she could get a good look at him. "What is it about you that strikes everyone as so strange?"

The infant didn't cry or even gurgle. The pale eyes stared fixedly.

"Zolkan doesn't want anything to do with you, but that is only normal. *Trilla* birds aren't noted for liking anything that takes away from their adulation. As for Molimo, he seems almost frightened of you, yet protective enough. What secrets do you hold in that tiny little body?" Kesira bounced the boy up and down in synchronization with the rolling of the boat.

No answers came. Kesira fed the infant, sighing as she felt the hungry mouth begin its meal.

Later she slept on the hard bunk, more from exhaustion than from normal need. The tossing and wallowing motion of the fishing boat awoke her near sunset. Kesira rocked the baby but he still slept, even as she put him into the sling around her shoulders. Wobbling, the nun made her way to the deck, now washed constantly by the heaving green water from the Sea of Katad.

"Stay below," shouted the captain. "The *Foul* is a staunch boat, but this miserable, demon cursed weather..." The rest of his words were swallowed by the high wind singing through the masts.

Kesira needed no urging to return to the relative safety below decks. She found Yinzan and Zolkan still engrossed in complex bird arguments. Molimo held on to a brace in the boat's hull and looked more than a little sick. Kesira dropped down beside him, hand resting on his shoulder.

"Try not to fight it so," she said. "The motion is violent, but you get used to it. I almost have." Even as she spoke Kesira knew that she lied. Her stomach tensed into a small fist, then tried to rush up her esophagus and erupt from her mouth. It didn't do her any good when Molimo laughed at her discomfort. The odd croaking noise had to be a laugh, she thought.

Together they sat and rode out the storm, each lost in deep thought. The two *trilla* birds conversed loudly and unintelligibly. From the expression on Molimo's face she doubted that he understood what passed between the birds, either. Kesira's mind wandered away: from the baby, from Molimo, from Zolkan and the boat, and back to the fight on the sandbar. She had *heard* a voice inside her head, and that voice had triggered her speed and power. It was her body, her muscle, her reaction, but the voice had released it when the nun had thought herself totally drained.

What had it been?

Kesira looked up at Molimo, but the man-wolf sat with eyes squeezed shut and lips pulled into a thin line. She couldn't help but feel proud of him. He had worked hard to keep control of the transformation, and had, for the most part, succeeded. The few times he had slipped and let out the animal, he had killed—and saved her life.

"Yinzan says boat founders."

"What?" Kesira's attention snapped to Zolkan. "What are you saying?"

"*Foul* is doomed ship. Prepare to sink."

"What about you?" Kesira demanded. "Can you fly in this weather? The wind? The rain?"

"Captain works us toward shore. No problem for *trilla* birds," Zolkan assured her. "But you and Molimo must prepare."

"Does the crew know?"

"Only four of them. They know. They are sailors and

no fools. Storms left from Ayondela's curse, Yinzan thinks. Smart bird, that Yinzan. Runs *Foul* and keeps captain in line."

Kesira shook Molimo awake, if he had been sleeping at all, and quickly repeated all Zolkan had said. The man heaved himself up on unsteady legs, checked Kesira and the baby, then led the way to the deck. Below, Kesira had doubted the bird's appraisal. When she saw the broken spars and the way the decking pulled up to expose the slowly filling cargo holds, she believed.

"Captain!" she shouted into the gale-force wind. "Should we take to the skiff?"

The man either didn't hear or he ignored her. He continued pulling at the rudder, muscles bulging and his own curses shoved back down his throat by the wind.

"What are we going to do?" she called to Zolkan. The *trilla* bird stood in the doorway with Yinzan. The two conferred. Zolkan took to wing and landed ponderously on Kesira's shoulder so that his beak pressed hard and wet against her ear.

"To skiff. Try to stay afloat for another hour. Storm nears peak as demons battle."

"What? Demons fighting?"

The *trilla* bird stared at her with one beady black eye, as if she were demented. "What else do you think causes such storm winds? Demons everywhere—and their spawn litter ocean depths. Beware sea, Kesira. Beware!"

Kesira and Molimo lurched toward the skiff just as the *Foul* split in half. Curtains of cold green water rose up on either side, waiting to swallow them without a trace.

Chapter Four

THE *FOUL* BROKE apart with a deafening roar. One half of the fishing boat twisted crazily and floated away, caught on high waves. The other half started straight for the bottom of the Sea of Katad—Kesima and Molimo clinging to its railing.

"The skiff!" the woman cried. She felt Molimo's strong hand gripping her skirt, pulling her along. Her own arms cradled the baby nestled against her breast. Together the three managed to get to the tiny skiff bouncing like a cork on the stormy sea. Sputtering, swimming, flailing, Kesira fought her way through the water, keeping on her back to prevent the infant from drowning. Molimo pulled her into the small boat.

She examined the infant. While awake and aware the boy did not cry out. Kesira wondered if the baby bore Molimo's affliction, but she remembered the feel of the tiny tongue, and this wouldn't affect crying. In a way, the infant's fortitude shamed her. She reacted more strongly to all that happened than to the baby—and babies were supposed to cry whenever something angered them or they grew fearful or scared.

Molimo just sat in the boat, slumped forward.

"Shouldn't we row?" Kesira called over the roaring winds. The cutting edges of the storm raked at her cheeks and brought tears to her eyes. While summer had reasserted itself after Ayondela's curse had been lifted, the water only slowly warmed. She felt every droplet of salty spray that hit her as a cold, wet fist. Kesira flinched and dodged the blows, but it did her no good. She kept her arms wrapped tightly around the baby, protecting him the best she could.

Molimo pointed: no oars. During the storm they had been washed away. Kesira wiped the water from her eyes and looked for them. The sight of what remained from the *Foul* convinced her that they were lucky to be alive.

"We must look for survivors," she said. Then it struck her; they had no choice in the matter. The wind and wave action carried them like a fallen leaf in a millrace. Without oars they were at the mercy of the elements. If they happened on one of the fishermen, fine. But they had no way to actively seek out those who might still be alive.

Kesira watched in mute horror as the part of the *Foul* that had stayed afloat broke into smaller pieces under a twenty-foot-high wave's crushing fall. In minutes no trace of the fishing boat could be found in the heaving ocean.

"See anyone?" she shouted.

Molimo shook his head.

Kesira settled down in the tiny boat, praying that the waves wouldn't inundate them, that the storm would die down, that they'd sight land soon. Most of all she prayed that the baby would survive. Kesira carried a heavy burden with the child. Not only had she seen the boy's parents killed, but also she had been directly responsible for their deaths.

Even deeper, she had a debt to repay. Sister Fenelia had taken her in when she had scarcely eight summers to her credit. Kesira had to see the boy placed in a good home where his upbringing would follow the moral teachings of Gelya. As the boat bucked and jerked in the storm she wondered how she would accomplish such a noble goal. Her mission had died with Lenc's attack on the nunnery.

The sight of Lenc's cold, white flame burning hungrily on Gelya's altar had become indelibly etched on her consciousness. No matter how long she lived, how quickly she died, that memory would fester within her.

"Oh, Gelya, you were too good," she said, sobbing. "The power of the jade made Lenc the stronger, and your integrity didn't allow you to truly fight him."

Arms circled her. She blinked away the salty mat forming over her eyes and saw Molimo. She snuggled closer, his strength flowing into her. If she died, she would do so knowing that her life had not been lived totally in vain. She had friends, she had performed duties for Emperor and her order the best she knew how. Never had Kesira Minette disgraced their name or her own.

Molimo holding her, and she holding the baby, they went to sleep.

Hot sunlight poured over her, drying her skin and caking on itchy salt. Kesira stirred. A voice demanded, "Will you pay their freight or not?"

"Zolkan?"

"Who else?" the *trilla* bird said, obviously irritated. "Yinzan will negotiate, but you must assure them of good seas. Superstitious lot, those sailors."

Kesira struggled to sit up in the unsteady boat. They had taken a considerable amount of water. Even with Molimo's constant bailing they sat ankle-deep. She supposed some of the boat's seams had opened during the storm. It amounted to nothing less than a miracle that a huge wave hadn't engulfed them and sent them to the bottom of the sea—like the *Foul*.

"They will haul you into port if you promise them clear sailing."

"I can't do that. Even when my order existed, we didn't converse directly with our patron. How am I supposed to say whether there'll be another storm?"

Molimo dug in his pack and pulled out his tablet. A quick move of his stylus produced, "Promise them. We sink."

"But what if there *is* another storm?"

"No storm," assured Zolkan. "Yinzan and I both see nothing but clear skies all way to horizon."

Kesira looked at the bird skeptically, then stood and put cupped hands to her mouth. "Hello!" she shouted. "Will you grant us passage to Lorum Bay?"

"The bird's relayed our terms. Will there be fair weather or nay?" came the reply. A short, gray-haired man clung to the side rail. Nothing differentiated him from the other sailors except for the snap of command in his voice.

"I am a sister of the Mission of Gelya," Kesira called back. "The power to cast the rune sticks is vested in me. There will be no adverse weather for..."

"Tell him two weeks," said Zolkan.

"...for a fortnight."

"A full fortnight?" the captain shouted back.

"One day less," said Kesira, deciding that this sounded better than simply agreeing. The authority in her voice as she told the lie impressed even her—and it carried with the fisherman.

"Catch the line. We are bound for Lorum Bay. But there is one more matter to decide."

Molimo pulled the battered skiff along a line toward the fishing vessel and tethered it to a dangling, rusted metal ring. Even as one of the sailors helped Kesira onto the main deck, the skiff started to sink. Molimo had to tread water before shinnying up the rope lowered for him. With a careless whack a sailor used his long knife to sever the rope binding the skiff to the ring. Tiny bubbles rose to mark the watery grave that might have been theirs.

"Never seen wood sink," muttered the captain. "Strange times, strange beasts out here in the sea."

"What was the other condition?" asked Kesira, settling the baby in her arms as she glanced around.

"Might be more'n you're willing to trade," the man said. "But you got little enough choice. Might heave you back into the drink if you don't agree."

"This matter is one you feel strongly about?"

"Aye, that I do. I want the *trilla* bird."

"Zolkan!" she said in surprise. "I can't barter him away. Even if it means swimming for shore."

"Shore's a long ways off. A good three leagues."

"He is not mine to give. He—"

"Agree," came Zolkan's broken squawk. "Captain does not mean me. He talks of Yinzan. Yinzan wants to be aboard another boat, now that *Foul* is sunk."

Kesira let out a gusty sigh of relief. The other *trilla* bird's motives were unclear to her, but he had obviously found himself a post aboard the fishing boats that made him indispensable.

"Certainly," she said to the captain. "Yinzan will be happy to continue on with you, and I give you my blessings on this also." Zolkan launched himself into the air and flapped hard to gain altitude. In a few seconds he joined a second green spot aloft. They circled one another for a full minute before a loud caw sounded and both Zolkan and Yinzan fluttered down from the sky, zigzagging around one another, forming a chain pattern of emerald-green feathers as they came. Zolkan landed on the deck railing and began to preen. The other *trilla* bird perched on the captain's shoulder, peering curiously at Kesira, as if she had taken on the appearance of some odd deep-sea creature washed ashore.

"How long till we reach Lorum Bay?" she asked. "I think my friends and I need a good rest."

The captain squinted and rubbed a stubbled chin. "We struck a good bargain, so we'll head directly for the port. Three days. Less, if the winds favor us." He hesitated, then asked, "That your boychild?"

Kesira stiffened; his tone was all wrong. "Yes," she answered. "He is in my care."

"Lost my own son." The captain hesitated, then moved closer, staring down at the infant. Bold, pale eyes peered up at the weather-beaten sailor. "Shame he's not an orphan. Give you good money in exchange for him. Raise him as my own."

Molimo stood behind the captain and slowly shook his head, but Kesira didn't require the prompting.

"We have family in Lorum Bay we haven't seen in some time." The captain seemed to know that Kesira was lying but did not pursue the matter. He turned and began bellowing out orders to get the boat moving.

With Molimo close by her side Kesira said, "Strange. He was more interested in the baby than he ought to have been. I didn't believe him when he said he'd lost a son, either."

Molimo hastily wrote, "We are better off away from this boat."

Kesira agreed. And she got nothing when she questioned Zolkan. Neither he nor Yinzan had any explanation for the captain's roundabout request to adopt the infant. And, through it all, the baby watched silently, never emitting even a whimper.

"They look as if they are coming out to meet us," Kesira said uneasily. Four longboats filled with armed men slid through the calm waters of Lorum Bay's smelly harbor.

"Routine, nothing more," said the captain. "The harbormaster's an old friend of mine. He and his drinking cronies a'times come to personally greet me."

The man moved away to tend to lashing down some small boxes on deck. Kesira turned to Molimo and said, "The captain's lying. I don't know why, but those soldiers come for us."

Molimo hurried below decks to get their sparse belongings. He returned carrying the infant, as if the child might break at any moment. Kesira laughed and took the baby, slinging him in front. She stretched and settled the straps, then motioned for Zolkan to join them. The *trilla* bird dropped to the railing in front of the nun and nervously sidestepped back and forth.

"What do you make of the captain's visitors?" she asked the bird.

Zolkan turned his head around fully and cast a biased

eye on those rowing out to the fishing boat. "Yinzan knows nothing of them," the bird said. "I am inclined to believe him. Captain is nothing more than pigeon shit—Yinzan will soon enough change that. But these?" Zolkan let out a mournful squawk.

"You don't trust the captain? Does Yinzan?"

"All humans untrustworthy," said Zolkan. "Yinzan can remake captain. But these do not look peaceful."

Molimo tugged at her arm and motioned for her to join him on the far side of the deck, out of sight of the long-boats. Strangled noises came from Molimo's throat, indicating his extreme agitation. He pointed to the water. Bits of garbage and other harbor debris slapped against the side of the fishing boat.

"I don't understand," Kesira said. "What do you want me to see?"

On the wood railing Molimo outlined "Off!"

Without even tensing he jumped flat-footed over the railing and into the water. He surfaced and motioned for Kesira to follow. She looked over her shoulder and saw that the captain's attention focused on those in the approaching boats. The man yelled his greetings and lowered a rope ladder. Kesira slipped over the railing and kicked free, falling into the water.

She surfaced and floated on her back to allow the baby to breathe. The infant smiled at her, seeming to enjoy the unexpected bath.

"What now?" she asked. Molimo pointed toward a rocky breakwater, then began swimming with powerful, slow strokes. Kesira found herself hard-pressed to keep up with even this slow pace because of her need to hold the baby's head above water. But they had reached the largest of the boulders and were pulling themselves up when the cry rose from the fishing boat. Armed men stormed about, screaming and cursing, brandishing their swords and having at the sailors.

Snippets drifted across to where Kesira and Molimo crouched.

"... lied to me!" The soldier lifted a heavy-bladed sword and brought it down with a meaty *thunk!* Kesira winced as red exploded from the captain's neck. The sailor half turned, to tumble over the railing and into the bay.

"Are we the cause of that?" she wondered aloud.

Zolkan alighted on a nearby rock and stretched one cramped wing. He carefully tucked it back before saying, "Yinzan apologizes for this. Shit for brains thought this treacherous captain good man. He sold us to soldiers."

"But how?" asked Kesira, confused. "We just dropped anchor an hour ago."

Zolkan snorted and shook his head at her stupidity. "Semaphore. Flagman relayed message to shore."

"Are those mercenaries?"

"Not Steel Crescent," said Zolkan. "Others. Many seek us now."

"Wonderful," Kesira said, sinking down to the ground. "Two jade demons seek to kill us, the entire Order of the Steel Crescent hunts us like rabbits, and now a new player comes into the game. And we don't even know who it is or why they want us!"

A tiny hand clutched at her blouse. Kesira looked down into the baby's pale eyes. No matter who sought them, it was suppertime. Irritated, Kesira allowed the infant to feed.

"Yinzan wants nothing more to do with us," explained Zolkan. "Bird thinks we are jinxed." The bird landed heavily on the street after an hour's reconnaissance of the village. He yawned and clacked his beak, then settled down as if to roost.

"He might be right," grumbled Kesira. "Nothing has gone our way since we came ashore." All day had been spent tramping along the cobblestone streets of Lorum Bay looking for—what? The woman couldn't say, but she figured that she'd know it when she saw it. A friendly face, a tiny mission to Gelya or another sympathetic patron, even a chance meeting in the street.

All of Lorum Bay walked as if it had been sentenced to die within the month. No one smiled. Children hunkered fearfully in doorways, not laughing or playing or begging. The street vendors listlessly pointed to their wares instead of actively hawking them. What few entertainers lined the byways sang off-key or juggled poorly. If Kesira hadn't known better, she would have thought that everyone in Lorum Bay had died and only their bodies inhabited the streets and alleys.

Never before had she seen a town without soul.

Even the thieves refused to ply their trade.

"Well, Zolkan, you're the one who insisted that Ayondela could be found in Lorum Bay. Where is she?" asked Kesira, not certain that she really wanted to find the female demon.

"Many talk secretively of clouds," said Zolkan. "Do not understand it. Foolish humans know nothing of clouds, of soaring through them, of feeling icy tingles along your feathers. Wondrous sensations." The bird waddled back and forth, doing a little dance. "They wet the wings so that—"

"Never mind, Zolkan," Kesira said, forestalling further discussion of how it felt to soar. "Did you happen across any information about those soldiers who met the boat?"

"Not of Ayondela's service," he said. "Nor of Steel Crescent."

Kesira gently rocked the baby as she thought. Finally she said, "There's no evidence Ayondela is here. Let's leave the village and see if we can't find more information in the foothills. Lonesome farmers tend to accumulate gossip from any traveler. These tight-mouthed city folk aren't any help at all."

A nearby man gasped and then let out a wordless cry of alarm. He levered himself to his feet and raced down the street, his boots click-clack-clicking as he ran. Others hearing the outcry hurried indoors, slamming shutters and barring their entryways.

"What did he see?" Kesira asked. Neither Zolkan nor

Molimo seemed to know. She had to trust their more acute senses.

"Fog drifting down street, nothing more," said the bird.

A wolf's howl cut the stillness. Kesira spun. Molimo had transformed into his wolf form and surged forward, fangs snapping at the foggy tendrils reaching out with mist-damp intent.

If Molimo's first cry had been one of challenge, the second, when he entered the fog, turned to pain and fear. The sleek gray wolf bolted from the fog, covered with a myriad of tiny cuts. Kesira tried to grab him as he ran past and failed. Her arms came away covered with the other-beast's blood.

"What happened?" she asked.

"Stay back," cautioned Zolkan. "Fog deadly."

"Why? How?"

"Leave *now.*" Zolkan took to wing, not waiting to see whether Kesira followed his advice. She stepped toward the silent fog, frowning at the texture. In the Yearn Mountains, where she had been raised, fog banks were common. She remembered fun-filled days as a child romping in them, she and the other sisters laughing and hiding, letting the floating clouds veil them as they acted out passion plays.

A tiny hand tugged at her blouse. "I'm not going to enter," she told the infant. "I saw what happened to Molimo." But Kesira held out a hand as the vaporous wisps drifted closer.

She screamed as wet droplets lacerated her flesh. She jerked away, almost stumbling. In confusion Kesira stared at her injured hand. It looked as if some demented demon had taken razors to it. Long, thin streaks of blood sprang up and dripped to the paving.

"Enough of this," she said, backpedaling from the mist. The woman turned and found only locked doors. And at the other end of the street came a new bank of fog, moving with a relentless pace toward her.

Kesira yelped as the other blanket of fog stroked over

her arm. Cuts only a fraction of an inch deep appeared wherever the mist touched her.

She didn't have to be told that she'd discovered yet another magical weapon of the jade demons.

"Ayondela!" Kesira called. "This will not stop me. You will not triumph. *You will not!*"

Like the jaws of a vise, the clouds of floating death closed on her.

Chapter Five

THE MIST TOOK ON an ominous life of its own, gray tendrils turning into grasping hands that followed Kesira's every move. She dodged; the vapor flowed to block her escape. She clutched the baby to her chest as she sought a path away from the deadly, cutting fog.

Kesira saw no escape.

All the doors had been securely fastened, and not even a curious eye peered through cracks or knotholes in the shutters.

"Help me!" she called out. No response. Kesira yelped in sudden pain as a thin tendril of the mist wrapped around her ankle. Where it touched, bright red blood sprang from new wounds. Another thready line of gray dampness sank from above, lightly brushing her cheek. This time Kesira experienced no pain, but the blood trickling down her face told her that she would soon perish unless she found shelter.

"What's wrong with you?" she called. "I will *die* if you don't let me inside!"

Kesira kicked on door after door. Behind one, she heard angry voices: a woman wanting her let in, a man protesting. Kesira had to hurry along because of the encroaching fog. She found fewer and fewer doors to knock on, fewer shutters to try to open with her fumbling fingers. The mist circled her now, moving closer and closer with every light puff of breeze off the harbor.

"No," she said in horror. "Not this way." Kesira had

survived battles with two jade demons. Dying in a magical mist mocked her earlier successes.

"The little one," came a broken, gravelly voice. "Is he all right? This is important!"

Kesira whipped around. Pressed into a niche in the stone wall stood an old man with long, flowing white locks; rheumy eyes; a nose the size of a potato, complete with sprouts; and a face that seemed kindly, concerned.

"The boy is unharmed—so far. There's nothing I can do to get away from the fog. What is it?"

"A curse," the old man said. He gusted a deep sigh of resignation. "If I could make it vanish, I would. But, alas, this is beyond my feeble abilities."

"Then there's no hope for us," Kesira said. Already her mind turned inward and sank quickly to the depths where her darkest nightmares lurked. She sought them now, facing them squarely so that death would not be feared.

"Wait!" the old man said. He hobbled forward, making an impatient gesture with his hand when a wispy column of fog swirled around him. The fog slid away from him, refusing to touch his flesh, just as oil and water refuse to mix. "You must come with me."

Without waiting for an answer the old man forged ahead, ignoring the fog. Kesira hesitated. A small wake of safety formed behind him as he went. Kesira knew she would have no better chance than this. She plunged into the deadly fog, cringing as occasional moist fingers probed for her flesh. While she sustained a few bloody streaks, the fog seemed unable to do more serious damage as long as she pressed close to the old man.

"Who are you?" she asked. "How is it that you know about the baby? How do you keep the fog at bay?"

"I watched you earlier with the boychild dangling around your neck. It must be a fearsomely tiring way to go through life, burdened thus."

"It's comfortable enough. More so than holding the baby in my arms."

"Ah, so it is, so it is." The white-haired man turned

and made a quick ninety-degree turn that confused Kesira. She had tried to keep a mental image of their path through the fog, but now she saw only gray swirls and the cobblestones beneath her feet. She pressed even closer to her guide.

"How do you keep the mist away from us?"

"The mists," he said, never slowing his pace or looking at her, "are magical. You knew as much. Lenc sends them to cow the good people of Lorum Bay."

"Effective," Kesira said bitterly.

"Aye, effective. Lenc is quite astute in knowing another's weakness. Remember that. He sniffs out weakness the way a hunting dog follows a spoor."

Kesira frowned. The old man spoke too intimately of Lenc to be a simple citizen of this coastal village.

"You are quite correct," he said, answering her unspoken thoughts. "I know Lenc. Ayondela also. Actually it is she who sends these cursed mists. Poor Ayondela, gone astray. The death of her son unsettled her fragile mind."

"Who are you?"

"Which demon, is that your question?" The old man laughed delightedly as they emerged from the fog and into the wan sunlight that was trying to instill some joy to Lorum Bay's fear-cloaked streets.

"I have met several," Kesira said, carefully choosing her words. "Some have been very nice."

"Gelya? No, you never met your patron, did you? Pity. He was an exceptional one, Gelya was. One of the few who bothered with dropping down among you mortals to impart some small gems of wisdom."

The old man—the demon—pushed open a rickety door and bowed low, indicating that Kesira should enter first. She protected the infant with her arms and bent body, then went inside. The dimness brought her up short. She imagined that she had walked into a black velvet curtain, but when her eyes adapted to the low light, she saw a nicely appointed, if somewhat Spartan, dwelling. On a low table stood a ceramic water pitcher and several glasses.

"Those are special," said the demon, following her in and closing the door. "Crystal from the Emperor's very own supplier. You mortals do some things very well and making leaded crystal is one. I envy you this art."

"You've tried it?" Kesira asked in surprise.

"Of course I have. Isn't creation of beauty one of Gelya's teachings? It is certainly worthy of anyone's time, whether they be mortal or demon. My crystal, however, never quite attained such clarity or tone." He thumped a finger against the rim of one glass. The pure, clear note seized Kesira and shook her gently, evoking pleasant memories, inciting a riot of tastes on her tongue, softly stroking her cheeks, summoning memories of first love. A single tear ran from the corner of her eye.

"That's the prettiest sound I've ever heard," she said, wiping away the tear. "It . . . does things to me."

"The maker of the glass is imbued with a gift unlike any other mortal's," said the old man. He settled down into a chair. Kesira couldn't tell if the sounds she heard now were from joints creaking or the wood protesting its slight burden.

"And your gift," the demon continued, "is even more amazing to one such as I."

"What? But you're a demon," Kesira blurted.

"A minor one, a very small one in the pantheon of the great." The demon stroked over his bare chin, then ran long, bony fingers through his white hair. "If I had any true power, I'd not be long in this body. Every movement is a trial for me." He straightened his legs. The popping sounds confirmed what Kesira had guessed at before. Joints too arthritic for fluid motion plagued him.

"I don't even know your name. I am—"

"Kesira Minette," he interrupted. "I have followed your path with some interest since you came to my attention on Ayondela's Isle of Eternal Winter." He poured water from the pitcher into one of the crystal glasses. "I am Cayabbib."

Kesira took the water gratefully. It had been too long

since she had eaten or drunk. But as thirsty as she was, she found it impossible to swallow more than a single mouthful; and even stranger, this one swallow sated both her thirst and hunger.

"Don't feel guilty that you have never heard the name. Cayabbib is hardly rolling off everyone's tongue these days."

"What's your interest in me?" she asked, putting down the glass with great reluctance. Kesira wanted to sample the strange brew further, even though it had slaked her thirst and hunger. She remembered all too vividly the times when she and Molimo had suffered from starvation. A single pint of this elixir would have carried them over nicely.

"You remember Toyaga?" the demon asked. He shifted around and moved to a more comfortable chair. He settled with obvious relief. Again sounded the crackling of his joints. "He summoned me for a small chat while running from Ayondela and Eznofadil. This was before your friend Zolkan convinced him to return and battle the jade power."

"So?"

"I am a minor demon, worshiped by some, ignored by the rest. Here in Lorum Bay rose a tiny group of followers loyal to me. I visited them on rare occasions, but it satisfied them. Unlike Gelya, I placed no stringent teachings upon my disciples. Perhaps I was too lenient. They seemed to prefer it that way, and I was only too happy to oblige."

"Why bother at all? Many—most—demons never sought worshipers or proselytes."

"My dear one, I felt a duty to humankind. Foolish, yes, time has shown that. I did too little, contributed too little time to the effort. Gelya created a positive force in this world. You are proof of that. But I?" The old man snorted in self-deprecation. "I had nothing to offer and gave of it stintingly."

"Why did you save me from the fog?" Kesira perched uneasily on the corner of the low table, trying to decide whether she really faced a demon or a demented old man lost in the wandering corridors of senility. The only tangible fact that remained was the way the mist had parted for him, and this might be some simple trick anyone could learn.

"You have a destiny far outshining anything I can offer this poor world. Do you think Ayondela and Lenc have stopped visiting their terror on humanity because you broke Ayondela's spell?"

"I didn't really break it. The white flame faltered. I . . . I had nothing to do with that."

Cayabbib shook his head sadly. "You do not believe that. You are intelligent and fearless. Your courage broke the flow of evil feeding the Lenc's flame. And thus was broken the spell. On my most potent day I could never have accomplished a fraction of that awesome deed. You did it. You and your friends."

"You must possess some power. You know so much about me."

"Even this, my dear, requires no great skill. I listen. The Steel Crescent seeks you. The Emperor's guard seeks you."

"What?" Kesira shot to her feet. The baby stirred, both tiny fists gripping the edge of the sling and shaking angrily at the upset. "What has Emperor Kwasian to do with me?"

"There are nodes of power, lines of flow, spots where nothing occurs—and other areas where all the magical worldlines coalesce. Inside you there is such a spot. You lack the power of jade, but there is something more, something different from the jade that Lenc fears."

"And what Lenc fears, others seek, is that what you're saying?" Kesira sat down again. "I don't believe your ravings."

Cayabbib smiled benignly. "I can do nothing to make you believe. That is beyond my power. Everything is, these days. As the power of the jade demons mounts mine declines.

"Listen," Cayabbib continued earnestly. "You have immense ability in casting the runes. Do you know its source?"

"From within. Gelya taught that we are able because we think that we are able."

"Sounds like Gelya's double talk," muttered Cayabbib. "Your ability is not shared. You of an entire world can accurately read the rune sticks. But the power is not yet refined and your control is spotty."

Kesira said nothing. She knew this better than Cayabbib ever could. The feel of the five bone sticks slipping from her fingers to fall was one thing, the interpretation of their positions another matter altogether. Sensations rose within her as she gazed at the lay of the bones, and the feelings hinted at vast wildernesses of meaning only vaguely comprehensible to her. But truth rested in those throws of the rune sticks.

Once, she had sensed another's presence guiding her.

"Merrisen," said the demon in a voice almost too low to hear.

"He died," she said, tiring of this. "He perished in battle with Lenc."

"A demon's body can die while his spirit lives on. Merrisen might have chosen this path to confuse his enemies. The power of jade is too great, even for one such as Merrisen."

"You speak in riddles. I must go find my friends." Kesira cradled the baby in her arms and went to the door. She saw the light mist forcing its way inside through tiny cracks and knotholes.

"Open the door and the fog will slice you to bloody rags," Cayabbib said. "I can part the fog, but that is the limit of my power. Ayondela seeks your death. The fog is her way of doing it. The crystal clouds do her bidding."

The infant bubbled and spat at the door. Only drool ran down his chin. Kesira absentmindedly wiped it away, her attention on the mist sliding into the room.

"You're saying I'm trapped here?"

"Ayondela wants you. Lenc wants more." The old demon took on a more substantial air, as if he had made a decision and knew it meant his death.

"You want something from me. What is it?"

"Poor Kesira Minette, your burden will be more than I could bear. But you will triumph—as long as you do not doubt yourself. Fear kills small parts of your mind, but doubt will play the traitor and make you lose the good that might be won by action."

"You're starting to sound like Gelya." Kesira had to smile, but Cayabbib's expression chilled her. He meant all he said.

"You need powers not yet within you," Cayabbib declared.

"And how am I supposed to get these powers? By . . ." Kesira's words trailed off. She remembered how she had filled Wemilat the Ugly with the strength to fight Howenthal—and how some of that good demon's power had been transferred to her because of the lovemaking.

"It is your decision. I can promise you nothing. I can say this, however. Unless you accept the feeble skills I can give to you, Lenc will rule the world. This I know with absolute certainty."

Kesira stared at Cayabbib. She was a sister of the Mission of Gelya. More than the gold sash and the knotted blue cord around her waist proved that. While Gelya's death meant less to her than his life and teachings—and how she venerated those—Kesira carried the seeds of revenge within her bosom. Gelya had not approved of revenge.

Sister Dana, her best friend. Dead by Lenc's hand, burned by his cold, white flame. Sister Fenelia, a surrogate mother to her. Dead. And all the others that had become her family.

Kesira owed fealty to the Emperor, but most of all she owed an obligation to her slain sisters. Honor required that. Deep down she felt that carrying out her duty would benefit the world. The power of the jade would be crushed.

"The Time of Chaos is near," Cayabbib said in a low, quaking voice. "I have no will to survive it—or even see it arrive. The Time after will be yours, my dear. Seize this chance while I am still able to offer you what I can."

"You said Merrisen still lived. He opposed Lenc and the others. Can he aid me?"

The expression on Cayabbib's face was unreadable. "He is—or was—a force for good. You must discover much before you can tap powers as great as his."

"But he lives?"

"That is not for me to say. With the energies I can pass to you perhaps you will know." Cayabbib slumped. "Or perhaps not. I can't say. Even as we speak my abilities fade into darkness, and I slip silently behind them."

Kesira looked down at the baby. Those all-knowing eyes stared up at her. She wished the baby could speak, could tell her what thoughts ran through the tiny mind. What she sought was an answer.

That had to come from her own soul.

Kesira slowly pulled the sling straps off her shoulders and placed the baby in a padded chair. Cayabbib watched as she began to disrobe.

When they were finished, Kesira sat up in the soft bed and stared at the demon's husk beside her. All his energy had passed into her in a single rush of ecstasy—and dread.

For a long while Kesira simply sat and stared at the fallen demon. She had known him only a few minutes. This short span had not allowed her to come to like or dislike him, but she felt a certain sorrow for his plight. To be powerless and still see wrongs being committed tore a feeling person apart inside.

Kesira knew. She had witnessed the death and destruction wrought by the jade demons and had been able to do so little.

For another demon to see it and be unable to stop them, it had to be even worse.

For Cayabbib, Kesira held no emotion. For the future, she exulted. She now *knew* more than before. Skin shining whitely in the dim light, Kesira rose from the bed and fumbled through her clothing. She took out the box containing the five rune sticks. A single swift cast sent them tumbling onto the tabletop.

Gone were the horrors associated with the reaching and finding of arcane answers. No longer did Kesira feel danger at every step. She read the runes with an accuracy that seemed more than human to her. And it was. She had absorbed Cayabbib's essence and now used it.

Brown eyes lifted from the runic pattern to the bundle lying silently in the chair. Pale eyes stared unblinkingly back at her.

"The runes are positive on two points," she said to the baby. The infant's head bobbed slightly, as if agreeing with her. "Ayondela's death is within my power." Kesira swallowed hard. "And you are the key to her death lock."

The baby smiled and clenched one fist, waving it.

Silently Kesira dressed and slung the baby into his usual position. Molimo and Zolkan wandered about in Lorum Bay's streets. She had to find them. Hesitant at first, then with mounting confidence, Kesira went to the door and flung it open. Gray hammers of mist surged forward to envelop her—and failed.

As Cayabbib had done, Kesira now held the mist away. The magicks employed were small, but she had gained use of the simple trick. Unhindered, she strode out into the fog and down the street seeking her friends.

Mists parted and fell away. The pale sun shone down upon her with tentative rays made lukewarm by the harshness of the sea breeze. Kesira looked behind her and saw the fog whipping away in the face of such adversity. She canted her face to the sky and let the cold wind carry her short brown hair back from her head. For the first time in weeks Kesira experienced a serenity born from strength rather than tiredness. Cayabbib had perished; she had gained.

"One by one," she said to the baby, "the good patrons are used up and discarded. Why does it fall to me to witness this sadness?" Left unspoken was her equally eloquent plea to be free of the jade demons.

"Come, my little one, let's go find Molimo. He must be in desperate need by now. The fog cut him badly, and there's no predicting what devilment he might have found in his wolf form." While her words were light, heaviness lay within Kesira's heart. Molimo's condition boded only ill. If any of Lorum Bay's fine citizens saw the transformation, they'd kill Molimo without hesitation. The other-beasts produced by the power of illicit jade roved the plains and mountains, some changed permanently, and others were doomed to half existences like Molimo's. Never had Kesira found another who sympathized with the other-beasts or who tried to aid them in escaping their affliction.

Kesira swallowed hard. She denied it aloud, but her spirit spoke with a truthfulness that pained her. She loved Molimo, transformations to wolf or not.

"Is it pity?" she muttered. "Do I pity him the lack of tongue and the shape-changing? Or do I love him for his loyalty, bravery, the nobility hidden within his soul?"

The baby gripped her blouse and tugged gently. She smiled and stroked over the virtually hairless head. The baby turned and nestled closer to her breast, a contented smile on his face.

"Finding Molimo is important," she said, "but we must give you a name." She heaved a sigh. "We must find you a home."

Pale eyes shot open and stared at her with unflinching directness.

"The rune sticks," Kesira muttered. "How can a mere babe in arms be the weapon against Ayondela?"

The rattle of weapons startled her. Kesira looked up. Fear clutched at her throat, constricting it, making her giddy. The soldiers, marching along the street crossing perpendicularly to the one in which she stood, were all too familiar.

They followed the banner of the Steel Crescent.

Trying not to appear to hurry, Kesira walked to the storefront and peered into the tiny window, as if she were only a young matron out seeking a new dress. She used the glass as a mirror. The reflections of one mercenary after another marching along showed that Nehan-dir had mustered his full complement. Sounds of metal clashing against metal echoed down the deserted street. Wood creaked and splintered, and a woman shrieked in pain. Deeper voiced protests rose, only to be silenced with a quick dagger slash.

The Order of the Steel Crescent plied their trade in Lorum Bay. They killed and looted and raped.

Kesira's anger boiled, but the nun restrained herself from seeking open confrontation. Against armed soldiers she stood no chance at all. She turned and walked away, seeking Molimo or Zolkan. So intent was she on eluding the soldiers behind her and finding her friends that Kesira walked into someone.

"Sorry," she said, not paying any attention to the short man.

"Why? You have saved me much hunting. I was prepared to burn this village to the ground to find you." Kesira gazed in horror at the pink cobwebbing of scars on Nehan-dir's face. The diminutive mercenary's smile spread crookedly until his thin, cruel lips pulled back in a sneer.

Kesira turned to run, but fingers like steel bands closed on her arm and spun her around, slamming her hard into a stone wall.

"Don't run. There's so much we have to talk about," Nehan-dir said. His evil laugh mingled with the sounds of death created by his soldiers. Kesira stood motionless in his grip, too frightened to respond.

Chapter Six

"YOU HAVE DISGRACED ME for the last time," Nehan-dir said in a voice colder than a demon's curse. The man's scars began to pulse with the intensity of his emotion. Kesira tried to pull free, but the mercenary gripped down even harder, bruising her upper arm.

"I have no reason to attack you," Kesira said. "My fight is with Ayondela and Lenc "

"I serve Lenc."

"Don't," she pleaded. "Not all patrons are like Tolek the Spare."

"Never mention his name," Nehan-dir snarled. Lips pulled back and yellowed teeth revealed, the soldier looked more like a beast than a human. Kesira sensed the wrath bubbling up from the injury caused by the profligate demon. Tolek had traded all his worshipers to another demon in exchange for a small island and cancellation of his gambling debts. When those still loyal to Tolek discovered the trade, they had abandoned their patron and sought only those demons holding real power. Thus was born the Order of the Steel Crescent.

"Will there be any place for you in a world ruled by Lenc?" asked Kesira. "He is a cruel master now. What will happen when total power rests in the palm of his jade-green hand?"

"Even a demon cannot be in all places at once. He will require human captains to rule in his stead." Nehan-dir obviously considered himself a candidate for this exalted rank. "We of the Steel Crescent do our jobs well. We will be rewarded."

"As Tolek rewarded you?" Even as Kesira said the words, she knew she'd made a mistake. Nehan-dir doubled his fist and struck her squarely on the jaw. Only his other hand, still gripping her arm, prevented her from falling to the pavement. Nehan-dir jerked the nun erect and slammed her against the stone wall.

The buzzing in her head deafened her and turned her stomach. "Can't stand," Kesira muttered. She winced as pain shot into her jaw from even those few words.

"Killing you will be such a pleasure. I admired your stand against Ayondela on the Isle. True courage is seldom seen outside my order. But you go beyond courage to foolhardiness." Nehan-dir spun her around. All Kesira could think of was protecting the baby. Both arms cradled the child slung at her breast as she lost balance and went tumbling into the middle of the street.

As short as Nehan-dir was, he towered above her. Merciless eyes bored into her. "The only question is whether to kill you immediately or to allow my troops some small amusement with your body before you join your sisters."

Kesira hunched over to keep the infant from harm as Nehan-dir raised his fist to land another blow.

Zolkan launched himself into the air, flapped hard to hold position, then plummeted to land on the wolf's back.

Molimo twisted agilely and snapped at the *trilla* bird. Zolkan used both wing and talon to leap up and avoid the snapping fangs. With a movement even more dextrous, the bird dropped forward and sank his claws into Molimo's neck. Powerful pinions creaked and snapped as Zolkan lifted Molimo off his front paws by force of wing. A twist, a lunge, and Zolkan exposed the wolf's soft underside.

"Rip out your throat," promised Zolkan. "Calm yourself. Now. Do it *now!*"

The thrashing subsided as the gray wolf gave in to the inevitable. Zolkan's claws relaxed when he felt fur changing to human skin, steely tendons shortening and becoming heavier human muscle. Zolkan hopped off the supine figure and watched the last stage of transformation back to human with an air of resignation.

It could be so difficult keeping Molimo in a usable form.

"All right?" the bird asked.

No, spoke Molimo, his answer ringing inside the bird's skull. *I* tried *to keep from changing when the mists rolled down the street. I failed. I tried and failed!*

"Ayondela's magicks are potent," said Zolkan. "Never have I seen a spell like this one."

Molimo snorted and shook his head. *Of all beings I ought to be able to confront her magicks.*

"As you confronted Lenc's?"

Molimo shoved himself to a sitting position and glanced around. The street was still deserted, even though it was just an hour past midday. The cutting fog had driven the citizens of Lorum Bay indoors to stay. For that Molimo gave a quick but fervent thanks. When the transformation had seized him, he had slipped free of his clothing. Upon returning, he couldn't remember where his clothes were.

"Half a mile back in that direction," said Zolkan, lifting one wing and pointing. His heavy beak clacked several times. "Forget clothing. Get new."

Kesira?

"Concentrate," ordered Zolkan.

Molimo pulled up his knees and circled them with his arms. Naked in the street, he let his mind drift like a leaf on a softly flowing brook. His entire body stiffened when his questions found answers.

Cayabbib is dead, he told Zolkan.

"Cayabbib?"

A minor demon, hardly of Ayondela's stature. He . . . gave of himself to aid Kesira.

"She has partaken of his energy, as she did with Wemilat?" The *trilla* bird's voice carried a tone of disdain with it. "Human mating rituals are silly enough. Demon and human make even sillier pairing."

Molimo got to his feet and looked around for a few seconds. His dark eyes fixed on one small house set apart from the others. His hard fist pounded on the door. From inside came the tremulous voice, "What do you want?"

Molimo emitted a croaking noise that produced even more fear on the other side of the door. Zolkan fluttered to rest on the man's shoulder. The *trilla* bird let out a loud squawk of indignation. "Let us in! How dare you keep His Imperial Majesty waiting!"

The door almost shot open. The mousy man inside stared with saucer-round eyes. "Y-you're not the Emperor."

By then Molimo had pushed into the house and left Zolkan to explain.

"Stop that," protested the owner of the house. "You can't steal my belongings. Stop!"

"Be of good cheer, kind sir. Know you and His Puissant Majesty in most delicate mission."

"But he's not the Emperor." The words came with less conviction. "Is he?"

"Would you admit to having seen His Majesty naked?" Zolkan asked. "When this is capital crime?"

"I . . . why, no."

Molimo found a cloak, breeches too small but adequate, and a long tunic of soft, staple cotton. He donned what he could and hid the poor fit with the cloak.

"Your name, good sir, your name," demanded Zolkan. "How else can His Imperial Majesty properly reward you?"

"T'gobe," the man got out. "Oldfar T'gobe."

"Your Majesty," Zolkan said, landing on Molimo's shoulder. "Your beneficence ought to grant this good citizen at least a small duchy. At least."

"A duchy?" T'gobe bowed deeply as Molimo whirled past. The man was awed by such a dignitary blessing his humble abode with the Imperial presence.

You should go into politics," Molimo told the *trilla*
bird. *That poor soul believed you.*

"What is not to believe? Are you not of nobility?"
Hardly.

"Gelya said belief is triumph of hope over reality."

Gelya prattled on too much for my taste. Molimo's long
legs began pumping faster, his strides longer in his haste
to find Kesira. Cayabbib's death assured Kesira of additional powers, but Molimo was at a loss to say exactly
what those powers might be. He feared that the woman
might feel invincible and attempt to confront Ayondela
directly.

Cayabbib had never possessed powers adequate for more
than trivial matters. Kesira might find herself in deadly
trouble if she believed otherwise.

"Ahead," cawed Zolkan. "Soldiers."

Molimo frowned. These were not troops of the Steel
Crescent.

"Emperor's guard," said the *trilla* bird.

This is why you were able to dupe the man so easily.
He saw the Emperor's soldiers in town and believed it
possible Kwasian himself commanded them.

Zolkan shrugged, sending a small flurry of green- and
blue-tipped feathers to the ground. "Sometimes luck is
better than skill."

"You there, halt!" called out an officer marching beside
the squad. Gold braid gleamed in the strengthening midday
sunlight. Several gaudy campaign ribbons on the officer's
chest attested to a remarkable career—this was no palace
dandy sent on a whimsical scavenger hunt.

Are there other soldiers nearby?

Zolkan took to the air, spiraling upward. The singsong
speech he used when communicating directly with Molimo
showered down: troops everywhere.

"You're not a local," the officer stated. "Who are you?"

Molimo pointed to his sundered mouth. The officer's
attitude didn't change. Captain Protaro had seen worse
during his military career. He only had three fingers on

either hand, the others lost to battle and gangrene. The Sarabella campaign had reduced his regiment to seventy-three. By the time reinforcements came at Reun, the barbarians had slain all but four of his men. Not one was left whole, in body or mind. Oh, yes, he had seen worse than a clipped-out tongue.

"You can write. Who are you?" Protaro impatiently motioned for a tall, husky soldier and a companion to join them. The smaller soldier held out a pad with a stylus while the larger fingered his sword, obviously awaiting the command to slay.

"A poor peasant escaping the unnatural winter," Molimo wrote.

Protaro knocked him to the ground with an openhanded blow. "None of that. Who are you?"

Molimo shrugged. Protaro kicked him hard in the ribs.

Zolkan landed heavily on a rail and watched. The Guard captain studied the *trilla* bird, connecting his presence with Molimo.

"These might be the ones we seek," Protaro said to his clerk. "Has a more detailed description arrived?"

Zolkan began the singsong speech with Molimo, saying, "Can they truly identify us?"

Yes. Lalasa aids the Emperor. Just because she opposes Lenc does not mean she looks favorably on us. Her goals are not necessarily ours. Take to wing.

Some subtle muscle twitch warned Protaro. The Guard captain dived forward, fingers reaching for Zolkan. The *trilla* bird snapped at the hand and missed or he might have removed another or.Protaro's fingers. By the time the captain recovered, Zolkan had jumped and become airborne. Heavy flaps took him beyond reach of the Emperor's Guard.

"Seize this one," Protaro commanded, indicating Molimo. "He must be the one Kwasian seeks."

The soldiers circled Molimo but did not consider him dangerous. He looked more like a clown in his ill-fitting clothing than a dangerous man. Joking and laughing, the guardsmen reached for him. Molimo kicked, spun, grabbed, and came away with one corporal's sword.

The corporal stood for an instant, stunned at being disarmed. Then he did the only honorable thing. He threw himself forward, oblivious to Molimo's thrust. The corporal's body wrenched the sword from Molimo's hand, even as it robbed the young soldier of his life.

"To left," squawked Zolkan from his aerial post. "You can escape them. And hurry! Kesira is captive of Nehan-dir."

Molimo damned himself for being so feeble. Once powerful, he was now trapped in weak flesh. Time healed him but slowly—too slowly.

He sprinted away from the soldiers, to their surprise; they had expected him to attempt to regain the fallen weapon. But Molimo had evaluated his chances and discarded any idea of rolling the corporal over and jerking free the sword from its bloody sheath.

The corporal had redeemed himself in the eyes of his comrades. Losing his weapon disgraced him; subsequent actions proved his devotion to the Emperor. None of this helped Molimo, however. Without sword he had little chance to fight off either the Emperor's Guard or stop Nehan-dir.

"Ahead," came the singsong direction from Zolkan. "Steel Crescent mercenaries ahead."

Molimo slowed his pace to allow Captain Protaro and his men to catch up. Even though he courted death, he had to keep the Guardsmen close. As he ran for where Nehan-dir held Kesira, Molimo began the spell given him by the demon Toyaga.

The world about me . . .

Molimo dodged a well-swung sword. A lock of his raven-dark hair leapt from his head as the backswing almost decapitated him. Protaro yelled that he should be captured, not slaughtered.

There are no eyes.

The second line of the spell rattled in his head, as if

parts had come loose. Power welled as he tapped the magicks known by the demons. "See her?" asked Zolkan. "Hurry! Oh, hurry! Nehan-dir will kill her!"

Freedom of the air and sky,
I fade into nothingness.

The spell finished, the power surging, Molimo was no longer visible. Not invisible, but non-noticeable. Protaro and his men found it difficult to focus on Molimo when Nehan-dir and a dozen other Steel Crescent mercenaries lined the street.

"The woman," snapped Captain Protaro. "She is the one. Stop those mercenaries. Attack!"

Molimo slipped across the street and under a low overhang to watch as the Emperor's Guard rushed forward in a broken line to meet the scattered followers of the Steel Crescent. To his surprise both sides proved equal in battle. Protaro and Nehan-dir squared off, the sounds of steel ringing against steel as they dueled. Well matched, they fought with silent competence.

Zolkan dropped into the middle of the fray and landed on Kesira's shoulder. Molimo heard the *trilla* bird say to her, "Escape now. Hurry! No time to dawdle."

The demonic spell began to fade as Molimo's strength waned. He motioned to her to join him, but the battle still separated them. Molimo agonized over aiding the woman.

Zolkan, he sent the silent message, *is she able to flee unaided?*

"Yes," came the immediate reply. "She was not harmed."

Molimo fumed. He saw the dark purple bruise forming on her chin where Nehan-dir had struck her. But the injury was minor compared to her fate if she stayed in the street.

Get her away when I create a diversion. .

Zolkan thrust his beak close to Kesira's ear. When Molimo saw her nod, he acted. He ran from cover and dived, body level with the street. He smashed hard into two of the fighters. Both went down in a struggling pile. Molimo rolled on top of them, forced them back into a heap, then scooped up one's sword. A quick slash severed a hamstring muscle and produced a geyser of slippery blood.

Molimo darted here and there through the fray, not caring which side he attacked. Confusion was his ally. His fighting style left much to be desired, but Molimo accomplished his goal.

Zolkan called out, "All clear. Flee!"

The man-wolf gasped as a Guardsman's sword opened a shallow gash on his chest. Molimo fought to control his shape. Pain often triggered the other-beast change. He had to remain in possession of his human faculties if he wanted to escape and rejoin Kesira.

Dizziness passed and, with it, the urge to transform into wolf. Molimo lunged, parried, twisted free. His deft riposte robbed a Steel Crescent mercenary of life.

And then Molimo was alone in an alley. Sounds of battle dwindled as he staggered along. Panting, he halted and carefully checked the wound on his chest. Even though it was shallow and hardly more than a scratch, it produced a continuous trickle of blood that wouldn't clot. Molimo ripped off his stolen shirt and crudely tied it tightly around his chest as he exhaled. This restrained his breathing but kept constant compression on the wound.

Zolkan? went out his summons. *Where is Kesira?*

He received no answer. Cursing, Molimo doubled back to find the woman and the *trilla* bird.

"Down street. Hurry. Now!" urged Zolkan. The trilla bird almost fell from the woman's shoulder as she lurched to her feet and began running.

Zolkan craned his head around and saw Nehan-dir kick the feet out from under the Guard captain. And Zolkan never paused when he flung himself forward to intercept the blow intended for Kesira's head. The *trilla* bird met the flat of Nehan-dir's blade squarely. It sent Zolkan tumbling through the air, unconscious. He landed in a clump of lore weed, barely distinguishable from the bright green spines.

Kesira thought her friend had simply taken off in protest to her uneven gait. She fought to right herself, to get back the ground-devouring stride she normally used. Carrying the infant around her neck threw her off-balance, but Kesira kept moving.

In less than a minute she had thoroughly confused herself. Down alleys, through littered streets, past the deserted central market, she stumbled and ran, more unconscious than aware. When she stopped, she had the feeling she was near the harbor. Odd sounds drifted on the breeze, sounds she associated with wooden ships and saltwater-soaked hemp rope mooring them to piers.

Kesira rubbed her temples and eased some of the tension. The baby stared up at her, eyes accusing.

"Hungry?" she asked. "Not now. You'll have to wait until there's time. I've got to find Molimo." Kesira frowned. "And Zolkan. He took off in a way different than he usually does." She rubbed the spot on her left shoulder where the bird perched. Tiny spots of blood soaked through her blouse, showing how precipitous Zolkan's launch had been.

She sought shelter from probing eyes, then settled down to compose her thoughts. As she did so she let the baby suckle.

"Those were the Emperor's Guard fighting Nehan-dir," she decided aloud. "Molimo led them to me, but he fought both sides." Kesira frowned. Trying to sift through so much confusion left her with a new headache that threatened her composure. Meditation techniques eased the tension and brought forth a clearer mind. By the time she had regained her composure, the baby had finished his meal.

"You never cry, do you? So strange, after all you've seen in your young life," she said, soothing herself as well as the baby. "And you deserve a name."

Kesira felt a new bleakness in her soul. The baby did not belong with her. Duty forced her to battle the jade demons; this was no place for an infant. Only the powers she'd received from Wemilat's kiss on her breast allowed her to nurse the baby. He wasn't hers, and she ought not become too attached to him. Along with this, Kesira realized she had not given a name to the boy because, had she done so, parting with him would have been impossible.

"If only a mission remained. You would have flourished under Gelya's gentle hand," she told the boy.

"There is a place for the infant," came a deep voice. Kesira started to rise but found a sword point at her throat. Her gaze worked from the flat of the blade along the blood gutter, to hilt, to deformed hand holding the sword. "The Emperor orders your presence. Or rather, Kwasian orders the baby's. I see that the two of you are inseparable, if the youngling is to feed."

Kesira looked past Captain Protaro at the ring of Guardsmen. She had gone from being Nehan-dir's prisoner to the Emperor's in less than an hour. She wasn't certain this was any improvement in her condition.

Chapter Seven

"THERE'S NO NEED to cut my throat by inches. Either do it or take that thing away." Kesira Minette reached up and shoved Captain Protaro's sword from under her chin. The soldier's slow smile showed that he approved of her courage.

"The Emperor requests your presence."

Kesira blinked in surprise and then shook her head. She felt the muzzy clouds of fatigue circling her brain, hemming in her thoughts, dulling her senses. No matter where she turned, someone wanted her killed or imprisoned.

"What does the Emperor desire from a poor nun belonging to the Order of Gelya?"

"Nothing," replied Protaro. He motioned. His Guardsmen formed a circle around them. Kesira saw several hurrying on ahead to accomplish some unspecified task. She guessed they went to stables and mounts ready for a long journey. Emperor Kwasian's capital of Limaden lay many weeks' journey to the west. Just thinking of those tedious miles and days in the saddle tired Kesira further.

"If the Emperor wants nothing of me, then why arrest me?"

"No one has arrested you," Protaro said, too quickly for Kesira's taste. He spoke as if he had memorized this portion of his orders. "You are to be Kwasian's guest at the palace for the equinox."

Kesira's mind almost stopped functioning entirely. Only the highest nobility received invitations to the Equinox

Festival. Never in her wildest dreams did she imagine she'd attend—nor did she believe for an instant that the Emperor intended to honor her. Lowly nuns were not permitted into the most festive of courtly events, even on the Emperor's whim. Society demanded that everyone know everyone else's standing so that all stayed in their correct place and acted accordingly.

If Kesira had met this Guard captain on the road, they would have nodded politely but never spoken. If he had entered a shrine where she worshiped, the Guardsman would not have spoken, but she might have ventured words to him had some wrong been committed that the Emperor's Guard was responsible for punishing. The code of social interaction, even though unwritten, held strict sway over all citizens.

The lower in social standing, the freer one became. The Emperor barely spoke without his every word being ritualistically required and ordained.

Kesira violated all social conventions by asking, "What does Kwasian really want of me? Not my presence. He can have a thousand sisters of the Mission, should he feel the spiritual urge. And never would he invite one of us to the equinox."

Protaro's face set into an unreadable mask. He almost drew his sheathed sword to run her through for this affront to decency. Kesira had passed caring about breach of etiquette. She wanted nothing more than a warm bath, a soft bed, and a long sleep. If decent food accompanied it, there was little more she could ask of life.

"The Emperor desires the company of the baby." Protaro lifted his head slightly and pointed with his chin, indicating the infant strapped around Kesira's body. Tiny pale eyes fixed on Captain Protaro's ribbons and glistening gold rank braid. The baby shifted to peer up and study the officer's lined face. Such scrutiny unsettled the battle-hardened veteran.

"The Emperor did not take me into his confidence. My orders are simple. Return the infant to the Imperial Court."

Kesira fought a silent battle with herself. Ever since she could remember, it had been ingrained in her how duty was paramount in everyone's life. Without honor and duty the realm disintegrated. Each person knew the role to be filled and did it. Whether one died as a result did not matter. Duty was carried out, honor was never besmirched with cowardice or inattention to the niceties of proper behavior.

Duty to family ranked high. For Kesira this had become shifted at an early age. With parents dead during a brigand attack, her family had become those with her in the nunnery. Gelya had become her teacher, Sister Fenelia a mother, Dominie Tredlo a father, Dana and the others her siblings. Lenc's destruction of the nunnery had made her duty clear. Honor demanded revenge on the jade demon and all his allies. No matter if the task looked impossible; the attempt had to be made. Those she had considered family must be allowed to rest in peace, knowing their own flesh and blood had fought and won—or fought and died nobly.

But above familial duty lay obeisance to regional lords and Empire bureaucrats. Kesira had none. As a member of a religious order, she owed fealty to no lord.

Above a regional lord, however, sat the Emperor and his Court. To the Court Kesira had no duty, but the Emperor reigned supreme in the land. His power extended from the highest lord to the lowest peasant. Duty to Emperor carried the greatest moral responsibility, greater even than duty to family.

Kesira walked beside the Guard captain and worked through the intricate maze that detailed her duty. For the naive nun recently gone from convent, duty seemed simple: Obey the Emperor. Kesira Minette had fought and defeated two of the jade demons, had lain with two more demons, and had assumed responsibility for a boychild. In all but the strictest sense the baby was her family, and her duty to him conflicted with the Emperor's request.

Folklore held obedience to the Emperor above family duties as the sign of true courage. Kesira wondered.

The rune sticks had shown her to be the one best able to fight Ayondela and bring the jade demon crashing to defeat. Didn't her duty to the Emperor require her to do all in her power to help him maintain his throne? By wasting time in the long journey to Limaden and allowing Ayondela and Lenc to consolidate their power, she doomed Kwasian. If she felt real devotion to the Emperor and wished to uphold his position, she had to ignore his edict.

Kesira's head ached from such contorted logic. To aid the Emperor she had to disobey a direct order. Duty—to destroy the jade demons—started with resisting the Emperor's Guard, normally an offense of the severest order.

Her world and rules had turned upside down, but Kesira knew it had been this way ever since the demons partook of the jade. They were the ones responsible for disrupting the smoothly running social fabric of the Empire. If Lenc, Eznofadil, and Howenthal had not aspired to more than their due, Kesira would still be safely sequestered in her nunnery, learning Gelya's teachings, making occasional trips to Blinn for provisions, and enjoying the company of her sisters.

Kesira made her decision quickly and with no regrets. Treasonously she sought the weaknesses in Captain Protaro's squad, looking for a path to escape.

"Will the smaller mare be adequate for you?" Protaro asked. Three of his soldiers rode up, leading enough horses for Protaro and the others. "It is sturdy and has a gait not too unsettling for someone unused to riding."

"I've ridden a great deal."

This surprised the officer. "My apologies. The mare is still a fine choice."

"I would rest before we leave Lorum Bay," she said. "I only arrived off a fishing boat. The storm that tossed us prevented me from sleeping and..."

"There will be ample time to sleep once we are on the road," the captain said brusquely. Kesira wondered if she detected even the slightest hint of sympathy in the man's cold eyes. She doubted it. Protaro knew his duty to the

Emperor and performed it well. If he had to die accomplishing his mission, he would, without a qualm.

Fleeting admiration for Protaro passed through her mind. Why couldn't she be more like the stern officer?

"You realize that the Order of the Steel Crescent is trying to kill me?" she asked.

Protaro shrugged it off. To him Nehan-dir meant nothing more than another obstacle to be overcome. He might not even know it had been Nehan-dir he'd fought in the brief street skirmish.

"Your ribbons attest to fierce battles with the barbarians," she said. Kesira remembered Rouvin's stories of the Sarabella front and the horrendous losses there. "A friend of mine fought at Sarabella. He was a captain of cavalry. Soon after the barbarians had been driven back into the sea, he resigned. No chance for advancement."

"I understand that," Protaro said. "My chances of attaining the rank of commander are nil." He frowned, previously hidden scars popping out in the furrow across his forehead. "Who is your friend? I knew most of the survivors."

"Rouvin the Stout."

"Rouvin? I knew him. A daring captain."

"He is dead," Kesira said carefully, trying to judge Protaro's reaction. "He fought the jade demons and it cost him his life." That wasn't the precise truth but neither was it a lie.

"Lalasa will want to hear more of this from you," the officer said. "She advises the Emperor but is unable to gain proper intelligence concerning the other demons. As a result, not all our forays have ended in victory. General Dayle was sorely wounded after attacks across the Quaking Lands."

"I know," Kesira said. "I watched from within Howenthal's castle. Your general did not realize the power he faced."

"*You* watched?" Protaro did not believe her. Kesira shook off the indignation of being thought a liar.

"I joined forces with Wemilat the Ugly and we killed Howenthal," she said, taking no joy in the telling. "Then I invaded Ayondela's fastness and killed Eznofadil."

"You, a slayer of demons?" Protaro laughed heartily. "I was wrong. Kwasian might desire your company. You are finer with the jest than his fool. You will be the talk of the Equinox Festival with your tall tales."

Kesira glanced down to make sure the baby rested comfortably. A small smile split his face and the eyes twinkled. He seemed to understand what decision she had reached and approved. This made it easier for Kesira to evade the Guard captain.

The runes had foretold that the baby was the key to stopping Ayondela's rampage. The only way Kesira could conceive of that being possible was a trade—the infant to replace Ayondela's lost son Rouvin. If she had another son to care for, to love, to nurture, the female demon might give up the power of the jade and abandon Lenc.

To offer the baby Kesira had to avoid being taken to Limaden.

In the saddle she waited for her chance to escape. It came sooner than she expected. Kesira saw Molimo crouching near a drainpipe, sword in one hand and dagger in the other. She put her arms around the infant, then spurred her horse forward at a pace faster than the Emperor's Guard. Protaro kicked at the flanks of his horse to catch up, and as he passed Molimo's position, the man-wolf leapt.

"Aieee!" the captain shrieked as a dagger drove into his left arm and a sword raked across a muscular thigh. The Guardsman lay writhing in pain on the pavement, unable to stand because of his wounds. Molimo hit and rolled to his feet, sword and dagger flashing toward new targets.

Kesira jerked around in the saddle when she thought she heard Molimo scream *Ride!* at her. She pushed such foolishness away. Better than anyone else, she knew Molimo had no tongue. Kesira bent forward and rode with the wind, taking the streets of Lorum Bay with reckless abandon. As she rode she worked out what might happen. Retaining the horse for too long would prove her downfall. She saw no way to outrun the Emperor's Guard. Better to hide and force them to search for her. That way, the Steel Crescent and the Guardsmen might clash again.

"Pit one enemy against the other," she said aloud. The idea appealed to her.

She rode for several more minutes, then vaulted from the saddle to land heavily in the cobblestone street. Kesira stumbled a bit until she regained her balance. The mare galloped on, as she'd hoped it would. That would leave a false track for the Guardsmen while she went in the other direction.

On foot she sought out the marketplace. Fear of the slashing mist had passed, and the citizens of Lorum Bay now conducted business in tiny stalls, stores opened to the sea air, and from pushcarts dotting the market area. Few took note of her and then only as a potential customer. These merchants were used to seeing strangers passing through their port town. No cry lifted, and for that Kesira breathed a sigh of relief.

"Many fine rugs," one merchant cried. He rushed out of his store and grabbed her arm. "Come inside. Look. Aheem the Rugger is honest and sells honest merchandise. Ask anyone."

"Aheem's a cutpurse and a fraud," yelled a neighboring merchant. "Come, noble lady, come to Yeeramian's store and see *real* bargains. Even the Emperor himself walks barefoot on such rugs."

"If the Emperor bought Yeeramian's rugs, he'd *have* to walk barefoot," countered Aheem. "That bandit's shaggy rugs would cut boot leather to ribbons!"

"Not interested," Kesira said, laughing. She enjoyed the friendly byplay between the rug sellers. When the day ended, Kesira thought it quite possible that Yeeramian and Aheem got together for a few friendly mugs of ale to discuss the day's business and how to squeeze an extra coin from unwitting customers.

Kesira found herself wobbling along, dizzy and disoriented. She sat down. It had been too long since she'd had a meal. The baby had eaten well enough, but she had neglected her own food. A pushcart passed close by. Kesira hailed the food vendor.

"Flayed rats on a stick?" the vendor asked. "Special-sized ones we got this fine day. Caught 'em in the fog. Freshly dead, they are."

"Something else," Kesira said, feeling queasy at the idea of eating wharf rats.

"Got some good *trilla* bird meat."

"Fresh?" she asked, afraid of the answer. She heaved a sigh of relief when the vendor admitted that his supply had been brought in from the tropics and might be a month old.

"Aged, I call it. Good 'n' aged *trilla* bird meat."

"I have very little money. A hunk of bread and some cheese is all I can afford."

The young vendor took this in stride. For three coppers Kesira bought a large piece of dark bread and a sharp cheese "from the monastery of Gelya in the Yearn Mountains," the vendor assured her.

Kesira had no idea where the cheese had been produced. Her nunnery had not exported any cheese and wasn't likely to have started in the past few months, not with the buildings reduced to rubble and Lenc's cold white flame burning in the stone altar once sacred to Gelya.

As Kesira ate she overheard the gossip between merchants. One conversation held her full attention.

". . . never deal with demons. Bad business. How can you collect?"

"I've had no trouble," answered another. "Ayondela buys much from me and always pays."

"In the past she has. The fog will visit you one day and leave your bloody carcass for all to see. What good, then, will your profits do you?"

"You're jealous of my contracts with her. The fog is rather pretty, if you look at the sun through it. Glistens like the finest of crystal."

"There's no fool like a greedy fool," said the second. He turned and called to another merchant, inquiring of business. The one who had dealings with Ayondela turned back to his store and sat on a three-legged stool, biding his time as he waited for prospective customers.

Kesira studied the man. The merchant looked prosperous but no more so than others scattered around the market. But Kesira saw a furtiveness in the man's gaze that troubled her. She could believe that he aided Ayondela knowing fully what evil the she-demon visited on the land. This was not an honorable person: the fleshy face, the beady eyes, the weak chin, all told Kesira of the man's venality and absorbed self-interest.

She went to him.

"Ah, gracious and lovely lady, how can Esamir assist you this fine day? A brass chamber pot engraved with designs beloved of the demons? No? A woman of your breeding needs candleholders formed of the purest onyx. I have just what you need. Come inside, please, this way." Esamir rose and bowed deeply, ushering Kesira into the dim interior. Kesira's nose wrinkled at the heavy incense burning in three separate brass urns. The best she could tell, each odor differed just enough from the others to produce a totally unpleasant sensory confusion.

The effect fit Esamir well.

"Your merchandise is outstanding," she said. Kesira glanced around, back into the market, hoping to catch a glimpse of Molimo. While she doubted that the Emperor's Guard had caught him, he might have been wounded— or undergone a shape-change into his wolf form. With the general populace as nervous about other-beasts as they were, this might prove fatal for Molimo.

"There is something I can show you that will warm your heart and bring a song to your finely shaped lips."

Esamir maneuvered around so that he stood between Kesira and the exit.

"Something worthy of . . . a demon," Kesira said. Her words almost broke with emotion.

"You know of my dealings with Ayondela?"

"It is common knowledge," Kesira said. She believed this to be true. If Esamir talked openly about it outside his shop, many others might know the details also.

"What is it to you?" the flowery words had been replaced by pointed questions.

"I would talk with Ayondela. I have something that might interest her."

The merchant's eyes narrowed. He seemed to take a good look at Kesira for the first time. When Esamir noticed the baby slung at her breast, he smiled. Kesira shivered in response. This man would betray his own grandmother if it netted him a bent copper.

What he would do for a pouch of gold Kesira didn't even want to consider.

"I do have minimal contact with her," Esamir said. "Rather, she contacts me when supplies are needed."

"Supplies for what?" asked Kesira. "No, I am sorry. I have no reason to ask that of you. All I need is the opportunity to speak with Ayondela."

"She knows you?" The cunning expression flickered across Esamir's face. Kesira knew he would not make a good gambler.

Kesira nodded curtly.

"She has only recently accepted delivery of certain goods," the merchant said. "It might be weeks before she asks for more. However, there is one path to follow that will gain you an audience almost immediately."

"What is it?" Even as she spoke Kesira knew that she betrayed her eagerness. If Esamir would make a terrible gambler, she was an even worse one.

He smiled broadly. "Coastal traders venture far to the south. Ayondela, it is rumored, has abandoned her Isle of Eternal Winter in favor of another mountain peak. The

Sarn Mountains are the loftiest on this continent and Ayondela now rules from the tallest of them. She claims to be able to see into the Emperor's bedchamber from there, though why she bothers is a mystery." Esamir smiled and spread his hands to show he only jested. Not even greedy merchants maligned the Emperor.

"You have the names of traders willing to take me south?"

"Of course, noble lady." Esamir fell silent.

"Well?" Kesira demanded. "What of the names? Who are these venturesome sailors?"

"Everything has a price. Even information."

Kesira clutched the child closer to her body.

"If I give you the name of a trader, will you carry a message to Ayondela for me?"

"What message?"

"Business matters. I have been seeking a courier, but the people of Lorum Bay are afraid to leave their cozy homes. They grow too complacent. Nobody will accept this minor inconvenience for me."

Kesira leapt at the chance. "Gladly will I deliver a sealed note to Ayondela if you—"

Esamir interrupted. "You must not read the contents of the message. Some intelligence requires the utmost secrecy, even in a simple business such as mine."

"I understand. I will not open the message and will deliver it personally to Ayondela."

"I can trust you?" Esamir asked, more of himself than Kesira. "Yes, I feel that I can. I have not remained in business for so many years without developing a sense of people. You are one I can depend on in this matter."

"Yes, yes," she said impatiently.

"One moment while I get the letter. Then I will guide you to the harbor where you can get passage south."

Esamir vanished into the back room. Kesira edged toward the exit, peering out into the sunlit market. Customers now thronged the stalls doing last-minute shopping, all fear of the deadly mist gone. But of Molimo she saw no trace.

"Here," Esamir said, startling her. He held out a thick packet of brown paper sealed with a sigil impressed in green wax. "Come along now and I shall take you to Leter. A knave of a man but the best sailor in all of Lorum Bay."

Just as they started to leave the store a small boy rushed from the back, yelling, "They come, master! The shipment from Chounabel has come a day early!"

Esamir cursed under his breath, then turned to Kesira. "I am sorry. My delivery demands an accounting. I cannot trust a thief such as this one." He cuffed the boy and knocked him into a pile of brass candlesticks. "He is both stupid and clumsy."

"How long will it take? To inventory the merchandise?" Kesira fretted that Protaro or Nehan-dir might find her.

"Well?" Esamir demanded of the boy.

"Four wagons, master. They bring four wagons."

Esamir gave an eloquent shrug. "Many hours, I fear. But you have the message. Go to the harbor and seek out Leter aboard the *Poxy Shrew*. Tell him of your mission and that I implore him to make great haste to the south-lands."

"Very well." Kesira relaxed as Esamir bowed deeply and hurried into the rear of the shop, the urchin close at his heels. She hadn't liked the idea of the sly merchant accompanying her. Now she could choose her own path to the harbor and hope Molimo found her soon.

Kesira sucked in a deep lungful of air and relaxed even more. The day blossomed warmly around her, and the fresh sea air invigorated her. She hurried toward the harbor, doubling back several times to make sure she was not being followed.

The harbor in view, she turned toward the nearest docks to seek out Captain Leter. She never heard the man behind her, nor did she feel the sharp impact of the club on the side of her head.

Kesira Minette slumped to the cobblestone paving, unconscious.

Chapter Eight

WATER SPLASHED on Kesira Minette's face. She snorted and sent a salty plume back into the sea. Sputtering, struggling in the damp embrace of the waves, she pulled herself erect to sit on the beach, the incoming tide lapping around her body.

For long minutes she simply sat and tried to get her world puzzled back into a coherent whole. Snippets of memory returned but not enough for Kesira to understand. The merchant. A ship. What was its name? She had been seeking Ayondela, but where was Molimo?

The pain in her skull changed from sharp stabs to a dull aching. Kesira closed her eyes and lay back, the sea washing away her misery. Slowly it all came back to her.

Kesira sat bolt upright again, clutching at the empty sling around her neck. "The baby!" she gasped. "Gone!"

She got to her feet and forced herself away from the sucking surf. A quarter-mile away ships of all descriptions bobbed and rocked gently against the docks—someone had carried her that distance and left her to drown. Or had they merely left her, not caring if she drowned or not? And who were "they"?

Quick hands searched for her pouch. It still rode at her hip, the bone box inside containing her rune sticks. Kidnapping, not robbery, had been the motive for the attack.

Kesira pushed aside the despair that rose within her. Gelya had taught that despair was a trap for fools: one could sit and bemoan her fate or one could act. Kesira

Minette acted. Returning to the spot where she had been attacked, she dropped to hands and knees and studied the cobblestones for some small clue to the identity of the kidnapper. Molimo with his animal-acute senses might have been able to understand the scuffs and nicks in the paving stones, but all Kesira could figure out was that heavy traffic passed over this spot daily.

"Pardon," came a hesitant voice. "You lookin' for somethin' in particular?"

Kesira looked up and saw a shabbily dressed man holding a small plate. A few small coins rested within it.

"I was attacked here some time ago." She peered at the sun and estimated times. "About two hours ago. They left me with a head feeling like a burst melon and no child."

"They stole your youngling?" This evoked real emotion on the beggar's part. He obviously didn't understand why any would kidnap another mouth to feed.

"Did you see anything? I don't have much." She reached into her pouch and took out the remaining four coppers and a silver centim embossed with Empress Aglenella's profile. "These are yours, if you did witness the crime."

"I'd like to be able to claim this fine reward," the beggar said, only a hint of sarcasm in his voice, "but the truth is that I saw nothin'. I work up and down the embarcadero. Sailors just in from long cruises tend to be more generous to the needy than other folks. They count it a payment to luck that they returned in one piece—or with coins jinglin' in their pouches."

"Who would kidnap an infant?"

The beggar laughed harshly. "No one. Feedin' yourself's a major concern for most people in Lorum Bay. Only the last few weeks have seen the Sea of Katad free of ice. Fishing has been poor, and no one's growin' crops yet." He restlessly rattled the paltry coins on his plate, as if in practice.

"Do you know a merchant named Esamir?"

Again came the harsh laugh. "That one? Steer clear of

him. He's bad weather, no matter what port you're hailing from."

"I know he deals with Ayondela."

"That'd be an improvement over the kind he normally has truck with. Now, I'm not one to go talkin' out of turn, but Esamir's been rumored to deal in human flesh."

"A slaver?"

The beggar's eyes widened, then he laughed. This time the sound rang out as genuine amusement. "Good lady, no! He sells people by the pound—for their flesh. He's a cannibal, he is. Expect the worst of him and you'll still be surprised at his evil ways."

Kesira had no reply. Lorum Bay had not seemed that badly damaged by Ayondela's wintery curse, but it had obviously driven some past the brink of acceptable, honorable behavior. Esamir a dealer in human meat? While Kesira had not liked the man and had believed him possible of any perfidy, this was more than mere crime against the Emperor. Cannibalism had to be a crime against society. Such a man lacked even the smallest portion of honor.

"Thank you," she said in a choked voice. She dropped the silver centim onto the beggar's plate. The man shrugged and moved on, not even thanking her. Kesira stared after him in wonder. What odd folk these were in Lorum Bay.

Or were they equally as odd throughout the Empire? Kesira had to admit that she had only recently burst upon the world outside the walls of her convent. How she longed to return to those pacific days with Sister Dana, picking the yellow wild flowers sacred to Gelya and lying in the field, hands clasped beneath her head, watching the wondrous fluffy patterns of clouds in the sky. Life had been easy before the jade had lured Lenc and the others to the ways of evil.

Kesira made her way through alleys and along shadowed lanes, avoiding the main thoroughfares of Lorum Bay. She finally discovered the service door to Esamir's shop. From the rubble in the alley, she knew that no large delivery had been made in some time, much less one totaling four entire wagonloads. He had instructed the urchin to lie.

Something niggled at her mind. Then she had it. Kesira reached inside her blouse and pulled out the packet Esamir had given her to deliver to Ayondela. She ran a ragged thumbnail under the green wax seal and popped open the pages. The pages were all blank. Holding one sheet to the sun and peering at the faint shadows cast by the watermark, Kesira decided that it held no secret message. Sister Kai had taught her much of the lore surrounding various juices and inks. Some even permitted invisible writing until the proper chemical or heat was applied, but Kesira had noted that while the message was hidden, the paper always wrinkled slightly from the ink.

No such wrinkles appeared on this sheaf of parchment. She tucked the voluminous pages away against the time when she might better study them, but she believed that this had been nothing more than a cunning ruse on Esamir's part. He had seen the baby and wanted it. The merchant's agile, devious mind had concocted a plot on the spur of the moment and had executed it perfectly.

Even if she went to the local authorities, Esamir had an alibi for the time when the attack took place. She had no doubt that he had picked a fight with another merchant or had otherwise created a ruckus to mark him in peoples' minds. One of his henchmen had performed the kidnapping—after all, he knew where Kesira was headed.

She wondered if there was even a Captain Leter and a ship called the *Poxy Shrew.* Possibly. The ring of fact in Esamir's voice had come through when speaking of them. Kesira had learned that the best lies were those interwoven with the truth. Buy an ounce of the tale, buy a pound.

She skillfully avoided the piles of debris in the alley and went to Esamir's back door. She gently tried the latch. Locked. Kesira pressed her fingers against the thin, unpainted wood and felt strong steel behind it. Esamir had well hidden the real strength behind this flimsy-looking entrance. Kesira would keep that in mind when dealing with the merchant again.

On the outside he might be a poor, simple merchant. Below that facade beat the heart of a cunning blackguard.

Kesira edged down the alley and peered around the corner toward the marketplace. The bustling crowds had thinned once more, taking time for afternoon meals. The few vendors lounged around, not pitching to those walking by.

Kesira shrieked when a heavy hand clamped on her shoulder. She jerked around as another hand shut off further outcries.

"Oh, Molimo," she said, relaxing when she saw the young man. "You startled me." Heart beating like a drum, she slumped against the cool brick wall of Esamir's store.

"Sorry," he wrote on his tablet. "Did not want you calling out to attract attention."

"What of the Guard?" she asked. "Do they still hunt for us?"

He nodded. Kesira heaved a deep sigh. Dealing with Howenthal and Eznofadil had not been this complex. And as dangerous as it had been, breaking the power of Ayondela's spell had been far easier than avoiding the Steel Crescent and Emperor's Guard on her trail.

"Someone has kidnapped the baby. I think it was the merchant inside." She tapped the brick wall. "His name's Esamir, and he claims to have dealings with Ayondela."

The accusing glare she got from Molimo chastised her. It had been foolish to approach a scoundrel like Esamir alone, and she knew it. But foolish self-reproach now accomplished nothing. They had to work to get the baby back.

"The runes say that the baby is the key to stopping Ayondela. I fear that she might harm the boy unless we are with him." Molimo vigorously nodded at that. Kesira closed her eyes and let the waves of tiredness sweep over her. "It is so strange. I read the runes with more clarity since my union with Cayabbib, but my strength wanes so quickly now. In some ways I am stronger, in others so much weaker."

Molimo's hand rested on her shoulder, reassuring her. She leaned forward and threw her arms around him, hugging him close. The weariness still plagued her, but it seemed minor now.

"Molimo, I need you so. Don't ever leave me. Please don't leave me."

He pushed her away even as she tried to hug him tighter. Kesira opened her brown eyes and saw his attention focused out in the market. She scanned the small crowd quickly, then paused when she saw a short man strutting like he owned the town.

"Nehan-dir," she said without real surprise. "Is he in league with Esamir?"

Molimo shook his head. The cocky leader of the Steel Crescent's mercenaries swung past Esamir's brasswares shop and continued on, hardly paying attention to anything inside. Whatever Nehan-dir sought—and Kesira believed it was she and Molimo—he hadn't seen it around the brass shop.

"Nehan-dir wanted the baby and so did Captain Protaro," she said. "Apparently Nehan-dir still seeks us. Unless there is a third party eager for the boy's company, it would seem Protaro has been the victor in this scavenger hunt."

"Would Esamir sell him to the Emperor's Guard?" wrote Molimo.

"I'm guessing. Why does anyone want the boy? By now he is getting hungry. I see no way they can feed him unless they find a source of mother's milk." Kesira touched her left breast, gravid with milk where Wemilat's kiss burned in the white flesh.

If anything convinced Kesira to continue the struggle against the jade demons, it was this sign. Wemilat's touch granted life. All that Lenc and Ayondela touched withered and died.

"We must be swift," Molimo wrote.

"One moment," she said, restraining him. Molimo had started out into the market area. "How did you escape from Protaro?"

Molimo stared at her, his eyes dark and lacking emotion. She swallowed hard. It was difficult when Molimo closed in on himself, shutting out both her and the world.

"You care for the captain?" he scribbled.

"Yes, of course I do," she said, a flush rising to her cheeks. "I care for all honorable men. He is the Emperor's emissary and . . . I care," she finished in a rush.

"He is injured but not mortally," wrote Molimo. "Others are dead. I escaped in the confusion."

"Good," she said, almost too softly for him to hear. A tear beaded at the corner of her eye. "Molimo, you are very special to me." He pulled away before she made eye contact. From his determined steps she knew he went to confront Esamir. Kesira trailed behind, casting furtive glances in all directions, fearful of what she'd see. Nehandir had gone; of the Emperor's Guardsmen she saw no trace. She followed the man-wolf into the brasswares store.

Already Esamir greeted Molimo, not seeing Kesira.

"Good and noble sir, how are you? Welcome to my humble shop. It is lucky for you that this very day I have on sale . . ." His voice trailed off when Molimo did not respond—or perhaps the merchant felt himself impaled by the icy gaze. When Kesira closed the door and latched it, Esamir bolted for the rear of the store.

One quick hand grabbed his tunic and lifted him into the air. His feet kicked inches above the carpeted shop floor.

"My friend is strong and quick. He also has a nasty habit of killing when someone lies to him."

Esamir's frightened stare told Kesira that he had already come to this conclusion about Molimo.

"The baby. Where is he?"

"I know nothing of this baby!" Esamir shrieked in fear as Molimo heaved him hard against the back wall of the store. The merchant smashed into the brick wall hard enough to rattle his teeth. He slumped into a pile next to a display of brass chamber pots. Molimo shoved him back down as he tried to stand.

"Molimo is very strong. Or hadn't you noticed?" Kesira said, taking a perverse joy in tormenting the merchant. She knew it was morally wrong to do so, but something deep inside pushed back all of Gelya's teachings and required this to maintain her sanity.

Molimo picked up one of the brass pots and held it between his hands. Muscles bulged as he began to squeeze. The pot flattened. Molimo took the newly wrought disk in one hand and flung it hard against a side wall. The edge of the brass dug into the brick and hung there, a testament to berserk strength.

"The baby. I want him back. Tell us or you'll not live to kidnap another child."

"This is beyond my power. I cannot say what happened. Oh!"

Molimo took Esamir's head between his hands and began to squeeze, just as he'd done with the pot. The merchant's eyes began to bulge. He beat feebly on the man's muscle-knotted belly.

"Hurry. Your tongue sticks out already. In another few seconds your head will be as flat as this."

Kesira dropped a brass serving tray in front of the struggling merchant.

"He, oh, the pain! He came to me, he bought my services."

"Who?"

Esamir let out only incoherent squeaks. Molimo lessened the pressure to allow him to speak. "The Guard Captain Protaro. He came to me. This was a duty put' upon me by the Emperor himself! Kwasian demanded it of me! I had no choice."

"How much were you paid?" asked Kesira, anger rising. Bartering in babies struck her as odious, no matter how it was couched.

"F-fifty gold sovereigns."

"Some duty."

A loud rattle from the back of the store caught her attention. Kesira spun in time to fend off a mountain of a man. Arms bulging with prodigious muscles groped for her; she ducked beneath the deadly circle, kicked, and squirmed free. The dirty, blond-haired man grunted and kept after her. Kesira picked up a brass platter and flung it at him. The edge produced a thin red line in the center of his kettle belly. He came on, not noticing this slight wound.

"Kill the bitch, Wardo!" screamed Esamir.

Kesira backed away slowly. Tiredness no longer dogged her every step. She came alive in ways alien to her. Kesira felt Cayabbib's presence welling up, guiding her, giving her strength that had never before been hers.

Wardo lunged forward just as Kesira launched a round-about kick. She landed it squarely in the pit of the man's belly. He doubled over, but the blow hardly slowed him.

"Molimo," she begged. "This is more than I can handle."

Wardo grabbed her. Kesira whirled around, caught the man's weight in just the proper spot, and hurled him over her shoulder. He landed heavily, crushing a display of wicker chairs.

"I need a staff." Longingly she eyed Molimo's sword, dangling at his waist. To draw it, to run Wardo through with it. But Kesira balked at this blasphemy. Gelya had not approved of steel weapons. She'd never received a clear answer when she'd asked Sister Fenelia and Dominie Tredlo about this prohibition, but it had been one she'd scrupulously obeyed, nonetheless. To go against it now proved more than she could do, even with the newfound strengths given her by Cayabbib.

Wardo's heavy fist smashed into the side of her head, knocking her sprawling.

"She still falls when I hit her," Wardo said, gloating. The eyes burned with small intelligence and great hatred.

Kesira had no doubt now who had committed the kidnapping. She faced him.

Wardo rushed her. Insane strength flowed through Kesira. She caught the hulking beast of a man and lifted him bodily. Swinging him around, using both his momentum and her anger-fed power, she slammed Wardo into the wall. But this did not deter him. And her own stamina drained all too quickly.

"Kill her now, Wardo! Quickly!" screamed Esamir.

A low, feral snarl pulled her attention from Wardo to Molimo. The man-wolf had become a wolf-man. Green eyes flashing, savage fangs agleam in the dim light of the shop, the gray wolf padded forward as he sized up his prey.

"No, Molimo, don't," Kesira cried.

A gray blur rocketed past her. Wardo threw up a meaty arm to protect his throat. Molimo's fangs sank deep into that arm and then began to rip and tear. Blood spurted from a severed artery. Wardo rolled over and over; Molimo followed his every move, fangs ripping, back leg claws pawing ferociously at the man's soft belly.

Wardo might have lived, had he reached the back room and bolted the door, but before he got halfway to safety, he exposed his throat for the briefest of times. Molimo's quick head jerked around, and teeth buried in the vulnerable carotid artery. Red fountains geysered over the combatants.

"The w-wolf's killed him," stuttered Esamir. "He was Lorum Bay's champion and the wolf killed him."

Kesira pulled herself together and took a deep breath. She reached out and caught Esamir's throat. Her fingers tightened.

"He doesn't like to be annoyed," she said. "You've annoyed him also." Strength flowed like a clean, pure river into Kesira's arm. She lifted. Esamir was pinned against the wall by the fragile-appearing woman's right hand. His feet kicked futilely above the floor once again.

"You have a demon's power," he gasped, the air not finding its way to his straining lungs.

"I want the baby," she said.

"I s-sold him to—I can't breathe!"

Kesira reached over and gripped a handful of fabric. Using this two-handed grip allowed her to release a bit of pressure on the merchant's throat.

"Where is Protaro keeping the baby?"

"The Guard captain will take the boy directly to Limaden and the Emperor. I am not lying!"

The way Esamir's eyes bulged and his tongue lolled told Kesira that he probably spoke the truth—or the truth as he knew it.

Kesira turned and heaved the merchant into the display of chamber pots. He seemed quite at home there.

"Do you actually deal in human flesh? For cannibalism?"

Esamir's eyes widened even more. He stuttered so badly, no coherent words formed. The fear she read in his eyes and his soul told her that the beggar near the harbor had not passed along unfounded rumors. She lost all compassion for Esamir and his gut-wrenching fears. He deserved nothing but punishment for his crimes.

Kesira didn't even try to stop Molimo as the gray wolf stalked by her, blood dripping from his muzzle. One single, loud, heart-rending shriek sounded. New blood dripped from Molimo's fangs.

Kesira sat and stroked Molimo's furry head until the transformation again seized him. Anguish showed in the man's dark eyes. Kesira's brown ones had lost any softness they once had.

"Come," she said, "we must find Protaro."

Kesira Minette never looked back at the two ravaged bodies as she stepped out into the sunlight and clear, salt-laced air of Lorum Bay's market.

Chapter Nine

THE IDEA OF BLATANT theft of such magnitude would once have appalled Kesira Minette. But not now. With cool, appraising eyes she studied the stables and evaluated their chances for making away with two of the better horses.

The chances looked good.

She motioned for Molimo to go around to the back of the barn while she confronted the owner.

Boldly she walked up to the man and asked, "Where might I find the merchant Esamir?"

The man frowned. "What would the likes of you be wantin' with scum like him?"

"He owes me a goodly amount of money. We dealt fairly and he cheated me. I've just arrived from ... the south."

"There's naught to the south, save for Ayondela's peak hidden off in the Sarn Mountains," the man said. He frowned even more. The deep furrows in his brow showed his displeasure at having to speak with someone who dealt with a female demon and a thieving merchant reputed to be selling human flesh.

Kesira saw Molimo moving silently in the back of the stable, soothing horses to keep them quiet, finding tack, choosing the best of the sorry lot. She turned her full attention back to the stable hand.

"My business is no concern of yours. However, I see that I must prove my claim. Here. Look." She reached into her blouse and found the blank sheets of paper Esamir had decoyed with her. She thrust them out for the man to examine. The man took them, as if he expected the pages to burst into flame.

"There's naught written here. What kind of game do you play with me now?"

Kesira looked perplexed as she took the pages back. "What are you saying? Of course there's something written on the sheets. Look more carefully."

As the man examined the blank pages, Molimo led two horses out of the stable. One of the animals spooked and emitted a shrill whinny. The stable hand glanced around. It took him long seconds to understand what happened.

"This knife will spit you if you move a muscle," Kesira said, thrusting the callused tips of her fingers into the man's back. "Tie him. Hurry!"

Molimo smiled as he obeyed. With the stable hand carefully tucked away in the back, the pair of horse thieves rode out. Kesira turned to Molimo and asked, "What were you grinning about back there? Did I say something funny?"

On his tablet Molimo scratched out the words, "You sounded like Zolkan. Always in a hurry."

"I did, did I?" Kesira said in mock anger. Then she, too, laughed, but the laughter died. "Where is Zolkan? I haven't seen him since the Emperor's Guard fought Nehandir's mercenaries."

Molimo frowned and made unintelligible gurgling noises. He appeared to be lost in deep thought, his eyes unfocused and his mouth slack with the effort of whatever it was he did. Finally the man-wolf shrugged and shook his head, indicating that he had no idea where the wayward *trilla* bird had gone.

"He'll have to find us," Kesira said firmly. "He takes off for days on end. I have never found where he goes or what he does, but . . ."

She stared at Molimo's guilty expression. The realization dawned on her that Molimo knew where Zolkan went when the bird vanished. It also hit her that asking for an explanation was wasted effort. The two of them shared a secret that excluded her.

"The trail," she said on a different tack. "Can you find the trail followed by Captain Protaro?"

Molimo pointed ahead, then made a snaking motion with his arm to indicate the turnings of the trail. In less than an hour Kesira found how exact that undulating description was. The trail switched back repeatedly as they climbed into the foothills—and then the foothills became full-fledged mountains.

But the woman had learned well during the past few months. While her eyes weren't as sharp as Molimo's in picking up the signs of passage, she detected bright, fresh nick marks in the rock where steel-shod hooves had recently passed, tiny leaves crushed but still damp with undried sap, the bending of twigs and branches near the path. A large party had preceded them by less than a day.

Captain Protaro and the Emperor's Guard. And a small baby who never cried.

"He must be starving," she said, her thoughts working into her words. "I'm sure Protaro would not willingly mistreat the boy, but he is a soldier. He can't know how to care for him." Kesira rode along and laughed ruefully. "We still have to call the baby 'him.' So young, and without a name."

Molimo held up the tablet for her to read.

"I know. Raellard Yera thought someone else had fathered the child, and Parvey named a demon as the father. Even if true, that's no reason not to give a name to the boy."

"Name him," Molimo wrote.

Kesira didn't answer immediately. She knew why she had neglected to baptize the boy. A name meant attachment. It would be more difficult to give him over to a foster home if "boy" became a person distinct with name. Yet this had worked against her. Now she had to find the baby, and she found it difficult to think of him as anything more than a commodity to be bartered, the rune-foretold key to breaking Ayondela away from the power of the jade.

"I am changing, Molimo," she said. "And not in ways I like. Life without honor is an abomination. So taught Gelya; so I've learned from others. But where is the honor in turning over a tiny infant to appease a demon? I consider this now without hesitation. I watched Esamir die and felt only relief that such a fiend is removed."

"He lacked honor. His actions dictated his death," wrote Molimo, his face set into a mask.

"You did well. I am not criticizing," Kesira said. "He forfeited all right to life for the things he did. But my feelings. They . . . have changed."

"Life is change."

Kesira wondered how Molimo meant that, considering his shape transformations. Would he die if he could not alter form? Or was it merely a response to progress in learning as she went through life?

"I have hardened, Molimo. That is what I fear. Inured to death, I come to despise life. It comes cheaply, as it did to Esamir. I don't want that. I won't become like that death merchant or Ayondela or Lenc or even Nehan-dir."

His hand lightly brushed over hers. She looked up. For the first time in weeks compassion shone forth from his eyes instead of the coldly emotionless stare. He squeezed lightly, then faced forward and spurred his horse to a faster pace. The trail narrowed rapidly and forced them to ride single file.

By nightfall they had reached the summit. Looking back at Lorum Bay, Kesira saw lanterns winking on and off throughout the village. The twilight cast an eerie gray over the Sea of Katad and turned it into a heaving, restless beast straining to break free of its bonds. And moving in from the south, devouring streets and buildings, sucking up human lives as it came, the oddly glistening magical fog dropped its tendrils and dug in for the night.

"Ayondela keeps a strict rein on her minions," Kesira

said, staring at the mist of death. "She enforces a curfew more stringent than any human watchman."

Molimo tugged at her sleeve, indicating a good place to camp. She shook her head, short brown hair swinging away from her face. "No. We will keep on. The baby grows hungrier, if I am any judge." She cupped her left breast, feeling the gathering weight of milk within. "He's missed two meals already. More and he will turn weak and die."

His birth in the middle of Ayondela's winter curse and his survival spoke of the baby's strength. The way he had endured the journey across the sea, the shipwreck, and all that followed told of more than strength. Kesira could almost believe that a demon *had* sired the boy.

Although their mounts had long since tired from the steep climb into the hills, Kesira pushed them on. Often she had to walk her horse to allow it a chance to catch its breath. Several times over the next hour Molimo looked back at her, an expression of concern on his face. Kesira saw the turmoil boiling within him. He wanted to speak and couldn't. Not for the first time, she cursed the jade demons and the affliction forced upon Molimo. She only barely understood how he must feel, wanting to speak to her, trying to make more than inarticulate gurgling noises. Everyone carried a different burden through the world.

Kesira had to admit that hers had compounded from simple revenge for all Lenc had done to her order to protecting the infant. If the baby had been her own flesh and blood, she wouldn't have felt more for him.

"What is it, Molimo?" she asked when the man stopped and just stood in the middle of the tiny path. He cocked his head to one side, as if listening. Strain as she might, Kesira caught nothing but natural sounds. *Trenly* crickets warbled and croaked their mating cries, a bit of wind whispered off the sea and carried with it the smell of salty water and fish, and tiny pops and creaks told where rock, heated by the summer sun, now cooled in the darkness. All natural, all expected.

Molimo came to her side and held out his tablet. He erased the words almost as quickly as he wrote them.

"Who could be following us?" she said, astounded. "Not the stable hand? Do you think he told the town constable of the horses we took?" Molimo shook his head. "What, then?"

"Steel Crescent" was all Molimo wrote.

Kesira heaved a deep sigh. Ahead rode the Emperor's Guard, and behind came the implacable Nehan-dir with his surviving mercenaries. Kesira experienced a curiously detached feeling, as if she floated atop the world and looked down emotionlessly on all that happened. Captain Protaro had the Emperor to command him, and Emperor Kwasian listened to the counsel of the demon Lalasa. Nehan-dir sold his sword to the highest bidder, the strongest jade demon. Lenc commanded him.

No one commanded Kesira Minette.

"What am I to do? How can I tell when I am right?" she muttered.

Molimo nudged her and pointed to his tablet. On it he had written, "Doubt others but never doubt yourself."

"One of your patron's maxims?" she asked. Kesira pulled back a step when Molimo started laughing. "What's so funny?"

"We must hurry on. We dare not be trapped on this stretch of trail," Molimo wrote, ignoring her question. Kesira saw the wisdom in the man-wolf's words. Nehan-dir's soldiers would slay them without effort here. The heavy wall of granite lay to their right, and a sheer drop of over a hundred feet vanished into darkness at the left side of the narrow trail. They had to keep advancing; to retreat—or to remain where they were—would bring them face-to-face with the Steel Crescent.

The horses protested but finally allowed Kesira and Molimo to push them at a faster gait. Soon the trail widened, mountain pastures stretching out to either side. And ahead Kesira saw tiny camp fires blazing.

"Protaro?" she asked Molimo. He solemnly nodded.

Kesira let out a low whistle, then sat astride her horse sucking at her cheeks. Now that they'd overtaken the Guardsmen she had no plan. The soldiers would not simply allow her to ride into camp to claim the baby. Even if Protaro did permit her in, he would never allow her to leave. She was the only source of nourishment for the baby.

Molimo made encompassing motions with his arms, indicating that they should circle the camp and approach from the far side. Kesira silently turned her horse to do so. If Protaro posted guards, they'd be alert on the trail leading back to Lorum Bay. She and Molimo spiraled in to the camp fires. As they rode silently she assayed their position and formed a plan.

Dismounting on the far side of Protaro's encampment, she tethered her horse and said softly, "We must move by stealth. I will enter the camp and get the baby."

Molimo protested but Kesira ignored him. "I do not mean to be cruel, Molimo, but you must stay behind. I can't chance a transformation. The other-breast is unpredictable. If only you controlled the shape-shifting better." She sighed. "You don't. I must go in alone. Watch and guard my back."

Molimo tried to stop her. He ran to his horse and pulled the tablet from the pouch slung behind his saddle, but the woman didn't wait to read his scribbled message. Kesira melted into the inky night that cloaked the mountain meadowland, her full attention turned to Captain Protaro's camp.

She measured every stride, tested every footstep before putting full weight down. No twig cracked. No leaf crumbled to betray her. Softer than any wind, Kesira Minette drifted through the trees, merging with nature to become a random sound, a dark shadow, a being more elemental than human.

"We'll be out of the mountains and onto the prairie by tomorrow noon," said one battered-looking man crouching near the fire. "I tell you, Cap'n, these hills aren't for the likes of me and you."

"Why not?" Protaro lounged back, propping himself up on one elbow. He gnawed at what meat remained on a small bone. "We've been through many mountain passes before, Tuwallan. You only ever get this edgy when we face up to magic."

The man—a scout?—chuckled. "I remember the Pinn Campaign. Couldn't kill those animated black boulders for love of the Emperor. Never did hear how you countered their attack."

"Pits. The men dug pits all night long. What makes you uneasy about this fine evening?" Protaro leaned back and stared up at the diamond points of stars in the sky. Involuntarily Kesira's rocked her head back and followed his gaze. Was the Guard captain staring at the constellations? The Jeweled Scepter just poking up over a dark mountain crag or the Throne of Azzica half turned in the sky?

"We ought to have left a few stragglers to guard our rear. We're traveling blind back there, Cap'n. Let me send a couple of the eager ones to check."

"Speed is more important. If we spent our time looking to our tails, the Emperor might not get his bundle before the Equinox Festival."

"What makes that brat so important?" Tuwallan duck-walked a few steps and peered down at a dark form in swaddling. "Doesn't even cry out."

"He's not taking the goat's milk too well, is he?" asked Protaro, concerned. Kesira felt some of the tension flow from her. The Guard captain at least cared for the boy and wasn't permitting him to be maltreated. But it sounded ominous that the infant refused to take the milk offered.

"When he gets hungry enough, he'll eat. But I never saw one so young that didn't cry out. He'll make a fine Guard in another fifteen summers."

"That's your trouble, Tu'lan. All you think about is the service."

"You do different, Cap'n?"

"No."

Conversation died down along with the fire. Kesira carefully studied the sentries, their posts, how they patroled, and when their watches changed. The Throne of Azzica made a half turn in the sky before Kesira moved into the camp, going directly to the baby.

Eyes so pale that they seemed luminous in the dark peered up at her. She smiled and stood the boy in her arms. Rocking him gently, she turned and began her slow journey back into the darkness.

Tuwallan stirred in his sleep, pulling his trail blanket up over one exposed shoulder. Kesira paused, thinking herself to be part of the night, willing her form to blend with dark shadows. But whatever it was that made the man Protaro's most expert scout alerted him. He rolled onto his back and stared straight at her.

Kesira knew better than to bluff her way out of this. She took three quick steps forward and dropped beside the soldier. The baby lowered to the ground, she struck with a short, hard punch to the prone man's throat. Tuwallan gagged. Thumb and forefinger closed his nostrils. Her other hand clamped firmly on the damaged windpipe. She squeezed. Not only her own life depended on it but also the life of the baby.

Tuwallan struggled feebly, trying vainly to get air into his tortured lungs. Then all movement ceased. Kesira held the grip for another minute to make certain that he wasn't bluffing, then released him. For all the battles he had survived, he had died relatively peacefully in the midst of his friends.

Kesira picked up the infant and forced herself to walk carefully into the darkness. Any sudden movement or incautious sound might alert the guards. Ten minutes later Kesira let out pent-up breath she hadn't known she held.

She looked down at the bundle in her arms. "You missed me, didn't you?" The baby's hands fumbled at her blouse. "No, you didn't miss me, you little imp. All you missed were a few meals." She sighed as the baby began to nurse greedily. "I don't blame you. Goat's milk can't be as satisfying."

The baby's appetite sated, Kesira continued on through the sparse mountain meadow, keeping low and taking advantage of the grassy contours. Only when she rejoined Molimo did she again feel safe.

That sensation passed.

"What is it?" she demanded, seeing the man's dour expression. He started to hold up his writing tablet, but an all-too-familiar voice stopped him.

"The negotiations will go more quickly if I deal with her directly, other-beast."

"Nehan-dir!" she gasped. Her hands opened and closed on nothing. How she wished for her stone-wood staff. Two quick spins, a thrust, and Nehan-dir's head would be crushed on both sides and the carcass knocked into a ravine.

The short, skinny leader of the Steel Crescent moved into view from the deep shadows that had hidden him from sight. He held his sword out and leveled it at Molimo, but Kesira saw no real intent to use it. Whatever weapon Nehan-dir wielded now, he thought it more effective than his vaunted steel blade.

"You ride well," he complimented. "We were hard-pressed to keep up with you. And to rescue the baby? A stroke of genius."

"You won't get him—not without a fight!"

She cast a quick glance at Molimo. The man sat slumped forward, as if he'd been defeated already. This was so totally unlike him, she wondered what Nehan-dir had done.

"I have learned my lesson, noble lady," Nehan-dir said mockingly. "I haven't come to fight you for the child, though the idea appeals to me. Lenc has ordered the baby delivered to him, and fighting you might not accomplish that."

"Nothing will," Kesira retorted. She clung to the baby with such fervor that he stirred and tried to push himself away. Tiny fists gripped at her until she relaxed enough to allow him to breathe again.

"There is a price for everything, even people," said Nehan-dir.

"Power is yours. You have yet to find mine!"

"Ah, you are wrong. At least I have told my followers that I have penetrated that facade of iron surrounding you so totally." Nehan-dir reached into the front of his tunic and pulled forth a handful of blue-tipped green feathers, then cast them in front of him as if paving the way for a tender-footed nobleman.

"So?" Kesira saw nothing in the mercenary's action to menace her.

"Those are *trilla* bird feathers. From your friend Zolkan."

Kesira said nothing. Molimo let out a strangled gasp that began deep in his chest and died in his throat.

"We have the *trilla* bird. If you do not agree to exchange the baby for your Zolkan, well," Nehan-dir said, smiling wickedly, "I have been told that *trilla* bird meat is quite tasty."

Molimo's ebony-dark eyes filled with tears and then overflowed. Kesira watched in silent horror as they stained the dirt on the man's cheeks. She might have called Nehan-dir a liar, but the sight of Molimo crying like this convinced her that the Steel Crescent did hold the bird captive. Whatever communication existed between Molimo and Zolkan had confirmed it.

But to give up the baby for Zolkan?

Kesira fought back tears of her own as she shook with impotent rage.

Chapter Ten

"THE TRADE IS QUITE simple, even for one such as you."
Nehan-dir openly sneered at her now. "The baby means
little to you. How can it be any other way? It isn't even
your flesh and blood. But the *trilla* bird..." The mercenary leader's voice trailed off suggestively. Kesira had no
doubt that Nehan-dir would perform the vilest of tortures
on Zolkan, given the chance.

"A few tail feathers cast on the ground does not mean
you actually have him," Kesira said.

Molimo handed her his tablet. On it he had written,
"Nehan-dir speaks the truth. Zolkan is their prisoner."

Kesira didn't bother to ask Molimo how he knew. That
odd communication between him and the *trilla* bird might
have come into play. If so, she had to believe that the
worst had happened.

She took a deep, settling breath and forced calm upon
her turbulent thoughts. Panic now spelled death for those
she loved—and perhaps even herself. Nehan-dir did not
deal honestly if he could find a more devious path to
follow. Kesira imagined herself drifting on the gentle summer winds, tossed as lightly as one of Zolkan's feathers,
drifting, floating, coming to rest on the good earth. This
gave her the needed tranquillity for deeper thoughts to rise
within her for examination, thoughts otherwise hidden behind the static of her fear.

"I want to discuss this with Molimo."

Nehan-dir made a deprecating gesture. "Take all the

time you want. Just don't be longer than one minute." He gave an ugly laugh. "How you can discuss anything with a cripple is beyond me."

Kesira wasted no time on Nehan-dir. She huddled close to Molimo and pressed her trembling lips to his ear. "We cannot let Zolkan stay in *his* hands."

"Boy is important. Without him there is no way to defeat Ayondela." A tear fell from Molimo's cheek to spot the tablet. He brushed it away self-consciously.

"Zolkan is more than a friend to you, isn't he?" she asked. Molimo only nodded. Kesira looked at Nehan-dir standing indolently, his sword balanced on its tip near the toe of his right boot. She kept her calm—and knew she had the answer.

She stood in front of Nehan-dir. Shoulders squared, Kesira looked him directly in the eye. For a moment her attitude perplexed the mercenary. The cobweb pattern of scars on his face throbbed pink, and his eyebrows lowered in a frown. Whatever response he'd expected, it hadn't been such boldness.

"I won't turn the baby over to you," she said in measured tones.

This did surprise Nehan-dir. "Then the bird's life is forfeit."

"That gains you nothing."

"Satisfaction. Some small pleasure watching the feathered one die." The small mercenary shrugged. "It's a hard life. I take what enjoyment I can, where I can."

"You'd still not have the baby."

"There are other ways."

"I offer you one," Kesira said. She forced herself not to nervously lick her lips and so betray her fear. "Zolkan and the infant are to be the stake in a winner-take-both duel."

"Oh? They're the stakes, are they?" Contempt rippled through his words, but Kesira saw that she'd won. Interest glowed in the man's narrowed eyes. She had embarrassed him too many times in their past meetings for such an offer to go unheeded. His finest warriors had died at her or Molimo's hand during their cross-country flight. Their escape from Ayondela's Isle of Eternal Winter had been the crowning humiliation for such a proud fighter.

"Do you accept the challenge?"

"If I don't, the *trilla* bird dies."

"If you don't, the baby will never be yours," Kesira countered hotly.

Nehan-dir smiled wickedly. "That's not necessarily true. While I can't bring my full force to bear at this moment"—he tipped his head in Captain Protaro's direction—"there is nothing to say that I won't be victorious later, down the trail, after you have left the Guard's protection."

"I can always decide that the boy is better off in the Emperor's hands than in yours."

"You have already made that decision once. Why make it again?" he asked. His eyes darted to where the infant lay, pale eyes watching closely in an uncharacteristically old and wise fashion.

"Single battle. At dawn."

"Where? I do not cherish the idea of combat so near to the Guard's camp. They won't take the loss of the child easily."

"Down the trail. A few miles. The fight won't take long." Kesira hoped it would never come to pass. She was only angling for more time and the possibilities it might offer.

"There is a small well. Be there at sunrise." Nehan-dir vanished into the ebon night as silently as if he'd never been present. Kesira stood and stared at the emptiness—and felt an equally large hole within her.

"We cannot fight by his rules, Molimo," she said. They hurried to their mounts, her mind racing all the while. "I'll cut myself a staff and engage him."

Molimo shook his head.

Kesira ignored him. "While we're fighting, you sneak into his camp and steal away with Zolkan, just as I've done with the baby."

Molimo looked skeptical. Kesira didn't blame him. The idea seemed too fragile to bear close scrutiny, however, and it was the best she could come up with under such pressure of time.

An hour down the trail Kesira stopped and went to a small sapling about her height. She motioned. Molimo chopped and hacked at it with his sword until she had a smooth staff. Kesira shivered as she ran her fingers along the supple green length. Gelya would never approve. The wood had been hewn with steel, thus robbing the staff of any mystical power that might otherwise have been imparted to it. Its balance did not pleasure her, either. One end was heavier than the other.

Kesira ran agile fingers down its length, frowning as tiny buds popped out along it. She hacked them off, stroked over the wood to test its smoothness, and again found incipient limbs sprouting. On impulse, she held her hand over one recent amputation. Her touch restored life to the staff.

Molimo watched silently. She shook her head and carefully scraped away the new growth she'd inadvertently fostered.

"It will have to do."

"This plan will never work," wrote Molimo. He underlined his words with a quick flourish to emphasize his worry.

"Can you think of anything better? All Nehan-dir's followers will want to watch the fight. Only if they do will their attention shift away from Zolkan. You *must* rescue him then."

"What of you?"

Kesira ran one hand through her short brown hair. "I don't know. Maybe I can defeat him." She saw the man's sour expression. "I don't think I can, either, but you told me that self-doubt is the great killer. Let's get on with it. I want to be away from both Protaro and Nehan-dir before noon."

Molimo trailed and dismounted when they came to the

small artesian well Nehan-dir had mentioned. Already three of the Steel Crescent soldiers stood by their leader. Their attention turned to Kesira as she walked up. She laid the baby down in a lightning-struck tree trunk, carefully filled with a few patches of moss, to make a small, comfortable cradle.

"Where's Zolkan?" she called to Nehan-dir.

"We have him. Do not fear on that point. I give you my word of honor that he will be released if you defeat me."

Nehan-dir slid his sword from its sheath. He accepted a small, round shield from one of his men and turned down the offer of a heavy helmet from another. Kesira smiled at this. After almost drowning in the Sea of Katad, Nehan-dir had learned that armor carried its own penalties. While he wasn't likely to fall into the shallow pool of clear water bubbling from the depths of the planet, he didn't want her superior mobility to work against him. No armor.

Kesira thought that his sword and shield would prove more than adequate against her unseasoned staff. Her eyes flickered in Molimo's direction, then came back to Nehan-dir. She could only hope that Molimo had sidled toward the copse surrounding the well and was making his way to Nehan-dir's encampment to rescue Zolkan.

"Haieeee!"

Kesira dropped into a defensive stance as Nehan-dir's shrill war cry shattered the tranquillity of the morning. He rushed her, sword held high. She deftly avoided his headlong rush, turning her back toward the rising sun. But she found this did her no good. He used the brilliantly polished shield to reflect light into her face. They circled warily, looking for any advantage.

"Give me the baby and save yourself," Nehan-dir said.

"We fight. To the death, if necessary."

Kesira easily fended off his thrust and swung her staff around to soundly thump Nehan-dir in the ribs.

The battle had begun in earnest.

* * *

Molimo watched as Kesira and Nehan-dir squared off. He began reciting the spell given him by Toyaga. Molimo saw the warriors' eyes blink and come unfocused as the magicks took hold and turned him into an object not easily stared at. The magicks made it easier for the mercenaries to watch their leader than to obey Nehan-dir's orders not to let Molimo out of their sight.

He worked his way up into the jagged rocks above the battle site, then across the face of a cliff, continually repeating the spell to keep prying eyes away.

Zolkan? his silent message went out. From below came the singsong speech Molimo had hoped to hear.

"Only two guard me," warned the *trilla* bird. "How degrading. They have me caged!"

Zolkan sounded more peeved than angry at his treatment.

"They pluck my feathers for their amusement! I will peck out their eyes for this affront! My lovely feathers, *gone!*"

Remain calm. Kesira fights Nehan-dir so that I can rescue you.

"Be quick about it." A loud squawk of protest allowed Molimo's sharp ears to pinpoint the bird in the Steel Crescent's campsite. One of the mercenaries had shaken Zolkan's cage to silence the bird.

Metamorphosis began inside Molimo. He stopped, sweat beading his forehead. He pressed himself into the cool, substantial rock, wincing at the slight pain as an outcropping cut into his flesh. He didn't want to transform into a wolf. Not now. He had to retain this form to rescue Zolkan.

His friend. Zolkan. Kesira fighting. Pain. Molimo fought to focus his thoughts on human concerns and not on animalistic ones. But the pain, the pain!

The dizziness passed, and he held on to the human shape. He gusted a sigh of relief, then turned his attention back to the camp. Two guards stood, one on either side of a crudely constructed cage. A dirty rag had been tossed over the top, but Molimo saw a long, brightly colored tail feather protruding from between the bars.

Carefully working his way down the rocky slope, Molimo came within ten teet of the guards before one turned and saw him. Gone was all hope of using Toyaga's spell to advance within striking distance.

Molimo whipped out his sword and took three quick steps forward and lunged. The tip of his blade found a bloody berth in the man's throat. Jerking free, Molimo slashed viciously at the other guard. She had time to respond.

Steel met steel.

But the contest ended swiftly when Zolkan got his head out between two of the wooden bars and fastened his beak firmly on the woman's leg. She yelped in pain as the serrated edges severed a greave and found flesh beneath. Molimo gave her no chance to recover. His blade arced up, down, into her shoulder, to sunder important arteries. She died without uttering a word.

Release her, Molimo commanded. *I can't get you out of the cage unless you do.*

"Satisfying," Zolkan said. "She tormented me constantly. Bitch. Pigeon-shit bitch!"

Kesira is facing Nehan-dir. We must get back and tell her you are safe.

"How are we to escape?" squawked the bird.

Molimo said nothing.

"Another of her fine plans, eh?" muttered Zolkan. "Great start, no finish. Pigeons plan better!"

Go, my friend. Show yourself to Kesira and let her know she can disengage.

Zolkan stretched cramped wings and legs, then waddled along clumsily until he found a downhill stretch. Racing along, flapping hard, the *trilla* bird became airborne. Molimo watched Zolkan spiral upward, then begin descending to warn Kesira. To his dismay Zolkan returned immediately, landing heavily on his shoulder. He knew the bird had only bad news to impart when sharp claws cut carelessly into his shoulder.

"They are gone. All of them," announced Zolkan, bitterness seeping into the words.

How?

"Why did you think Nehan-dir would fight fairly? He wanted baby, he took baby. Ground looks as if Kesira fought when all surrounded and took her prisoner."

They took her to insure food for the baby, Molimo said.

"Weakling child," grumbled Zolkan. "Not like *trilla* bird hatchlings. A few weeks in nest, then out. Only way to learn to fly."

Don't sit there, get aloft. Find them. They can't be more than a few minutes away.

"You run after them. I saw no horses."

Nehan-dir wastes nothing, said Molimo. *But I have two mounts. Theirs.* He pointed to the fallen soldiers. *Go. Find them and return to let me know where.*

"Others seek you. Squad of men coming from direction of Lorum Bay."

Protaro and the Emperor's Guard. Kesira killed one of them to recover the baby.

"Brat is going to get us slaughtered. Leave it with Nehan-dir."

No! You know why we cannot do that. Now go, damn your beak. Go!

Zolkan took wing again and strained up the meadows until he found morning thermals to ride. Quick black eyes scanned the ground for signs of Kesira and her captors. Zolkan found them in less than ten minutes. He wheeled to return to Molimo.

"Their horses tire," said Zolkan.

Kesira holds them back. See how she purposefully chooses the worst path?

The *trilla* bird cawed and hunkered down on Molimo's shoulder to watch. Molimo pulled his horse around abruptly and took a higher path through the meadow to keep a stand of trees between him and Nehan-dir's party. The man had been all too aware of the Emperor's Guard slowly narrowing the distance between them throughout the day. The collision of the Steel Crescent mercenaries and Captain Protaro's men was not something Molimo wanted to see again. If luck held, he and Kesira and the baby would be far away by the time the Emperor's fire mixed with the Order of the Steel Crescent's tinder.

"They stop. I hear sounds of dismounting," said Zolkan.

Molimo vaulted from the saddle and tethered both horses to a low shrub. He hurried into the lightly forested area bordering the meadow, feeling as if some force pulled him toward Nehan-dir.

Power fills me, he told the *trilla* bird. *It is a sensation similar to that I get when I use Toyaga's spell.*

"Compulsion magicks?"

I . . . it may be. It is so difficult for me to tell. If only I were stronger!

Molimo dropped to hands and knees and traversed the last twenty yards in this manner. Through bushes fragrant with blossoms and buzzing with pollen-dusted insects, Molimo peered out to see Kesira nursing the infant. Beside her stood Nehan-dir, hand on his sword hilt. The others in the band prepared fortifications.

They realize Protaro is close behind, he said. *They must not be able to outrun the Emperor's Guard.*

"Should I attract Kesira's attention?" asked the bird.

Wait. She . . . she knows we are here.

"How?"

The baby tells her. The baby summons me. Me! *How is that possible?*

"It has more power than the pink worm it resembles," Zolkan said with ill grace. "Trouble. It only brings us more trouble."

Molimo pushed Zolkan back into the wooded area and fell flat onto his belly. Even his sharp ears did not catch all that Nehan-dir said to Kesira. Whatever it was, the words obviously distressed the nun. She shot to her feet, only to be shoved back to the ground. Molimo closed his eyes and concentrated on retaining his human shape. As before, it did him no good to become his wolf self.

Power from without aided him. When he opened his eyes, he saw that Nehan-dir had sent away the others guarding Kesira. Only he stood over her.

Molimo began the magical spell that would allow him to approach unseen.

> The world about me,
> There are no eyes.
> Freedom of the air and sky,
> I fade into nothingness.

He inched forward as quietly as he could. One hand reached out and tugged at Kesira's sleeve while his other gripped his dagger. Nehan-dir died if he penetrated the veil of magic.

Kesira frowned as she looked down, then smiled. She shook her head slightly to indicate that this was not the most opportune time to escape. Molimo knew they had no choice. Protaro and his Guardsmen would arrive within the hour. If they were caught up in the ensuing battle, it would bode ill for everyone.

"They will not recapture the baby," said Nehan-dir to Kesira. "Lenc has ordered the infant's presence and promised vast rewards when we are successful."

"The Emperor will grant you equal riches," she said.

"Riches? Lenc promises power. What else is there? With power all riches can be mine." Nehan-dir half turned to survey the hasty construction work on the battlements. Molimo flowed upward, the hilt of his dagger aimed directly at the man's prominent chin.

Metal struck bone. The mercenary leader fell to the ground, stunned.

"No!" Kesira said as Molimo reversed the knife to slit the exposed throat. "Leave him."

Molimo was not going to obey. Never leave behind a weapon or a living enemy. Those were hard lessons recently learned. But he had no time to finish even a quick cut now. Nehan-dir's soldiers had seen him, and Kesira tugged at his arm.

"Leave him!" she cried. "We must get away. Why couldn't you have waited?"

Molimo shoved the woman toward the sparse forest. She stumbled but held on to the child. The rattle of weapons kept them moving until the thicker stands of trees sheltered them. Molimo jerked her to one side and pointed to a game trail running at a right angle to their current path. Without hesitation Kesira took it. Molimo started to continue on, then heard the uproar from behind.

None of the Steel Crescent mercenaries followed. The Emperor's Guard had attacked, successfully decoying the mercenaries into believing that their main body still rode the trail. This diversion might be enough to let him slip away with Kesira.

Zolkan! he cried, reaching out to find the *trilla* bird.

"They won't be after you for several minutes," the bird responded. "Stay with Kesira."

Molimo darted along the trail, feet pounding heavily until he overtook her. He looked at her dirty face, the matted hair, the scratched arms and battered clothing and had never seen any woman as pretty.

The baby's pale eyes fixed on his dark ones. Power flowed. Molimo croaked, but no audible words came.

Kesira halted and stared curiously at them. "Are you all right?" she asked Molimo. The man nodded. Kesira reached out and touched his cheek. "You're flushed. You're not running a fever?"

Zolkan battered his way through the overhanging branches and perched on a slender limb just above their heads. "Horses dead. Protaro's soldiers killed them."

"What? Why?" Kesira asked.

"Thought they were Nehan-dir's. Battle goes against Steel Crescent. Nehan-dir still unconscious." Zolkan looked disparagingly at Molimo. The mercenary leader ought to have died with a quick slash of the dagger.

"Without horses, what are we going to do?" Kesira asked. "We must go back and steal some. That's the only way. The confusion, we can——"

Molimo took her by the elbow and turned her to face a shallow depression in the side of a low, rocky hill. He went to it and began digging, dirt and greenery flying. In a few minutes he revealed a low cave entrance. Molimo pointed.

"Well, it might work," she said, frowning. "If we hide long enough, they'll think we escaped. But I don't like the idea of hiding in a cave." Memories of all that had happened to her in the Abbey of Ayondela returned with haunting force.

Molimo scooted in on his belly. Reluctantly Kesira followed close behind—and just in time.

The heavy tread of boots echoed down the game trail they'd just abandoned. Zolkan awkwardly pulled loose bushes up to cover the entrance, but he didn't work fast enough.

"There," called a loud voice. "There they are. In that cave!"

Kesira and Molimo exchanged looks. Fighting in the narrow confines of this rocky shaft was out of the question.

"Let's get on with it," she said. "I don't like it, but we have no other choice." On hands and knees Kesira Minette crawled deeper into the cave. From the sides and above she felt the ponderous weight of rock waiting to crush her to a bloody pulp.

Chapter Eleven

"WAIT! STOP! Don't leave me!"

Kesira looked back over her shoulder the best she could in the low-ceilinged rock passage and saw a green lump of rumpled feathers waddling along behind.

"Zolkan!" she cried. "Why didn't you fly off?"

"Trapped. Pigeon-shit soldiers trapped me!" The *trilla* bird hopped up and landed on Kesira's back. She sagged under the additional weight. With the infant slung under her, so that she could barely move, and the large bird's bulk pressing her down, Kesira felt as if she truly carried the weight of the world on her shoulders.

From the pursed mouth of the cave came the sounds of pursuit. Kesira took a deep breath and continued after Molimo. No matter where this passage led, it would be paradise compared to being captured by either Captain Protaro or Nehan-dir. Both would share her death for what she'd done to them.

An eternity later Kesira banged into Molimo. The darkness had turned absolute, and claustrophobia closed in on her, making it difficult to breathe. She knew that this was only a failure of her mind, not of the air itself, but that did not make the problem any less significant.

She snapped at Molimo, "What are you stopping for? Keep going!"

He crawled another few feet. Kesira sensed a widening in the tunnel, as if it turned into a large chamber. She rushed forward as fast as she could on hands and knees, then cautiously explored with her hands. The low ceiling vanished abruptly. Like a blind beggar, Kesira started feeling for the limits of this chamber.

She shrieked when she found Molimo.

"You startled me," she said, trying to still her racing heart. When the pounding in her temples died down, she heard the scratchings of metal on rock back in the passage. Someone came for them—and she had no idea whether it was the Steel Crescent or the Emperor's Guard.

Even worse, it didn't matter. She had to fight to the death to keep them from taking the baby. Kesira cradled the infant and rocked it gently, soothingly. She felt one fat little fist clutch at her, but no sound rose from those lips. Weights even greater than before descended on her. The child had to be afflicted in some fashion—possibly by the evil power of jade. All her troubles stemmed from Lenc and the others. All Molimo's did also. It seemed only reasonable to blame any problems of the baby on the jade demons.

"We don't have much time," she said. "They're not more than five minutes behind us. How long do you think we can hold them back, Molimo?"

She tensed when the man fumbled at her pouch, then relaxed when she saw what he wanted. He withdrew the last of her magical powder used for starting fires.

"Do you have any fuel?"

The sudden blinding flare of white answered her question. He had found some dried cave moss. It burned rapidly, but the ample piles of it in the medium-size cave provided fuel for all the time they'd need. She closed her eyes and tried to calm her raging emotions. All the time they'd need: less than five minutes now.

Sounds of pursuit came closer.

"That," squawked Zolkan. "Move it! Move it!"

"What?" Kesira swung around to see what the bird meant. At the rear of the cave a large, circular stone plug filled—what? A new passage? To where?

Kesira went to the plug and ran her hand over it. In

the guttering light cast by the burning moss all color vanished. She squinted and ran her fingernail across the surface.

"*Tulna* stone. This cost an Emperor's treasury to make!"

"Open it, open it. No time to steal it. Hurry!" urged Zolkan. The bird waddled back and forth nervously. "They come soon, too soon. They eat *trilla* meat!"

Kesira's fingers tensed, and her shoulders ached from the attempt to push the stone door, or pull it, or move it in any direction. Sweating, eyes burning with acrid smoke from the burning moss, she sank to the floor.

"Too heavy," she said.

She glanced up at Molimo, who stood strangely transfixed. Kesira started to touch him, to urge him to resist the shape-change to wolf. But his expression was subtly different from that seizing him prior to a shape-altering. She thought a change was occurring but not of form.

Molimo walked to the orange *tulna* stone, widened his stance, and put his hands flat against the smooth gateway. Muscles expanded along his upper arms and shoulders, knotting so hard that his tunic began to bulge. Sweat popped onto his forehead, but his face kept the same odd lack of expression.

The stone door moved inward. Molimo shifted, and the door swung away to reveal a corridor walled in ceramic tiles decorated with intricate dancing figures, finely drawn geometric patterns, and colors so brilliant, they almost hurt Kesira's eyes. It took her several seconds to realize why.

"The tiles glow!"

Molimo stood motionless, eyes fixed on something at the far end of the newly revealed corridor. But on what Kesira couldn't tell.

Zolkan had already flapped his way into the passage, cawing loudly. Kesira followed, taking Molimo by the hand and gently pulling him after.

"Can you close the door?" she asked. Her eyes darted to the low tunnel soon to be filled with the soldiers pursuing them. Having the door between them and the soldiers would further hinder capture.

Molimo did a smart about-face and leaned against the orange door, getting it into ponderous movement once more.

Kesira put her weight against the door, too, when she saw the first soldier stagger upright in the smoky chamber they'd just left. A loud battle cry rang in her ears—almost as loud as the slithering of steel against sheath.

"Oh, faster, faster," she moaned, straining. Kesira doubted that her efforts aided Molimo one iota, but she had to try. All the power she had felt when she fought Esamir pulsed through her, but it was still too small an effort to move so ponderous a door. She saw that the advancing soldier, one of the Emperor's Guard, evaluated the problem facing him and acted instinctively. He threw his sword forward to prevent the door from smoothly meeting the jamb. By the time they got the blade free to lock the door, his comrades would have joined him.

The shiny steel clanked noisily as Molimo pushed the stone door closed.

Kesira watched in mute horror as the blade began to smoke. It melted and ran down the walls to form a puddle of hissing, molten metal. She danced away to keep the metallic spray from burning her.

"What caused that?" she asked.

Molimo motioned for her to accompany Zolkan down the corridor.

"They'll have the door open soon," she said. "You're right. We must be away when they get through."

For the first time Molimo's expression changed. He smiled, then laughed silently. With a soot-smudged finger he wrote on one of the snowy white tiles lining the walls.

"No one opens that door."

"But you did."

"I am feeling stronger now. I heal. Away from jade I heal!" His words trailed into illegibility as the soot finally rubbed free of his fingers, and Kesira couldn't read the rest.

Molimo may have felt stronger, but Kesira's legs buckled under her. She sagged. Molimo caught her and half carried her along the glowing hallway. The pictures flowed beside her as if they had taken on a life of their own. Kesira fought to stay alert and failed.

"Rest," ordered Zolkan, hopping up beside her. "We can go on soon. When it arrives."

"It? What are you talking about? What *is* this place?" she asked. But her strength faded more and more. Kesira lay back, the baby snuggling serenely at her side. She drifted off to a deep, dreamless sleep, the last thing she remembered being Molimo saying, *We can reach Ayondela before dawn.*

Kesira stirred and opened her eyes. Molimo sat just a few feet away, watching her. His expression defied her powers to describe, but it was a tender look. Love? She couldn't say for certain.

"Hello," she said, stretching her arms and legs to get circulation back. "I had the strangest dream—or not-dream—just before I went to sleep. I thought you spoke to me."

Molimo looked at Zolkan, then back at her. He shook his head slowly, thoughtfully.

"Not likely, not likely," the *trilla* bird squawked. "When do we eat? So hungry. Can't stay clean, don't get fed. What life is this to lead?"

"One of us gets fed," she said, picking up the infant.

Molimo dropped to the floor and pressed his ear against the cool ceramic tile. For long minutes he listened, then quickly motioned to Zolkan. The bird let forth a long string of the singsong speech that excluded Kesira before saying to her, "Ride comes. We go faster now. Be sure to hang on."

"Ride? Our horses are outside—dead, you told me."

"No horses. Faster. We go to Ayondela. Come along, hurry, hurry!"

Kesira settled the baby over her shoulder and gently patted him as she went to stand beside Molimo and Zolkan. The bird cawed and vaulted to her right shoulder.

"Put it away. No time for hobby."

"Zolkan, he's not a hobby."

The sudden change in air pressure made Kesira clap hands over her ears. She cried out and neutralized the inner pressure, and finally a long, wide yawn finished the job. Kesira stared in amazement at the device causing her the discomfort.

"It's like a wagon," she said, "but there aren't any wheels. What manner of magical device is it?"

"Demons hate travel among humans," said Zolkan. "This is demon's private transport system."

Kesira examined it carefully. The short, padded bench mounted on a circular plug of *tulna* stone had come through an irising hole in the wall. Other than this she saw nothing at all. Molimo took her elbow and guided her toward the bench. With some trepidation she sat down, Molimo beside her. Zolkan muttered to himself, then jumped to the seat, wedging himself between them.

"Hate this. Why can't we fly?" the bird grumbled.

The sudden acceleration took away Kesira's breath, even as a scream formed on her lips. The bench and circular stone behind it shot forward toward a solid wall. A fraction of a second before they'd have become jam, the wall irised open to a diameter large enough to accommodate their strange vehicle. They blasted through and into a long, dark shaft. The sense of speed mounted, and wind seared at the woman's face.

"I can't see anything!" she shouted past the rush of air. "What if we hit something?"

"We die," came Zolkan's hardly cheering words. "Hate this. Better to soar and look down on miserable humans."

Kesira gulped as a tiny point of light grew and grew. Another doorway irised open; they stopped as quickly as they had started. Kesira tumbled forward, not prepared for the braking. Molimo grabbed her in time to save her from a nasty fall.

On shaking legs Kesira walked away from the bench. A gust of wind blew past her, and the magical vehicle vanished on its imponderable way beneath the ground.

"Who conjured that?" she asked, staring at the empty space where the vehicle had been. "It must have been a mighty demon."

"Not so strong but a good demon," said Zolkan. "Merrisen honeycombed world with these pigeon-brained things for his own use. Other demons use them sometimes."

"He waited for one of those carriages to come, then just rode it? How'd he control where it went?"

"Merrisen powerful enough to summon, then direct," explained Zolkan. "But no longer. Some roam, going from spot to spot. We caught one of those."

Kesira shook her head in amazement. She had never suspected that such a network existed. "Do these tunnels reach into the Yearn Mountains?"

"Within ten miles of your nunnery," said Zolkan.

"How do you know this? You've never shown such knowledge before."

"No need to tell all I know, is there?" The *trilla* bird jumped from her shoulder and flapped a few feet to land in front of another large diameter of *tulna* stone. He made pecking motions at it, anxious to be under way. Kesira went to the stone and laid her hands against it. Try as she might, the stone door refused to budge. Only when Molimo came over and began pushing did it move slowly.

Kesira boldly walked through to the chamber on the other side, not expecting the reception she received. Hairy arms grabbed at her hair and face. Clawed hind feet came up to savage her belly. And the creature's bulk made her stagger backward into Molimo.

An inarticulate cry erupted from Molimo's throat. The almost human sound turned to a wolf's snarl. Kesira slumped to the floor, hands clutching her belly, thankful the claws had missed the baby. In the center of the chamber Molimo and the ape creature faced each other, snapping and dodging, venting noisy challenges, looking for the other's weakness in order to end the battle.

"Zolkan, help him!" she cried.

But the *trilla* bird perched on a broken tile, not moving. Disgusted with her friend, Kesira shucked off the sling holding the baby and put him out of harm's way. She rushed to Molimo's discarded clothing, her hand almost closing on the sword hilt, but though her indoctrination had faded, she could not ignore Gelya's edict against using steel. Instead she grabbed Molimo's tunic and rushed forward, swinging it in front of her.

The ape creature turned large, luminous brown eyes in her direction. Yellowed, broken teeth clattered together, and an unearthly howl filled her ears. She didn't wait to see what further devilment this monster might give. She tossed the tunic as if it were a fisherman's net. It spun open, then fell over the creature's head, momentarily blinding it.

A gray streak passed her. Molimo's fangs found the beast's throat. Strong neck muscles bulged as Molimo ripped and tore, even as the ape creature's claws opened bloody streaks on the wolf's flanks. That raking motion weakened, then stopped when the last of the creature's life fled its carcass.

Molimo threw back his lupine head and howled in triumph. Kesira watched, sick to her stomach. Even though she would have died without the other-beast transformation seizing Molimo, she wished it could be otherwise. It was so difficult to care for someone who might view you as dinner.

The howling cut off in midnote. Quick green eyes darted about. The sensitive wolf nose sniffed the air.

Kesira almost fainted when she saw the bat fluttering crazily into the chamber. She had never been afraid of bats—real bats. This one robbed her of all feeling but dread.

A human girl's face had replaced the usual ratlike one.

"Kill you, kill you!" cried the bat, swooping low. Tiny fangs opened and closed just a fraction of an inch away from Kesira's nose. She swatted at the odious other-beast, then saw that it flew directly for the baby. Kesira's feet slipped on the blood-slickened floor and sent her sprawling facedown. She screamed and fought to get to the baby before the bat-thing.

Zolkan dropped like a stone, talons catching the bat just behind the neck. The *trilla* bird jerked sideways, lost airspeed, and fell heavily to the tile floor, still clinging to the bat. Another hard jerk produced a tiny snapping noise. The other-beast shrilled and died. Zolkan cast it away with obvious distaste.

"Jade infects too many," he said.

"That had been a little girl? A child?" asked Kesira in shock. The idea that the baby—*her* baby—might end up like that stunned her. "I've seen adults caught in the transformations but never a child. Why?"

There had been no reason for her to exclude small children from her mental image of those afflicted with the jade evil, but she had. Those either switching totally, like Molimo, or permanently caught or trapped halfway, had all been adults.

"This is a travesty," she muttered between clenched teeth. "Ayondela will pay for this. And Lenc—curse you, Lenc! If I desired your death before, it fades before the hatred I hold for you now!"

"Shush," cautioned Zolkan. "Jade power lets them hear anything, anywhere."

"Come for me now if this is so," Kesira challenged. "I'll meet you!"

A hand on her shoulder broke her insane rage. Molimo had undergone the transformation once more and had donned his clothing. The tunic had been tattered by the ape's claws, and blood soaked everything. He went to the white tile on the walls and wrote in blood, "Do not summon them until we are ready. Please!"

"But this is awful." Kesira sat cross-legged and stared at the girl-faced bat.

"Bad," agreed Zolkan. "Worse if we die."

"Did Merrisen always guard his chambers with the likes of that?" she said, forcing herself to look away from the bat-thing and toward the ape.

"It is other-beast too. Great power flows nearby. Ayondela is atop her mountain."

"We'll be battling their ilk?"

Zolkan's head bobbed up and down.

"Then let us get to it. My nerve might not last much longer." Kesira saw that the baby had watched their struggles with inhuman calm, but then, what did a mere babe in arms know of such atrocities against nature? She slung the boy comfortably and followed Molimo down the glow-tiled corridor.

They passed another of the orange *tulna*-stone barriers and into a cave. Kesira Minette left the cave to emerge into the bright light of day.

She gasped at the sight dominating the landscape.

Chapter Twelve

"THAT'S IMPOSSIBLE," Kesira Minette whispered. She took a step forward and stood, arms hanging at her sides. The single spire rose up with beauty so breathtaking, it couldn't be real. Pure white snow decorated the ebony trail spiraling up the dark red granite column like a portrait lifted from a master painter's canvas. No detail marred the perfection, but the mountain itself accounted for only a small portion of Kesira's awestruck gaping.

A tiny toy of a jade palace capped the peak. Sunlight reflected off the green sides in a dazzling display that highlighted the other stark colors.

"How large must it be?" she said, her voice returning to normal. "It looks so small, but the peak is immense. The palace must be larger than the Emperor's!"

"More, much more," agreed Zolkan. "Deadly too. Everywhere Ayondela has traps. No one invades. Thousands died constructing her hideaway." The *trilla* bird turned bitter. "She had birds fly up much. All died. All."

"Do you mean *trilla* birds? You're not large enough, Zolkan."

"Magicks made many large enough. Many thousands. All dead. The spells killed all, noble hearts bursting from effort." Zolkan made a spitting noise. "She is shit. Worse! Ayondela not fit to live."

Kesira wobbled slightly, light-headed. Her inchoate plan to offer the baby to Ayondela in exchange for her neutrality

135

seemed naive. But her rune sticks had indicated that as the solution to the problems posed by the female demon.

"I can't comprehend such magic," Kesira admitted. For the first time she had an inkling of the forces she opposed and how lucky she had been to defeat both Eznofadil and Howenthal. Wemilat had given her some protection, and Kesira had to admit that only demons unseen and unmentioned opposing Ayondela had brought victory.

Who were her allies now? Wemilat the Ugly had died. Toyaga had perished. Left were a molting *trilla* bird and a young man whose tongue had been ripped out. Kesira wanted to cry when she looked down and added Raellard and Parvey's infant.

A bird, a baby, and a mute, together with a nun from an order whose patron had perished. The mighty conquerors!

Molimo snapped his fingers in front of her nose and broke her self-pitying reverie. In the dirt he etched the words, "We can do it. Doubt yourself and fail. Believe and succeed."

"You're sounding more like Gelya all the time," Kesira said, smiling weakly. "But there's not much choice, is there? If we don't try—and as bad as it looks, we've got the best chance—no one will. The Emperor is off in Limaden tending to the concerns of running the Empire. We've defied him because we thought we could do a better job of fighting the jade demons."

Kesira looked again at the majestic spire rising to stab the very clouds. White, fluffy cumulus clouds built below the summit, then rose.

She frowned when she noted the odd swirling of those clouds. They looked more like the product of a tornado than mountain-wind-whipped clouds.

"Those," she said. Molimo nodded.

Zolkan said, "Worse than mist in Lorum Bay. That was just practice. Those clouds are deadly. No one flies to the summit, not past clouds."

"Can we even climb the trail?" Kesira knew she had

received power enough from Cayabbib to dissipate small clusters of clouds—but those! She witnessed hurricane-force winds churning at a mile-deep layer of cloud ringing the mountaintop.

"We must."

Visions of the clouds surging around her, crystalline knives slashing at her face and hands and arms and any exposed portion of her body rose in the woman's mind. Such magical protection provided Ayondela more security than legions of soldiers. Who could mount an upward assault on the jade fortress in strengths enough to conquer?

"Stealth is our only hope. Can we sneak past the clouds?"

"Only go through. Very, very dangerous," said Zolkan.

The slick granite walls of the shaft hadn't formed naturally; they had been scoured clean by the slicing action of the clouds.

"We have a long way to go on foot," Kesira said. "I've lived in mountains all my life and know how deceptive distances can be. This looks so close—and lies so far away."

They began the trek to the base of Ayondela's fortress.

"The other-beasts haven't bothered us for the past four days," Kesira said. "Any reason why not?"

Molimo drew the answer in the dirt. "They fear Ayondela's power. No one stays this close to the heart of her magicks."

"But her power created them—or at least the power of the jade did."

"Come too near jade and it twists you," spoke up Zolkan. "Even I feel its awful influences when I wing closer. What must those with true power feel?"

"You mean other demons?"

"The jade pulls them like lodestones draw iron. Then it destroys." The bird shifted uneasily on her shoulder. Kesira reached down and plucked a blueberry from a bush and held it for Zolkan. His quick beak snared it from her palm without even touching her flesh. "Berry unripe.

Phooey!" Zolkan spat the skin and a few seeds out and rubbed his beak against her blouse.

"You complain too much."

"You complain more if this gives me shits." Zolkan wiggled his tail feathers above her shoulder to make his point.

"Do you feel the power of the jade? If it holds the other-beasts at bay, it must be immense." She glanced around nervously. Kesira imagined pressures mounting, but they were all in her mind. No physical pressure assailed her, and she didn't detect any magical one.

"I don't. Molimo might."

"Do you, Molimo? Feel Ayondela's magicks?"

Molimo had been leading the way down the winding trail. He stopped and looked back. Kesira swallowed hard when she saw his normally dark eyes flashing jade-green. Only when he transformed into wolf did he have such a feral, predatory look. But even as she watched the light died, and midnight eyes peered up at her.

Molimo shook his head, but Kesira knew he lied.

The other-beasts had dogged their steps, but she worried more about Protaro and Nehan-dir. While the quick transport under the mountains and far to the south had given her and the others many days' lead on both the Steel Crescent and the Emperor's Guard, she did not doubt that their determination and wrath at her would goad them into inhuman speeds. She had never made any secret of her destination. Protaro had to know—and Nehan-dir need only inquire of his jade patron.

"Is Lenc up there with Ayondela?" she asked.

"Who knows? We find out when we knock on front door," said Zolkan.

Kesira jumped when a bass voice said, "Such information might be had for a price."

She spun, whirling the pitiful staff she had fashioned from a small sapling. Like the other she had made, this one's wood proved too green for real strength. She needed hardness, not suppleness. And every time she tried to strip off the fledgling limbs, new ones grew. Her slightest touch generated life, not the death she wanted.

But this accounted for only a part of her problems. The baby slung in front of her body hindered her too. She silently thanked Molimo for his quick retreat along the path. The man-wolf stood at her side, sword drawn.

Kesira frowned. How had the stranger escaped Molimo's keen senses? And her own were scarcely less acute.

The man sat cross-legged on a boulder, looking down at them. The amused expression on his face irritated Kesira more than anything else. He wore a long, dark brown robe embroidered with silver-thread-contrived beetles. On his head he wore a floppy cap pulled down low over his left eye at what he no doubt thought a jaunty angle. From beneath the hat poked shocks of sandy hair.

But his expression, those laughing blue eyes, that damnable way he had, all made her feel inferior.

"Who are you?" Kesira demanded.

"Such manners. One expects more from a nun of your order. Gelya's order, is it not? I detect the fine nuances in your speech, the way you walk along the trail—most delightful when observed from the proper angle, I might say." He leered at her openly.

"Molimo, Zolkan," she said. She began backing away and motioned for Molimo to do likewise. Zolkan buried his head under his wing and refused to look from his perch on her shoulder.

"Don't leave. Please! Have I offended you? What did I say? I get so lonely in these hills. No one comes along this way anymore, not since *she* built *that*." He pointed at the jade palace on the summit of the spire.

Kesira didn't follow the man's gesture. She had grown suspicious and noted that many warriors used such a motion to distract. From the corner of her eye she saw that Molimo didn't look away, either. Kesira felt vindicated. Molimo suspected this man, too, but of what?

"You live nearby?"

"Oh, yes, of course I do. For many years. It is so

peaceful in the hills, except during the winter months. Then there're continual snowstorms. Nasty ones but you grow used to them. I have. I even like them a little now. But for this time of year! Ah, nowhere in all the realm is there a finer spot."

"Who are you?"

The man slid down from the boulder and landed lightly. He made a bow Kesira thought more mocking than courtly.

"I supposed everyone knew me. How could I have been so mistaken, eh? I am Norvin. There are other names that go along with it, but you'd never remember them, so why bother?"

"Pleased to meet you," Kesira said insincerely.

"Your friend must be the doughty Zolkan, this one without tongue is Molimo, and you are Kesira Minette. And the baby." Norvin started to touch the child, then stopped, his face losing all expression. He glanced over at Molimo. "This one's power is ... ample," Norvin said. Before Kesira could ask what he meant, the brown-robed man danced away.

"You must come and dine with me. Such a feast it will be. Never has anyone tickled your palates like I will."

"How do you know our names?" Kesira asked.

"You are famous throughout the realm. Aren't you the sister of the Mission? Yes! The gold sash, while the worse for wear, shows it. I was right!"

Kesira saw that she'd get no straight answer from Norvin. She tried a different approach. "You mentioned paying for information."

"But of course. All is for sale. I am the ultimate broker of any and all information. You need to know of Ayondela's palace? I have explored far into the cutting clouds and can sell you a map. Farther? You need only ask— and pony up the appropriate amount of coin. *I can be bought!*"

Norvin made it sound like a virtue.

"I'm not sure you have anything worth purchasing,"

Kesira said. "Come, let's be on our way. We still have a few hours of sunlight before the mountains rob us of day."

"It is worth more than the mountains themselves, what I can sell you. For, you see, I am a mage of some power. Some *immense* power."

"Why do you stay in Ayondela's shadow?"

"It . . . feeds me. I take what she discards and grow wiser from it."

"You," Kesira accused, "are not a demon?"

"I? Hardly. Oh, that is rich. She thinks I am a demon." Norvin shook his head and laughed at her. "While I am powerful, I am not *that* powerful. Except in one way."

"We have no need to listen to his blitherings," she said, turning to leave. If he intended to stab them in the back, Kesira decided that this might be better than having Norvin bore them to death with his egotistical bragging.

"You might have noticed that I use words well. I am a very oral person."

"I'm sure," Kesira said, tiring rapidly.

"I speak well, I sway the masses, should I ever encounter any—and I offer Molimo the power of speech. I have the power. I can restore his tongue."

Kesira stopped dead in her tracks. Turning slowly, she stared at the self-proclaimed mage in amazement.

"Yes, Lady of Gelya's Mission, it is true. Every word of it," Norvin said.

"You can give Molimo back his speech?"

"I can—and I will. For a price."

"No price can be too high for this."

What Norvin named was too high. "I want the baby," the mage said, his blue eyes gleaming.

Chapter Thirteen

"IT'S EVER SO SIMPLE. I would think even one as clever as you could understand my proposition." Norvin stood with arms crossed and a superior look on his face. "You give me the child, I give back Molimo's tongue and his power of speech."

"That's not possible," Kesira said in a low voice.

"But of course it is!" exclaimed Norvin. He bounced around. "The power is mine. I am a mage and very good at what I do. Or," he said, cocking his head to one side as he stared at Kesira, "do you mean you won't surrender the baby?"

"Both."

"It can't be both," the mage said firmly. "No, absolutely not. I get so lonely out here. I see you wandering through with a child you don't really care a whit for, and I think to myself, 'Norvin, you master mage, what is missing from your life?' The answer is ever so easy to come by. Companionship."

"Get pet," grumbled Zolkan, daring to look out from under his wing for the first time.

"I had a *trilla* bird once," Norvin said lightly. "I ate him."

"He'd do same with baby," said Zolkan. "Never trust any who eats bird flesh. Cannibals! All are cannibals!"

"A young one to learn my trade, to grow with me, to share the experiences of this wondrous life. Imagine living in such splendor *and* being trained by the foremost mage

142

in all the world." Norvin swept his arm around to indicate the panoramic beauty of the countryside. Kesira couldn't help but follow that arm—partway. Her eyes stopped at the base of the spire holding Ayondela's jade palace. Slowly she studied every rock, every imperfection in the column until she came to the jade structure atop it.

Living in the shadow of such evil was no fit life for anyone, even a braggart like Norvin.

"Ah, you fear the young one's life because of Ayondela. Do not. She never notices that which is so close at hand. Her gaze goes out to the rest of the land. She fails to see me. She overlooks me as she looks over me. The baby would be safe to grow into manhood here."

"What magicks do you control that you can restore a tongue magically sundered?"

"My patron is noted for healings. You've certainly heard of him. Dunbar?"

Kesira said nothing. Close ties with a demon explained Norvin's knowledge. She had no doubt that the elevated society of demons buzzed with all that happened concerning Lenc and the others. Their existences were threatened, but most were powerless to fight the jade. She had considered most demons' desire to ignore all that happened and decided that the demons were just like humans—all too willing to believe conditions would improve without their help. Was Dunbar different?

Molimo caught her eye. He slowly shook his head. Kesira wondered if the man-wolf read her mind. At times it seemed so. At times it seemed that she read his thoughts.

"What use is the child to you? A burden, nothing more. He'd be a cherished part of my household. But come, I promised dinner such as you've never tasted before. Come and see how I dine in gourmet style every night."

"Eats *trilla* birds," complained Zolkan. "Eat shit before you dine at his table."

Norvin laughed in delight. "No *trilla* meat on this day's menu. Come and see for yourself."

The brown-robed man almost danced down the trail.

Kesira tried to understand his motives and failed. He seemed a happy enough sort, even addlepated, but she detected undercurrents of something more. No man in his right mind lived this close to the bastions of Ayondela's power without being touched—adversely.

"Come and look, see the sky? Those clouds mean nothing to the sky. The vast azure vault is limitless, Ayondela's power limited to a few paltry clouds of crystal knives."

Kesira let Norvin rattle on with his pointless speech. The beauty of the Sarn Mountains affected her, but her mind kept returning to the spire and the jade palace atop the spire. *That* was her goal; *that* might be her death.

"Wait," the mage said, thrusting his arms out straight on either side of his body. From behind he took on the aspect of some brown-winged bird of prey. "There is movement all around us. Evil stalks us."

Molimo shook his head and tapped his ears. He saw and heard nothing. In her ear Zolkan whispered, "Crazy as pigeon shit. Let him be. We can go on without him. Lies about Molimo's tongue."

"What is it you see?" Kesira called to Norvin. "We don't see anything."

"What?" the man bellowed. "How is that possible? You, the demon killers, do not detect them? They're everywhere. Everywhere!"

Even as the mage stomped around, flapping his arms and making odd gestures, Kesira sensed the presence of *others*. Not other-beasts but something deadly—and magical.

Whirlwinds exploded into flesh-searing violence all around. Dust blasted forth to blind and sting, and feathery fingers of mobile air ripped at Kesira's clothing. Her wolf-skin skirt flapped wildly and tripped her, bringing the woman to her knees. Zolkan was blown off her shoulder in a spray of green- and blue-tipped feathers, and the baby's hands clutched at her with as much strength as any full-grown adult.

"Molimo!" she shouted into the teeth of the wind. "Where are you?"

Of the man-wolf there was no trace. Kesira squinted into the dust storm and sought out Molimo. Zolkan could find shelter behind a small rock; Molimo might change to wolf form. She wanted to avoid that transformation in the mage's presence. While Norvin probably knew of this additional affliction, Kesira wanted it kept secret if he didn't. People reacted with instinctive hatred for the other-beasts.

She found Molimo and clung to him. But even through the cloaking of the brown dust she saw the man's eyes change from coal-black to glowing jade-green. Power emanated from his body in palpable waves, but he fought the shape-change. Kesira felt his body quivering as he used every ounce of his being to prevent the animal metamorphosis.

"Good, Molimo," she shouted. "Fight it. Fight it!"

Even as she spoke Kesira thought she heard Molimo say to her, *Wind devils. Norvin summoned them!*

Hands grabbed for her. Kesira struck out and landed a fist on her unseen attacker. Molimo's arm snaked around her waist. Together they stood against the wind's onslaught.

"It's getting stronger," she cried. "Find shelter."

There is none.

Kesira wiped dust from her face and stared at Molimo. "You spoke," she said, not quite believing it. The man-wolf shook his head. Kesira was distracted by the baby trying to crawl up the front of her blouse. She held the infant in her arms, astounded at the baby's strength. Only a few months old and he possessed the coordination of a three-year-old.

Pale eyes stared at her and turned her queasy. Was it Molimo speaking or the baby? Intelligence shone from the child's eyes. She believed in that instant that he was the offspring of a demon father and a human mother.

"No!" she cried. Metaphor turned to reality. The whirlwind of dust developed visible teeth, snapping, opening and closing ever closer. Teeth of rock and dust and debris surged up and plummeted to engulf her. Kesira screamed, turning her back and hunching over to protect the child. Molimo twisted around and interposed his body between her and the disembodied teeth.

Kesira cringed, waiting for the impact. It never came. She opened her eyes and saw nothing of the churning dust. Cautiously relaxing, she discovered nothing but a tranquil trail.

"What happened?" she asked.

Molimo sat down heavily, green eyes fading to a more normal black. He shook, and sweat soaked his clothing. Whatever effort he had expended, it had been prodigious to drain him like this. From behind a rock a few yards distant came a familiar squawking noise. Zolkan pulled himself up to the top of the rock, unhurt but minus a few more feathers. The *trilla* bird staggered around as if drunk, then righted himself.

"There," came Norvin's satisfied voice. "Took care of the devils. Awesome expenditure of magicks on my part too. Did you not cherish the skill with which I wielded the spells?"

"You didn't get rid of those . . . things. They just went away."

"Nonsense. Of course I dispersed them. Frightful strain, but there's no mage who can honestly call himself my peer. One sorceress might be able to claim an equal skill, but that is neither here nor there. Come along. I did promise you a fine dinner."

"Do these whirlwinds come often?"

"Only since Ayondela finished her jade palace. I think they might be the souls of some of the workers killed during the construction. Thousands died. Then again, it might be nothing of the sort. What's the difference? With me you are safe. Come, come!"

Norvin skipped down the trail like a schoolboy. Kesira

and Molimo followed, more fearful of disobeying the demented mage than anything else at the moment.

"Here. Isn't it lovely? All mine. Years to build but worth it; well worth it, yes!"

The quaint house did have a certain charm. Norvin had used the side of a mountain for one wall and followed the contours of the land with the rest of the structure. Tasteful, sedate, it seemed at odds with Norvin's flamboyant—and insane—nature.

"Come in. We'll be perfectly safe from those terrible wind devils. They never stray too close to the mountain slopes. Breaks them apart into eddies."

The inside of the house was as neatly appointed as the exterior. If Kesira hadn't met Norvin she would have thought this house belonged to a prosperous farmer or landowner.

"Your rooms are at the top of the stairs. Go clean up. Pick whichever rooms suit you—or room, eh?" Norvin winked broadly, a lewd leer rippling along his full lips. He left them standing in the entryway without uttering another word.

Molimo fidgeted, but Kesira took his hand and led him up the stairs. "We might as well enjoy this," she told him. She opened the first door on the right and gasped. Even the Empress's bedchamber couldn't have been so sumptuous.

"Look at the bed. It . . . it's so comfortable. And there's a bath!" Hot water steamed in the ceramic tub. "And the wardrobes have clothing." She took out one Imperial ball gown and held it up. If a tailor had spent days working on this gown, it couldn't have been more perfectly suited for her in style and color and fit. "It's as if we found paradise."

Molimo shook his head. He went to the full-length mirror, dipped his finger in a washbasin next to it, and quickly wrote, "Norvin is not to be trusted."

"I know that. The whirlwind? He caused it?"

Molimo nodded. Kesira didn't ask how the man knew.

He sensed magicks more easily than she, having been touched by the worst of the jade rains when Lenc destroyed Merrisen.

"You will not give up the child?" wrote Molimo.

"No," she said. "I do not deal in human flesh. Not even if it restores your tongue."

"I heal faster now," Molimo continued. "Soon I will be able to speak again."

Kesira worried at this illusion so dearly held by Molimo. Bodies did not regrow severed organs or limbs, yet he no longer appeared the fuzzy-chinned youth. He had developed—aged—rapidly. Kesira frowned as she realized for the first time that Molimo now looked years older than she, rather than years younger. This had occurred within the span of a few months.

"Good water," came Zolkan's squawk. The bird dived into the warm bathwater and washed the grime from his feathers. When he emerged to perch on the edge of the tub, what feathers he had left shone with a brilliance that dazzled Kesira. "Now to eat. No decent meals on the trail. Blueberries, pah!"

"They kept you alive," chided Kesira. "Be thankful for them. A hungry person never listens to reason—not that you do even when your belly's full."

"Listen to reason," Zolkan declared. "Seldom hear it, though."

From below came Norvin's loud shout, "Dinner is served in one hour. Don't be late or I throw it to the animals."

"Your big chance, Zolkan," said Kesira. "Keep us locked in and you get all the meal."

The bird didn't appear pleased at that prospect.

Bathed and clothed in finery from the wardrobes provided by Norvin, they sat down to dine at the elegantly appointed table. Candles burned with fragrant softness, delicate china and silver flatware graced each setting, and effervescent wine bubbled in crystal goblets.

"It is so seldom that anyone blunders in my direction.

A feast to celebrate!" Norvin clapped his hands. Floating unattended from the side of the room came trays heaped high with steaming viands of every description. Zolkan hopped to the table and pecked at one suspicious dish presented in a circle of *trilla* bird feathers. He turned a beady eye toward Norvin but said nothing. Zolkan settled down and began eating, making no attempt to show good manners.

"This is all so elaborate," Kesira said, "for you to have prepared by yourself. You must have a staff of a dozen or more to maintain the place."

"Just myself," Norvin said. "And a spell or two to aid me."

Norvin waved his hand indolently and brought forth a new round of floating dishes. Kesira watched, remembering the dust storms that had come upon them so suddenly. She knew nothing of magicks and spell-casting, these being rare traits even in such power centers as Limaden, but it struck her that only a matter of degree separated this display from the miniature tornadoes.

"My patron is quite generous in imparting spells to me," Norvin went on. "That's why I am so sure I can restore Molimo's tongue."

"In exchange for the baby."

Norvin lifted his crystal goblet and inclined his head in Kesira's direction. He sipped, the bubbly wine apparently tickling his nose. Norvin smiled, then laughed. "I do so love this wine."

"Trading a life for Molimo's tongue is not to my liking," Kesira said.

"Ah, I detect Gelya's light touch in your answer. Human dignity, nobility of soul, never trade a life for a life. What a bore Gelya was. Not that I am glad to see him go, mind you." Norvin finished off his wine with one large swallow. "Go rest, sleep on this weighty matter. Come the morrow, you might see differently."

Norvin looked from Molimo to Kesira. "Imagine what

it would be like hearing his lover's lies whispered in your ear at night, eh?"

Norvin stood and left abruptly, not giving Kesira time to retort.

"Food tastes like shit." Zolkan spat out a mouthful on the intricately woven gold tablecloth.

"It took you three helpings to decide that?" Kesira said, her mind on Norvin's offer. She dismissed it. While she felt some responsibility to Molimo, he had healed enough to be able to look after himself. The infant was another matter.

"*Pah!*" Zolkan wiped his beak on a napkin and fluttered to sit on her shoulder. "Time to sleep." With that, the *trilla* bird tucked his head under a wing and dozed off.

Kesira and Molimo ascended the stairs, self-consciously hand in hand. "Sleep well, Molimo," she said. He started to protest, but she gently pushed him away. Inside her room she closed the door and leaned against it, tears in her eyes.

"Duty," she said. "I have my duty to perform. Revenge. Nothing else must intrude." Kesira hated the idea that she would ever consider trading another's life for Molimo's tongue, yet Norvin's offer tempted her sorely. It showed the depths of how much she did care for the man—love? Dare she deny that it was love that produced such thoughts? And how badly she had been disturbed by all that had happened since Lenc destroyed her nunnery, her friends, her patron, her universe.

She went to the baby and gently rocked him. He slept soundly. She placed him back in the wood cradle, thinking that here he would be safe and cared for. Surely Norvin's magicks could feed the baby.

Kesira forced such images from her mind. The boy was not hers to barter with like a sack of oats. And the rune sticks had said that Ayondela's rampage would be halted because of the baby.

She reached into her battered leather pouch and pulled out the bone box containing the five carved rune sticks.

With a quick toss she sent them flashing across the slick bedspread. They landed with soft plops, their pattern meaningless. Again Kesira cast. Again no reading was possible.

"Too close to Ayondela?" she wondered aloud. "Too confused on my part to read? Or is it Norvin's meddling?" She had no clear notion which of those answers might be true.

Tired, she took off the elegant gown and hung it in the wardrobe. Kesira slipped between the satin sheets on the soft bed and let her body relax totally. She floated off to a deep sleep, resting better than she had in weeks.

When she awoke the next morning, the baby was gone.

Chapter Fourteen

KESIRA MINETTE LAY in bed staring at the empty cradle. Her mind tumbled and spun without direction until she forced herself to sit up. No emotion rose. All feeling had become deadened by the loss.

Molimo burst into the room, sword in hand.

What . . . ?

Kersira looked up, her listless attitude such that she didn't even question that she'd heard Molimo speak.

"Norvin must have kidnapped the baby. They all want him. Why is he so important? Captain Protaro had him kidnapped. Nehan-dir tried to steal him away. Now a mage without a sane thought in his head takes him from under my nose." Kesira spoke in a voice devoid of emotion. "It might be best to let Norvin keep him."

"No!" squawked Zolkan, fluttering around. "Rune sticks say baby is needed for Ayondela's defeat."

Kesira stretched to where she'd placed the carved bone box. She tossed out the engraved sticks again. This time they fell into a readable pattern.

"The baby is the key to Ayondela's rampage," Kesira said. "That's what the runes tell me."

Angrily she jumped from the bed, throwing back the covers. She stormed around, emotions flaring uncontrolled now. "Why do the runes sometimes speak to me and other times say nothing? What is *wrong?*"

Zolkan landed on her shoulder and dug in his talons

until she calmed down. "It is art, not science. You cannot always expect total success."

"I feel as if someone is *sending* me the messages. I am not responsible for them. I only act as a conduit." She slumped to the bed, head in hands. "It's as if the times I am unable to read the rune sticks are when the sender is not noticing me. Other times, the message is clear. That must be it. It must be!"

"Demons communicate in odd ways," muttered Zolkan. The *trilla* bird looked over at Molimo, who crossed the room and sat beside Kesira, his arm snaking around her shoulders.

"They all want the boy. The boy. We haven't even given him a name. Why don't I call him Raellard after his father?"

"Boy's father was a demon," pointed out Zolkan. "Raellard and Parvey Yera both agreed on that."

"Or Masataro or something else?" Her voice turned shrill with mounting hysteria. "He deserves a name. He's being used as a punting ball in this madness. Why shouldn't he have a name?"

Molimo's arm tightened. She fought, but the man proved too strong for her to easily break away. Instead she turned and buried her face in his shoulders. Hot, salty tears dampened his shirt. Molimo held her awkwardly and made soothing sounds deep in his throat.

It will be all right.

Kesira jerked away, eyes wide. "You spoke!"

Molimo shook his head.

"I *heard* you."

"I heard nothing," said Zolkan. "You imagined it. You are distraught by loss of baby. If we are to recover pink wormy thing, we must seek Norvin's trail. A mage will not be easy to track down."

"I didn't imagine it. I *heard* him speak. Molimo, you did speak, didn't you?" She looked into the dark eyes. Tiny sparks of green danced in the depths, unreadable in their meaning. "Not with words for my ears, but I still *heard*. Didn't I?"

Molimo took her by the arms and lifted her. Gently he pushed her toward the pile of her travel clothes draped over a chair, then he spun and left the room. Kesira heard him rattling around, fastening his sword belt, preparing his pack for the trail. She sank back to the bed and simply stared after him. She had reached a point where nothing made sense, everything confused her, and she didn't have the slightest notion of what to do. Gelya had not given any succinct maxims to cover her present condition. Kesira realized, perhaps for the first time, how alone in the world she was.

She had slipped out of the neat order imposed by society. No longer did she have an order to provide stability and guidance. By denying Emperor Kwasian's soldiers when they came for the baby, Kesira had dissociated herself from an even greater social structure than family. She had disobeyed the Emperor's direct order.

To whom did she go for guidance? Where did she turn for reassurance? Kesira knew now she had clung to the baby with the feeble hope that this might turn into a family for her. The structure the child gave to her existence far outweighed any usefulness against Ayondela.

"We are your family," said Zolkan, as if understanding perfectly what troubled her. "Molimo and I and baby are all family."

Kesira dressed silently, her mind still in turmoil. Life had turned into a giant puzzle for her, with most of the pieces missing. Worst of all, she had no idea where the boundaries were anymore.

Every footstep cost her that much more of her precious energy. Kesira felt she had come to the end of her life's journey. Too tired to think, she settled down and began humming to herself. Zolkan craned his head around and stared at Molimo, who listened.

"Your death song?" asked Zolkan.

"It will be completed soon," she answered. "I had only a few lines written before. When I left the nunnery to go to Blinn, three lines had suggested themselves. Now I've added ones about the Quaking Lands and Wemilat and Eznofadil and Howenthal. And Rouvin, yes, about him— and my own failure."

"Failure?"

"Something prevented me from loving him as he loved me. He died with my name on his lips. I mourned his loss but nothing more."

"He was a braggart," said Zolkan. "He loved only himself."

"He was a hero."

"Molimo is hero. He faces with courage his affliction every day. You do heroic things and you have no idea of what is heroic. *Pah!*" The *trilla* bird launched himself from the nun's shoulder and flapped hard until he became a tiny green dot in the cloudy sky. Then even this reminder of the bird vanished.

"I've insulted him. Why?" she asked.

Molimo dropped to the ground beside her and rapidly wrote, "A useless life is an early death. Yours has meaning."

"What meaning? Sister Fenelia and the others are gone. I have disobeyed the Emperor. I can't even properly tend an infant."

"He is the focus of much power. Power beyond our comprehension."

"Mine, yes," Kesira said thoughtfully, "but yours? I often wonder."

"My power returns after being caught in the jade rain, but slowly, too slowly," Molimo wrote.

"What power? Speech?"

He nodded. Kesira sighed. Molimo was deluding himself; just as she was, trying to convince herself that the world would return to the peacefulness she had known within the Order of Gelya.

Molimo pointed to the faint scuff marks on the dusty trail they followed into the hills. Every step took them closer to the base of the spire holding Ayondela's jade palace. For this Kesira felt some small relief. Norvin's hurried flight had been in the direction they needed to go.

"The boy is getting hungry by now," she said. In spite of her intention to name the baby, she hadn't. Something stopped Kesira short of actually putting to voice the "proper" name. It had to be more than the idea that a name bound them together. As far as Kesira was concerned, the baby might as well have been her natural-born son.

"Norvin's magicks might hold hunger away," wrote Molimo. "The mage goes to meet another."

"How do you get that from the spoor?" For the first time in the three hours since leaving Norvin's neatly appointed house, curiosity got the better of her.

"The baby is of no use to a mage, any more than he is to Emperor Kwasian."

"You're saying that it was the Emperor's demon Lalasa who wanted the baby and therefore it must be Norvin's patron who does also?"

"Yes," Molimo wrote. "The baby is a focal point for demonic interest."

"Norvin's patron," mused Kesira. "Dunbar, he said. Do you know this one?"

Molimo shrugged. What this gesture meant Kesira couldn't say. She heaved herself to her feet and told Molimo, "We'd best be on our way. There're still many hours of light left, even here."

High peaks to the west shortened the summer day by several hours. Kesira knew that Molimo could track as well at night as in the daylight, but she preferred to be able to see the tracks herself. She believed implicitly in the man-wolf's ability but saw no reason to take chances; on herself she could always depend.

The loud warning caw from above brought Kesira's green staff whipping around and into a defensive pose. Beside her Molimo drew his sword. Zolkan flashed into sight, beating his wings so hard in a braking action that his pinions creaked and snapped with effort.

"Many other-beasts ahead!" he warned. "Norvin has made them angry. They come along trail. Flee! Hurry, hurry!"

Kesira had just pulled herself onto a dusty boulder when the first of the loping jackal creatures came into view. It stopped and turned to look at her and Molimo standing on the rock. Jet-black, the jackal looked more like a shadow come to life than a living, breathing animal. It threw back its head and let forth a mournful cry that stirred hidden emotions within Kesira.

"That sounds so much like the 'Lament of Lost Souls,'" she said wistfully. "We used to sing it when we were depressed." The jackal looked up at her, agony in its eyes. The howling took on more musical overtones—this other-beast remembered its human origins.

"Is it afflicted like you?" she asked Molimo. "Can it change back into human form?" So many of the other-beasts had become trapped in mid-transformation. She thought of the bat with the small child's face and repressed a shiver of dread.

Kesira saw a legion of the beast-humans lumbering along the trail. One man pulled himself along on arms; from the waist down he had become a diamond-patterned snake. Another's body had remained untouched by the changing evil of the jade; her head was that of a *prin* rat. All members of the pack showed both animal and human features. Only the jackal seemed to have made a complete metamorphosis into animal—and Kesira wondered. Did the brain still function as human?

She found that it did not matter. No matter what condition these poor creatures had been cursed with, they all had one thought in their brains: *Kill.*

The jackal yipped sharply, then leapt. Kesira swung her staff around, off-balance. The woman realized that she had become so used to carrying the baby that she now compensated for his weight—and the weight was gone. Kesira fell to her knees, skinning both of them, but the hard end of her staff crashed soundly into a lupine head.

No real damage was done, but the jackal fell back to the ground, piteously yelping.

The other creatures attacking did not yelp in pain or surprise. They attacked with a silent ferocity that startled Kesira.

Molimo's blade swung in a red arc, blood spraying as he defended her right side. Zolkan dipped and darted, talons seeking eyes, beak ripping at any flesh exposed overlong. But the three of them together could not hope to withstand the onslaught of so many other-beasts.

"Leave us, Molimo," she shouted. "Use your spell and get away. You must save the baby. Please! Do it!"

Zolkan's strong neck twisted and ripped off a bit of fur, part of an ear still attached to it. The *trilla* bird spat it out and ducked, fluttering away from a snake beast that struck and landed heavily, split tongue flicking in anger at its failure.

"What of me?" the bird protested. "Do I matter so little?"

"I hoped you would stay with me for a while longer," the woman said. "Then you can go."

Kesira's elbow snapped as she swung her staff around as hard as she could, missing her target. Impact of wood on rock sent a shock up into her arm that caused pain every time she moved.

"Go now," she urged.

Kesira felt a curious mixture of relief and betrayal when she noticed that Molimo had vanished. Irrational as it was, she hoped he would stay with her. But that would only have meant his life also. She had no way to escape; he did. One of them should survive to continue the fight against the jade demons.

Still...

Kesira swung her staff low and broke a *chillna* cat's leg. It tumbled off the boulder and disturbed the attack of two other creatures. She took the brief respite to gasp in deep lungfuls of air. And then the attack came again, from two sides now that Molimo had left.

She forced calm onto herself. As she fought she concentrated on her death song. Kesira hadn't thought it quite finished yet, but she knew she had to be wrong. A final verse, then death. If only she could have included one about Lenc's demise and how she had exacted revenge for his killing of Gelya.

Kesira shrieked in surprise as the huge boulder beneath her feet moved. Slowly at first, then with increasing speed, it rolled forward onto the attacking other-beasts. Like an acrobat at the Spring Fair, she danced along quickly to keep her balance atop the rock. Cries, human and animal, and a mixture of both human and animal, echoed up as the rock caught many of the attacking creatures by surprise. Others, including the jackal, darted out of range, but their spirit had been broken. Not even the most vicious of nips and barks from the jackal rallied his forces to stir up the attack to its former intensity.

Zolkan pecked out an eye. Kesira broke one creature's neck with a vicious swing of her staff and kicked another in the belly. Molimo scooped up a creature and snapped its spine.

The jackal eyed her, then backed off. Turning tail, it ran down the path.

Kesira carefully walked along the top of the boulder and looked behind it. Some immense force had moved the rock at the precise instant it'd do her the most good. At first Kesira saw nothing. She frowned as sunlight caught faint depressions in the bedrock. Sliding down and scraping her knees further, Kesira bent to look at the depressions.

"Footprints," she said in wonder. "It's as if someone pushed against the boulder so hard, he left footprints in solid rock."

Zolkan squawked and alighted on her shoulder. "Molimo's strength grows," the bird said.

"*He* did that?"

A presence made her spin, staff ready. Molimo smiled broadly. Kesira's eyes dropped to the man's boots. The soles had been worn off—by the effort of pushing a boulder as large as a peasant's hut?

"How did you do it?" she asked. "You *did* move the rock?"

He nodded, then motioned that they must hurry. Kesira agreed but still wanted an answer. It wasn't forthcoming. No human could have started the rock rolling.

"Did Toyaga give you more than the non-noticeability spell?" she asked. Molimo turned slightly, the slight smile on his lips both ethereal and mocking. Kesira went cold inside when she saw that his coal-black eyes burned with emerald brilliance.

"He does not partake of jade," said Zolkan, seeing her frightened reaction. "Do not worry about Molimo. He is..." The *trilla* bird's words trailed off. Another joined them.

Kesira stopped to glare at Norvin. The mage held the infant as if the child were nothing more than a sack of potatoes. In spite of what must have been an uncomfortable position, the baby did not cry out. If anything ever disturbed his calm, Kesira had yet to discover it.

"You really ought to have stayed and savored the hospitality of my manor," Norvin said. "The magicks would have kept you comfortably for many years."

"I want the baby back." Her words snapped out, as brittle as glass and as sharp-edged as a knife.

"Now, Kesira, you know that's just not to be. We all have our mission in this world. The game must be played to its end, and I have taken the marker. Do return and let us be."

"Your pack of other-beasts didn't stop me. You won't, either."

"That bothers me." Norvin frowned. "Usually they are very proficient. Not too many returned from this foray. You are more than you appear, Kesira. And your friends surprise me also." Norvin's eyes fixed on Molimo.

Kesira gave the mage no chance. She shoved down hard on her staff, using it to help launch her attack. Four steps, five, six. The staff whipped around at knee level. Seven steps, then eight, and the wood rod impacted on Norvin's thigh. The mage dropped, howling in pain. She used the recoil off his thigh to whirl the other end back around to crash into his upper right arm. From the way it turned flaccid, she knew she'd meted out a good blow.

A foot planted in the middle of the kneeling man's chest sent him tumbling onto his back. She reached for the baby. Pale eyes looked up at her with faint displeasure.

"You can't take him, you can't!" shouted Norvin.

"You won't," came a softer, more menacing voice. "I have plans for the boy that do not include one of Gelya's proselytes."

Kesira found herself frozen as she reached for the infant. Molimo came to her side, unhurried, and helped her straighten up so that she could face the newcomer.

The old man's long white beard came to his waist. Warts and mottled skin made him uglier than any other human Kesira had seen, and gnarled hands with knuckles the size of pecans reached for the baby. Insane thoughts flashed through her mind. What dice those knucklebones would make!

"Stop," the old man commanded. Kesira glanced around to see Zolkan fall from the sky as if dead. The heavy bird crashed to the ground a few feet away.

"He can do the same to you if he wants," said Norvin, painfully getting to his feet. He leaned heavily to protect his injured thigh, and his right arm still dangled uselessly. "My patron Dunbar is a greater mage than I."

"You fool," the demon Dunbar said without rancor. "All you know I have taught you."

"You can't take the baby. He'll starve."

"This is a matter of some interest," said the old man-demon. "How is it that you nurse the infant? But this is of only passing importance. I can suspend its life function to prevent starvation."

"But why? What is so vital that you'd do this to a poor orphaned child?"

"I expected more from you." Dunbar dismissed her out of hand.

Kesira saw that argument would not sway either Dunbar or Norvin. She reached down inside herself and found the old faith engendered by a lifetime of adherence to Gelya's teachings. Wemilat's kiss burned on her breast. And all that she had obtained from Cayabbib as he died now rose within her. She felt like a cauldron with uncooked portions of stew boiling around inside. Kesira pushed aside any confusion that might weaken her—and she acted.

Her staff arced up and came down squarely on the top of Dunbar's head. Even though the demon appeared to her as an old man, she showed him no mercy. The magicks locked within his frail-appearing body more than offset any physical disability.

The impact caused her to drop her staff. Pain lanced into her injured elbow and made her stagger slightly. But Dunbar dropped to the ground, unconscious.

"My patron!" shrieked Norvin, all pretense of urbanity peeled away. The mage swung on her, right arm shaking. He dropped the baby and used his left to steady his damaged right.

Molimo interposed his body between the mage and Kesira just as the miniature tornado took form. Teeth of wind and dust snapped and clacked and tore at Molimo's frame, but Kesira avoided the worst of the magical attack.

She rubbed her elbow and picked up her staff. They fought demons and mages and won! For an instant this revelation disabled her more than her injuries. Then she rejoined the battle. Norvin sent his whirlwind against Molimo; he couldn't break it apart and send it after both of them. Kesira attacked the mage with fervor, all her anger coming out as her staff rose and fell on his arms and shoulders.

"You can't do this!" screamed Norvin. "Stop this instant!"

"The baby," Kesira said with grim finality. "We're taking the baby."

A quick blow to the back of Norvin's knee sent him sprawling. While Molimo kept the whirlwind at bay she scooped up the baby.

"Come on. Let's get Zolkan and get away from here!"

Kesira took two steps toward the fallen *trilla* bird when all sensation left her body. She fell facedown in the dust, almost crushing the infant. Eyes focused on the rock beneath her face, but nothing else seemed functional. Kesira wanted to scream, but her lungs held no air. She suffocated by slow measures.

The vibrations in the rock told her that someone took the baby from her nerveless arms.

"Do you wish to live?" came the demon's angry words. "Yield to me!"

"I . . . I yield," she said in a voice almost too choked to be audible. Her lungs filled with life-giving air, and her limbs responded. The paralysis that had fallen over her like the first chilling snowfall of winter vanished.

Dunbar held the baby in his arms in a more reasonable fashion than Norvin had. The infant did not look happy at this turn of events, but neither did he cry.

"For what you've done I ought to kill you out of hand."

"Do it and be cursed," flared Kesira, angry at both the demon and her own failures. "You can't steal the baby!"

Bars of flame surged skyward between angry woman and demon. "Starve in there," Dunbar shouted. The demon stalked off, baby in his arms. Norvin licked his lips nervously, then hobbled after his patron. Through the shimmering, intense heat of the fiery bars Kesira saw the mage look back several times before rounding a curve in the trail and disappearing from sight.

Within the circle of flame both Molimo and Zolkan lay, unmoving. Kesira approached the barrier and cringed from the fierce heat. They were truly prisoners in Dunbar's magical prison. She saw no way to escape. None.

Chapter Fifteen

KESIRA MINETTE TURNED from her futile attempts to breach the flame barrier and knelt beside Molimo, hopelessness rising within her. Whatever spell Dunbar had used to paralyze her also held Molimo in thrall. She sat, legs crossed, Molimo's shaggy head in her lap. Ebon hair spilled out to cover the wolfskin skirt. She softly stroked the man's forehead, reflecting on how fate had doomed Molimo. He so easily became the wolf wearing a skin similar to her skirt, a hunter's prize, unable to control the animalistic instincts.

But Kesira wondered at the man. Both Norvin and Dunbar had hinted that Molimo's powers were not to be taken lightly. All evidence pointed to him pushing the boulder over onto the other-beasts. No amount of effort on a dozen men's parts could have budged such a massive stone, and yet he must have been responsible.

"Does the jade possess you so?" she asked softly. The blazing emerald in his eyes hinted that it might.

His eyelids fluttered; dark eyes stared up into her softer brown ones. "Welcome back to the world of the living," she said. "Don't try to move. Just rest for a few minutes. The spell wears off quickly enough, but you'll be a little queasy. I was."

Kesira knew that the effects passed almost immediately. She just didn't want for this moment to pass. But it had to. Molimo forced himself to a sitting position, studying carefully the flame bars holding them to this spot.

He quickly wrote in the dirt, "Have they left? I no longer *feel* Dunbar nearby."

"You sense him?"

"Not now."

"No," she said, "that's not what I meant. You mean, you can detect him in some way other than seeing or hearing?"

Molimo nodded, then pointed to his tongueless mouth. Kesira understood.

"A talent you can now use because of the action of the jade rains," she said. "If something is lost, there must be gain elsewhere. Balance, symmetry in the world, always exists. Gelya said that this was the fate of the universe."

"Fate?" he wrote.

She laughed. "My interpretation. If all things balance, then the sum must always be zero. Isn't it distressing to think that the best one can average between birth and death is mediocrity?"

Molimo stared at her curiously, then turned to examine the tiny columns of fire rising a hundred feet and more into the air. The extent of their circular prison came down to a diameter of less than ten paces. Molimo cautiously moved closer and closer to the dancing tubes of orange flame, testing every inch of the way. When he lacked but a few inches of touching, he winced and moved away. Blisters sprang up on the palm of the venturesome hand.

Kesira started to tend it, then stopped, watching in surprise as Molimo glared at his injured hand. The blisters sank back into the skin, and pinkness marking the sites of the wounds deepened and melted into the tanned area until no trace of damage remained. Molimo looked disgusted at the time wasted tending such minor problems, then began walking the circular area, less than an arm's distance from the flaming bars.

"Molimo, how'd you heal yourself so quickly?" Kesira asked. "Answer me!"

"I just do," he wrote. "Do you know how you heal yourself?"

"No, my body does it through its own knowledge. But I don't do it as fast. Why, you healed in seconds!"

He shrugged. "A second, a day, what's the difference? I still have no idea how my body does it." He continued his circling.

Kesira stared at him, then shook free of her mounting dread. Molimo changed daily—hourly. This hardly seemed the same man she knew a few months earlier lying beside the road, more dead than alive from the showering jade. This one moved boulders as large as huts, commanded spells given him by demons, and healed with a glance. He had aged visibly, now approaching middle age, but with this added age came power and ability. He had been touched, but how?

The imprint of evil jade burned too brightly for Kesira to bear it. She turned from Molimo and his surliness.

Kesira bent down and gently turned Zolkan over onto his back. The *trilla* bird lay as if dead. She tried to pry open one of his beady black eyes and failed in the attempt. While Molimo stalked around more like a wild beast than a man, she stroked over Zolkan's feathers and gently probed for some sign of injury. The bird still breathed; she thought he only experienced the effects of Dunbar's paralysis.

"Zolkan, are you awake?" she asked softly.

Wings twitched, then fluttered. Instinct took over. The bird curled his head under one wing. Kesira carefully pried the wing up and found the familiar black eye peering up at her.

"Let this bird die in peace." Zolkan moaned like one nearing death.

"The demon used a spell on you. You're all right, just a bit battered from the fall. You were twenty feet in the air when he paralyzed you with his magicks."

"Pig-shit demon," muttered Zolkan. Kesira knew then that he'd be fine. With a twitch of the tail feathers and an awkward twist, Zolkan got to his feet, then settled down like a hen roosting. He still lacked strength to do more than glare.

"Fry us," he grumbled. "Dunbar tries to cook us inside his oven and eat *trilla* bird meat. Damn cannibal!"

"You'll be able to get free," Kesira told him. "When you're strong enough, you can fly straight up and over the top of the flames."

"Catch fire and die," insisted the *trilla* bird. "Dunbar wants me fried, that . . . that product of diarrhea!"

"Calm yourself," soothed Kesira. "Molimo and I might be caught here, but you can get away." In a more desolate tone she added, "You might be our only hope for escape. I see no way for either Molimo or me to get through those bars."

The orange flames danced and licked at one another, scant inches apart. The heat reddened her skin and caused her to sweat profusely. Kesira took only one look at the ground to know that tunneling free was out of the question. They had the misfortune to be trapped in a particularly rocky stretch of the trail.

Kesira sat heavily in the dust and began running it through her fingers. Every time a tight, dry clump of dirt landed, a green sprout poked up. Curious, she stroked over the buds and saw new growth. Her touch accelerated growth.

"Sister Kai would have kept me in the fields all summer if I'd been able to do this at the convent," Kesira said, a little awed at how her mere touch seemed to foster life. It finally occurred to her that the staff hadn't grown its new limbs by itself; she had aided the growth.

"Isn't this amazing?" she asked of Zolkan. "It must be part of Cayabbib's legacy to me." She ran more dirt through her fingers and produced neat rows of weeds foolishly attempting to survive on the rocky path. This was a gift of great importance, but it did no one any good now. They were still trapped within the flaming prison.

Zolkan sputtered and swore, talons clicking against rock as he paraded around. Kesira started to lash out, to tell him that he made her nervous with his restless pacing. Gelya had always preached that those with patience received all that they desired. She failed to understand how simply sitting and waiting proved anything in her present situation.

The woman shifted the blue, knotted cord around her waist and took off the golden sash, now tattered almost beyond recognition. With loving care she straightened it the best she could, then wove it around the blue cord of her order. Idly she pulled out the bone box containing her rune sticks. A quick casting could hurt nothing.

Kesira's attention focused immediately on the result of the fall.

"Molimo, Zolkan, look," she said.

Zolkan waddled over, but Molimo continued his tireless circuit of their prison. "What do you read?" the bird asked. One wing reached out tentatively to point at the stack of five sticks.

"Ayondela. I see a female jade demon," she said. Kesira's face furrowed as she concentrated. Words and images bubbled up inside her head, unbidden. The casting of the rune sticks worked to free her inner senses, the ones she had such small control over.

Eyes closed, Kesira said, "I see myself facing Ayondela."

"Where?"

"In a room constructed entirely of jade. It might be inside her jade palace. I meet her, but there is no fear. Confidence rides at my shoulder."

"What happens?"

"Ayondela fears me. No, not me, but someone with me. I cannot see who it is. Perhaps Molimo."

"She does not fear him," Zolkan said with finality.

"The picture wavers." Her entire body floated with sweat now. Kesira kept her eyes screwed shut so tightly, her face began to ache with the strain. "I see no more of the confrontation. But the fear on her face!"

"What else?" prompted Zolkan.

"I . . . nothing. I can't see how to escape this imprisonment, but I must have if I am to meet Ayondela in her palace." Kesira opened her eyes and felt the sting of perspiration running into them. She wiped at the corners of her eyes, then peered through the flame bars to the majestic tower of granite holding Ayondela's jade palace.

Somehow she would make the journey to the top of that mountain. And Ayondela would fear her once she arrived.

Bleakness replaced her little thrill of precognition. Kesira Minette realized how tantalizing this glimpse had been and how it only served to make her more depressed over her imprisonment. Life had always been this way for her, ever since her parents had been slaughtered by brigands. The elder Minettes had been on their way to market. Their bountiful harvest insured an easy winter. With the profits from their grain they'd be able to stock in enough supplies from Blinn's fine merchants to weather any snowfall in the Yearn Mountains. But the brigands had foolishly struck as they went to market rather than waiting until they returned. With no solid coin or luxury goods to buy off the thieves and only a wagonload of grain to offer, both Rudo and Jensine Minette had been slaughtered by the brigands. All the while Kesira burrowed between the sacks of grain, fearfully peering out.

She had seen one thief slit her father's throat. What the rest had done to Jensine Minette had been forever burned into Kesira's memory.

Catatonic, she had sat and stared long after the brigands had left. Sister Fenelia had found her late that day and taken her into the Order of Gelya.

As kind as the sisters of the Order of Gelya were, nothing erased the evil memories of that autumn day. Kesira had spoken again and even laughed and frolicked with others her own age in the order, but the underlying sense of despair had been a constant companion, reminding her that Gelya's teachings were ideals and not necessarily attainable in a world populated with brigands. Now that emptiness rose within her and cast her into an arid desert without end.

"Can't fly over," squawked Zolkan.

"Eh? What's that?" she said, turning to the *trilla* bird.

"Spell turns flames inward near top. No flight out."

Kesira stared upward but failed to see what Zolkan meant. Her despair mounted, however, and she did not question him further. If he said he couldn't escape, he couldn't. And what good would the bird's escape do either her or Molimo? They had run out of allies. Toyaga had perished; so had Cayabbib; and Wemilat the Ugly had died defeating Howenthal. This Merrisen Zolkan spoke of so highly had been vanquished by Lenc in the battle that had robbed Molimo of his tongue and dropped bits of jade across the land; she had even been given a vision of Merrisen's destruction. Worst of all, her patron was no more.

"Dead," she murmured. "Gelya is dead."

"Despair doubles strength," said Zolkan.

Kesira turned her listless brown eyes to the bird. She frowned. "What are you talking about?"

"Did not Gelya say as much? Do you surrender this easily? You escape. You know that."

"But how?"

"You do," insisted Zolkan. "Runes say so."

"The rune sticks," Kesira said, shaking her head. "I have no idea what to make of them. Ever since Gelya was killed, the power seems to have grown within me, but what credence do I put on my interpretations? It's as if someone else is telling me what to say, slipping clues into my mind."

"Not all demons are strong," said Zolkan. "Most cannot oppose jade demons openly. Some sly. Some sneaky, but good too."

"You're saying there might be demons aiding me by giving hints through the rune castings?" Kesira almost laughed at this. "Why do they choose me? I am the last member of a dead order. The jade demons cannot fear me."

"Howenthal and Eznofadil do not fear you."

"They're dead."

"All more reason for Ayondela and Lenc to oppose you. No one else battles them. Human Emperor chases own concerns. Nehan-dir wants only power. You have slain two jade demons."

Kesira tried to force away the tenuous threads of Zolkan's ensnaring logic. So what if she had been successful to that extent? The most powerful of the demons rampaged throughout the land, usurping power and tightening control.

But she had aided Wemilat well. And Toyaga had been destroyed before Kesira battled Eznofadil. The power grew within her.

"Never mind," said Zolkan. "Nothing you can do. Sit, wait. Let Dunbar have baby."

"Damn your feathers," she snapped. "I am honor-bound to protect the baby. His father and mother died because of me." Kesira didn't question the truth of this. She used emotion to whip herself up into righteous indignation. "How dare Dunbar try to prevent me from following the honorable course through life? How *dare* he!"

Kesira shot to her feet and walked directly to the flame barrier. Her eyes watered as she stared unblinkingly. Resolve firmed—and something hidden deep inside stretched and stirred and came to life. Kesira reached out, her hand trembling. Then all nervousness passed. She knew what had to be done and how to do it.

She *knew*.

One hand gripped a bar. No flesh seared. No pain drove her back. Fingers wrapped around the flame bar; the woman began to tug. The stirring deep inside her soul became a writhing, seething, churning creature that gave her renewed determination. She thrust out her left hand and gripped the adjacent bar of pure orange flame.

Kesira sensed Molimo and Zolkan beside her. They added to her strength through their presence, but the true power came from reservoirs inside. Kesira began drawing the flame bars apart, not through force of muscle but through force of spirit. She was greater than any spell Dunbar might cast. Duty drove her. Honor demanded performance.

The bars parted. An inch. Two. Five. A foot. More.

Kesira looked past the barrier and to the mountain cradling Ayondela's palace. Surges of will allowed Kesira to separate the bars further. The nun saw a gray body jump past her: Molimo. A loud squawk, followed by a cascade of bright feathers, echoed back to her: Zolkan.

She took a step forward until the bars arched on either side of her body, bending at fluid angles never attempted by iron. For a moment she stood and stared in wonder. She had done this. Kesira Minette, orphan, alone in the world, her sisters slaughtered by powers beyond her comprehension. She had battled back and won.

Kesira took another step forward and dropped her arms to her sides. A loud hissing behind her caused her to yelp and jump away. The wolfskin skirt had begun to smolder and stink.

The brown-haired woman turned and stared in disbelief. She felt as if she had come out of a lifelong coma into a world brighter, more vibrantly alive, better. Kesira stared at the flame bars and saw how Dunbar had performed his magicks. While she could not duplicate the feat or destroy it, she knew full well how it had been accomplished.

"So simple, so elegant," she said, more to herself than to Zolkan, who fluttered down to land on her shoulder.

The *trilla* bird peered at her, then said, "You learn of worlds beyond your world."

"What do you know of that?" she asked. "You seem to know so much more than you reveal. Tell me! What's happened to me? How can I walk through spells of such potency?"

"Cayabbib. Wemilat. You accumulate demon power. You will never be demon, but now you use their gifts. You glimpse their world."

Kesira spun around, almost dislodging Zolkan from his perch. She narrowed her eyes and pointed down the trail. "They return. Dunbar and Norvin are coming back."

"Dunbar might have sensed your escape," said Zolkan. "Let's fly."

"Go on without me," Kesira urged. "I am going to get the baby back. I've not escaped from Dunbar's prison simply to turn my heel and flee like a craven."

"He is demon. Too strong!"

"You're the one who said I've accumulated Cayabbib's and Wemilat's power. Zolkan, I *feel* it within me. If I don't use it, I'll never know. Better to oppose Dunbar now than to meet Ayondela later and be unsure of myself."

"Wait for... Molimo." Zolkan sidestepped back and forth along her shoulder. His beak clacked when Dunbar and his tame mage, Norvin, holding the baby, walked into view.

Dunbar frowned when he saw Kesira and Zolkan outside the spell prison. "I sensed something amiss with my prison. It is good that I returned. You astound me with your resourcefulness. Or am I congratulating the wrong one? Where is your companion?"

"Molimo had nothing to do with our escape."

Dunbar laughed, obviously not believing her. "It is of no concern. I misjudged your ignorance of demonic matters. I shall tell you this once and only once. Do not attempt to interfere. You awaken angers best left slumbering."

"In the jade demons?" Kesira tried to hold back her own anger and failed.

"There, yes," said Dunbar. He shuffled forward until he stood squarely in front of the nun. "The order of the universe is shifting. These are uneasy times. If you find yourself a hidey-hole, you might weather the storms of change and survive in your pathetic way. Otherwise..." The demon shrugged thin shoulders to indicate that Kesira would be killed without any thought of mercy.

"You've been kind once," she said, her words laden with sarcasm. "You will be again."

"No." Dunbar missed her meaning, but Norvin caught it. The mage stepped forward and whispered hurried words into the demon's ear. Dunbar brushed him away as if the mage were nothing more than an annoying fly buzzing around.

"Now that the baby is in my control I have no need of anyone." Dunbar pulled himself erect. Kesira felt twinges in her joints. The demon cast another spell to immobilize her.

"What is the baby to you? To the jade demons? If they fear an infant so, why haven't they killed him before now?"

"Insane pride, belief that they were invincible. Lenc and the others refuse to believe that we enter the last days of their power. We have long debated the Time of Chaos, those of us who even dare mention it. Lenc does not believe it will ever happen—especially not with him in total power."

"You claim that Chaos is gripping the world now?" asked Kesira.

"Not yet." Dunbar glanced toward the baby. "Soon, unless the proper order of life is restored."

"Please," pleaded Norvin, holding the baby as if the child might turn into a snake and squirm free at any instant. "Let's not carry on like this. Please!"

"He is useful—to a point," Dunbar said of Norvin. Kesira blinked. The demon spoke to her as an equal and to his mage as if Norvin were nothing more than a menial laborer. "He does yeoman's work tending the child until I can instruct it properly."

Dunbar heaved a deep sigh. "Enough of idle chatter. Even a worm like Norvin can be right. I have suffered your presence too long."

Kesira fell to her knees as pressure engulfed her. From all sides came crushing planes, compressing her, trying to compact her to Zolkan's size. The full power of a demon turned against her.

Chapter Sixteen

KESIRA MINETTE GROANED in agony from the magicks compressing her. Nowhere did she find succor. Zolkan lay as if dead, one glassy eye staring up at the azure sky littered with fleecy, rapidly moving clouds. Of Molimo she saw nothing. And the pain! It mounted gradually, but simple twisting and turning did nothing to alleviate it.

"Norvin," she called. Her teeth clacked shut as Dunbar increased the pressure to the point that she almost passed out. "Norvin! The demon only uses you. Listen to his words. He scorns you!"

Her eyes blurred. Curtains of dark drew silently at the perimeters of sight, but still Kesira fought. The depths of her strength did nothing to fight off the crushing insistence of Dunbar's spell, but she detected weakness in the demon's rank: Norvin.

"Wait. She can be useful," said Norvin.

Dunbar waved his mage away, shooing him away like a noisome puppy following too closely.

"See?" Kesira grated out between clenched teeth. Her innards turned to jelly. Bones protested and threatened to break. Worst of all, her head felt as if Dunbar had placed it within the jaws of a vise. Every pass of his hand clamped down that much more firmly.

Had it all come to this moment? Kesira's death song lacked verses. She had composed many new ones to tell of her travails, but of Ayondela she had written too little.

And what of the baby? Nothing. She had concentrated on Eznofadil and Howenthal.

How could she die when she wasn't prepared? It wasn't Cayabbib's energy or Wemilat's protection that held back the demon's spell now; it was her own innate courage and strength of character. Dunbar tried to force her into early death, but she had obligations to meet.

Revenge had to be taken on Lenc for what he had done to her patron. Only Kesira Minette remained to do it.

Dunbar's eyebrows arched when he felt the stiffening of her resolve and the failure of his spell to further crush her.

The elderly appearing demon swung around when the sleek, gray form of a wolf flashed past. Kesira's eyes were filled with stinging sweat, but she caught sight of Molimo's vicious jaws closing on Norvin's throat. The mage gurgled hideously as he died. Molimo tossed his head and sent a spray of blood over Dunbar.

"He was mine!" shrieked the demon. "You . . . you're not an other-beast! You're—"

Dunbar never finished. Molimo whirled around, lithely stepped over the baby lying in the dust, and launched himself at the demon. Whatever spells Dunbar commanded held Molimo at bay. But the break in the demon's attention freed Kesira from her crushing, invisible prison. For a moment she fell forward onto hands and knees and panted, doglike.

Then she rose.

Within her burned anger fed by mistreatment at Dunbar's hand. Energies surged *through* her from no discernible source. She acted as a conduit and diverted them at Dunbar.

"Aieee!" The demon's beard exploded into wild, consuming orange flames. Dunbar staggered away. Molimo tried to follow but hesitated, then fell back to stand guard over the baby. The infant's pale eyes watched with intelligence and interest too old for such a small child. No sound came from his lips. He let Molimo's growls speak.

"You are no different than Lenc and Ayondela," accused Kesira. "While you have not followed the path offered by the jade, your intentions are evil. You'd deal in human life as if it meant little more than this." She snapped her fingers. Power erupted from within her, and Dunbar's long white hair turned to ash as the dancing blue-orange flame worked up toward his chin. The demon shrieked and tried to beat out the fire.

"Stop it! My head! Inside, it burns. My brain burns!"

Kesira had no idea what she did, what magicks she commanded or how this transformation had come about. Something about the punishment she had endured triggered an artesian well of strength and ability far surpassing even a demon's.

"Your lack of caring betrayed you," she said. "You sought only safety for yourself. Selfish lives deserve selfish death."

Dunbar fought now. Kesira turned gelid inside as the pressures from all sides mounted once more, but this time the spell lacked true conviction. With a careless toss of her hand she pushed aside the invisible planes seeking to crush her like a leaf placed between the vellum pages of a book.

The coldness left Kesira as she fought on. She came to realize that she was a match for the demon. But the nun battled only to a draw. Dunbar's initial panic had faded, and the fires adance on his head had sputtered out. Demon and woman faced each other, realization slowly dawning that neither would triumph in this battle. For all her newfound powers, Kesira could not vanquish Dunbar, nor could the demon make any further headway against her.

From her left came the sputters and squawks she knew so well. Zolkan rolled onto his side and used a shaky wing to regain his feet. The beady black eye slowly focused. The sound of his voice shocked Kesira. The *trilla* bird cut loose with singsong so rapid and high-pitched that she winced.

"Zolkan!" she shouted. "Quiet!" Her warning did no good. If anything, the bird's shrillness increased. Kesira felt as if he drove white-hot needles through her eardrums.

"He works for me," said Dunbar, a smirk crossing his ancient lips. "The bird is mine!"

The demon sought only to unnerve; no truth rang in his voice. Kesira saw the effect of Zolkan's words on Molimo. The wolf shape flowed and faded, human arms and legs and torso reappearing. In seconds Molimo had fully transformed into human. He came to stand beside her. Kesira, in spite of the continuing duel of magicks with Dunbar, blushed as she saw Molimo's nakedness. While nursing him to health after the jade rains, she had seen him thus many times. Now it was ... different.

Before, he had been a boy. Now he had become a mature man.

Energies of subtly different composition filled her. Sexual energies. They merged with the magical energies instilled in her by Cayabbib and Wemilat. Molimo held the baby. New dimensions came into play. Her heart went out to the poor child left an orphan by the jade demons. Pale eyes bored into her softer brown ones. As steel is tempered by fire, so did her powers become tempered by the infant's penetrating gaze.

Dunbar toppled face-forward, like a tree with its trunk sawed through. The demon lay twitching feebly, arms and legs aflutter as if he were the newborn and not the ancient.

"You rightly oppose the Ayondela and Lenc," Kesira said to the fallen demon, "but your methods were doomed to failure. You placed personal concerns above those of duty and honor." She let out a long, gusty breath. "If only Gelya had lived instead of you."

"My body is afire." Dunbar moaned. "Put out the fire, I beg you!"

Kesira had no idea what she had done to him. As a hose only carried liquid, so she had been a pipeline for the magical energies debilitating Dunbar. She made a few passes with her hand but sensed nothing. Dunbar's agony did not lessen.

"This is your punishment for kidnapping the baby, for treating Norvin so shabbily, for not living up to your responsibilities."

"Please!"

Kesira turned and jerked her head toward the mountain of granite dominating the landscape. Atop it gleamed the green dot showing where Ayondela awaited them. Without further word to the fallen demon she and the others started on the journey that could only end with a far deadlier confrontation.

"Ayondela," she said softly, "I am coming for you." Kesira's eyes narrowed as she saw the path winding up the side of the mountain.

"How do we know Ayondela is in her palace?" asked Kesira, panting from the long day's hike up the steep, rocky road carved from solid stone. She sat down heavily, rested her staff against a boulder, and unslung the baby from his position in the pack on her back. She rocked the infant until he drifted off to a peaceful sleep.

How she envied the child. His world was so simple, hers so complex. In the nunnery Kesira had lived a peaceful life uncomplicated by concerns basic to others outside Gelya's walls. The farmers nearby would never let them starve, even in lean years, taking away any fear on this account, not that such aid had ever been needed. Their own farming efforts had been blessed, and their charity kept many others alive. Of politics and the affairs of the Empire, Kesira knew vanishingly little. The Emperor commanded their loyalty. That basic tenet had been driven home repeatedly. Duty to family was second only to duty to Kwasian.

For Kesira her sisters in the order were her only family.

A tear formed as she thought of them, dead. Kesira brushed the tear away and heaved a deep sigh as she thought of how she had disobeyed the Emperor's Guard

captain. Family—sisters—gone, open flaunting of the
Emperor's command, all she held most basic had vanished.

The baby nestled against her breast, eyes screwed shut
in sleep, one tiny thumb thrust into his mouth. Zolkan and
Molimo rested a few paces away. The *trilla* bird harangued
Molimo constantly with the singsong speech. Whatever
he said did not make Molimo any happier. The man-wolf
frowned and gestured, dark eyes buried under a squint that
turned him bestial.

She rose and joined them, her legs protesting any movement at all. The steep climb had taken its toll on her, yet
they had covered only a quarter of the distance to the
mountaintop.

"Don't you like the view?" she asked, trying to lift the
others' spirits. "Look. There's the valley leading back into
the mountains. Somewhere in that direction is the marvelous transport we used to get here from Lorum Bay."

Molimo began writing in the dust. Zolkan hopped down,
and quick claws obliterated the words. More singsong
protests erupted from the *trilla* bird's beak until Kesira
lost her temper.

"Speak so that I can understand!"

Both bird and man turned to stare at her.

"I will *not* be excluded like this." Tears began misting
her vision again. "We are in grave danger and might find
ourselves confronting Ayondela at any instant. I do *not*
want the last thing I hear to be a deafening, shrill bird."

"Sorry," said Zolkan, but his tone carried no hint of
contrition. "Ayondela knows we come."

"How are you so sure?"

"At the end of road she awaits us." The bird shivered.
Tiny puffs of green feathers dropped from his body. He
quickly preened and then canted his head around to peer
up at Kesira. "Going to die looking a mess. No good. No
good. Hungry too."

"How you look when you die has nothing to do with
it," she said tartly. "How you've lived your life is all that
matters."

"Want to look good when I die."

Kesira turned away. The vista spread before her would have brightened her spirits under other circumstances. She hadn't been lying when she commented on the stark beauty of the mountains, the burgeoning green of the stunted summer growths, the vibrant yellows and velvety browns of wild flowers in bloom months late. Kesira sighed as she drank in the sight. Those were the flowers sacred to her patron. But the vision of paradise held those flowers as only a small portion of true loveliness. The air came crisp and sharp and clean in her nostrils, and the gentle stirrings of birds far off in the trees rode the wind to her ears. All this and a myriad of other details stretched away from her. Along the road she found only rock—and more rock. The chunks of gravel along the road had been designed to give purchase to draft horses and large wagons, not foot travelers. Kesira had to be continually on guard or she'd turn an ankle on the too-large gravel. But what troubled her the most was the lack of vegetation. Everywhere else she looked, blushes of summer finally touched the land. This ominous, dark red granite mountain jutted above the other mountains, devoid of life. The only hint of green was Ayondela's palace at the top of the road.

Jade green. Death green.

"We've come so far, and I'm still unsure of what we will do when we find Ayondela." She sank down to a rock beside Molimo. "What can we really achieve?"

"Do not doubt," he wrote on a small portion of dusty rock. "Ayondela can be stopped. She and Lenc consolidate their power. Zolkan is wrong; she does not know we come. Not yet."

"How do you know? How does Zolkan know Ayondela is even in her palace? She might have fled to another. Didn't she abandon the Isle of Eternal Winter? Perhaps she's somewhere else now, leaving this palace behind."

"Lenc's flame faltered," wrote Molimo.

Kesira nodded. She had interrupted its magical continuity, but why was this enough to drive away Ayondela?

There were so many unanswered questions. The source of her new power troubled her. She did not feel—*feel*—that the power stemmed from evil, but how could she know? The ways of magic had not been her training. No one in the Order of Gelya knew such things. The casting of the rune sticks had been the most remarkable ability among all her sisters, and she was the one capable of the reading.

Where did her interpretations come from? Kesira had always felt that the vivid pictures, the subtle hints, the niggling uneasinesses had originated outside her mind and not from within. Who or what planted those beguiling glimpses of the future?

Unbidden, she turned and studied Molimo's strong profile. Scars marred his handsome good looks, and he appeared to carry burdens as great as hers. Gone was all trace of the callow youth she had known. And replacing it?

Power? Yes. Worry? Definitely. Was he the source of her rune-casting skill? If true, that only raised more questions than it answered. Molimo had been touched by the jade and become an other-beast, but she knew that he transcended that affliction often enough to alert her to a strength of character surpassing most humans.

"Molimo, you deal so easily with demons. Are you one of them?"

"Ridiculous," piped up Zolkan. "He is caught in jade curse. You see him change to wolf. Would a demon permit that?"

"Toyaga gave him a spell he has no trouble using. Ayondela acted as if she recognized him. . . ."

"Not so. She did not recognize him. Impossible." The bird waddled around self-importantly. Kesira saw this as an attempt to turn her away from the topic. "Why would jade demon know mere mortal?"

Kesira stared hard at Molimo. He took no notice. She shook her head. Molimo was more than a poor, afflicted farmer unable to control the other-beast changes. He had a nobility lacking in others, and there was a mystery too. She wanted to pull away the veils of mystery surrounding him and reveal the true nature behind the lies and half truths and misinterpreted appearances.

"Molimo," she said softly, touching him lightly on the arm. "I don't care what you are. I love you." Emotions within her stirred and fought for supremacy. She feared for him; she feared him. Dominating everything else, she loved him.

A small smile rippled Molimo's lips. His dark eyes sparkled for a moment, then turned icy. He gestured, indicating that they must continue their climb.

Kesira kept the baby slung in front of her. She hefted her staff and leaned heavily on it as she began the tedious journey upward. They traveled for another hour before Kesira called out for Molimo to rest.

"Just a few minutes," she begged. "I tire quicker now." She considered letting Molimo carry the baby but always stopped short of asking. Molimo had not offered, either, which struck her as odd. Always before, he had been solicitous of her.

Kesira reflected. Molimo didn't show the outright contempt for the baby that Zolkan did, but the man also seemed leery of the child. Protective, yes, but also . . . frightened?

"Hurry," urged Zolkan. "We must go upward quickly. Night comes. We dare not be on road after dark."

"Why not?" she asked. "We haven't seen any other travelers, much less guards."

"What need does jade demon have of human guards?" demanded Zolkan. "Magicks abound. All around, all around!"

"What are you blathering on about?" Kesira said. "There's nothing." Both up the curving road and back along the bend she saw only rocky emptiness. Now the road presented a much finer view: hundreds of square miles of heart-stopping beautiful land stretched before her. Kesira could almost imagine herself Empress, commanding all this terrain.

But of guards or ward spells she saw no trace.

"Clouds!" The *trilla* bird flapped his wings in real agitation. Molimo shied away from the pummeling.

"We've climbed high enough to be among the clouds," Kesira admitted. "While it's getting chillier, we're clothed heavily enough to keep from freezing. Are you cold, Zolkan?"

"Clouds!" the bird repeated. "So soon you forget. Like the mists in Lorum Bay."

Kesira stopped and stared at the green bird. Of ordinary clouds she held no fear. Mists of invisible razors that slashed at her flesh filled her with dread, even if she had successfully walked through them in Lorum Bay after laying with Cayabbib. Anger at Zolkan's secrecy burned away fear.

"Why didn't you say something sooner? We could have made better time. Come along!" Kesira placed staff to rocky road and levered herself forward. She hadn't taken a dozen paces when the first wispy tendrils of fog drifted down from above. They had reached the spot where low-scudding clouds had appeared level with them out over the valleys and drifting into other peaks in the Sarn Mountains. Now she found the slightest hint of those soft, wetly caressing puffs frightening. Gentle reminders of summer changed to fanged, vaporous dragons intent on killing.

Kesira shook off the fantasy building in her mind. "Don't distract me," she told Zolkan. "Give warning when necessary but don't build this into something it's not. See?"

Kesira thrust out her hand. One gray finger of mist swirled downward and wrapped around her wrist. Even though she tensed at the touch, no burning came. Only clammy dampness.

"It is nothing more than fog. As you pointed out, the day is almost at an end, and mountains draw clouds like lodestone pulls iron. Come along."

With a boldness that she didn't really feel, Kesira strode off through the gathering fog. Quickly enveloped in its gelid arms, she fought the insane urge to break into a run.

At her breast the baby stirred, one tiny hand gripping her blouse so that he could turn and see what was happening. Behind her, Kesira heard Molimo and Zolkan. The bird rode on the man's shoulder and protested vigorously such blatant foolhardiness.

The fog chilled but did not cut. Kesira hurried on before her courage flagged.

"Look out. To the left," she said to Molimo as the man came level with her. "The sunset. Doesn't the mist make it all the more lovely?"

Rainbows gleamed, and one began to form a perfect circle behind them, as if forming a colorful exit. In front, the setting sun turned the mist gold and silver and, in places, ominously dark.

"There!" squawked Zolkan. "Ahead!"

Kesira stopped and gripped her staff, ready to fight. Then she relaxed. "It was only a trick of the light," she assured the *trilla* bird. "Nothing is there." Kesira brushed the sweat from her upper lip. She had also seen the dark, swiftly moving phantasm. But she and her friends were the only beings of substance in the fog. What both she and Zolkan had glimpsed had been, as she had explained, a trick of the setting sun.

Only a trick. Over and over Kesira told herself that until she believed it. In gathering darkness they continued up the road, often not able to see more than a few feet ahead because of the dying light and the blowing waves of gray fog.

The baby stirred. She placed a hand on his head to soothe the boy, but for the first time since she had "adopted" him, the child fought. Weak struggles made Kesira rock him and say, "There's nothing to worry about. Nothing, nothing." Her voice calmed Zolkan; the baby's fists pounded futilely against her chest.

Kesira frowned. Something disturbed the infant. She looked behind her, down the road, past gravel and granite to the emptiness of the verge. One misstep would carry her thousands of feet to her death. But the road was wide. Such a mistake couldn't happen, even in pitch blackness.

From ahead drifted more clouds.

Molimo let out a gurgling sound that almost put his pain into words. A feeble tendril of the fog reached out and swirled around his leg. Where the cloud touched appeared lacerations.

"The clouds!" she cried. "Zolkan, get away. Hurry. Save yourself!"

"Cannot. Look above! Cloud banks everywhere. We are englobed. They eat our flesh!"

The *trilla* bird fluttered around, wings whipping at the clouds, dispersing them a little—but not enough. Overhead, behind, ahead, the crystal clouds billowed with deadly, silent intent. Even as Zolkan tried to fly, the invisible razors within the clouds slashed off portions of wing and tail and crest. The air filled with feathery debris from the bird's futile escape attempt.

Molimo had ripped off his tunic and flapped it wildly. The sudden breeze, pitiful as it was, forced away a tiny portion of the clouds. Kesira rushed forward, staying as close to Molimo as she could. The woman didn't even protest when the heavy *trilla* bird alighted on her shoulder. The burden of the child and the bird caused her knees to buckle, but Kesira fought every step and kept pace as they forged ahead.

But Molimo's arms tired, and the insidious fog wormed its way past his gusty shield.

Tiny incisions bled with increasing profusion on exposed arms and legs and faces.

She closed her eyes and tried to summon whatever power it was that allowed her to walk through the fog unscatched. Kesira winced as her pitiful spell failed and new cuts appeared on her hands and face.

"Back, back down the road," Kesira urged. "There's no way we can reach the summit. Not fighting these damnable clouds." A quick swipe removed a tiny rivulet of blood from her forehead and kept it out of her eyes. Molimo shook his head. "Why not? Let's retreat and try again later."

Again Molimo shook his head. He kept a steady pace upward. Zolkan spoke for him, saying, "We near top. More chance to die retreating."

Kesira protected the baby the best she could, but the fog slipped through her fingers and found tiny fists and bare arms and silken-haired head. The baby stirred more and more. Kesira found herself hard-pressed to control such a small child.

"We can't!"

"Must," insisted Zolkan. The bird cut loose with a shrill singsong that Molimo understood. The man picked up the pace even more but at a price. More of the fog slipped past his flapping tunic. All around them hideous figures loomed. Kesira swallowed hard as she thought she saw direbeasts of impossible size opening and closing their fiercely fanged mouths. Darting shadows like wolves nipped at her legs until her boots turned slippery with her own blood. She stumbled and would have fallen, but for Molimo's arm supporting her.

"No!" she gasped, fighting to regain her balance. The clouds had swirled around in such a way that the woman thought she fell headlong into a gaping mouth lined with diamond teeth. As Molimo's tunic sent gusts toward the apparition, the teeth changed into water droplets and the mouth became nothing more than dark rock.

Illusion it might have been, but their wounds were all too real. Kesira felt herself weakening by the second. The trek up the mountain had depleted much of her stamina; dying the death of a thousand cuts pushed her closer to collapse.

Zolkan's claws added to her injuries when the bird tightened down on her left shoulder. Blood flowed in twin rivers.

"Stop it!" she cried. "You're worse than the clouds!"

"Stay on road. I can fly. You cannot."

Kesira wiped blood away from her eyes. Sweat stung

and made her blink. The blood blinded her as surely as if
a dark silk bandage descended over her eyes. She saw how
close she had strayed to the edge of the rocky road. Another
step and she would have been tumbling for many long
seconds until she smashed into the base of the sheer cliff.

"Thanks," she murmured. "But it'll take more than this
to get us away." She sobbed as a damp finger of cloud-
stuff stroked over her eyelids. Pain. Blood. Blindness.
Kesira reached the end of her endurance. No amount of
faith in Gelya and his teachings readied her for this insistent, all-pervasive torture.

"I can't go on. I can't, " she sobbed as the cloud billowed with increasing insistence around them. It was as
if Molimo fanned the deadly clouds into existence now,
rather than chasing them away.

"Can't go on. Can't, can't." Kesira sank to her knees.
Agony assailed her from every direction. Eyes bled.
Her blouse dripped blood. Every square inch of exposed
skin had a dozen tiny scratches, a score, hundreds.

Breaking the eerie silence of the crystal clouds, a small
voice rose. Wordless, crying in pain and rage, it mounted
in intensity. At first Kesira thought it echoed from ahead.
Then she imagined that the cries came from Molimo's
sundered mouth.

She shook when she realized that the baby cried for the
first time.

"Poor thing," she said, trying to soothe it. But the child
had passed the point of being so easily calmed. The frustration locked in that tiny voice tore at Kesira's heart.
Shrill, the thin, young voice rose until it passed the limits
of her hearing and made her flinch away. Zolkan cawed
in protest, and Molimo clapped hands over his ears to hold
back the awful, penetrating cry.

"The clouds! Molimo, keep..." Kesira's voice trailed
off. Molimo had stopped waving his tunic, but the clouds
no longer encroached upon them. They stood as if enclosed
in an invisible, protective bubble.

Louder, ever louder, came the baby's cries. Face screwed

up tightly, fists clenched, the baby turned red with the effort of crying.

The bubble around them expanded.

"It . . . the crying is driving away the clouds!" Kesira struggled up from her knees. The baby's voice strengthened. "To the top. Hurry. We can reach the palace. Hurry, oh, please, hurry!"

Zolkan no longer weighed her down. Molimo aided her. And the baby cried. Never before had a child cried so loudly, so powerfully, with such stunning effect. The jade demon's deadly crystal-edged clouds parted and made way before such might.

Chapter Seventeen

"THE JADE PALACE," Kesira whispered in awe. She clutched the baby to her breast as if he would sprout wings and fly away but fixed her full attention on the slender towers at either end of an immensely tall, intricately carved jade wall. Those towers, also of white-veined jade, moved in subtle, eye-confusing ways that disturbed her. From the corner of her eye Kesira saw movement. The tower to her left. Spinning to face it, she saw only the solid, dully phosphorescent green, but she had the impression of sinuous twisting. As soon as she faced it and confirmed its solidity, more motion attracted her. The tower to the right.

No matter how she turned, the tower on the other side of the palace moved.

"The jade is alive," she said, louder. Zolkan flapped from Molimo's shoulder to hers. She gripped her wooden staff more tightly. As her fingers pressed to the wood she felt tiny buds sprouting. How she envied them their mindless life. If only she could keep from thinking, from knowing her fate! Inside those walls Ayondela awaited her. But as she had foreseen in her rune casting, she felt no fear for herself. For Molimo and Zolkan and the baby Kesira fretted, but not for herself. The power had come to her.

But the woman had no inkling as to its source. All Kesira knew for certain was that the power opposed that of the jade and that it would have been given Gelya's blessing, had her patron lived.

"Clouds try to cut us," the *trilla* bird protested. "We must escape soon."

"The baby's crying holds Ayondela's foggy messengers at bay," said Kesira, more interested now in getting inside the palace. She walked to the wall and examined the carving. Untold workmen had spent lifetimes on these decorations—perhaps even lifetimes cut short by Ayondela's wrath.

"Palace built on bones of workers," said Zolkan. The bird clucked nervously. "Too near jade. We must hurry."

"For once I agree with you." Kesira started walking along the wall, eyes seeking the slightest crack that might indicate an entrance. As she approached the tower at the corner her steps slowed. She cast her gaze upward. From the slit windows cut high in the jade tower gushed forth more of the deadly clouds. The stars twinkling in the darkening sky played hide-and-seek through those crystalline billows, beguiling her, holding her captive to her own imagination.

Kesira saw creatures both mighty and pathetic trapped with the clouds. Some were punished with hideous cuts while others romped with wild abandon, feeding off the souls of those dying from the magicks. Ayondela's clouds soared into the vault of the sky and carpeted the heavens with death. And always, no matter how the winds dissipated those clouds, the slits in the tower pumped out more of the killing vapors.

Kesira jumped when Molimo placed a bleeding hand on her shoulder. He pointed to the clouds gusting forth and shook his head.

"I didn't think we could get in those windows," she assured him. "But what a favor we would do the world—and ourselves—if we could plug the vents."

Again Molimo startled her. He reached out and used a bloody forefinger to write on the jade wall. Wherever his blood touched, the jade came alive, burning with an intensity almost too great for human sight. Kesira slowly read the blazing words.

"I agree," she said. "Ayondela must know we have reached the top of her mountain. Why does she always seek mountaintops for her place of power?" Kesira glanced back through the bubble of cloud around them. Just beyond, she knew, the edge of the granite spire looked down on a five-thousand-foot precipice.

"Demons prefer privacy," squawked Zolkan. "For Ayondela this is perfect. She can work her evil and see all."

Clouds of shining crystal continued to spew forth from the tower. Kesira shivered at the thought of the death and suffering those slashing puffs of mist might cause. Uneasily she looked around and saw that those very clouds edged closer. The baby's angry cries had quieted to more contented mewlings now—and the clouds crept up on Kesira and the others.

Molimo wiped away more blood from his forehead and etched more flaring letters into the jade. "Only demons can enter this palace," he wrote.

Kesira sensed undercurrents boiling within her. She was no demon, or even half-breed, such as Rouvin had been. But entry posed no problem for her. She had seen the runes. She confronted Ayondela. Inside the walls of jade.

"How would a demon enter?" she asked. Kesira stiffened as she saw Molimo write out the instructions. Whether the words burned in eye or brain, she didn't know. The swiftness of his answer reinforced what she had come to suspect.

"Very well," the nun said. "We shall attempt an entry through the use of some minor magic." Molimo had indicated that this small token separated the curious—and mortal—from those of more exalted—and demonic—birth.

Kesira faced the carved wall and tapped her staff against the solid jade. Dizziness assailed her. She felt Molimo's supporting arm, but she brushed it away. A curious detachment filled her like water fills a jug. Magicks previously untapped welled up and spilled over. All that Cayabbib had imparted now aided her. Wemilat's kiss burned hot on her breast. The skills used to read the rune sticks came into play, and the nun began reading the hitherto random carvings on the wall. Just like the runes, they spelled out messages to her. Patterns shifted; she altered them, read them, exulted in them.

"Only demons may pass?" she asked quietly. Kesira's laugh echoed forth. The solid jade dissolved into mist. She stepped forward *through* the wall, just as Wemilat had traveled through solid rock. A coldness brought out gooseflesh. Kesira took another step and passed into the great hallway leading to Ayondela's throne room.

Beside her stood Molimo. On her shoulder Zolkan quivered in fear, the physical proof of the *trilla* bird's fright running warm and liquid down her back. And cradled in her left arm quietly rode the baby, eyes wide and cries stilled.

"My staff may not be of Gelya's sacred stone-wood, but it appears potent enough when I use it." Tiny limbs again sprouted from the shaved wood rod, leaves a living green countering that of the cold jade surrounding them.

Molimo wiped away more blood from his eyes. On impulse Kesira reached out. The fire of magicks burning within her had not yet died down. Sparks arced from her fingertips to the man's open cuts. He winced as fat blue discharges played along his wounds, but as Kesira's hand passed, the effects of the crystal clouds vanished. He was healed.

Kesira stepped back, as surprised at this as Molimo. She started to speak, to tell him of all the things burning inside her. Molimo motioned her to silence, pointing down the long corridor to the doors opening onto Ayondela's audience chamber.

"You're right," she said softly. "Later. After we speak with Ayondela."

"Speak?" protested Zolkan, his heavy body shaking as if he had the ague. "She will not *speak!* Ayondela will *destroy!* Can you match her power?"

"I no longer fear her." Kesira had read the runes; it had been difficult to believe that facing Ayondela would not instill great fear in her, but Kesira now experienced powers beyond her comprehension. She had lain with demons and absorbed their powers. And had there been more, a dormant seed within her, that only now came into full blossom? Kesira drifted along on winds too strong for any mortal to fight. Where that gale was taking her, she didn't know.

Staff thumping soundly with every other step, Kesira walked boldly toward the lofty arch and the jade doors. Beyond them awaited Ayondela.

"Foolish," muttered Zolkan. "We cannot go on."

"The runes told me I had nothing to fear."

"Runes?" shrieked Zolkan. He batted his wings against her face and head. "Lies! You have no power to see the future. All that was sent by Merrisen."

"What?" Kesira swung about and poked at the bird with the tip of her still-blossoming staff. "Merrisen is dead. I saw the battle with Lenc. Merrisen died."

Molimo grabbed for Zolkan, missed, sent the bird awing. Zolkan squawked in fright and continued up, wings straining.

Kesira rapped her staff against Molimo's shoulder. "Explain his words. Does Merrisen live?"

Molimo solemnly nodded.

"Why doesn't he aid us directly? Is he afraid?" Kesira lost some of the bravado she'd felt. "Does he use us as a cat's-paw while he performs other deeds? Or is he sacrificing us to weaken the jade demons?" Fear gripped her heart tightly, keeping it from beating. Kesira's mouth turned to cotton, and she found it impossible to swallow.

Molimo's stricken look did nothing to restore her confidence. He grabbed her by the upper arms and pulled her close. The light brush of his lips against hers sent an electric thrill throughout her body. She jerked back, the baby stirring restlessly. Tiny fists gripped her blouse and demanded her full attention.

Molimo glared angrily at the baby.

"It's too late, Molimo," she said, her voice harsh and alien in her ears. "Before, yes. But not now. Not here." The words grated even more as she said, "I *do* love you." Tears ran down her cheeks. She resumed her steady progress toward the huge doors.

Outside the doors she had only the sense of vast rooms and sullen quiet. Passing under the arch and into Ayondela's chamber took away her breath. The room had no walls. Kesira looked out into infinity in all directions. She staggered slightly, vertigo seizing control of her senses. She quieted herself using techniques taught by Gelya. All that was of substance around her allowed Kesira to focus. Her staff. The baby. The sound of Molimo's harsh breathing. Distant flapping of Zolkan's wings. Faint, musty scents caused by the sealed room.

Sealed?

Hesitantly Kesira opened her eyes again. This time she mastered her giddiness. Each wall presented a different view. Directly in front of her, framing a jade throne that seemed to float in midair, she saw a vast plain, checkered with green and brown squares of farmland. Clouds jetted to and fro, touching lightly before soaring back into the azure sky. Everywhere those clouds touched they left deep, ragged furrows. Closer examination showed Kesira the misery locked within the beauty.

Peasants died in Ayondela's deadly clouds. The land itself was raped and ravaged by the slicing actions of those deceptively innocent puffs of moist white.

Kesira shuddered slightly, turning to the left. A city cloaked in night and streets lighted by occasional gas lamps lay like a perfect jewel. But the perfection contained no joy. Dark clouds gusted between buildings like a vaporous assassin seeking out victims. One tiny figure ran pell-mell along the street—only to be cut off.

No sound reached Kesira, but she knew that the small child died with shrieks of total agony on his lips.

The vista to the right proved even stranger but not less

appalling. Darkness as complete as any mineshaft turned the wall into a mystery. Gradually Kesira realized that she did indeed peer into the bowels of the planet along a cruelly driven tunnel. Cowering at the far end of the shaft like rats chevied by terriers was a small group of people, too indistinct for individual recognition.

They shared the fate seen on the other two walls. Crystal clouds glittering in their deadliness, billowed along the tunnel and brought a slashing, vicious end. Again no sound reached Kesira's ears, but she fancied that she could smell the fear, the death.

And above? Kesira Minette looked aloft to seek out Zolkan. There in the heavens arched not a roof or the sky but a view of the Emperor's palace in Limaden. Kesira recognized it from descriptions. What mortal dwelling could be so grand? Clouds lunged like a master swordsman, only to vanish in wetness before reaching the walls of the Imperial city. Fascinated, Kesira craned her neck to watch. Long minutes of the duel convinced her that Emperor Kwasian still resisted, that Ayondela had yet to force the ruler to abdicate.

Odd thoughts drifted through her mind. Was Captain Protaro safely within the zone of protection used by the Emperor, or did the guard Captain still seek out the baby? Why did she care?

Kesira jerked in surprise when Molimo pointed downward. Kesira had resisted the urge because of the new waves of vertigo it produced. No solid floor existed beneath her feet. She floated, just as Ayondela's throne seemed to be suspended in thin air. Miles below bobbed a fleet of ships flying garish banners decorated with animal totems.

"A barbarian invasion fleet?" She looked at Molimo, unable to come to any other conclusion. The man solemnly nodded.

"They take advantage of the unrest throughout Kwasian's realm," came a soft, pleasant voice. "They think to gain ascendancy, but, of course, that is absurd. *I* am victorious. *On every front!*"

"Ayondela!" Kesira hadn't seen the female demon enter the room, but amid the confusing jumble of pictures, such an entry could have been made easily.

"You enjoy the display? I am pleased with it. The ... magicks are so easy for me now." The demon sat on her jade throne, icy blue scepter in hand. The long canines had become even more pronounced, turning her once considerable beauty into a travesty. Even as the demon spoke, those fangs grew in length and pulsed with a soft inner light; the teeth were of the purest jade.

Before Kesira could respond, Ayondela went on in her conversational tones, "Lenc had no difficulty convincing me of the power of the jade. Why hadn't any of us seen it before? It is so simple to embrace its power. You come to join me?" For the first time Ayondela focused her full attention on Kesira and Molimo.

She frowned, as if trying to remember the answer to a difficult question.

"I know you," she said. "You are not demons. *You* are not!" The scepter of blue ice pointed directly at Kesira. The woman staggered under the magicks pouring forth from that gelid wand.

"Ayondela, we come to plead with you. There is no need to bring such misery to the world. Lenc only uses you. He—" Kesira was slammed back by the force of a spell cast by the female demon.

Kesira watched in abject horror as Ayondela's aspect altered from one of tranquillity to total insanity.

"You murdered my only son. *You* killed Rouvin." The demon's entire body pulsed with a pale verdant light. She rose, arms crossed over her breast. Water ran down her arms from the melting scepter. Ayondela took no notice. She stepped forward, away from her throne—and grew.

Kesira tried to convince herself that the rune casting had been accurate, that she would meet and defeat Ayondela. She put all the magical power into her words that she could, hoping they might sway Ayondela. Kesira had to repeatedly thrust away the mind-numbing fear that threatened to seize her. But the effort became increasingly difficult. Ayondela had been crazed when they'd met before. Kesira saw nothing but burning, jade-fueled insanity in those demon eyes now.

"Lenc lies to you," Kesira shouted. "You visit your clouds on the land and create death and destruction—and the people hate *you*, not Lenc. He uses you for his own purposes!"

"Rouvin died. You killed my son!"

Whatever shred of sanity that had lingered in Ayondela after her son's death had fled. Kesira knew better than to explain the circumstances. True, Molimo had ripped out Rouvin's throat with wolf fangs. But the jade gave birth to Molimo's other-beast transformations. And Rouvin's death had been necessary to free Wemilat. Only with this kindly demon's aid had it been possible to combat another jade demon, Howenthal.

"No amount of suffering among the mortals brings Rouvin back to me," Ayondela raged. "But the jade gives me the power to make the suffering continue for all eternity." Ayondela staggered slightly, righting herself.

"For all eternity?" shouted Kesira, taking a different tack. "In human terms you were immortal—but not now. Don't you feel the jade sucking away your vitality? Your life is drawing to an end because of the jade. The more you rely on its power, the sooner you will die."

"Lies!"

"Lenc is the liar. He knows that he will perish quickly if he relies heavily on the jade to subjugate humankind. That's why he lets you do it. He is duping you, Ayondela. Reject him. Reject both Lenc and the jade. It's not too late!"

But Kesira knew that it was. The green pulsations bathing Ayondela's body told as much. The addiction to power was great, but the insidious nature of the jade had worked its way into every nerve, every artery, every brain cell of Ayondela's being. Removal of its power would reduce the female demon to a mere husk.

Kesira summoned her newfound energy, coaxed it, nurtured the sensations of power, and then loosed it.

Ayondela staggered, but Kesira couldn't tell whether from the potency of her magical thrust or simple infirmity brought about by the jade.

"You killed Rouvin," Ayondela said single-mindedly. "For that you will suffer. Oh, how you will suffer! No mortal has ever felt what you will endure. You will beg me for death."

"I beg you for life, yes," said Kesira, trying to reform her thoughts and devise a new method of attack. She had hoped her power had grown to such an extent that the thrust would have ended the conflict. Ayondela had shrugged it off. Now Kesira needed new ploys. But what? She realized with a sinking feeling in the pit of her belly that she knew so little about such warfare—or any warfare.

"Worm! Slut!"

"For the rest of the world. Take my life, do what you will to me, but let everyone else live. Stop your assaults on the farmlands, on the Emperor, on the people."

"On the barbarians sailing so diligently for the coasts of this continent?" Ayondela's lips curled into a sneer around the deforming tusks of glowing jade.

"Even them. The Emperor can deal with them. Return to the old ways, Ayondela. Think how it used to be." Kesira felt the imponderable weight of Ayondela's spells crushing her. She shifted the baby so that she could sling him on her back and leave her hands free. Kesira's knuckles turned white on her staff as she hoisted herself back to her feet. But even this simple movement took more effort than she had expected. Ayondela battered at her strength constantly, and Kesira had no effective way of fighting back.

"The old ways?" Ayondela's madness faded slightly. "The old ways," the female demon mused. "They were so nice. Separate from the annoying presence of mortals, dealing among ourselves, demon to demon with our concerns."

"Yes!"

Ayondela snapped from her reverie. "That has passed. A new order must be imposed. The other demons—other than Lenc—are fools! We have power. What good is power unless it is used?"

"The jade perverts your power," Kesira said. Where was Molimo? How she needed his support now!

"The jade *gives* the power," bellowed Ayondela.

An invisible hand pulled Kesira into the air and tossed her toward the far wall, the one showing the ravaged farmlands. She shrieked as she knew she would fall miles to her death. Kesira groaned as she smashed into invisible—and substantial—walls. She sank down, bleeding from nose and split lip.

"The jade gives me the power to see what effect I have on the land. Me! Ayondela!"

For an instant the image just beyond Kesira's nose shimmered and turned into the solid green of jade. As quickly as the flickering had come, it vanished and again showed the destroyed farms and ruined lives produced by Ayondela's clouds.

Kesira mustered what power she could. Dimly she heard the baby begin to whimper. The woman pushed aside such worries. She would die quickly unless she found the power to resist the jade demon. But try as she might, Kesira failed to find the proper combinations of power from Cayabbib and ability from Wemilat. The kiss Wemilat had placed on her breast burned with manic fury, making her sob with lancing pain every time her heart throbbed another frenzied beat.

"You resist?" asked Ayondela. "There is power within you—where does it come from?" Ayondela pointed her scepter at Kesira, and the woman lost all sense of time and space. She hung suspended in a world of her own, blackness wrapping her in numbness, her senses gone.

One by one Ayondela restored those senses. Pain shot through Kesira's body in ways hitherto unknown to the woman. She thought she had known suffering, but real pain visited itself on her now. Odors so hideous that she flinched away assailed her nose, and tastes combining bitterness and acid tang gagged her. Light burst with painful brilliance, flaring jade-green to remind her of her tormentor. And then sounds returned, choking cries from the infant, strangled gasps from Molimo, outraged squawks from Zolkan, and another sound, unrecognizable.

Finally Kesira knew that those awful noises were produced by her own throat, that Ayondela's tortures wrested the ultimate in protest from her.

Then Ayondela began the punishment for her son's death.

"The flesh that sprang from my loins is no more," she heard Ayondela say. "You robbed me of a millennium of pleasure from his company. He was more than half demon. Rouvin was special. He was my son!"

Kesira's back arched as needles of white-hot pain shot into her belly, seeking out the most sensitive of her nerve endings, over-stimulating until she wanted only the surcease of death. Ayondela did not grant it.

"My precious crystal clouds. See them? See how they love to caress your fine body?" Cackles totally lacking in mercy or sanity echoed in Kesira's ears. And then she felt the misty dampness washing over her body. The clouds had cut and slashed physically before. Ayondela added a psychic dimension to the torture. Not only did the cloud flay Kesira's skin, they also tore at her deepest-held beliefs.

She bled and hurt—and doubted.

The crystal clouds cut away at her most cherished desires, her belief in Gelya and herself, her position in society. She doubted herself and Zolkan and even Molimo.

Kesira Minette began to curl in upon herself. At first she only pulled her body into a fetal position. Then her mind contracted, struggling to fend off the feathery touches against her consciousness. She retreated to the darkness of catatonia even as a distant, buried part of that living spirit that made her *her* protested.

But no effort on her part held Ayondela at bay. Kesira began to die physically and emotionally.

"Molimo," went out her thought. "I *do* love you. And you, too, Zolkan. And my baby, my baby..."

The clouds dragged mistlike tendrils across the fringes of her mind, forcing her to collapse ever inward. A hard, bright spark burned as she made one last effort to fight. Then even this spark faltered and diminished until it was only an ember.

The runes had lied. She had not defeated Ayondela. And she had known soul-numbing fear.

The last thing Kesira Minette experienced was the crying of the baby. This only added to her defeat. She had failed not only her order and herself but even an innocent child.

Chapter Eighteen

SWADDLED IN HER own madness, Kesira Minette sank deeper and deeper into her own mind. She wandered lonely corridors, blind and lost, but strangely she experienced no fear. Fear had assaulted her, but now Kesira existed in a realm beyond mere terror.

Or had Gelya's teachings prepared her for this isolation? Never in her life had Kesira imagined such punishment. Seldom had she ever been alone. Her sisters in the order always had been there to help and cajole, to aid and amuse. And after Lenc's destruction Kesira had found solace in Molimo's company. And Zolkan! The *trilla* bird never failed to entertain her with his odd ways and insistence on hurrying, no matter how delicate or precise the matter.

Solitude was alien to her. Kesira found out exactly how frightening it could be to someone so dependent on others.

She curled up tighter, retreating further into herself. Ayondela's crystalline clouds had slashed and maimed, but their effect on Kesira's mind far transcended physical abuse. Kesira recoiled from the clouds in the only way she could.

Oh, how she had approached Ayondela with great faith in her own abilities! How she had erroneously assumed that the power gained from Cayabbib and Wemilat would be adequate. Kesira had misjudged Ayondela's insanity, fueled by the death of her son—and the jade.

The jade. Kesira wondered how she had ever believed it possible to confront the power of the jade and triumph.

Now she paid the price with total isolation from the world. All senses were stolen from her, and she was alone, *alone*, ALONE!

No sight, no taste or touch, no smell, no sound.

Except...

Some part of Kesira seized on the tiny sound filtering down the corridors of her mind to find her in the absolute blackness. It came as a cry, hardly more than a whisper. But it mounted in intensity. Kesira's hopes rose like a geyser surging toward the heavens. She was alone, but the sound had to be...

...the baby.

The infant's wailing cut through the barriers around her. Kesira dared to believe that escape from this inner prison was possible. She turned and followed the whimpers and choked cries—and met resistance.

Ayondela's clouds battered against the periphery of her mind, trying to force her back down into herself. Feathery touches, vicious slashes, drifting insanity all crashed against mind and body in a never-ending onslaught. Kesira used techniques learned over a lifetime to ignore, to accept, to continue on. She sought the baby and its dear cries. Once the child had repelled the clouds with his cries, Kesira had to believe that he could do it a second time. How, she didn't know or care. That it happened was enough.

Dim light. Touch. The feel of the wiggling child in her arms.

"I'm not alone," she whispered, almost crushing the child in her embrace. She blinked and saw the familiar room. All that had changed was the expression on the female demon's face. Before she had forced Kesira into lonely inner exile, madness had run rampant. Now fear touched the greenly complected face.

"Fear!" shouted Kesira. "Know what it is like, Ayondela. Renounce the jade. Do it and you need never fear again." Even as Kesira spoke she knew that the female demon was too deeply influenced by the magical green stone. Ayondela's tusks shimmered and burned with intense green light. The shadows cast on the planes and ridges of her face gave her a curiously mixed expression: fear and triumph.

It was as if Ayondela had realized what the jade did to her and yet still reveled in the power, unable to follow any other path.

"What is that *thing?*" the demon demanded, pointing her scepter at the baby. The air froze in a solid bar between scepter and child. Kesira interposed her body to prevent the icy thrust from reaching the infant. Such solicitude was unnecessary. The baby's sobs and whimpers shattered the column.

Tinkles of ice against jade filled the chamber as a small rain began. No matter how Ayondela cast her spell at the infant, his crying thwarted the effect.

"No!" Ayondela blasted to her feet. Green tusks working up and down as she tried spell after spell, Ayondela betrayed stark fear. Kesira took advantage of the she-demon's preoccupation to rise and approach. As the runes foretold, Kesira felt no panic, held no fear of a jade demon who had locked the world in winter, then slashed and cut it with her devastating clouds. Kesira squarely faced her adversary.

"Stop your attacks against those below," Kesira ordered. "We have come to help you, Ayondela, not to harm you. Your son's death was unfortunate, but the jade caused it. The *jade*. Forsake its corruption."

Ayondela sidestepped, moving away from throne and Kesira, then let out a shriek and bolted. Kesira grabbed for the demon, but the baby slowed her reactions. Ayondela escaped.

"Doors!" Zolkan warned from above. "Beware all doors. Traps. Ayondela has set traps everywhere!" Zolkan spiraled down and landed on Kesira's shoulder.

"Where have you been?" she asked. "I needed you, and you abandoned me."

"Saw it all," admitted the *trilla* bird. "Could do nothing. Such power! All turned against me. I . . . I defecated in fear! Like frightened pigeon, I shit everywhere!" Zolkan tucked his head under one wing, mortified at his craven behavior.

"Her power is immense, isn't it?" soothed Kesira. "But she fled when the baby cried. Just as her clouds were held back, so is Ayondela."

Zolkan peered out from under his wing, glaring at the baby. Even when the child saved him, Zolkan appeared to hold little affection for the child. Kesira hugged the baby closer to her breast where Wemilat's kiss pulsed and warmed her.

"Where's Molimo?" She looked around the chamber, head spinning in confusion at the scenes flashing by. She still felt disorientation every time she glanced at the floor—or where she knew the solid floor to be. Only emptiness stretched under her feet. Kesira forced the thought away. She would show no fear. The casting of the rune sticks had told her that she would show great courage facing Ayondela.

"There," said the bird. "There he is. Oh, wounds! Molimo is wounded!" Zolkan flew over to land beside Molimo. Kesira approached more cautiously. The man looked unharmed, but the green light burning in his half-opened eyes warned of the other-beast transformation. The nearness of so much jade pushed Molimo's control to the limit, but did it push him beyond that limit?

"Molimo," she said gently. "We are in grave danger. Ayondela has fled. But I know she will return as soon as she has regained her composure."

"Jade," said Zolkan, shuddering. "Jade gives her back determination. We must flee. Now!"

"If we go now, there'll never be another chance," said Kesira. She wobbled as blood rushed from her head. Feeling faint, she sat down beside Molimo. "What happened to you?" she asked Molimo. "I . . . I needed you, and you were gone."

The man drew an index finger across one of the new wounds that had appeared on his arm and dripped the blood seemingly onto the scene stretched out so far below. Every spot where a drop of his blood touched, burning jade appeared. Molimo quickly wrote, "I used the spell Toyaga gave. The jade weakens me. It is dangerous for me to be here. Dying. I am dying."

At that, Kesira had to laugh. "It's dangerous for anyone to be here," she pointed out. Anger flared on Molimo's face; she reached out to lightly touch his cheek. "I meant nothing by that."

"You can't know the danger," he wrote. Turning to get new space, he continued. "Ayondela can destroy me, in spite of my returning strength."

"Worse," cut in Zolkan, "she might identify him because of power."

"She knows Molimo?"

The *trilla* bird squawked. Molimo nodded.

"How?"

"Every second we stay in this palace adds to our danger. We must kill Ayondela if we can." Molimo's face turned paler. Kesira stroked over the wounds caused by the latest onslaught of the maiming clouds and eased some of the hurt. Beneath her fingertips she felt power surging, and, as she healed his cuts, so did a measure of his strength enter her, patching over the festering wounds left by her brief isolation.

Shivering, she pulled away. The healing was almost as bad as the loneliness.

"Ayondela's pretty pictures are fading," she said, looking around. From the burning droplets of Molimo's blood spread wave after wave of solid green: the floor returned to normal. When those ripples of solidity struck the corners, the scenes of farmland and Imperial capital and the night sky began to flicker.

The baby let out a tiny shriek that snapped off all the pictures and gave an unrelieved view of only shiny green walls. For the first time since entering the chamber Kesira got a good look at the way it truly was. Unlike the exterior walls to the palace, these walls carried no ornamental carvings. Only the delicate veining of jade broke the monotony of three-story-high walls and ceiling. The floor showed some small traces of scuff marks—and the place where Molimo had burned in his message. Those fiery letters still blazed with eye-searing intensity.

Ayondela's throne stood atop a foot-high pillar of jadeite, whiter and less intricately marbled than the walls. Of the female demon who had so recently occupied the throne Kesira saw no trace.

Zolkan pointed one bedraggled wing in the direction of an arched doorway. "There. She went there. Traps! Everywhere!" Zolkan didn't have to tell Kesira how frightened he was. She felt the continuing stream of semi-liquid warmth down her back. Her nose wrinkled at the idea of her blouse being further defiled, then pushed such thoughts away. Ayondela had fled; she must be found and stopped.

Kesira stood and stared at the archway Zolkan indicated. She saw not only with her eyes but also with senses other than sight. More important than the snippets of information she gleaned, Kesira's confidence built again. Doubt had assailed her when she had confronted Ayondela. Her pride and mistaken belief in her own abilities had led her to the brink of disaster. Now Kesira put the newfound powers into perspective. She might face a jade demon, but defeating one single-handedly was impossible.

For her it was impossible. Kesira looked down into the infant's pale eyes.

"You've kept from crying all this time, haven't you?" she asked softly. "You saved it for the moment when it mattered most. You saved me, you know?"

The baby gurgled contentedly, hands opening and closing on her blouse. Kesira lifted the infant and kissed him on the forehead. A smile wrinkled the corners of his lips and crinkled his nose and eyes.

"You've done well. Now we must continue the battle. Rest," she told the baby. To Molimo and Zolkan she said, "How do we track Ayondela? Any traps she's constructed would be the end of us if we sprang them."

Molimo swayed slightly as he walked. Kesira frowned, worrying over his endurance. All the way up the mountain—even through the deadly clouds on the road—Molimo had been a tower of strength. Entering the jade palace had taken more than a small toll on him; he looked as weak as when she'd first come upon him after the jade rains.

"We must hurry," said Zolkan. "He cannot take more. And if Ayondela discovers him..." The *trilla* bird's sentence trailed off. Kesira didn't ask him to finish it.

"If the doorway is booby-trapped, how do we find her? She might have gone to summon Lenc. The pair of them will be far more than we can cope with."

"Lenc has worries of his own," said Zolkan. "He would come only as last resort."

"Another door?" asked Kesira. "Do we have to directly follow Ayondela?"

Before Zolkan could answer, Molimo stumbled forward—through the arched entryway. From lips that had forgotten words came a shriek that froze Kesira as surely as any magical spell cast her direction by Ayondela. Molimo arched his back, head tossing from side to side, that hideous sound pouring from his lips. Flaring green bathed his body, causing his limbs to twitch spastically, turning him into a crazed marionette.

Kesira started forward to rescue him, but Zolkan prevented her by leaping from her shoulder and deftly spinning in midair, his wings pounding at her face. She was forced a step back to keep the bird from harming the infant she so lovingly cradled in her arms.

"What are you doing? We've got to save him. Look at him!"

Zolkan said nothing. The *trilla* bird whipped around and dropped downward slightly, claws fastening into Molimo's shoulders. Bloody spots sprouted on the man's tunic at every puncture spot—and tiny emerald fires blazed as the blood met and mixed with the magical curtain holding Molimo in thrall.

The bird's feathers began to smolder as he struggled amid the magicks to pull Molimo free. The bird finally twisted and flapped with his long wings, using both weight and flying power to jerk Molimo free. They fell into an unmoving heap on the floor.

For the span of a heartbeat Kesira didn't move. She stared at them. Zolkan lay on his back, eyes open and sightless. Molimo lay facedown. She saw no sign of life in either.

Shock gone, Kesira hurried to Zolkan's side. The bird's breast rose and fell softly. She ignored him as she rolled Molimo supine. The green witch-fire that always accompanied his shape-change to wolf blazed in his glazed eyes. She stroked over his forehead, using what power she could summon to restore him.

"Live, Molimo. Live as a man. Reject the other-beast inside you. But live, damn you, live!" Tears dripped onto Molimo's chest; Kesira didn't bother to brush them away. More rolled down her cheeks and onto his body until she viewed the world through wavering vision, as if water rippled between her and Molimo.

Molimo's lips moved silently now, voice again lost. Kesira started to speak, to give thanks, but the baby reached up to silence her. Molimo nodded. He mouthed the words, "Play dead. Ayondela will return now. Lie beside me."

Kesira slipped to a prone position, her hand clutching Molimo's. The man gently squeezed back. Kesira had to rearrange her position several times until she found a comfortable one on the the hard floor, the baby nestled between her and Molimo. Again Kesira wondered at the man's reaction. He didn't quite flinch away from the baby, but he definitely showed aversion.

She had no more time to consider this odd behavior on Molimo's part. The echoing click-click of sandals against the jade floor filled the chamber. Through partially opened eyelids Kesira saw Ayondela return to the throne. The jade demon strode with assurance again, secure in the mistaken belief that her booby-trapped doorway had done its job.

Kesira worried as to the next step. Ayondela had returned. But how did they go about attacking her? Molimo had been drained by the force of the magicks guarding the doorway. Zolkan stirred restlessly, but the bird's abilities had never amounted to that much.

Kesira Minette knew the full burden of doubt. No fear—the rune casting held her away from fear—but how was she to combat Ayondela's evil? Kesira felt sympathy for the people's lives blighted by the crystalline clouds Ayondela visited upon them. She even sorrowed for the destruction wrought on the land. The elements of nature had been disturbed; nature had never been unfaithful to humanity, but the power of the jade had changed that. Now only perversion of nature existed in the world. For all that, Kesira felt her anger rising.

Was anger enough? Kesira doubted it. Even relatively rested, she had not possessed sufficient skill or power to turn Ayondela from her wanton course.

All Kesira could do was try.

She mustered her strength, prepared herself as Gelya himself would have, and waited for the precise instant

Ayondela shifted on her throne, nervously switching the ice-blue scepter back and forth in her hands. Kesira thought that the demon peered too intently at her—or at Molimo.

Ayondela rose to her feet but did not leave the throne's small platform. "Who are you, you who endure my fiercest magicks? You who are so familiar? You!" Ayondela thrust out her scepter. Frosty spears launched themselves from the rounded top to fly directly toward Molimo. The man moaned loudly as the ice penetrated his body. He propped himself up on one elbow, staring at Ayondela.

His eyes burned with a green deeper and purer than Ayondela's own. Her tusks began to pulsate, and fear cast a dark shadow over her once again.

"This cannot be," the female demon muttered. "You did not die. But the magicks, the spells—you did not die!"

Ayondela's scepter began to melt under the energy she

funneled through it. Kesira dared wait no longer. She threw up what barriers she could against the spells. For a moment hope flared. Then Ayondela's superior power and skillful conjuring ripped apart Kesira's feeble efforts at defense.

To Kesira's surprise the demon did not attack her. She focused her assault entirely on Molimo. Before Kesira's eyes the man withered, diminished. Whatever the spell, it sucked away Molimo's vital forces like pulling juice from a succulent fruit. The green glow in the man's eyes dimmed. No longer able to support himself, even on one elbow, he collapsed back to the jade floor.

Kesira shouted, "Stop it! You can't hurt him. You can't!"

"He is weaker than I," gloated Ayondela. "There might never be another opportunity. I loved once but no longer. I will accomplish more than Lenc ever dreamed of!"

All around Ayondela's throne billowed her frightening clouds. The vaporous masses huddled together, hesitant at first, then with growing boldness. They floated at knee-level across the broad floor, leaving behind a shimmering on every bit of jade they touched. Kesira saw creatures writhing in the clouds, half seen, totally frightening. Did those beasts produce the savage cuts with bared talon or were they only products of Ayondela's demented mind sent to horrify her victims even more?

Kesira tried her feeble powers against the clouds and failed. They roiled with internal storm winds now. Then they crept away from Ayondela's throne, stalking Zolkan, Molimo, Kesira.

The *trilla* bird let out a muffled cry that stopped as soon as the clouds boiled over him on their way to Molimo. Again Kesira tried to halt that advance. Again she failed.

Clouds rustled wetly on her arms and cheek and neck. Blood sprouted in red rivulets. She struggled to her feet. The clouds encircled her, then rose. Of Molimo she had no sight. The man had been covered totally by the shining magical mists.

"These are a perversion of nature," Kesira called out.

"Is there anything you do which isn't against the normal flow of the universe?"

Ayondela laughed, dementia seizing her in its grip once again. Green tusks throbbed with inner light. Her scepter pointed, and the clouds obeyed.

Kesira steeled herself not to cry out in pain. Her resolve vanished the instant the clouds stroked up the insides of her thighs and blood ran in torrents down her legs. Her cry lifted and reverberated in the audience chamber.

And was drowned out by another.

The baby began to cry again.

Chapter Nineteen

KESIRA MINETTE HELD the baby close to her body, but insistent, small fists beat against her. She relented, and the baby cried even louder. His rich, oddly full voice rose to drown out Ayondela's chanted spells. The intensity mounted until Kesira was forced to put the baby on the floor and clap protective hands over her ears. And still the cry grew.

Ayondela stopped gesturing with her scepter and fell silent. Her spells died. The clouds trembled and began creeping away from baby and nun. The expression of fear that came over Ayondela heartened Kesira, but the woman found it difficult to explain. What was it that the female demon feared so? The way the baby's cries repelled the clouds? Or was there more to it?

"Stop it." Ayondela groaned.

She staggered back and sat heavily on her throne. Weak hands failed to lift her scepter. The ice wand fell from nerveless fingers and shattered to glistening shards on the floor. "The sound. Stop it, stop it!"

"Release the land from your spells," demanded Kesira. "Bring back your clouds. Stop the death and destruction."

"I can't stand it. I . . . I curse you!" Ayondela lifted one trembling hand of gleaming jade and pointed at Kesira. Once, this would have terrified Kesira. Not now. She saw how debilitated the demon had become. And still the baby cried.

"That accomplishes nothing," Kesira said. "Give up the

214

power given you by the jade. Only by returning to the old ways can you live happily."

"Rouvin," the demon whispered. Anger—insanity—returned to Ayondela's face.

The baby's cry reached a crescendo.

Ayondela exploded, scattering fragments of jade in all directions.

Kesira dropped over the baby to protect him from the shower. Off to one side Kesira heard Molimo whimpering as the new jade rain cascaded on him. Her heart went out to him, but to protect the infant she had to stay where she was. When the fragments of jade demon stopped falling, she straightened. Zolkan tended Molimo; Kesira took the baby in her arms and slowly walked to Ayondela's throne.

Huge cracks had appeared in the solid jade where Ayondela had touched it. Kesira stared in mute amazement at how completely the demon had been destroyed—by an infant's cry.

The baby tugged at her blouse. She looked down into his pale eyes and failed to read the emotions churning there. Elation? She doubted it. Fear? Not a trace. It was as if the child had done a workmanlike job and was content with the result.

"What are you?" she asked softly. The baby turned his head as he tugged once more. Kesira looked away to a spot just behind the throne. One of Ayondela's tusks lay on the floor, softly pulsing with green light. She bent and lightly ran her fingertips over the tusk. Power rushed into her body, renewing her, making her whole once again.

Kesira backed away from it, but the baby protested.

"You want me to take it?" she asked. The baby nodded, showing mature intelligence in his infant's body. Kesira gingerly reached out and touched the long tooth. Pleasure filled her, but she had grown. She had tasted the power of other demons and knew that, somehow, this remnant of the jade demon posed no threat to her.

If anything, it offered solace—and hope.

Gelya had given strict orders against carrying steel

weapons. Kesira hefted the tusk like a knife blade. It lacked much as a slashing weapon, but as a thrusting one, it carried good balance and a point both deadly and seemingly unbreakable. She tucked the jade tusk into the knotted blue cord and gold sash at her waist. The baby smiled at her and all was well.

"Zolkan," she called out. "Is Molimo all right?"

"More dead than alive," came the grim words. "Hurt. Jade hurt him badly."

Kesira rushed to Molimo's side. The man's face was drawn and the pallor frightened her. She helped Zolkan move the man; he had fallen uncomfortably over her staff. Kesira pushed the staff to one side and stroked Molimo's forehead, summoning what healing powers she could. The wounds caused by the crystal clouds vanished, but the grayness remained, making him appear as if someone had cut his throat and drained all the blood from his body.

Molimo's eyelids flickered, then opened. His lips moved, but Kesira made no sense of what he tried to say.

Zolkan dropped between them and beat her back with his wings. "Jade tooth!" the *trilla* bird protested. "It kills Molimo."

"What?" Kesira looked down to her waist where Ayondela's tusk still pulsated a soft green. She reached for the tusk to throw it away, but the baby's cry stopped her. Kesira found herself caught between Molimo's infirmity and the baby's insistence that she keep the artifact. Before she could sort it all out, a clap of thunder filled the jade chamber. The shock wave bowled her over. Kesira grabbed frantically for her staff, only to find herself rolling along the floor slick with blood. She slammed hard into one wall.

Groggy, she turned to see what had caused the thunder.

Kesira Minette had experienced no fear facing Ayondela. She quaked inside now that she faced Lenc. Around the remaining jade demon's feet burned small white flames, flames akin to one desecrating the altar of Gelya in her nunnery. Lenc, powerful and arrogant, stood with arms crossed, wearing an expression of complete disdain.

"*You* have caused Ayondela such ... discomfort?" His mocking words were accompanied by a slow, dramatic sweep of a heavily muscled green arm.

Kesira fought to get to her feet. Using the staff helped, but fear robbed her of true steadiness.

"You turned her against the world. You used her."

"Of course I did." Lenc laughed at Kesira's surprise. "You thought I would deny it? Hardly." His booming laugh rivaled any thunder in the Yearn Mountains. "For every use of the jade power a few seconds is nibbled away from a demon's lifespan. The others—Eznofadil and Howenthal and poor, troubled Ayondela—all performed their tasks well while I stood by and supervised their efforts."

"You do not mourn their passing?"

"Mourn? I *sought* their deaths. No one dares oppose me now. I alone can rule supreme. No demon remains with a fraction of my power. And Ayondela has virtually completed subjugation of the mortal world with her delightful clouds."

"Emperor Kwasian still opposes you!"

"So? His power is limited. All his farmlands are destroyed. How does he feed those who are still loyal? They will drift away when I offer them food."

"In exchange for what?"

"Why, in exchange for worshiping me, of course!"

Lenc laughed boisterously. Kesira fingered Ayondela's tooth in her sash. The warmth of the jade might have perverted Ayondela, but in a mortal's hand it might return the world to its natural order. Kesira took a few steps forward, thinking to draw the tusk and use it as a dagger aimed directly at Lenc's heart.

Jade destroying jade. It seemed to satisfy the symmetries of the universe.

"Hold!" bellowed Lenc. White flame replaced the demon's fingers. The leaping tendrils of cold fire pointed directly at her. Ayondela's ice scepter had sent freezing waves up and down her spine; now Lenc's fire burned her every nerve ending.

"You are only a poor mortal. One of Gelya's pets. Nothing more. You cannot hope to harm me, the supreme ruler of this entire world!"

Kesira started to boast of the other three jade demons' demise, then bit back her hot words. For all she knew, Lenc had maneuvered her into the position of killing pawns he found no longer useful.

"Ah, you see something of my schemes. Do you enjoy the visitations I have made upon you through the rune sticks?"

"You?" The revelation was almost more than Kesira could bear. "You sent me all those visions?"

"All? I can hardly claim all. Some. The ones I found most beneficial. It hardly mattered whether you showed fear or not in front of Ayondela, but it amused me if you destroyed her."

"I didn't," Kesira said before she could check herself.

"Oh?" Lenc looked around the room. Molimo lay like a corpse on the floor, Zolkan nested down on his chest. The baby quietly rested a foot away. Kesira ran to the child.

"He destroyed Ayondela? My son is more powerful than I had thought."

"*Your* son?" Kesira refused to believe it.

"It happened soon after the full power of the jade filled my arteries. The sexual thrill couldn't be denied. I visited dozens of peasants along the Pharna River. I think I recognize something of this one's mother in him."

"You can't take him!" Kesira swung her staff around and planted her feet firmly for the fight.

"Take him? Why should I even *want* him? My bastards will overpopulate the world. I can have any mortal I want— and any demon!" Lenc leered and stroked along one cheek with his flame-tipped forefinger. "I can even have you."

Kesira didn't respond. She would die defending the baby and herself.

Lenc appeared to know her every thought. "Die you will, foolish mortal. But I waste precious time. I must consolidate all that my three late allies have so graciously created for me and left as their dutiful legacy to the one destined to reign."

"Lenc, stop!" shouted Kesira.

"Thank you for destroying them for me. You saved me some little annoyance." Lenc flashed out of existence, a second peal of thunder filling the jade chamber.

Kesira stood like a statue, the enormity of all that had happened seizing her mind and emotions. Deadened inside, the nun simply stared at the empty spot where Lenc had been. The jade had ignited, and tiny white flames licked at the floor.

"We must flee! Feel it! Feel it!"

Kesira shook free of her shock enough to ask Zolkan, "What are you talking about?"

"Palace crumbles. We die if we stay!"

Kesira looked up and saw huge cracks widening in the ceiling. Smaller fractures from the walls joined them. The sound of stone *tearing* filled her ears.

She scooped up the baby, noting that the child wasn't responsible for this added destruction. He looked up at her with a quiet confident smile that warmed her.

A huge chunk of jade smashed onto the floor not ten feet away. The fragments, more brutal than those from the Emperor's artillery shells, ripped at her flesh. She winced and stumbled over Molimo. Kesira righted herself and slung the baby in the harness around her shoulders so that both her hands would be free.

"Up, Molimo, up! I can't carry you!" She tugged at the man. His eyelids fluttered and opened, but the stricken look showed that all his physical strength had vanished. Somehow the jade had sapped him totally. Molimo lay closer to death than life.

She dragged him along for a few feet before realizing how futile this was. Pieces of Ayondela's audience chamber rained down all around them. When the throne exploded and sent shards arrowing outward, Kesira knew they were doomed.

Hugging the baby close, she said, "I'd hoped for more for you. I'm sorry it has to end this way." But the baby smiled and pointed a pudgy finger toward her staff.

Kesira frowned, then dodged another large cross beam falling from the roof. The baby showed no fright. Was he really Lenc's son? Kesira couldn't doubt that, but if so . . .

She had no further time for reflection on the baby's lineage or the father's motives. The immense jade walls started to shatter, to explode, to send jade bullets throughout the room. The small injuries she and Molimo sustained would soon become major ones as the destruction mounted. Instinctively Kesira fended off a flying hunk of sharp-edged jade with her staff. She missed by fractions but still deflected it when a willowy branch sprouted.

The baby cooed. Pale eyes locked with her brown ones, and Kesira *knew*.

She planted the staff firmly on the floor and turned her healing powers on it. At first nothing happened. She brushed away the blood and jade dust settling on her and concentrated. Wemilat. Cayabbib. Even the tusk taken from Ayondela. All contributed to her flow of energy from deep inside to her staff. Just as she had once caused tiny leaves to spring forth, now she urged the limber wooden staff back to life.

Branches sprouted. Leaves popped out. The staff thickened and became a true trunk. And the fledgling tree grew. Almost faster than she could comprehend, the limbs turned bigger and thrust out protective branches able to stop the jade from raining down on them.

"Molimo, help me. I can't carry you. We must get under the tree." He feebly kicked and slipped as she tugged on his arm. They eventually crouched near the now-massive brown trunk, Ayondela's palace crashing in ruin all around them.

The destruction accelerated, and the protection given by the towering tree increased in proportion. In less than five minutes the cold, crisp night sky showed through the tree's leaves. Kesira and Molimo ventured out to stare at the harsh pinpoints of stars.

A knee-high mound of jade dust was all that survived from Ayondela's once-massive palace.

"I can't believe the destruction was this complete," Kesira said in wonder.

"Lenc's doing. Lenc thought to kill us all," said Zolkan from the lowest branch of the tree.

"Perhaps so." Kesira saw the tree surge once again, roots spreading like dark brown snakes through the jade dust. The intense churning action showed that the tree assimilated the jade and forced it into the dirt. In a few minutes only a patina to the soil marked where Ayondela's jade castle had been.

"The tree is going to be permanent. I can hardly believe the way it's taken root," she said. "And I don't even know exactly what I did to trigger its growth."

Molimo motioned weakly toward the gravel road spiraling back down the granite mountain. Red splotches marked his cheekbones, but his color still looked unhealthy.

"The jade did this to you?" she asked. He nodded. She lightly touched the jade tusk. Molimo backed away from her. "I'll get rid of it." Kesira grasped the tooth and started to pull it free.

The baby cried. Kesira started to calm the infant but found herself paralyzed. As the child had disrupted the substance of Ayondela's body with his cries, so now did he force her to his will. Try as she might, Kesira couldn't remove the tooth from her sash.

"Down the mountain," she said in a choked voice. Molimo nodded and stumbled ahead of her, seeming to understand that the child forced her to keep the jade tusk. A soft shower of feathers and a loud flapping told her that Zolkan had taken wing.

Kesira started down the winding road, weary in both soul and body. Lenc had used her to eliminate his competition—the other jade demons. He now had only to consolidate his power and rule however long the jade permitted him to survive—which might be centuries. Those long years would mean abject slavery for all humankind, unless she found some way of fighting Lenc.

Kesira Minette looked over her shoulder at the sturdy tree reaching for the cloudless heavens. Somehow, in that symbol, she found hope. Lenc would be destroyed. How, she didn't know, but he would be.

4: THE WHITE FIRE

This one's for Dick Patten and Peter C. Rabbit

Chapter One

THEY CAMPED at the base of the towering granite spire, tired in body and spirit. Kesira Minette dropped to the ground, almost forgetting to cradle the infant she carried so gingerly. So much had changed, she thought. So much. She brushed a dirty strand of brunette hair back from her eyes and stared down at the baby boy.

His pale gray eyes boldly met hers—challenged her. No trace of child existed, save in body.

"What goes on inside your head?" she wondered aloud. Kesira cringed, waiting for the baby's answering cry, but it did not come. Atop the mountain, she had met the jade demon Ayondela and had almost perished in the conflict. If it hadn't been for the baby's shrill, shattering cries that had disintegrated the demon like a dropped pane of window glass, Kesira knew that she—and the world—would have been ground under Ayondela's heel.

Not that the outcome proved any better for either Kesira Minette or the world in general. One of four jade demons still lived, and Lenc was the worst of the lot. More cunning, stronger, more insane, he ruled now without opposition. He had used Kesira and her companions Molimo and the *trilla* bird Zolkan for his own evil ends. Cat's-paws. They had fought and destroyed Lenc's enemies without even realizing what they did, and now the jade demon ruled supreme.

Even worse, the baby she held, the one who eyed her so sagely, the one whose slightest cry brought death and suffering, this little one had been sired by Lenc.

"True," sputtered the green-plumed *trilla* bird. Zolkan fluttered to a bare tree branch overhead. The crunching of his powerful talons into the wood beat a counterpoint to the

1

soft sighing of wind through the leaves remaining on the tree's highest limbs. "Bratling is Lenc's spawn. Kill it before it kills us!"

"I . . ." Kesira stilled her rampaging emotions. "I can't," she said, swallowing hard. "The boy may be Lenc's son, but he is also half human."

"You call that charwoman Parvey Yera human?" Zolkan spat out a thick red gob of bark he'd been gnawing. "Lucky I am *trilla* bird. Filthy human."

"We owe it to her to tend her son."

"We owe bitch nothing!" screeched Zolkan. The bird turned one harsh black eye toward the infant, then broke the gaze. The *trilla* bird could not outstare the boy.

Parvey Yera had been driven mad by deprivation, and her husband had given his life aiding them in destroying another of the jade demons. Eznofadil would have slain them but for the man. If for nothing else, Kesira owed something to Raellard Yera, and she'd have to repay the debt by caring for the baby, even if this boy weren't his son.

"We owe her," Kesira said firmly. "And the Order of Gelya is not to be accused of turning away the needy. Never has one of my order wantonly killed a child."

"Not human child. Demon spawn!" squawked Zolkan. The bird settled down, hunching his sloping shoulders and pulling his wings up to shield his head. In a few minutes, he tucked his large head under the left wing and snored loudly.

Kesira busied herself making a small cooking fire. Now and then she turned to peer over her shoulder at the red granite massif that had held Ayondela's jade palace like a jewel in an emperor's crown. Clouds drifted slowly around the cap, alternately veiling and revealing silently. She shuddered. Ayondela had commanded those clouds to cut and slash. Kesira still bore dozens of deep cuts from the demon's crystal clouds and hundreds of shallower scratches.

"Ayondela is dead. So are Eznofadil and Howenthal," she said quietly, firmly, trying to convince herself that she had done well. In one respect, she had. No one else might have opposed the power of the jade for so long. Her fury at Lenc's destruction of her patron Gelya had fueled her quest for vengeance, at first, but now she felt only hollowness. So much of what she'd accomplished had been abetted by Lenc himself. The demon had needed Ayondela and the others to bolster his power until the jade totally dominated his body, as it did now.

Now Lenc alone ruled the world. His slightest whim had to be obeyed, in violation of the eons-old pact between human and demon. Kesira felt the ember of hatred being fanned back into full blaze at the unfairness of it all. Humans should rule humans; demons were supposed to tend to their own affairs, asking only for minor obeisances and tributes.

No longer. Lenc wanted everyone to worship him. Kesira clenched her hands into tight balls and ground her teeth together so hard it triggered shooting pains up and down her neck. Consciously relaxing, using the meditative techniques of her order, she eased the tension. But after doing so much, to find only ashes...

Soft footfalls caused her to turn. A tall, dark-haired, dark-eyed man of middle years worked his way up the small ravine over which she camped. Clutched in one hand was a rabbit, fat from a delayed summer's feasting. Molimo dropped the animal beside her, then knelt.

"Will one be enough?" she asked. Molimo pointed to his mouth and rubbed his stomach, indicating that he had already eaten. Kesira tried to hold back the tears and failed. Molimo reached out and touched her. She flinched away.

"I cannot help it," he wrote on a small tablet. "The changes are too strong now, since confronting Lenc. I am stronger, but so is the shape alteration urge."

"I'm sorry, Molimo. I know you can't help yourself." Kesira wiped away the tears and found dirty smudges where the salty drops had mixed with dust on her cheeks. Molimo, caught in a rain of jade, had been cursed not only with having his tongue ripped from his mouth but also an inability to hold human form. When he least wanted, he changed into a wolf, without the slightest control over animalistic urges. He had never harmed her or Zolkan, but Kesira knew that the intensity of the transformation into other-beast now overwhelmed Molimo.

"You can control it," she said. "You can, Molimo!" The man shook his head. For the first time she saw red sunlight glinting off silver strands. After the jade rain, when she had tended his wounds, Molimo looked hardly older than seventeen. Now? Kesira guessed forty. The nearness of jade had taken its toll on him, even as he regained physical strength.

"Does Lenc age this way, also?" she asked, before she could still her words. Molimo nodded, then wrote quickly.

She peered over his shoulder, reading, "The jade makes him invincible in human terms, but it also robs him of virtual immortality. He has traded longevity for power."

"But you're not a demon. The effect of the jade . . ." Her voice trailed off.

"I have been touched by the jade." He pointed at his sundered mouth. "Its mere presence makes me feel faint." Molimo pointed at the jade tusk thrust through Kesira's belt. His hand shook.

"I don't know why I took Ayondela's tooth," Kesira said. "The baby—he forced me to do it." The words grated and caused her almost physical injury, just uttering them. How did the baby influence her? He was Lenc's son; Kesira could offer no other explanation. "I don't want to keep it because I see what it does to you, but I can't get rid of it! I just can't!"

Her hand flashed to the six-inch-long fang. To prove her point, Kesira pulled it free and threw it as hard as she could. The baby watched impassively, the only indication he even noticed being the small upturnings of his lips in a faint smile. The green fang cartwheeled into the sunset, stopped and hung suspended in midair, then slowly turned and curved back. It landed in the dirt at Kesira's feet, sharp point in the ground. Struggle as she might, Kesira couldn't prevent herself from bending over and pulling it free. She thrust it back into her dirty yellow sash. Only then did the compulsion die and give her a moment's surcease.

She blacked out. When she came to, the sun had dipped behind the Sarn Mountain range and chill night breezes stalked her. Kesira pulled her tattered robe more tightly around her thin frame, then moved closer to the fire Molimo had maintained. Of the man-wolf she saw no trace, but Zolkan still perched on the tree limb.

As if reading her thoughts, the *trilla* bird said, "Gone. He hunts. You are to eat."

Molimo had dressed and roasted the rabbit, but Kesira found she had little appetite. Zolkan flapped down and hit the ground hard enough to send him staggering. The *trilla* bird waddled over to her and shoved a portion of the meat forward with the tip of his long wing.

"Eat."

Silently, Kesira obeyed. The baby reached out and gripped her robe when she had finished, demanding his own dinner. She found a rent in the fabric and allowed the infant to nurse contentedly at her demon-kissed breast. Kesira sighed with the simple pleasure of the feelings inside her; the spot where the demon Wemilat's lips had touched her breast now burned with an inner warmth. Wemilat had died so that the jade demon Howenthal might also perish.

Death, always death, Kesira thought, suddenly bitter. Her patron Gelya had died, killed by Lenc. The jade demon had left behind his mocking sigil, the cold, dancing white fire that desecrated all it touched. Wemilat had been ugly and misshapen, but his spirit had been beautiful. He, too, had died. And so many others, both demon and human.

"Do not dwell on it. We have much to do," said Zolkan. Long trip. Long and tiresome."

"Why leave?" Kesira asked. The listlessness fell over her like winter's first soft snow blanketing the forests. "With Lenc invincible, one place is as good as another. Or as bad. The Sarn Mountains have a beauty to them that appeals to me."

"More than your nunnery?"

"No," she said. "But what is there for me? Lenc's flame consumes Gelya's altar. Sister Fenelia is dead. Dana, Kai and the others—all dead."

She brushed dirty fingertips across the knotted blue cord indicating her sisterhood in the Order of Gelya, then traced along the once-gold sash proclaiming her to be the Sister of Mission. Kesira laughed without humor. She had become

Sister of Mission simply by being the last of Gelya's worshipers. The others had died or lost faith.

"Why do I still believe? Gelya is dead by Lenc's hand.
Why do I continue? Why not stay here for the rest of my
days? The land is rich enough. I could grow some vegetables
and perhaps even start an orchard of fruit trees. Game
abounds. Molimo finds no difficulty in hunting."

"You would allow Lenc to enslave everyone?" asked
Zolkan.

"How can I stop him?" Kesira morosely poked at the
fire with a slender twig picked up from the ground. "You
say it wrongly, also. Lenc already *has* enslaved everyone.
Even my rune castings were dictated by his whim." Her
only talent had been revealed to her as a fraud, as signs sent
by Lenc to guide her in the directions he desired.

"Are you so sure?" pressed Zolkan. "Why must jade
demon speak truthfully? Lenc lies for agony it causes others."

For a moment, Kesira brightened; but the hope sputtered
and died just as the fire in front of her did. She made no
effort to rekindle the fire—or her faith.

"Feel sorry for yourself," Zolkan taunted. "If this is all
Gelya taught, pah!" The *trilla* bird spat. A tiny, quivering
column of steam rose from the fire's embers.

"I feel for the world," Kesira said softly, more to herself
than to Zolkan. Then she said, "That's not entirely true.
How can any mortal embrace all the world? I care for what
has happened to me and those I know."

Her eyes darted to the peacefully sleeping baby. In repose
he appeared no different from any other child—but no ordinary infant shattered the jade flesh of a demon and brought
down an entire palace with a single outcry. Truly, he had
to be the spawn of a demon. And so, even this small thing,
this newborn life, this simple joy, was tainted.

Live according to the tenets, simply and well, Gelya had
promised, and the future was assured. The universe had
order and everything was in its place. She need never want.
Obey the Emperor, worship Gelya, know her place in society
and the world, execute her duty to the best of her ability,
and life would be kind and good. Those were the things
she had been taught.

Those were the lies.

"Go to Limaden." Zolkan waddled back and forth, his fluttering wings fanning the fire to new life. Kesira listened to the bird with only half an ear as her thoughts turned inward.

She had done much in the past few months. When she had returned to the nunnery from Blinn with the lamp oil requested by Sister Fenelia, Kesira had composed only a few lines of her death song. A few lines describing her parents' death at the hands of brigands and her loyalty to Gelya—and nothing more.

Since that ill-fated day when the skies rained jade and she found mute Molimo, much had happened that must be included. Kesira began composing the lines. When the death song was finished—and only she would know that instant—her life would end.

Kesira mentally wrought and turned and twisted the words to her own particular scansion, music finding its way between words and phrases to illuminate and lend substance and emphasis. New verses told of Molimo and Zolkan, of the jade demons, of despair and triumph, sacrifice and death, daring Howenthal's Quaking Lands, the frozen waves of the Sea of Katad, the crystal clouds cloaking Ayondela's final resting place. All those fell neatly into her death song.

Kesira's brown eyes again checked the baby. He slept soundly now, a smile on pink lips. She couldn't bring herself to compose the verses dealing with the boy. The rhymes failed; she became confused and even the notes turned flat.

"My time is not at hand," she said.

"Foolish human. You know nothing," grumbled Zolkan.

"There is no need to go to Limaden," she said. "The Emperor Kwasian is there. He of all mortals might be able to hold out against Lenc. But what is there for me in the Emperor's capital?"

"More than there is here."

Kesira shook her head; she felt dull with fatigue. To stay here . . . the land was favorable and the tranquility appealed to her. She had seen too much death and suffering—had caused too much by her actions. Kesira Minette wanted only to rest. . . .

Her eyelids sank like the setting sun, slowly, inexorably, and she entered a land where dreams were stalked by nightmares. Kesira sat upright, eyes wide, sweat pouring down face and body. Her fingers gripped harsh, rocky soil and she looked around fearfully.

"What is it?" she demanded of Zolkan.

The bird had again perched on the denuded tree limb. Even in the darkness she saw his beady eyes glistening. "Molimo," the *trilla* bird said simply.

Kesira pushed herself to her feet, propping herself up unsteadily with the staff she had fashioned from a green sapling. She longed for her old, stolid stonewood staff, but even that—Gelya's sacred wood—had been destroyed. Since then, she'd had scant opportunity to season a new staff. Not for the first time she cursed Gelya's prohibition against using steel weapons.

Unbidden, her hand went to the jade tusk sheathed at her belt.

"What trouble has Molimo found?" she asked, fighting down guilt as she fleetingly hoped Zolkan would not answer and that she could go back to sleep.

"Humans do not tolerate other-beasts. Bands of your kind hunt those like Molimo."

Kesira flinched as if the *trilla* bird had physically struck her. Never before had he used phrases like "your kind" to indict the men and women trying to cope with the afflictions brought by Lenc and the power of the jade the demon had ingested. In doing so, Zolkan put her in what she had unconsciously always considered an inferior group.

"Where? Maybe I can help him."

"Why bother?" the *trilla* bird squawked. "He goes on to fight Lenc. He must. You have chosen another path."

"Molimo's in trouble. Curse you if you won't help!" Kesira cocked her head to one side and strained to hear the slight sounds that had awakened her. A wolf's mournful yelpings were drowned out by the ululation of what she thought at first to be a pack of animals. Then the noise became clearer: human voices. A hunting band, seeking out the other-beasts, planning to vent its collective rage and frustration on the poor creatures trapped between human and animal.

Like Molimo.

"Watch after the boy," she said, getting her feet firmly under her now. She didn't even pause to see if Zolkan would obey. It hardly mattered. The boy had proven he could take care of himself. Hadn't he destroyed Ayondela?

And who would ever threaten the son of Lenc? Kesira pushed that from her mind, beginning the settling exercises that had given her tranquility through much of her life. Gelya had taught that fear sprang from uncertainty; tenseness was caused by fear. She relaxed. Slowly, muscles unknotted and confidence returned. While Kesira knew she was no match for a trained fighter, she could more than hold her own against a peasant brandishing a crude spear or a hay fork.

Her sisters in the Order of Gelya had never taken vows of nonviolence, nor had Kesira ever believed such pacifism possible. Gelya preached that violence spawned violence. Kesira tried to avoid conflict, would not initiate the attack if she could prevent it; but often, especially in these times of death and disorder, violence was the only saving response to violence.

Kesira crashed through low shrubs and made more noise than a dozen marching soldiers for a few hundred feet, until she was sure that those in the hunting pack had heard her approach. Then she changed tactics. On feet as silent as if she'd swaddled them in cotton, Kesira advanced, staff clutched so hard her forearms began to knot with the strain. She forced her muscles to relax. Over and over she went through the litany that would give her the needed mental and physical tranquility to react with maximum speed. Only when the nun was sure of herself did she begin circling.

Eventually Kesira found a rocky perch overlooking a sandy pit. Molimo snapped and yelped and dashed about inside a ragged circle formed by the hunters.

"Filthy beast," snarled one man in a voice more animal-like than the wolf's howls.

"It's an accursed other-beast," shouted another from the far side of the circle. He took the opportunity to poke Molimo in the side with a spear. The man-wolf spun; his strong jaws clamped on the spear's haft. The loud *snap!* as it broke echoed through the night, reverberating off stony buttes and down lonely canyons.

For a moment the men stood, stunned, as if it had never occurred to them that the other-beast they chevied might prove truly dangerous. Kesira almost cheered; but before she could, the men stiffened their resolve and surged forward as one, intending to overwhelm Molimo.

The wolf ducked under their probing spears and sticks, found a fleshy thigh and ripped. The man's screams did nothing to deter the others this time. If anything, it goaded them on. Red stripes crisscrossed Molimo's gray fur as they swung spear and knife, stick and rock at him.

"Stop!" Kesira shouted, rising up on the rock. They had heard—and forgotten—her noisy approach. Now they drew back fearfully to appraise this new danger.

"What do you want? Get you gone!" shouted the man with a large, jagged scar running diagonally across his face. Even in the dark, the cicatrice seemed to glow with an inner light.

"Where did you get the scar?" Kesira asked, deliberately pitching her voice lower to give an air of authority. She softened her words and spoke so that all had to force themselves to hear.

"Ayondela!" the man shouted. "She cut me with jade!"

The others nodded and murmured. They'd heard the story, no doubt told many times around the communal fires. And who knew? Kesira thought that the man might speak truthfully. The scar's odd inner light indicated no ordinary wound.

"She cut you? With one of her tusks?"

"A fingernail," the man said, almost as if this were an admission of cowardice.

"Let the wolf go."

"It's an other-beast," someone shouted. The leader with the scar motioned for silence.

"Aye, that it is. An other-beast. They steal our children and slay our women. They were touched badly by the power of the jade. They must be destroyed!"

"Let him go or you'll feel the true power of the jade." Kesira pulled the tusk from her dirty gold sash. Clutching it like a dagger, she held the jade high for all to see. The tusk's faint glow brought instant silence.

Then, "She's a demon!"

"No!" Kesira shouted. "I am no demon. But I killed Ayondela, and this is her tusk. This other-beast aided me. Molimo, join me."

The men milled around, uncertain. For a fleeting instant Kesira thought she and Molimo might escape without further argument. But the jade-scarred man brought the others around too quickly.

"She lies to save the other-beast! You, Cord, didn't you lose wife and two children to the shape changers? And you, Exas, what of your mother? Doesn't she hobble on one leg because of the other-beast that attacked her?" The knowing, fearful mutters convinced Kesira that she had lost control.

"Molimo, hurry!" she shouted.

The men attacked again just as the wolf leaped to the rock beside her. Kesira had the advantage for a few seconds, and her staff cracked open several foreheads and broke some exposed wrists. But there were too many of them, and her arms quickly became leaden. She had been through too much, with little rest and even less food. A strong, meaty hand gripped her ankle and pulled her to the sandy pit.

She had replaced Molimo as the object of their hatred. Spears gouged and rocks pelted her. Kesira doubled up and tried to pull away, but she quickly realized that if she tried only to defend herself, she would die.

"No!" Kesira roared. She rose, spinning her staff so fast it became a virtual wall of green sapling encircling her, knocking away spear thrusts and bony fists.

When one man knocked the staff spinning from her hands, Kesira stood defenseless. Again she withdrew the jade tusk from her sash. Now it glowed a vibrant green. Wielded like a dagger, it didn't do much harm—but it *was* Ayondela's tusk. The men backed off.

As they retreated, Molimo attacked, biting and snarling. And from above came a green rocket bursting noisily above Kesira's head. Feathers floated down around her as Zolkan's pinions cracked under the strain of his dive and the sudden midair stop. Talons raked and the *trilla* bird's sharp beak ripped at exposed flesh. The threefold attack, by nun and bird and wolf, drove the men back.

"Run!" shouted the scarred man, when he saw his companions fleeing.

The men crashed off into the brush, and eventually the sounds of their boots against rocks and scrub faded away.

Kesira sank to the sandy ground and cradled her head in shaking hands. There could be no rest, not while even one of the jade demons walked the land.

"Zolkan," she said in an uncharacteristically weak voice, "how far is it to Limaden?"

"Far," the *trilla* bird replied. "Very far."

Kesira didn't know whether Zolkan meant in distance or in what they must endure. It hardly mattered either way. If the land of her birth was to again find peace, she must confront Lenc and destroy the remaining jade demon.

That was her fate; that was her accursed destiny.

Chapter Two

THE OTHER-BEAST hunters dogged their steps like a carrion eater waiting for its intended dinner to finally die. Kesira couldn't remember feeling more driven, more tired, less able to cope with the pressures of such dogged pursuit. But somehow she kept on moving toward Limaden, although she had no idea what lay in the Emperor Kwasian's capital for them.

"If these ignorant peasants are so vehement about killing unfortunates like Molimo," she asked Zolkan, "why won't the citizens of the capital seek his hide, also?"

"Might," admitted Zolkan. The bird fluttered and swooped and finally came to rest on her shoulder. Kesira didn't exactly wince when the *trilla* bird's sharp talons dug in; but she sagged from physical exhaustion. They had spent four hard days a'trail after fighting off the other-beast hunters. While they hadn't encountered another band as large or as determined, the nibblings of those smaller bands were almost as deadly: A cut here, a reopened wound there, and strength fled.

Strength none of them had.

"We should be glad we find only farmers," Zolkan remarked. "Nehan-dir and his Order of the Steel Crescent would make fine dinner of us. They eat *trilla* bird meat." The large bird shuddered hard enough to unbalance Kesira. She regained her stride, but with even less confidence. What Zolkan said was true.

Nehan-dir and his mercenaries had been left on the far side of the Sarn Mountains engaged in mortal combat with a small company of the Emperor's Guard. The Order of the Steel Crescent would sell its loyalty to whatever patron offered the greatest chance for power. Nehan-dir, as leader, had selected poorly. Their original patron, Tolek the Spare, had sold them to another demon for cancellation of a gambling debt. Even among the demons, with their extremes of emotion, desires and angers and loves many times magnified over those of humans, this unseemly behavior had brought only scorn. The Order of the Steel Crescent had abandoned its new patron in favor of another offering more raw power—the jade demon Howenthal.

Kesira had been responsible for Howenthal's destruction, again leaving the Steel Crescent without a patron. Going with the gusty winds of change, they had sought out Ayondela. Now that their newest patron had perished, Nehan-dir commanded that they worship Lenc.

This time Kesira thought they had chosen well. Lenc could grant them infinite power—or sudden death. But whatever the jade demon commanded, he would not simply cast them off or trade them in payment of gambling debts. She allowed a faint smile to cross her lips. A chance existed that, for a third time, she would personally rob Nehan-dir and the Steel Crescent of a patron. Howenthal and Ayondela had become jade dust on a devastated palace floor; she might still find a way to destroy Lenc.

The woman realized, even as she smiled at these wondrous thoughts, that they were sheer fantasy. When every footfall threatened to be her last, when her body ached and wounds burned with gelid fire and her own kind sought her death because she consorted with other-beasts, what chance did she have of destroying the last jade demon?

"Do you anticipate Nehan-dir finding us?" she asked Zolkan. The bird didn't answer, but Molimo dropped back from his position as scout. The man—he had stayed in human form for almost two days now—pulled out his tablet and wrote quickly.

"If Lenc informs the Steel Crescent of our whereabouts, we can expect visitors at any time," Kesira read.

"Can't we use the underground transport system?" she asked. Molimo had revealed a marvelous magical-powered cart that shot through tunnels dug with cruel power. They had dipped under the Sarn Mountains and reached the very base of Ayondela's cloud-capped stronghold in the wink of an eye. Zolkan had later remarked that this array of tunnels extended throughout the Empire and that one terminus lay less than an hour's walk from her destroyed nunnery in the foothills of the distant Yearn Mountains.

"Lenc destroyed it. He was angered after we used it to reach Ayondela," explained the *trilla* bird. Not for the first time Kesira wondered how Zolkan came by these snippets of information. He was seldom out of her sight. His occasional flights to reconnoiter and to scout for food provided no chance to exchange such data with others. But Kesira's lethargy prevented her from again questioning Zolkan. The bird always ignored her direct questions or cleverly turned the topic to one less interesting.

"How much farther to Limaden?" she asked.

Molimo wrote, "We go to Kolya."

"What? Why? Zolkan was adamant about going to the capital. He said that Emperor Kwasian would be the focal point for resistance against Lenc."

Molimo nodded. His dark eyes retained some of the blazing green highlights they took on when he altered form. Kesira shivered, even though the afternoon wasn't yet chilly. Every time Molimo's eyes shone green, he found it harder to keep human shape, and he took a little longer to shift back after he became a wolf.

"Kolya holds our destiny. We either destroy Lenc there— or not at all."

"May all the demons curse you forever!" Kesira shouted, anger animating her. "You and Zolkan prattle on and on about these things. How do you *know?* Tell me your source of information. Don't keep me ignorant. Haven't we shared enough for you to trust me?"

Kesira was shocked speechless when Molimo stared her directly in the eyes and slowly shook his head. His stride lengthened and he outpaced her, leaving her with the *trilla* bird weighing her down.

Before she could protest, Zolkan cut her off. "Do not ask. There are matters too dangerous for you to know yet."

"Yet? You mean one day you'll deign to tell me? What am I? Your servant? Your toady doing all the menial chores?"

She glared at the green-plumed bird. Coldness gripped her soul when she read the answer in the bird's unblinking beady eye.

"That's all I am to you—and to Molimo," she said in a stunned voice.

"You are more. Always," the bird said. "One day you will know. One day."

She clutched the baby closer to her breast and stumbled along in the dying afternoon light. She hadn't believed such cruelty existed in the world as this just shown her by Molimo and Zolkan. Kesira had taken the *trilla* bird in and nursed him back to health after he flew into the nunnery's sacristy one wintry night. And Molimo? She had kept him alive after he'd been caught in the jade rain. What did they refuse to tell her after all they'd shared?

The sounds of another pack of other-beast hunters drove these thoughts from her mind. Her pace quickened, and they were soon free of their pursuers.

Kolya lay nineteen days' travel to the west.

Kesira Minette entered Kolya, uneasy at the crush of people around her. It had been many months since she had seen such crowds, and she had never frequented cities larger than provincial Blinn while at her nunnery. Zolkan's head swiveled around as the *trilla* bird took in the exotic sights and sounds that made Kesira queasy.

"Good place," the bird pronounced. "Not like cities where they eat *trilla* birds."

"How can you tell?" she asked. "There might be stalls over in the central market."

"I know." Zolkan's smugness told her that he was probably correct. How he could know with such certainty was another of the mysteries surrounding the bird.

Kesira pulled her tattered robes around her ankles and moved through the crowds, unsure where she headed. The paved streets felt unnatural to her after having trod so long on dirt roads, but the lack of dust rising to make her sneeze and cough soon offset any discomfort from the hardness of the surface.

She cradled the baby closer when a parade pushed its

way through the populace. Two small platforms carried by well-dressed servants sported altars. Behind each platform walked a priest with head bowed low, chanting incomprehensible words, censers pouring out noxious fumes. Kesira was well versed in worship of most patrons, this having been a required portion of her education at Sister Fenelia's hand, but this ceremony did not seem at all familiar.

"What patron do they worship?" she asked an onlooker. The woman turned and glared at Kesira, leaving without speaking. Contempt and even suppressed hatred radiated from her as she rounded the corner and vanished from Kesira's sight.

"Not one of their followers," Kesira guessed. "If we find out what patron they worship, we might be able to invoke aid and . . ."

Her words trailed off when she saw Zolkan shaking his head sadly, as if she were the village fool.

"They worship Lenc," she said, understanding bursting upon her like the blooming of an ice flower.

"Who else remains?"

Kesira sank to the paving, pulling her legs up close. The baby protested by reaching out an unnaturally strong hand and tugging at her robe. She ignored him. The world swung around her in crazy circles, the people stumbling over her and going on, muttering about derelicts. Kesira closed her eyes and tried not to cry. Every turn presented new and more fruitless paths to follow; all led to Lenc.

"Seeds of rebellion need nurturing in Kolya," said Zolkan so low that only she could hear. "You can stir them against the power of jade."

"Why bother? A pitiful rabble waving pointed sticks will not topple Lenc from his lofty throne. He is invincible now. He rules with an iron grip." Kesira smiled mirthlessly. "I should have said that he rules with a jade grip."

"He cannot be in all places at same time," Zolkan said. "Kolya is ripe for uprising against him. Few like yoke he places around their necks."

Kesira fought her way to her feet and stood with tired back against a cool stone building. A hint of autumn entered the city on the soft summer wind and chilled her. Summer had been delayed because of Ayondela's curse. Once she had broken the demon's curse, summer arrived quickly, but the natural roll of seasons now shortened the warmth and promised bleaker winter.

"We must find a place to stay. The night will be cold without shelter."

Kesira looked around, trying to locate Molimo, but the man had disappeared into the crowd. She shrugged this off. He'd have to be careful. The slightest hint of shape change would bring down the wrath of Kolya's citizens, of that she was sure. All across the plains on the way from the mountains they had seen roving bands of marauders intent on slaying other-beasts. Some even offered generous bounties for other-beast pelts. Kesira knew that this served only as an excuse for the brigand bands to pillage and rape as they had always done, but the general populace now believed these lies.

That bespoke a real fear on the part of ordinary people concerning the other-beasts.

"Molimo," she said softly.

"He scouts. He will return. Shape change will not overtake him. He fights it hard in city."

"I hope you're right." Kesira walked aimlessly down the main streets, through alleys to lesser thoroughfares; and finally she located the quieter residential sections of Kolya. She saw a small inn with neatly swept walkway, freshly painted sign and the air of caring about it.

"There," squawked Zolkan. "We stay there."

"You take to wing. They'd never allow me in with a *trilla* bird on my shoulder."

"Bigots," the bird grumbled, but he leaped and quickly flew to the peaked roof, where he perched to glare down at Kesira.

Kesira's purse hung limp and empty. Getting a room and food would prove difficult even without the big bird's presence. With him, Kesira didn't want to consider the problems.

The interior of the inn proved as neatly kept as the exterior. The low wooden tables had been waxed laboriously and shone like mirrors. The flagstone floor felt cold beneath her feet but better than the dusty trail that led to Kolya. At the back of the small public room ran a waist-high counter laden with foods that made Kesira's mouth water. She took two quick steps toward the banquet before her fingers brushed over her empty purse again. She stopped and simply stared in longing.

"Help you?"

Kesira spun guiltily and faced a portly man with a scarred, florid face. "I did not mean to sneak in like this. I . . . I saw the food and I am very hungry after long days on the trail," she finished weakly.

He studied her with practiced eyes, taking in the robe and its tears, the brutalized flesh beneath, the knotted blue cord and dirty yellow sash, the staff, the baby quietly suckling at her breast through one of the tears.

"Been awhile since you ate?" he asked.

Kesira nodded.

"You got the look of a nun about you. Which order?"

"Gelya," she answered simply. Kesira felt no need to add that Gelya had been slain by Lenc. Most of the patrons who had perished were killed by the jade demon.

"Rough times, eh?"

"They are, good sir."

"You willing to work around here for your meal?"

"And a place to sleep? We just arrived. Traveled through from the Sarn Mountains."

"You and the youngling crossed the plains what with all the brigands running free and wild?" The innkeeper appeared skeptical at this, but Kesira's condition finally convinced him. "You're a tough one, tougher'n me. Never leave the boundaries of Kolya these days. Used to roam free, I did. No more. Too many willing to cut your throat just for the sick thrill it gives 'em."

Kesira cared little about the man's past or his philosophy. His food drew her as a lodestone pulls iron, however. He saw, and waved her to the counter. She put the baby down behind the counter in a blanket-swathed box intended for a pet, sat and devoured the simple food until she felt ready to burst. Kesira leaned back and smiled.

"You eat like there's no tomorrow," the man observed.

"And who knows, you may be right, what with Lenc visiting his anger on us all the time. Not a fit place for a man nor beast—nor other-beast—these days."

"Lenc personally comes here?" she asked, surprised.

"He does. What he finds in Kolya is any mortal's guess." The innkeeper turned grim. "Would that he go away for all time." The grimness metamorphosed into fear, as if Kesira were Lenc and would still his hammering heart with a single pass of a jade hand.

"Lenc killed my patron," she said. "I have no love for the demon."

The man nodded as if his head bobbed on a rubber cord. Three men entering the inn claimed his attention; he put on a happy smile that Kesira knew had to be insincere.

The innkeeper spoke briefly with the three men. Finally, the man seated farthest from the entryway gestured to Kesira. She sighed. This wasn't the first time she had acted as servant. Her first five years at the Order of Gelya had been spent waiting on the elder sisters. They were harsh taskmasters; now Kesira was glad for that. Any customers in this placid inn would seem tame by comparison.

"What's your pleasure?" she asked the small, slender man. She stared at him boldly, not liking what she saw. He had a head that was too thin and a face like the nicked edge of a hatchet blade. Dark, cruel eyes studied her even as she stood waiting for his order. A tiny mustache, hardly more than a dirty smudge, disgraced his upper lip. In the shadowy interior of the inn, Kesira couldn't tell if that mustache hid a deformity. She thought that it did. Quick, jerky movements told of the man's inherent nervousness. He tapped fingertips against the table in front of him.

"Sit. Join us, my dear," he said in a tone both oily and edged in cold steel.

Kesira glanced at the innkeeper, who nodded. Kesira sat, stiffly erect and waiting.

"You've come from the Sarns?" the thin man asked. Kesira didn't speak. He wouldn't have asked if he hadn't already known the answer. "How did you avoid the hunting bands?"

"There are only so many of them. With enough agility and cunning one can avoid them."

"There's more," he said. "I know there's more. *How* did you come to be on the plains?" He leaned forward eagerly, fingers drumming in wave patterns on the shining tabletop.

"The jade demons forced the trip upon me," she said, wary of revealing too much. "Ayondela perished high atop her mountain. The power used by Lenc forced me to flee. We came to Kolya because there was nowhere else for us to go."

"You and the baby?" The man frowned so hard his head turned into a land more rutted than any farmer's prized acreage.

"The pair."

"You weren't touched by the jade? There are those in the city worried over Lenc's son. The demon claims this bastard spawn will one day rule Kolya and all the rest."

Kesira turned icy inside. No matter how she turned, Lenc blocked her escape. Such tales spelled not only her death but that of the baby as well. She moved so that the folds of her robe hid Ayondela's jade tusk. No one had noticed it yet; Kesira wanted to keep it that way.

"People always worry," she said simply.

"You avoided both jade demon and brigand?" The man's gaze turned harsher, more accusing.

"I am not in league with Lenc. He killed my patron. But the innkeeper's already told you of this." The way the portly innkeeper flushed showed the truth of her words. Kesira also saw that they were not satisfied with her explanation about avoiding the bands of homeless hunters on the plains.

Kesira knew that she dared not tell these men of Molimo. They looked no better than the hunters they'd already avoided. Speaking of Zolkan seemed safer, but still she hesitated. Kesira picked the one thing most innocuous.

"I can read the rune sticks," she said. "This allowed me to pass among the hunters unscathed."

The men sat back, eyes wide. They quickly recovered their senses and huddled, muttering among themselves. Finally, the thin man with the dark mustache turned back to

Kesira and said, "My name is Kene Zoheret. I represent a small group of citizens who, uh..."

"Get on with it, Kene," snapped another. "Tell her. If she can cast the rune sticks, she'll be able to find out."

"You," cut in Kesira, "are part of a group opposed to Lenc." They stared at her as if she were Lenc himself. Kesira laughed at their shock. "It takes no reading of the runes to figure that out." These men were rank amateurs in intrigue. She saw no purpose in joining with them, but then, where else might she turn? Even a sorry rebel might be better than none at all.

"We do take ourselves rather seriously," said Zoheret. "But you can read the runes?" Kesira silently pulled the carved box out from under her robe and opened it. The gleaming white engraved knucklebones spilled forth and rattled noisily against the hardwood table. Zoheret pointed, then demanded, "Read the cast."

Kesira swallowed hard and wiped the back of her hand across her mouth. Lenc had sent her the visions before, had used her, had made her believe she possessed powers only a handful do in any generation. Now that her usefulness had passed, the skill had to be lost.

But Kesira felt the wellings of a force deep inside similar to those she had experienced before. Visions flashed before her eyes, behind and in her head. She reeled a little, gripped the edge of the table for support and finally settled her mind in the ways taught by Gelya.

Clarity of image came then.

"You control some meager magicks," she said in a voice unlike her natural one. "You, Zoheret, are a minor adept at spells of fire. There is more." Kesira fought against an inky cloud veiling a profound truth about the rebel.

"That's enough," he said, shaking her arm and pulling her from the reverie. "You've convinced us. We need you to aid us in what we attempt this evening."

"What?" Kesira sat in a mist of confusion, her mind unable to snap back from the intensity of the vision. Always before she had just *known*. This time it was as if she watched reality unfolding at an accelerated pace. The *texture* of the rune casting seemed alien to her, different and—friendly.

"We will attack Lenc's temple," Kene Zoheret said with ill-disguised eagerness, misinterpreting her reaction. "We will storm the gates, burn them down, set fire to the priests— show the people of Kolya that resistance is possible!"

"You will only provoke Lenc. Killing his mortal pawns does nothing to weaken him."

"Something *must* be done," Zoheret insisted. "The tyranny of the demon is intolerable. Right?" He hastily checked his companions. They all agreed. Zoheret rushed on. "You can't know how terrible it is in Kolya. Lenc rapes our women, then tortures them to an agonizing death—and forces us to watch. His power holds us enthralled. We watch as he mutilates our children, destroys crops and stores with the pass of his hand, and we are powerless.

"Individually," Zoheret said with passion, "we are helpless. Together we can make a stand. We *must* fight him. We *will!*"

"Do you have alliances with those who follow other patrons?" Kesira asked.

"Why bother?"

"They might be in a position similar to mine. Their patrons dead by the hand of the jade demons. They might bring needed abilities—gold—to your rank."

"You can foresee the future. *That* is a skill we desperately need," said one of the other men.

Kesira didn't try to explain that she had no control over her visions. Ever since dealing with Ayondela, the feeling of power within had grown stronger, but it had died when Lenc told her haughtily that he had sent her the rune readings. Now, she didn't know. It felt right, but Lenc's insidious lies had, also.

"We have her approval for what we do this night," crowed Zoheret. Before Kesira could protest, say that she had seen nothing of their venture, the men slapped their hands ringingly on the table and stood. "To the staging area. We attack in one hour!"

Kesira grabbed Zoheret's sleeve as the man started after his two friends. "I saw nothing of your success—or failure—in this. Even without the rune cast, I can tell you it is a mistake. Attract Lenc's attention and he'll destroy you!"

"We strike for freedom!" Kene Zoheret's expression came closer to a sneer than a smile. Kesira edged away from him. "Come and watch us in our victory," the man went on. "See how we strike fear into that bastard's jade heart!"

"No," Kesira said, shaking her head and backing away.

"I'll tend the child," said the innkeeper. "It's needed for you to aid us. What few patrons are left to us must have sent you. Please." Kesira looked into the innkeeper's eyes and saw only sorrow there. In a low voice he said, "Lenc took my w-wife. Elounorie was one of the f-first he u-used. My daughter was the next."

"I'll go," Kesira said. She turned and followed Kene Zoheret.

"Soon, very soon," Zoheret gloated. He hunched over the crude map he'd sketched in the dust on the warehouse floor and stabbed his finger down at a spot marked with an X.

"This strikes me as pointless," Kesira protested. "So you kill a few of his loyal followers. So what? Has it ever occurred to you these priests might perform their services because they're more frightened of Lenc than obedient? That you might recruit them for your own purposes? A mortal spy in his confidence could provide more than a few dead priests who only mouth platitudes."

"They are the symbols Lenc uses in Kolya to keep us in check. Destroy them, and we show the citizens there is a rebellion against the demon!"

Zoheret's words rang hollow in Kesira's ears. She studied the thin man and worried about his motivations. He couldn't be swayed from this suicidal attack, and he kept his pitiful band of followers firmly in line with promises of the adulation and support they would receive after the night's activity.

"I can conjure just well enough to bring down the entire temple. The use of my burning spell will show Lenc he's up against more than a few sickly old women waving sticks at him."

Kesira had listened to Zoheret's stories of how Lenc had marched forth on the Plains of Roggen and destroyed the

Emperor Kwasian's entire army with lightnings drawn down from the sky, jade bombs that burst inside the commander's skull, turbulent storms that swept cavalry from their saddles. General Dayle had perished and left the army—or the fearful few who survived—in the command of a junior captain. All other officers had died hideous deaths.

And Zoheret thought to frighten Lenc with petty vandalism?

"Now, we must go now!" Kene Zoheret insisted. The fear had become a miasma cloaking the room, but none of the men dared admit he lacked the courage to venture forth on this mad escapade. She knew that the slightest sign of resistance would send these would-be rebels racing for the safety of their homes. Not a one had the courage that marked a real warrior. She thought about those she had seen who had this courage: Rouvin, now dead; Molimo, somewhere in the city; Captain Protaro of the Emperor's Guard, left behind in the Sarn Mountains. They were fighters to be trusted.

Kesira closed her eyes and settled her seething emotions. Somehow, even the most advanced meditative techniques refused to quell the hammering of her heart. They were going to their deaths, and only she seemed to understand it.

Single-file, they slipped from the dingy warehouse and into a square facing the temple Lenc had ordered constructed. Bits of jade sparkled in the night, illuminating the front steps leading up to the massive carved wooden doors. Kesira's anger rose when she saw that the doors were hewn from stonewood, the substance sacred to Gelya. Even in forcing others to worship him, Lenc mocked the other demons.

Zoheret motioned for the men to split into two groups, one circling to the left and the other going right. He and Kesira stayed in the square, directly in front of the ominously silent temple. Zoheret dropped to his knees and began the magical incantations needed to produce the fire spell. Kesira felt the air stir around her as the magicks condensed behind the guard spell holding them in readiness.

Zoheret clapped his hands and a minuscule fireball burst

forth to crash into the stonewood doors, which shed the fire in a molten cascade. Zoheret launched a second fireball but this one was even smaller than the first. Already his powers waned.

As weak as Zoheret's magicks had become, fate worked against those within the temple. Just as Zoheret's last, pitifully small magical fire sped through the night, a priest opened the door to peer out into the square. The fireball hurled past the priest and into the temple, to smash against fringed tapestries on the back wall. Kesira saw orange tongues of flame begin licking their way up the walls. Frantic shouts came from within. The priest in the door rushed out to find the public watering tubs.

A dagger found his heart before he got ten paces. Those of Zoheret's band who had lain in wait now jumped up brandishing their pitiful weapons. The other priests rushed outside and died on the points of those inexpertly used weapons.

"Now what?" asked Kesira. Her stomach churned with nausea at the sign of the wanton killing. It was bad enough when demon slew human. For one human to kill another defeated the purpose of any rebellion against the jade power. Didn't these men have families who would mourn their passing—and demand revenge on those responsible? How could a man, in good faith, join with those who had killed a friend and neighbor in the name of peace?

Perhaps this was Lenc's plan, to turn one human against another. Kesira knew the demon might find infinite pleasure in the petty squabblings and vendettas. Such misuse of the power Lenc controlled would not seem wanton to a demon befuddled by jade that slowly perverted him to its own mysterious ways.

"They're dead, they're all dead!" cried Zoheret. He danced around like a madman made even eerier by the shadows from the flames leaping twenty feet and more into the nighttime sky.

Kesira edged out of the square and pressed herself into an alcove of a small dry-goods shop. Because of their celebration, not one of the rebels had noticed the odd coloration of the flames engulfing Lenc's temple. They had begun as a normal orange. They now turned a deep green and changed from insubstantial gases rising into the darkness to a form she know all too well.

A form of the purest jade.

Unwittingly, Kene Zoheret had summoned Lenc.

Chapter Three

MOLIMO PURPOSELY left Kesira behind. The woman struggled through the thick crowds along Kolya's main street, trying to keep strange shoulders from crashing into the baby's head, dodging those moving slower, failing to keep up with Molimo's long-legged pace. Molimo made a quick right and ducked into the portal of a coppersmith's store. Kesira blundered along a few minutes later, looking lost. Zolkan weighed her down and, seeing Molimo, shifted a heavy, green-feathered body to prevent the woman from spying him.

Molimo held back a pang of regret at treating Kesira in such a cavalier fashion, but her presence would only prevent his doing the distasteful tasks that lay ahead.

Kesira spun around, vainly looking for him. She stamped her foot and started off down a side street Zolkan indicated. Molimo had to smile. The *trilla* bird proved his friendship repeatedly. Molimo waited until he no longer saw the dirty brown top of Kesira's head and the flashing green of Zolkan's feathers before he left his post.

Heaving a deep sigh, he looked up and down the street. Molimo closed his eyes and almost staggered under the imponderable force emanating from the center of Kolya.

Lenc's temple. No other explanation matched the facts. He had led Kesira to this city because Lenc had decided to make this his final battleground. If Kolya fell, so did all the world. Limaden meant nothing after Lenc's defeat of General Dayle and the Emperor Kwasian's entire force on the Plains of Roggen. Molimo concentrated and saw the march of ghost battalions before him. The entire battle fought through in only a few minutes, but speeding it up gave

Molimo the chance to see the errors made by the human commanders. Dayle was good—had been good. But never before had he faced a demon of Lenc's power.

Even the jade demon could be slain. The deaths of the other three proved that. Lenc might be the strongest, but the jade made him more vulnerable than any human thought—even Kesira.

Lenc had traded virtual immortality for power. Molimo choked down the incoherent cry of anger rising within his throat. He might outlive Lenc now, because of the adverse effect of the jade on Lenc's longevity, but even so, Molimo knew that the other demon might live for hundreds of years. Far too long for Molimo to continue suffering the indignities heaped upon him. If Lenc wanted supreme power, he was going to have to fight for it.

Molimo flexed his muscles. Many women passing by, and not a few men, watched enviously; but Molimo knew that his real strength dwelt within. For a human, he was well muscled, but his real power derived from force of character. It was that power the jade rain had stolen from him, and only now, after these long months, did he regain a significant portion of what had once been his.

He turned and stared into a small windowpane at his reflection. A man a score of years older than he remembered peered back at him. The healing had taken its toll and added enervating years to his appearance. Molimo brushed one quick-fingered hand through his hair and came away with strands of silver. When Kesira had found him, he'd been scarcely more than seventeen. Now? Twice that and more.

But he had healed.

Molimo made sure his sword hung freely in his sheath, and he skirted the center of town, heading for the far side of Kolya. The crush of the market fell behind. His pace quickened. The streets narrowed and the houses brushed along his arms. Only occasionally now did he sight another. This was the sorriest section of Kolya, that part no one spoke of in polite company. Molimo had entered the Festering.

Rubble filled the small walkway, forcing him to climb up and over, but his sense of direction remained secure. He unerringly followed the twisty, turning path through the slum region until he came out into a small courtyard.

Molimo paused when the quiet rattle of small-link chains echoed down the tight streets. He fingered the hilt of his sword but did not draw as eight scrawny youths crowded into the small area. One, wearing an elaborately embroidered eyepatch with a shining gemstone sewn in the center, stepped forward.

"You're a well-fed-looking one, now aren't you?" he called out to Molimo.

When Molimo failed to answer, the youth stepped forward and swung a short length of silver chain in a flashing figure-eight pattern. "You can make it easy or you can make it hard," the youth said. "Not that we care. In fact, fool, we haven't been getting enough excitement in our lives down here in the Festering. Certainly not with the likes of you."

Molimo pointed to his mouth and tried to indicate that he lacked a tongue. The leader of the scavenger pack seemed not to care.

He motioned, and two others joined him, one on the left and the other on the right. They held short, wicked daggers.

"Now, the boys and me, we been wondering about how you rich folks live over in—what would you say? In Quo? Genrer? Maybe near the Slurries? It might all be part of Kolya, but we never see it. We're stuck down here puking out our guts and starving to death and getting the rots.

"Think he'd like to make a small donation to charity, my good men?"

The two on either side of their leader moved with practiced coordination. Molimo didn't draw his sword. In the confines of this tiny courtyard, its length would be a hindrance. He waited. When the one on the left feinted, Molimo moved right. His fist traveled only a few inches, but connected squarely with the boy's solar plexus. The scavenger turned green and spiraled to the ground, gasping for air. Molimo half turned and lightly backhanded the other. The youth slammed with impossible force against the wall, then toppled forward like a felled tree. He lay facedown on the dirty pavement, unmoving.

"Stay back. This one be mine," the leader said. His chain whistled with menace. Molimo let him attack. The chain wound itself around a brawny wrist, then began to smoke. When molten droplets of the steel chain dripped to the pavement, the gang leader's eyes widened in horror.

"It's Lenc!"

He bolted for a side alley, but a flash of green intercepted him. Strong talons caught the back of his tunic and lifted until his kicking feet were inches above the pavement. Molimo motioned, and Zolkan twisted mightily in midair, slamming the youth hard against one wall. The bird's strong wings pulled the half-dazed youth around and smashed him into the opposite wall. Only then did he drop his victim.

"Prefer not to eat this one," Zolkan said contemptuously. "Take too long to clean."

You saved me a footrace, friend. This is the urchin I sought. The communication flashed between Molimo and Zolkan without words, touching the surface of their minds, imparting eddies of thought that never shared a verbal counterpart.

"Turn him loose and let me hunt him down again. I need practice. Being with Kesira has turned me into a pigeon-shit carrion eater, not a hunter."

The youth heard Zolkan's words but not Molimo's silent reply. He jerked away. Molimo took two quick steps and caught him.

"You got me wrong, good sir," the scavenger leader stammered. "We meant you no harm. Just a prank it was. A prank!"

Ask him where I can find it.

Zolkan fluttered down and landed on the boy's arm, talons gripping so tightly they drew tiny pinpricks of blood. "We seek the Order of Lalasa. Where is the priestess?"

"Lalasa?" he stammered. "I know nothing of demon doings."

"Lenc will eat you if you don't answer," Zolkan promised.

Molimo scowled at the crude threat. But it worked. The floodgates of information opened and the youth babbled, telling them all they needed to learn between pleas not to feed him to the jade demon.

Have him lead the way, Molimo ordered. *I do not trust him. I read deception in his every movement.*

"He is good friend. He would not think to lie." Zolkan's talons closed until the youth winced at the pain. "Lead us, good friend. Lead us to Lalasa's place of worship."

"All other patrons, save for mighty Lenc, are outlawed. We can be punished mightily for seeking out Lalasa."

Tell him he'll die here and now unless he obeys us.

Zolkan didn't have to translate for the youth. The expression on Molimo's face bespoke the threat more eloquently than any words. With servile bobbings of his head, the youth turned and scurried off, motioning for them to follow. Zolkan fluttered along warily, but Molimo strode without fear.

As befit a demon.

"It is long since any came to our worship," the frail old woman explained. "We cannot keep the shrine in proper repair." She smiled, showing broken yellow teeth. "In fact, we prefer it in the Festering. Only the most faithful seek us out—and we have ample opportunity to decide to whom they are faithful as they wend their way here."

She patted the scavenger leader on the arm. He pulled away and held it; Zolkan had clawed him several times as he tried to escape.

"The boys are loyal enough. They do not seek gain by turning us over to Lenc."

"He has served purpose. Send him on," said Zolkan. The youth smiled weakly and looked at the old woman. At her gesture, he left.

"He will die before another year passes," the woman said sadly. "The Festering does not permit long life."

"Nor does Lenc. We come to seek others who share our concern."

The old woman peered myopically at Molimo, then lightly brushed calloused fingertips over his arms and chest.

"He is no meat in market," protested Zolkan.

"No, that he isn't. He is much more. He seeks Lalasa?"

Tell her I want any of the demons still actively opposing

Lenc to come. We must forge an alliance if we are to defeat the jade-wielder.

The woman seemed to understand before Zolkan could put the thought into words. She said, "Lalasa is far distant, in Limaden conferring with Emperor Kwasian. Lenc has dealt the Emperor a severe setback militarily, and they must regroup if they are to defend the capital. She is a kind patron, but not good at military matters."

"Other demons," Zolkan pressed. "What of them?"

"So few," she said, sighing heavily. "So very few remain. They always were a distant lot, but now they are fearful, too. The Time of Chaos is truly at hand." She emitted a sigh that sounded like a volcanic fumarole venting its noxious gases.

Not kindly disposed to us, is she?

"With good reason," Zolkan said. Louder, to the priestess, the *trilla* bird said, "We desire a room where we might summon them and meet with those answering the call."

"Lalasa cannot come. I do not know if others will."

"We must try. Only here—and in Limaden—is there a shrine still consecrated. Lenc is thorough in destroying other patrons and their worshipers."

"That he is." The priestess muttered some curses as she led them to a tiny chapel. A small block of dark orange *tulna* stone served as the altar. To the left in a red clay pot adorned with mystical symbols grew the fern sacred to Lalasa. On the other side of the altar stood a triptych carved from a rich oak, the wood most beloved by Lalasa. Somehow, in these settings, in the center of the Festering, the pathetic trappings inspired pity rather than reverence.

"I will leave you. I have no part in such a gathering." She bowed low and left. Zolkan fluttered around the tiny room twice before coming to rest on the back of a pew.

"Will any come when you summon?"

We can only find out by trying, Molimo indicated. He sank to his knees in front of the altar, another supplicant. But the force building around him could belong to no mere worshiper. The power grew, surged out, became directed, hidden from Lenc, aimed at any other.

For hours Molimo knelt before the altar. Zolkan watched

and worried. His friend lacked time sense when he entered this state. The *trilla* bird had seen him vanish within himself for weeks on end. If Molimo hadn't roused himself now and again for food, he might have starved. This particular body carried frailty to the limit, but the jade rain had locked Molimo within it, just as it had stripped him of his power and robbed him of his tongue. The bird began to seriously worry when Molimo stirred.

Lalasa will not come. Not immediately, Molimo reported. *But there are others.*

"How many?"

Too few. Four, possibly five. None I know well. A tear beaded at the corner of Molimo's eye, threatening to run down his cheek. He did nothing to stop the salty flood when it finally occurred. So few demons still lived—Lenc and his allies had slaughtered legions. And those who had survived possessed only minor abilities, insufficient to fight Lenc. The jade demon kept these few around for his entertainment; any true rivals had long since been eliminated.

A tiny *pop!* sounded. Zolkan swiveled his head around and peered at the tall, emaciated demon. Zolkan finally recognized him, and spat the gobbet of red pulp he had been chewing onto the demon's unpolished boots.

"What an unmannerly oaf you are!" protested the demon.

"I spit only on those I despise," Zolkan answered. "Of all demons, I should have known Tolek would live. Cowards and wastrels prevail, in any climate."

"One gets by however one must," Tolek said, feelings hurt. "I don't even know you or this knave abasing himself in front of Lalasa's altar. Who are you and how is it you can summon a demon?"

"A pathetic demon," snapped Zolkan. "Once I bore messages for only mightiest of demons. Now I must greet the likes of you." Zolkan spat again; Tolek had to dance away to avoid a second red-staining gob.

"That's no way to speak."

"When you gambled away your worshipers, you spawned Order of Steel Crescent. Caused countless miseries throughout empire as a result. I loathe you for that."

"The debts were staggering, bird. The trade seemed fair

to me. A few idle worshipers of no intrinsic value, in exchange for expiation and a rather nice island, too."

"Nehan-dir seeks only those patrons able to give Steel Crescent power. They *worship* power because of you."

"Oh, really. Not *because* of me. Don't try to blame the failings of mortals on *me*, bird. And don't try to change the subject. Who is this knave who managed to summon me so handily? He seems vaguely familiar, but..."

Another entrance silenced Tolek the Spare. A demon with arms thicker than ale kegs loomed in one corner of the room. Misshapen and immensely strong, the demon lumbered forward, knuckles dangerously close to the floor.

"Who calls Baram?"

"Welcome, friend demon. A moment, and all will be explained," said Zolkan.

A final *pop!* produced a dwarf with too-short arms, a head twice that expected for decent proportions, and a bulging forehead that settled into a bony ridge over his deep-set gray eyes.

Welcome, Noissa, greeted Molimo. *And you, Baram, and even you, Tolek.*

"Who are you, mortal? You speak as we do, but I do not recognize you." Noissa stepped back fearfully, hiding behind the orange stone altar.

We all have changed, Molimo said. *Most of all I. The jade changed me—luckily.*

"You are not Lenc," growled Baram. The massive demon knocked over a row of pews as he carved an area to hunker down in. "Only Lenc has contact with the jade."

I am aware of that. Eznofadil, Howenthal and Ayondela exist no more. I have aided the Sister of Gelya's Order in this. When I fought Lenc I was unprepared for the strength given him by the jade. He thought he destroyed me, but the jade altered my substance instead. I found myself trapped—disguised—in a mortal's form.

Molimo paused. *After all I have endured, I am a mortal, doomed to live out a short life in this form.*

Noissa edged around the altar, still fearful. "This might be a trick. Lenc is cunning."

"No trick, no trick," insisted Zolkan. "You know me. I stand by those words."

"Aye, you are familiar. You are the *trilla* bird who delivered messages and arranged for trysts." The dwarf relaxed visibly. "You even passed a note along to darling Leoranne for me."

"Your wife is still healthy?" asked Zolkan.

"For a mortal. Her days are limited but our joy still grows."

"Then listen, if you want more days for joy to grow. Listen well to him."

Molimo stood. He had hoped for a more auspicious turnout of demons. He found it almost impossible to believe that only these three—four, if Lalasa was counted—remained of those who had once frolicked and debauched with such abandon. Baram, for all his physical prowess, lacked real mental capacity. Noissa, on the other hand, was all intellect—and fear. For Tolek, Molimo had nothing but contempt; he expected no help from the lean demon. Any patron who traded his worshipers for a gambling debt deserved more than a *trilla* bird spitting on his boots.

But they were the survivors, the ones Lenc had permitted to live.

We must fight Lenc and kill him. The power of the jade will do that eventually, I know, but before that happens his evil will ruin this world.

"So?" asked Tolek. "We've had scant contact with the mortals for thousands of years. Why the sympathy for them now? Let Lenc do his worst. As you say, the jade destroys him daily, even as it augments his power. Let it burn him out like a guttering candle." Tolek produced a small flame dancing on one fingertip. "We can wait until he is snuffed out." The flame vanished in a twisting column of black smoke. The demon looked inordinately pleased with his minor magicks.

The Time of Chaos is at hand, Molimo communicated. *We must deal with this. To survive, we must prevent the coming of the new gods.*

"Superstition," rumbled Baram. "No puny god will replace me!" He picked up the one long pew he hadn't destroyed and crushed it to splinters in his meaty hands.

"This we must consider, Baram," said Noissa. "Perhaps the old legends are more. Perhaps the myths speak truly. Gelya seemed to think they did."

"All myth. Nothing more," roared Baram. "I do not die. I am demon!"

But Molimo had begun to think, as had Gelya. The world had formed from void and light, air and water decorating the surface of the planet. From these grew animal life. Humans came to coexist with animals, and their offspring were the demons, all human and animal traits magnified a hundredfold. Strength and weakness permeated the demons, and they lived apart, different from both animals and humans. The humans came to worship that which was strongest in their patrons, but few of the demons deigned to come into contact with the world beneath them.

So said the myth of creation. The myth of destruction told of mating between demon and human to produce true gods possessing only the finest traits of demon and human. And surrounding this birth whirled the Time of Chaos, the war in which demons perished and the gods flourished.

The Sister of Gelya's Order, Kesira Minette, Molimo continued, *carries a boychild that Lenc claims for his own son. There is indication the infant was born of a coupling between Lenc and a peasant woman named Parvey Yera. Do any know of this for certain?*

"Vague rumors only," said Noissa. "Lenc boasts his bastard son will carry on the rule of jade and found a dynasty stretching down through the eons."

He knows the jade robs him of life?

Noissa shrugged. "Perhaps. Perhaps he only says these things because they are more understandable—and thereby more frightening—for the humans. Without them, whom can he rule? He *needs* the mortals, lest he rule a world populated only with memories."

The boychild must be destroyed, Molimo replied.

"Kesira will never allow it!" cried Zolkan. "She thinks of the bratling as her own."

Lenc has deluded her. He uses her as a surrogate mother

until the child grows large enough to accept his role as Lenc's heir. We must convince her of this. The baby must die!

"So, kill the pink worm," said Tolek. "Why the discussion? If this is something you must do, then do it." He settled down, frowning at them. Baram flexed his muscles until joints snapped like breaking twigs. Tolek refused to let his fright show—too much.

For a mortal, Kesira Minette possesses profound powers. She casts the rune sticks and accurately reads them. Not even Lenc's lies can cloud her vision of the future.

"She sees the Time of Change upon us?" asked Noissa, shaking like a leaf in a whirlwind. The dwarf shrank back to the protection of the altar.

I know little of what she sees. It is blocked to me. Until I regain my full power, I cannot force her to do anything against her will.

"Why hasn't Lenc destroyed you? After all, you were the strongest of the lot of us," said Tolek.

The jade altered my form and robbed me of the power Lenc might trace to me. Only slowly have I recovered. And, Molimo communicated grimly, *others of our rank have given their lives to aid me. Toyaga died after giving me a spell of non-noticeability.*

"*That* one?" scoffed Tolek. "No one is fooled by it. You don't even vanish from sight. You just make yourself harder to see."

When Lenc and the other jade demons did not expect to find me at all, thinking me long dead, Toyaga's spell worked well enough.

Tolek only shrugged disinterestedly.

Are we agreed? We'll band together to destroy Lenc?

Baram grunted, then vanished without giving a definite answer. Tolek tried to hide the fear that illuminated his face.

"Don't be ridiculous. Lenc won't harm us. He could have slain us at any time. Since he's let us live . . . well, he must like us." Tolek smiled weakly, then vanished.

Old friend—Molimo turned to Noissa—*you do not believe that, do you?*

"I believe only that attracting Lenc's attention also draws

his wrath. You have not seen what he's done to the others.
Not Baram and Tolek, but to Berura-ko and Roas and all
the others." Noissa cringed, tiny arms unconsciously rising
to protect his misshapen head. "He tore them apart. He
tortured them horribly. He used the jade power in ways that
made their agony last for an eternity even as they died in a
split second. What he does to humans is a pale imitation of
what he has done to those who opposed him in our ranks."

"You do not join with us?" asked Zolkan.

"I agree that the boychild should be destroyed. But this
will anger Lenc. Perhaps... after my beloved, all-too-mortal
Leoranne is no more... perhaps then I might be of some
assistance."

But she might live for fifty more years! protested Molimo.

"Perhaps that long. I hope so. Please be careful—you
always were the most impetuous among us. Now you are
no match for Lenc."

Noissa disappeared as the other demons had. Molimo,
shaking with frustration, sank to the floor once again and
growled deep in his throat. The power that had returned to
him was worthless unless he could use it—and he still
wasn't strong enough to face Lenc alone. If only there had
been other demons able to help!

"Your shape," cautioned Zolkan. "You change. Fight it,
fight it!"

Halfway through, Molimo managed to stop the transformation. Sweating, straining, he forced his reluctant body
back into its human form. The jade had hidden him from
Lenc, but the cost had been so great. If he couldn't control
his own form, how could he possibly defeat the other demon?

The path to Lenc's destruction must lie in the infant
Kesira wet-nursed. Destroy the boy and Lenc's dynasty died
also. A faint hope, but Molimo knew he had to nurture it.

We must find Kesira.

Zolkan said nothing as he perched on Molimo's shoulder.
The *trilla* bird knew better than his master the danger in
trying to separate Kesira from the boy. Even Lenc's wrath
would pale in comparison. But Zolkan said nothing.

Chapter Four

THE LICKING TONGUES of flame coalesced into the figure Kesira Minette knew and feared. Lenc stretched out long green arms in a mocking embrace and threw back his head. Chilling laughter drowned out the crackling fire consuming the temple. Lenc's hands clenched into tightly balled fists, and his head lowered to study the small square in front of his ruined place of worship.

"Who dares oppose me?" he boomed. Kesira pressed deeper into shadows made less inky by the firelight. She summoned her courage and held her position. To run would reveal her to the jade demon.

Kesira let out her pent-up breath and tried to relax. Tenseness brought error; so taught Gelya. She watched in mute horror as Lenc pointed his finger and made stabbing motions. Every time he affixed his attention on some poor wight, he died. Those who had gathered around Kene Zoheret perished, one by one. Of the rebel leader Kesira saw no trace.

"You dare use puny magicks against me? Against *me?*" The demon strode out of the fire and brushed away burning debris from his shoulders and arms. "I will show you real magic."

The demon clapped his hands. The thunder rumbling down the streets of Kolya deafened Kesira. She fell to her knees, sobbing with the pain lancing into her head. Even putting fingers in her ears failed to stop the hideous noise ripping away at her soul. And just when she thought it might be bearable, Lenc clapped his hands again.

And he laughed. How the woman hated that mocking, tormenting laughter!

41

Kesira fought to clear her head, to keep control of her fear. It would eat away inside her and force her into view if she didn't conquer her emotions. The sight of Kene Zoheret scuttling away helped her find the focus for her hatred. That weasel of a man had created this maelstrom of death and destruction; now the craven ran from it.

Kesira edged back and watched Lenc run amok. The demon tortured those unfortunate men he found. When he used his prodigious, jade-driven might to rip off the roof of a house and drag forth a poor woman for his sexual satiation, Kesira ducked away and ran in the opposite direction. She allowed fear to rise up within her now, to lend speed to her flight, to show her heels to the one enemy in the entire world capable of intimidating her.

Out of breath, she rested against a cool wooden door. Sweat stained the wood, then began trickling down in a rivulet. She pushed back her lank hair and wiped her forehead, clearing it of the fear-sweat. Kesira opened the door and entered the inn. Zoheret had already arrived and sat in the far corner, clutching a mug of ale with two trembling hands. He spilled more than he got into his mouth.

"You left them to die," Kesira accused. "You launched the magical fire spells, then you ran, leaving your friends to be slaughtered by Lenc."

"I didn't know the demon would appear. How could I? I thought it would be a symbol, a gesture to show all Kolya that we could fight back and win."

"You turned it into disaster. As soon as word of what actually happened gets out, no one will dare oppose Lenc. Your action cost us the chance of any effective move against the power of the jade."

"You," snapped Zoheret, pointing a trembling finger, "did nothing to aid us. You read the runes wrong. You promised victory. You let this happen!"

"Now then, Zoheret, she did nothing of the kind." The portly innkeeper came out and perched on the end of one of his polished tables. "If 'n I remember a 'right, you stopped her before she read more than a few simple things about you. Not once did you ask if she saw victory this night in her castings."

"You two are in this together!"

Kesira snorted in contempt and sat heavily in a chair. The innkeeper brought her a small mug of the ale, but Kesira barely tasted it. Her mind was working to find a way to salvage a victory from this monumental blunder. With Lenc's attention drawn to the city's feeble rebellion, it wouldn't be easy.

She downed the ale in one long gulp, when her thoughts turned to the baby. Had Lenc somehow managed to detect his son? Was this the reason for the demon's presence? The burning of a single temple would hardly anger the jade demon so much. Whatever he did, he did for a reason. He *chose* to come to avenge the blasphemy.

Kesira couldn't put the coincidence of Lenc's presence and her own in the city to rest. Gelya had said that facts were stubborn. Kesira had been well trained in not assuming luck and ability were the same—she could change the course of all that happened, if only she proved smart enough to find the proper path. But to find that path required the knowledge of why Lenc had appeared now.

"Zoheret," she called over to the thin rebel leader, "what are your plans now? Most of your men died this night."

"I have a few more. And word has come that the Emperor Kwasian will support us with his personal troops."

"Soon?"

"Soon enough to count. We will regain Kolya. I feel it." The man, his hands shaking, sloshed more ale into his lap and didn't even seem to notice. And this was the mage Kesira had half hoped would provide the impetus to a real uprising against Lenc.

"Is the baby all right?" she asked the innkeeper.

The man nodded, but his expression changed as he asked, "Is this a normal child? He never cries. And his eyes..."

"What of his eyes?" demanded Zoheret. "Are they the green of jade?"

"No, quite the opposite. They are pale, almost colorless. But the boy's expression is so . . . so old. It's as if he's seen the world and knows it all, for a fact."

Zoheret shot to his feet and rocketed across the small public room to peer over the counter. Kesira followed a step behind. Before Zoheret could reach out and touch the child, Kesira grabbed the rebel leader's arm and spun him around. Her own normally soft brown eyes hardened into daggers.

"Leave the child alone." Her tone brooked no challenge. Zoheret stepped back in fright, startled at her vehemence. He recovered his wit slowly.

"What makes you so defensive about your son? He *is* your son, isn't he? Or is he of another's flesh?"

"He is an orphan."

"And his father? Might his father be the demon? Did Lenc spawn this miserable little worm of pink flesh?" Zoheret shoved Kesira out of the way and vaulted the counter. He landed heavily in a crouch. Before he could reach out to touch the child, Kesira hurried around the counter and clamped her hand firmly over the infant's mouth to prevent him from crying out.

Not only might Zoheret be killed—and the innkeeper and perhaps even herself—but that cry would draw Lenc's attention. The jade demon sought something in Kolya. What else could it be except his son?

"The innkeeper said he never cries, and yet you stifle him. Why?" Zoheret's curiosity got the better of him.

"The sound of an infant crying annoys me. I know how to discipline him to prevent his cries. And," Kesira said, rising and shoving Zoheret away, "you do not want to annoy me. Perhaps I do more than simply report what I see in the runes. Has it ever occurred to you that I might be able to affect the future through the rune readings I give?"

"But . . ."

"Is it death I see for you? Or something else? The casting was not sufficiently detailed to tell. Do you want me to do another?" The panic on Zoheret's face startled and pleased her. She had found the lever to move him to her will, but why the fear? Was the soft spot fearing his own death, or fearing what her rune casting might reveal?

Kene Zoheret rounded the counter and went to sit where his spilled ale frothed on the table. Kesira nursed the boy, and fought down her own feelings of panic at his calm acceptance of everything around him. Nothing disturbed the infant. The only hint that all was well came in the warmth of the spot where Wemilat the Ugly had kissed her breast. The lip print left by the hideous, kindly demon reassured her that no evil came from feeding the baby.

"We can attack again, burn down the monster's strongholds. He can't stop us," muttered Zoheret. "I can get the entire underground movement together for one huge strike. Even the Emperor's soldiers can take part when they arrive. Yes, that's it. One big attack. Lenc'll never recover!"

Still mumbling to himself, Zoheret left the inn.

"He is doomed to failure, and he'll bring down Lenc's wrath on everyone," Kesira said.

"You see this in the runes?" asked the innkeeper.

"I need only logic, not magic. Zoheret's spells are few and weak. He cannot hope to match Lenc. And to mere force of arms the demon is invulnerable." She paused, thinking about this. Was Lenc truly invincible? Would a sword thrust end his jade-driven life? He had forsaken virtual immortality for power.

Kesira stopped trying to wrestle with imponderable questions. It was futile; Gelya would not have approved. She must find the actions that'd be most productive, then follow that course to the end.

To the end . . .

It sounded too final for her to appreciate. Kesira called out to the innkeeper, "Is there anything else you want of me before I turn in? The place looks spotless. Not much business this evening?"

The man stared at her in disbelief. "After all you've been through this awful eve, you ask about polishing and cleaning?"

"I am Sister of the Mission of Gelya. I made a promise to trade work for room and board. Never have I gone back on a promise made willingly. Whether I am tired matters little. For what is given me I will work." Kesira waited. The innkeeper waved her toward the back of the public room.

"There's a fine little cot for you in there," he said. "You can sleep out of the cold and elements for the night."

The way he said it indicated he now considered her a liability. Kesira didn't blame the innkeeper. He'd lost wife and daughter to Lenc. Even allowing her to stay under the same roof might anger Lenc further. After all, she had taken part in the abortive attack on Lenc's temple and had drawn the jade demon back to Kolya. She began to appreciate the idea of being the small mouse, doing nothing to draw the tyrant's gaze, and possibly escaping harm.

But to live in fear at the same time?

Kesira picked up the baby, went to the room indicated and settled in. Before she had lain down, her mind had fixed firmly on the concept of never bowing to a tyrant's whim. She might play the mouse, but for her own reason: to muster her forces, take advantage of any chance, however slim, to defeat Lenc. Living in the dark shadow of fear for the rest of her life held no appeal. The test of courage was in the living, not the dying.

Kesira tossed and turned on the cot, unable to sleep. The more she tried to relax, the tenser she became. Finally yielding to insomnia, she rose and paced the tiny room. This soothed her; the room reminded her of the first cell she'd been given when she arrived at the nunnery so many years ago. As she'd grown older, she was allowed a larger room and a few possessions.

But her only true possessions were those she carried within her breast and spirit. Everything else could be stripped from her—and had been. Even Molimo seemed to have abandoned her, and of Zolkan she'd seen not so much as a pinfeather.

Idly, Kesira pulled out the box containing the carved knucklebones. She opened the hinged lid and tapped the bones out onto the cot. They fell softly, silently, like snow on a cold winter's eve.

The pattern confused Kesira for a few minutes. She had never seen this precise alignment before, and almost picked up the knucklebones to make a second cast. But she stopped before touching them. Closing her eyes, Kesira began to meditate, to seek out every morsel of information that had ever been imparted to her. Sinking down within her own mind produced the result she'd hoped for.

Unbidden, the single name rose to her lips: Lalasa.

Louder, she called, "Lalasa, your rune appears in my

casting. I need you—we need you." Kesira cast a hesitant glance in the direction of the sleeping baby. He lay with eyes tightly screwed shut, thumb in his mouth. If she hadn't known differently, Kesira would have thought he was simply another infant.

A human infant.

"Lalasa," she said a third time, "I would speak with you. Give me your counsel."

The air shimmered and turned mirrorlike. Stirrings like bugs crawling along autumnal leaves moved the length of the room, returned, became more distinct. Kesira felt her pulse racing. Never before had she summoned a demon.

"You are Kesira," the demon said. The shimmery curtain slowly faded to reveal a tall woman lavishly attired in purple velvet and a soft, delicate, lavishly expensive white fur. The demon's face was the feature, however, that startled Kesira the most.

Lalasa possessed no overwhelming beauty. If anything, Kesira would describe the demon as plain. And yet she consorted with rulers and advised Emperor Kwasian on the running of the empire.

"You have suffered much, but you hold up well. There is a chance," said Lalasa. "One I would have ignored previously, but seeing you, one I now endorse wholeheartedly."

"You will help us destroy Lenc?"

"Of course," Lalasa said impatiently. "Everything I have done since he, Eznofadil and Howenthal first placed the jade within their mouths has been directed to his defeat. You cannot know the agony of the jade. I have watched friends become greedy and turned into monsters capable of any perversion to satisfy the urges of the jade."

Kesira's anger flared. "*I* do not know the agony caused by the jade? My patron, Gelya, died. My order was destroyed. I have battled those demons and Ayondela—Ayondela who lost her son because of the power of the jade and was then seduced by revenge. It has ruined my life and my world, and you say I know nothing of the agony?"

Lalasa sniffed contemptuously. "Touch that jade tusk hidden in the folds of your robe. Go on, touch it." Kesira did. The tusk felt cold, quiescent. "It does nothing to you because you are human. If I were to touch it, the sensation might overcome me. I might follow Lenc. I might go insane—many demons did over the past thousand years. They thought to rule as Lenc has done, but they lacked whatever lies within his breast. The jade destroyed them instantly."

"Lenc it destroys slowly. Over the span of years, he grows insane."

Lalasa nodded.

"What aid can you offer?" Kesira asked. "The rune sticks gave no hint."

The tall female demon pushed both hands through her long hair. She crossed the small room in two strides and seated herself on the cot next to the rune sticks. She studied them for a few seconds, then shook her head.

"I read nothing in them to aid either of us."

"You didn't send this message to me?" asked Kesira, startled.

"You have the gift. Why do you ask?"

"Lenc told me that he sent all the readings."

At this, Lalasa laughed until tears rolled down her cheeks. "And you *believed* him? Demons can influence, but the talent is human. No demon casts the runes and foresees the future. I can read, but the casting skill is denied me. In that lies most of the ability."

Kesira considered this. Her flagging spirits began to rise as she realized her power was crucial in defeating Lenc. How she would stop the jade demon, she didn't know. But she would!

"I was called by another, but chose to speak with you. The other's meeting was futile," said Lalasa.

"Other demons will aid us?"

"Perhaps the greatest," said Lalasa. "But those few remaining in our rank provide him scant support. Baram is physically powerful, but lacks even a small human child's intellect. Noissa, brilliant in his way, is but a coward who flees his own shadow. Afraid of the dark, suspicious of the light—he can do nothing." Lalasa's expression turned to one of extreme distaste. "Tolek is another."

Lalasa's eyes crackled with hatred, and Kesira felt a sense of loss. She had learned of Tolek's perfidy long ago, even

before entering the Quaking Lands to do battle with Howenthal. That such a coward should be among those left in
demonic rank stripped away the veneer of confidence she
had felt.

"I see you know of dear, precious Tolek," Lalasa spat.

"But if none of these can help us . . ."

"There is still Merrisen."

"But Merrisen died!" cried Kesira.

"What? When? I recognized his call only minutes ago.
Rather than speak with him, I sought you."

Kesira shook her head. "He and Lenc fought months
ago. Lenc turned Merrisen into jade and then shattered him.
The rain of the shards preceded the destruction of my order.
It severely injured a friend of mine caught in the rain. He
even lost his tongue because of the shower of fragments."

"Merrisen lives," Lalasa said firmly. "I know the . . . the
feel of him. I cannot describe it to a mortal."

"He will help us?" Kesira sat cross-legged on the floor
like a new acolyte listening to her master's every word. A
weight lifted from her shoulders. Zolkan always spoke so
highly of Merrisen. The handsome demon would return and
do battle again with Lenc. He *would!* Lalasa guaranteed it.
This time there would be support for his fight. She would
provide it!

"He must. Without him, we are lost. I can do nothing
against Lenc. Even before he took the jade, I presented no
threat to him. Now?" Lalasa shrugged.

"What are your powers? Zolkan tells me every demon
has some human trait but magnified a hundredfold or more."

"True," the female demon said. She settled the velvet
gown about her thin shoulders and stroked over the fur collar
as if this soothed her. "Tolek is more venal than any mortal,
Baram physically stronger, Noissa more knowledgeable,
Wemilat kinder—and I am possessed of inherent ability to
be a diplomat."

"You can make people agree?"

"Come to mutually agreeable terms." Lalasa's smile was
wan. "With Lenc, there can be no negotiation. I am helpless
against him. Instead of fighting him directly, I use my power
to hold Emperor Kwasian to the throne, to keep the factions

in the Empire welded into a unified front. Even though physical means are as nothing, still I make the attempt."

"But Merrisen?"

"Merrisen is the most balanced of all demons. He has no single outstanding talent. Every demon outshines him in one area, just as he outshines them in all others. Merrisen is unique. Only he saw the danger Lenc posed, only he had the power and wit and courage and selflessness to try to battle him."

"Merrisen still lives? How do I contact him?"

"I will find him and have him come to you. He is, after all, in Kolya. It was from my temple that his summons came." Lalasa stood. "Let me get Merrisen and bring him here."

"Wait, before you go," Kesira said, tugging at the demon's velvet gown. "I must know. Why is Kolya important? Emperor Kwasian makes his stand in Limaden. Why does Lenc come to *this* city?"

Lalasa looked at her with pity in her eyes. "All threads of power end here. Life, death—all."

"I don't understand."

"Lenc comes here because you are here. And because his son is with you." Lalasa looked at the sleeping baby, fear and loathing fleetingly shown on her face.

"He won't get him! I won't give the child over to Lenc!"

"Do not worry on that score. No one wants Lenc and his son reunited. Like the other demons, I want them both · dead!"

Lalasa vanished behind the shimmery curtain, leaving Kesira staring at the cracked plaster on the back wall. Everyone wanted the boy dead—even the demons she had counted on for aid.

Kesira Minette sat and cried—for her dead patron, for herself, for her baby.

Chapter Five

KESIRA MINETTE slumped forward onto the cot where Lalasa had sat, head cradled by her crossed arms, and cried
until the sleep that had been denied previously claimed her.

But the sleep wasn't peaceful. It seemed as if Lalasa
visited her dreams to reveal the horrors wrecking the Empire. Kesira seemed to float a thousand feet above the Plains
of Roggen, watching the antlike creatures moving about
below. A quick swoop, much as she imagined Zolkan making, brought her breathless and excited to a spot less than
a hundred feet over the heads of Emperor Kwasian's soldiers. General Dayle rode along their rank, nodding, pointing out minor infractions, generously heaping praise on
officers and foot soldiers alike.

The world tore apart in a crazy kaleidoscope. When it
reformed, Kesira saw the battle lines marching forward,
spears lowered, grim expressions on every face. A shout
went along the front line and the soldiers broke into a run,
sprinting for a hillock where Lenc stood.

With amused superiority, the jade demon watched the
thousands of men advancing on him. A casual pass of the
hand sent his fireballs tumbling amid the ranks. The gaps
caused by his wholesale destruction closed with new troops.
Lenc again released the destruction with a nonchalant gesture, as if he did nothing more than swat an annoying insect
buzzing around his head.

General Dayle attempted a retreat. It turned into a rout.

Kesira turned away, but only found herself staring at
another aspect of Lenc's cruelty. She saw cities aflame,
women ripped apart by the demon's huge jade penis, men
blasted apart when fireballs appeared inside mouth and

belly—and what Lenc did to small children caused bile to rise into her throat. She choked back the burning vomit.

Spinning through space, she found herself on a circuit of the empire. Limaden with its majestic streets and noble rulers might have been a city deserted for a hundred years. No commerce crowded the markets; caravans camped at the fringes, not daring to move; and the citizens peered out from behind locked windows with a fearfulness that brought tears to Kesira's eyes again.

Limaden no longer presented a face of confidence to the world. Lenc had broken the empire's spirit.

"Oh, Gelya, how I pray for you." Kesira hardly dared to voice the thought that came on the heels of her involuntary outcry. "You are the lucky one, Gelya my patron. We who yet live now have to face this horror."

Over the Yearn Mountains she flew. Blinn no longer existed: the small town nestled in the foothills smoldered as cold, dancing white flame consumed stone and dirt and bone and flesh. Just a few miles farther she saw her nunnery. No one had entered since she had left so many months earlier. The front gates still hung awry and the altar was still desecrated by Lenc's mocking sigil: white fire. That cold light had eaten away the altar to half its original size.

When Kesira forced herself to look away, all she saw were graves covered in the yellow wildflower sacred to Gelya.

"My sisters." To release the anger rising within her, Kesira shouted, "Lalasa, why do you show me this? Why?"

Kesira's breath was taken away by the sudden transit to the Quaking Lands. Those once undulating plains now stretched quiet, inert. Farmers even dared run their furrows and plant along the extreme edges. The magicks brought to the terrain by Howenthal had died along with that jade demon. A solitary spire of rock rose in the center of what had been earthquake-tossed land. Sparkling green dust caught sunlight and reflected it to Kesira.

"You are gone, Howenthal. Along with Wemilat, you are gone." For Wemilat the Ugly, she mourned. No such gentle emotion reminded her of Howenthal.

Kesira blinked. Waves lapped across a sandy shore below

her feet. A gull sounded its mating cry; another swept back its wings and plunged seaward, snaring an incautious *gnar* fish. The Sea of Katad had never been more majestic, even when it had vanished under the frozen waves brought by Ayondela's curse of eternal winter.

The spire rising where Kesira had met and bested Eznofadil was no more. Lenc's cold fire had destroyed it totally.

The huge granite peak where Ayondela had perished replaced the seascape. Nothing remained of the demented female demon, not even the cutting clouds of purest crystal she had used as her weapons against humanity. High winds had whipped up the powdery dust of her shattered body and spread it over the Sarn Mountains. The land she had cursed now accepted her substance willingly.

The land, the sea, the air—Kesira had met the jade demons and defeated all in their strongholds.

She jerked back, surprised to find herself once more in the tiny room at the back of the inn. The blanket on the cot had become soaked with her perspiration and tears. Kesira stood on shaking legs. She had traveled around the empire and seen the destruction wrought by Lenc—and the destruction she had wrought on the jade demons.

"Thank you, Lalasa," she said, hoping the female demon could hear. "I understand now. I *have* mattered."

Kesira silently promised both Lalasa and Gelya that she would not stop in her attempts to defeat Lenc. She had no inkling how it could be done, but then she'd had no idea how to slay any of the other three jade demons before she did so. Wemilat had aided her, Zolkan and Molimo with their sudden insights, the baby with his destructive screams—all had made the difference between victory and failure.

She had not anticipated any of them. They had been there when she needed them. Lalasa had shown her that continued struggle against Lenc need not be futile, that she had to oppose the power of the jade until the proper instant.

But the one thing she would not do, not for Lalasa or Lenc or Kene Zoheret, was forsake the baby. She picked the boy up and allowed him his breakfast. The infant might be Lenc's son, but she would fight to the death to prevent any harm from coming to him.

Pale eyes stared up at her, knowing. The smile on his tiny lips both chilled and relieved her.

Kene Zoheret sat in the corner of the public room with a half-dozen conspirators. Kesira despaired at the snatches of their talk she overheard. Zoheret passionately urged another foray against Lenc's temples, something she saw as futile and self-destructive.

They refused to face the issues Kesira considered most vital. How were they going to act on their own and accomplish anything? Change of any meaningful sort could only come from concerted effort, in harmony with the others in the city. The Emperor Kwasian ruled because he commanded respect—and because he earned it through his wise orders and caring for those in the empire. Kesira had no doubt that the Emperor agonized every night over the fate of so many of his subjects, not because they had died, but because he had failed them.

Zohert addressed none of the real issues. He insisted on acting secretively, alone; on being in charge when others seemed better suited to the task. His sole claim to planning lay in his minor uses of magic. The pitiful fire spells had failed against Lenc. Kesira saw no reason for them not to fail a second time, yet Zoheret continued with his earnest, if misguided, planning.

"...all Kolya will notice us and rally around," Zoheret finished, smashing his fist into the table and looking at the small group.

Kesira frowned. Something struck her as amiss in the way Kene Zoheret spoke and acted. Not only did he violate the social strictures that had allowed the the empire to exist, he was openly contemptuous of the Emperor.

Zoheret acted as if he held back some vital fact. Kesira began to distrust him more and more.

"More ale!" he called. "We have made our decision. Now let us toast it!"

Kesira silently carried a tray of frothy mugs to the table. The men stared at her oddly, as if Zoheret had spoken of her in slighting terms. They took the ale and drank deeply, quickly finishing and scurrying off like rats afraid to face the sunrise.

When only Zoheret remained, he motioned her over to the table. "Sit," he said, as if he were the Emperor offering her the greatest boon imaginable. "That child with you—"

"I have no wish to discuss it." Kesira moved to leave. Zoheret grabbed her arm and jerked her back roughly enough to keep her at the table.

"It is Lenc's spawn, isn't it?"

"He is an orphan. I told you that already."

Zoheret eyed her, then released his grip. Kesira rubbed the spot where his fingers had cut like steel bands into her flesh.

"You must look into the future and scry it for me. We expect the Emperor Kwasian to send reinforcements soon. We must know when they will arrive."

"The Emperor sends troops?" This puzzled her. She had seen—Lalasa had shown her—the destruction wrought by Lenc on the Plains of Roggen. Why did the Emperor dare send forth even a small band away from the defense of his capital? Limaden had to rank more highly in the hearts and minds of the empire than Kolya. It was a symbol of unity as much as anything else.

"Not many," confided Zoheret. "A few. A company at most. But they will be adequate."

Kesira didn't ask "adequate for what." She had the idea Zoheret meant adequate for his own purposes. He was no better than Lenc, plotting and scheming for personal gain rather than for the betterment of all citizens.

"I'll cast the runes," Kesira said. She saw surprise cross Zoheret's face. He had expected her to refuse, but she had her own motives. There were too few soldiers left for the Emperor to dispatch even a company to Kolya's rescue. These had to come from somewhere else—and she thought she knew. The reading from the rune sticks would confirm her suspicions.

Kesira retrieved the bone box from under her gray robe, and flipped open the lid. Zoheret fell silent as she tossed the knucklebones onto the table.

Kesira settled her mind and let the images well up from

deep within her. Lalasa had claimed that this was a true talent, one having nothing to do with Lenc. The jade demon had lied to her, or had only influenced a few of her readings. Kesira Minette had the talent.

Use it, she told herself.

Images twisted and turned into more solid pictures. A soldier covered with scars and glory came riding from the Sea of Katad at the head of a squadron of men, numbering fewer than twenty. But the set to their leader's face, the familiar lines and planes, told Kesira what she needed to know.

"Captain Protaro comes," she said.

"The Emperor's Guard?" Fear and anxiety intermixed in Zoheret's question.

"A small detachment. They have been patrolling along the seashore. They met opposition with Nehan-dir and his mercenaries."

"They fought the Order of the Steel Crescent?"

"Yes."

"The outcome. What was it?" Zoheret shook her so hard the images blurred and went away. Kesira blinked; the public room replaced the vision of Protaro astride his mangy horse, leading his pitiful band to Kolya.

"Captain Protaro prevailed," she said simply.

"Nehan-dir is dead?"

Kesira stared at the rebel leader. His interest in the mercenaries following the Steel Crescent's banner seemed out of place. As if realizing he'd shown unseemly curiosity, Zoheret quickly said, "I need to know. The mercenaries are strong in this region. We must know if they are to be a factor in our fight."

"Nehan-dir lives. The battle was of little consequence, except that Nehan-dir was forced to retreat. Little damage was incurred by either side." Kesira considered lying to Zoheret and telling him that Protaro had completely eradicated the mercenaries. It might be instructive to see the man's reaction. But out of long habit, she told only the truth.

"When does this Protaro arrive?"

"By sundown. He rides on the outskirts of Kolya already.

He will circle the city before entering to find needed supplies and potential escape routes."

"He plans to show his heel and run like a craven?"

"Not at all," Kesira said, tiring of this. "He is a good soldier and scouts out strong and weak points. If he must retreat, he will retreat to a position of strength, not weakness."

Kene Zoheret nodded quickly, rose and left Kesira alone in the inn. The innkeeper was nowhere to be seen, so Kesira went into the back room. The baby lay in his makeshift cradle. She picked him up and rocked gently, more to soothe herself than the boy. Protaro's arrival would not be good for her, not after she had killed his sergeant and disobeyed the Emperor Kwasian's direct order to go to Limaden.

Kesira might have argued this latter point successfully. After all, she *was* heading in the direction of the capital. Zolkan had urged it, and so had Molimo. But of the sergeant's death as the guard pursued her in the mountain passes above the sea? Kesira would never be able to placate Protaro. Those two had been more than friends; they had been comrades in arms.

She rocked, and the baby drifted off to sleep. Kesira wished her own view of the future allowed her such peace.

"Where are you, Zolkan?" she cried out loud. Kesira paced the small room that had become more like a prison to her. The evening crowd had already left the inn. A pair of exceptionally thirsty customers stayed, but the portly innkeeper tended them. In fact, when last Kesira had glanced out into the room, the innkeeper had joined them. She doubted many coins slid into the till from that party. The innkeeper had relieved her and told her to rest.

Kesira needed the break. The strain of watching the colors change outside from bright day to ruddy sunset to ebony darkness had taken its toll on her nerves. Captain Protaro would arrive soon. Not only had the rune sticks foretold his coming, she *felt* it deep down.

And it frightened her. In ways Kesira couldn't put into words, she knew that Protaro's coming would trigger events in Kolya that no mortal could control.

"Where are you, you filthy, featherbrained bird?" Zolkan had vanished on their first day in Kolya and she had not seen him since. Calling out his name had drawn only strange stares from passersby in the street. And contacting Molimo was impossible. She had tried.

Kesira settled her rising panic the best she could and tried to sift through what she knew. Lalasa had told her that one demon who might aid them all had survived: Merrisen.

Kesira began meditating, working her mind around in such a fashion that an unspoken prayer went out to wherever Merrisen might be. At first, Kesira had to push away the sensation of being foolish. What if Merrisen were dead? She prayed for succor from a dead demon.

She realized then that she had done the same with Gelya, even though her patron had perished. This eased her mind. She concentrated, and allowed her thoughts free rein. A curiously disconnected feeling overwhelmed her. Kesira fought it, then encouraged it.

"Merrisen!" she called out. With that name went her hopes and fears, her need, the need of all in the world to be free of Lenc and to return to a normal, well-ordered society.

Feathery tickles brushed her soul, but no firm contact was made. Sweaty, tired, she sagged forward onto her cot. Kesira wiped her forehead and stretched out. Something soft touched her hand, causing her to jump.

"Trouble. Hurry, hurry," squawked Zolkan.

"Where have you been?" she cried. "I've been worried about you. Don't just go off like that again."

"You cast me out. You said no way to get room here if ugly, awful *trilla* bird like me came along." Zolkan sniffed and turned his head to one side, trying to look hurt.

"Don't be like that. Where have you been? Is Molimo all right?"

"I have been digging through trash to find small scraps of food to keep me alive. Horrible," the bird declared. "Ruins the oil on my feathers. So hard to preen when you are covered with garbage."

Kesira looked closely at Zolkan. The plumpness and glossy condition of his feathers put the lie to his statements.

Whatever he had been doing for the past few days, it hadn't been digging through refuse.

"Where's Molimo?"

"Around. I have come to tell you of the guard captain's arrival. Protaro enters city even as we speak."

"We must reach him before Zoheret."

"Zoheret?"

"He's leader of a band of rebels. He wants Protaro to aid him in some foolish scheme to burn down all Lenc's temples."

"Not bad plan, if you roast your dinner over flames," said Zolkan. "Otherwise, why antagonize Lenc to no purpose?"

"I see you share my sentiments in this, Zolkan. I hope we can convince Protaro not to throw away any real chance he has at defeating Lenc."

"One soldier—even Protaro—cannot defeat Lenc."

"He can fight. *We* can fight. And joined, we might be able to do an even better job. But after our last brief meeting, I doubt Protaro will listen to me. What do you suggest?"

Zolkan let out a loud, wordless squawk. "You ask me, an outcast from polite society?" The *trilla* bird craned his neck around, taking in not only the small room but the public room beyond.

"Stop it!" Kesira snapped. "There's no time for petty squabbling."

"Always time," Zolkan muttered. Louder, he said, "Protaro bivouacs a half-hour's walk outside Kolya. Should I inquire as to the captain's intentions?"

"A half hour?" Kesira considered. "I'll go personally. The distance isn't too far. If I hurry, I can be back here before dawn."

"Why bother?"

"The innkeeper has been good to me. I promised to work for my room and food." A twinkle came to her eyes, and for the first time in days, she smiled. "You have me to thank for placing all that succulent garbage outside for you to dine on."

"Fool's errand," said Zolkan, scowling at her. He shook

his head and caused a minor snowstorm of bright green and blue feathers. "Protaro aids only Emperor Kwasian."

"Our goal is the same—defeating Lenc."

"Sooner you start, sooner you find out how wrong you can be," said Zolkan. The heavy bird perched on her shoulder as if daring her to brush him off. If anything, the familiar weight and nearness comforted Kesira. She picked up the sleeping baby, slipped out the back way and, following Zolkan's earthy directions, found the road on which Protaro camped with his men.

As she walked in the night stillness, Kesira noted that no one shared the road. Even at night Kolya had bustled with activity, and the night wasn't old enough yet for all citizens to be in bed.

She grew increasingly uneasy as she walked. Finally, Kesira said to Zolkan, "Where is everyone? I...I don't even hear insects chirping. There are no night sounds at all!"

"Lenc has worked well," said the *trilla* bird. "All bugs gone. Hungry times. I enjoy a good, juicy bug now and again." Zolkan clacked his strong beak shut.

"Lenc drives the people indoors, too?"

"He kidnaps unwary travelers. When you hold unchecked power, you must use it. Otherwise, what good is it? Lenc abuses his."

Even the insects had been destroyed? Kesira's stride lengthened until she almost ran into the darkness. The sight of a dozen small campfires blazing and valiantly holding back the emptiness of night made her heart skip a beat. She paused for a moment to collect her thoughts and regain her breath. It wouldn't do to confront Protaro acting as if she'd run all the way from Kolya—even though she had come very close to doing so.

"Mistake," said Zolkan. "Let me talk with captain."

"You're always urging me to hurry. Now is the time. Let's go." She straightened her tattered but clean robe and leaned on her staff. The baby still slept, snugly cradled in the knapsack she'd slung on her back.

She'd gone only a dozen paces when a guard challenged her.

"I have come to see Captain Protaro," she responded.

"Your name and business?"

"Kesira Minette, Sister of the Mission for the Order of Gelya. The business is—"

A sharp command cut off her explanation. Striding out of the shadows and standing with his back to a nearby fire was a commanding figure of a man. Even though the shadows hid his features, Kesira knew him.

"Captain, I want to apologize for all that happened at our last meeting."

"You disobeyed the Emperor Kwasian's command," Protaro said without preamble. No mention was made of Sergeant Tuwallan's death. Kesira thought that he might have accepted his friend's death as a battle casualty; in this way he might be able to remember without undue mourning.

"Ayondela is dead. That was more important than an audience with the Emperor." Even as she spoke, Kesira knew how hollow the words sounded. Everyone knew his place within society. Even something as vital as destruction of one of the jade demons ought to rank second to a direct order from the Emperor. Duty to family and Emperor took precedence over all other things.

The baby stirred in her backpack, rubbing tiny eyes with equally tiny fists.

Kesira gripped her staff. She had to explain quickly. "We need your help. Lenc is—"

"Sentry?" snapped Protaro.

"Sir! There is a small child in the knapsack." Kesira looked to her left where the guard still stood, sword drawn. Silvery glints shone off the long blade, showing where nicks hadn't been properly honed, giving the deep blood gutter an ominous appearance of fingers reaching from its shallow depths.

"Kill the child!"

Kesira's attention jerked back to the guard captain. Protaro drew his sword and advanced. Already, the camp had awakened. No matter where she looked, Kesira saw only naked steel and determined soldiers advancing on her.

"Kill the child!" The shout went up through the soldiers'

ranks. Kesira swung her staff and batted away the sentry's sword, but there were too many for her to fight.

But she could do nothing else. Kesira Minette stood her ground grimly, ready to die defending the baby's life.

Chapter Six

KESIRA MINETTE'S staff swung just above knee level. The snap when it connected with the guardsman's leg echoed through the night until his scream drowned it out. He clutched his knee and sank to the ground. Kesira finished him off with a thrust of the butt end of her staff to his temple. He jerked once, then lay still on the ground, the campfire light showing that his open eyes already clouded with death.

"Back," ordered Protaro. He stood, sword leveled, studying her. "We want the baby. It is evil."

"How can such a small child be evil?" she countered. But Kesira's thoughts turned to an old saying Dominie Tredlo had been fond of repeating: Evil events come from evil causes.

The baby had been spawned by Lenc. Nothing in Kesira's world touched evil more. The Emperor's demon Lalasa had spoken against the baby, Zolkan wanted him dead, all Kolya thought the baby evil, and now Protaro would kill the child unless she acted.

"You will have to kill me to get the infant."

"You think that deters me?" snapped Protaro. She read the hurt and need for vengeance in his eyes. The way his entire body settled down completed the picture. He would strike like a snake with that well-used sword and she would die.

Kesira parried the first thrust and landed the tip of her staff in his belly. The shudder ran the length of the staff. For an instant Kesira thought she'd smashed the wooden rod against a stone wall, but Protaro grunted and danced back. Her eyes widened. The man's stomach must be protected by steel bands!

Kesira began retreating, thinking to run even though she was bone-tired from her trip from Kolya. The others in Protaro's company circled her, cutting off her escape. Then they began moving inward to restrict her movements. She swung the staff in wide circles now, holding them at bay. But it was only a matter of time before she tired. They numbered more than fifty. Like a pack of dogs worrying its prey, they would have her soon enough.

But not without a fight!

Protaro's quick sword engaged her staff and knocked it from her hands when she became careless.

"Surrender now," the captain said, "and I will let you live."

She saw the immense concession he made; he wanted her death to atone for the loss of his friend and comrade in arms. Kesira heard no hint of duplicity in the words, either. Protaro was a man of honor and would defend his promise to the death.

"For that I thank you, Captain," she said, "but I cannot allow you to slaughter an innocent baby. You'd be no better than the one we both fight."

"Lalasa says the child is Lenc's son. We have been ordered to kill it!"

Kesira wondered why Lalasa hadn't simply taken the child when the female demon had visited her at the inn. Every indication of physical presence had shown Lalasa to be in the room. The cot had sagged. A faint hint of unidentifiable perfume had lingered for hours. And there could be no question of a demon's being unable to overpower a mortal.

Or was there? The idea shook Kesira. Had she somehow grown so powerful that even the demon advising the Emperor Kwasian feared her? Kesira pushed this idea from her mind as absurd. A more likely reason was Lalasa's fear that, if the baby awakened, it might use its loud cry on her.

Even this rang hollow and untrue in Kesira's mind. Lalasa was not of jade; she would not shatter as Ayondela had done. The baby's wail brought down palaces, but it affected only jade.

Kesira yelped when Protaro's blade nicked her arm. The

guard captain advanced, step-slide, step-slide, as if she were still armed.

The tusk taken from Ayondela's mouth came into her hand more from desperation than considered thoughtfulness. The tusk gleamed dully in the firelight. Whatever power dwelt inside had long since gone out. All Kesira had was a hard, round, sharp-tipped tooth of little value in a real fight.

"Back! She has jade!" cried one of the men. Even Protaro took two quick steps back. The captain eyed her with real hatred now. Kesira brandished the tusk, hoping no one noticed it was capable of inflicting only the most superficial of injuries.

"The witch tool will avail you naught," Protaro said. "Give us the child and you can still go unmolested."

Kesira said nothing. She edged to her left, swinging the jade tusk in a wide arc. The men fell back in an orderly fashion, not allowing her even the smallest gap to escape through.

Wait. Hold them off for a few minutes more.

Kesira jerked as if someone had touched her with a burning coal. The words had seared across her mind, but no sound reached her ears. She desperately searched for the source and found no clue.

"Zolkan!" she cried out. The *trilla* bird had taken to wing when Protaro advanced on them. "Help me, Zolkan!"

"She calls down her evil patron's wrath," muttered one of the men facing her. Kesira stabbed in his direction with the jade tusk, but succeeded only in tiring herself just a little more. From the corner of her eye, she saw Protaro motioning for the ring to again tighten around her. Without her staff, she couldn't keep them far enough away to prevent an occasional lunge from touching her flesh. They would attack and attack again until she bled from a thousand cuts.

Crystal clouds, soldiers' swords—what was the difference? The pain burned her soul in the same way.

"She calls for the *trilla* bird," said Protaro. "No demon, no evil patron. Get her!"

The world about me,
There are no eyes.

Freedom of the air and sky,
I fade into nothingness.

Kesira heard the spell within her skull. Once before she'd caught snippets of this, but what it meant she had no idea.

Just as the ring constricted to the point where any of the soldiers might impale her on spear or sword tip, she felt a stirring at her elbow. She blinked, trying to focus her eyes. It was as if her vision slipped to one side or the other off—Molimo.

Her momentary lapse signaled the soldiers to attack.

Run. Now, run and find Zolkan. He will guide you back to Kolya.

She fought to see Molimo. With extreme concentration, she saw his sinews rippling in the firelight, casting deep valleys of shadow and revealing broad plains of muscles tightening in combat. His sword flew like a silver bird, slashing, singing, fluttering on to knock away thrusts meant to kill her. He fought—and Protaro's men couldn't see him.

"She's ensorcelled us!"

"She doesn't touch us but we die!" another shouted in fear. Even Captain Protaro appeared confused. Kesira stood and watched while the guard captain's men were driven back.

Flee now. *Hurry!*

The source of that potent command had to be Molimo. But how? This wasn't speech as she knew it. The words came with too much clarity and force—and they boomed inside her skull. Molimo hadn't grown a new tongue in the few days he had been absent, but he seemed to have found a better method of communication.

Kesira fought the niggling sensation that she'd experienced this before. From Molimo? In Ayondela's palace she had felt something similar, but she hadn't recognized it as coming from Molimo. Now, there could be no one else originating the word-thoughts.

Still having trouble focusing her eyes on the man cloaked with the demon's spell of nonnoticeability, Kesira ducked through the break in the circle around her. She hadn't run fifty feet when she heard Protaro yell, and a dozen men start racing after her.

One by one, they screamed, and she heard their heavy footfalls no more.

Kesira gasped in pain when a heavy body crashed into her left shoulder. She stumbled and almost fell face-forward into the soft, yielding dirt. The nun managed to keep her feet, and continued at a slower pace.

"I could run faster if I didn't have to carry you, too," she told Zolkan. The *trilla* bird sat complacently on her shoulder again, flexing his talons into her fleshy shoulder. Dampness soaked her robe under Zolkan's feet. She hazarded a quick touch: blood.

"I am uninjured," the bird assured her. "Many of good captain's men lack an ear or an eye now, though."

"They wanted to kill the baby."

"Don't know why Molimo insisted on rescuing you," answered Zolkan. "Let them have bratling. Be for best. Nobody but Lenc wants the baby alive."

"He didn't take the child when he had the chance back at Ayondela's palace."

"Why bother? You provide better transportation. Also, how would Lenc feed bratling?"

Kesira swallowed and tasted ashes. All the *trilla* bird said was true. Until the baby grew and could be weaned, she provided his only reliable source of nourishment. Wemilat's kiss had turned into a curse burning like a brand into her breast. She wanted to claw out the mark and heave the baby into the night.

She could do neither.

"I don't understand," she gasped out, her strength beginning to fade. In the distance she heard the thunder of horses' hooves. Protaro had mounted and come after her. Not even Molimo, using his spell, could protect her now. She looked around for a hiding place.

Zolkan held out one long wing and pointed to a small ravine. Silently, Kesira turned toward it. When the bank caved in beneath her feet and sent her tumbling, Kesira twisted so that she scooted down the dirt on her belly, instinctively protecting the baby strapped to her back. The whole while, the infant didn't let out even a tiny murmur.

That action on her part, done totally without thinking,

convinced Kesira that she'd never allow anybody to kill the boy. She reached behind and pulled the tiny bundle around to where she could hold it. Rocking slowly, she soothed the infant. Those damnable pale, laughing eyes stared up at her, as if thanking her—and mocking her for her gullibility.

"Why don't I name you?" she said aloud. "A good name would save you from being forever called 'it' by Zolkan."

"Impossible to give name to it," said Zolkan. "What can be right?"

Kesira's head ached horribly. She cooed to the baby, as if it needed comforting, and tried to think this through. The *trilla* bird was right. No name she came up with fit the boy. Try as she might, names slipped off the infant like gentle spring rains off a tiled roof. The name formed, built, then vanished, leaving behind only the reality.

"All right, no name," she said, chagrined. "But you'll not end up spitted on any guardsman's sword."

The baby graced her with a soft chuckle. He reached up and tugged at her robe, then began nursing when he found a convenient tear.

"Protaro will ride past. Darkness hides your track," said Zolkan. "Molimo will join us soon."

"Good. I want to talk to him. I had the most unusual experience back in Protaro's camp. It was as if Molimo spoke directly to my mind. I'd had similar feelings on the way up to Ayondela's palace—and even before that. But these were stark, clear words."

"Quiet!" squawked the bird.

Hooves clumped along down the road at a pace slower than a gallop but faster than any walk. The voices mingled and became indistinct, but one rang out over the others.

"Lose her, and I'll have you walking sentry for a year!" Protaro's anger burned in his every word. Kesira caught her breath and barely dared to breathe as the guardsmen trotted by on the road. For a long time after the last sounds of their horses' hooves had faded to silence, Kesira maintained her strained, expectant pose.

"They are gone," said Zolkan. The bird jumped from her shoulder and waddled about, pecking and hunting through the debris caused by her fall down the ravine bank. "No good food anywhere in this miserable place. Want to go back to where pigeons don't get everything first."

Kesira tended to the baby while Zolkan continued to look for some small tidbit for his supper. The baby turned against her, and she felt a warmth beginning at her sash. Kesira put the baby aside and looked at the jade tusk.

It glowed with its inner light again. The baby had touched the jade tooth, and it recovered whatever power had been drained. Kesira turned cold inside. She dared not let the power of the jade overwhelm her or seduce the infant. The woman tried to grasp the tusk and throw it away.

It sailed through the night like a green comet, only to return as if it were on a string. Repeatedly, Kesira threw the jade tusk, and it always came back. She fell to her knees, sobbing with frustration.

"This can't be happening. I don't want it, I don't want it."

"Baby is sign of Time of Chaos," said Zolkan. "Evil. Change is evil."

"I know," sobbed Kesira. Her entire world had been structured so that each person knew his or her duty and performed it. Alter the world, and the roles changed. She didn't want the disruption the jade demons had brought, and she didn't want what the baby promised.

"If only it could all go back to the way it was."

"Change has started," Zolkan said glumly. "No turning back now. We must forge ahead. But kill bratling. That will help stop flood of changes."

Kesira held the glowing jade tooth in one hand and reached out hesitantly with her other hand. She touched the baby's head. He smiled. All she had to do was lift the jade dagger and bring it slashing down to the tender body. The tooth would penetrate and kill instantly. Kesira's hand quaked with indecision.

"I can't do it," she said finally, the tears drying on her cheeks. "Gelya taught us never to squander precious life. I can't murder an innocent."

Zolkan sniffed. "Some innocent. Pigeon shit! It forces Time of Chaos upon us. All we know will vanish. Do you want that?"

"No." Kesira tucked the jade tusk into her sash. "And I can't kill him, either."

Zolkan made a rude noise.

Before Kesira could reply, she heard the crunch of boots on the dried soil near the ravine bank. Kesira scooped up the infant and spun so that the overhang shielded her from sight. Zolkan stifled a squawk and waddled beside her. The way the *trilla* bird held himself, a quick leap would have him airborne and away from danger.

"Trail's already cold," came a voice. "She must be back in Kolya by now."

"Protaro's going to have our balls if she got away from us. You're supposed to be the best tracker in the outfit, Tamun. What do you read?"

Another voice piped up, shrill and almost feminine. "Not far. I don't read the trail, I sense it. I *feel* her nearby, and the baby's with her."

Kesira stilled her racing heart and kept her mind ready to respond to any attack. She pushed the baby from her when he reached out and touched the jade tusk once again. The brilliance from it now cast a faint shadow out into the dried riverbed.

Even as Kesira started to worry about the ghostly light being seen, she saw the two dark figures falling through the air. They landed in crouches not five feet away. Both had their daggers drawn.

"You'll win a promotion for this, Tamun," said the shadowy figure on the right as they moved forward with practiced ease.

But neither expected the loud complaint and the burst of feathers and beak when Zolkan launched himself into the fray. Kesira sat for a few seconds, stunned by the soldiers' sudden appearance, but when she heard a meaty fist strike Zolkan, she sprang into action.

The tusk came lightly to hand. Jade met steel—and shattered the tempered blade. Kesira never hesitated. She kicked out, found a vulnerable kneecap and broke it. Spinning, she caught Tamun's blade. Again, steel proved no match for the delicately veined jade dagger. As the two touched, the steel exploded into a million fragments like one of the Emperor's artillery bombs.

Tamun shrieked as his knife turned molten in his face. Kesira pressed the advantage and drove the jade tusk straight for an exposed throat. The tooth entered easily. As blood frothed around the wound, it stained the tusk and began to sizzle. Steam rose, causing Kesira to jerk back.

She stared at the jade stupidly, as if doubting any of this could have happened. But the two men on the ground gave mute testimony to the power of the blade—the jade weapon that had been activated by the baby's feeble touch.

Kesira stared at the infant. What might Lenc's son do when he became full-grown?

"Help me," came the low plea for assistance. Kesira hurried to a bramble bush where Zolkan had become entangled. She pulled the bird out gingerly, trying not to damage his precious, well-groomed feathers too much. He had told her once that he needed as much wing surface as possible for flight; his heavy body nearly overtaxed his wingspan even at the best of times.

"Pigeon lovers," grumbled Zolkan. "Why do they skulk about like that?"

"You're all right," Kesira said, checking out pinions and tail feathers. "Just a little dignity missing."

"Bruised. Hurt inside." Zolkan stretched, and used one wing to point off into the darkness. "Hurry off. They find us soon."

When Kesira bent to pick up the baby, the one whose knee she'd broken tried to grab her. Zolkan flapped over, ripped with his talons and produced a fountain of blood that quickly vanished into the thirsty sand.

"Doesn't make me feel better," the bird confided. "Might, though, if I get enough of them."

"They are the Emperor Kwasian's personal guard," she said. "They aren't our enemy. Lenc is. We ought to try to make our peace with them."

"Easy for you to say. You killed one, crippled another. What peace is Protaro likely to offer?"

Kesira shut up. She hated it when the *trilla* bird came this close to pointing out how wrong she could be. Baby safely tucked away in the backpack, she trudged through the darkened countryside, intent on the faint necklace of gaslights showing the entry portals to Kolya.

"Where's Molimo?" she asked. Zolkan sat in the corner of the room and sulked. He hadn't said a dozen words all the way back from their encounter with Protaro's guardsmen on the road.

Kesira began pacing the small room, then stopped, heart leaping to her throat when she heard a hard banging on the inn door. The innkeeper grumbled and shuffled his way across. Kesira heard the portly man mumble something, but the response froze her.

"Emperor's Guard. We seek a woman with a small child." Protaro was searching Kolya door by door, seeking her out. She clutched at the jade tusk, for once glad that Gelya had forbidden the use of steel weapons. If she'd relied on a sword against the guardsmen, she'd've been dead. As it was, the magicks inherent in the jade had saved her.

But at what cost? She felt no different from using the evil jade, but then she wasn't a demon. The demons were easily—quickly—perverted by the jade. How long would it take before a mortal succumbed?

Kesira didn't want to consider that.

The jade tusk rested cool and reassuring in her hand as she listened to the innkeeper arguing with the guardsman.

"You can't search my place. Damn fool shame to disturb any of my customers. Too few, now that Lenc's come into Kolya. Why don't you concern yourselves with the likes of him, why don't you, eh?" The innkeeper jabbed a stubby finger into the soldier's chest. Kesira sucked in her breath in surprise. To touch one of the Emperor's troops was an act tantamount to treason.

The guardsman said nothing. He spun and left without demanding a thorough search—or the innkeeper's head for his action. Kesira relaxed.

"Protaro looks everywhere," Zolkan said. "He won't find us. He looks as if you leave a trail in forest. Must look for trail in city. Different. Pigeon-shit bratling."

The sudden change in topic confused Kesira for a mo-

ment, then she realized he spoke of the baby sleeping peacefully on the cot. Kesira ran a gentle hand over the baby's
wrinkled, almost hairless head, then gusted a deep sigh.

Her life had become too confused, too far from the norm
that society demanded. She no longer knew her duty—and,
from the innkeeper's actions, neither did anyone else. The
soldier, in turn, had acted wrongly in not slaying the man
instantly. And all people were slaves to Lenc.

Where would it end?

Without even noticing what she did, Kesira pulled out
the bone box and tossed the rune sticks. She disliked doing
this too often for fear of "wearing out" whatever talent she
had. But she needed guidance to know the proper path to
follow.

Her eyes widened as she read the runes. Lenc—that one
she knew all too well. But this time it showed strength
followed by abrupt weakness. Protaro—he wove through
the pattern. Nehan-dir and even Molimo.

"Molimo is everywhere in the new patterns," she muttered.

"What of demons?" asked Zolkan, peering over her
shoulder, trying to find a comfortable perch on her arm.

"Only Lenc and Molimo. Some of Lalasa, but little, very
little."

"Those?" Zolkan asked, pointing out a strange pairing
of sticks.

"Victory. I read a monumental battle with Lenc—and *I*
win." She sat on the floor, astonished. There was no equiv-
ocation in these runes. No vagueness. No ambiguous runes
to be misread.

She would fight Lenc—and win.

Kesira experienced an inner glow of triumph at this—
but the runes left out some crucial information.

They didn't tell her where to battle Lenc, when, or most
important of all, how.

She would triumph ultimately. But how?

Chapter Seven

THE SMALL, scrawny man with the pink spiderweb of scars across his face pointed off to a cloud of dust indicating a troop of soldiers hard a'ride toward Kolya.

"There," Nehan-dir said. "That must be the damned guard captain and his sycophants."

Nehan-dir's lieutenant wiped a dripping nose on her sleeve, then stifled a yawn. To those of the Steel Crescent, it mattered little whether they fought the Emperor Kwasian's guard or some ragtag band of other-beast hunters out on the plains. A battle brought out the best in a warrior, gave definition to life, set bounds and presented opportunity to display courage and talent. Under Nehan-dir, there had been many fine battles for the order, even if their accursed bad fate decreed continual loss of patronage.

"So?" asked Famii Bren-ko, wiping her nose on her other sleeve. "Their blood spills just like any other."

Nehan-dir half turned in the saddle and glared at her. "Lenc wants his son returned to him unharmed. What will an enraged demon do to us if we allow Protaro to kill the child? A demon's blood *doesn't* spill like any other."

Bren-ko grinned wickedly, showing yellowed, broken teeth. "In such a case, our loving patron might not take out his wrath on all the order. Just our leader." She rocked back in her saddle and hefted a sturdy leg up and around the pommel. "Might be a good opportunity for a strong second-in-command to move up, eh?"

"You'll be smiling from a second mouth before that happens," Nehan-dir said, moving his index finger along the woman's throat to indicate where his dagger would go before Lenc could slay him.

Famii Bren-ko jerked away and stared at the vanishing dust cloud.

Nehan-dir's attention turned inward, to plans, to schemes, to ways of entering Kolya without arousing much ire or creating a stir. Even though Lenc controlled the city with the power of jade, the populace still rebelled at odd times. Nehan-dir chuckled at this. Even in rebellion, Lenc ruled. But that was another concern, one beyond the scope of Nehan-dir's orders.

Even the battle-hardened mercenary shivered at the thought of his meeting with Lenc. The demon had appeared in a cloud of choking vapor. The thunderclap accompanying his arrival had deafened the Steel Crescent leader and had driven him to his knees with pain. Only then had Lenc spoken to him.

"Worm!" the jade demon had roared. "You disgust me. You are a pathetic nothing. Why do I tolerate your continued existence?"

"I seek only to obey, Master!" Nehan-dir had shouted, his words louder than he'd expected because of the ringing still hindering his hearing.

"Then know this, low one. I have allowed Gelya's whore to keep my son by the mortal Parvey Yera. She suckles my heir when no one else can. But the time for this charity on my part draws to an end. I want my son beside me in my hour of total triumph. You will go to Kolya and retrieve my son from Kesira Minette."

"Why Kolya?"

Lenc had strode back and forth in front of the kneeling mercenary; the demon's eyes flared a brilliant green and tiny sparks danced off his arms and legs. When the demon clenched his fists, Nehan-dir had thought he would die for asking an impertinent question. To have come so far, to have endured Tolek's bartering of his worshipers, to sorrow over the loss of Howenthal and Ayondela, only to die at an angered patron's hand!

Lenc's rage subsided. "Why not Kolya? For my purposes, it is ideal. Emperor Kwasian still commands the populace in Limaden. Lalasa is no threat, but she manages to annoy me."

Nehan-dir sucked in his breath as the thought occurred to him that Lenc might actually fear what the Emperor's demon might be capable of accomplishing with only mortals at her command.

"Further," Lenc had gone on, "I have decided my main temple will be constructed in a city untainted by other demons. Kolya is my choice. To have throngs come and pay me homage. To hear their voices uplifted in prayers beseeching me not to destroy them. To know that I of all the demons rule supreme!"

"The Order of the Steel Crescent will not fail you, Master!"

The demon had snorted and pointed a green-blazing finger at him. "Fail and die, worm. Succeed and you will be my vicar to the people of this world. Of all mortals, you, Nehan-dir, will be elevated above even the Emperor."

Nehan-dir had bowed deeply, hardly daring to believe such grandiose promises. Tolek had promised; he had lied. The other patrons sought out by the Steel Crescent had proven weak and had perished before delivering their payments. The thunderclap had repeated itself, and the noxious odors vanished with the jade demon. Nehan-dir had risen on weak legs and staggered away to mount and ride hard for Kolya.

Nehan-dir decided that the soldiers under Protaro's command numbered fewer than a hundred. Perhaps even less. The mercenary leader worried over ambushes, attacks, the proper method of attack. Those following his banner had grown in the past weeks to over seventy. Power drew power. With the structure of society weakening, the Emperor Kwasian unable to provide the services of defense and leadership, many drifted, unsure of their places.

Nehan-dir told them their places, and they rejoiced to again know their duties.

If only he could find another to replace Famii Bren-ko. Her allegiance was plain to any who even dared ask: she fought for herself. Nehan-dir didn't understand this or her need for personal power. He sought only to serve his order and give them the best he could. When another came along able to give the Steel Crescent more, Nehan-dir would step aside.

This would not come willingly, true. He would be dead, the other having triumphed in individual combat. But it would be an honorable death, and Nehan-dir could find his rest knowing that a stronger leader rode at the front of the Steel Crescent's battle column.

Service to his order came first, always. But what of Famii Bren-ko? He mistrusted her motives.

"We ride south, then into Kolya."

"Why ignore the guard?" the woman demanded. "Let's engage them now, while they are still worn out from their long ride across the plains. We won't have any of those accursed Kolyans getting in our way. Waste of time, hacking through a crowd of peasants armed with nothing more than daggers and spit."

"We are tired, also," Nehan-dir said. "The battle might go against us since Protaro holds higher ground. We enter Kolya. We rest. We pick our target well, *then* strike."

The woman shrugged as if it were a matter of total indifference to her and pulled a filthy cloak tighter around her well-fleshed body. Nehan-dir started to reprimand her for such disobedience, then stopped. Bren-ko had a small but loyal cadre among the order's newer members. This was neither the time nor the place to challenge her for complete control.

But Nehan-dir knew it had to come soon, if the order was to survive.

"We find Lenc's son, then we fight," he promised.

"Bastard," came the faint, derisive word. Nehan-dir didn't know if Famii Bren-ko meant Lenc's son or him, though the epithet was true in both cases. The small leader spurred his horse toward the distant city, glad once more to feel wind whipping against his face, robbing his ears of the words of those behind him. No other feeling rivaled the sensation of galloping at the head of a column of mercenaries intent on battle.

None.

The newly promoted sergeant failed to replace Tuwallen, in either friendship or ability, but he was the best of the surviving guards. Protaro listened to the report with only half an ear, more intent on considering the ramifications of those who'd been following them for almost a week.

"Thank you," Protaro said, breaking off the scouting report. "I am convinced that only the Steel Crescent could mount a troop the size of those to the south."

"Should we prepare for battle, Captain?"

Protaro snorted. The silvery lace of his breath hung in the cold night air until a slight breeze grabbed hold and carried it away, a captive of approaching winter. He slapped himself on the upper arms and restored what circulation he could. Ayondela's curse had laid a snowy blanket across the land for most of the summer. What brief respite there'd been counted more as autumn. Again, for the second time in less than three months, winter's frosty grip squeezed and shook the land.

The only consolation lay in that this winter came naturally and not at the beck of a jade demon.

"Nehan-dir wants the boy sheltered by the nun," Protaro said, more to himself than to the newly promoted sergeant.

"Why should the Steel Crescent fetch the infant for Lenc? Why doesn't the demon simply take the boy himself? He has the power of jade to enforce any whim."

"Perhaps it is nothing more than that—a whim. Or it might be more." Protaro kept thinking along those lines, and came to the unsettling conclusion that Lenc might be afraid of Kesira. What power did Gelya's nun command that a jade demon feared? The woman had claimed to have slain the other three demons, but Protaro discounted this as wild ravings. Lenc had eliminated competition for sole rule. Kesira had not mattered.

But many things about the nun struck Protaro as odd. The *trilla* bird with her, for instance. Such birds were often the messengers of the demons—or had been, when a significant number of demons had existed. And the tongueless youth. Molimo, the woman had called him. He seemed familiar to Protaro, and the soldier didn't know why. The youth was too young to have been a soldier serving along the lines when the barbarians had launched their final attack. Protaro knew few others outside the Emperor's service.

Where lay Kesira Minette's power? Protaro found it hard

to swallow the notion that Lenc feared her. She commanded no powerful magicks, or she would have unleashed them against him and his men when she'd blundered into their camp the night before. Kesira had fought her way free, the *trilla* bird aiding her in some mysterious fashion. Protaro thought it had been as if another battled on the nun's side, one unseen by even the keenest-eyed of his sentries.

The guard captain shrugged this off. He had been given a mission to accomplish, the orders signed by the Emperor's own hand. Protaro touched the now almost disintegrated paper hidden inside his tunic. Emperor Kwasian's own chop made it official: the boy with Kesira Minette must be returned to Limaden. Barring this, the child must die.

Protaro didn't like the idea of being executioner to such a small one, but his duty shone bright and clear through the murk cast by Lenc's ambitions. The Emperor desired the boy's death. Protaro was a good soldier. He would obey even if he did have a grudging admiration for the nun's courage. Still, the vision of his good friend and comrade Tuwallen lying dead back in the rocky Sarn Mountains returned to haunt him. Kesira had caused that sudden death.

Now she taunted him by dangling the boy in front of him while they camped outside Kolya.

"Lenc fears something," Protaro told his sergeant. "Even with his immense power, he is fearful. Why pick a city like Kolya for his capital?"

"It is untainted by other demons," suggested the sergeant. The man shuffled uncomfortably. These matters lay beyond the realm of his thoughts. Such considerations, however, obviously engaged much of his commander's time.

"A better symbol would be crushing Emperor Kwasian, humiliating Lalasa, then assuming the throne in Limaden. Lenc comes here for a reason—Kesira Minette is still some weeks distant from Limaden. Does Lenc fear her joining forces with the Emperor?" This made no sense to the captain. Lenc ought to be able to stop any single traveler along the empire's roads. Only the capital remained in Emperor Kwasian's power. Even more to the point, Kwasian wanted the boy dead, something Kesira fought bitterly against. Sel-

dom had Protaro seen one of any religious order more adamant and in violation of the Emperor's direct command.

The sergeant shrugged, it being a matter of no real im-
port. He cared more about a full belly and a good night's
sleep, both of which had been in short supply. He told his
captain this.

"We'll enter Kolya by the west gate. The nun can't have
gone far. We will track her through the streets, if necessary,
but the baby will be ours before the sun reaches zenith today.
Prepare to ride."

This the sergeant understood. He spun and began barking
orders, getting the men into formation, checking gear,
readying them for what had to be a battle.

Protaro watched in silence, his brain churning with the
infinity of possibilities generated by Emperor Kwasian and
the demons. He gave up finally, convinced it was a fool's
game. He would obey his orders, and Lenc take the reasons
behind it.

"The guardsman has left," Kesira said, peering out into
the moonlit street. One moon hung just above the rooftops
and cast a pewter glow over Kolya. Nobody but the Emperor's Guard strayed this night, making it easier for her to
determine her own safety. "They won't be back soon. There
are too few of them and too many places to search."

"Some search. Pigeon-brained soldiers didn't even poke
around inside," said Zolkan.

"Whose side are you on?" she demanded angrily. "If
they'd found us, they would have killed the baby."

"No loss. Need bratling dead. Bad, very bad."

"He's too young to be bad," she said, her confidence
eroding as she watched the baby stir. Those penetrating pale
eyes opened to affix firmly on her. Intelligence unlike any
she'd known blazed within those cool eyes. Kesira saw now
that this was no mortal baby but the true offspring of a
demon.

Why did he have to be Lenc's son? She cursed her weakness in not giving in to Protaro—Emperor Kwasian!—and
Lalasa and Zolkan and even the citizens of Kolya who
wanted the baby dead. Stubbornness had always plagued

her. Sister Fenelia had cautioned her repeatedly about obstinance, but Kesira had chosen her own path over that dictated by her superiors. This made her a misfit, a social outcast in many ways. As much as she tried to obey, to know her place in society, the more it rankled.

"I will *not* give up the child."

Zolkan made a rude noise and an even ruder gesture.

"And if I catch you trying to harm him, you'll end up in a stewpot."

"No need to get nasty," Zolkan said with ill grace. "I cannot harm baby. But bratling must die. Too dangerous."

Kesira settled down on her cot, the door into the public room open slightly to allow her a view of the large window in the outer room. Shadows fluttered across the window, often nothing more than clouds obscuring the rising moon; but now and again she saw the harsher shadows of soldiers.

"Zolkan," she whispered. "Protaro's men are outside. They've tracked us down!"

The bird fluttered around the small room, then smashed into the door, knocking it open. Like a nocturnal bird of prey, he darted out into the public room and sailed directly for the window. Perched there, he pressed one beady eye against the dirty pane. For long minutes, he did not stir. Then he returned.

"Not guardsmen. Steel Crescent mercenaries. I saw Nehan-dir at end of street. Somehow, he senses your presence. He follows *that*." Zolkan indicated the baby with the tip of his long wing.

"Can we flee?"

"Where? All seek you, all want bratling dead. Protaro, Nehan-dir, even people of Kolya, if they find you harbor Lenc's son."

"Where's Molimo? If we can only..." Kesira's words died when she heard the click of steel against steel.

"Outside. Many soldiers. Hurry, flee, flee!" urged the *trilla* bird.

Kesira's mind raced, awash with the paths of escape open to her. They all amounted to little more than hope. The only one giving her even a modicum of a chance was Kene Zoheret and his rebel underground. If Zoheret could smuggle her to the outskirts of Kolya, she might be able to steal a horse and ride.

But to where? Molimo and Zolkan had urged her to go to Limaden. She doubted her own safety there—and she knew what the baby might expect at Kwasian's hand. Even Lalasa sought the infant's death.

"Can we get out across the roof?" she asked Zolkan. The bird flapped away to scout. Kesira edged out of the room, her few belongings already gathered. For a weapon she had nothing more than the jade tusk taken from Ayondela's mouth. She longed for the firm, secure feel of a thick, well-seasoned stonewood staff in her hand. At least, having the wood—sacred to Gelya—nearby would have allowed her to more easily calm herself.

". . . inside," came the thin, reedy voice of a woman. "I can slit the bitch's throat for you, if you've no stomach for it, Nehan-dir."

"I don't care what you do to her," came the Steel Crescent leader's voice. "Just leave the boy untouched. So much as scratch his precious hide and yours will be tanning in the sun."

The laugh that answered told Kesira that Nehan-dir had trouble on his hands. The woman with him fought for the joy of killing, not for the joy of serving.

The door exploded inward as a heavily booted foot kicked against it. Standing silhouetted was the woman.

"Get her, Bren-ko. Don't block the way for the rest of us," came Nehan-dir's impatient command.

The woman—Bren-ko—laughed, and charged forward, swinging her sword. Kesira crouched, ready to react to whatever form Bren-ko's attack took. Before the warrior woman reached Kesira, however, a flash of green from above exploded in a mass of feathers and slashing talons. Zolkan's claws embedded firmly in Famii Bren-ko's right wrist and caused a fountain of blood to spray outward.

Bren-ko swore as she jerked back, swinging sword and arm and Zolkan hard into a wall. The *trilla* bird let out an almost human squeal before sliding to the floor, unconscious. Famii Bren-ko had lost her sword, and her right hand hung, limp, at her side, but the feral glow in her eyes told Kesira that the woman had just begun to fight. She would attack and attack and attack until the last breath was driven from her lungs by death's cold grasp.

Kesira helped Bren-ko along that path. Two quick steps, a feint, a lunge. Bren-ko almost parried the lunge, but her injured hand betrayed her. The tip of Ayondela's tusk entered the warrior woman's leather armor and plunged into flesh beneath. As it traveled, it sizzled and popped, like grease dropped into a hot skillet.

Bren-ko opened her mouth in a silent scream of pain. She clutched at the tusk's point of entry, her fingers charring when she touched the tusk. Famii Bren-ko stepped back a half-pace, pulling herself free of the jade weapon. Then she fell face-forward onto the floor. Kesira knew that her opponent had died in terrible agony.

"Thank you," came the soft, menacing words. Nehan-dir stood in the doorway, sword drawn. "You saved me the trouble of dealing with poor, ambitious Famii. Now, give me the boy."

Kesira said nothing. She held the tusk in front of her, point up and dancing lazily in wide circles, as if she held a real knife. The baby had been securely strapped down in her backpack, and Kesira thought she could get by Nehan-dir. The mercenary twisted to his right, then swung his sword in an arc aimed at her knees—a maiming stroke.

Kesira lightly jumped the edged weapon and confounded Nehan-dir when she didn't come back down to the floor. He had jerked hard on the sword and brought it back in a move designed to cut her off at the ankles. To his surprise, Kesira swung in midair, hands gripping an overhead beam. She kicked out and caught him on the shoulder. The leader of the Steel Crescent stumbled and gave her the chance to dart for the stairs leading to the second floor.

Kesira took the steps in long strides, whirled quickly at the top and kicked. She again caught Nehan-dir by surprise and sent him tumbling back down into the common room. Kesira looked about frantically. Zolkan had seen a way out. She had to find it in the next few heartbeats before Nehan-dir summoned the others of his order.

Already, heavy footsteps below warned her of the dangers of lingering.

Through a door, lock it, through another and out a window. Kesira felt as if she had sprouted wings and was flying. Onto the roof she tumbled. Kesira tried to keep from rolling over onto the baby and barely succeeded. The baby's tiny fists grabbed at her robe and tugged. She ignored him. There wasn't time.

Frantically, she looked for an escape route. Not finding it, she dashed across the sloping roof and leaped to the next building without breaking stride. Kesira's footing proved too tenuous; she slipped on her belly all the way down the tiled roof and crashed into the street not fifteen paces from where a tight knot of the mercenaries stood, hands on weapons and muttering among themselves about what transpired inside the inn.

"There she is! And the baby!" The cry went up before Kesira regained her feet.

She rolled over and came to hands and knees, but the feel of a dozen blades poking into her body halted any further attempts at escaping.

"Get Nehan-dir. Bring him here. He'll want to see the bitch brought to her knees like this!"

Sword points prodded her back to her knees when she tried to stand. Panting, angry at herself, Kesira Minette crouched on hands and knees and waited for Nehan-dir to come.

She expected a slow, lingering death at his hands. And for the baby? She didn't even allow herself the slightest thought of the child's being given over to Lenc.

Chapter Eight

KESIRA MINETTE winced as a sword pinked her upper arm.
A slow trickle of blood ran down her bicep, across her
forearm and dripped onto the cobblestone paving. Worse
than the pain was the humiliation the mercenaries forced
upon her. Gathering her strength, she tried to stand, only
to be driven back to the pavement with the flats of their
swords and their derisive laughter.

"Good work," came the all-too-familiar sound of Nehan-
dir's voice. The small man strutted around and planted his
feet wide apart. With a flourish he drew his blade and rested
the point on the ground just inches from Kesira's face.
Nehan-dir leaned on the blade, bending slightly at the waist
so that he could whisper to her.

Kesira roared in rage at the man's words. She flushed
when he straightened, laughed and pointed at her. She had
done nothing but feed the man's reputation for toughness
among his followers. Kesira had forgotten one of Gelya's
prime tenets: pride and weakness are twin sisters. She allowed her own pride to betray all she stood for. Not only
were those of the Steel Crescent seeing her humiliated, they
saw weakness, too.

No more.

Kesira stood, ignoring the pain and the solid blows descending on her from all sides. She looked Nehan-dir directly in the eye, with courage now, secure in the feeling
that he had done all he might to her. She would permit
nothing else.

"Back, stay your swords," he ordered sharply. "She is
vanquished."

Before Kesira could say a word, the clatter of horses'

hooves echoed down the night-darkened street. Moonlight caught on the flashing war spurs worn by the horses and sent messages of death to those of the Steel Crescent.

Screaming, they scattered when the Emperor's Guard crashed through the sentry lines in the small street. Protaro's men reined in their animals, caused them to rear and kick out with their hooves. Each spiked hoof struck one of the Steel Crescent mercenaries, to rip open a bloody wound— or worse.

Kesira whipped around and backed into a doorway, making sure the infant had the protection of her body against the fight raging now. She saw one man, mounted and swinging a longsword, and knew Captain Protaro had once again found her. Kesira's mouth turned to gummy cotton. If the Emperor's order carried and Protaro won this skirmish, the baby would lose his life. If Nehan-dir won, the baby would be raised as heir to the evil generated by Lenc and his abominable jade.

Either way, Kesira saw little future for herself.

Nehan-dir brought his sword up and around in a wide arc, blade meeting one guardsman's horse just above the leg. The sword edge slashed open the horse's shoulder, spilling blood, innards and rider to the ground. The hideous death sounds from the horse filled the cold night air. And not a single citizen of Kolya ventured even a frightened glance outside to see what disturbed the silence of the night. Lenc had prowled the streets too long, perpetrating his horrors, for any to be unduly curious.

Kesira held down her rising gorge only through extreme effort of will. Nehan-dir had been bathed in blood, both animal and human. His scars gleamed pinkly as he fought, standing out through the gore besmirching him. The small man stood with legs spread far apart, swinging his sword with a power that belied his stature. Guardsman after guardsman fell to the mercenary's blade—and Kesira saw this scene repeated everywhere she looked.

The initial attack by Kwasian's guard had caught the Steel Crescent by surprise. The flailing horses' hooves had gouged and cut and destroyed at will. But then the tide turned when Nehan-dir wrested control of the battle by sheer effort.

Whether he did it out of fear of Lenc's retribution if he failed or because he was the superior fighter, Kesira couldn't say.

More and more of the guard fell.

"Kesira!" came a cry. "To me!" She peered out of the doorway and saw Protaro waving to her. For a moment, the nun almost ran across the blood-slickened street to join him. Then she paused. Finally, she ducked back into the relative safety of the portal. Protaro would kill the infant. She couldn't allow herself—and the baby—to so easily fall into the man's hands.

The cry had alerted Nehan-dir to his adversary. The small man grinned. The effect of blood over his face—the white teeth shining, the pink network of scars glistening—all turned Nehan-dir into something less than human. Even when Molimo became a wolf and ravaged the countryside, he seemed more human than this swearing, fighting juggernaut.

Nehan-dir slashed his way through the few remaining guardsmen until he reached Captain Protaro.

"Again we meet," Nehan-dir said, and without any further words he launched a vicious attack. Protaro countered easily, but then lost ground when Nehan-dir pressed in savagely, ignoring the risk of personal injury. Protaro fell into a more stolid defensive stance and battled head-to-head with Nehan-dir. Kesira saw that the pair was well matched. What Nehan-dir lacked in skill he more than made up for with intensity—and she also saw that Protaro was exhausted. His long days on her trail had taken their toll.

She darted away from the doorway and into the inn as the tide of battle moved down the street. Kesira squinted in the dark room, then dropped to hands and knees and began searching. She bumped her head into the wall in her excitement when she found the huddled mass on the floor.

"Zolkan!" she shouted. The ringing of steel from Protaro and Nehan-dir's battle filled her ears. "Are you all right?" She tenderly touched the limp bird. He didn't stir. She pressed her fingertips into his side and felt the rapid beating of the *trilla* bird's heart, the slow rise and fall of his chest. Stroking, cuddling, she held the heavy bird close. "Be all right, please," she sobbed. "I need you so. You're the only friend I have left."

The bundle of feathers stirred, then one wing brushed across her cheek. "Molimo is your friend, too," Zolkan said weakly. She clutched him tightly to her breast and received an outraged squawk for her trouble. "You smother me. You mash me. Isn't it enough I crash into pigeon-shit wall helping you?"

Kesira placed the bird on her shoulder. She noticed right away that Zolkan's claws didn't grip her shoulder as strongly as in the past. She'd have to be careful not to unseat the battered creature.

"Nehan-dir fights Protaro."

"And?" the bird asked.

"Nehan-dir is winning."

"That ought to make you happy. This way the bratling lives."

"I don't want want him raised by his father." Even mouthing the word *father* in connection with Lenc and the boy struck Kesira as vile. "I want him to live a normal life, free of threats from the Emperor, free of Lenc's jade influence."

She expected Zolkan to protest as before. It was a mark of his injury that he said nothing. But his claws tightened on her shoulder, reassuring her that his strength was slowly returning. Kesira rushed to the door and peered out. The two soldiers fought, but the outcome was apparent from the onlookers.

All were Nehan-dir's followers. Every last guardsman had been killed or routed. Only Protaro fought on. Even granting the valiant man the strength and cunning of a demon, Kesira saw no way Protaro could survive.

Unless she helped him. Kesira worried over this decision. Protaro wanted the boy dead. He was an honorable man and his Emperor had ordered the deed done. In spite of this, Kesira dared not let Nehan-dir capture the infant and turn him over to Lenc.

"Run," urged Zolkan. "Find back door and run. We can find Molimo. He is somewhere in city. We can find him."

"I can't leave Protaro out there. He'll die."

"Always help the foundlings, is that it?" said Zolkan.

"I helped you when you flew into our sacristy more dead than alive. You'd nearly frozen to death. In spite of Sister Fenelia's complaints, I kept you and nursed you back to your cantankerous self. And Molimo. What of him? Didn't I help him after he got caught in the shower of jade fragments? Where would he be without my help? And the boy. He is an innocent."

"Point made. Do what you must. But don't expect me to like it." The bird burrowed down and found what remained of her cowl. He burrowed deeper and completely hid himself in the folds of her robe until she looked like a hunchback. But no hunchback's hump ever quivered and squawked to itself like this one.

Decision made, Kesira faced the problem of actually rescuing Protaro from the Steel Crescent. Too many mercenaries ringed Protaro and Nehan-dir for any easy escape. She didn't think any simple diversion would work against the battle-trained order, either, but she carried one weapon which might prevail.

If only she could use it.

Kesira swung the baby around and saw the pale gray eyes looking up at her. "I need your help," she said simply. "Nehan-dir would take you away from me. Protaro would kill you, but Protaro is a good man. I cannot let him die. If you won't aid me, I'll have to try to save him on my own. I will in all probability die if I do that."

The tiny boy pulled a wet thumb from his mouth. Kesira saw that white ridges of teeth formed; he had the look of a child teething for some time, yet she had felt no teeth when last she'd breast-fed him. Growth came in giddy spurts— giddy for Kesira Minette.

"Help me," she repeated.

The baby opened his mouth. A tiny gurgle came out. The gurgle turned to a chuckle. The chuckle rose in pitch and power until window glass broke in all nearby buildings. The fighters paused, and all attention turned to Kesira and the boy.

The cry rose until Kesira wanted to clap her hands over her ears and never listen to it again. When it began to undulate, she heard a new, more resonant snapping sound.

All the steel weapons borne by the mercenaries became brittle and broke, just as the jade in Ayondela's palace had, just as Ayondela herself had. The shattered weapons fell to the street in shards. As soon as the last dagger had been reduced to metallic dust, the baby stopped his shattering scream.

Kesira stood stunned by the cry's intensity, but so did the Steel Crescent. Their weapons had been stripped from their hands in the span of a dozen heartbeats. Nehan-dir stood covered with blood and gore, a confused look on his face. Whatever Lenc had told him about the baby, this had not been mentioned.

Protaro seized upon the chance to push Nehan-dir aside, cuff another behind the ear and kick a third in the groin to get free of the imprisoning circle. He spun out of the grasp of a fourth to join Kesira.

"To the rear of the inn. Run!" he ordered. Protaro slammed the door and saw that the bar had been broken earlier. He grabbed a low bench and braced it against the door to make a crude barricade. Even as he ran to the back of the inn, the Steel Crescent mercenaries crashed through the remains of the window, bypassing the door.

"Where now?" panted Kesira, waiting for Protaro in the alleyway.

"They'll be around in seconds. Down there. Through that warehouse and out onto the street beyond."

They ran in silence, the only sounds their own pulses hammering in their temples and the harsh grating of gasping lungs pushed beyond all reasonable limits. Protaro provided the muscle to smash through locked doors, and Kesira's quickness through tightly stacked rows of crates got them to the far side of the warehouse long before the pursuers even found the building.

"Almost sunrise," Protaro said. "This hasn't been a good day. I have let Emperor Kwasian down."

"Not your fault," Kesira said, trying to catch her breath. "There were too many of Nehan-dir's soldiers. Too well armed, trained. Rested." She put the infant into the back-pack, then leaned forward, her hands on her knees. Air came into her lungs more easily now, even as sweat dripped onto the paving from her forehead.

"What happened?"

Kesira looked up, not sure of the question's intent.

"My sword. Theirs. Even my dagger." Protaro touched his empty leather sheath. Faint metallic sprinkles remained.

"Gelya warned against the use of steel weapons," Kesira said. "I'd never understood why before. Now I know." She had said this in a flip tone, intending to divert Protaro's attention from the baby and his incredible power, but her own mind turned down different roads. Had Gelya known the future, that such would happen? She touched the jade tooth thrust through her sash. It had escaped undamaged. Kesira pushed this from her mind. The boy had destroyed Ayondela and her jade palace with his cries; jade was not immune to his power.

But wood? It must be impervious to the baby's sonic attacks. Stonewood in particular. Kesira vowed to replace her trusty staff at the earliest opportunity. Items wrought by man might fail, but natural implements couldn't. All things fit together into a harmonious whole. It was up to her— using Gelya's teachings—to find how the infant met some need.

"It was no dead demon's warning that reduced my sword to powder," Protaro said. He eyed her curiously, then changed the subject. "We need to find refuge. Any ideas?"

Kesira had one or two, but she didn't know if Protaro would agree to them. "I know of one group, a rebel group, that might give us shelter. They seek Lenc's downfall, but their efforts have been pitiful so far."

"They set fire to the temple? We passed it on our way through the center of Kolya."

Kesira nodded. She remembered all too well how that destruction had brought Lenc's personal attention to the city. The jade demon had strode along the streets, killing, maiming, raping at will. If anything, it seemed better to keep activities against the demon to a low point until the killing stroke could be administered.

"Sounds as if they need someone to do their planning for them," Protaro said. "Since I have failed Emperor

Kwasian so grievously, do you think these rebels would accept me into their ranks?"

Kesira looked sharply at the guard captain. His tone indicated he sought absolution for his failure—the absolution of death. Kesira didn't know the man at all well, but this hunched, dejected figure squinting into the rising sun was not the confident warrior she had met previously.

"I've even lost my sword." His hand fluttered like a dying butterfly over his empty scabbard.

"You still live. In that lies hope."

"But I don't live by my own hand. Another saved me." He frowned, as if returning to a difficult topic. Kesira cut him off before he again asked how she had reduced all the weapons to dust.

"We must find Kene Zoheret soon," she said. "Nehandir will be searching the streets for us. He might even appeal to Lenc to seek us out."

"Lenc comes," Zolkan moaned. "Find Molimo. We need help. Lenc is coming!"

Protaro stiffened at the disembodied voice.

"Be calm," Kesira said, resting her hand lightly on his shoulder. "Zolkan is a friend. Come on out. It must be stuffy in that cowl." The green-feathered *trilla* bird shook himself free and returned to his usual perch on her left shoulder. "See?" she asked of Protaro. "Only a *trilla* bird."

"Only!" exclaimed Zolkan. "Is that all you think of me? Only?"

Kesira stroked gently over the brilliant blue-and-green feathered crest, soothing her friend's injured feelings. "You are more. Always."

Zolkan snorted and settled down, his feathers sadly in need of preening. The bird tucked his head under one wing and slipped off to sleep as Kesira hastened through the slowly awakening city streets.

"They are the messengers of the demons. Does he spy on us, or for us?" asked Protaro.

"I nursed him back to health. He and Molimo are my only true allies."

Protaro nodded, remembering the fracas in the mountains. "I know of this Molimo. No tongue. You say you trust him, but what of this Zoheret we seek out?"

"He is prone to rashness. He is harmless otherwise." Even as she spoke, Kesira wondered if she believed this. For all his apparent impracticality, Kene Zoheret struck her as something more. But how much more? And Protaro's words needled her. Did she truly consider Zoheret a friend to trust with her life? While she had no choice, it seemed to her that Zoheret would sell her out to Nehan-dir for a few bent coins.

"Zoheret mentioned coming to an inn when he left the one where I worked."

"You *worked* at that public house?" Shock rolled over Protaro's features. It had never occurred to him that Kesira might seek employment. "As a means of hiding out?"

"As a way to earn my keep. I have no money. The Emperor Kwasian does not pay me a regular fee for my services." Kesira grew impatient.

"The Emperor doesn't pay me now, either. Not after I have so severely disgraced his service."

"You failed," Kesira said brutally. "That doesn't make you worthless."

"I should have prepared better. We had the advantage. We timed the attack poorly. We failed. I may be the only survivor."

"Battles against overwhelming numbers shouldn't be anything new for you. I've heard the tales of fighting during the barbarian invasions."

"Thousands were reduced to tens," he said. "But we triumphed, even at such a great cost."

He fell into a moody silence that suited Kesira. She worked along the slowly filling streets, not daring to inquire after Zoheret. By sheer chance, the nun sighted a battered wooden sign dangling above the entrance to an inn.

"The Falling Leaf," she said. "This is the place." Cautiously Kesira looked up and down the street. They had moved quickly enough to stay ahead of Nehan-dir's methodical house-to-house search; but with the Steel Crescent's power ascendant in Kolya, it could be only a matter of hours before Nehan-dir located them.

Inside the dimly lit inn they found a mug-ringed table in the dank back corner. The place smelled of spilled ale, and the innkeeper took no pride in maintaining a high standard of cleanliness. Kesira's nose curled at the odors and she repressed an urge to take up a rag and start tidying.

"What'll it be?" the innkeeper called out from his position near the fireplace. "Got some breakfast cooking." He prodded the contents of a stewpot on the fire and peered inside. From his expression, Kesira wasn't sure if she even dared ask what he prepared.

"We're looking for a friend," she said.

The innkeeper turned and faced them, studying them more closely. "In Kolya, no one's got a friend anymore."

"Zoheret," Kesira said softly. "We need his help."

The innkeeper turned back to his pot, gave it a few tentative stirs, then ambled over to the grimy window and peered into the street. He stood watching for several minutes, assuring himself that the shabby nun and the bloody man weren't out to trap him. Finally sure than no one dangerous lingered in the street, he came over and perched one fat buttock on the edge of their table.

"Zoheret's not here. Why not come back later and see if he's made it here? Ofttimes he won't put in an appearance for days, even weeks." The innkeeper rocked to and fro on the table. Kesira started to comment that there were better ways of cleaning a tabletop, but she held her tongue.

"We're fleeing Nehan-dir," Protaro said, taking the initiative. "The Order of the Steel Crescent," he added when he saw noncomprehension in the man's face. This produced a tiny spark of fear. "Lenc's mercenaries," Protaro added, finally fueling a definite response.

"Zoheret's not here. Hasn't been in weeks."

Even before the innkeeper's words faded in the room, Kene Zoheret entered, trailing three of his lieutenants. Seeing Kesira and Protaro, Zoheret motioned the three to posts.

"Good work, Sandor," Zoheret said loudly, slapping the suspicious innkeeper on the back. "We've been out hunting these two. Just the ones we need!"

The innkeeper smiled weakly and went back to his cooking, glad to be free of such intrigues. Noxious green vapors rose from the stewpot and the odor of burning garbage filled the room.

"They're hunting everywhere for you!" cried Zoheret. Protaro and Kesira exchanged glances. To this man, it was all a game.

"Then you know the guard company has been wiped out. The Emperor doesn't have another to send," Protaro said honestly. "Whatever response to Nehan-dir and Lenc will have to come from the citizens."

"From *my* underground!" gloated Zoheret.

"Yes." The way Protaro said it told Kesira that the man sought an honorable death to ease the humiliation of his lost command and failure to carry out Emperor Kwasian's orders.

"A captain, oh, good, very good," crowed Zoheret. "We need a tactician for what I have in mind. We will strike at Lenc's jade heart this time, when the demon comes to secure his rule over Kolya."

"It's already in his control," Kesira said. "We must wrest it from Lenc."

"Not his," contradicted Zoheret. "He must make a public appearance and openly destroy all the other patrons."

"No great problem. Kolya has never been famous for its piety," said Protaro. "Even Lalasa has found no great acceptance in Kolya."

"Here's our plan," Zoheret said, reaching into his jerkin and pulling out a tattered piece of paper. With nimble fingers he pressed out the wrinkles. To Kesira, the squiggles on the paper were meaningless. She saw that they meant little more to Protaro, even when Zoheret explained their significance.

"So," said Zoheret, "we gather in front of Lenc's temple. His new one hasn't been completed yet, so he still appears in the one on the Street of Colored Paper. That's where we attack."

"With your bare hands? Against a demon relying on the power of jade?"

Zoheret ignored Kesira, turning his full attention to Protaro, who seemed more interested and less skeptical. "Even demons can die. Lenc can be killed, if we attack him when he least expects it. He can only direct those fireballs

in one direction at a time. He is tricked into releasing one—
we attack. Simple!"

Kesira's head threatened to split with the inconsistencies
and outright mistakes Zoheret proposed. But she kept silent.

"I agree that Lenc can be destroyed," she heard Protaro
saying. "The jade weakens him, even as it gives him power.
His immortality was forfeit when he first used the jade. A
sword thrust through the midriff will dispatch him."

"Yes, right!"

"But I need a sword. We all need weapons. Can we get
them before Lenc appears to proclaim his complete power
over Kolya?"

Zoheret frowned. "The only remaining source of weapons is the Steel Crescent; Lenc destroyed the city guard.
Few others have even a dagger, much less a sword. Yes,
definitely, we must steal arms from the Steel Crescent."

Kesira stroked Zolkan's greasy, broken feathers. The *trilla*
bird cooed like a dove, stirring in her hand without waking.
She shifted about on the bench, keeping the knapsack out
of Zoheret's sight. Protaro had mentioned nothing about
turning the infant over to Emperor Kwasian since she had
rescued him, but the thought might intrude at any time if
she reminded the captain of the baby's presence. Protaro
might see this as a way to regain lost honor.

And Zoheret? She didn't want the overzealous underground leader thinking the baby was an easy road to even
greater power over Kolya's populace. Publicly execute Lenc's
son and be proclaimed a hero. No, she didn't want him
thinking along those lines.

Mostly, Kesira felt an incredible lassitude settling over
her. Too much had happened. Now she listened to crackbrained schemes that had no chance of succeeding. Without
casting her rune sticks, she knew these plans would fail.
Lenc might be demented due to the jade, but he hadn't lost
his analytical powers. The demon had to know any meaningful resistance against him had to come when he proclaimed his regency over Kolya.

Crush all civil disobedience in plain view of the city, and
he had achieved what he wanted most: power. Anyone who
secretly considered rebellion would then forget it.

Kesira agreed on the need to raid the Steel Crescent's armory for weapons, but afterward? What must happen then? Only magicks could match Lenc's magicks. The burning white fire that was his sigil had to be dealt with, using—what?

She didn't know.

Chapter Nine

"WHAT IF their headquarters is protected by magic?" Kesira Minette asked. She crouched next to Protaro and Kene Zoheret. Both men peered at a map spread on the ground, corners held by small rocks. Zoheret held a sputtering torch overhead so that they might be able to interpret the map's wondrous information.

Kesira sighed. They had memorized this worthless map back at the Falling Leaf. Now they mistrusted their memories to the point they endangered the entire mission by lighting the torch and revealing their position, should any of Nehan-dir's patrols be close enough to wonder what cast such horrid illumination. If they couldn't mount a successful assault on a human-manned base, what would they face going against Lenc?

She preferred not to consider that horror at the moment.

"Do you sense magicks?" asked Zoheret, not looking up from the map. He and Protaro made arcane notations on the margins.

"I'm no witch, no sorcerer able to command vast spells and create a demon's magicks. Peering occasionally into the future with the rune sticks is the best I can do."

"You foresee disaster?" Zoheret quickly focused his full attention on her. Whatever he feared in the future, she had never seen it. In fact, she had never cast the rune sticks specifically aimed at finding out a modicum of Zoheret's future.

"No," she said, "but this is obviously a poor plan. You just walk up and knock? Is that it? You expect Nehan-dir to meekly offer you all the swords and spears you can carry off?"

101

"Nehan-dir is away patrolling the city," said Protaro. "His lieutenants are in disarray. Apparently, his second in command was killed in the foray this morning."

Kesira started to tell of Famii Bren-ko's death, then bit back the words. Protaro wouldn't believe her, and why should he? He didn't even believe she'd had anything to do with Howenthal, Eznofadil and Ayondela's deaths.

Kesira closed her eyes and turned all her training on devising a workable plan of attack. After all, she *had* been responsible for the death of three jade demons. Mounting a raid against the Steel Crescent's armory ought to be simpler than fighting her way across the Quaking Lands or enduring the agonies meted out by Ayondela's crystal clouds.

The more she considered their position, the more it seemed that the two men plotted with the sole purpose of losing their lives. Protaro she understood. He had been a captain in Kwasian's fabled guard and had failed to live up to his high office. The dishonor that went along with losing so ignominiously to Nehan-dir had to make him think in terms of death. But Zoheret was another matter. Was the man merely stupid? Protaro certainly played to that idiocy with this wild scheme for breaking into the Steel Crescent's headquarters.

"We number a full twenty," Zoheret said. "More than enough."

"Stick against sword. A good match," Kesira said sarcastically. She didn't try to keep the contempt from her voice. Even a handful of the Steel Crescent mercenaries ought to be able to repel any attempt to breach their walls.

The men continued to ignore her. Kesira moved away, reached over and pulled Zolkan from his perch on her shoulder. "Can you fly?" she asked.

"Poorly. Wings hurt."

"Go scout. Return with a count of the mercenaries inside the building."

"You don't want much, do you? It's not enough I am battered in your defense. Now you ask me to kill myself on *trilla* bird eaters' sword tips."

"It'd be an easier trip for Molimo," she said, "but you

seem to have lost him." Kesira baited Zolkan, but he ignored it. "Go. We need the information."

Zolkan protested with a wordless squawk, then launched into the air. The force of his takeoff staggered Kesira. She watched worriedly as Zolkan wobbled and dipped through the air separating them from the mercenaries. He hadn't been pretending when he claimed to be injured sorely.

Kesira waited. In less time than it takes to cross the square to the armory, Zolkan returned.

"Bad," he said. "Twelve inside. Two more with bow and arrow on roof. All alert. No sign of disarray. Need to make strong attack to overcome opposition."

"I was afraid of this." She smoothed Zolkan's head feathers and let him crawl back into the safety of her cowl. Kesira rushed back to talk with Protaro.

"Not now. We are almost ready for the attack."

"You'll go against a dozen inside, two sentries with bows and arrows on the roof. How do you plan to escape them?"

Protaro blinked. "We didn't know of those on the roof. How did you find out?"

If he'd thought on the matter for even a fraction of a second, he'd have known of Zolkan's abilities. That he didn't showed Kesira how suicidal this attack would become. Whether Protaro still reacted to his loss or had lost permanently any tactical ability he once possessed, she declined to say.

"You'll have to infiltrate, sneak up close and take out the rooftop patrol before continuing. If you don't, they'll fill you with arrows before you get halfway." Kesira took a long breath, then hunkered down by the crude map. "Here. Buildings. They'll shield you most of the way. The risk in crossing this space is great, but men dressed in dark clothing might blend with the shadows, if they don't hurry. Slow movement, coupled with vagrant breezes, might lull the bowmen into thinking they see nothing. Those reaching the base of the armory must climb here and here. With skill they can remove the bowmen and open the way for the rest."

"Might work," Protaro said.

"We have to use our original plan. It's too late to switch. We'll get confused!" Zoheret almost screamed in agitation.

"We'll do it her way," Protaro said, the snap of command in his voice. "Look. See? A careless sentry on the roof."

A dark outline occluded the stars, then slowly disappeared behind a low wall.

"Get me the men you claimed were hunters."

"We dare not change now. We have no time to change plans. Nehan-dir will return before we can—"

"Do it."

Kesira saw that Protaro wanted a decisive victory. No longer would he agree to anything Zoheret said. Now Protaro wanted the coppery smell of blood in his nostrils and the sweet taste of winning on his tongue.

The men arrived, received their new orders, then went on their way. Kesira peered out from her hiding place, straining to see in the shadows between the two buildings. To her, the rebels' progress was as obvious as if they'd banged gongs and shouted praises of the Emperor, but to the sentries they were virtually invisible. Kesira wished she knew the spell Molimo used to make him so hard to detect.

As the men reached the armory wall and began their painful ascent Kesira's thoughts strayed to Molimo. Where had he gone? Once in Kolya, the man had vanished. She hoped fervently that he restrained his shape changes. The other-beast hunters on the plains had been vicious; what would city crowds be like? She had visions of Kolyan citizens taking out their wrath on Molimo, skinning him alive, the wolf fur changing to human skin even as they stripped it from his body. She shuddered.

Molino had helped her escape Protaro when they were on the road, but where he had gone afterward remained a mystery. If only Zolkan weren't so close-beaked about what the pair of them did. Not for the first time, Kesira felt like an outsider. Molimo and Zolkan could communicate in ways she did not understand. A minute of the shrill singsongy words used by Zolkan conveyed more to Molimo than an hour's talking. And in some fashion beyond her ken, Molimo spoke to Zolkan without uttering a word.

But she loved Molimo, in spite of everything.

"One is at the top. Another . . . now the third!" whispered Protaro. "There—they attack."

The sounds of muffled combat drifted across the square. Kesira worried that those inside the armory had overheard, but the men of the Steel Crescent weren't straining to hear the smallest of sounds. They joked and argued boisterously, thinking themselves safely guarded by rooftop archers.

"Now," said Protaro, waving his arm. The small band made more noise than a Spring Fair celebration, but they reached the door to the Steel Crescent's headquarters without being filled with sharp-pointed arrows.

Zoheret knocked on the door, nervously shifting weight from one foot to the other. When one of the mercenaries opened the door a crack, Protaro smashed into Zoheret and sent the man reeling into the mercenary, who toppled; and the rabble burst into the main room.

Kesira hardly believed that the Steel Crescent's sentries could be surprised so easily. The fighting turned fierce, but only for a few minutes. Then Protaro grabbed a fallen sword and slashed and thrust like an invincible fighting machine. Half of Zoheret's rebels perished, but Protaro made sure all the Steel Crescent mercenaries died, steel ripping through their guts or across their throats.

Kesira walked through the carnage, placing her feet carefully. She finally stopped trying to keep from getting blood on her boots or robe. It had sprayed everywhere in the battle. She had seen so much killing, but it still sickened her. The Order of the Steel Crescent sought only what others had found in a patron. Guidance, a sure knowledge of their place and duty in society, occasional encouragement. That their original patron had been Tolek and that he'd exchanged his worshipers for a gambling debt was unfortunate. Since then the Steel Crescent's search for its place in society had been pathetic, but not truly evil in the way Lenc was. Kesira wished she could talk with Nehan-dir and see if they couldn't come to terms with the small mercenary's need for power.

If only Gelya hadn't died. If only Lenc hadn't killed off most of the demons.

Kesira smiled humorlessly. If only she had Zolkan's wings she could fly. She didn't, she never would, and she had to live with her own limitations. Kesira had worked to overcome her faults; but Nehan-dir had come to look on his as virtues.

"Such fertile fields for your philosophy, Gelya," Kesira said softly.

The nun took no part in the raid. The steel weapons sought by the others were prohibited by her dead patron, and with good reason, as she had learned. But a stout staff—not of the stonewood sacred to Gelya—leaned against the far wall. Kesira took it and poked through the debris, trying not to touch the cooling corpses on the floor.

"What do you seek?" Protaro asked.

"There must be some hint as to their purpose in coming to Kolya. They want the . . . baby." She hardly got the words out. Protaro's eyes showed no desire to fulfill that order to kill the child. Perhaps it was his earlier failure or maybe just a symptom of the Time of Chaos, but somehow Protaro had decided that he need no longer serve the Emperor as he once had. His duty had changed.

"You think there's more?"

"Lenc chose Kolya for some reason. It might be merely a desire not to confront the Emperor in his stronghold. Lenc could establish Kolya as his, then march on Limaden later."

"Forever is a long time," Protaro said. "With no opposition anywhere in the empire, Lenc might get bored. Leaving the Emperor's capital intact and heavily defended might give the accursed demon years of pleasure."

Kesira nodded. She'd considered this. Even though Lenc had forfeited his longevity for the power of the jade, he could still outlive any mortal now walking the empire's land. Forever was a long time, indeed.

"Look," she said, thrusting with the tip of the staff. The body of a woman who'd been sitting at a broad table toppled to the floor. Bloodsoaked papers littered the table. "Organizational plans. I'm not familiar enough with Kolya to know the locations."

"Lenc's new temple," Zoheret said, pointing. "There. That'll be the new center of Kolya where Lenc's temple is being constructed."

Kesira's quick eyes worked over the columns of numbers. "A date only six days hence."

"The work must be nearing completion," said Protaro. "These are troop placements. They have ordered in a full company and more to be scattered around the square. To keep the crowds in close, from the look of it. Many minor governors do the same when they make speeches. It wouldn't do having a bored populace wander off."

"Lenc wants all the populace present," mused Kesira. "He must be planning to appear on the steps of his new temple. Why else arrange such a show of force?"

"Lenc returns in six days." Protaro's eyes lit with excitement. "This is our chance. We can attack then. We have the weapons from this raid. We can recruit the soldiers we need before then. One swift, sure thrust, and Lenc dies!"

Kesira hardly believed Protaro deluded himself in such a fashion.

"The demon throws fireballs," she pointed out. "Any massive attack must deal with Lenc's magicks. None of us can even construct a defensive shield."

"Is that possible?" asked Zoheret.

Kesira started to tell of the mysterious force that had protected her, Zolkan and Molimo in Ayondela's palace, then stopped. Something in the way Zoheret asked the question kept the truth from her lips.

"I've heard stories—but they might have been rumors or tall tales meant to amuse the children on cold nights."

"We can't waste time searching for spells when no one can use them," said Protaro. "We must practice, plan, get every detail worked out. There's so little time. If we don't stop Lenc at what he considers the moment of his triumph, we may never be strong enough to fight him effectively."

Kesira left the room, the others hurriedly looting whatever else they could find. She walked into the night, colder than ever before. In her backpack the baby stirred.

Kolya bustled with activity as its citizens prepared for the ceremony, but Kesira Minette saw no gaiety. The people seemed grim. Children didn't play their usual games but listlessly sat and watched their elders, absorbing the gloom.

Commerce continued, but not with its usual boisterousness. Street vendors didn't seem to care if they sold their wares; merchants in stalls sat and stared into space, their vegetables spoiling from lack of attention; friends passing in the street hardly acknowledged each other.

And everywhere stood the mercenaries of the Steel Crescent. Nehan-dir had been recruiting heavily over the past week since the raid on his armory. The hirelings annoyed the citizens and occasionally killed one, just to keep in practice. Nobody objected openly. The muttering done behind closed doors amounted to little.

"The people are ready to rise in revolt to aid us," said Zoheret. He peered out the dirty window of the Falling Leaf. "Give them back the leadership that has been taken from them and they'll follow. This will be memorable, oh, yes, very memorable." He rubbed his hands together as if they were cold.

Kesira wondered at Zoheret's motivations in this. He seemed an unlikely sort to play the rebel. If he thought to supplant the Emperor in anyone's heart or mind, he knew very little of the empire and the bonds that held it together. No one blamed Emperor Kwasian for Lenc's victories. Whoever defeated Lenc might earn the Emperor's gratitude; but that mattered little to Kesira. It was merely her responsibility as a loyal servant.

Loyal servant? Hardly—not now that she'd openly flouted Kwasian's command to give the baby to Protaro. Kesira twisted about on the hard wooden bench and saw the soldier standing in the corner, eyes focused on distant memories. She had been responsible for his defeat. If she had obeyed the valid command and turned over the boy, Protaro wouldn't have followed her to Kolya and run afoul of the Steel Crescent. Still, she couldn't part with the boy. While he wasn't family in a blood sense, she considered him as precious as her own son.

If only the boy hadn't been born to a mortal mother, with Lenc his father.

"My scouts report that the Square of All Temples has been decorated according to Nehan-dir's order. Nehan-dir claims that Lenc will appear at sunset." Zoheret continued to rub his hands together and peer outside, as if he might spot Lenc a few minutes earlier than anyone else.

Kesira checked the shadows marching slowly across the room: a few minutes past zenith. Almost six hours before Lenc would come to bless Kolya with his jade presence.

She rose silently and slipped out the back way. Even though Nehan-dir's hirelings patrolled constantly, Kesira had found a safe route through the streets. No handful of armed soldiers might hope to check all byways, especially those leading into treacherously turning dead ends where ambushers might lurk. Kesira walked quickly to the inn where she still maintained a room. As she entered the deserted public room, the innkeeper looked up. His smile at seeing her was genuine.

"You've come for a spot of ale?" he asked.

"I've come to ask a favor." She settled down at the table near him. "Will you look after the boy for me?"

The portly innkeeper nodded.

"I know it is a great deal to ask, but keeping him out of the crowds tonight is of great importance to me."

"You're going to see Lenc's arrival?" the innkeeper asked.

"I must. And that's why I don't want the boy hindering me. I . . . I fear Lenc might be able to sense the boy's presence. Here, you'll both be safe."

"Give him over to me now. There," the innkeeper said, holding the baby. Pale eyes stared up emotionlessly. "Such a big one he is now."

"He eats solid food." Kesira almost choked as she said it; her hand went to the spot on her breast where Wemilat had kissed her. The baby no longer suckled. Like Molimo, he grew older even as she watched. In a short week, the boy had taken a few hesitant steps. While he still preferred to be carried, Kesira thought he might be able to walk on his own. What changes would another week bring?

"We'll be fine here. I have no urge to see Lenc lord it over us. He seeks only our humiliation."

Kesira had nothing to say. The innkeeper was right. Lenc came only to show his true power. He had no reason to formalize his rule because everyone obeyed without question—or they died.

"I haven't cast the rune sticks," Kesira said. "I fear the outcome, yet one casting shows..." She looked at the innkeeper. It wouldn't do to burden him with the details of what she'd read. She would emerge victorious over Lenc; the rune sticks told her this. Kesira had pondered the question regarding Lenc's possible influence over the runes. While he might have sent her false visions in the past, this one carried the ring of truth.

She *would* defeat the jade demon, just as she'd vanquished the other three. But how? And when? Life might prove very long under Lenc's rule, waiting for the proper instant to destroy him.

"Keep him safe, and I'll return when I can. Perhaps by midnight." She bent down and lightly kissed the baby on the forehead. Pale gray eyes watched her, almost pityingly. She pushed such thoughts away. The baby couldn't know what lay ahead. Even the rune sticks remained clouded on that at times.

"Be...until you return," the innkeeper said. Kesira smiled. He had almost told her to "be careful," a whimsical order in this dangerous city.

Kesira ducked into a storefront doorway just in time to avoid a mounted Steel Crescent patrol. She bent double and hid behind a low row of baskets to keep Nehan-dir from spotting her. The small, scarred leader rode proudly at the head of the column, banner fluttering in the sluggish afternoon breeze. Kesira let the column turn and pass down a side street before she emerged.

While more than four hours still remained before Lenc's promised arrival, she found herself walking toward the Square of All Temples. A huge fountain in the center of the square had been torn out and paved over to make room for the throngs that would begin crowding in a few hours later. At one time the square had been the focal point for most of Kolya's orders. No longer. Most of the temples and altars to the other patrons had been razed; some remained as burned-out husks. Nor did Kesira see anybody venturing close to worship or even meditate.

She closed her eyes and sank down into her churning inner thoughts. Meditation brought relaxation, and with the relaxation the opportunity to consider what might happen here a few hours in the future.

Lenc had ordered the other temples destroyed. Only the one built of ugly black volcanic stone remained—Lenc's. She did not for an instant consider entering it. Sitting on the edge of the square was enough for the moment. Kesira saw nothing but trouble ahead, but she knew she would triumph. The rune sticks said so.

People passed through the square, not speaking, not joking, shooing away small children. It was as if this was a monument to war. Kesira sighed. In a way, it was. The war had been fought, and the losers were the patrons of the empty temples.

Those demons had already perished. Now it was time for the souls of every person in Kolya to die, also.

As the afternoon wore on, shadows grew long over the buildings. Gaslights popped on and cooking fires flared, only to be quickly extinguished when the Steel Crescent's mercenaries came through, rousting everyone they could find from their homes and crowding them into the streets. They herded the people like cattle toward the Square of All Temples.

Kesira sat and watched, grieving. She tried to find where Protaro and Zoheret would stage their attack, and failed. Somehow, the square didn't seem the same as the one on Zoheret's maps. What she'd thought to be the rebel assembly point lay too distant for the quick attack they had planned.

"All hearken!" came a crier's ringing voice. "All hearken, the mighty lord of all demons demands your presence. All hearken!"

Kesira levered herself to her feet using the staff. With back to a stone wall, she watched as the square became crowded, then overcrowded. People jammed together shoulder to shoulder. If anyone should faint for lack of air, it would be impossible to ever fall to the ground.

A cold, wintry wind blew through the assembly now, making Kesira even more aware of how Lenc had planned all this. The jade demon had left nothing to chance. His appearance would be dramatic, memorable.

The mercenaries blocked off the streets leading into the

square. Long minutes dragged by. The crowd began to mutter. Twilight turned into night, and the evening stars gleamed like twin beacons just above the horizon. Even more stars above popped into existence. Kesira began to wonder if Lenc had misjudged the crowd's acceptance.

He hadn't.

The clap of thunder drove the thousands huddled together to their knees. It was as if they had a single mind, a single body.

Kesira edged along the wall and dropped to her own knees to avoid unwanted attention.

Another thunderclap, then a bolt of lightning crashed into the hulk of a temple on the west side of the square. Fragments of stone rained down; nothing but a smoldering crater remained of the building that had once been consecrated to Toyaga. Another bolt: more destruction. The air filled with a garlic stench. The actinic glare of the lightning forced Kesira to squint and shield her eyes.

Then, silence so absolute she thought she'd lost her hearing.

She clutched her staff until her knuckles turned white. Even though she told herself Lenc was manipulating her emotions, she felt a surge of fear and anticipation. She stared at the black temple, the only one still intact.

The force of the words hurled her against the wall.

"People of Kolya," boomed the voice Kesira Minette knew and loathed. "From this day forward, you will worship only me.

"I am Lenc!"

Dazzling jade-green light bathed Lenc as he strode forward, arms raised.

"Worship me!"

Chapter Ten

LENC'S WORDS reverberated off walls and buildings, down streets, into alleys. Kesira almost fainted from the impact of his cry, "Worship me!"

A nimbus of green swirled around Lenc's head, bathing the planes of his face in a harsh jade light. Tiny bolts of lightning jumped from his arms and shoulders to the cloud, to be swallowed there by the miniature storm brewing.

"You are my subjects. You will worship me!"

The people kneeling closest to the bottom steps of Lenc's temple withered and died like autumn leaves caught by an early frost as the flesh burned off their bones. They screamed as they died.

The demon pointed and the next rank of people died also.

"You will cast aside all other patrons. No other demon will be allowed within the bounds of Kolya!" Lenc gestured.

Another group of people died.

"Any who insist on opposing me by continued belief in other patrons will receive no mercy."

"All praise mighty Lenc!" the cry went up. Kesira watched the Steel Crescent mercenaries raise their weapons high. They began to push through the crowd, shouting, inciting others to join in the calls of approbation for the new lord of Kolya.

Never had a demon meddled in mortal affairs to this extent. They might be petty, venal, malicious, but Kesira knew of none who ordered worship on pain of death.

Gelya had never wanted to be worshiped. He dispensed his wisdom because he was good. His goodness carried over into his order, and his disciples ventured forth to carry on other works needed in society. Kesira's dead patron had helped them define their places in society, then gave them the training and inspiration to fulfill the roles.

Lenc wanted only power. And anyone who refused his whim received only death.

Kesira craned her neck to try to find where Protaro and Zoheret were assembling their men. According to the battle map she had memorized, the rebels ought to be in sight now. She shifted and peered in the other direction. Coldness seized her belly and twisted, threatening to nauseate her.

"No!" Kesira tried to warn Protaro. "Don't attack from there!" But the crowd's roar swallowed her words. If the guard captain tried to rush directly down to where Lenc stood basking in the cheers from the captive crowd, Nehan-dir's men would slice the rebels to bloody ribbons. It was almost as if the mercenaries had deliberately opened a corridor for the rebels, to make the tube through which Zoheret and the others would run.

Kesira toyed with the idea of defectors in the Steel Crescent's rank. She pushed that aside when she saw Nehan-dir using the flat of his sword to drive back some of the crowd.

Nehan-dir had set up a trap—and Protaro was going to run headlong into it.

Kesira grabbed her cowl and shook hard. Zolkan protested, then tumbled heavily to the ground. The fall stunned the *trilla* bird, but he quickly recovered.

"Haven't I suffered enough at your hand?" the bird complained.

"Zolkan, be quiet. Listen carefully. The rebels are heading into a trap. Nehan-dir *wants* them to attack Lenc. See?" She grabbed the heavy bird and lifted him above the heads of the crowd around her, making sure he saw what she meant. "If they don't retreat immediately, Lenc will seize them all."

She tossed the bird into the air and yelled after him, "Stop Protaro!"

Green feathers flashed and vanished into the darkness just as Zoheret's voice carried clear and strong across the square.

"Death to traitors!"

Kesira stared in disbelief as she saw Protaro rushing

forward, sword in hand. He and several dozen rebels met no resistance as they dashed down the strip cleared for them. Only Kene Zoheret hung back, a strange exultation in his expression.

Kesira didn't have to read her rune sticks to know that Zoheret had betrayed the underground to Lenc.

The crush of the crowd prevented her from charging forward to aid Protaro in his futile attack on Lenc. She saw the captain reach the slagged lava steps and start up them. Lenc turned, an amused look on his hard jade face. The cloud whirling about the demon's ears took on more substance, flowed, formed an arrow. The green mist solidified and sailed straight for Protaro.

Kesira watched in horrified silence as the jade shaft impaled him. It moved in slow motion, entering his body an agonizing inch every dozen seconds. Protaro twitched and jerked, dropping his sword. Some acoustical quirk allowed Kesira to hear the metallic click-click-click as the fallen sword clattered down the temple steps.

No sound in the world could have drowned out Protaro's shriek of pain. At first Kesira thought the baby had been brought to the square and had begun crying. Then she realized it was Protaro. The jade shaft passed halfway through his body, then stopped. The soldier stood, trying to pull the misty arrow free and failing.

"See, loyal worshipers?" bellowed Lenc. "See how I punish those who dare offend me!"

Protaro's body levitated and spun in midair, the jade arrow still embedded in his chest. Poised above the spot where the old fountain had been, the man rotated slowly on the spoke of magic. Whatever spell held him had to be one of the greatest potency. His pain seemed to grow instant by instant—and death was denied Captain Protaro.

"He will live forever, a captive of jade," bragged Lenc. "See how he suffers. Know you that I can grant anyone within my hearing even worse agony if they oppose me."

Lenc spun, his stubby finger pointing to the edge of the crowd. "You. You are a Senior Brother in the Order of Toyaga. No more!"

A pillar of cold white fire enveloped the man. His screams

mingled with those Protaro still mouthed. Then the flame consumed him and black ash descended on the crowd. But the pillar of white fire still burned, turning the volcanic rock molten beneath it, yet giving off no steam, no heat. That white flame burned with the fury of a polar hell.

Kesira's ears shut out Protaro's cries for mercy; her eyes became blind to the mass of people. She saw only the dancing flames on the temple steps. Similar white fire had consumed Gelya's altar—and still desecrated the nunnery hidden away in the Yearn Mountains.

With a shout, Lenc gestured at the other rebels. Tiny bits of jade spewed forth from the demon's hands. Each shard flew directly for the left eye of a rebel. No matter how the men ducked, no matter how they tried to protect themselves, a splinter of jade buried itself in each brain. Those poor wights kicked and moaned in agony long after ordinary men would have ceased struggling. It took them long minutes to die.

"*That* is how I treat rebels," said Lenc. "And this is how I reward those loyal to me. Behold Kene Zoheret, the one who betrayed his friends." Lenc's tone carried extreme scorn for Zoheret, but the traitor seemed not to notice. Proudly, the man strode down the cleared corridor toward the temple. He fell face-forward and gave himself willingly to Lenc.

Kesira didn't know how any man could barter his soul so cheaply, yet Kene Zoheret had. She clenched her staff firmly in her hand and used it to beat her way through the milling crowd. She had not been with Protaro when he had begun his abortive attack, but she could bring Zoheret to some measure of the justice he deserved.

"Back," squawked Zolkan. "Lenc awaits you. Go back!"

Kesira hazarded a quick look above her head. Zolkan fluttered about like a crippled bug, green feathers raining down from body and wing. She impatiently motioned him away. Nothing seemed left to her but revenge on Zoheret for his betrayal.

Her order was dead. Lenc had consolidated his power in Kolya—and throughout the realm, except for Limaden. And nothing awaited her in Limaden save the Emperor's wrath for disobeying his direct command to hand over the baby.

For a moment the thought of the boy slowed her, then she pushed it away. He no longer needed her. The innkeeper could find a foster home for him. She had finally decided the only mission worthy of her meager talent lay in killing Zoheret.

Gelya wouldn't have approved, but Gelya was dead, too.

Kesira got through the crowd, passing not a dozen paces from Nehan-dir. The leader of the Steel Crescent didn't see her in the sea of faces. She came close to the spot where Zoheret stood so proudly, relishing the attention he got from Lenc.

Kesira took her staff and swung it with all her might. Never had her aim been more precise, her arm so strong. The impact shattered the stout wooden staff, sending splinters flying. Shock numbed Kesira's hands and arms and drove her to her knees.

She blinked, expecting to see Zoheret's bloody, ruined head in front of her. Instead, he stood there, a startled expression in his face. A column of white fire had formed between the man and Kesira's staff. She had dashed her staff against the pale, dancing tongues of flame and not the traitor's skull.

"I wondered where the little nun was," mocked Lenc. "You joined the rebels, I see. A mistake. You have suckled my son. For that I owe you a debt of thanks."

Kesira stayed on her knees, too shaken to move or speak. Lenc fashioned another spear from the jade cloud encircling his head. The shaft hardened and then drove directly for her breast. She tried to scream, but the words jumbled in her throat. Only tiny trapped animal noises escaped.

"I will now repay that debt. I will *not* leave you as I have Captain Protaro." Lenc laughed at her. "Am I not the most generous patron who ever sullied his hands with you silly mortals?"

"Master, allow me to kill her!"

"Silence, worm," Lenc snapped at Zoheret. "Compared to her you are a nothing, a failure, a mistake of nature. Look upon her courage and learn—if you can."

"Wh-what are you going to do?" Kesira's voice firmed, but inside she was quaking.

"I shall continue doing as I please: toy with the Emperor. Lalasa provides another diversion, but she is too weak to give me much opposition or pleasure. Ruling the empire will give me another instant of delight. I will find others."

"What of me?"

"You, my little whore of Gelya? You shall be forced to watch my son mature and grow into my successor!"

Kesira used all her training and forced her way to her feet. Tottering, she advanced. The expression on Lenc's jade face spurred her on. He stared at her in complete amazement that she could do more than twitch. Kesira's fingers tensed in anticipation of closing on Lenc's throat. She had no idea if a demon could be strangled to death; since her hands were the only weapon left to her, she'd use them.

"You disobey my command!" Lenc roared. "For that you will die!"

The misty green spear formed once more from the clouds circling Lenc's head like a crown. But again the spear didn't find her body. She heard a strange clicking behind her.

Kesira gasped when a gray form flashed past her, intent on Lenc's throat.

"Molimo!" she cried. "Don't!"

The man-wolf's fangs snapped against Lenc's hard jade arm. Sparks of blue and white danced off into the night as Molimo swiveled and jerked about, trying to find a vulnerable spot on the demon's throat.

With a pass of his hand, Lenc tossed Molimo away. The wolf tumbled down the black lava steps and lay snarling at the bottom. Kesira saw eyes greener than the jade of Lenc's body fill with hatred. The shape change altered Molimo in so many ways she didn't dare think about it—but those eyes! They rivaled Lenc's in cruelty.

"Don't Molimo, please. You can't harm him."

"She's right, boy. I am invincible!" Lenc sent his fireball searing toward Molimo. To the demon's obvious surprise, the fireball exploded at the tip of the wolf's nose, leaving the sleek gray body unscathed. Molimo launched himself once more, attacking an exposed leg, pawing hard at a jade belly, seeking out the throat again.

Once more, Lenc used his magicks to toss the wolf away. They stared at each other like adversaries who knew each other. A curious expression crossed Lenc's face, then vanished.

"I ought to know you, wolf. You are so familiar."

Before Molimo tried another time to destroy the demon, Lenc erected a barrier of white flame between them. Molimo dodged, but column after column of cold, soul-burning flame rose to block his path.

"There, wolf, see how you enjoy my hospitality." Lenc clapped his hands. The circle of fire began to shrink, to move in on Molimo. The wolf howled piteously. Then the cries turned more human as Molimo transformed himself back into man form.

"You are a versatile one, other-beast. Cease your crying. I have a reward in store for you. For you and the nun."

Kesira paid little attention to the jade demon; she was staring openmouthed at the way Molimo cried out in a most human fashion."

"Your tongue," she said.

"'Row bath,'" Molimo said. It took Kesira an instant to realize he was trying to say, "Grow back."

Strong hands lifted her and hurried her forward. Kesira saw Nehan-dir's scarred face off to the right. He motioned to the soldiers of the Steel Crescent to put her inside the white fire circle with Molimo. As she passed through the barrier, Kesira thought she'd go mad with pain. Deep within her soul the burning refused to stop. It gnawed and ripped and ate until she wanted only to die.

The sensation passed as abruptly as it had begun. She clung to Molimo.

"How did you endure it?" she asked. "It felt as if every inch of my body, inside and out, had been roasted."

It affects me differently.

Kesira looked up sharply, knowing Molimo hadn't spoken. Deep in his black eyes burned tiny flecks of green. She saw the heavy worry lines, the aging, the burdens Molimo carried written on his once-youthful body. The Molimo she had first nursed back to health had been hardly past seventeen. This man had seen forty summers—more.

"What's happening to you? How is it you can speak?"

"No worrs," he said, slurring heavily.

"You don't want me to talk?" He nodded. Kesira obeyed, feeling secure in the circle of Molimo's strong arm as she turned to face Lenc. The jade demon continued to harangue from his position at the top of the lava steps.

". . . all will worship in my temple once a week. Those failing to do so will *die!*"

To punctuate his command, Lenc fell silent and let the crowd listen to Protaro's unceasing misery.

"You might die," the demon continued, "or worse." He pointed needlessly to the spot where Protaro twisted slowly in midair, the magical spear turning him over and over to increase his agony.

What tore at Kesira the most was the lack of obvious physical damage done to Protaro. No blood dripped from the entry or exit points. No wound gaped. Only pain etched the man's face.

"You think you have thwarted me," Lenc said, directing his awful gaze at Kesira. "Try to hide my son from me. Try to destroy me. Try—and fail!"

Lenc signaled. The crowd split apart as mounted Steel Crescent mercenaries trotted forward. Immediately behind them stumbled the portly innkeeper, tightly clutching the baby. Tears rolled down the man's cheeks. Kesira knew he did not enter the square willingly. Lenc's coercion obviously tore at the man's heart.

"All behold! My son!"

As one, the crowd dropped to their faces. The closeness caused many to fall on top of others. Kesira wondered what Kolya—and the rest of the empire—would be like in a year. Ten? Lenc misused his power constantly; Kesira couldn't see the empire surviving past that. Lenc, in his boredom, would have killed off everyone by then.

"See how I punish those who oppose me."

"No!" Kesira strained forward. Molimo held her back. The innkeeper's entire body came awash in Lenc's white fire. The innkeeper sputtered and burned, producing a greasy black smoke that rose and found wintry upper air currents. The sickening stench of human flesh afire vanished mercifully as a result. But the sight of the man's imploring gesture, not blaming, turned Kesira dead inside.

Was life to come to this? A slave for a demon and nothing more? That wasn't what Gelya taught. And what of the rune sticks? They'd told her she would triumph over Lenc. Kesira saw no way to destroy the demon from the interior of this magical prison.

"My son," cooed Lenc, holding the baby awkwardly. Even in her present straits, Kesira marveled at how the baby had grown. She had left him only a few hours earlier, and already he was toddler size. Guiltily, she looked up at Molimo. His lined face showed the same aging. Whether this rapid growth was the product of the unleashed jade or something more, Kesira couldn't say. It affected those around her in ways she didn't like.

She wondered if she was as young, and young appearing, as she had been.

"Worrs come," Molimo said. She had to agree. There had to be even worse times ahead. The only bright spot Kesira saw lay in Zolkan's continued freedom. The *trilla* bird had tried to alert her to the trap, then had taken to wing. Where he might be, she didn't know, but as long as he had escaped Lenc's wrath, Kesira would rest easier.

"You will worship my son as you do me!" roared Lenc. The ripple passed through the crowd. They rose up, then flung themselves prone once more in abject obeisance.

"Take these two away. To my *special* prison." Lenc spun and stormed back into his dark temple. As he went, he made casting motions. Everywhere he pointed, tiny white fire sputtered and grew to a soul-burning foot-thick column. Lenc vanished within the temple, and a huge sigh of relief rose from the crowd.

For the moment, their ordeal was over.

Nehan-dir trotted up next to the pen where Molimo and Kesira stood. He saluted his departed demon patron.

"Take them to the prison," Nehan-dir ordered.

A full score of mounted soldiers came forward, lances lowered. Kesira again felt the tearing fear and pain as they forced her through the barrier of white fire. Molimo came through more stoically, but even though he did not cry out, he sagged to his knees. Kesira had to help him to his feet.

Like animals they were herded through the streets of Kolya.

Kesira felt rather than saw the citizens watching from behind closed shutters and partially opened doors. She didn't blame them for not attempting a rescue. They had just witnessed Lenc's wrath. Not to want to draw it down on their families by a precipitous act like rescuing failed rebels seemed only right to the nun.

She still wished someone would have tried.

The lancers forced them into a cold stone building sitting in the center of a large field. On the grounds camped hundreds of Steel Crescent mercenaries who all curiously watched as Nehan-dir rushed Kesira and Molimo to the building.

"This isn't the same building you used before," she said.

"Lenc demolished the other, on my suggestion. It doesn't pay to allow reminders of failure to exist." He stared down at her. "In a way, I am sorry you will die. You've shown extreme bravery. No sense, but bravery. For that I salute you."

"There's still a chance," she began. Molimo's grip on her arm bruised her flesh. She subsided. Kesira had thought to sway Nehan-dir, but she knew how impossible that was. The man sought and had finally found his position in society. That it meant the destruction of her society was secondary to the Order of the Steel Crescent.

"Inside," Nehan-dir ordered.

They entered the low stone building, then spiraled down ramp after ramp into the bowels of the planet. Kesira lost track of how far they went, but she guessed it had to be a hundred feet or more. Escape from this prison would be impossible if they had to fight their way back to the surface.

It was impossible on all scores when she saw the prison-cell doors. They burned with bright green light similar to that encircling Lenc's head. He held his prisoners securely with magic, as well as with force of arms.

Nehan-dir held the door. Both Molimo and Kesira entered. The iron clang as Nehan-dir closed the door might have been a judge dealing out an execution order.

"Molimo," she began. He pulled away and sank to the cold, rocky floor, head on curled-up knees.

Kesira shared his despair. She dropped into another corner of the cell and stared at the green glow barring their exit without really seeing it. Gelya had taught that defeat was nothing but a new lesson to be learned, that the defeated might emerge stronger and wiser.

Kesira felt no wiser.

Her mind tumbled and roiled about until one snippet from what Lalasa had said came to her: Merrisen lived. Had the Emperor's demon meant that literally or figuratively, in the same way that Gelya still lived because he and his teachings had not been forgotten?

"Merrisen," she said softly. "If you live, hearken to my words. The world cannot long endure Lenc. We need your strength, your wisdom. You, who are called the greatest of demons, aid us!"

Merrisen didn't respond. Kesira soon fell into a troubled sleep populated by leering demons and Lenc's cruel tortures.

Chapter Eleven

KESIRA MINETTE cast her thoughts back through the years, to her parents dying at the hands of brigands, to Sister Fenelia and Sister Dana and Kai and Dominie Tredlo and her years in the nunnery. Bad times, but good ones, also. Kesira refined verse after verse of her death song, honing it, making it lyrically say the exact things she desired. Without doubt, she would die soon.

Kesira touched the box containing her rune sticks. The casting showing her unconditionally triumphant over Lenc had been a lie. Perhaps Lenc had sent the vision so that her defeat would be even more intense. She thought any cruelty possible for the demon. He had used his friends and seduced them into the awful power of the jade so that they would do chores he shied away from.

Ayondela, most of all, had been lured to evil by her need for vengeance. Kesira sighed at the sad memory of the female demon. All Ayondela had wanted was revenge for the death of her half-demon, half-human son.

Kesira had watched Molimo rip out the throat of Ayondela's son and had been unable to prevent it. Cold-numbed fingers touched the warmth of Wemilat's kiss on her breast. Through the death of Ayondela's son, Wemilat had been freed; he had subsequently given his life to slay Howenthal. But Ayondela saw only the fact of her mortal son's death.

Kesira had come far to have her life end in a small prison cell a hundred feet below the surface. Humming her death song to herself, she repeatedly went over every lyric, every word. When the verses satisfied her, she wrote a new verse dealing with all that had occurred in Kolya.

The saddest lines were those relating Protaro's fate.

"Molimo?" she called out softly. "Are you awake?"

"Wake," he mumbled.

"Tell me how your tongue regenerated. I've never heard of anyone growing a new one. This is as fantastic as sprouting a new arm or leg." While Kesira was interested, she sought only to pass the time.

In the dank, windowless cell time had ceased to have meaning. The only illumination came from the green-glowing doorway that Kesira could barely force herself to look at. It reminded her too much of Lenc and how the demon now held the baby she had carried for so long.

"Magic. Demon magic."

"Which demon? Lalasa?" Molimo nodded. "I met with Lalasa," Kesira said, almost dreamily. "She came to me while I hid at the inn. She wanted the baby killed, too. She was the one who had suggested this to Emperor Kwasian. I refused her this, but she must have strong principles if she helped you with your tongue."

"Good demon. But die soon," Molimo said.

"What? Why?" Kesira sagged. "Oh, you mean Lenc will kill her soon. I suppose so. A shame. I liked her, even if she was a demon."

"You haf strong powers." Molimo obviously strained to form the unfamiliar words. As he did so, Kesira watched the man age. White streaks shot through his ebony hair and turned him even older. While Kesira saw no hint of physical weakening, it had to come soon. Molimo would die of old age soon, very soon.

"Are you this way because of the jade?" she asked. Molimo nodded. She had seen the way Ayondela's jade palace had affected him. The man had turned infirm and required help to retreat down the road away from the jade. Not for the first time, Kesira wondered that she wasn't similarly affected. The more she thought about it, the more puzzling it became. No human she had seen reacted only to the jade.

"You spoke to me in the square, but not with words. How did you do that?"

At times, it is easier, came the thought inside her skull.

"You've spoken to me this way before. I caught only

fragments then. But now I can understand more, perhaps all."

Some, Molimo corrected.

"Is this how you 'talked' to Zolkan?"

"Yisss," Molimo said. "Zolkan speech birdlike, mine in head."

"Don't tire yourself. Why not speak inside my head all the time? I . . . I like it." Kesira found herself saying this almost shyly, as if such admission had to be perverted. The intimacy it gave, fleetingly, aroused her in many ways. Molimo had stayed distant from her because of his other-beast affliction, but Kesira found herself wishing for more from the man.

Much more.

"Tiring. Har-hard talk this way."

Kesira settled back. Talking with Molimo helped her pass the time, and kept her mind off their predicament. She didn't want to consider how long it would be before Lenc decided on their fate. Since he could have left her spinning in the square as he had done to Protaro, she decided the demon had something more in store for her. Something even worse than the magical impalement.

"Why does jade give such power to the demons?" she asked, almost to herself rather than to Molimo.

Vibration enhancement, came the thought. *Jade increases vitality of a demon, even as it robs life. Insidious.*

Kesira rose and stood facing the barrier. Reaching out, she brushed her fingertips along the periphery of the green glow. She bit back her cry as agony arrowed up her arm and into her shoulder. The lightest touch had set off more pain than she could endure.

"Not like the cell we occupied in the Quaking Lands, is it?" she asked. "There I managed to—well, I don't know what I did. I managed to hold the magicks at bay long enough for you to slip through. Should I try it again?"

Molimo shook his head.

"I thought not. This spell *feels* different. More deadly." The woman walked back and forth until she realized she was acting like an animal in a cage. Then the nun settled back down on the floor, concentrating on escape.

"What bothers me the most," she said, "is Kene Zoheret. You don't know him—he's the one Lenc rewarded with whatever it was. I never thought he'd betray us all to Lenc the way he did."

Zoheret is Lenc's high priest now, Molimo supplied.

"Zoheret prospers, we die. The man only sought to unite opposition to Lenc so that he could remove it all with one quick cut." Kesira snorted in derision. "And we believed him. There's probably not a single man or woman in Kolya willing to oppose Lenc now. Even if there are, they'd be hesitant about revealing their intentions to anyone else for fear of betrayal."

Lenc comes.

Kesira sat up straight. She heard nothing, but began to sense what Molimo already had: a tension building in the air, making her edgy. When the flickering green barrier winked out of existence, she had no chance to rush out of the cell. Lenc's huge green form barred her exit.

"Stay on your knees, slime," Lenc roared. Kesira winced but tried not to make any show of her raging fear. "You have angered me, but I am merciful."

"You are a tyrant. Insane and a tyrant," Kesira said without rancor. She was too exhausted to work up a good hate toward Lenc.

"A lesser demon might have slain you out of hand for such words. Not I. Rather, I intend that you will live for some time. For exactly a year and a day."

"Why so long? You don't give me the chance to prepare my death song."

Lenc laughed. Kesira tried to told back the involuntary shudder and failed. Against such power she was little more than a pawn. Lenc could do with her as he pleased.

"It will take you that long to die. Slowly, a bit more each day, you will suffer. That much more of your life force will vanish. Pain will haunt you. All hope will flee. You will beg for death—but I will not grant it."

"What have you done with the boy?"

"My son? You ask after my son when your life is being bartered away?"

"I barter nothing. You can kill me whenever you choose.

I cannot stop that. But I will never beg you for my life. Nothing you do can demean me."

"Oh?"

Kesira rolled on the floor, screaming, whining, choking to keep from pleading for mercy. As suddenly as the pain began, it stopped.

Trembling, she pulled herself to her feet; managed to remain upright by leaning against one wall. "Do it a thousand times and I will still not give you the satisfaction of breaking my spirit."

"You make this claim today. There will be a full year more. Of this, and *this,* and even *this!*"

Kesira lost consciousness from the brutalities Lenc heaped upon her. Somewhere in the muzzy fog swirling through her brain she heard Molimo calling to her. She struggled for that sound, the tiny point of light that his voice promised.

"Passed out, didn't I?" she asked. He cradled her head in his lap. He nodded. "The pain was almost more than I could bear. I . . . I don't know if I can endure a full year of this. Lenc will get more and more diabolical as the days go by." Again Molimo agreed.

She tried to push herself into a sitting position, but Molimo held her down. Kesira decided she liked it.

We must escape now. No more hesitation. Within you is the power. We can break through the barrier.

Kesira studied the glowing mist where the door was. She had no idea how to penetrate that jade fog. Even with another piece of jade.

This time she sat bolt upright, her hand going to the jade tusk tucked away in the folds of her robe. She ran clumsy fingers along the tooth that had once belonged to Ayondela.

"This way?" she asked.

"Yesss," Molimo said. "Cannot touch it. You can. Use it. Must escape soon or Lenc will wear us down."

"He didn't torture you, did he?"

"Lenc unsure of me. He knows I have been touched by the jade but doesn't know how."

"Can you use this?" She held out the tusk for Molimo to take. He recoiled.

"No! I would perish if I tried. You must. The jade gave

me other-beast change, took away power. I regain my strength slowly, but the cost is dear."

Kesira saw the lined, aging face and knew the cost. Molimo had grown old in the span of a few months. He would be dead from infirmity within another few months. The touch of the jade had done this to him.

For Molimo, death would come relatively soon. For the rest of the world, Lenc's cruelty might linger for decades as he destroyed the very fabric of society.

"Why didn't Lenc sense this jade?" she said, taking the tusk firmly in her hand and holding it like a short dagger.

He is too far into the mind-warping power of the jade to sense other fragments. This piece is too minute. Use it!

Kesira approached the curtain of shimmery magicks and tentatively thrust out the jade tusk. She jerked away when the brilliance flared at the tip of the tusk. Nothing had happened. Bolder, she again thrust with the tusk. As if she had pulled the plug from a drain, the tusk sucked in the power of the barrier.

"Molimo, hurry. Get through the door. I don't know how long this will last." Kesira watched in fascination as green mist flowed *into* the tusk. She shivered and knew that the tooth alone did not perform this miracle. Something within her commanded the tusk to rob the barrier of its energy. Kesira tried to isolate that portion of herself and failed. Too many responses had become instinctual with her. The teachings of Gelya had been drilled into her over a lifetime. Now she responded without knowing how.

Molimo pushed past her, went to the iron door. Weakly he banged against this physical barricade. Kesira's heart crept up until she thought it had lodged firmly in her throat; she feared Lenc had barred the door as well as placed this spell upon it.

Molimo shoved the door open, using his weight more than his strength, then tumbled out into the corridor and fell heavily to the rocky floor.

Carefully Kesira held the tusk stationary while she moved around and got out of the cell. With incredible caution, she pulled the tusk out of the green mist. The barrier snapped back into place with a blinding surge that left her eyes watering and seeing blue and yellow dancing spots.

"We're out!" she exulted.

"Still underground," Molimo said.

"You're worse than Zolkan. Always looking at the bleak side. Now I know why you two get along so well."

But Kesira's enthusiasm died when she realized that Molimo spoke the truth. To regain their freedom, they'd have to fight their way up the spiral ramp—and they dared not set off any alarm. Hundreds of Steel Crescent mercenaries were camped overhead.

"We may not make it, but we can try—and we can make certain that a few of them won't live to aid Lenc."

Almost crawling, Molimo began the ascent. Kesira followed warily, fearing detection with every step. She tried to help Molimo, but the man shook off her assistance.

Need to concentrate. Need to locate him.

"Him? Who? Lenc?"

The answer became obvious a few minutes later when the powerful flapping of wings sent currents of air down against Kesira's face. The nun looked up, ready to fight, until she recognized Zolkan.

"Pretty sight," grumbled the *trilla* bird. "Hurry now. You can still reach fifth level."

"What's there?"

Both Zolkan and Molimo said as one, "Zoheret."

It took Kesira a few seconds to realize what they meant. Escape to the surface wasn't possible, but wreaking vengeance on the traitor might be.

"He has personal office on fifth level," Zolkan said. "Not well guarded. Lenc dislikes traitors as much as any human. Doesn't trust Zoheret."

"He'll die by my hand," Kesira said, thrusting the jade tusk into her tattered yellow sash. She unfastened the knotted blue cord that told of her selfless devotion to Gelya. It seemed fitting that this would be the instrument for Zoheret's death. The symbol of faith used against the faithless.

"Quiet," said Zolkan. "Guards on next level. Sentries everywhere. Nehan-dir takes no chances."

"We can get up to Zoheret's level," Molimo managed to say. "Must escape, though. Must stop Lenc."

Kesira focused all her attention on the one task: killing Kene Zoheret. The man's treachery had removed any chance for effective resistance to Lenc in Kolya. That alone made him a target for her wrath—but it went deeper. Zoheret had violated the precepts of society, had betrayed all Kesira held as dear by embracing Lenc and the ways of the jade.

She and Molimo started up the spiral ramp, only to halt when the scrape of boots sounded above them. Pressing themselves flat against the wall did little to hide them. Anyone who looked over the railing would spy them instantly. Realizing this, Kesira continued her climb, forcing tired legs into action. Molimo followed at a slower pace, obviously worn from his exertions.

"Sentry, take me to Nehan-dir," she called out when she came within a few feet of the guard. The man turned, started to salute and then saw who commanded him.

Caught midway between salute and sword hilt, the guard couldn't effectively stop Kesira's short, hard punch to his throat. He staggered back, gagging. Zolkan fluttered down and fastened hard talons into the man's jugular. In less than a minute the guard lay dead.

Kesira started to pick up the dead man's sword, then hesitated. She still carried Ayondela's tusk. That seemed a more potent weapon, and didn't violate Gelya's edict against steel. Molimo scooped up the sword and pulled it free, checking its razor edge. He smiled wickedly.

"Better. My strength returns, but too slowly. This helps." He made a few whirling cuts through the air.

"More guards come. Hurry, hurry!" squawked Zolkan.

The *trilla* bird's warning alerted the sentries. Four rushed forward while a fifth held back. Brawny arms grabbed Kesira, intent on flinging her to the floor. She twisted, found her center and upended the Steel Crescent mercenary, sending him over her hip. He crashed to the floor and lay there, the wind knocked out of his lungs. Kesira could see the crescent scar on his chest where the man had accepted his order's cruel sigil. Kesira used it as a target for the jade tusk.

The mercenary twitched once, then died.

And Kesira found herself knocked away by the flat of another's sword. Had it not been for Zolkan's claws closing on the tall, stringy-haired woman's sword wrist, the blade would have sliced through Kesira's hamstrings.

"Fight!" bellowed Zolkan. "Can't do it all by myself!"

Kesira needed no such urging. She regained her balance and swung around, inside the sword's arc. She closed with the woman and hammered a hard fist into an exposed temple. The mercenary jerked away, stunned. Kesira and Zolkan both followed quickly with kicks and raking talons until the woman lay dead on the floor. Panting, Kesira bent double to regain her breath.

"Two dead," Molimo said.

Then, inside her head, she heard Molimo tell her, *Another escaped. We have only a few minutes before all of Nehandir's order floods into these levels. Do we try to flee or do we seek out Zoheret?*

For Kesira there was no question.

"Zoheret!"

Up two more levels, they ran. Zolkan wobbled in midair and indicated a side passageway leading away from the spiral ramp. "He is down there."

Even as the *trilla* bird said the words, Kene Zoheret appeared, rubbing sleep from his eyes and mumbling to himself.

"What's going on?" he demanded, irritable at having been awakened by the noise of combat. Zoheret's eyes grew wider when he saw Kesira and Molimo. For an instant he seemed frozen to the spot, then he turned and bolted back into the room.

Zolkan prevented the traitor from barring the door behind him. Then Molimo's powerful kick sent the heavy iron door slamming open against the wall.

"Wait, I can explain all this. It . . . it's a trick. I'm finding out what I can about Lenc to use that knowledge against him."

"You betrayed your comrades. You told Lenc where to find the baby. You are responsible for Protaro's fate, the death of the innkeeper, the subjugation of all Kolya. Worst of all, you have not lived up to your responsibilities as citizen of the empire. You have failed your city and your Emperor."

Zoheret spun to the side and pulled forth a short sword. Molimo started to engage him, but Kesira's grip on his upper arm stayed him. His dark eyes, now flecked with green, bored hard into her brown ones. No longer were Kesira's eyes softer. She had purpose. Zoheret had betrayed much of what she had struggled for over the past months since the reign of jade terror had begun.

Zoheret was solely responsible for Lenc's regaining his son.

Molimo stepped to one side.

This action, more than anything else, drained the color from Zoheret's face. He looked at the small nun in the tattered robe and read his death in her eyes.

"Give yourselves up," Zoheret said, his voice cracking with strain. "You can't hope to escape. The alarm's been sounded."

Kesira moved with deliberate steps toward the traitor. Zoheret lifted his sword, then made a clumsy lunge. Kesira let it go past, between her arm and body, then trapped it and lifted. She caught Zoheret's elbow in a lock that raised him to his toes and forced him to drop the sword.

"You'll break my arm. Stop! I submit!"

With a deft twist, Kesira released the arm and stepped behind Zoheret. The knotted blue cord around her waist came free. She whipped it into a quick loop and dropped it around Zoheret's neck. For a brief instant, Kesira thought he might have thwarted her. He succeeded in getting two fingers of his left hand between cord and throat.

She jerked hard on the cord; the action severed Zoheret's fingers. The doomed man let out a tiny cry, then sagged as the knotted cord cut deeper into his flesh, shutting off air and blood. His tongue protruded and swelled and his eyes bulged.

He is dead, Molimo communicated. Kesira hung onto the cord grimly. *Release him. You can do no more.*

Only when Zolkan landed on her shoulder and nipped at her cheek did she let Zoheret's body fall to the floor.

"It doesn't regain the baby, does it?" she said, staring at the corpse. "Gelya had always said that revenge is thought sweet by fools." She released the cord and refastened it around her waist. "I'm not so sure."

"He deserved his fate," Zolkan said. "But we must hurry, or share it."

Molimo stood silently by the door, listening intently. Kesira heard nothing, but as she went into the corridor she saw the rush of guards down the spiral ramp. Ducking back out of sight, she waited.

"They have gone back to level where we killed other guards," said Molimo. "Let's go before they return."

Kesira hardly believed their good luck. Foolishly, the Steel Crescent mercenaries had all hastened down to where their comrades had been killed. She started up the ramp, and knew instantly that escape was not possible.

Lenc stood in front of her, mighty arms crossed on his bare chest. The jade demon's tiny nimbus flickered and crackled with lighting. If the demon's looming presence hadn't blocked their path, the bolts of lightning blasting from the cloud would have.

Kesira turned to retreat, only to find that the mercenaries had already started back up. She and Molimo were trapped between a score of armed guards and their patron.

Even worse than the sinking sensation of failure was Lenc's mocking laughter.

Chapter Twelve

LENC'S LAUGHTER first robbed Kesira of courage, then filled her with the need to confront the demon. He stood so complacent, so assured, so all-powerful, that she wanted to scream.

"You allowed me to kill Zoheret," she accused.

"Of course I did, little one," Lenc said. When he smiled, he revealed twin rows of jade-green teeth. Kesira fingered the jade tusk hidden in her robe and discarded the notion of using it. The time would come for an attack on Lenc. But not at this instant.

"You grow bored already?"

Don't goad him, came Molimo's thought. The man appeared to have aged another ten years. White streaks ran through his once black hair, turning him into one of advanced middle age. Kesira would have guessed him to be fifty if she hadn't known otherwise. *He is dangerous. To you, to me, to the world.*

Kesira smiled wanly to reassure Molimo that she knew the full extent of the danger in dealing with the demon. His capriciousness walked hand in hand with insanity caused by the jade. While Kesira had not known Lenc before he'd partaken of the awful green magic, she guessed that he hadn't changed—he'd just acquired more power. Now he could do as he pleased with no one to check him.

"What a burden it is, being so powerful. Is there nothing else but death and wanton destruction to keep you occupied?"

"Perhaps . . . when I tire of seeing insects such as you killing other insects." Lenc gestured, and a fireball raced from his fingertips. White flame burned through the rock

137

walls and exposed the chamber where Kene Zoheret lay.
Already the corpse provided a feast for scavenger beetles.
"Fascinating, the way they clip and saw their way through
flesh, don't you agree?"

Lenc clapped his hands. The ringing sound reminded
Kesira more of stone against stone than flesh on flesh.

"You are becoming a statue," she said. "The jade is
transforming you."

"It alters my flesh. A minor price to pay for the power
I get."

"All your functions now depend on the jade," she guessed.
"Do you enjoy another's gentle caress? Can you even feel
it?"

Take care, came Molimo's warning. *This is dangerous
ground. He is insane.*

Lenc laughed. "What are those to me? I enjoy the sensation of complete power. Mere animal functions are secondary now. I transcend such concerns."

"And what are your concerns?" she demanded. Kesira
glanced back toward the Steel Crescent soldiers. They stood
fingering their sword hilts, ready to attack the instant their
patron ordered it. Kesira wondered how far she could goad
Lenc before he ordered that—or if it was possible to go
that far under any circumstances. He obviously enjoyed
keeping her captive—for the amusement value, if nothing
else.

"You transcend such functions? Yet you are the worst
predator in all of the empire."

"All the world," the demon corrected with some gusto.
"I take pride in this accomplishment. My fellow demons
proved too cowardly to take the step to greatness. I shall
be remembered for all time. Every human who ever walks
the face of the planet, from this day forward, will quake at
the mere mention of my name. No one will ever forget me."
Lenc's laugh shook the foundations of the prison around
them.

"Why is it so important to be cruel? Use your power for
good!"

The jade perverts him. Stop this!

Kesira shook her head, not bothering to look at Molimo. Her brown eyes fixed on Lenc.

"Good, evil—what are those but meaningless noises," scoffed Lenc. "I do as I see fit. There is nothing evil or good in that—it is merely my will."

Before Kesira could answer, Lenc thrust out his hands and then spread them slowly in front of his ponderous body. For a moment the woman thought Lenc had turned entirely to jade and had started to topple, but it proved only an illusion caused by the rippling air around him. The magicks he commanded confused her senses and brought home exactly how powerful the jade demon was.

"Witness!" he cried.

Kesira no longer stood on the spiral ramp. She floated a thousand feet above the ground. The brief instant of vertigo passed. This was similar to the illusory tricks Lalasa had shown her when the female demon had spirited her to the Plains of Roggen and the defeat of Emperor Kwasian's most valiant general.

"How like bugs they are. Less than the beetles feasting on Zoheret's flesh," said Lenc. "Look at them and tell me you can't feel the same contempt for them I do."

Kesira swallowed hard. She saw what it meant for Lenc to be in absolute control of the empire. Outside of Limaden, in plain view of Emperor Kwasian and those huddled fearfully within the capital, Lenc had ordered thousands of men and women to begin construction of a towering monument—to the jade demon. The gleaming sides had been covered with sheets of jade, and the lofty central spire rose up to impudently challenge the sun for supremacy. Even as Kesira watched, hundreds died from their exertions.

"You haven't fed them!" she cried. "They need water, food, rest. Why do you drive them like this?"

"Insects deserve nothing more. When they have finished this tribute, perhaps then I shall allow them respite. Or perhaps I will require them to build a second monument, one even larger and grander."

"To what purpose? You kill them for no reason!"

"For every good purpose. I *desire* the monument. It pleases me. What else ought there to be? I have the power. I must use it. Otherwise it is pointless for me to have risked all to obtain it."

"You mock Emperor Kwasian with this monument."

"He can't do anything to prevent it from being built. Yes, it is a thorn in his side. That also amuses me."

"There's more," Kesira said, suddenly suspicious. Lenc shifted her in the air, causing cold winter winds to bite into her flesh and rob her of breath.

"There's more," Lenc confirmed. "Lalasa still opposes me. I will draw her into battle with this outrage. I can then enjoy the exquisite feel of slaying her as I have so many other demons."

Kesira said nothing. While Lalasa had hardly proven herself a worthy ally, Kesira bore the demon no malice. What she witnessed, what Lenc showed her so gleefully, was nothing less than genocide. Lenc had killed off most of his own kind, singly and in small groups, ever since the jade demons had fought for ascendancy. Now that Kesira had helped destroy Ayondela and his two other cohorts, Lenc sought to be the sole demonic survivor.

"She'll be lured out soon," Lenc predicted. "If I destroy enough of her precious pets, she will come to oppose me. Then I'll slay her as I have all the others!"

"Why show me? What am I to you? You claim to be all-powerful. Why try to impress me with your brutality?" Kesira's anger mounted with every passing instant. The workers on this pointless monument tumbled and fell to their deaths even as she watched. To Lenc this was nothing more than an experiment in torture.

Torture. Kesira's mind seized upon that. He had shown her everything to evoke this very response. He wanted her angry, confused, aroused at the indignity and horror. The demon fed on this. The more emotion he stirred within her breast, the headier his experience.

"You are different," Lenc said unexpectedly. "Somehow you managed to nurture my son. No other human female could have done that, save the weak thing I chose as Dymek's mother."

"Dymek? You call the boy this?"

"A strong name for one who will succeed me."

"You know the jade destroys you, and yet you continue to embrace it?"

"I'll last a thousand years, a million! To you that is inconceivable, but I must plan ahead. After that million years when I am no more, Dymek will reign in my place. The dynasty I establish will rule through all eternity."

"The jade kills you daily. You won't even live a hundred years." Even to Kesira her words sounded spiteful and petty.

Lenc was amused. "Ha! Look. Lalasa can take no more. She agrees to do battle with me. You deserve to see her fate."

Kesira had the sinking feeling that Lalasa might have been right. Perhaps the baby Dymek—the name tasted bitter on her tongue—ought to have been killed. The nun knew it might be considered weakness on her part that she couldn't do such a foul deed, but Gelya's teachings did not permit it under any circumstances. Dymek had not proven himself evil. The infant hadn't partaken of the jade and become a menace to demon and human alike.

What he might become depended more on the upbringing his father gave than on what he was at this instant.

Kesira whirled downward so fast she screwed shut her eyes in fear. The cessation of the fall caused her to peer out fearfully. She had alighted with the softness of a floating feather. A dozen paces away stood Lenc, green skin gleaming in the sunlight. The perpetual storm cloud above his head crackled and boomed with lighting, making him into a miniature mountain peak. Lalasa had appeared and stood nearby.

"The monument is pointless, Lenc," Lalasa said. The homely female demon appeared drawn, haggard. She shuffled forward and pointed accusingly at the jade demon. "Your soul will wither for this offense."

"I have no soul but the jade," snapped Lenc. "And what do *you* care for these pitiful humans? Weren't you the one who advised Kwasian and his generals in their battles against the barbarians? You oversaw the deaths of hundreds of thousands over the span of twenty years. Compared to your record for destruction, I am a piker."

"Count them as insignificant if you will," said Lalasa, "but they have not wiped out most of their own kind."

"No thanks to you."

"Sometimes it is necessary to prune a branch so that the tree may live—however distasteful the action. What *you* have done is destroy the whole tree. How many demons remain? How many, Lenc?"

"Only those I have permitted to live. Baram muddles about, roaring his unintelligible nothings against mountains and listening to the echoes. Tolek cowers on a distant island. You remain, darling Lalasa."

Lalasa frowned. "Noissa? What of him?"

Lenc laughed. "I killed him as he lay with his human slut. No demon ought to couple with lower life forms."

"As you did with the peasant woman?"

Kesira saw that Lalasa's swift retort stung. Lenc roared in anger. "Who among the demons would have me? You and those like you forced me into that perversion. Now suffer my vengeance for making me an outcast among my own kind!" Insanity flared and caused the small lightnings to sing and crackle in the cloud above the demon's head.

Kesira settled her emotions and began going over her death song, line by line. She doubted it would be much longer before she composed the final verse.

"My powers are no match for yours. Even when there were many of us to oppose you, there could be no real contest between us, Lenc."

"Yes, darling Lalasa, roll over, play dead. Let me have my way with you."

"Never! I know where my duty lies. You shall never... oh!"

The female demon sagged with the pain of Lenc's mighty attack, her face rippling and flowing into something not even vaguely human. For the first time Kesira realized how different the demons were.

Lalasa showed a truly alien aspect as Lenc increased the suffering he visited upon her.

"You will perish before your time, Lenc," moaned Lalasa.

"Not by your hand, weakling."

Lalasa made a small, almost unnoticed gesture. The air around Lenc began to swirl, a new storm forming to rob the one above his head of its virulence. At first Lenc ignored this, then fought against the swirling winds of the vortex. Kesira saw Lalasa gesture again; ice formed around Lenc's body. Green arms froze into a solid block of polar ice. When his halo of cloud winked from sight, the slow encapsulation sped up.

More and more of the jade demon's body vanished in the encasing ice.

Lalasa sank to her knees, expression drawn and complexion gray from the exertion. "Die as you have permitted so many others to die, Lenc. Die, curse you, die!"

The transparent block of ice began to turn frosty. The demon hidden within vanished. Lalasa fell face-forward to the ground, arms and legs twitching feebly. Kesira rushed to her.

"You did it," Kesira cried. "You stopped him. I never knew you had such power. You were magnificent. No wonder Emperor Kwasian listens so closely when you advise him. You—"

"Stop babbling," Lalasa said, letting Kesira help her sit upright. The nun had to prop the frail demon against her knee. The physical weakness appalled her even as the spiritual strength buoyed her.

"You succeeded when all others failed."

"Merrisen," said Lalasa, eyelids drooping. "So great. The greatest of us all."

"And he failed," came Lenc's voice, "just as you have failed."

Kesira jerked around and stared in disbelief at the giant block of ice. Already Lenc's face had melted free of the cold prison. Inch by inch, more of his jade body escaped until he stood in a puddle of cold water, totally free of the icy bonds.

"Do it again, Lalasa. You stopped him once. Do it again!"

"She did nothing, weak one." Lenc sneered. "Do you not see the exquisite torture I give her? She thinks me impotent, no longer a threat. Thereby she dares to hope.

Then I snatch away her hope. This makes her defeat all the more bitter."

"Lenc," Lalasa sobbed.

"Let my name be the last word to cross your lips." Lenc thrust his hands in front of him. Cold white fire leaped forth to engulf Lalasa. She gave one convulsive shudder, then fell from Kesira's grasp. The flames danced with polar delight, dining on demon flesh. In a minute only a skeleton remained. Then even these bones vanished. A few charred spots and myriad tiny white fires marked the ground where Lalasa had lain.

"No," Kesira whispered—so softly the word was almost drowned out by the beating of her heart.

"Baram!" screamed Lenc. The very sky quivered with the intensity of the demon's summons. "You are next to die!"

A roar like an enraged bull pulled Kesira's attention away from the spot where Lalasa had fallen. A giant demon had materialized: arms thicker than Kesira's waist, taller and heavier than any mortal she'd ever known, Baram bellowed forth an inchoate cry of rage and pain and frustration.

Lenc stood his ground, waiting.

"You are evil. You must die," said Baram. Kesira knew the outcome of this battle. Baram might be physically strong but lacked the required cunning and intelligence to defeat Lenc.

Baram and Lenc smashed together, arms around each other. Baram roared again and held the jade demon in a bone-crushing grip around the small of the back. Kesira dared hope for an instant when she heard Lenc's bones snapping and crackling loudly. She prayed that Baram would crush Lenc's spine.

Then Lenc reached out and took Baram's head in his hands. With a grin on his face, the jade demon started to twist. Baram finally had to release his grip on Lenc to avoid the excruciating pain in jaw and neck.

Baram kicked free, one massively thewed leg tensing so much that his leather trousers split. Lenc smashed a jade fist into Baram's face. The other demon took no notice of the thin trickle of blood coming from his crushed nose.

Kesira hoped that Baram was beyond pain; she feared that he hadn't sense enough to feel pain.

The powerful demon reached out and seized Lenc's arm, trying to break it. Lenc pulled free. They continued to wrestle, each giving as much as he received until Kesira saw the subtle change in Lenc's face. The jade demon tired of this new amusement.

With a twist both agile and adroit, Lenc got behind his adversary. A thick forearm circled Baram's throat and a heavy hand pushed down on the top of the struggling demon's head.

"Die now, Baram, you stupid oaf." Lenc applied more pressure, and the giant demon's neck snapped like a dried twig. Head canted at a sickening angle, Baram lay unmoving on the ground. Lenc's breath came in deep, gusty drafts, and perspiration shone on his green skin.

Kesira felt only numbness when Lenc pointed, and his white fire danced across Baram's body. In seconds only those flames remained.

"What now?" the nun asked. "Do I suffer the same fate? Twist my head off? Let your flames devour my body?"

Lenc's laughter told her that more subtle tortures lay in store for her.

"You still have a year of exquisite agony," Lenc told her. "FIrst we begin with breaking your will. Then we proceed to . . . more imaginative torture."

Kesira gasped as blackness swirled around her. She clutched her robe tightly around her spare body and tried to keep her teeth from chattering. As quickly as the darkness had swallowed her, it spat her out. She tumbled forward, skinning her knees and elbows on the rough floor of the prison cell.

Are you all right? came Molimo's comforting thought. His gentle hands helped her rise. She brushed off the dirt the best she could.

"Such a nice couple they make. The other-beast and the nun." Lenc barred the doorway with his massive frame, looking none the worse for his bouts with Lalasa and Baram. "I think you will make an even nicer pair when you do my bidding."

"Kill us and be done with it," Kesira said angrily. "We aren't toys."

"Ah, but you *are* interesting toys. For now. Outlive that, and you will die horribly."

Kesira bit her lower lip as pain drove into her body from all sides. One of Lenc's white fireballs had exploded in her gut, doubling her over. As the cold fire continued to burn, she knew she'd die then and there. But she didn't. The fire extinguished itself and left her physically unscathed.

"Obey and you will live—for at least one more day."

Do not anger him, Molimo sent to her.

Kesira still couldn't speak.

"Make love. I would watch you couple with an animal."

"You're more of an animal than he is, even when the change takes him."

Kesira's insult only amused the jade demon, who ordered, "Do it. Now!"

Kesira glared at Lenc. Then she heard a sound behind her—and it chilled her as much as anything ever had. Molimo's control had slipped again. Gray fur rubbed against her legs, moved up her body.

"No, please, this isn't . . ." The jade power controlled by Lenc flattened her on the floor and held her motionless.

"Go on," Lenc urged the wolf. "Mate with her."

The force holding Kesira in place eased somewhat and she escaped it, only to find this was what Lenc intended. She found herself on hands and knees, Molimo behind her. Savage teeth ripped at her robe to expose her flanks. Tears ran down her cheeks as she tried—and failed—to escape this degradation.

She gasped as the wolf jerked forward. Her emotions whirled: hatred, fear, shame, arousal.

Kesira hated herself for this blatant sexual arousal she experienced. Her passions mounted; the thrill of feeling the wolf enter her turned to something more. Ecstasy, yes, but more. She tensed and strained against the furry body.

All the while Lenc kept up a crude commentary.

Finally Kesira recognized the sensation underlying her

ecstasy. Power. Power flooded her arteries, blasted brightly into her brain. Power seared every nerve in her body.

And Kesira Minette knew that the rune sticks had not lied. She knew she could defeat Lenc. She now had the power.

Chapter Thirteen

KESIRA MINETTE collapsed onto the floor and felt the gray-furred wolf behind her change back into human form. She rolled over and touched Molimo's head. He flinched away.

"I understand. Lenc forced us to do this for his amusement. He *forced* us."

I wanted to. *That was why it was so easy for him.*

A tear formed in the corners of Kesira's eyes. "I wanted it, too," she whispered.

"How touching. A wolf mating with the last of Gelya's whores." Lenc laughed so hard he had to hold his sides. "This is rich. The finest I have arranged yet. Killing Lalasa provided me with much less pleasure than I'd thought it would. Removing Baram was more like stepping on an insect."

Kesira glared at the jade demon but said nothing. Any response she made would only amuse Lenc more. The horrifying thought occurred to her that the world was truly doomed if Lenc was already this bored with his existence. What would happen ten years hence, or fifty? Lenc would have tried every petty cruelty, every major perversion.

Kesira wondered that she wasn't more shamed by what Lenc had just forced her and Molimo to do. Instead of being degraded, she experienced an inner peace unlike any she'd known before. Even her deepest meditations had failed to achieve such a beatitude. Self-doubt and worry had assailed her before. No longer. Kesira had felt worn down and on the brink of exhaustion. Now exhilaration made her every nerve sing.

"Go on," Lenc urged. "Enjoy his furred body once again. Go on!"

Molimo let out a strangled cry and began the other-beast transformation into wolf. Kesira threw her arms around the thickening neck and hugged Molimo close. Lenc snorted in derision and left.

"Don't let the change take you over, Molimo. You can fight it. You can! I know it. I...I feel the power within me. Feel it within you."

Even as she spoke, the thick gray fur rippled and changed back to smooth skin. Molimo the human stayed within the circle of her arms.

"Wrong. I shouldn't have let him do that to us. So weak then. Still weak, but better."

"Don't talk," Kesira said. "Lenc still doesn't know you have regained your tongue. It might be better if he doesn't learn, unless he's spying on us."

"He's not. More I speak, the easier it becomes. Want to. So long. So much horror."

They kissed, and Kesira sank down against Molimo's strong body. He might have aged dramatically in the past few months, but this didn't stem the tide of her passion for him. If anything, Lenc had done them a favor. He had lowered barriers they had erected. She had tried to convince herself Molimo was nothing more than a poor, mute youth trapped by the jade rain. The strength of character, the kindness, the caring were still within him no matter what age the body. She loved him and had from the first time she'd spied his bloodied, battered body.

Afterward, Molimo asked, "Why did you hide your feelings for me all this time?"

"Why'd you hide yours for me?"

"Who wants a half-man? The shape change takes me too unexpectedly."

"I rather enjoyed you that way, also," she said.

The shock in Molimo's expression made her hug him close. "I love you for *you*, not just your shape."

"There's more."

"The jade ages you rapidly, that I can see. And you hide other details from me. No," she said, putting one finger across his lips to still the protest, "I've seen the way you

and Zolkan talk. There's a bond between the two of you
that doesn't exist between us. But I love you."

"You didn't love Rouvin?"

"No." Kesira had fought long, emotional inner battles
with this. Rouvin had been gallant, brave, a warrior second
to none—and she had had strong bonds with him. But not
love. Friendship, yes. When he had died—his throat ripped
apart by Molimo's wolf fangs—she had grieved, but more
for the psychic pain it caused Molimo than the passing of
Rouvin.

"Others?"

"There have been others," she said. "Gelya preached
moderation, not celibacy. All sisters of the order leave the
nunnery for five years before returning as Senior Sisters. I
had several more years to go before my journey into the
world to find more of life than that taught by Gelya, but I
had known others. In Blinn. Dominie Tredlo, our Senior
Brother. Others in my order."

Molimo said nothing. Kesira wiggled as feathery caresses
brushed over the surface of her mind. It seemed that
Molimo's words ought to be forming as they had before,
but no coherent message came. When she realized what he
was doing, she jerked free from his arms and glared.

"You can see my thoughts. Stop it!"

You detected my prowlings?

"Yes!"

*Unusual for one such as you to be able to know when I
touch you.*

"I see nothing odd in it," Kesira said. "In fact, since . . .
since Lenc forced us to . . . to do what we did, I've been
stronger. I got a great deal from you, just as I did from
Wemilat." Kesira frowned. "Yes, that's it. I'm stronger now,
just as I was after being with Wemilat. A vitality flowed
into me."

And into me, said Molimo.

"I can almost believe the rune reading."

"Wh-what rune reading?" Molimo struggled to put his
thoughts into speech.

"I didn't tell you. While you were off doing whatever it
was you were doing in Kolya, I cast the rune sticks and

asked about the future. Never have I seen a more positive reading. Each one indicated triumph over Lenc. Until now, I'd passed it off as another of his cruel tricks."

"Lenc s-sent you false castings?"

"That's what he claimed. But I don't think this one was his doing. Lalasa had just left me in the inn, and the casting went so easily. Nothing but victory indications over Lenc."

"I didn't send it, either."

Kesira looked at him. "Of course you didn't. But this power suffusing my every nerve . . . I don't know how to use it."

"Remember when we escaped from Howenthal's prison?" Molimo swallowed hard, then licked his lips. Speaking posed problems for him, but Kesira thought he remastered the skill well. "Your meditations opened the curtain. It was similar to this."

Molimo went to the green barrier and held out his hand. He jerked back as tiny green sparks arced over to bite him. Molimo silently inclined his head in the direction of the magical wall.

"You think my skill works against Lenc? I don't even know what it was that I did, Molimo. The demon is a master of his magicks. I can't even say I dabble. I don't know *anything!* What if I make a mistake?"

"Try. You are much stronger than you think."

"Molimo . . ."

"Do it for Gelya, for Emperor Kwasian, for yourself." In a lower voice, Molimo added, "Do it for the baby."

"Dymek," she said in a choked voice. "That's the name Lenc gave him. Dymek. An ugly name."

"Do it!"

Kesira took one hesitant step, then another, and a bolder third one. She closed her eyes and ran through the litanies taught her by her sisters. When she felt tiny pinpricks against her skin, she knew she approached the barrier and that her only reward would be excruciating pain. Kesira forgot the litanies and began humming her death song.

So many verses had been written in the past few months. How many to go before she gave voice to the song and let those at her deathbed hear her life's story?

"Molimo, it's not going to work. I—Molimo!"

Kesira Minette stood on the far side of the green barrier. Molimo stood beside her.

"I followed when you walked through. There is nothing you cannot do. Nothing. You have the power now, and it isn't the power of jade."

"Where does it come from, then?"

Molimo paled. "The Time of Chaos feeds your energies. The flux from the death of all the demons gives you power, just as the jade does Lenc."

"But all the demons aren't dead," she protested. "Lenc said Tolek still lived."

"No gain," Molimo said grimly.

"And Lalasa was sure that Merrisen had survived."

Molimo grabbed her arm and pointed up the spiral ramp again. "Guards. I can use the spell taught me by Toyaga so that they won't notice me, but you—I can't protect you with it."

"But when I walked through the magical barrier, you came along."

"My powers are different from yours. And being so near your jade dagger prevents me from full recovery."

"But why?"

Kesira had no chance for further questions. Two of the Steel Crescent guards overheard her and came to investigate. Kesira rushed forward, sidestepped one guard's clumsy sword thrust and jerked him around so that she could kick his foot from under him. He tumbled head over heels down the ramp to land in the midst of the green barrier still covering the cell door. He screamed once in stark agony, then died.

The other guard tried to run, but Molimo overtook him halfway to the next level. A hard fist to the side of the skull silenced the mercenary permanently. Molimo stripped the guard of his sword and dagger.

"Not much, but better than bare hands."

A wan ray of light caught Molimo and highlighted the white streaks in his hair. Kesira swallowed, trying to get rid of the tight knot in her throat. So handsome he was to be afflicted with the curse of accelerating age. First he had lost his tongue, had it regenerated mysteriously, still changed into an other-beast uncontrollably, and now this. Fate was unkind to the man.

"Fire tries gold, misery tries men," she said softly. The delicate touches over her mind told Kesira that Molimo had heard and understood.

Whether he communicated to her on an even more elemental level or she simply knew it, Kesira couldn't say; but the misery Molimo lived with only strengthened him.

"Four more levels to the surface," he said. "Few guards. They are in Kolya for ceremonies."

She didn't bother asking how he knew. Like Zolkan, he always managed to come up with needed facts.

They reached the top level of the underground prison before the heavy tramping of boots echoed down to them. Kesira stopped, knowing they couldn't possibly fight their way through so many soldiers. Above ground, they might be able to slip away; but in the prison area they'd be crowded back down, level after level. Fighting uphill was bad, but the designer had done even more. Any person wielding a weapon in the right hand found it pressed hard against a circular wall.

All the advantage lay with those above.

Even worse, Kesira knew the man they faced: Nehandir.

For the span of five heartbeats, Nehan-dir simply stood and stared at them. The disbelief flowed across his face, then turned into unbridled anger.

"Slay them!" he shouted to the dozen armed mercenaries behind. "Slay them both!"

"But Lenc wanted them for torture," a woman immediately behind Nehan-dir said. "To kill them means our own death. Lenc would see to it!"

"Fools! Don't let them past. I'll take care of them myself." The small, scarred mercenary drew forth his sword. Expression one of complete concentration, Nehan-dir came down the ramp toward Kesira. "How you got past the magical barrier, I can't say. But you'll never get by my cold steel."

He ripped open his tunic and showed the cruel half-moon brand on his chest signifying his membership in the Order of the Steel Crescent. As if this were a shield, Nehan-dir rushed forward.

Kesira had learned not to act but to react. She did not initiate, but waited for her attacker, knowing that in every offense there is a weakness, a method of defense. While Nehan-dir was skillful and determined, Kesira instantly saw the vulnerable point of his attack.

Nehan-dir slashed down powerfully—and found only empty air. Kesira had stepped just enough to one side to let the deadly blade miss. She hopped forward, her arms encircling Nehan-dir's small body. She gasped at the power locked within such a tiny man, but she held on long enough to unbalance him. Turning to one side, she succeeded in getting one foot out from under him. When she released him, he had no choice but to curl up in a ball and roll down the ramp.

"Get Lenc," shouted the woman who seemed to be Nehan-dir's second-in-command. "Get him! We'll hold them here."

Kesira started forward empty-handed, but Molimo's touch on her shoulder stopped her. He handed her a long, stout spear he'd wrested from another mercenary before breaking the man's neck.

"No steel," Kesira said. She placed the razor-edged point against the wall and applied leverage. A loud *snap!* marked the breaking of the spear. "A staff is better."

Kesira proved that it was. The months of starvation and deprivation lay behind her. The power she had acquired by lying with Molimo now flooded her as soft spring rains cover a meadow. Every nerve responded fully. Each muscle screamed with power. Never had her mind been clearer, more settled, readier for the task ahead of her.

She fought. She won.

She and Molimo stumbled out into the crisp evening air. "The stars," she said, panting. "Never have they looked so good to me."

"Enjoy them, slut. You'll never see them again. After this, I will pluck out your eyes and force you to eat them!"

Kesira straightened and turned to face Lenc. The jade demon towered above her, thick biceps tensing. She had seen him kill the vastly more powerful Baram with little effort. He had worked his way out of Lalasa's most effective magicks. He had destroyed almost all of his fellow demons. Lenc ruled supreme in the land.

She faced him and felt no fear.

"You think I will rip out your eyes and then let you die?" he screamed. "Is that why you fail to quake in fright? I won't *kill* you, I'll torture you even more. I said I'd let you live for a year and a day. I'll stretch that into two years. Five! A decade!"

Kesira took two quick steps forward and swung her staff. The hard wood butt smashed into Lenc's leg just above the kneecap. The vibration traveling back along the wooden length told her the demon had become more jade than flesh, but the impact staggered him.

"You dare touch me? Worm!"

Kesira settled into a fighting pose. As Lenc came toward her, she estimated distances, then struck. The staff hit repeatedly, against head, on wrist, on knee, on ankle.

Lenc's bull roar told her she damaged not his body but his pride.

"Burn with my fire in your guts!"

Kesira kept her death song running through her mind, occupying her, forcing away fear. Everyone died eventually. Death was nothing to fear, unless death came by dishonor. She fought with a cold savagery she hadn't known she possessed. All that Lenc had done he would atone for. The tortures, the misery, the way he had taken Dymek away from her.

The staff crashed into the side of Lenc's head, sending him to his knees. For a brief instant, hope replaced the fighting calm that had taken over her senses.

"The runes spoke truly. You *are* vulnerable."

The expression on Lenc's face defied description. "I sent you no message of victory."

"You confused me before. No longer. I *can* read the rune sticks. I read your defeat."

Lenc laughed. "You think that I, killer of demons, cannot defeat a mortal? I play with you, nothing more."

Again he tried to send his fireballs to explode within her,

and again they failed to form properly. Kesira didn't question the source of her good fortune. That Lenc failed was enough to drive her forward. The nun slid both hands together on the staff and brought it up and then down in a vicious downward blow that ended on the top of Lenc's head. The sharp cracking noise told the tale.

His jade head had developed a small fissure. Like a man wounded and bleeding, Lenc reached up to touch the spot. He shook his head and got to his feet.

"You will die now, whore. No more toying with you."

Kesira measured her blow and landed it squarely on a jade kneecap. Lenc lurched to one side, off balance, but she didn't slow his advance. Massively powerful hands that had broken Baram's neck seized the end of her staff and wrested it away. Lenc held the stout quarterstaff so that one hand rested on each end of the rod. His chest expanded and he bent the ends downward, trying to force them together.

The staff exploded like lightning before he accomplished the feat. Lenc tossed aside the splinters.

"Come here. Let me kill you quickly. I will even be merciful and not let you suffer—long."

Curiously, Kesira kept calm. Fear was the killer, of mind and body and soul. She permitted it no entry into her thoughts. Lenc grabbed for her. She deftly ducked under his clumsy groping and slid her arm past. With a mighty heave, she threw the demon over her hip. He landed heavily, but unhurt.

"The rune sticks did not lie. I can best you."

Lenc's eyes blazed with the purest jade light. His lips curled back and ruined whatever handsome features he might have possessed. Kesira knew fear then. She could not hope to destroy the demon now that the full power of jade clouded his mind and robbed him of his soul. Lenc had succumbed to the lure of power untempered by wisdom.

He grabbed her by the arms and lifted. Feet free of the ground, Kesira could only feebly kick and twist. She tried to scratch and claw, but the power in the demon's grip proved too much for her to break.

"I'll pull you apart as I would a bug."

She gasped as he began pulling on her arms. Pain shot

into her shoulders. She knew that her arms would pop free of her joints at any instant.

"Merrisen, please, oh, Merrisen!" she cried. "Lalasa said you had survived. Help, Merrisen, help me!"

"Merrisen?" roared Lenc, sensing her pain and defeat. "I killed him. He was one of the first. I used a bolt of my white fire to sear him, then I turned him into the hardest of jade and shattered him. You might as well summon Gelya. I killed him with my fire, too!"

Kesira passed simple pain. Numbed, she stared directly into Lenc's face. The demon continued to apply the tension on her arms. Only seconds remained before he would rip them from her body.

The cessation of the pain took Kesira by surprise. Her pitiful kicks couldn't have caused Lenc to drop her as he did. She stared up into his contorted jade face and wondered at the confusion written in the planes and valleys.

"No," Lenc said, "it's not possible."

"You'll be defeated. The runes foretold it!" Kesira shouted. But Lenc looked not at her but past her. Kesira rolled over on the ground and saw Molimo standing quietly, arms dangling at his sides. In one hand he loosely held a sword. The expression on his face was unreadable.

Looking back at Lenc, Kesira saw the confusion replaced by sheer fright. All the panic and fear he had instilled in legions of others now boiled to the surface. The jade of his face turned noticeably whiter, showed more veining, actually began to chip away around the fissure she had started.

"It's not possible," Lenc muttered. "You're dead. You died by my hand, Merrisen!"

"No," said Molimo. "I did not die. But you will. You will die now!"

Lenc's scream of fear rattled Kesira's head and shook doors and windows in Kolya as Molimo advanced.

Chapter Fourteen

"MERRISEN!"

Kesira couldn't decide whether to watch Lenc or Molimo. The stark terror now seizing Lenc fascinated her, but the transformation in Molimo was even more astounding.

He grew in stature as he advanced.

"You're dead!" the jade demon screamed. "I turned you into jade and you shattered into a million pieces. You rained down on the mountains. I saw you die!"

Molimo shook as if he had been caught in a high wind. Kesira saw gray fur popping out around the collar of his tunic, the legs tightening and the arms changing.

"No, don't, Molimo, don't let the transformation take you!" she cried. But it happened. Molimo changed into the sleek gray wolf she had come to love and hate.

The wolf launched himself directly for Lenc. The jade demon fell backward under the impact of the heavy body. Savage jaws closed on Lenc's throat. Sparks jumped and scattered into the night like giant red cockroaches. No matter how hard Lenc hammered with his heavy fists on the wolf's flanks, those ripping teeth continued to tear at the rock-hard throat.

Lenc succeeded in rolling over. With a mighty blow, he sent Molimo reeling. The wolf hunkered down, green eyes matching those of the towering demon in intensity and promised death.

To Kesira's surprise, everywhere Molimo—Merrisen?—had bitten, tiny fractures appeared. If he had kept at Lenc's throat for even another minute, he would have decapitated the demon.

"How did you survive? How, curse you, Merrisen, how?"

Lenc's fear couldn't be denied now. Kesira looked for an opportunity to join in the fight again but saw nothing. Molimo circled warily, steaming saliva dripping from his fangs. Lenc tried repeatedly to send forth his fireballs. Each died a sizzling death just inches from his fingertips. Even the storm cloud that had followed the demon with its forbidding lightnings had abandoned him.

"Don't let him escape," Kesira called. "Kill him!"

Even as she shouted encouragement to Molimo, she wondered. The rune sticks had shown her to be the victor over Lenc, not Molimo—not Merrisen. If Lenc had not sent the message to give her false hope and then snatch away even this shred from her, had Merrisen sent the prophecy?

That struck Kesira as wrong, also. Molimo had been startled when she told him in the cell of the rune casting. There could be no other possibility than that the reading had been accurate. She, rather than Merrisen, would destroy Lenc.

How?

Kesira looked around for a weapon, something to use against Lenc. The low stone building that provided shelter for the Steel Crescent beckoned to her. She left Merrisen and Lenc and rushed to the doorway and peered inside. Rude bunks lined the walls, and the weapons racks down the center of the room stood empty. All of the Steel Crescent had gone into Kolya for whatever ceremony Lenc had ordered. Those not at the ceremony walked sentry duty elsewhere and had taken their weapons. She started away from the empty room when a white flash caught her eye.

The nun raced into the deserted room and reached under one of the bunks.

"A staff. Of stonewood! Gelya be praised!" She hefted the quarterstaff of wood sacred to her dead patron. She had experienced a surge of power when she'd made love with Molimo . . . Merrisen. The staff of the sacred wood in her hands made Kesira think she floated inches off the ground.

Racing back to where Lenc and Merrisen still battled, she stood close, waiting for the proper opening. When Lenc turned sideways to her, she swung the stonewood staff with all her might. A tiny explosion marked the spot where she connected with the jade demon's rib cage. His screech of pain signaled the damage she'd done.

"You've committed enough foul deeds," she said, moving closer. "For what you've done, you will die, Lenc. Die!"

She attacked. And missed. Lenc quickly turned and got her between him and Merrisen. With a brilliant burst of light, Lenc vanished.

Kesira stood, openmouthed. She turned and faced the gray wolf. The other-beast transformation worked its magicks and the wolf form vanished, to be replaced by the aging figure of Molimo she knew and loved.

"You're all right?" she asked.

"You fool!" Merrisen shouted. "I held him here. If you hadn't gotten between us, I would have finished him!"

"I didn't know," she said weakly. The man slumped and took her in his arms.

"Yes, all this must be confusing for you."

"You're Molimo? Or Merrisen?"

"Both. You know me as Molimo. When Lenc and I fought the first time, I underestimated his power. I thought the jade had only barely augmented his abilities. I erred."

"He really did turn you into a statue of jade?"

"And shattered me, sending me raining down all over the Yearn Mountains. But he grossly underestimated *my* power. While he had stripped me of all but the most feeble of mortal abilities, I was able to recover slowly."

Kesira stared at the man—the demon—in silence.

"I had lost my tongue; it regenerated over the months. All my power had fled, but it has now returned."

"That's why the jade affected you so strongly. You're a ...demon."

"Yes," Merrisen said softly. The green light in his eyes had died down, but flecks still showed in the ebony. "Power gone, I was invisible to Lenc. He believed I had perished and had no reason to hunt me down."

"That's why so many of the demons thought they recognized you."

"Wemilat did know me. He was a wise demon, one of the finest. And at the end, my lover Ayondela also knew me. By then, much of my power had returned, but her jade kept me weak."

"Your lover?" Kesira said in a choked voice.

"Ayondela was, at one time." Merrisen smiled. "Among demons, time passes slowly, and amusing ourselves is of paramount importance. Our liaisons are everything you mortals rumor them to be—and more." Sadness filled him now. "I speak as if nothing had changed. All that is past. The Time of Change is upon us."

"I don't understand."

"Remember what Gelya taught you of the Time. Gelya and I had our differences, not the least of which was the nature of the Time of Chaos. He instructed his followers differently than I did the few of mine." Merrisen straightened, his stature growing. "I admit my error now. Gelya has been proven correct."

"The demons are all gone? But you're still here." Fear caught at Kesira. "You can't go. You can't!"

"Moment by moment, my power returns. Our coupling provided the trigger for its full return—or perhaps I tapped a reservoir deep within you, a power source unlike another in mortal or demon. It matters little the cause. I am again able to confront Lenc. I must."

"I felt the power, too. I thought it came from you."

"A mutual exchange. It is as it should be, neither taking from the other but each giving to the other."

"But you're still growing older." Kesira reached out and lightly brushed her fingers along the heavily graying streaks in Merrisen's hair. The texture felt coarser to her than what was left of his dark black strands.

"I must hurry." Merrisen chuckled. "I begin to sound like Zolkan. Always in a hurry. For one with such a short lifespan, hurry is necessary. I realize that now."

"Zolkan's life might be limited. So might mine. But you're a demon."

"Look at me and tell me you don't believe I will soon die. That's why I must find Lenc quickly. Age takes my body, not my spirit."

"I want to help. Let me. You can't leave me behind. Not after all we've been through together."

He looked at her, green dancing with midnight-black in his eyes. "I am touched by the jade. It's an insidious canker chewing away at me. You see it most when I change shape. Don't let yourself become contaminated, too."

"I'm going with you."

Merrisen smiled. "Determination always was your strong point. Very well, Kesira. But don't make the mistake of getting between Lenc and me again. I can bind him to one spot as long as no one breaks the magical bond."

Kesira shrieked as the ground vanished beneath her feet. But she didn't fall. Again she found herself transported through space. Higher and higher she and Merrisen went. Kesira clung to his strong arm and marveled at the lines in his face, the aging. All that mattered little to her. When they had given Lenc the end he deserved, she would find a remedy for the evil jade's touch on Molimo . . . *Merrisen*, she quickly corrected.

"Terrible," Merrisen said. "Look at what Lenc has accomplished in such a short time." They swooped down over the capital of Limaden. Those in the streets walked with a listless shuffle. No children played. Vendors sat silently beside stands filled with rotting foodstuffs. All commerce had ceased. Worst of all, many of the fine monuments and temples had been razed.

"Lenc destroyed any shrine belonging to another patron," she said. Virtually every street, every block of buildings suffered Lenc's cruelly burning fire.

"He is still here. I sense his presence."

Kesira gasped again as they rocketed down to Emperor Kwasian's palace. The usual contingent of guardsmen stood about in ragged ranks holding unpolished weapons. One or two pointed at the strangers but none of them reacted with the usual swift challenge. Merrisen and Kesira landed lightly and walked under the alabaster arch leading to the inner courtyard of the palace.

"All my life I've heard of this," Kesira said in a whisper. "Never did I think to see it."

"Lenc stalks these halls. He thinks to reduce our will by torturing the Emperor and the Empress. No matter what he does to them, remember that he must be stopped now or his reign will echo down through the corridors of time."

"I know." Kesira's quick eyes darted about, taking in the splendor of Emperor Kwasian's court. The paving beneath her feet gleamed with mother-of-pearl. The walls were hung with the finest of tapestries—or so Kesira thought until she neared them. Vines of surpassingly fine leaf had been trained to grow in intricate patterns to form murals. To her even greater surprise, the coloration was provided by different types of vine; no one had painted the lovely pictures. The living tapestries stretched over three of the high walls enclosing the courtyard. In the center rose a carved marble fountain spraying four different-colored fluids in a continual rainbow that confused sight and appealed to other senses as well. The liquids were perfumes, mixing in fragrance as well as color. The fourth wall of the courtyard glowed with enough inner light to illuminate the entire area.

"It's like Lenc's fire," she said, staring at the wall. "Cold light. Dare we go through the portal?"

"That is Lalasa's doing. Her magicks were benign, cosmetic. And we must go inside. Lenc awaits us."

Merrisen walked quickly to the portal and passed through, but Kesira thought a slight hesitation came to his step the instant he came even with the archway. She followed more slowly, more cautiously. Once inside the palace proper, she stopped and simply gawked at the richness like a country bumpkin.

"Never have I seen such majesty."

The hallway to the audience chamber sported more gems than Kesira had imagined to exist in the entire world.

"It's said that Emperor Kwasian can stand on this very spot and peer into the jewels and see any point in his realm, any suffering no matter how minor, and be able to correct it."

"No longer," said Kesira. She pointed to the thrones Emperor Kwasian and Empress Aglenella had once occupied. In their places burned tiny white fires.

Merrisen closed his eyes and slowly turned through a full rotation. He went through a small passageway hidden from sight by a screen hand-painted with intricate scenes of the empire's victory over the barbarians. Then Merrisen hurried down the corridor and to a room, where he kicked open the door.

Kesira had thought herself invulnerable to shock. Lenc's evil had touched her and everyone else: what more could the jade demon do? But now Kesira found out.

Empress Aglenella hung naked in delicate golden chains. Thousands of tiny cuts riddled her skin—not deeply but enough to produce a sluggish flow of blood. The pain had driven her insane. She drooled and chuckled to herself in spite of her condition.

"Molimo—Merrisen," Kesira said, "is there anything you can do? She's our Empress. All her charities, all the good she's done for the empire . . . It's not right for her to end like this."

"I can do nothing. She has been damaged far beyond those wounds you see. Her skin is breached. So is her soul. Lenc has shown her atrocities beyond even my demonic understanding. There's only one gift we can give her."

For a moment Kesira didn't understand what he meant. When she did, lightheadedness assailed her. She had to support herself against one heavily jeweled wall.

"Do it, then. I have no heart for it." Tears streamed down Kesira's face as Merrisen stepped forward. The demon grasped Empress Aglenella's nose between thumb and forefinger. Tightening, he cut off her air. As she opened her mouth, he clamped his palm over it. She died quickly, relatively painlessly.

"She is beyond Lenc's control now."

"What else did he do to her?"

"He started with her sexual abuse by every guardsman." Merrisen held up his hand to forestall Kesira's protests. "The guardsmen might not even remember they did it. Probably not, or they would have killed themselves from the shame. Lenc probably found it amusing to be able to restore such memory at random and see the guards' reaction."

"He *started* her torture with rape by hundreds?" Kesira turned numb. "I don't want to know the rest. I just want Lenc dead."

Merrisen got a far-off look in his eyes. "He is near. With

Emperor Kwasian. In the rear of the palace. A makeshift dungeon, since the Emperor didn't have one of his own."

The demon walked off without even a glance at Kesira or Empress Aglenella. Kesira couldn't show such restraint. She had to take one last backward look at the Empress so adored by all in the empire. Her eyes refused to focus properly; all Kesira truly saw were the specks of blood staining the gold chains.

A bull-throated roar filled the palace. Merrisen hurried along toward it and burst into a room at the back of the throne room. A spiraling ramp downward had been crudely cut into the wood inlaid floor.

"Lenc's prison?" she asked.

Merrisen had already started down. "He won't escape this time. I drained him of a considerable portion of his power before. He hasn't had time to regenerate, even using more jade." Merrisen laughed without humor. "If he tries to use more jade, he'll cast himself into an immobile state. Our only problem then will be finding a sledgehammer to smash his head to powder."

"The Emperor," she gasped. What Lenc had done to Empress Aglenella was terrible. The horrors he continually applied to Emperor Kwasian were a thousandfold worse. Kesira took an involuntary step toward the man dangling upside down in the cruel chains before she realized Lenc was also in the room.

The jade demon tried to position her between himself and Merrisen. Kesira doubled up and rolled like a ball to one side.

"She knows my power, Lenc. And yours," said Merrisen. "You escaped by accident once. Not this time."

"I have recovered my strength. You are losing yours," accused Lenc. "Look at you. Already your hand shakes with age. Liver spots stain your flesh. Your hair turns white with the years."

"Such is the penalty of coming so close to the jade."

"That's the penalty of not embracing the jade! You could have ruled with me, Merrisen. The jade has made me invincible!"

"It's made you crazy." Merrisen sighed. "It might have

been inevitable. The Time of Chaos has been precipitated by your insane urge for power. Now all the demons are dead or dying."

"I still live. Tolek, also. But you, Merrisen, you will die!"

Kesira threw up her hand to shield her eyes from the brilliant flares as the two locked in combat. While they locked like a pair of mortal wrestlers, their battle became both physical and magical. Arms might break, but the real conflict came in the bursts of white fire, the flashes of intense jade green.

"They do go at it, don't they?" came a light, almost mocking voice. At first Kesira thought Emperor Kwasian had spoken, but the man still hung upside down and incapable of speech. The ruler's glazed eyes told of the tremendous psychic trauma he had endured.

Kesira pulled her eyes away from the battling demons and found the speaker. He sat cross-legged to one side of the crude torture chamber. It took several seconds for her to decide who this had to be.

"You're Tolek." The statement came out as an accusation.

"None other than. My, don't they make a majestic sight? Where are the sculptors when something truly dramatic happens? This ought to be captured for the mortals to ogle later."

"Help him, curse you!" Kesira cried. "Merrisen needs your help. Destroy Lenc!"

"Are you joking?" The demon appeared uneasy at the suggestion. "Lenc has allowed me to live. Granted, it gets lonely on that island where he exiled me, but I still live, which is more than I can say for the others." Tolek eyed her slyly. "Your Gelya, for instance."

"Do something. Help him! Fight your exile. Be brave!" She realized this was similar to begging the dirt to be water or the air to be stone. It wasn't in Tolek's nature. He had sold out his worshipers. Without his cowardice, Nehan-dir and the Order of the Steel Crescent would never have fallen into Lenc's power.

Kesira reached down to her blue knotted cord. She had used it on Kene Zoheret. It might work on Lenc, though she doubted it. She remembered how Merrisen had changed into wolf form and been unable to rip out Lenc's jade throat. But cracks had appeared. She had put them there herself with her staff. A chance still existed. Hope could not die so easily.

"If you won't help me, I'll try by myself."

If Kesira had thought to shame Tolek into aiding her, she failed. The tall, thin demon pointed and said, "Be my guest."

The tide of the battle ebbed and flowed, bringing the combatants back to where she stood. Kesira didn't understand the weapons used by either, but she knew Lenc could be stopped. The rune sticks had told her she could do it.

"Watch out!" Merrisen shouted. Kesira threw herself flat on the floor and avoided one of Lenc's cold, white fireballs. The screech from behind her, however, told that it had found a target.

Tolek burned in the center of a column of the pure white flame. He crumpled, leaving behind only dark, greasy ashes.

The two remaining demons continued their battle. Merrisen's arms locked around Lenc's body and held his arms at his side. This seemed to prevent the jade demon from launching his fireballs. But Merrisen took a brutal beating as Lenc smashed his head repeatedly into Merrisen's face. Bloodied, weakening—aging, to Kesira's horror— Merrisen could not survive long.

The knotted cord slipped from the nun's fingers when she remembered she had another weapon. From under the dirtied yellow sash proclaiming her to be Sister of Mission, she took the jade tusk. Lenc had been unable to see it, or perhaps he had discounted its danger. Kesira remembered how it slashed through steel and bone.

As she would lift a dagger for a downward stab, Kesira held Ayondela's jade tusk. Merrisen's eyes widened when he saw her. He grunted and whirled Lenc about in a tight circle so that the jade demon's back was exposed to Kesira. She lifted her jade weapon and brought it down on the base of Lenc's skull with all the power locked within her body.

The tip sparked when it touched jade flesh, and she realized mere physical strength wouldn't deliver the killing stroke. From inside, all of the goodness she possessed rushed upward to stiffen her resolve, to give her the energy needed. Added to this came the full force of her wrath for all that had been done to her and her world. Her nunnery destroyed by Lenc; her life in shambles because of the demon; Howenthal and Wemilat's death; Rouvin and Molimo's otherbeast affliction; Eznofadil and the frozen waves on the Sea of Katad; Ayondela driven mad by Lenc and the jade; the horrors Lenc perpetrated once he had triumphed.

The Time of Chaos.

Jade dagger point entered jade flesh at the base of Lenc's neck. The demon stiffened, then screamed. A sound like an explosion replaced the jade demon's death agony. Green dust erupted like a blizzard and finally settled across the room.

Lenc was no more.

Shaken, Kesira staggered back and found a wall. She slid down it and doubled up, hugging her knees. She felt as if nothing remained inside. Like a water jug during a drought, she was empty and dry.

"He's dead," she said in a flat, emotionless voice. "Dead."

When Merrisen didn't answer, she snapped out of her shock. "What's wrong? Molimo, please, Molimo!"

"Merrisen," he said weakly. "Molimo was only a name to keep you from suspecting. I had to hide from Lenc and the others until I regained my power. Now, there's no need."

"I'll never call you Molimo again."

"No," the demon said. Even as Kesira watched, he aged. His skin turned to parchment and the blue veins beneath pulsed spasmodically. "The Time of Chaos is at hand. We demons have had our day. Now it's time for . . . something more."

"Don't," Kesira cried, clutching his frail body as if she could prevent his death by force of will. "I love you."

"And I love you," Merrisen said. The green light in his eyes faded. "You have much to do. I see it now. You have so much to do. Zolkan will help you."

"Zolkan?"

"He was a messenger for many demons, and remained loyal to his ideals even when many demons did not. He will see your future clearly now that there are no more of us."

"Merrisen."

"My final gift. I will return you to Kolya. If you are truly the one I think—and you must be—you will know what must be done." His voice faded.

Their eyes locked and told more than simple words.

Do what you must, came the final words.

"No, Merrisen, no!"

Kesira grasped thin air. The aging body had vanished, replaced by the crisp cold of the field outside the Steel Crescent's headquarters. Alone, Kesira Minette sat in the field and cried for all that she had lost.

Chapter Fifteen

KESIRA MINETTE clutched herself tightly and sat in the field, crying. It hadn't been enough to have her sisters and order destroyed. The man she loved turned out to be a demon, and now he too was dead.

"Molimo," she sobbed. "Merrisen."

Kesira wiped the tears away and stared up into the cold darkness of night. Merrisen had returned her to Kolya for a reason. With Lenc dead, that could only mean one thing. She had to find what Lenc had done with Dymek. The bond between her and the boy strengthened even as she thought about it.

What else did she have left?

The world might be free of the evil posed by the jade demons, but everything else had turned to ash. Emperor Kwasian couldn't possibly survive his terrible wounds. Empress Aglenella hadn't. The empire lay in ruins.

"But demons are gone," came Zolkan's voice. The *trilla* bird waddled up to her and cocked his head to one side so he could study her. "You live. Bratling lives."

"Merrisen died," she said in a voice without emotion.

"I know. We were always closest. Of all demons, I loved Merrisen most."

"You could have told me."

"No," said Zolkan. "Merrisen did not want it that way. When Lenc first accepted jade, I carried message to others and was thrown into blizzard for my trouble."

"That's when you came into the sacristy? Even then you were allied with Merrisen?"

"Always," said Zolkan. "He watched me hatch and raised me from fledgling. I failed to warn him and found myself

171

trapped in your order's nunnery. Merrisen fought Lenc and . . ."

"I know the rest," Kesira cut in. "The jade rain, him posing as Molimo. He died of old age. He just kept getting frailer and frailer until he died."

"Time of Chaos," agreed Zolkan.

Kesira started to rise, then doubled over with pain in her belly. She dropped to one knee, arm across stomach. Dizziness almost cast her back to the ground.

"I've been through too much, I guess," she said. "Never felt this strange before."

"It gets worse," Zolken said. "You will find out."

"What are you talking about?"

As he had so many times in the past, Zolkan changed the subject. "Nehan-dir knows his patron is destroyed. There seemed to be some thread binding him and Lenc."

"Is he aware that *all* the demons are gone?"

"Doesn't matter to Nehan-dir. Events have driven him insane. Or maybe he sees opportunity to consolidate all of empire under his rule. Emperor Kwasian is dead, after all."

"He is?" Kesira wondered how Zolkan might know this. It didn't surprise her.

"Yes," squawked Zolkan. "I felt him die. Awful pain. Awful. Be many weeks before new Emperor can be chosen. In that time Nehan-dir can do much to forge his own domain."

Kesira stood and tried to straighten. She again bent double. "I don't feel well. Nausea. Everything's spinning."

"It happens quickly," Zolkan said. "You will be fine. Must go and save bratling."

"You've changed your mind about Dymek." She shivered. The name still didn't seem right to her. It had been given by Lenc, and that alone tainted it with evil.

"Merrisen showed new future. Time of Chaos must be ridden through with minimum problem. Then . . ." The *trilla* bird shook all over, sending a feathery shower in all directions.

Kesira saw that chaos would reign in the empire. Emperor Kwasian dead, all the demons gone, society itself would need an anchor. Where to look for it? She had no idea on that score. The foundation of society had been duty to Emperor and family. Everyone has known his duty, his place, and had performed his duties to the best of his ability. Whether it was a simple farmer, a moneylender dealing in exotic currencies, the Emperor or a beggar, all knew what was expected of them—and they did it.

The demons aided with philosophy and occasional intervention, but always before the aid had been intended to maintain the stability of society. Now that the leaders were gone, everyone would have to find new ways of keeping the fabric of the country together.

"I feel a little better now. Such a burning deep inside me. It churned, almost as if someone had shot me with an arrow." Kesira rubbed her stomach. All pain had vanished and a peace settled over her. Without even knowing she did so, her hand went to the tattered robe and the left breast below it. Wemilat's kiss glowed warmly, a comfort to ease any discomfort she might experience.

"Nehan-dir has whipped his mercenaries into a killing frenzy. They must cow all citizens in city before taking over. Without Lenc to enforce his will using his magicks, Steel Crescent might otherwise be deposed by angry people."

"What can we do?" Kesira hardly considered herself to be in any condition to rescue all of Kolya's citizenry, yet Dymek needed help. She had no idea where Lenc had sequestered the boy, but wherever it was, she had to be the one to arrive before Nehan-dir. The Steel Crescent leader would see Lenc's son as a threat to his own supremacy—or would use the boy as a figurehead to ensure that the Kolyans would buckle under to his reign. When the infant grew older, Nehan-dir would from necessity have to kill him.

Either way, Dymek would die. Kesira refused to allow that. She had already lost too much. Like a sailor drowning, she clutched at the feeblest of twigs.

As she and Zolkan began the walk into the deserted streets of Kolya, she asked, "What of Lenc's magicks? Do they linger or have they vanished when he died?"

"You think of Protaro?"

"No one should endure the agony he went through. The sight of him turning on that jade-green shaft tore at me almost as much as it did him."

"Jade power is big unknown. Protaro might have died or he might have been freed. We must see for ourselves."

"I hope he's all right."

"He is in disgrace," pointed out Zolkan. "He failed Emperor Kwasian. He did not do his duty."

"Against the jade demons? Against *us?*" Kesira laughed harshly. "We, the ones who have killed four jade demons, could hardly be expected to obey meekly."

"Danger, wait, wait!" the *trilla* bird squawked. Zolkan took to wing and quickly disappeared into the murky shadow of nighttime Kolya, now that its gaslights had flickered out from lack of attention. Only wan starlight and the occasional window that held a lighted oil lamp illuminated street and square.

Kesira kept walking, stopping only when she reached the corner of the Square of All Temples. The sight before her did little to convince the woman that her course was the proper one. Protaro still turned slowly in midair, the green shaft penetrating his gut. On the black slagged lava steps of Lenc's temple stood Nehan-dir. The short leader of the Steel Crescent waved his sword about wildly.

His words came to her as insane snippets. In a way she had hoped Nehan-dir had not succumbed to the madness of the jade. A rational leader might form new alliances, forge new bonds, bring the empire back to the old ways. If he understood his duty, she would not have been averse to seeing Nehan-dir as Emperor.

The thought flickered and vanished, a feather in a flame. Nehan-dir could never perform the duty of Emperor satisfactorily, she saw. He hadn't the total selflessness to place citizens above his own needs. He had been too warped by the Steel Crescent's poor choices of patron to think properly. Nehan-dir still saw the various patrons' actions and deaths as betrayal.

Gelya had not betrayed Kesira or his order when he died. His teachings lived on. Their truth or falseness would be the proof of the demon's worth. She mourned her patron's passing, but did not grieve over it to the exclusion of all else. It didn't matter how long anyone lived, but how well. Gelya had been kind, and everything he'd given humanity was proof of that.

A rush of air across her face brought Kesira around. Zolkan landed heavily. In spite of steeling herself for his landing, she sagged. The woman realized how feeble she actually was. Too much had happened too quickly to accept. She needed a long rest and time to meditate. Lenc's death seemed remote, Merrisen's a vaguely remembered dream. Both ought to be more, she knew.

"Well? What of Nehan-dir?" she asked.

"Bad, very bad," the *trilla* bird reported. "He has rousted out most of citizens for this rally. He executes any who dare voice opposition. Many are already dead."

"He's scarcely different from Lenc in that respect," she said.

"Nehan-dir has opposition within rank of Steel Crescent. Many others see opportunity for power. He has killed several, but others think to unseat little man."

"Stature has nothing to do with his determination." Kesira remembered the first time she had confronted Nehan-dir. The diminutive frame had fooled her into thinking he lacked strength. Both physical and spiritual strength lay within his scarred body. That she didn't agree with the course his spirit had taken did not detract from its power.

"How do we rescue Protaro? If we can't do anything about Nehan-dir right now, we ought to free the guard captain."

"You are expert when dealing with magicks. I always bowed to Merrisen on such matters. I report and little more." The bird rubbed his crested head against her cheek. She stroked over it, soothing him. For the first time she heard the pain of Molimo's loss in Zolkan's tone.

"You are much more. Always, Zolkan, always. Now, let's see about Protaro."

She slipped into deeper shadow and moved around the periphery of the sullen crowd. Nehan-dir continued to harangue, occasionally pointing at Protaro. The agony visible on the captive's face tore at Kesira's heart. The misery had not lessened. If anything, it had increased.

"Nehan-dir must leave square before rescue of Protaro is possible. Cannot go and take him down in plain view."

"I hate leaving him even an instant longer." Kesira considered. "I think I know how to free him, if we can get close enough. Somehow, I can interrupt the flow of magicks for a few necessary seconds. Twice Molimo—Merrisen— and I escaped the jade demons' prison cells that way."

"You destroyed Lenc's flame, too," Zolkan said, reminding her of how she had broken Ayondela's powerful curse that had laid an eternal winter on the land. "How close must you be?"

"I don't know. What did you have in mind?"

"Create diversion on far side of square. Nehan-dir chases me. You pull down rotating hero."

It sounded farfetched, but Kesira saw nothing else to try. If they waited for Nehan-dir to clear the square, he might declare it off-limits for all citizens. This would give Kesira no chance at all of rescuing Protaro. And, she had to admit to herself, thinking of him in such pain for even one second longer bothered her. How long could the man endure it without permanent damage?

Kesira didn't even consider the possibility that Protaro might have been driven insane already.

"Go," she said. "I must prepare. By the time you decoy Nehan-dir away, I will be ready."

"Don't fail. We get no second chance," said Zolkan. "Now, hurry, hurry! I go to annoy those pigeon shits!"

The *trilla* bird took to wing and circled. One or two of Nehan-dir's mercenaries saw and pointed. Nehan-dir ignored them—and Zolkan. Kesira closed her eyes and began the meditations that unleashed powers deep within her mind. She sank into the darkness of her soul and drew strength from Merrisen's memory. To her surprise, another hard, glowing point blazed inside. Unlike anything she'd detected in her meditations before, Kesira almost forgot about Protaro in an effort to probe this unexpected source of energy.

Zolkan's loud squawk pulled her back to her mission. The *trilla* bird dived down, then pivoted in midair, hindquarters pointed at Nehan-dir. The bird squawked as he deposited load after watery load on the top of the mercenary's head. Outraged at the soiling, Nehan-dir whipped out his sword and tried to impale the bird. Zolkan lightly flapped to one side, mouthing obscenities.

Nehan-dir's control was too tenuous for him to allow such open rebellion. He ordered his followers after Zolkan. The crowd squeezed into the square provided Zolkan the time needed for his escape. By the time the Steel Crescent soldiers forced their way toward the street taken by Zolkan, confusion reigned supreme.

Kesira silently walked into the square and stood where the old fountain had been. Above her slowly spun Protaro, the magical green shaft through his belly. His hands clung to the axle as he turned, but this did nothing to keep down the pain.

She looked up, her mind calm and ready. All the tricks she'd used before to rob the magical green barriers of their integrity came into play. And they failed. In frustration, Kesira summoned up the feelings when she had interrupted Lenc's column of white fire. It had been for only an instant, but it had released the world from the jade curse of perpetual winter.

"Almost," she sobbed, just missing it. The sensations within her defied description. Ineffable, they bordered on magic without actually entering that realm. "Again. Again!"

This time the brilliance blazing within her surged upward. She guided the seething power and focused it on the green shaft.

Protaro fell heavily to the square, freed of Lenc's magical punishment.

He rose to hands and knees. She had always thought the expression "sweating blood" had little basis in reality. Blood dotted the soldier's forehead. So extreme had been his pain that his insides oozed through his skin.

"Words can never say enough," Protaro gasped out. "My life is yours."

"I give it back—on one condition."

"Anything."

"Your life must be devoted to the teachings of Gelya."

Protaro stared at her as she helped him to his feet. "Even at this juncture you proselytize? You amaze me."

"Do you agree?"

"I'll need a teacher. I've been a soldier and know little of philosophies."

"I can instruct you. After all, I'm Sister of the Mission now."

"And we'll both be dead if Nehan-dir returns and sees I've been let down. If your patron's words show me how to perform such miracles, I'll happily learn anything you can teach me."

The people still milling in the square began to gather around Protaro and Kesira. The unwanted attention drew Nehan-dir's mercenaries back.

"Go away, go on!" Kesira shouted at the Kolyans, but it took the mercenaries' hard-swinging swords to clear a path.

"Up the steps to the temple," said Protaro. "Our only chance to get away before they reach us."

The pair raced up the black lava steps, only to find that Nehan-dir blocked their way. The Steel Crescent leader had wiped off the humiliations Zolkan had dropped on his head and stood with sword drawn.

"I wondered at the bird's timing. Where he goes, you have always trailed." Nehan-dir advanced on Kesira. "I felt it the instant Lenc died. While I do not know for certain, I feel you had a part in my patron's death."

"All the demons are dead," she said. Then, seeing this did nothing to placate Nehan-dir, she said, "Yes, I killed him. With my own hand I killed him. Lenc lies beneath the Emperor's palace, nothing more than powdered jade now."

"You killed him and Howenthal. Every patron of the Steel Crescent, you kill."

"Tolek died, also. Lenc turned him to ash with a single speck of white fire."

Nehan-dir spat. "So be it. Tolek sold us. We don't need them. Any of them. Good riddance to all demons! We have the chance now to take our own destiny in hand."

"You won't be the one guiding that destiny," said Protaro. "The Emperor won't permit it."

"The Emperor's dead," snapped Nehan-dir. "Oh, you didn't know that? But of course not. You were swirling around and around, letting your guts turn to mush."

"You'll never replace Emperor Kwasian. There are others," said Kesira, seeing the train of Nehan-dir's logic.

"I'll carve my own empire. Let those in Limaden do as they please. Let them rot! Here in Kolya I'll build the foundation for a kingdom of my own!"

Protaro rushed the small man, giving him no chance to use his drawn sword. Fists hammering, feet kicking, Protaro attacked with all his might. Although weakened by his ordeal, Protaro proved a worthy opponent. But Nehan-dir was rested, and stronger than his thin frame suggested. They locked together and rolled over and over on the rough lava, lacerating backs and arms, knees and hands.

Kesira had started to help Protaro but halted when a sharp pain lanced into her side. One of the mercenaries blocked her, dagger ready. "Let them fight," the man said past a harelip. "If the wrong one wins, well, then I'll have to kill Nehan-dir myself!" He laughed with his twisted mouth; but the look in his eyes stayed ice cold.

Nehan-dir got one leg between his body and Protaro's. A powerful kick sent the guardsman somersaulting through the air to land heavily at the foot of the lava steps. Protaro swung back, facing Nehan-dir's sharp sword.

Just as the mercenary lunged, a green streak plummeted to strike at his wrist. Zolkan's talons raked four long, bloody gashes along his forearm. Nehan-dir screeched, more in surprise than pain. He spun to engage Zolkan; Protaro dived and knocked Nehan-dir to the ground.

When the man holding his dagger at Kesira's side tried to kick Zolkan as he waddled back from the fray, Kesira acted. One slender-fingered hand gripped a brawny wrist. She pulled slightly. Placing her other hand on the wrist she jerked backward, using her entire weight against that arm. The mercenary yelped with pain as his arm popped from the shoulder socket. She finished him with a kick to the throat. He lay gasping for a few seconds until Zolkan ripped repeatedly at throat and face.

"That wasn't necessary," Kesira chided.

"He tried to kick me. Pigeon-shit mercenary."

Kesira waved back others coming up the steps. They stared at her, then at their leader locked in mortal combat with Protaro, and then they obeyed.

A shove from Protaro sent Nehan-dir stumbling' back. When Zolkan plucked up the fallen dagger that had been aimed at Kesira's heart and tossed it to Protaro, the odds became more even.

Nehan-dir with his sword circled warily around Protaro and the dagger.

Kesira expected Protaro to be at a disadvantage, even with his longer reach. But she underestimated the man.

The nun blinked, and in that split second Protaro made his move. Kesira opened her eyes to see Nehan-dir stiffen, his face devoid of expression. The tiny webbing of pink scars on his face glowed, then faded. His sword clattered to the lava steps and down to the square. Nehan-dir toppled after it like a felled tree.

Bloody dagger in hand, Protaro stood on the steps. Long years of command came into play. He pitched his voice in the proper fashion to ensure swift obedience.

"Go home, citizens of Kolya. Go home and rest from your ordeal. It is over. And mercenaries of the Steel Crescent . . ." he said, pausing. Kesira saw dozens of them tense. "You are not responsible for leader or patron. I grant you amnesty. Take it or die."

"What are we to do?" demanded one of the Steel Crescent at the side of the steps.

"The empire needs rebuilding. Emperor Kwasian is dead. So are all our patrons, the demons. We are alone now, and much depends on the next few years, how they are spent, what steps we take to maintain order."

"We can become brigands," muttered one.

"Do, and we will hunt you down like animals," shouted Protaro, angry. "Be productive, not destructive. We have all suffered enough. Do not add to the confusion and misery still stalking our land. Now go!"

Those living in Kolya drifted away, silent. The Order of the Steel Crescent left at a slower pace, talking quietly among themselves. Only when the square was entirely deserted did Protaro collapse.

Kesira ran to him and propped him up, head in her lap. For a heartrending moment, she thought he'd suffered a fatal wound at Nehan-dir's hand. A quick examination showed only superficial injuries from the fight. To her amazement, not even a red spot showed where Lenc's green shaft had penetrated the soldier's body and left him suspended in the air. The only evidence of that cruel torture Protaro carried within him as memory. Kesira was glad to see that the exhaustion that caused the weakness was due to all that had happened and not to weakness of spirit.

"They listened," he said in wonder.

"You are a potent leader."

"A leader of nothing. My troop is dead. I failed Emperor Kwasian."

"And you owe your life to Gelya. You've made a good start to restoring peace to a land twisted by suspicion and death."

Protaro said nothing for a few minutes, then, "You still seek the boy?"

Kesira nodded.

"He is within the temple. I heard Nehan-dir mention it."

"He may be Lenc's son, but I have been a mother to him. I cannot abandon him now. Without Lenc's evil, there is hope. Gelya can guide Dymek, with words if not presence."

Leaning on each other, Protaro and Kesira went up the last of the steps to the temple door. There Zolkan huddled, grumbling loudly to himself.

"Did you find Dymek?" she asked.

"Didn't look. Best to leave."

"That isn't what Merrisen wanted for the boy. It's not what I want, either. Get out of my way." Kesira pushed past the *trilla* bird.

She stopped, heart rising to clog her throat.

"I warned you," squawked Zolkan.

Dymek, Lenc's son, stood encased in a pillar of the jade

demon's white fire. Even from a distance of a hundred feet, Kesira felt the evil fire's power.

For all eternity the boy would be trapped inside that magically raging inferno.

Chapter Sixteen

"IT CAN'T BE. No!" Kesira screamed. She dropped to her knees and stared. The dancing pillar of flame totally engulfed the boy. What horrified Kesira even more was Dymek's size. He was no longer the infant to be carried in her arms and suckled at her breast. He might have been four or five years old, standing trapped in the center of the white flames.

"Lenc wanted his son safe. This is how the demon did it," said Zolkan. "No way to free bratling."

"There must be. We did it before."

"Merrisen was there before. He might not have possessed full power, but he did have some left after first battle with Lenc."

Kesira feared that the *trilla* bird spoke the truth. Why should she have any power? She was nothing but a nun from an order long since destroyed. Even if Gelya had lived and her order had survived, what made her think she held the reins of any power at all unusual?

"The rune sticks. I can cast them and read the future," she said, clutching at the thinnest of hopes. "Molimo— Merrisen—said that was a skill few had, even in the demons' ranks."

"True," said Zolkan, "but that is far from being able to free boy from Lenc's magicks."

Kesira stood and slowly advanced. The crackling sounded louder. Only cold radiated from the flames, but she felt a fire burning within her. Kesira had to squint a little to see Dymek standing unconcerned and even expectant.

"We have to get him out. Remember how I destroyed

Eznofadil's power? How I destroyed the white flame powering Ayondela's spell?"

"You didn't destroy it," said Zolkan. "You only interrupted flow of magicks. Much different."

"Can you do that again?" asked Protaro. "Interrupt the flow for a few seconds? I don't know what you're talking about, but if you can release the barrier around the boy for even five seconds, I can go in, grab him and get back out."

"No," Kesira said. "That's too dangerous. The times I've thwarted the demons' spells have been for very brief durations. Less than two or three seconds."

"Let's get closer." Protaro tried, but the force of the white fire drove him back.

"You can never reach boy in three seconds. Or five," said Zolkan.

"And you'd never be able to fly in, grab him in your claws and fly out, either," Kesira told him firmly.

"Not thinking about it." The bird looked hurt that she'd believe him possible of such an altruistic act. "Merrisen wanted boy to live, for some reason."

"Why not?" asked Protaro.

"Would you be willing to hasten your own death?" Zolkan squawked. "Boy is at front of Time of Chaos. Demons die, humans muddle along, gods arise. No one likes to become obsolete, even a demon."

Kesira didn't bother listening to Zolkan and Protaro discuss possible means of entry. She circled the column and found no weakness. The spell had been wrought perfectly. Closing her eyes, she settled herself for the effort. She'd done it before. Calmness. Find the proper spot, twist with that portion of her soul so well trained by Gelya.

She remembered the feelings when she had blanked out the magical cell door in Lenc's dungeon. She duplicated it. The power rushed through her, into the fire—and away.

"Brief flicker," said Zolkan. "Nothing more."

"Maybe I do need Merrisen," she said glumly. "But we can't just *leave* him there. We can't!"

"Tunnel in from below?" suggested Protaro. "I don't see any chance of dropping in from the temple roof. It's too high, and the flames come together in an arch."

Kesira didn't have to try it to know that tunneling beneath the column wouldn't work. The *feel* was wrong. She had matched wits with the jade demons for long months now, and such an easy solution would reveal traps carefully laid by Lenc.

"Is there no one else who can perform such spells?" she asked out loud, not wanting an answer. She quickly ran through a list of all who had even a passing hint of magic at their command.

Most were dead and buried. Not for the first time did she miss Molimo.

She turned when she heard Protaro dragging something across the stark black temple floor. He had several long wooden beams which he dropped at her feet.

"We build a barricade," he said. "The flame can't chew through these thick beams too fast. And if they do, then you just shove a bit more into the flame and force the fire to digest that, too. We make a tunnel from the beams and I crawl down the center. When the fire wall is breached, I go and get the boy."

Zolkan only snorted from his perch on Kesira's shoulder.

"The fire is different," she said, trying to explain to the guardsman. "It doesn't take time to burn the wood, even wood soaked with water. It'll come directly through."

"What have we to lose?"

Kesira watched in silence as Protaro sweated over the exact arrangement of the beams he lugged in from outside. The man constructed a tunnel hardly wide enough for his broad shoulders. When he'd finished, he began sliding it toward the fire.

"Tell me when I break through the fire. Maybe the boy can crawl out on his own and save me the trip."

Protaro kept shoving and Kesira stayed silent. When a full five feet of the crawlway had vanished through the fire, Protaro stopped and simply stared. The fire didn't merely burn; it evaporated the wood. The lightest caress of wood to fire brought about instant destruction.

"How does the boy live inside?" marveled Protaro.

"Might be different inside. Lenc's magicks were not often subtle, but he could do it when he tried," said Zolkan.

Kesira wobbled a bit on her feet. Protaro grabbed her around the shoulders and supported her. "Are you ill?"

"Dizzy again. Was like this when . . . when I got back from Limaden. Must be the effect of Lenc's death. Magicks everywhere. Got caught in some residual spell."

"Pigeon-shit idea," muttered Zolkan. "No such thing as residual magic."

Kesira sagged and Protaro caught her up in his arms. "Let's get out of here," he said to the *trilla* bird. "Nothing we're going to do for the moment. If we rest, eat and then have the chance to think on it, we'll do better."

"Good idea. Glad *someone* cares about his belly. Haven't eaten in days." The *trilla* bird hopped over to Protaro's obliging shoulder and rode out on this new perch as the soldier carried an unconscious Kesira.

"Where?" Kesira jerked erect in the bed, afraid. She didn't know where she was or how she'd gotten here. The last she remembered was the hypnotically dancing white flame encasing Dymek.

"You're all right," came Protaro's soothing words. "You slept for almost a full day. It's just now dusk—the day after our skirmish with Nehan-dir."

"The inn," she said, finally recognizing the place. "Where's the innkeeper?" When she remembered how he had died, she dropped back to the soft bed. "Lenc killed him. It's all clear now. All of it."

"Want some food? There haven't been any customers at the inn, so I've been helping myself to the food rather than let it spoil. I cook a good trail stew."

The thought of food made Kesira's stomach churn uneasily. "No, not right now. I just want to lie and rest."

Kesira drifted off to a troubled sleep, a sleep populated with a burning Dymek and a leering Lenc, gentle Merrisen turning ancient before her eyes, small children frolicking in a grassy meadow. When she again awoke, the thought of food pleased her, and she ate voraciously.

"My cooking's not that good," Protaro commented. "So you must be hungry." He leaned back and hiked his feet up to the immaculately clean tabletop. The innkeeper had done well here. His presence would be missed.

"What are you thinking?" Kesira asked.

"Things are different for me," the guardsman said slowly. "My debt of honor requires repayment, but the death of Emperor Kwasian and Empress Aglenella erases that. I owe you my life and have pledged myself to learn the teachings of Gelya." Protaro idly wiped up a droplet spilled on the table. "Never thought about running a tavern before. Don't see that the innkeeper had any relatives, and no one seems to mind that I've been running this place."

"You want to stay?"

"Being a soldier is all I know. Might be able to find a local militia that requires some leadership to fight off the brigands. No matter who's Emperor, that's always going to be a problem."

"But you don't think so?"

Protaro shook his head. "Kolya's not a bad city. Been through hard times, but haven't we all? I don't think the life of chasing across the country holds the appeal for me that it once did."

"Your commission wasn't inherited?"

"Earned it. I had risen as far as I could unless I somehow found myself elevated to nobility. Not likely, not for a beggar's son. If I died in service, then I might have made one more promotion."

Kesira knew the dilemma faced by most in the Emperor's Guard. The highest posts were hereditary offices. No one could work through the ranks and achieve more than Protaro had. If he'd died nobly, the Emperor might have seen fit to promote him posthumously to commander. There was no other way for Protaro to rise.

"Innkeeping is an honorable profession."

"Any is, as long as it fulfills a need," Protaro said. A long silence descended.

Finally, Kesira said, "You want me to free you from your vow to serve Gelya, don't you?"

"Innkeepers have little need for intricate philosophy, other than that spouted drunkenly over the rim of a frothy mug of ale. That's not the same, is it?"

"No." Kesira heaved a deep breath. "You are released. I should never have bound you. I erred. Gelya taught that promises freely given are always observed but those extorted are always regretted. Learn what Gelya taught, if it pleases you."

"The demons are dead," said Protaro. "We must stumble along our own path, without their guidance."

For the first time Kesira faced the fact that her order was gone, as were all the others. She and she alone remained of the hundreds once devoted to Gelya. She would never be able to recruit enough novices to found a new nunnery, a new order. A different path had to be found.

"The old times are dead," she said quietly.

"Yes," sighed Protaro. "Every morning offered a noble chance, and every noble chance brought with it someone willing to seize the opportunity."

"That can be again," Kesira said. "Hope cannot die this easily. The demons are gone, our Empire lacks a leader, but soon, like water seeking its level, all will settle down into a new pattern."

"I've ceased desiring to make waves in the pattern."

Kesira shook herself and knew that Protaro had changed. So had she. "Where's Zolkan? I haven't seen his green feathers since I awoke."

"He said he was going out to kill a pigeon or two. Work off his frustrations."

"I need him. If we are to pry loose Dymek from his father's infernal spell, we must get at it again."

Kesira turned and stared at Protaro when he didn't respond. She read accurately the expression on his face.

"What's changed since yesterday? Dymek hasn't been freed, has he?"

Protaro stood and began wiping at the already clean table. "The people. They've decided that no one will be allowed to even try to free Dymek. Lenc drove it home to them constantly that Dymek was his son, his successor. They don't want to release another demon on the world."

"They can't stop me from trying!"

"Right now, a dozen armed guards patrol the base of the temple. No one can enter for any reason."

"I will."

"I agree that this fanaticism on their part will fade as the months wear on. Once Kolya is again a thriving town, there'll be no reason to waste time prowling about and thrusting spears at shadows near Lenc's dark temple. But until then, isn't it best that you leave Dymek where he is?"

"What would you have answered if Dymek had said, 'Isn't it best we leave Protaro with that shaft through his guts?'"

Protaro sank down to one of the benches. He shrugged and tried to smile. Even his second attempt failed.

"What do you want me to do?"

Kesira's mind began turning over various plans, examining and discarding them, then moving on to others. Somehow, she'd free Dymek. She would!

"Bad hunting now," complained Zolkan. "No pigeons about."

"We don't want activity, we want sleep," Protaro said in a low voice. "Only two hours till dawn. I've seen sentries fresh on their post fall asleep at this time of night."

"Three of them," Kesira reported, "all in front of the temple on the square. They're sitting with their backs to the temple—seem to be nodding off."

"See?" Protaro ruffled Zolkan's feathers, and the *trilla* bird replied with a vicious clacking of his beak just inches from the offending fingers.

"How will this be different?" asked Zolkan. "We get inside, and then what? We sit about and stare at the trapped bratling?"

"I . . . it'll be different," Kesira said. "I sense that it will."

"You're still sick," said Protaro. "You're drawn, and your hands shake. Let's wait until you've had a chance to rest some more. Another day or two. That'll aid us also in getting past the guards. In only one day they've fallen off from a dozen to only three. In a week, no one will guard this place."

"Now. Let's go."

Protaro started to argue, but found himself talking to Kesira's back. "She knows her own mind," said Zolkan. "Always gets her into bad trouble."

"Us, too," said Protaro.

"I can fly away. What about you?" Zolkan appeared smug that he had gotten back at Protaro for ruffling his headcrest.

As silent as three shadows, they drifted along the black lava steps and up to the opened doors leading into the temple. The cold light emanating from within told them that Lenc's magic still fired the column imprisoning Dymek.

"Keep watch," Kesira told Protaro. She and Zolkan hurried to within twenty feet of the white fire. Through the shifting curtain of flame she saw Dymek's gently smiling face. The boy waved to her, as if preparing to go on a short trip.

Kesira moaned suddenly, then bent double. Protaro rushed to her side.

"Get back there. Don't let anyone in. I'll be all right. It's just something I ate. Still nauseated."

Kesira pushed Protaro away and turned her attention to the pillar of fire. She straightened, her mind taking control of her body. All discomfort vanished. She worked on the litanies Gelya had taught; she found the verses to her death song, now likely to run much longer. The rhythms, the flows, the urgencies all were hers.

She struggled to regain the power she'd had when she thwarted the magical barriers. She struggled and she succeeded. Kesira didn't let herself exult in it; she needed concentration, a negation of self in favor of the power. It flowed; she used it.

The white fire Lenc had used as his sigil and as his weapon flickered.

"Close. Almost. More, more!" urged Zolkan.

Sweat beaded her forehead even though the coldness from the fire chilled her to the bone. Emotions crippled her efforts. She pushed them away and concentrated totally.

For what seemed hours, Kesira fought to lift the magicks surrounding Dymek. She fought and failed. There wasn't enough left within her. She'd used it all. But the nun refused to give up. She again settled her emotions and reached within herself, but the needed energy simply wasn't there.

And then it was.

From a bright, burning point in her abdomen came a rush

of power that dazzled her. Flowing like the ocean, like the winds whipping across the world, it erupted and touched Lenc's pillar of fire.

As a candle is extinguished by a hurricane's full force, so did the white fire vanish into nothingness.

Dymek walked forward as if nothing had happened. The little boy—already waist high when measured against Kesira—held out his hand and smiled.

"Thank you," he said simply.

"Dymek!"

She dropped to her knees and hugged him. In that instant she knew the name Lenc had given him was the proper one. No other name fit.

"Kesira! One of the guards heard us. He went and fetched the others. There must be hundreds of them now. We've got to get out of here. Right now!"

Kesira jerked Dymek along by his arm, his short legs barely able to keep up. She didn't question him about his rapid growth. She had seen Merrisen age almost before her eyes. She hoped Dymek wouldn't grow old and die within weeks or months, too.

"There's only the front way out." Protaro skidded to a halt. More than fifty armed men blocked the way to freedom.

"They've freed the demon child. Kill them! Kill them all!"

"Wait!" shouted Protaro. "This isn't the demon's son. Lenc lied. Dymek is the son of peasants. He's just a child. How can one so young be a threat to you?"

Protaro's face paled when he pointed to what he'd thought would be an innocent-appearing child. Dymek's piercing gray eyes bespoke of infinite wisdom and experience, of sophistication far beyond any of the mercenaries threatening him. Only in size did he seem like a human child.

The crowd shoved Protaro out of the way in their haste to get to Kesira and Dymek.

"Stop," Kesira said, her voice almost too low to be heard. It was as if a mighty hand grabbed those in the crowd and restrained them. "You do not know me, but I am a sister of the Order of Gelya. Of all those in Kolya, I hated Lenc the most for what he'd done."

"No!" "Impossible!" came the cries.

"True," she said. Her voice carried the snap of authority. "My sisters, my order, my entire world were destroyed by the jade demons—and I destroyed them, each of them. Eznofadil and Howenthal and Ayondela and finally Lenc. I slew *four* jade demons."

Absolute silence greeted this statement.

"Believe me or not, I went into Howenthal's Quaking Lands. I met and defeated Eznofadil. I climbed Ayondela's accursed mountain and there she died."

Dymek tugged on Kesira's sleeve. "You forget," the boy said. "I'm the one who killed Ayondela. I cried and she shattered. Her entire temple came down in a rain of jade dust."

This caused the crowd to begin muttering again.

"I am beloved of demons," Kesira said, motioning Dymek to silence. "Wemilat gave me his mark. You all know Wemilat the Ugly, a good and kind patron." She exposed her breast where the lip print glowed warmly. "This mark ensures that Dymek will never be touched by evil. Lenc imprisoned him, but this mark proclaims him free of any taint of jade."

"She might be lying," came the uneasy words. "That *is* Lenc's son."

"I am," Dymek said in his unsettling voice. This created another stir.

"He is Lenc's son, but I protect him. I have fought alongside the finest of the demons. Wemilat and Merrisen. I loved and was loved by Merrisen. Lenc killed him with the jade. I cannot ever allow that green curse to happen to another."

"Kill them. Kill them all!" The cry started out as a ragged chant, then grew in volume as more and more got caught up in the power of a mob.

Dymek started to speak, to cry out. Kesira clamped her hand over his mouth to stifle his death-giving shrieks.

"Let us go!" she shouted. "Let us leave Kolya and we will never return."

The bright spot glowing within her flared once more.

The same power that had snuffed out Lenc's fire now bowled over those in the crowd. They stumbled and fell, leaving a pathway for Kesira and Dymek.

Zolkan fluttered back down to her shoulder. "What of Protaro?" he asked.

"They didn't even notice him. He'll be fine. We must find horses and ride from here, ride and find a place to live."

"Know good spot," said Zolkan. "One where you and Dymek and Suzo can live."

"Suzo?"

Kesira walked more rapidly to get away from Lenc's temple. The threat of the crowd diminished, but she felt the need for haste. The sooner they left Kolya, the easier she'd feel.

"Suzo is her name. Daughter Merrisen sired. One growing inside you."

"I'm pregnant? By Merrisen?"

Hurry, came the command within her.

"Yes, Suzo is right. Let's hurry," said Dymek.

Kesira obeyed. She could do nothing less.

Epilogue

GENTLE BREEZES laden with the sharp tang of sea salt blew across the meadow and up the slopes of the low mountain. Below, in a misty fog, rolled the blue Sea of Katad. Above, cloaked in the purple haze of distance, rose the lofty peaks of the Sarn Mountains. All around Kesira Minette were peaceful, grassy pastures bursting with the promise of warm summer and just beginning to catch spring-fire with brilliant blossoms and verdant leaves.

Kesira sighed as she sat back against a dead stump and looked downslope to the sea. It had been only three years since that lovely expanse of bright water had been frozen into viciously edged cutting waves. No more. She saw a few fishing boats working the shoals and bringing in their catch. Above drifted white and pink seabirds, wary of predators like Zolkan.

Try as she might, Kesira couldn't find the green-plumed *trilla* bird in the air. He might have tired of soaring on the thermals and come to rest. Or, knowing him, he'd gone down the coast to one of the ports to trade improbable stories with other *trilla* birds shipping on the freighters as navigators.

She plucked a juicy blade of grass and sucked on the bitter juices. Mouth watering, Kesira wondered if it were possible for life to get any better. Here she had no worry, no want; she passed the time as she saw fit and everyone was happy and healthy.

Tipping her head up to catch both the liquid warmth of the burgeoning sun and to see the puffs of white cloud, Kesira felt a lethargy creeping over her. So peaceful. She just wanted to sleep.

She did, and when she awoke it was to the sound of heavy bootsteps tramping on the freshly rain-dampened ground.

"Kesira!" A figure dressed in a crimson tunic and leather breeches waved. She waved back.

"Up here, Protaro."

Protaro climbed the slope and, out of breath, dropped beside her. "I'm not used to exertion like this. The life of an innkeeper appeals more and more to me."

"It was good of you to come and see me. You didn't have to."

"You never come to Kolya. If I want to see you, I have to come here." They sat side by side, silent, lost in their own thoughts.

"There's no need for me to leave here. I am content," she said after a while. "Such harmony not even Gelya preached. Every insect knows its place. Look." Her fingernails dug into the stump she'd used for a backrest. Termites squirmed under the sunlight, diving back down well-drilled tunnels into the heart of the rotting stump. "They know their duty, do it and live well. In a year the stump will be returned to the soil."

"It's always been that way. This isn't something new."

She noticed the man's uneasiness. "This is the way it is with *all* things now. Men do not fight men. There's harmony once more in the empire. Emperor Benniso rules wisely and well. Everyone knows his station and duty; everyone performs it."

"Are you happy with your duties?" Protaro's discomfort grew. His eyes darted around the peaceful meadow as if looking for a band of brigands. The last of the roving thieves had died over a year prior, at the request of the children, but Kesira didn't tell Protaro that. It would only add to his restlessness.

"My duties are few now. The children are mature."

"I saw Suzo but not Dymek. She looked to be eleven or twelve."

"Dymek is a handsome young man. He told me the other day that he wasn't going to allow himself to age any further. He might pass for seventeen." Kesira smiled. "That will change. In a few years he'll prefer to look older. That'll give him more credibility."

"Does a god need credibility?" asked Protaro.

"Even a god," she said. Again the silence fell between them. *Trenly* crickets chirped, and flying insects intent on pollination flitted from flower to bright flower sucking nectar. "Especially a god. Being all-powerful isn't enough. Coercion is never as good as allowing your followers to ... follow."

"Lenc tried to force worship. His son does better?"

"Dymek knows—and he cannot make the mistakes of his father. Lenc was a demon; Dymek is a god." Kesira sighed. "The Time of Chaos, they called it. The demons' name, and a poor reflection of what has actually happened."

"For them it was chaos. They died."

"And the gods were born. You know that Dymek and Suzo talk of their children? Not any time soon, mind you. Thousands of years from now, but already they talk of their successors. That was something the demons couldn't."

"Their human traits got in the way," said Protaro. "The demons were shortsighted, even more than humans, because all their traits, both good and bad, were magnified."

"That might be. I doubt it. The demons were imperfect, a steppingstone to ... them." Kesira pointed to where Dymek and Suzo walked on the far side of the meadow. Deep in discussion, they seemed oblivious to the world around them, yet faint touches of thought brushed over Kesira's mind.

"They say hello," she said. Protaro jumped as if someone stuck him in the side with a dagger. "Don't be like that, dear friend," she said, reaching out to touch Protaro's arm and calm him. "They are gods and have a god's interest, but that doesn't mean they ignore everyone around them. They seem aloof only because we cannot understand their concerns. Would you believe that Dymek actually worries over the extinction of a single species of insect on the far side of the empire? And it won't happen for another four hundred years."

Protaro shook his head. "They make me uneasy."

"But they will not harm you."

"That bug they talk about might be us. It might be all of us."

"Yes," Kesira agreed softly. "It might be."

She took his hand and led Protaro down the slope to the small house where she lived. Dymek and Suzo had long since moved out to live under the sun and stars, to feel the elements against their skins and be that much closer in contact with their world.

"My ale suffers in comparison to yours, I'm sure, but will you have some anyway?" She poured a mug of the frothing brew and slid it across the table to Protaro.

"It's good, but you're right; that which I buy for the Stonewood Inn is better." This struck Protaro as ludicrous. "You can have *them* conjure anything you want. Why settle for second-best in anything?"

"Live like the Emperor, you mean? In a fine palace, with servants waiting on me every instant of the day, satisfying any whim I might have? It doesn't suit me. I was raised a nun and have simple tastes. Even now, I haven't changed that much."

"What of the bird?"

A loud squawk announced Zolkan's arrival. He flapped through a partially opened window without touching the frame and landed heavily on the edge of the table. Zolkan found the spot where his talons had left familiar marks and formed a rude perch.

"Saw you coming but wanted to finish hearing from Zeeka. She travels the coastline all way to Clorrisai. Need new victuals for inn? She can provide them at a discount through her humans. Rare foods. But you must hurry. She leaves soon. Hurry, hurry."

Protaro laughed for the first time. "Zolkan, you never change. No, I'm content with what I have."

"Content. All humans are only content. Is no one happy? Sad? Always content. Damn bratlings."

Protaro recoiled, waiting for the gods to strike the *trilla* bird down. Nothing happened.

"They are kind, Protaro. It is so hard to believe that after the atrocities done to us by Lenc and the other jade demons, but these are gods."

"Born of human and demon, just as the demons were born of animal and human."

"They have transcended most of the faults in humans. Only the best is there, and magnified, as in the demons. They are more than human, but only in the good ways." Kesira sipped at her ale. "And I think they have abilities unknown to humans. Even I cannot guess at them."

"How long do you stay, Protaro?" asked Zolkan.

"I am only passing through, just for the single day. I've been to the coastal fisheries to arrange for fresh catch to be iced and then shipped overland to Kolya. Good prices. I'll make the Stonewood Inn the best in the city or know the reason." Protaro took a large drink, then dropped the mug to the table with a loud, ringing bang. "Why not join me on the way back to Kolya, Zolkan?"

He addressed the *trilla* bird but looked at Kesira.

"Good change of pace. I tire of not being able to understand Dymek and Suzo. Demon talk was plain. Not theirs." Zolkan launched himself and deftly turned in midair. "Let's be off. Much distance to travel this day."

"Patience, Zolkan. How about you, Kesira? Will you join us, too?"

More than a simple request for company went with Protaro's words.

"You two go on. I may decide to join you later in the summer."

"You aren't needed here. They can care for themselves."

"Go on. If I decide I can leave, I'll see you in Kolya. Later."

Protaro nodded and quickly left, Zolkan perched on his shoulder and chattering away about the sea, about Zeeka and her pet sailors, about a thousand other things. Seeing Protaro reminded her of Molimo—Merrisen—and brought a tear to her eye. She wiped it away quickly. The past was so sad, so strange—and gone.

Kesira watched them go down the winding gravel path and finally vanish from sight in the direction of the village, knowing she'd never join Protaro. Zolkan might return someday. Or he might not. It didn't matter any longer.

Kesira Minette was content. And mother to gods.

ALSO AVAILABLE FROM
HODDER AND STOUGHTON PAPERBACKS